ALFRED HITCHCOCK

THE BEST OF
MYSTERY

ALFRED HITCHCOCK

THE BEST OF
MYSTERY

BARNES
&NOBLE
BOOKS
NEW YORK

Published by Galahad Books
A division of BBS Publishing Corporation
450 Raritan Center Parkway
Edison, New Jersey 08837

By arrangement with Dell Magazines.

This edition distributed by Barnes & Noble Books.

Library of Congress Catalog Card Number: 82-83239

ISBN: 0-76074-592-7

Printed in the United States Of America.

ACKNOWLEDGMENTS

The editor hereby makes grateful acknowledgment to the following authors and authors' representatives for giving permission to reprint the material in this volume:

Mary Barrett for *One for the Crow* by Mary Barrett, © 1973 by H. S. D. Publications, Inc.

Lawrence Block for *With a Smile for the Ending* by Lawrence Block, © 1965 by H. S. D. Publications, Inc., and for *Pseudo Identity* by Lawrence Block, © 1966 by H. S. D. Publications, Inc.

Wenzell Brown for *Death by Misadventure* by Wenzell Brown, © 1964 by H. S. D. Publications, Inc.

Margaret Chenoweth for *The White Moth* by Margaret Chenoweth, © 1969 by H. S. D. Publications, Inc.

Robert Colby for *Voice in the Night* by Robert Colby, © 1969 by H. S. D. Publications, Inc.

Borden Deal for *A Try for the Big Prize* by Borden Deal, © 1961 by H. S. D. Publications, Inc.

Charlotte Edwards for *Television Country* by Charlotte Edwards, © 1962 by H. S. D. Publications, Inc.

Ann Elmo Agency, Inc. for *Pattern of Guilt* by Helen Nielsen, © 1958 by H. S. D. Publications, Inc.; for *Nothing but Human Nature* by Hillary Waugh, © 1969 by H. S. D. Publications, Inc.; and for *Galton and the Yelling Boys* by Hillary Waugh, © 1970 by H. S. D. Publications, Inc.

Paul Fairman for *Panther, Panther in the Night* by Paul Fairman, © 1959 by H. S. D. Publications, Inc.

Ron Goulart for *Undertaker, Please Drive Slow* by Ron Goulart, © 1967 by H. S. D. Publications, Inc., and for *News From Nowhere* by Ron Goulart, © 1971 by H. S. D. Publications, Inc.

Edward D. Hoch for *Winter Run* by Edward D. Hoch, © 1964 by H. S. D. Publications, Inc.; for *Warrior's Farewell* by Edward D. Hoch, © 1967 by H. S .D. Publications, Inc.; and for *A Melee of Diamonds* by Edward D. Hoch, © 1972 by H. S. D. Publications, Inc.

International Creative Management for *Countdown* by David Ely, © 1962 by H. S. D. Publications, Inc.

Alex Jackinson Literary Agency for *Ghost of a Chance* by Carroll Mayers, © 1965 by H. S. D. Publications, Inc.

Lenniger Literary Agency, Inc. for *Blind Date* by Charles Boeckman, © 1964 by H. S. D. Publications, Inc.

William Link and Richard Levinson for *Child's Play* by William Link and Richard Levinson, © 1958 by H. S. D. Publications, Inc.

John Lutz for *Games for Adults* by John Lutz, © 1971 by H. S. D. Publications, Inc.

Kirby McCauley, Ltd. for *The Cost of Kent Castwell* by Avram Davidson, © 1961 by H. S. D. Publications, Inc.

McIntosh & Otis, Inc. for *Death Overdue* by Eleanor Daly Boylan, © 1959 by H. S. D. Publications, Inc.; for *Variations on a Game* by Patricia Highsmith, © 1973 by Patricia Highsmith; for *Murderer #2* by Jean Potts, © 1960 by H. S. D. Publications, Inc.; and for *The Pursuer* by Holly Roth, © 1959 by H. S. D. Publications, Inc.

Dan J. Marlowe for *Art for Money's Sake* by Dan J. Marlowe, © February 1970 by Elks Magazine.

Scott Meredith Literary Agency, Inc. for *Glory Hunter* by Richard M. Ellis, © 1970 by H. S. D. Publications, Inc.; for *Murder, 1990* by C. B. Gilford, © 1960 by H. S. D. Publications, Inc.;

Bank Floor by James Holding, © 1961 by H. S. D. Publications, Inc.; for *The Montevideo Squeeze* by James Holding, © 1973 by H. S. D. Publications, Inc.; for *The Vietnam Circle* by F. J. Kelly, © 1964 by H. S. D. Publications, Inc.; for *Final Arrangements* by Lawrence Page, © 1961 by H. S. D. Publications, Inc.; and for *A Very Cautious Boy* by Gilbert Ralston, © 1961 by H. S. D. Publications, Inc.

William Morris Agency for *Sadie When She Died* by Ed McBain, © 1972 by H. S. D. Publications, Inc.

Harold Ober Associates, Inc. for *Perfectly Timed Plot* by E. X. Ferrars, © 1958 by H. S. D. Publications, Inc.

Bill Pronzini for *The Running Man* by Bill Pronzini, © 1967 by H. S. D. Publications, Inc.; for *I Don't Understand !!* by Bill Pronzini, © 1972 by H. S. D. Publications, Inc.; and for *Here Lies Another Blackmailer* by Bill Pronzini, © 1974 by H. S. D. Publications, Inc.

Raines & Raines for *A Real, Live Murderer* by Donald Honig, © 1960 by H. S. D. Publications, Inc.

Paul R. Reynolds, Inc. for *Damon and Pythias and Delilah Brown* by Rufus King, © 1958 by H. S. D. Publications, Inc.

BP Singer Features, Inc. for *An Interlude for Murder* by Paul Tabori, © 1958 by H. S. D. Publications, Inc.

Henry Slesar for *Case of the Kind Waitress* by Henry Slesar, © 1958 by H. S. D. Publications, Inc.; for *You Can't Blame Me* by Henry Slesar, © 1961 by H. S. D. Publications, Inc.; and for *Happiness before Death* by Henry Slesar, © 1974 by H. S. D. Publications, Inc.

Pauline C. Smith for *A Flower in Her Hair* by Pauline C. Smith, © 1967 by H. S. D. Publications, Inc., and for *Linda Is Gone* by Pauline C. Smith, © 1973 by H. S. D. Publications, Inc.

Richard Stark for *Just a Little Impractical Joke* by Richard Stark, © 1961 by H. S. D. Publications, Inc.

Larry Sternig Literary Agency for *#8* by Jack Ritchie, © 1958 by H. S. D. Publications, Inc.; for *The Third Call* by Jack Ritchie, © 1961 by H. S. D. Publications, Inc.; and for *That Russian!* by Jack Ritchie, © 1968 by H. S. D. Publications, Inc.

Lawrence Treat for *Dead Duck* by Lawrence Treat, © 1958 by H. S. D. Publications, Inc.

Nedra Tyre for *Murder between Friends* by Nedra Tyre, © 1963 by H. S. D. Publications, Inc.

James Michael Ullman for *Night of the Twisters* by James Michael Ullman, © 1972 by H. S. D. Publications, Inc.

Bryce Walton for *Doctor Apollo* by Bryce Walton; originally appeared under the title *My Name Is Apollo*, © 1958 by Fosdeck Publications, Inc., and for *All the Needless Killing* by Bryce Walton, © 1960 by H. S. D. Publications, Inc.

Austin Wahl Agency for *Pressure* by Roderick Wilkinson, © 1967 by H. S. D. Publications, Inc.

Donald E. Westlake for *The Best-Friend Murder* by Donald E. Westlake, © 1959 by H. S. D. Publications, Inc.; for *Come Back, Come Back . . .* by Donald E. Westlake, © 1960 by H. S. D. Publications, Inc.; and for *Never Shake a Family Tree* by Donald E. Westlake, © 1961 by H. S. D. Publications, Inc.

Kate Wilhelm for *A Case of Desperation* by Kate Wilhelm, © 1964 by H. S. D. Publications, Inc.

CONTENTS

ALFRED HITCHCOCK

THE BEST OF
MYSTERY

EDWARD D. HOCH

Winter Run

Johnny Kendell was first out of the squad car, first into the alley with his gun already drawn. The snow had drifted here, and it was easy to follow the prints of the running feet. He knew the neighborhood, knew that the alley dead-ended at a ten-foot board fence. The man he sought would be trapped there.

"This is the police!" he shouted. "Come out with your hands up!"

There was no answer except the whistle of wind through the alley, and something which might have been the desperate breathing of a trapped man. Behind him, Kendell could hear Sergeant Racin following, and knew that he too would have his gun drawn. The man they sought had broken the window of a liquor store down the street and had made off with an armload of gin bottles. Now he'd escaped to nowhere and had left a trail in the snow that couldn't be missed, long running steps.

Overhead, as suddenly as the flick of a light switch, the full moon passed from behind a cloud and bathed the alley in a blue-white glow. Twenty feet ahead of him, Johnny Kendell saw the man he tracked, saw the quick glisten of something in his upraised hand. Johnny squeezed the trigger of his police revolver.

Even after the targeted quarry had staggered backward, dying, into the fence that blocked the alley's end, Kendell kept firing. He didn't stop until Sergeant Racin, aghast, knocked the gun from his hand, kicked it out of reach.

Kendell didn't wait for the departmental investigation. Within forty-eight hours he had resigned from the force and was headed west with a girl named Sandy Brown whom he'd been planning to marry in a month. And it was not until the little car had burned up close to three hundred miles that he felt like talking about it, even to someone as close as Sandy.

"He was a bum, an old guy who just couldn't wait for the next drink. After he broke the window and stole that gin, he just went down the alley to drink it in peace. He was lifting a bottle to his lips when I saw him, and I don't know what I thought it was—a gun, maybe, or a knife. As soon as I fired the first shot I knew it was just a bottle, and I guess maybe in my rage at myself, or at the world, I kept pulling the trigger." He lit a cigarette with shaking hands. "If he hadn't been just a bum I'd probably be up before the grand jury!"

Sandy was a quiet girl who asked little from the man she loved. She was tall and angular, with a boyish cut to her dark brown hair, and a way of laughing that made men want to sell their souls. That laugh, and the subdued twinkle deep within her pale blue eyes, told anyone who cared that Sandy Brown was not always quiet, not really boyish.

Now, sitting beside Johnny Kendell, she said, "He was as good as dead anyway, Johnny. If he'd passed out in that alley they wouldn't have found him until he was frozen stiff."

He swerved the car a bit to avoid a stretch of highway where the snow had drifted over. "But I put three bullets in him, just to make sure. He stole some gin, and I killed him for it."

"You thought he had a weapon."

"I didn't think. I just didn't think about anything. Sergeant Racin had been talking about a cop he knew who was crippled by a holdup man's bullet, and I suppose if I was thinking about anything it was about that."

"I still wish you had stayed until after the hearing."

"So they could fire me nice and offical? No thanks!"

Johnny drove and smoked in silence for a time, opening the side window a bit to let the cold air whisper through his blond hair. He was handsome, not yet thirty, and until now there'd always been a ring of certainty about his every action. "I guess I just wasn't cut out to be a cop," he said finally.

"What *are* you cut out for, Johnny? Just running across the country like this? Running when nobody's chasing you?"

"We'll find a place to stop and I'll get a job and then we'll get married. You'll see."

"What can you do besides run?"

He stared out through the windshield at the passing banks of soot-stained snow. "I can kill a man," he answered.

The town was called Wagon Lake, a name which fitted its past better than its present. The obvious signs of that past were everywhere to be seen, the old cottages that lined the frozen lakefront, and the deeply rutted dirt roads which here and there ran parallel to the modern highways. But Wagon Lake, once so far removed from everywhere, had reckoned without the coming of the automobile and the postwar boom which would convert it into a fashionable suburb less than an hour's drive from the largest city in the state.

The place was midwestern to its very roots, and perhaps there was something about the air that convinced Johnny Kendell. That, or perhaps he was only tired of running. "This is the place," he told Sandy while they were stopped at a gas station. "Let's stay a while."

"The lake's all frozen over," she retorted, looking dubious.

"We're not going swimming."

"No, but summer places like this always seem so cold in the winter, colder than regular cities."

But they could both see that the subdivisions had come to Wagon Lake along with the superhighways, and it was no longer just a summer place. They would stay.

For the time being they settled on adjoining rooms at a nearby motel, because Sandy refused to share an apartment with him until they were married. In the morning, Kendell left her the task of starting the apartment hunt while he went off in search of work. At the third place he tried, the man shook his head sadly. "Nobody around here hires in the winter," he told Kendell, "except maybe the sheriff. You're a husky fellow. Why don't you try him?"

"Thanks, maybe I will," Johnny Kendell said, but he tried two more local businesses before he found himself at the courthouse and the sheriff's office.

The sheriff's name was Quintin Dade, and he spoke from around a cheap cigar that never left the corner of his mouth. He was a politician and a smart one. Despite the cigar, it was obvious that the newly arrived wealth of Wagon Lake had elected him.

"Sure," he said, settling down behind a desk scattered casually with letters, reports, and wanted circulars. "I'm looking for a man. We always hire somebody in the winter, to patrol the lake road and keep an eye on the cottages. People leave some expensive stuff in those old places during the winter months. They expect it to be protected."

"You don't have a man yet?" Kendell asked.

"We had one, up until last week." Sheriff Dade offered no more. Instead, he asked, "Any experience in police work?"

"I was on the force for better than a year back East."

"Why'd you leave?"

"I wanted to travel."

"Married?"

"I will be, as soon as I land a job."

"This one just pays seventy-five a week, and it's nights. If you work out, though, I'll keep you on come summer."

"What do I have to do?"

"Drive a patrol car around the lake every hour, check cottages, make sure the kids aren't busting them up—that sort of thing."

"Have you had much trouble?"

"Oh, nothing serious," the sheriff answered, looking quickly away. "Nothing you couldn't handle, a big guy like you."

"Would I have to carry a gun?"

"Well, sure!"

Johny Kendell thought about it. "All right," he said finally. "I'll give it a try."

"Good. Here are some applications to fill out. I'll be checking with the people back East, but that needn't delay your starting. I've got a gun here for you. I can show you the car and you can begin tonight."

Kendell accepted the .38 revolver with reluctance. It was a different make from the one he'd carried back East, but they were too similar. The very feel and weight and coldness of it against his palm brought back the memory of that night in the alley.

Later, when he went back to the motel and told Sandy about the job, she only sat cross-legged on her bed staring up at him. "It wasn't even a week ago, Johnny. How can you take another gun in your hand so soon?"

"I won't have it in my hand. I promise you I won't even draw it."

"What if you see some kids breaking into a cottage?"

"Sandy, it's a job! It's the only thing I know how to do. On seventy-five a week we can get married."

"We can get married anyway. I found a job myself, down at the supermarket."

Kendell stared out the window at a distant hill dotted here and there with snowy spots. "I told him I'd take the job, Sandy. I thought you were on my side."

"I am. I always have been. But you killed a man, Johnny. I don't want it to happen again, for any reason."

"It won't happen again."

He went over to the bed and kissed her, their lips barely brushing.

That night, Sheriff Dade took him out on the first run around the lake, pausing at a number of deserted cottages while instructing him in the art of checking for intruders. The evening was cold, but there was a moon which reflected brightly off the surface of the frozen lake. Kendell wore his own suit and topcoat, with only the badge and gun to show that he belonged in the sheriffs car, He knew at once that he would like the job, even the boredom of it, and he listened carefully to the sheriff's orders.

"About once an hour you take a swing around the lake. That takes you twenty minutes, plus stops. But don't fall into a pattern with your trips, so someone can predict when you'll be passing any given cottage. Vary it, and, of course, check these bars along here too. Especially on weekends we get a lot of underage drinkers. And they're the ones who usually get loaded and decide to break into a cottage."

"They even come here in the winter?"

"This isn't a summer town any more. But sometimes I have a time convincing the cottagers of that."

They rode in silence for a time, and the weight of the gun was heavy on Johnny Kendell's hip. Finally, he decided what had to be done. "Sheriff," he began, "there's something I want to tell you."

"What's that?"

"You'll find out anyway when you check on me back East. I killed a man while I was on duty. Just last week. He was a bum who broke into a liquor store and I thought he had a gun so I shot him. I resigned from the force because they were making a fuss about it."

Sheriff Dade scratched his balding head. "Well, I don't hold that against you. Glad you mentioned it, though. Just remember, out here the most dangerous thing you'll probably face will be a couple of beered-up teenagers. And they don't call for guns."

"I know."

"Right.   Drop me back at the courthouse and you're on your own.   Good luck."

An hour later, Kendell started his first solo swing around the lake, concentrating on the line of shuttered cottages which stood like sentinels against some invader from the frozen lake.   Once he stopped the car to investigate four figures moving on the ice, but they were only children gingerly testing skates on the glossy surface.

On the far side of the lake he checked a couple of cottages at random.   Then he pulled in and parked beside a bar called the Blue Zebra.   It had more cars than the others, and there was a certain Friday night gaiety about the place even from outside.   He went in, letting his topcoat hang loosely over the badge pinned to his suit lapel.   The bar was crowded and all the tables were occupied, but he couldn't pinpoint any underage group.   They were young men self-consciously trying to please their dates, beer-drinking groups of men fresh from their weekly bowling, and the occasional women nearing middle age that one always finds sitting on bar stools.

Kendell chatted a few moments with the owner and then went back outside. There was nothing for him here.   He'd turned down the inevitable offer of a drink because it was too early in the evening, and too soon on the job to be relaxing.

As he was climbing into his car, a voice called to him from the doorway of the Blue Zebra.   "Hey, Deputy!"

"What's the trouble?"

The man was slim and tall, and not much older than Kendell.   He came down the steps of the bar slowly, not speaking again until he was standing only inches away.   "I just wanted to get a look at you, that's all.   I had that job until last week."

"Oh?" Kendell said, because there was nothing else to say.

"Didn't old Dade tell you he fired me?"

"No."

"Well, he did.   Ask him why sometime.   Ask him why he fired Milt Wood-man."   He laughed and turned away, heading back to the bar.

Kendell shrugged and got into the car.   It didn't really matter to him that a man named Milt Woodman was bitter about losing his job.   His thoughts were on the future, and on Sandy, waiting back at the motel . . .

She was sleeping when he returned to their rooms.   He went in quietly and sat on the edge of the bed, waiting until she awakened.   Presently her blue eyes opened and she saw him.   "Hi.   How'd it go?"

"Fine.   I think I'm going to like it.   Get up and watch the sunrise with me."

"I have to go to work at the supermarket."

"Nuts to that!   I'm never going to see you if we're both working."

"We need the money, Johnny.   We can't afford this motel, or these two rooms, much longer."

"Let's talk about it later, huh?"   He suddenly realized that he hadn't heard her laugh in days, and the thought of it made him sad.   Sandy's laughter had always been an important part of her.

That night passed much as the previous one, with patrols around the lake and frequent checks at the crowded bars.   He saw Milt Woodman again, watching him through the haze of cigarette smoke at the Blue Zebra, but this time the man did not speak.   The following day, though, Kendell remembered to ask Sheriff Dade about him.

"I ran into somebody Friday night—fellow named Milt Woodman," he said.

Dade frowned.   "He try to give you any trouble?"

"No, not really.   He just said to ask you sometime why you fired him."

"*Are* you asking me?"

"No.   It doesn't matter to me in the least."

Dade nodded.   "It shouldn't.   But let me know if he bothers you any more."

"Why should he?" Kendell asked, troubled by the remark.

"No reason.   Just keep on your toes."

The following night, Monday, Johnny didn't have to work.   He decided to celebrate with Sandy by taking her to a nearby drive-in where the management kept open all winter by supplying little heaters for each car.

Tuesday night, just after midnight, Kendell pulled into the parking lot at the Blue Zebra.   The neoned juke box was playing something plaintive and the bar was almost empty.   The owner offered him a drink again, and he decided he could risk it.

"Hello, Deputy," a voice said at his shoulder.   He knew before he turned that it was Milt Woodman.

"The name's Johnny Kendell," he said, keeping it friendly.

"Nice name.   You know mine."   He chuckled a little.   "That's a good-looking wife you got.   Saw you together at the movie last night."

"Oh?" Kendell moved instinctively away.

Milt Woodman kept on smiling.   "Did Dade ever tell you why he fired me?"

"I didn't ask him,"

The chuckle became a laugh.   "Good boy!   Keep your nose clean.   Protect that seventy-five a week."   He turned and went toward the door.   "See you around."

Kendell finished his drink and followed him out.   There was a hint of snow in the air and tonight no moon could be seen.   Ahead, on the road, the twin tail lights of Woodman's car glowed for a moment until they disappeared around a curve. Kendell gunned his car ahead with a sudden urge to follow the man, but when he'd reached the curve himself the road ahead was clear.   Woodman had turned off somewhere.

The rest of the week was quiet, but on Friday he had a shock.   It had always been difficult for him to sleep days, and he often awakened around noon after only four or five hours' slumber.   This day he decided to meet Sandy at her job for lunch, and as he arrived at the supermarket he saw her chatting with someone at the checkout counter.   It was Milt Woodman, and they were laughing together like old friends.

Kendell walked around the block, trying to tell himself that there was nothing to be concerned about. When he returned to the store, Woodman was gone and Sandy was ready for lunch.

"Who was your friend?" he asked casually,

"What friend?"

"I passed a few minutes ago and you were talking to some guy. Seemed to be having a great time."

"Oh, I don't know, a customer. He comes in a lot, loafs around."

Kendell didn't mention it again. But it struck him over the weekend that Sandy no longer harped on the need for a quick marriage. In fact, she no longer mentioned marriage at all.

On Monday evening, Kendell's night off, Sheriff Dade invited them for dinner at his house. It was a friendly gesture, and Sandy was eager to accept at once. Mrs. Dade proved to be a handsome blonde woman in her mid-thirties, and she handled the evening with the air of someone who knew all about living the good life at Wagon Lake.

After dinner, Kendell followed Dade to his basement workshop. "Just a place to putter around in," the sheriff told him. He picked up a power saw and handled it fondly. "Don't get as much time down here as I'd like."

"You're kept pretty busy at work."

Dade nodded. "Too busy. But I like the job you're doing, Johnny. I really do."

"Thanks." Kendell lit a cigarette and leaned against the workbench. "Sheriff, there's something I want to ask you. I didn't ask it before."

"What's that?"

"Why did you fire Milt Woodman?"

"He been giving you trouble?"

"No. Not really. I guess I'm just curious."

"All right. There's no real reason for not telling you, I suppose. He used to get down at the far end of the lake, beyond the Blue Zebra, and park his car in the bushes. Then he'd take some girl into one of the cottages and spend half the night there with her. I couldn't have that sort of thing going on. The fool was supposed to be guarding the cottages, not using them for his private parties."

"He's quite a man with the girls, huh?"

Dade nodded sourly. "He always was. He's just a no-good bum. I should never have hired him in the first place."

They went upstairs to join the ladies. Nothing more was said about Woodman's activities, but the next night while on patrol Kendell spotted him once again in the Blue Zebra. He waited down the road until Woodman emerged, then followed him around the curve to the point where he'd vanished the week before. Yes, he'd turned off into one of the steep driveways that led down to the cottages at the water's edge. There was a driveway between each pair of cottages, so Kendell had the spot pretty much narrowed down to one of two places, both big rambling houses built back when Wagon Lake was a summer retreat for the very rich.

He smoked a cigarette and tried to decide what to do. It was his duty to keep people away from the cottages, yet for some reason he wasn't quite ready to challenge Milt Woodman. Perhaps he knew that the man would never submit meekly to his orders. Perhaps he knew he might once again have to use the gun on his hip.

So he did nothing that night about Milt Woodman.

The following day Sheriff Dade handed him a mimeographed list. "I made up a new directory of names and addresses around town. All the houses are listed, along with the phone numbers of the bars and some of the other places you check. Might want to leave it with your wife, in case she has to reach you during the night." Dade always referred to Sandy as Kendell's wife, though he must have known better. "You're still at that motel, aren't you?"

"For a little while longer," Kendell answered vaguely.

Dade grunted. "Seen Woodman around?"

"Caught a glimpse of him last night. Didn't talk to him."

The sheriff nodded and said no more.

The following evening, when Johnny was getting ready to go on duty, Sandy seemed more distant than ever.

"What's the matter?" he asked finally.

"Oh, just a hard day, I guess. All the weekend shopping starts on Thursday."

"Has that guy been in again? The one I saw you talking to?"

"I told you he comes in a lot. What of it?"

"Sandy—" He went to her, but she turned away.

"Johnny, you're different, changed. Ever since you killed that man you've been like a stranger. I thought you were really sorry about it, but now you've taken this job so you can carry a gun again."

"I haven't had it out of the holster!"

"Not yet."

"All right," he said finally. "I'm sorry you feel that way. I'll see you in the morning." He went out, conscious of the revolver's weight against his hip.

The night was cold, with a hint of snow again in the air. He drove faster than usual, making one circuit of the lake in fifteen minutes, and barely glancing at the crowded parking lots along the route. The words with Sandy had bothered him, more than he cared to admit. On the second trip around the lake, he tried to pick out Woodman's car, but it was nowhere to be seen. Or was his car hidden off the road down at one of those cottages?

He thought about Sandy some more.

Near midnight, with the moon playing through the clouds and reflecting off the frozen lake, Johnny drove into town, between his inspection trips. There wasn't much time, so he went directly to the motel. Sandy's room was empty, the bed smooth and undisturbed.

He drove back to the lake, this time seeking lights in the cottages he knew Woodman used. But all seemed dark and deserted. There were no familiar faces at the Blue Zebra, either. He accepted a drink from the manager and stood by the bar sipping it.   His mood grew gradually worse, and when a college boy tried to buy a drink for his girl Kendell chased them out for being under age.   It was something he had never done before.

Later, around two, while he was checking another couple parked down a side road, he saw Woodman's familiar car shoot past.   There was a girl in the front seat with him, a concealing scarf wrapped around her hair.   Kendell let out his breath slowly.   If it was Sandy, he thought that he would kill her.

"Where were you last night?" he asked her in the morning, trying to keep his voice casual.   "I stopped by around midnight."

"I went to a late movie."

"How come?"

She lit a cigarette, turning half away from him before she answered.   "I just get tired of sitting around here alone every night.   Can't you understand that?"

"I understand it all right," he said.

Late that afternoon, when the winter darkness had already descended over the town and the lake, he left his room early and drove out to the old cottages beyond the Blue Zebra.   He parked off the road, in the hidden spot he knew Woodman used, and made his way to the nearer of the houses.   There seemed nothing unusual about it, no signs of illegal entry, and he turned his attention to the cottage on the other side of the driveway.   There, facing the lake, he found an unlatched window and climbed in.

The place was furnished like a country estate house, and great white sheets had been draped over the furniture to protect it from a winter's dust.   He'd never seen so elaborate a summer home, but he hadn't come to look at furniture.   In the bedroom upstairs he found what he sought.   There had been some attempt to collect the beer bottles into a neat pile, but they hadn't bothered to smooth out the sheets.

He looked in the ash tray and saw Sandy's brand.   All right, he tried to tell himself, that proved nothing.   Not for sure.   Then he saw on the floor a crumpled ball of paper, which she'd used to blot her lipstick.   He smoothed it out, fearing, but already knowing.   It was the mimeographed list Sheriff Dade had given him just two days before, the one Sandy had stuffed into her purse.

All right.   Now he knew.

He left it all as he'd found it and went back out the window.   Even Woodman would not have dared leave such a mess for any length of time.   He was planning to come back, and soon—perhaps that night.   And he wouldn't dare bring another girl, when he hadn't yet cleaned up the evidence of the last one.   No, it would be Sandy again.

Kendell drove to the Blue Zebra and had two quick drinks before starting his tour of duty.   Then, as he drove around the lake, he tried to keep a special eye out for Woodman's car.   At midnight, back at the bar, he asked the manager, "Seen Milt around tonight?"

"Woodman?   Yeah, he stopped by for some cigarettes and beer."

"Thanks."

Kendell stepped into the phone booth, and called the motel.   Sandy was not in her room.   He left the bar and drove down the road, past the cottage.   There were no lights, but he caught a glimpse of Woodman's car in the usual spot.   They were there, all right.

He parked further down the road, and for a long time just sat in the car, smoking. Presently he took the .38 revolver from his holster and checked to see that it was loaded.   Then he drove back to the Blue Zebra for two more drinks.

When he returned to the cottage, Woodman's car was still there.   Kendell made his way around to the front and silently worked the window open.   He heard their muffled, whispering voices as he started up the stairs.

The bedroom door was open and he stood for a moment in the hallway, letting his eyes grow accustomed to the dark.   They hadn't yet heard his approach.

"Woodman," he said.

The man started at the sound of his name, rising from the bed with a curse. "What the hell!" Kendell fired once at the voice, heard the girl's scream of terror and fired again.   He squeezed the trigger and kept squeezing it, because this time there was no Sergeant Racin to knock the pistol from his hand.   This time there was nothing to stop him until all six shots had been blasted into the figures on the bed.

Then, letting the pistol fall to the floor, he walked over and struck a match. Milt Woodman was sprawled on the floor, his head in a gathering pool of blood. The girl's body was still under the sheet, and he approached it carefally.

It wasn't Sandy.

It was Mrs. Dade, the sheriff's wife.

This time he knew they wouldn't be far behind him.   This time he knew there'd be no next town, no new life.

But he had to keep going.   Running.

HENRY SLESAR

You Can't Blame Me

Now it was Beggs' turn. A generation had grown to manhood since he went behind the gates, and now they were opening for him. As he stood in the Warden's office, his skin itching in civilian tweed, he thought, First twenty-year-old I see, I'll go up to him and say, kid, I'm one guy you never laid eyes on before, I'm one guy you can't blame for anything, because I've been sitting out your lifetime.

Twenty years!

"Fifty's not old," the Warden said. "Plenty of men get new careers at fifty, Beggs. Don't go getting discouraged, because you know what that leads to."

"What?" Beggs said dreamily, knowing the answer, only wanting to keep the talk going, to delay the moment.

"You know. Trouble. You wouldn't be the first I've said goodbye to one day and hello to the next."

He cleared his throat and shuffled papers. "I see you have a family."

"Had," Beggs said, not with bitterness.

"Your wife wasn't much for visiting, was she?"

"No."

"That money you stole—"

"What money?"

"All right," the Warden sighed. "I remember now. You're one of the in-nocent ones. Well, fine. That's the kind I like to see leave." His hand was out. "Good luck, Beggs. I hope you find what you want out there. Only wish I had some good advice for you."

"That's all right, Warden. Thanks just the same."

"I'll give you one tip." He smiled benignly. "Dye your hair."

"Thanks," Beggs said. . .

He was out. He knew Edith wouldn't be waiting on the other side of the wall, but he stopped and looked up and down and sat on a hydrant to smoke a cigarette within ten yards of the prison gates. He heard a guard chuckle on the catwalk overhead. Then he got up, and walked to the bus stop. He sat in the rear seat of the bus and watched his white-haired reflection all the way into town. I'm an old man, he thought. But that's all right.

He used up most of the rehabilitation money in two days.   Some went for shelter, for new clothes, for food, and for train fare.   When he stepped onto the platform at Purdy's Landing, a taxi man solicited his business.   He said yes, and got into the front seat.   "Do you know the Cobbin farm?" he said.

"Nope," the cabdriver said.   "Never heard of it."

"Used to be on Edge Road?"

"Heard of Edge Road."

"That's where I want to go.   I'll tell you where to stop."

He told him, within sight of a small housing development.   He paid the man, but waited until he was driving off before he approached one of the houses.   When the car was out of sight, he turned out of the driveway and started walking down the road.   Nothing seemed familiar, but he wasn't worried.   Everything changes. Latitudes remain.   Stone endures.

He saw the jagged rim of the rocky slope ahead of him, and he knew he was in the right place.   He slid down the small embankment, bracing himself against a fall.   He had been nimbler twenty years ago.   There was a steep woodland at the end of the slope, and he entered the thick of it.   He stumbled around until he saw the rough circle of stacked stones, the old blackened tree stump, and the spot where he had hidden the money.

He began removing the stones.   There were many of them.   He had no fear that his hiding place had been discovered in his absence.   His confidence was as strong as faith.

It was there, still in the leather suitcase, all in cash, neatly bundled up by denomination, slightly damp but still new-looking and spendable.   He wiped off the suitcase—it had cost forty dollars, new—and clucked when he saw the mold damage on its edge.   But it was sturdy still, and hefted well by its stout handle.

He returned to the road, carrying the suitcase.   This time, he did stop at one of the houses, and knocked on the door.   A woman answered, looked dubiously at his suitcase as if expecting a sales pitch, and then relaxed when she saw his snowy hair and heard his question.   Could he have a drink of water?   Of course.   Could he please call a taxi?   Go ahead, phone's right over there.   She was a nice woman, not young.   With a shock, Beggs remembered that Edith would be the same age now.

He reached the old neighborhood at dusk.   The light dab of rouge on the tenements didn't improve their appearance; it was like makeup on a trollop.   Not much change here, he thought, only for the worse.   Dilapidation and decay, another twenty-year layer of dirt on the pavements and building stones.   Then he saw the difference: an all-glass front on the corner drugstore; an empty lot where a candy warehouse had been; a change in nationality in the street urchins; a new sign, neon, in front of Mike's Bar and Grill.   The sign read "Lucky's," and when it blinked, the "L" fizzled and crackled and seemed ready to burn out.

He went into the bar.   He had spent plenty of hours there in his youth, even after his marriage.   But only the latitude and longitude were the same.   Mike's place had been rough-furnished, honestly lit, and the bartender had had sweat on his forearms. Lucky's was another sort of place altogether. It was dark, too dark for an old pair of eyes, jeweled up with chrome and colored glass, a lousy cocktail lounge. There were even women: he saw a black dress and a string of pearls and heard hard, feminine laughter. The bartender wore a white uniform and had a ferret's face. He played the cash register like a Hammond organ.

"Yes, sir?" the barman said.

"Phone?" Beggs said hoarsely.

Contempt. "Back there."

He stumbled on something, righted himself, found the phone booth. He searched clumsily through the directory, marveling at its thickness, the smell of alcohol around him almost strong enough to make his head spin; there hadn't been whiskey past his throat in two decades. He found her listing, BEGGS, EDITH, the number different but the address the same. He felt almost weepy with gratitude towards his wife for being stubborn and changeless.

He went into the booth, forcing the suitcase in between his legs, dug a nickel out of his pocket and then saw that rates were different. He found a dime, but he didn't deposit it. His hands were shaking too much. He couldn't face the moment, couldn't sit here in this glass cell and hear the voice from yesterday tinny and disembodied in the receiver. He came out of the booth, sweating.

At the bar, he sat on a plush stool and placed his elbows on the bar and rested his head in his hands. There was nobody drinking. The barman moved in on him like a bird of prey. "What'll it be?" he said seductively. "You look like you need one, friend."

Beggs looked up. "Whatever happened to Mike?" he said.

"Who?"

"I'll—I'll have a whiskey."

The glass was in front of him, paid for, easing the strain between them. The barman relaxed and said: "You mean Mike Duram? Used to be his bar once?"

"Yes. "

"Six feet under," the man said, jerking his thumb downwards. "Maybe ten years ago. Place had four owners since then. You a friend of Mike's or something?"

"I knew him," Beggs said. "A long time ago." He downed the drink and it exploded in his head like a grenade. He coughed, choked, almost fell forward on the mahogany counter. The bartender cursed and got him water.

"What are you, a wise guy?" he said. "Tryin' to make out my whiskey's no good?"

"I'm sorry; it's been a long time."

"Yeah, don't give me that."

He walked off, injured. Beggs covered his face with his hand. Then he felt a touch in the middle of his back, and turned to see the cheap dead-white pearls and the slim throat severed by a low black neckline.

"Hello, Pop, you got a cold or something?"

"It's nothing," he said.   She came and sat on the opposite stool, a young, pale, pretty girl, her skin even whiter than the fake necklace she wore.   "I'm not used to it," he said.   "Can't take the stuff anymore."

"You need practice," she smiled.   Then he realized that this wasn't amateur cordiality; the girl worked there.   He reached for the suitcase handle.   "Stick around, Pop, you can't fly on one wing."

"I don't understand."

"Have another drink.   It'll taste better this time."

"I don't think so."

"I'll tell you what.   You buy one and try it; if you don't like it, I'll finish it for you.   It's like a moneyback guarantee, only you don't get your money back." She laughed gaily.

He started to refuse, but he hated to see even the false smile disappear.

"All right," he said gruffly.

The bartender returned, all prepared.   He set two shot glasses in front of them, and filled both to the rim.   He placed the bottle in front of Beggs, turning it to display the brand name.   Beggs, chastised, gave him a small grin.   The girl's thin white fingers closed around her glass, and she lifted it.

"Here's to you," she said.

The second went down easier.   It didn't relax him, but it made his depression easier to bear.   It made him remember what a drink was for.   He looked shyly at the girl, and she patted his shoulder.   "Nice man," she said, cute, patronizing. "Such nice white hair."

"You're not drinking," he said.

"Come to think of it, I'd like mine with ginger ale.   Couldn't we sit at a table?"

Beggs looked to the end of the bar; the bartender was wiping glasses and appeared contented.

"Sure, why not?" he said.   He picked up the suitcase and climbed off the stool. His foot didn't feel the ground when he touched it, and he laughed.   "Hey, what's going on here?   My foot's asleep."

She giggled, and looked at the suitcase.   Then she put her arm through his. "Gee, you're cute," she said.   "I'm glad you came in."

He was in the prison shop, the machines roaring, his body stiff with fatigue, his head hurting.   He rested it on the cool surface of the lathe, and the guard gripped his shoulder and shook it.

"Wake up, buddy."

"What?" Beggs said, lifting his head from the micarta tabletop.   His hand was still around a glass, but the glass was empty.   "What did you say?" he said.

"Wake up," the bartender grumbled.   "This ain't a hotel.   I got to close up."

"What time is it?"   He straightened and gongs rang in his ears.   His fingertips were tingling and there was glue in his mouth.   "I must have fallen asleep," he said.

"It's after one," the bartender said.   "Go on home."

Beggs looked at the other side of the booth. It was empty. He reached down for the suitcase handle and clutched air. "My suitcase," he said calmly.

"Your what?"

"Suitcase. Maybe I left it at the bar . . ." He got up, stumbled toward the stools and started pushing them around. "It's got to be here someplace," he said. "Didn't you see it?"

"Look, buddy—"

"My suitcase," Beggs said distinctly, facing the man. "I want my suitcase, you understand?"

"I didn't see any suitcase. Listen, you accusing me of—"

"The girl I was with. The one who worked here."

"No girl works here, fella. You got the wrong idea about the kind of place I run."

Beggs put his hand on the man's lapel, not rough. "Please don't fool around," he said. He even smiled. "Look, don't joke. I'm an old man. See my white hair? What did you do with it? Where's the girl?"

"Mister, I'll tell you this once more." The barman plucked off his fingers. "I didn't see your lousy suitcase. And no girl works here. If you got rolled by somebody, that's your business, not mine."

"You *liar!*"

Beggs hurled himself forward. It wasn't an attack; his arms were spread out in pleading, not violence. He shouted at the man again and the man walked away, disdainful. He followed him, and the man turned and said nasty words. Then Beggs started to sob, and the bartender sighed wearily and said, "Oh, that did it, that's too much." He grabbed Beggs' arm and began propelling him to the doorway. He scooped up his overcoat from the rack and threw it at him. Beggs shouted, but he kept moving. At the door, the barman gave one final shove that sent him into the street. The door slammed shut and Beggs pounded it with his fist, only once.

Then he stood on the sidewalk, and put on his overcoat. There were cigarettes in the pocket, but they were crushed and worthless. He threw the crumpled pack into the gutter.

Then he walked off.

He remembered the stairs. There were three flights of them, easy to take when he had been young and newly married and Edith was waiting for him upstairs. Steeper when he had been drinking at Mike's after a jobless day. Now they were endless, a wooden Everest. He was puffing by the time he reached the apartment door.

He knocked, and in a little while a woman who could have been Edith's mother opened the door. But it was Edith. She stared at him, pushing back the limp yellow-gray strands from her face, a bony hand fumbling with the dangling button of a soiled housecoat. He wasn't sure if she recognized him, so he said, "It's Harry, Edith."

"Harry?"

"It's kind of late," he mumbled. "I'm sorry to come so late. They let me out today. Could I come in, maybe?"

"Oh, my God," Edith said, putting her hands flat over her eyes. She didn't move for almost thirty seconds. He didn't know whether to touch her or not. He shifted from one foot to another, and licked his lips dryly.

"I'm awful thirsty," he said. "Could I have a glass of water?"

She let him in. The room was in darkness; so his wife lit a table lamp. She went into the kitchen and came out with the water. She brought it to him, and he sat down before drinking it.

When he handed her the empty glass, he smiled shyly and said, "Thanks. I sure was thirsty."

"What do you want, Harry?"

"Nothing," he said quietly. "Only a glass of water. I couldn't expect nothing else from you, could I?"

She walked away from him, fooling with her hair. "My God, I look terrible. Why couldn't you give me some warning?"

"I'm sorry, Edith," he said. "I better get going."

"Where to?"

"I don't know," Beggs said. "I haven't thought about it."

"You got no place to go?"

"No."

She took the empty glass to the kitchen, and then came out. She remained in the doorway, folding her arms and leaning against the doorframe.

"You could stay here," she said flatly. "I couldn't turn you out, without no place to go. You could sleep on the couch. Do you want to do that, Harry?"

He rubbed his palm over the cushion.

"This couch," he said slowly. "I'd rather sleep on this couch than in a palace." He looked at her, and she was crying. "Aw, Edith," he said.

"Don't mind me—"

He got up and went to her side. He put his arms around her.

"Is it okay if I stay? I mean, not just tonight?"

She nodded.

Beggs held her tighter, the embrace of a young lover. Edith must have realized how foolish it looked, because she laughed brokenly and pushed a tear off her cheek with the heel of her hand.

"My God, what am I thinking of?" she said. "Harry, you know how old I am?"

"I don't care—"

"I'm a woman with a grown daughter. Harry, you never even saw your daughter." She freed herself and went to a closed bedroom door. She knocked, and her voice trembled. "Harry, you never saw Angela. She was only a baby when— Angela! Angela, wake up!"

A moment later the door opened. The blonde girl in the loose-fitting nightgown was yawning and blinking. She was pretty, but her expression was cross.

"What the heck's going on?" she said.   "What's all the yellin' about?"

"Angela, I want you to meet somebody.   Somebody special!"

Edith clasped her hands together and looked at Beggs.   Beggs was looking at the girl, smiling foolishly, in embarrassment.   The smile didn't last.   Edith saw it go, and made a sound of disappointment.   They looked at each other, the old man and the girl, and Angela tugged nervously at the strand of cheap dead-white pearls still around her throat.

PAULINE C. SMITH

A Flower in Her Hair

"While you're here, I s'pose I better take you over to see Aunt Abbie."

"Aunt Abbie?" questioned the girl. "Who is she?"

"Well, she ain't really an aunt, but she's some relation . . ." Melinda's voice trailed off as her memory attempted to locate the offshoot on the family tree that was Aunt Abbie. "Bein' my second cousin, I guess she's pretty fur removed from you." She gazed at her visitor uncertainly, then her eyes turned resolute. "But she's blood kin, so you should see her."

"Why?" The girl was growing impatient of distant family ties woven to strangle her in this strange country of her mother's.

Melinda bustled. "She's the record keeper. Got second sight too."

"When do we have to go?" Tradition and folklore were losing their piquancy.

Again Melinda looked doubtfully upon the city-bred frailty of her guest. "Well, it's quite a piece. Rough ground. But I guess we better get over there today, you're leavin' so soon."

The girl sighed, mentally ticking off the hours left to her here.

In the hot sun she followed in the wake of Melinda's angular maturity, which plowed a furrow through weeds and thistle, over boulder-strewn hillsides bare of trees and bristling with prickly growth that offered no protection from the beating heat.

At last, Melinda turned to look at the girl behind her. "We better stop and rest awhile, I guess." She eased her bulk down carefully, watching her companion slump to the ground. "Tired, ain'tcha?"

The girl nodded.

"I shoulda remembered you ain't used to this kind o' country. Your face sure is flushed."

The girl thrust out a lower lip to blow cooling air across her cheeks.

"You redheads sunburn, don'tcha?"

Again the girl nodded.

Melinda turned reflective. "Don't know that there ever was a redhead in the family before . . ."

"My father had auburn hair."

"Oh. I never seen him. Your ma's hair was black's a raven's wing."

"I remember."

Melinda heaved herself to her broad feet. "Might's well get goin' if we want to get back by sundown. Ain't fur now.'' She pointed. ''Just up the hill and over to the ridge. See it in a little bit.''

The cabin finally appeared in the distance, like a lookout on the rim.

Staring curiously, the girl asked, ''Is that it?''

''That's it. Aunt Abbie's lived there now goin' on fifty year.''

''How old is she?''

They had reached the summit. The cabin squatted beneath bowed trees that held hands over its roof.

''She must be over seventy now. Spry, though. Spry's a chicken.'' Melinda took a sidelong glance at her weary companion. ''Climbs these hills like a mountain goat when she's a mind to.''

The girl knew even a gentle thrust when she felt one. Her mouth tightened. ''Well,'' she said flatly, ''I just hope she's spry enough to get me a nice cold drink of water.''

''She'll have grapejuice. Always keeps a pitcherful down in the cave.''

The girl paused to stare over the ridge and into the gorge below. She backed up, trembling. ''Are you sure she's home?''

''Aunt Abbie? Oh, sure. She don't go noplace. Always busy,'' Melinda said with certainty as she stepped through a broken gate and up a path hemmed in by weed-choked flowers.

The door was open. Melinda poked her head through. ''Aunt Abbie,'' she shrieked. Behind her, the girl stumbled over a claw hammer at the sill. She kicked it aside and into the weeds.

''Aunt Abbie,'' shouted Melinda again.

''Yes, yes, yes. I'm a-comin'.''

Erupting from the shadows, peering into the sunlight, Aunt Abbie strained forward. As Melinda had said, she was spry, as spry as a taut steel spring. Her meager nose projected itself before her. Her dark eyes were lodestones and her mouth an iron bar.

''Oh, it's you, Melinda. Who's that you got with you?''

Melinda stepped aside to give the girl an abrupt shove into the room. ''This here's Marty's girl. She's been stoppin' with us a coupla days.''

Aunt Abbie sifted relationships through her mind. ''Marty's girl.'' Inspecting her, she reached forth a clawlike hand with a feather touch. The girl drew minutely away. ''Come in. Come in and set down.''

Sidling into the room, the girl backed to a chair, feeling the slick, wooden arms of it with her fingertips. As she sat on the edge of the broken cane seat, Aunt Abbie stood before her. Again the claws reached out. ''Marty's girl. Such pretty red hair.'' Talons hovered over the girl's shining head, suspended there. ''Such awful pretty red hair.'' Aunt Abbie turned to Melinda. ''Did you ever see such pretty red hair?''

Melinda shook her head. ''Can't say I ever did. Guess I never seen any red hair in this family before. She says she got it from her pa.''

The girl shrank, her eyes moving cautiously from Aunt Abbie to the objects in the room—cluttered and stacked souvenirs—a chaos of remembrance.

''She's thirsty,'' suggested Melinda.

Aunt Abbie took another covetous look at the flaming hair. "Such a pretty red. Yes, Melinda. I'll fetch some grapejuice." She scuttled from the room.

The girl heard a door slam, quick, staccato footsteps descending.

The room grew brighter as her eyes adjusted. "So much stuff," she murmured.

"Aunt Abbie keeps everything," Melinda explained proudly. "All the family records too. Them rugs she made from relations' clothes."

As Melinda gestured with humble admiration, the girl looked down upon the oblongs, circles, hooked and braided, crocheted and cross-stitched; utilization of the rags of memory, placed in precision like an army, white pine boards between the battalions.

"She made all them samplers too."

The girl raised her eyes to stare at the walls with their exquisite needlework. Each square of cloth threaded with a MAY HE REST IN PEACE or derivative. "When they die," explained Melinda, "she stitches 'em up."

The girl shuddered, drowned in her own morbid fascination. Her eyes fixed themselves on the bright colors of death.

"I'll try and get Aunt Abbie to show you the wreath," Melinda whispered, her eyes rolling, her breast swelling beneath coarse cotton, her large spare body quivering with anticipation.

The girl offered no answering interest, intent only upon the sound of scrambling footsteps as they returned. Her every thought, every desire, was to get away from here, from the saffron face of Aunt Abbie, her nimble tread, the heavy cup pushed so gently, ever so insidiously, into her hand.

The girl sipped the cold, dark liquid.

"Good, ain't it?" prodded Melinda.

She nodded with a faint smile and a thread of purple parting her lips. Stiffly then, with eyes averted, she placed the half-full cup on the marble-topped table at her side.

Aunt Abbie stood lightly on a hooked memorial, watching her. "Your ma had black hair." She turned to Melinda. "Remember how dark Marty's hair was?"

Melinda nodded. "I thought maybe you'd show us your you-know-what . . ."

Aunt Abbie looked speculatively at the girl. She extended a hand, fingers curved, almost touching the bright hair. "I'll fetch it."

The girl was deep in the chair now, feeling the stiff, jagged ends of broken cane. Her stomach curled; streaks of cold hunched her shoulders. Sluggishly, she gazed out at the shaft of sunshine in the doorway.

"Oh, the book of records too," called Melinda, leaning forward as Aunt Abbie returned to squat before the girl.

Carefully, Aunt Abbie laid the large gilt frame on a braided rug. She opened a book upon her knees.

"That," explained Melinda, "is the family record. The first part shows the birthings. The last part, the dyings."

Aunt Abbie flipped pages, her sepia fingers fondling the last of them, clean and unwritten. "How old are you, my dear?"

"Twenty-four."

"Just twenty-four.   Well, well.   Your ma lived to be . . . let's see . . ."She leafed back.   "Thirty-two.   Your branch of the family always did go young. Your pa ain't in here.   He wan't kin."

"Dad died last year."

"You're all alone?"

"Well, yes . . ."

"Except for us."

The girl was hazily displeased with the tie-in.   "I'm just passing through here," she said in minor revolt, "on my way home.   To the coast," she added, feeling the necessity of identity, a longing for familiarity.

"Well, well, well," Aunt Abbie crooned absently.   Her mind seemed to wander as her eyes studied the girl.   "Well," and she smiled, her lips sucking her teeth briskly.   "So you want to see the wreath?"

"Wreath?"

"The hair wreath."   Aunt Abbie placed the book on the floor and picked up the oval gilt frame.   Its curves caught the beams of light from the doorway.   She held it up against her knees, her fingers holding it in place.   Steadily, she watched the girl.

The girl stared down and into a circlet of flowers painstakingly woven against the linen background.   Twined into the floral hoop bloomed the white of cherry blossom, the gray of cactus spine, yellow daisies, brown iris, ashen lilies, goldenrod . . .

Aunt Abbie bent her head, her liver-colored claw pointing out a portion of the wreath.   "See them?   Them are black-eyed Susans.   The centers come straight from your ma's hair.   Pretty, ain't they?"   The finger caressed the glossy black.

"My mother's *hair*?"   The girl drew back, held her breath and allowed her face to blank out in utter disbelief.

"This here's made of hair.   Didn't you know?"

The girl stared glassily at this incredible woman and her absurd handwork.   She felt the sharp gouge of broken cane and the hard rungs of the chair against her back.

"It's got hair in it from every one of the family that's passed on."

Melinda hitched closer, tipping her head as she gazed proudly down upon the wreath.   "Ain't it pretty now?   Ain't it just elegant?"   She shook her head with wonder.   "How she does it, I'll never know—all them fine hairs, the little bitty stitches.   I wouldn't never have the patience."

"You mean that's hair?"   The girl clung to the arms of the chair because here was substance, here reality.   "Human hair?   All of it?"

Aunt Abbie nodded, pleased.   "Just the family though," she qualified with dignity.   "I wa'nt never one to fool with any that ain't kin."

"And all those people are dead?"

Rising, Aunt Abbie leaned the frame against a table and stepped back to view it. "That's how I keep 'em.   It's a kind of memorial.   Shows my respect, sort of."

The girl stared at her, then back to the wreath.   Her lips stretched, her nostrils flared.

"See?" Aunt Abbie's long finger pointed. "I ain't got that rose in yet."
Reflectively, she gazed at the girl in the chair. "I just got the rose left."

The empty spot severed the circle like a break in a wedding ring. Outlines of
rose petals had been sketched upon the linen. "It's all that's left. Once I get
that in, the wreath'll be done."

The room began to swing, the wreath whirled concentrically, wreath within
wreath, circle upon circle. Heat held the girl's body; chill released it. She placed
an uncertain hand before her eyes. "I'm a little sick," she whispered weakly.
Attempting to rise, she stumbled, and was caught in Melinda's strong but gentle
grasp.

"She's a city girl," she faintly heard Melinda apologize. "She ain't used to
the walk we took. We'll lay her on your cot, Aunt Abbie."

She felt herself half-dragged, half-carried, through rolling blackness.

Melinda stepped from the sleeproom while Aunt Abbie tarried to stroke the
shining hair on the pillow. Melinda paused in thought.

"She's a pretty sick girl. Too much, sun, maybe. Her skin looks kinda green,
don't it?"

"Such pretty, pretty red hair," said Aunt Abbie.

"Could be . . ." Melinda hesitated, absorbed now with a problem, beset by
it and confused, "could be I best go home alone and get Tom to come back with
the truck and fetch her." She looked upon Aunt Abbie for confirmation. "She
couldn't never walk through them hills again the way she—"

"You do that." Aunt Abbie's decision was immediate and definite. She urged
Melinda to the door, through it, and out into the sunshine. "There ain't no hurry
now. Not a mite of it. I'll tend to the girl. Don't you worry on it. I'll see
she gets a nice long sleep."

Without a single backward glance, Melinda walked over the boulders in the
setting sun. Familiar with Aunt Abbie's competent hands and second sight, she
felt a sense of accomplishment. Hadn't Aunt Abbie cured Old Opal of the jumps?
And predicted the death of little Junie May? Nobody believed her that time, the
baby being so fat and rosylike. But lo and behold! Junie May died like *that!*
Melinda, in recollection, chopped the air with her hand. That child's hair turned
into the brightest yellow buttercups of them all.

When Tom arrived at near-dark, Melinda told him, "There ain't no rushin' hurry.
Aunt Abbie'll take care of the girl good. It's best we don't unsettle her rest tonight.
We'll fetch her first thing in the mornin' though, so's she can catch her train."

At daybreak, Melinda was pleased to relax on the seat of the truck. She spread
her dress down over her thighs and leaned back against the wooden brace. The
trip to Aunt Abbie's didn't take long this way, through dust-streaked fennel and
the cool clear dawn.

"We'll fetch her right back home so's she can pack up. It sure makes a girl
puny to raise her up in the city. You wouldn't think that a bit of walk like that
would get her to ailin', now, would you? She's a sweet little thing, though, even
if she ain't healthy. I've growed real fond on her."

Aunt Abbie's cabin crouched in the shadow of the trees, a dreary and somnolent recluse. Melinda walked around it to the open door. She kicked a hammer from the sill into the weeds, and bent over to pick up a pocket mirror from the warped floor.

Inside, Aunt Abbie formed a pale sickle of absorption in the shadows, intent upon her needle, the gilt frame propped before her.

"How is she?" called Melinda.

Aunt Abbie turned slowly to peer through the gloom. "How's who?"

"Why, Marty's girl, Aunt Abbie. She got to ailin' while we was visitin' yesterday. Remember?"

Aunt Abbie's mind seemed to reach back into all the yesterdays where it groped, fumbled, poked and pried. "Oh, the redhead." She turned back to her work and, with great care, slid her needle into the linen, the copper-red strand glinting against the half-finished rose. "Well now, Melinda, did I tell you I seen death on that girl?"

Melinda clutched her heart and knew sudden terror. Then she rocked back to awe and veneration. "You seen that, Aunt Abbie? Like you seen it in Junie May?" Melinda was hypnotized by the shine of a wondrous second sight.

"Just the same," said Aunt Abbie nodding. "Just the same," and took another stitch.

"You mean she's dead now, Aunt Abbie?"

"She's dead now."

Aunt Abbie's words impaled Melinda's mind, to send her glance, slant-eyed, around the shadows of the room, searching out, yet sliding from the girl's departed soul.

It was then Melinda discovered the mirror in her hand—the mirror she had found on the porch. With reverence, she placed it, clear as a circular pond, upon the marble-topped table. She felt a moment's sharp grief for Marty's girl, quickly followed by respect for Aunt Abbie's ever-accurate prognostications. Melinda's breast was full of sorrow and it almost burst with pride.

With humility, Melinda took a step closer to the wreath. The rose had begun to take form, bright and shining, under Aunt Abbie's able fingers.

"Where is she?" asked Melinda in hushed tones. "Did you lay her out on your cot, Aunt Abbie?"

"She went walkin' to death, Melinda." Aunt Abbie turned from her work and pierced Melinda with eyes that held the gift of knowledge. "Some folk do that, Melinda. They go walkin' out to meet their death. Marty's girl went out to meet hers and tumbled right over into the gorge."

Melinda could see it—the girl with outstretched arms—the gorge a black and yawning mouth.

"She's there *now*?" Melinda asked.

"Right down in the gorge. A broken flower." Aunt Abbie returned to the wreath.

Melinda watched the bright hair snake through linen. She was fully aware that Aunt Abbie never snipped a live lock. Never. How many times had she observed

Aunt Abbie's assistance to the dying?   The mirror held patiently near to parted lips until no further fog clouded the surface.   *Then* came the slash of scissors, and an aster grew upon the wreath, a russet chrysanthemum—now a rose.

Melinda's sorrowful, pride-filled mind knew perplexity.   If Marty's girl had walked to death, had toppled over the rim and dropped deep in the gorge to meet it, how had Aunt Abbie gone through the rites, those never-changing rites of the mirror, the slash of blades and the lock of hair?

Melinda retreated a reluctant step.

How?

Melinda's mind groped for understanding through its fog of indecision.   Aunt Abbie was spry, spry as a mountain goat, but Melinda hadn't known she was spry enough to spring up the sheer face of the gorge—with scissors, hair and a mirror in her hand.

Melinda heaved a final sigh of acceptance.   She guessed she was, though.   Aunt Abbie, with her second sight and her talent for keeping the record, could do most anything, Melinda guessed.

"That's a mighty pretty rose," she said at last.

"Mighty pretty.   And ain't it red?"

AVRAM DAVIDSON

The Cost of Kent Castwell

Clem Goodhue met the train with his taxi. If old Mrs. Merriman were aboard he would be sure of at least one passenger. Furthermore, old Mrs. Merriman had somehow gotten the idea that the minimum fare was a dollar. It was really seventy-five cents, but Clem had never been able to see a reason for telling her that. However, she was not aboard that morning. Sam Wells was. He was coming back from the city—been to put in a claim to have his pension increased—but Sam Wells wouldn't pay five cents to ride any distance under five miles. Clem disregarded him.

After old Sam a thin, brown-haired kid got off the train. Next came a girl, also thin and also brown-haired, who Clem thought was maybe the kid's teenage sister. Actually, it was the kid's mother.

After *that* came Kent Castwell.

Clem had seen him before, early in the summer. Strangers were not numerous in Ashby, particularly strangers who got ugly and caused commotions in bars. So Clem wouldn't forget him in a hurry. Big, husky fellow. Always seemed to be sneering at something. But the girl and the kid hadn't been with him then.

"Taxi?" Clem called.

Castwell ignored him, began to take down luggage from the train. But the young girl holding the kid by the hand turned and said, "Yes—just a minute."

"Where to?" Clem asked, when the luggage was in the taxi.

"The old Peabody place," the girl said. "You know where that is?"

"Yes. But nobody lives there any more."

"Somebody does now. Us." The big man swore as he fiddled with the handle of the right-hand door. It was tied with ropes. "Why don't you fix this thing or get a new one?"

"Costs money," Clem said. Then, "Peabody place? Have to charge you three dollars for that."

"Let's go dammit, let's go!"

After they'd started off, Castwell said, "I'm giving you two bucks. Probably twice what it's worth, anyway."

Half-turning his head, Clem protested. "I told you, mister, it was three."

"And I'm telling you, mister," Castwell mimicked the driver's New England accent, "that I'm giving you two."

Clem argued that the Peabody place was far out. He mentioned the price of gas, the bad condition of the road, the wear on the tires. The big man yawned. Then he used a word which Clem rarely used himself, and never in the presence of women and children. But this young woman and child didn't seem to notice.

"Stop off at Nickerson's Real Estate Office," Castwell said.

Levi P. Nickerson, who was also the County Tax Assessor, said, "Mr. Castwell. I assume this is Mrs. Castwell?"

"If that's your assumption, go right ahead," said Kent. And laughed.

It wasn't a pleasant laugh. The woman smiled faintly, so L.P. Nickerson allowed himself an economical chuckle. Then he cleared his throat. City people had odd ideas of what was funny. Meanwhile, though—

"Now, Mr. Castwell. About this place you're renting. I didn't realize—you didn't mention—that you had this little one, here."

Kent said, "What if I didn't mention it? It's my own business. I haven't got all *day*—"

Nickerson pointed out that the Peabody place stood all alone, isolated, with no other house for at least a mile and no other children in the neighborhood. Mrs. Castwell—if, indeed, she *was*—said that this wouldn't matter much, because Kathie would be in school most of the day.

"School. Well, that's it, you see. The school bus, in the first place, will have to go three miles off what's been its regular route to pick up your little girl. And that means the road will have to be plowed regular—snow gets real deep up in these parts, you know. Up till now, with nobody living in the old Peabody place, we never had to bother with the road. Now, this means," and he began to count off on his fingers, "first, it'll cost Ed Westlake, he drives the school bus, more than he figured on when he bid for the contract; second, it'll cost the County to keep your road open. That's besides the cost of the girl's schooling, which is third."

Kent Castwell said that was tough, wasn't it? "Let's have the keys, Nick," he said.

A flicker of distaste at the familiarity crossed the real estate man's face. "You don't seem to realize that all this extra expense to the County isn't covered by the tax assessment on the Peabody place," he pointed out. "Now, it just so happens that there's a house right on the outskirts of town become available this week. Miss Sarah Beech passed on, and her sister, Miss Lavinia, moved in with their married sister, Mrs. Calvin Adams. 'Twon't cost *you* any more, and it would save *us* considerable."

Castwell, sneering, got up. "What! Me live where some old-maid landlady can be on my neck all the time about messing up her pretty things? Thanks a lot. No thanks." He held out his hand. "The keys, kid. Gimme the keys."

Mr. Nickerson gave him the keys. Afterwards he was to say, and to say often, that he wished he'd thrown them into Lake Amastanquit, instead.

The income of the Castwell menage was not large and consisted of a monthly check and a monthly money order. The check came on the fifteenth, from a city trust company, and was assumed by some to be inherited income. Others argued in favor of its being a remittance paid by Castwell's family to keep him away. The money order was made out to Louise Cane, and signed by an army sergeant in Alaska.   The young woman said this was alimony, and that Sergeant Burndall was her former husband.   Tom Tally, at the grocery store, had her sign the endorsement twice, as Louise Cane and as Louise Castwell.   Tom was a cautious man.

Castwell gave Louise a hard time, there was no doubt about that.   If she so much as walked in between the sofa, on which he spent most of his time, and the television, he'd leap up and belt her.   More than once both she and the kid had to run out of the house to get away from him.   He wouldn't follow, as a rule, because he was barefooted, as a rule, and it was too much trouble to put his shoes on.

Lie on the sofa and drink beer and watch television all afternoon, and hitch into town and drink bar whiskey and watch television all evening—that was Kent Castwell's daily schedule.   He got to know who drove along the road regularly, at what time, and in which direction, and he'd be there, waiting.   There was more than one who could have dispensed with the pleasure of his company, but he'd get out in the road and wave his arms and not move until the car he got in front of stopped.

What could you do about it?   Put him in jail?

Sure you could.

He hadn't been living there a week before he got into a fight at the Ashby Bar.

"Disturbing the peace, using profane and abusive language, and resisting arrest— that will be ten dollars or ten days on each of the charges," said Judge Paltiel Bradford.   "And count yourself lucky it's not more.   Pay the Clerk."

But Castwell, his ugly leer in no way improved by the dirt and bruises on his face, said, "I'll take jail."

Judge Bradford's long jaw set, then loosened.   "Look here, Mr. Castwell, that was just legal language on my part.   The jail is closed up.   Hasn't been anybody in there since July."   It was then November.   "It would have to be heated, and illuminated, and the water turned on, and a guard hired.   To say nothing of feeding you.   Now, I don't see why the County should be put to all that expense on your account.   You pay the Clerk thirty dollars.   You haven't got it on you, take till tomorrow.   Well?"

"I'll take the jail."

"It's most inconvenient—"

"That's too bad, Your Honor."

The judge glared at him.   Gamaliel Coolidge, the District Attorney, stood up. "Perhaps the Court would care to suspend sentence," he suggested.   "Seeing it is the defendant's first offense."

The Court did care.   But the next week Kent was back again, on the same charge.   Altogether the sentence now came to sixty dollars, or sixty days.   And again Castwell chose jail.

"I don't generally do this," the judge said, fuming.   "But I'll let you pay your fine off in installments.   Considering you have a wife and child."

"Uh-uh.   I'll take jail."

"You won't like the food!" warned His Honor.

Castwell said he guessed the food would be up to the legal requirements. If it wasn't, he said, the State Board of Prison Inspectors would hear about it.

Some pains were taken to see that the food served Kent during his stay in jail was beyond the legal requirements—if not much beyond. The last time the State Board had inspected the County Jail it had cost the tax-payers two hundred dollars in repairs. It was costing them quite enough to incarcerate Kent Castwell, as it was, although the judge had reduced the cost by ordering the sentences to run concurrently.

All in all, Kent spent over a month in jail that winter, at various times. It seemed to some that whenever his money ran out he let the County support him, and let the woman and child fend for themselves. Tom Talley gave them a little credit at the store. Not much.

Ed Westlake, when he bid again for the school bus contract, added the cost of going three miles out of his way to pick up Kathie. The County had no choice but to meet the extra charge. It was considered very thoughtless of Louise to wait till *after* the contract was signed before leaving Castwell and going back to the city with her child. The side road to the Peabody place didn't have to be plowed so often, but it still had to be plowed *some*. That extra cost, just for one man! It was maddening.

It almost seemed—no, it *did* seem—as if Kent Castwell was deliberately setting himself in the face of New England respectability and thrift. The sacred words, "Eat it up, wear it out, make it do, or do without," didn't mean a thing to him. He wasn't just indifferent. He was hostile.

Ashby was not a thriving place. It had no industries. It was not a resort town, being far from sea and mountains alike, with only the shallow, muddy waters of Lake Amastanquit for a pleasure spot. Its thin-soiled farms and meager woodlots produced a scanty return for the hard labor exacted. The young people continued to leave. Kent Castwell, unfortunately, showed no signs of leaving.

All things considered, it was not surprising that Ashby had no artists' colony. It *was* rather surprising, then, that Clem Goodhue, meeting the train with his taxi, recognized Bob Laurel at once as an artist. When asked afterwards how he had known, Clem looked smug, and said that he had once been to Provincetown.

The conversation, as Clem recalled it afterwards, began with Bob Laurel's asking where he could find a house which offered low rent, peace and quiet, and a place to paint.

"So I recommended Kent Castwell," Clem said. He was talking to Sheriff Erastus Nickerson (Levi P.'s cousin) at the time.

" 'Peace and *quiet*?' " the sheriff repeated. "I know Laurel's a city fellow, and an artist, but, still and all—"

They were seated in the bar of the Ashby House, drinking their weekly small glass of beer. "I looked at it this way, Erastus," the taxi-man said. "Sure, there's empty houses all around that he could rent. Suppose *he*—this artist fellow— suppose *he* picks one off on the side road with nobody else living on it? Suppose *he* comes up with a wife out of somewhere, and suppose *she* has a school-age child?''

"You're right, Clem."

" 'Course I'm right. Bad enough for the County to be put to all that cost for *one* house, let alone two."

"You're right, Clem. But will he stay with Castwell?''

Clem shrugged. "That I can't say. But I did my best."

Laurel stayed with Castwell. He really had no choice. The big man agreed to take him in as lodger and to give over the front room for a studio. And, holding out offers of insulating the house, putting in another window, and who knows what else, Kent Castwell persuaded the unwary artist to pay several months' rent in advance. Needless to say, he drank up the money and did nothing at all in the way of the promised improvements.

Neither District Attorney Gamaliel Coolidge nor Sheriff Nickerson, nor, for that matter, anyone else, showed Laurel much sympathy. He had grounds for a civil suit, they said; nothing else. It should be a lesson to him not to throw his money around in the future, they said.

So the unhappy artist stayed on at the old Peabody place, buying his own food and cutting his own wood, and painting, painting, painting. And all the time he knew full well that his leering landlord only waited for him to go into town in order to help himself to both food and wood.

Laurel invited Clem to have a glass of beer with him more than once, just to have someone to tell his troubles to. Besides stealing his food and fuel, Kent Castwell, it seemed, played the TV at full blast when Laurel wanted to sleep; if it was too late for TV, he set the radio to roaring. At moments when the artist was intent on delicate brushwork, Castwell would decide to bring in stove-wood and drop it on the floor so that the whole house shook.

"He talks to himself in that loud, rough voice of his," Bob Laurel complained. "He has a filthy mouth. He makes fun of my painting. He—"

"I tell you what it is," Clem said. "Kent Castwell has no consideration for others. That's what it is. Yep."

Bets were taken in town, of a ten-cent cigar per bet, on how long Laurel would stand for it. Levi Nickerson, the County Tax Assessor, thought he'd leave as soon as his rent was up. Clem's opinion was that he'd leave sooner. "Money don't mean that much to city people," he pointed out.

Clem won.

When he came into Nickerson's house, Levi, who was sitting close to the small fire in the kitchen stove, wordlessly handed over the cigar. Clem nodded, put it in his pocket. Mrs. Abby Nickerson sat next to her husband, wearing a man's sweater. It had belonged to her late father, whose heart had failed to survive the first re-election of Franklin D. Roosevelt, and it still had a lot of wear left in it. Abby was unraveling old socks, and winding the wool into a ball. "Waste not, want not," was her motto—as well as that of every other old-time local resident.

On the stove a kettle steamed thinly. Two piles of used envelopes were on the table. They had all been addressed to the Tax Assessor's office of the County, and had been carefully opened so as not to mutilate them. While Clem watched, Levi Nickerson removed one of the envelopes from its place on top of the uncovered kettle. The mucilage on its flaps loosened by steam, it opened out easily to Nickerson's touch. He proceeded to refold it and then reseal it so that the used outside was now inside; then he added it to the other pile.

"Saved the County eleven dollars this way last year," he observed. "Shouldn't wonder but what I don't make it twelve this year, maybe twelve-fifty." Clem gave a small appreciative grunt. "Where is he?" the Tax Assessor asked.

"Laurel? In the Ashby Bar. He's all packed. I told him to stay put. I told them to keep an eye on him, phone me here if he made a move to leave."

He took a sheet of paper out of his pocket and put it on the table. Levi looked at it, but made no move to pick it up. To his wife he said, "I'm expecting Erastus and Gam Coolidge over, Mrs. Nickerson. County business. I expect you can find something to do in the front of the house while we talk."

Mrs. Levi nodded. Even words were not wasted.

A car drove up to the house.

"That's Erastus," said his cousin. "Gam should be along—he *is* along. Might've known he wouldn't waste gasoline; came with Erastus."

The two men came into the kitchen. Mrs. Abby Nickerson arose and departed.

"Hope we can get this over with before nightfall," the sheriff said. "I don't like to drive after dark if I can help it. One of my headlights is getting dim, and they cost so darned much to replace."

Clem cleared his throat. "Well, here 'tis," he said, gesturing to the paper on the table. "Laurel's confession. 'Tell the sheriff and the D.A. that I'm ready to give myself up,' " he says. " 'I wrote it all down here,' " he says. Happened about two o'clock this afternoon, I guess. Straw that broke the camel's back. Kent Castwell, he was acting up as usual. Stomping and swearing out there at the Peabody place. Words were exchanged. Laurel left to go out back," Clem said, delicately, not needing to further comment on the Peabody place's lack of indoor plumbing. "When he come back, Castwell had taken the biggest brush he could find and smeared paint over all the pictures Laurel had been working on. Ruined them completely."

There was a moment's silence. "Castwell had no call to do that," the sheriff said. "Destroying another man's property. They tell me some of those artists get as much as a hundred dollars for a painting . . . What'd he do then? Laurel, I mean."

"Picked up a piece of stovewood and hit him with it. Hit him hard."

"No doubt about his being dead, I suppose?" the sheriff asked.

Clem shook his head. "There was no blood or anything on the wood," he added. "Just another piece of stove wood . . . But he's dead, all right."

After a moment Levi Nickerson said, "His wife will have to be notified. No reason why the County should have to pay burial expenses. Hmm. I expect she won't have any money, though. Best get in touch with those trustees who sent Castwell his money every month. *They*'ll pay."

Gamaliel Coolidge asked if anyone else knew. Clem said no. Bob Laurel hadn't told anyone else. He didn't seem to want to talk.

This time there was a longer silence.

"Do you realize how much Kent Castwell cost this County, one way or the other?" Nickerson asked.

Clem said he supposed hundreds of dollars. "Hundreds and *hundreds* of dollars," Nickerson said.

"And," the Tax Assessor went on, "do you know what it will cost us to try this fellow—for murder in any degree or manslaughter?"

The District Attorney said it would cost thousands. "Thousands and *thousands* . . . and that's just the trial," he elaborated. "Suppose he's found guilty and appeals? We'd be obliged to fight the appeal. More thousands. And suppose he gets a new trial? We'd have it to pay all over again.

Levi P. Nickerson opened his mouth as though it hurt him to do so. "What it would do to the County tax-rate . . ." he groaned. "Kent Castwell," he said, his voice becoming crisp and definite, "is not worth it. He is just not *worth* it."

Clem took out the ten-cent cigar he'd won, sniffed it. "My opinion," he said, "it would have been much better if this fellow Laurel had just packed up and left. Anybody finding Castwell's body would assume he'd fallen and hit his head. But this confession, now—"

Sheriff Erastus Nickerson said reflectively, "I haven't read any confession. You, Gam? You, Levi? No. What you've told us, Clem, is just hearsay. Can't act on hearsay. Totally contrary to all principles of American law . . . Hmm. Mighty nice sunset." He arose and walked over to the window. His cousin followed him. So did District Attorney Coolidge. While they were looking at the sunset Clem Goodhue, after a single glance at their backs, took the sheet of paper from the kitchen table and thrust it into the kitchen stove. There was a flare of light. It quickly died down. Clem carefully reached his hand into the stove, took out the small corner of the paper remaining, and lit his cigar with it.

The three men turned from the window.

Levi P. Nickerson was first to speak. "Can't ask any of you to stay to supper," he said. "Just a few leftovers is all we're having. I expect you'll want to be going on your way."

The two other County officials nodded.

The taxi-man said, "I believe I'll stop by the Ashby Bar. Might be someone there wanting to catch the evening train. Night, Levi. Don't turn on the yard light for us."

"Wasn't going to," said Levi. "Turning them on and off, that's what burns them out. Night, Clem, Gam, Erastus." He closed the door after them. "Mrs. Nickerson," he called to his wife, "you can come and start supper now. We finished our business."

Pseudo Identity

Somewhere between four and four-thirty, Howard Jordan called his wife. "It looks like another late night," he told her. "The spot TV copy for Prentiss was full of holes. I'll be here half the night rewriting it."

"You'll stay in town?"

"No choice."

"I hope you won't have trouble finding a room."

"I'll make reservations now. Or there's always the office couch."

"Well," Carolyn said, and he heard her sigh the sigh designed to reassure him that she was sorry he would not be coming home, "I'll see you tomorrow night, then. Don't forget to call the hotel."

"I won't."

He did not call the hotel. At five, the office emptied out. At five minutes after five, Howard Jordan cleared off his desk, packed up his attaché case and left the building. He had a steak in a small restaurant around the corner from his office, then caught a cab south and west to a four-story red brick building on Christopher Street. His key opened the door, and he walked in.

In the hallway, a thin girl with long blonde hair smiled at him. "Hi, Roy."

"Hello, baby."

"Too much," she said, eyeing his clothes. "The picture of middle-class respectability."

"A mere façade. A con perpetrated upon the soulless bosses."

"Crazy. There's a party over at Ted and Betty's. You going?"

"I might."

"See you there."

He entered his own apartment, tucked his attaché case behind a low bookcase improvised of bricks and planks. In the small closet he hung his gray sharkskin suit, his button-down shirt, his rep-striped tie. He dressed again in tight Levi's and a bulky brown turtleneck sweater, changed his black moccasin toe oxfords for white hole-in-the-toe tennis sneakers. He left his wallet in the pocket of the sharkskin suit and pocketed another wallet, this one containing considerably less cash, no credit cards at all, and a few cards identifying him as Roy Baker.

He spent an hour playing chess in the back room of a Sullivan Street coffee house, winning two games of three. He joined friends in a bar a few blocks away and got into an overly impassioned argument on the cultural implications of Camp; when the bartender ejected them, he took his friends along to the party in the East Village apartment of Ted Marsh and Betty Haniford. Someone had brought a guitar, and he sat on the floor drinking wine and listening to the singing.

Ginny, the long-haired blonde who had an apartment in his building, drank too much wine. He walked her home, and the night air sobered her.

"Come up for a minute or two," she said. "I want you to hear what my analyst said this afternoon. I'll make us some coffee."

"Groovy," he said, and went upstairs with her. He enjoyed the conversation and the coffee and Ginny. An hour later, around one-thirty, he returned to his own apartment and went to sleep.

In the morning he rose, showered, put on a fresh white shirt, another striped tie, and the same gray sharkskin suit, and rode uptown to his office.

It had begun innocently enough. From the time he'd made the big jump from senior copywriter at Lowell, Burham & Plescow to copy chief at Keith Wenrall Associates, he had found himself working late more and more frequently. While the late hours never bothered him, merely depriving him of the company of a whining wife, the midnight train to New Hope was a constant source of aggravation. He never got to bed before two-thirty those nights he rode it, and then had to drag himself out of bed just four and a half hours later in order to be at his desk by nine.

It wasn't long before he abandoned the train and spent those late nights in a midtown hotel. This proved an imperfect solution, substituting inconvenience and expense for sleeplessness. It was often difficult to find a room at a late hour, always impossible to locate one for less than twelve dollars; and hotel rooms, however well appointed, did not provide such amenities as a toothbrush or a razor, not to mention a change of underwear and a clean shirt. Then too, there was something disturbingly temporary and marginal about a hotel room. It felt even less like home than did his split-level miasma in Bucks County.

An apartment, he realized, would overcome all of these objections while actually saving him money. He could rent a perfectly satisfactory place for a hundred dollars a month, less than he presently spent on hotels, and it would always be there for him, with fresh clothing in the closet and a razor and toothbrush in the bathroom.

He found the listing in the classified pages—*Christopher St, 1 rm, bth, ktte, frnshd, util, $90 mth*. He translated this and decided that a one-room apartment on Christopher Street with bathroom and kitchenette, furnished, with utilities included at ninety dollars per month, was just what he was looking for. He called the landlord and asked when he could see the apartment.

"Come around after dinner," the landlord said. He gave him the address and asked his name.

"Baker," Howard Jordan said. "Roy Baker."

After he hung up he tried to imagine why he had given a false name. It was a handy device when one wanted to avoid being called back, but it did seem pointless in this instance.   Well, no matter, he decided.   He would make certain the landlord got his name straight when he rented the apartment.   Meanwhile, he had problems enough changing a junior copywriter's flights of literary fancy into something that might actually convince a man that the girls would love him more if he used the client's brand of gunk on his hair.

The landlord, a birdlike little man with thick metal-rimmed glasses, was waiting for Jordan.

He said, "Mr. Baker?   Right this way.   First floor in the rear.   Real nice place."

The apartment was small but satisfactory.   When he agreed to rent it the landlord produced a lease, and Jordan immediately changed his mind about clearing up the matter of his own identity.   A lease, he knew, would be infinitely easier to break without his name on it.   He gave the document a casual reading, then signed it "Roy Baker" in a handwriting quite unlike his own.

"Now I'll want a hundred and eighty dollars," the landlord said.   "That's a month's rent in advance and a month's security."

Jordan reached for his checkbook, then realized his bank would be quite unlikely to honor a check with Roy Baker's signature on it.   He paid the landlord in cash, and arranged to move in the next day.

He spent the following day's lunch hour buying extra clothing for the apartment, selecting bed linen, and finally purchasing a suitcase to accommodate the items he had bought.   On a whim, he had the suitcase monogrammed "R.B."   That night he worked late, told Carolyn he would be staying in a hotel, then carried the suitcase to his apartment, put his new clothes in the closet, put his new toothbrush and razor in the tiny bathroom and, finally, made his bed and lay in it.   At this point Roy Baker was no more than a signature on a lease and two initials on a suitcase.

Two months later, Roy Baker was a person.

The process by which Roy Baker's bones were clad with flesh was a gradual one.   Looking back on it, Jordan could not tell exactly how it had begun, or at what point it had become purposeful.   Baker's personal wardrobe came into being when Jordan began to make the rounds of village bars and coffee houses, and wanted to look more like a neighborhood resident and less like a celebrant from uptown.   He bought denim trousers, canvas shoes, bulky sweaters; and when he shed his three-button suit and donned his Roy Baker costume, he was transformed as utterly as Bruce Wayne clad in Batman's mask and cape.

When he met people in the building or around the neighborhood, he automatically introduced himself as Baker.   This was simply expedient; it wouldn't do to get into involved discussions with casual acquaintances, telling them that he answered to one name but lived under another, but by being Baker instead of Jordan, he could play a far more interesting role.   Jordan, after all, was a square, a Madison Avenue copy chief, an animal of little interest to the folksingers and artists and actors he met in the village.   Baker, on the other hand, could be whatever Jordan wanted him to be.   Before long his identity took form: he was an artist, he'd been unable to do any serious work since his wife's tragic death, and for the time being he was stuck in a square job with a commercial art studio.

This identity he had picked for Baker was a source of occasional amusement to him. Its expedience aside, he was not blind to its psychological implications. Substitute *writer* for *artist* and one approached his own situation. He had long dreamed of being a writer, but had made no efforts toward serious writing since his marriage to Carolyn. The bit about the tragic death of his wife was nothing more than simple wish-fulfillment. Nothing would have pleased him more than Carolyn's death, so he had incorporated this dream in Baker's biography.

As the weeks passed, Baker accumulated more and more of the trappings of personality. He opened a bank account. It was, after all, inconvenient to pay the rent in cash. He joined a book club and promptly wound up on half the world's mailing lists. He got a letter from his congressman advising him of latest developments in Washington and the heroic job his elected representative was doing to safeguard his interests. Before very long, he found himself heading for his Christopher Street apartment even on nights when he did not have to work late at all.

Interestingly enough, his late work actually decreased once he was settled in the apartment. Perhaps he had only developed the need to work late out of a larger need to avoid going home to Carolyn. In any event, now that he had a place to go after work, he found it far less essential to stay around the office after five o'clock. He rarely worked late more than one night a week—but he always spent three nights a week in town, and often four.

Sometimes he spent the evening with friends. Sometimes he stayed in his apartment and rejoiced in the blessings of solitude. Other times he combined the best of two worlds by finding an agreeable village female to share his solitude.

He kept waiting for the double life to catch up with him, anticipating the tension and insecurity which were always a component of such living patterns in the movies and on television. He expected to be discovered, or overcome by guilt, or otherwise to have the error of his dual ways brought forcibly home to him. But this did not happen. His office work showed a noticeable improvement; he was not only more efficient, but his copy was fresher, more inspired, more creative. He was doing more work in less time and doing a better job of it. Even his home life improved, if only in that there was less of it.

Divorce? He thought about it, imagined the joy of being Roy Baker on a fulltime basis. It would be financially devastating, he knew. Carolyn would wind up with the house and the car and the lion's share of his salary, but Roy Baker could survive on a mere fraction of Howard Jordan's salary, existing quite comfortably without house or car. He never relinquished the idea of asking Carolyn for a divorce, nor did he ever quite get around to it—until one night he saw her leaving a night club on West Third Street, her black hair blowing in the wind, her step drunkenly unsteady, and a man's arm curled possessively around her waist.

His first reaction was one of astonishment that anyone would actually desire her. With all the vibrant, fresh-bodied girls in the Village, why would anyone be interested in Carolyn? It made no sense to him.

Then, suddenly, his puzzlement gave way to absolute fury. She had been cold to him for years, and now she was running around with other men, adding insult to injury. She let him support her, let him pay off the endless mortgage on the horrible house, let him sponsor her charge accounts while she spent her way toward the list of Ten Best-Dressed Women. She took everything from him and gave nothing to him, and all the while she was giving it to someone else.

He knew, then, that he hated her, that he had always hated her and, finally, that he was going to do something about it.

What? Hire detectives? Gather evidence? Divorce her as an adulteress? Small revenge, hardly the punishment that fit the crime.

No. No, *he* could not possibly do anything about it. It would be too much out of character for him to take positive action. He was the good clean-living, midtown-square type, good old Howie Jordan. He would do all that such a man could do, bearing his new knowledge in silence, pretending that he knew nothing, and going on as before.

But Roy Baker could do more.

From that day on he let his two lives overlap. On the nights when he stayed in town he went directly from the office to a nearby hotel, took a room, rumpled up the bed so that it would look as though it had been slept in, then left the hotel by back staircase and rear exit. After a quick cab ride downtown and a change of clothes, he became Roy Baker again and lived Roy Baker's usual life, spending just a little more time than usual around West Third Street. It wasn't long before he saw her again. This time he followed her. He found out that her lover was a self-styled folk singer named Stud Clement, and he learned by discreet inquiries that Carolyn was paying Stud's rent.

"Stud inherited her from Phillie Wells when Phillie split for the coast," someone told him. "She's got some square husband in Connecticut or someplace. If Stud's not on the scene, she don't care who she goes home with."

She had been at this, then, for some time. He smiled bitterly. It was true, he decided; the husband was really the last to know.

He went on using the midtown hotel, creating a careful pattern for his life, and he kept careful patterns on Stud Clement. One night when Carolyn didn't come to town, he managed to stand next to the big folk singer in a Hudson Street bar and listen to him talk. He caught the slight Tennessee accent, the pitch of the voice, the type of words that Clement used.

Through it all he waited for his hatred to die, waited for his fury to cool. In a sense she had done no more to him than he had done to her. He half expected that he would lose his hatred sooner or later, but he found that he hated her more every day, not only for cheating but for making him an ad man instead of a writer, for making him live in that house instead of a Village apartment, for all the things she had done to ruin every aspect of his life. If it had not been for her, he would have been Roy Baker all his life. She had made a Howard Jordan of him, and for that he would hate her forever.

Once he realized this, he made the phone call. "I gotta see you tonight," he said.

"Stud?"

So the imitation was successful. "Not at my place," he said quickly. "193 Christopher, Apartment I-D. Seven-thirty, no sooner and no later. And don't be going near my place."

"Trouble?"

"Just be there," he said, and hung up.

His own phone rang in less than five minutes. He smiled a bitter smile as he answered it.

She said, "Howard? I was wondering, you're not coming home tonight, are you? You'll have to stay at your hotel in town?"

"I don't know," he said. "I've got a lot of work, but I hate to be away from you so much. Maybe I'll let it slide for a night—"

"No!" He heard her gasp. Then she recovered, and her voice was calm when she spoke again. "I mean, your career comes first, darling. You know that. You shouldn't think of me. Think of your job."

"Well," he said, enjoying all this, "I'm not sure—"

"I've got a dreary headache anyway, darling. Why not stay in town? We'll have the weekend together—"

He let her talk him into it. After she rang off, he called his usual hotel and made his usual reservation for eleven-thirty. He went back to work, left the office at five-thirty, signed the register downstairs and left the building. He had a quick bite at a lunch counter and was back at his desk at six o'clock, after signing the book again on the way in.

At a quarter to seven he left the building again, this time failing to sign himself out. He took a cab to his apartment and was inside it by ten minutes after seven. At precisely seven-thirty there was a knock on his door. He answered it, and she stared at him as he dragged her inside. She couldn't figure it out; her face contorted.

"I'm going to kill you, Carolyn," he said, and showed her the knife. She died slowly, and noisily. Her cries would have brought out the National Guard anywhere else in the country, but they were in New York now, and New Yorkers never concern themselves with the shrieks of dying women.

He took the few clothes that did not belong to Baker, scooped up Carolyn's purse, and got out of the apartment. From a pay phone on Sheridan Square he called the air terminal and made a reservation. Then he taxied back to the office and slipped inside, again without writing his name in the register.

At eleven-fifteen he left the office, went to his hotel and slept much more soundly than he had expected. He went to the office in the morning and had his secretary put in three calls to New Hope. No one answered.

That was Friday. He took his usual train home, rang his bell a few times, used his key, called Carolyn's name several times, then made himself a drink. After half an hour he called the next door neighbor and asked her if she knew where his wife was. She didn't. After another three hours he called the police.

Sunday a local policeman came around to see him. Evidently Carolyn had had her fingerprints taken once, maybe when she'd held a civil service job before they were married. The New York police had found the body Saturday evening, and it had taken them a little less than twenty-four hours to run a check on the prints and trace Carolyn to New Hope.

"I hoped I wouldn't have to tell you this," the policeman said. "When you reported your wife missing, we talked to some of the neighbors. It looks as though she was—uh—stepping out on you, Mr. Jordan. I'm afraid it had been going on for some time. There were men she met in New York. Does the name Roy Baker mean anything to you?"

"No. Was he—"

"I'm afraid he was one of the men she was seeing, Mr. Jordan. I'm afraid he killed her, sir."

Howard's reactions combined hurt and loss and bewilderment in proper proportion. He almost broke down when they had him view the body but managed to hold himself together stoically. He learned from the New York police that Roy Baker was a Village type, evidently some sort of irresponsible artist. Baker had made a reservation on a plane shortly after killing Carolyn but hadn't picked up his ticket, evidently realizing that the police would be able to trace him. He'd no doubt take a plane under another name, but they were certain they would catch up with him before too long.

"He cleared out in a rush," the policeman said. "Left his clothes, never got to empty out his bank account. A guy like this, he's going to turn up in a certain kind of place. The Village, North Beach in Frisco, maybe New Orleans. He'll be back in the Village within a year, I'll bet on it, and when he does we'll pick him up."

For form's sake, the New York police checked Jordan's whereabouts at the time of the murder, and they found that he'd been at his office until eleven-fifteen, except for a half hour when he'd had a sandwich around the corner, and that he had spent the rest of the night at the hotel where he always stayed when he worked late.

That, incredibly, was all there was to it.

After a suitable interval, Howard put the New Hope house on the market and sold it almost immediately at a better price than he had thought possible.

He moved to town, stayed at his alibi hotel while he checked the papers for a Village apartment.

He was in a cab, heading downtown for a look at a three-room apartment on Horatio Street, before he realized suddenly that he could not possibly live in the Village, not now. He was known there as Roy Baker, and if he went there he would be identified as Roy Baker and arrested as Roy Baker, and that would be the end of it.

"Better turn around," he told the cab driver. "Take me back to the hotel. I changed my mind."

He spent another two weeks in the hotel, trying to think things through, looking for a safe way to live Roy Baker's life again. If there was an answer, he couldn't find it. The casual life of the Village had to stay out of bounds.

He took an apartment uptown on the East Side. It was quite expensive but he found it cold and charmless. He took to spending his free evenings at midtown nightclubs, where he drank a little too much and spent a great deal of money to see poor floor shows.   He didn't get out often, though, because he seemed to be working late more frequently now.   It was harder and harder to get everything done on time.   On top of that, his work had lost its sharpness; he had to go over blocks of copy again and again to get them right.

Revelation came slowly, painfully.   He began to see just what he had done to himself.

In Roy Baker, he had found the one perfect life for himself.   The Christopher Street apartment, the false identity, the new world of new friends and different clothes and words and customs, had been a world he took to with ease because it was the perfect world for him.   The mechanics of preserving this dual identity, the taut fabric of lies that clothed it, the childlike delight in pure secrecy, had added a sharp element of excitement to it all.   He had enjoyed being Roy Baker; more, he had enjoyed being Howard Jordan playing at being Roy Baker.

The double life suited him so perfectly that he had felt no great need to divorce Carolyn.

Instead, he had killed her—and killed Roy Baker in the bargain, erased him very neatly, put him out of the picture for all time.

Howard bought a pair of Levi's, a turtleneck sweater, a pair of white tennis sneakers.   He kept these clothes in the closet of his Sutton Place apartment, and now and then when he spent a solitary evening there he dressed in his Roy Baker costume and sat on the floor drinking California wine straight from the jug.   He wished he were playing chess in the back room of a coffee house, or arguing art and religion in a Village bar, or listening to a blue guitar at a loft party.

He could dress up all he wanted in his Roy Baker costume, but it wouldn't work. He could drink wine and play guitar music on his stereo, but that wouldn't work, either.   He could buy women, but he couldn't walk them home from Village parties and make love to them in third-floor walk-ups.

He had to be Howard Jordan.

Carolyn or no Carolyn, married or single, New Hope split-level or Sutton Place apartment, one central fact remained unchanged.   He simply did not like being Howard Jordan.

JACK RITCHIE

That Russian!

Ah, how Nadia could run—like a gazelle, like an antelope—for at least ten seconds; Mariska too.

For myself, I throw my weight around—which is the hammer.

On the upper deck of this Russian boat which travels to the sports meet in the United States, I stand and eat a sandwich while I watch these Russians at mass exercise, back and forth, right and left, and up and down.

It is not that we Hungarians do not exercise. It is simply that we are more individual about this. We do not want a loud-voice on a platform telling us what to do—especially if it is in Russian.

I observe the women's group down below and the overwhelming number of sturdy legs, but Nadia does not have sturdy legs. They are long and at a glance one sees that she can run and probably must, for she has lustrous black hair and violet eyes and one thinks of the ballet rather than the cinder track.

Mariska appears at my side. "You are watching Nadia again?" she asks. "That *Russian?*"

Mariska is the fastest woman in all Hungary. This is true also for events in Poland and Italy. However, in Western Germany and France, she comes in second to Nadia in the 100 meter dash.

It is obvious that Mariska is very jealous of Nadia's running—fifty percent of the time, at least—and from the narrowness of her eyes, I have the feeling that in America they will settle this once and for all.

"We should have defected in Germany or France," Mariska says. "Or even Italy."

I shake my head. "No, Mariska. Since our ultimate goal is the freedom of America, does it not pay to remain with the team until it arrives there? In this manner we are assured free passage."

We become aware that Boris Volakov has moved beside us.

Boris is a most unpopular man. He is commissar for the Russian team, plus in overall charge of the voyage. It is a rumor that his unfavorable reports have caused the disappearance of one high jumper, one long distance runner, and one hop, skip, and jump.

"You are attending the All-Nations Friendship Party on board tomorrow night?" he asks.

With the Russians, we speak English.   It is a beautiful language and besides it irritates them.

"I am sorry," Mariska says, "but I am developing a cold."

"I have this trouble with my sinuses," I say.   "This always requires forty-eight hours for the cure."

Boris smiles like a shark and is not disturbed.   "I have talked to the leaders of all nationalities and they will see that medical problems of that nature are cleared up by the time of the party."

He looks Mariska up and down.   "I have always admired the Hungarians.   I have spent some time in Budapest."

"Oh?" Mariska says with great sweetness.   "As a tourist?"

He clears his throat.   "Not exactly."

Now, on the deck below, the exercises have come to a close and the group is dismissed.

Boris excuses himself and walks toward the iron stairs which lead to the lower decks.

Nadia looks up and sees that he is coming down.   Very casually, but firmly, she begins to walk away.

It is interesting to watch—from my height—this pursuit and the evasion, this looking back over the shoulder, this increasing of the pace, this series of sharp right and left turns around lifeboats and funnels.

I study the situation and see that eventually she is about to be trapped—for this Boris is tricky and foresighted.

"I think I will go downstairs," I say to Mariska.

She looks at me, but says nothing.

I go down the stairs and after five minutes, manage to intercept Nadia.   "This way," I say, and take her arm.

"Oh," she says, "it is you again," for we have met and talked before whenever I was able to create the opportunity.

She comes where I take her, which is to crouch behind a winch, and we wait. Soon Boris passes by, the yellow gleam of pursuit still in his eyes.

Nadia takes a deep breath.   "So far I have been saved by one thing or another, but I am running out of miracles and excuses."

"Why are excuses even necessary?" I say.   "Is not a simple 'no' in his face enough?"

She looks at me like I am a child.   "Life is not always that simple.   Boris is a man of much influence."

"Ah yes," I say wisely.   "I understand that he has sent three men to Siberia."

She smiles, but tightly.   "They were not men and they were not sent to Siberia. We are no longer that primitive in the treatment of our athletes.   They were women who said 'no' and they were simply dismissed from the team.   Today they are teaching calisthenics to pre-school children in Kandalaksha, which is just beyond the Arctic Circle, but still in Europe."

"Nadia," I say, "France is a nice country and free—in a capitalistic way, of course—and this is true also of Western Germany and Italy.   Why did you not seek asylum in one of these places?   It is unlikely that Boris would have continued pursuit.''

She shakes her head.   "No.   I could not do anything like that.''

"You have relatives in Russia?   They would be liquidated?''

"We no longer liquidate relatives,'' she says stiffly.   "However, I do not wish to leave the team.   It is a great honor to be a member and this I would not willingly give up.''

I feel anger stirring.   "So remaining on the team is of greater importance than your honor?''

She looks frosty.   "I would prefer to have both.''

She thinks more on the subject of Boris.   "He is the commissar of the athletes,'' she says bitterly, "but in his life he has yet to run even the one hundred meter dash.   He is greedy and opportunistic.   He goes as the wind blows—wherever it is easiest, wherever he has the most to gain for himself.   This is how he has come to his present position, after beginning as the custodian of the uniforms.   Also, I think that in Russia he was a speculator in the black market, but has always been too clever to be caught.''

I rub my jaw.   To me has come the expression that if a mountain does not come to the Mohammedans, then it is necessary for the Mohammedans to go to the mountain.   "Do not despair,'' I say, "I will personally work on this problem.''

That evening in the dining room, I sit at Boris' table—which is easy, for there is always room—and over tea I ask, "Have you ever been to New York?''

"No,'' Boris says.   "I know nothing about America except that the poor are exploited by the rich.''

"How true,'' I say, and then sigh.   "It is unfortunate, but I will not be able to visit my cousin Stephen when we arrive there.   He is one of these rich exploiters.''

Boris is interested.   "Rich?   But why can you not go to see him?''

I smile sadly.   "Because he is a defector and as a loyal member of the party, I certainly would not want to be seen in his presence.   He fled from Hungary two years ago.''

Boris' mind fastened on one point.   "A *rich* defector?   Before he defected, did he somehow manage to—ah—transfer money to some Swiss bank?   Hm?''

"No,'' I say.   "When Stephen arrived in America, he was penniless.''

Boris thinks on this too.   "He defected but two years ago, but *today* he is rich?''

I nod.   "He has a large estate in Hoboken, a swimming pool, two limousines, three mistresses, and eight horses.''

Boris is impressed.   "Three?   But how did this all happen?''

"It is all the responsibility of his agent, who has the strange American name of John Smith.   This John Smith had Stephen's experiences written into a book which has become a best seller.   And also it will soon be made into a motion picture in which Stephen will hold a percentage.''

Boris is puzzled.   "But there are tens of thousands of defectors.   Surely not every one of them could write a book and expect to make so much money?''

"Of course not,'' I say.   "But Stephen was an important man behind the Iron—'' I clear my throat "—in our country.   He was a commissar overseeing the Fejer Building Institue. Perhaps you have heard of his book? *I Was a Commissar for the F.B.I.?"*

Boris frowns. "It is somehow vaguely familiar."

"People are extremely interested in Stephen," I say. "There is a shortage of commissars in America, for not many of them defect. They know when they have it good."

Boris agrees. "Good, yes. But riches, no." He looks very casual. "This John Smith agent, where does he live, this capitalist pig?"

"In Chicago at a place called State Street. Probably his name is in the telephone book."

When I rise to leave Boris is still thinking about my cousin Stephen, who does not exist.

The night of the Friendship Party there comes a thick fog upon the ocean and it is necessary for the ship to slow almost to a halt and blow its horns often. Even so, we almost run into other ships, for we are now near New York and the traffic lanes are heavy.

In the dining room, I find that Nadia, Mariska, and I have been assigned to Boris' table.

He talks hardly at all. Mostly he is preoccupied and he drinks a good deal.

It is a yawning evening until ten when there is trouble in the bar among the united Czechoslovakians. The Czechs and the Slovakians begin to fight and the Ruthenians watch and smile.

When order is restored, I notice that Boris has left his previous thoughts and is now looking at Nadia.

His voice is thick with the drink. "Nadia, let us, you and I, walk about the deck."

"No," Nadia says. "The fog is bad for my throat."

"You are not a singer," Boris snaps and then he glares at her. "How would you like to teach calisthenics to pre-school children?"

The band strikes up with dance music and I immediately sweep Nadia upon the floor.

"Nadia," I say, "this is not the moment to spill the soup in the ointment. You must cooperate with Boris for the time being."

She is shocked. "You, of all people, to say *that?"*

I explain hastily. "I mean only for this walk on the foggy deck. You can come to no harm, for I think that he has drunk too much to be dangerous. I even wonder whether he can still walk at all."

She studies me. "Just what are you up to, Janos?"

I smile. "I have a clever plan and I will tell you when it works. I have the feeling that soon you will never see Boris again."

When we return from the dance, Nadia is more friendly and soon she and Boris rise and move toward the door. He walks much better than I anticipate and so I begin to worry.

Finally I too rise and walk out into the fog. I hesitate. Where have they gone? To the right or to the left? I listen, but I hear nothing.

I turn to the right and after a dozen steps I bump into two people who are much close together. I recognize the man as a Czech high jumper and the woman as a Rumanian gymnast, which is bad politics at the present time, but they do not seem to care.

"Pardon," I say. "Did anyone pass this way recently?"

The man peers into my face and is relieved that I am not a commissar. "No," he says. "Not that we notice."

I go in the opposite direction, bumping into objects occasionally and listening. All I hear is the groan of horns near and far, and when there is no horn noise, it appears that I am in a vacuum of silence. I think that I may have taken the wrong direction after all, but then I hear the commencing of a scream. It is muffled by the fog and yet I feel that it is near.

I press on immediately and after only twenty feet I come upon Boris and Nadia, and I see that he is considerably less drunk than I had thought. When I see what could be impending, fury springs into my blood and I forget all about Mohammedans and their mountains. I spring forward shouting a nationalist war cry.

Boris is considerably surprised by my entrance out of the fog, but he becomes even more so when I immediately grasp him by one arm and one leg and swing him in a circle. . . once. . . twice. . . and then I let go.

It is a great fling, perhaps a world's record for this type of event. Boris and his scream fly through a thin patch in the fog and over the ship's rail.

Nadia joins me and we look into the swirling white gray which hides the water. "Was this your clever plan?" she asks.

"No," I say sadly. "There is many a slip between the cup and the ship."

We are now silent and I try to think about this predicament.

"Nadia," I finally say, "I will surrender myself and confess. I will say that you were not even here. It was a personal quarrel."

"Nonsense," Nadia says. "Since no one has rushed here, evidently the fog muffled his scream and he was not heard. We will simply walk away. Boris just disappeared, and we know nothing about it at all."

"But you were seen leaving the ballroom with him," I say. "There will be questions asked. And there is no Supreme Court to throw out the confession that will inevitably follow."

Nadia offers another idea. "We will say it was an accident which we both witnessed. Boris slipped and fell overboard."

I shook my head. "I do not think we will be believed. It is generally established that commissars do not meet death by accident."

We are silent again and then I sigh. "Nadia, I do not worry for myself. If no one heard the scream, I do not think that Boris will be missed before tomorrow and we will have arrived in New York by then. Freedom is but a leap or a dash beyond."

She is wide-eyed. "You are going to defect?"

"Yes," I say. "We have planned upon this for a long time."

The wide eyes become narrow eyes. "We? Who is we?"

"Mariska and I."

Her lips tighten.   It is strange how these women athletes are so jealous of each other's ability to run.   Among men, there is more sportsmanship.

"America is a big country," I say.   "It is big enough for *two* runners of excellence."

"I doubt this," she says, but sighs.   "However, I do not think I have much of a choice."

We arrive in clear weather at the Port of New York the next morning.   Soon we descend the gangplank while the ship's loudspeaker calls out for Boris to report to his contingent.

There is a rumor—which Nadia and I have started—that Boris has drunk too much and fallen asleep in some corner of the ship.

We step without trouble onto American soil and are taken to the hotel.

I would have preferred to participate first in the sports meet before defecting—as would Nadia and Mariska—but to postpone our defecting could possibly be fatal. So at the first opportunity, the three of us join and find the nearest police station and declare ourselves to be political refugees.

It is something I have never regretted, and three months later—at my wedding—I see Bela, a pole vaulter on our team who also defected, but after the meet. Evidently he has heard that I was to marry and wished to attend the event.

We shake hands and he smiles.   "So it was you who threw Boris overboard," he says.

Perhaps I pale a bit, for if this is made public information, I am ruined.   The Americans would not shield a murderer, even if the victim is a Russian.   "Did you witness the event?"   I ask quickly.

He shakes his head.   "No.   But I have just heard that Boris himself maintains that this happened."

I blink.   "Boris Volakov is alive?"

Bela smiles.   "You tossed him overboard just as a small freighter glided past in the fog, and Boris landed unnoticed on the canvas top of a lifeboat.   The length of the fall, however, rendered him unconscious for perhaps a half hour."

I take a breath of relief.

Bela continues.   "When Boris awoke and ascertained that he was alive and on another ship, he rushed immediately to the captain on the bridge and announced that he was declaring himself a political refugee who wished to remain in the west, and he also wanted to send swiftly a radiogram to a Mr. John Smith of State Street, Chicago."

I sighed.   "So Boris is now in America?"

Bela smiled again.   "No.   Unfortunately for Boris, the ship upon which you tossed him turned out to be a Russian freighter."

It was a successful wedding.   I was handsome and Nadia, my bride, looked beautiful.

The maid of honor, of course, was Mariska, my sister.

Galton and the Yelling Boys

"**H**uman nature," said Mike Galton, the captain of detectives, "is the key to man's universe. And," the old man went on, "if you want my opinion, a good, experienced cop knows more about human nature than a good, experienced psychiatrist."

Detective Bill Dennis, his young sidekick, said, "Oh, come on, Cap. That's stretching it a little."

They were having coffee with the desk sergeant and it was a mild May night with a full moon up. "I think he's right, Bill," the sergeant said.

"Given equal mentalities, of course," the old man cautioned. "But the reason I say that is because the opportunities are so great. We routinely encounter examples of human behavior the average man couldn't imagine, and psychiatrists have only read about."

The others couldn't gainsay that and were silent a moment, reflecting on personal experiences. Galton lighted his pipe and sat back enjoying the night. It had been a quiet one, with the citizens, for the most part, behaving themselves. There'd been a complaint of a fight over in the east end of town, but it was a husband and wife, and the appearance of a patrolman stopped it. There'd been a complaint south of City Park about a car full of boys helling it up, yelling and honking, but they were gone by the time the radio car went by. Even the missing child, reported by a frantic mother at six o'clock, had turned up fifteen minutes later. Violence had not gone abroad that night. The natives weren't restless and the police on duty could relax over their coffee, talk about non-cop things, and let the softness of the night steal through the open doors.

Then there was a screech of brakes, the slamming of a car door, and the clatter of racing feet on the outside steps. Galton sighed with regret, for the sounds told him peace was at an end even before the youth burst through the doorway and rushed up to the desk.

He was about nineteen, tall, with curly hair and good quality clothes. The clothes, however, were a mess, and so was his face. He was panting, and he looked in shock.

"Help me," he said, looking first at the detectives, then to the uniformed sergeant behind the big desk. "You gotta help me."

"That's what we're here for," the sergeant said easily.   "What's the problem?"

"Three men!" the boy panted.   "They kidnapped my girl."

"Whereabouts?"

"City Park.   Hurry, hurry."

"We will," the sergeant said.   "Relax, young fella.   Calm down and tell us your name."

"But she's in trouble."

"And when we hear your story we'll know what to do about it.   What's your name?"

The boy said impatiently, "Lawrence Wainwright."

"Where do you live?"

"Is that important?   My girl—"

"You're wasting time, fella.   What's your address?"

The boy told him, giving an address in one of the best sections of town.

"Now tell us what happened," the sergeant went on, writing in the blotter, keeping his manner calm.

"We were parked in the park, minding our own business, when all of a sudden three men appeared and dragged us out of the car.   I tried to fight them, but they ganged up and knocked me out.   And when I came to, they were gone and she was gone."

"When did this take place?"

"About twenty minutes ago.   About quarter of eleven."

"What's the girl's name and address?"

"What does it matter?" the boy cried.   "We've got to save her."

"We'll save her just as soon as we know she needs saving.   What's her name and where does she live?"

"Her name is Helen MacKenzie and she lives over on Wells Street.   Thirty-one Wells."

Galton moved behind the desk and thumbed through the phone book as the sergeant recorded the information and asked where the youth had seen the girl last.

"In City Park.   I told you."

"It's a big park, Mr. Wainwright.   Just where in City Park?"

"Near the pond."

"That doesn't help much.   It's a big pond."

"I've got my car outside.   I'll show you."

Galton dialed a number and while he waited, said, "Did you know any of the men, Mr. Wainwright?"

"No.   Of course not.   Please, we're wasting time.   Can't we go now?"

Galton said into the phone, "Mrs. MacKenzie?   This is Captain Galton of the police department.   I'm sorry to disturb you at this hour.   Is your daughter Helen there, please?"   He listened briefly, his face becoming still more sober.   "What's the name of the boy she's out with?" he asked, and then, "Do you know where they went?"   He listened for a bit and said, "When she comes in, would you have her call the police department?   The moment she comes in.   It doesn't matter what time." When he spoke again, it was to say, reassuringly, "No, she's not in trouble with the police, Mrs. MacKenzie. She hasn't done anything wrong. We just want to get in touch with her."

He put down the phone and said to Dennis and the sergeant, "It checks out and she's not home yet." To the boy, he said, "These men. What did they look like?"

"Two were dark and one was blond. They were my height but heavier."

"How old?"

"Maybe twenty."

"What were they wearing?"

"Sport clothes. Dark sport clothes. No jackets."

Galton's manner was brisk now. He took out a notebook. "Tell us exactly what happened."

The boy touched the blood on his cheek and absently wiped it on his shirt. "We were parked in the park doing a little—you know—smooching. All of a sudden I looked up and two men were staring at us through her window. Then, before I could do anything, they opened her door and at the same time the third man opened my door. He grabbed me and the others grabbed Helen. I fought with the one who grabbed me, but one of the others came and hit me and they both jumped on me and knocked me down and kicked me unconscious."

"What did Helen do? She scream?"

"No. I think they had a hand over her mouth. I heard her say, 'Stop it! Don't!' but that's all."

"You know if they had a car?"

"I think they did. I think they're the same men we saw when we went into the park."

The old man arched an eyebrow. "Tell us about that."

"Just when we were driving in, this cream-colored convertible went racing past us with three boys in it yelling and screaming. I think they were the same ones."

The desk sergeant said, "Say, that's the car we got a call on, Captain."

Galton turned. "When? What about?"

"We got a complaint." The sergeant looked back on the blotter. "Nine forty-two. Call from a Mrs. Stanley Turner on Westlake Avenue about a light-colored convertible with three boys in it driving around her neighborhood yelling and honking and raising hell. I sent Charlie car to respond, but they were gone."

Galton nodded. "Better alert all units." He said to the boy, "You didn't make the license plate, did you? Or notice what make of car?"

"No, sir. I just saw the three boys in it. Two dark and one blond."

Galton took a last swallow from his cup. "All right, we'll go out and take a look around. You feel up to it, son? Would you like some coffee?" he asked the boy solicitously.

"No, thanks. I'm all right."

"You'd better have a doctor look at your face."

"Later. Right now I want to find my girl."

Dennis finished his own coffee and tucked away his notebook. He and Galton led the way outside. A shiny new hardtop was against the curb with the lights on and the boy started toward it, but Galton stopped him. "We'll go in ours. It's got a radio."

They climbed into a black, unmarked cruiser, the detectives in front, the boy in back. They headed for the park, watching for convertibles. Dennis, driving, said, "What were you and the girl doing in the car?"

Wainwright hesitated and said, "A little necking."

"How were you making out with her?"

"Believe me, it's not what you think."

Galton said, "What was it?"

"We were kissing. That's all."

The detectives slid knowing looks at each other. Galton said, "You pick her up and take her out in the park and all you do is kiss?"

Wainwright swallowed. "No," he said. "We also talk. We sit and we talk and sometimes we kiss. When those men looked in the window, we were kissing."

"What kind of a girl is she?"

"A nice girl."

"What makes you so sure?"

"Well—what do you mean? I date her."

"What I mean is, she comes from another part of town. She comes from a different social station than you do. I'm not saying it's this way in your case, but usually when men date girls below their social class, it's for only one reason."

Wainwright said heatedly, "I'm not a snob. We happen to like each other. We've talked about marriage, if you really want to know. I mean, we aren't formally engaged and we haven't said anything to our folks, but we're serious."

Galton didn't push it. "Any chance she knew the boys? She call any of them by name?"

Wainwright said no, nor had her abductors used names. They hadn't said a word.

Dennis turned into the park and followed its winding roads. He looked at the moon and said, "If a bunch of boys want to raid neckers, Cap, this is the night to find them."

When they drove past the pond, Wainwright pointed to a stand of trees, black against the moonlit sky. "That's where we were," he said.

Dennis pulled off the road and crossed the fields some fifty yards to the trees. They got out and the detectives looked around by flashlight. Some grass had been flattened by wheels, but that was all.

Galton said, "You didn't see or hear anything before you saw them at the window? No car headlights? No motor?"

Wainwright shook his head. Dennis said, "They must have seen a girl in the car and doubled back with their lights off."

Galton agreed. He said, "In what direction did they drag her?"

Wainwright pointed toward black woods a hundred yards distant. "That way. At least, the last I saw."

"You see or hear a car any time after they slugged you?"

"No, sir."

Dennis said to the old man, "You think they might still be around?"

"It doesn't look like it.   They probably took off after he did."   Galton got back into the cruiser and picked up the microphone.

"Headquarters from Galton.   The girl been heard from yet?"

The sergeant came on.   "Negative."

"Anything on that convertible?"

"No, sir."

Galton depressed the mike button again and said, "Send all available units and all available men to City Park, the field opposite the pond.   I want search parties prepared to go through the woods."

"Affirmative, Captain.   All units.   Calling all units—" in a monotone.

When Galton got out of the car, the youth said, "You think she's in the woods?"

Galton's tone was heavier, his voice distracted.   "I don't know where she is, son, but you say that's where she was dragged, so that's the first place to look."

The two detectives and the boy reconnoitered the nearby areas while waiting and then, shortly after midnight, the squad cars began arriving and men poured out. By quarter past twelve, thirty policemen were on hand with flashlights and hand lamps, and the headlights of the cars gave a daylight look to the fields.

The men spread out and broke into the woods in a row, tramping through, throwing the beams of the lights in all the shadowy areas, calling the girl's name at intervals, looking for signs of her passing.   The youth hunted with Galton and Dennis, but they made him stay in back of them lest his inexperienced bumbling destroy a clue.

They pushed through briars and bushes and trees for a long five minutes and then, from far on the left, there came a shout.   Galton, Dennis and the boy started in that direction, following the others.

When they reached the spot, the other men were cluttered and mumbling, heads and shoulders bowed.   The air was black and electric.

"You find her?" the old man said, pushing through.

"We found her."

They stepped aside so Galton, Dennis and the youth could see.

It was a sad and ugly sight.   The young girl lay dead and cold under a tree. Her pants were down, her skirt was up and her blouse and bra were off.   Her once-pretty head was bloody and broken, and a red-stained rock, wrenched from the nearby earth, lay beside her.

The boy said, "No!   Oh, God, no!" and turned away moaning.   Dennis muttered a prayer under his breath, the captain shook his head and sighed.

"I was afraid of that," the old man muttered.   "When she still wasn't home, I was afraid."   He turned away and, with head down, started back.   Dennis, the distraught youth and the searchers followed.

At the car they gathered around as Galton radioed in.   The girl was dead, he reported heavily.   The medical examiner was to be notified, the photo lab and the morgue.   He got out of the car again, closed the door and leaned an elbow on the roof. He shook his head once, straightened a little and took a breath. "All right," he said wearily to the boy, "tell us what happened."

The boy said, "I did tell you."

The old mouth tightened and the tone grew firmer. "Tell it again, son. But this time tell it right."

The youth, glancing nervously at the large group of encircling men, said querulously, "What do you mean by right?"

"Tell it the way it really happened."

"I don't get you."

"You know, like this. You brought the girl into the park and a car with three yelling boys went by. You pulled off and parked under these trees. You took the girl down into the woods and started to pitch woo. Only she didn't want to go as far as you did and she tried to fight you off. But you were determined and you hit her with a rock to quiet her down, only, when it was all over, you found out you'd hit her too hard and she was dead. So you remembered the car full of boys and then you came in and told us the boys had kidnapped her." The old man turned his light on the youth's face. "That's pretty close to what happened, isn't it?"

The stunned boy blinked in the glare. "No," he whispered, his face white. "It's like I told you. They grabbed her. They hit me . . ." He looked around desperately, but all the faces were cold and disbelieving.

The old man shook his head impatiently. "Do you think you're the first person who's ever tried to sell the police a phony story? Do you think we con that easy? We get it all the time. All of us. I've heard so many phonies I could smell this one the moment you came in tonight. I hoped like hell you were telling the truth, but when she wasn't in by midnight, I was afraid you weren't."

The boy said heatedly, "You're crazy. I am telling the truth! I don't know what you've heard before, but this time you're wrong."

The old man snorted. "Are you kidding? All I have to do is look at her and look at you and I know the story's a lie. We all do."

"I defy you. What's not true about it? Show me what's not true!"

"The fact that you're alive and she's dead makes it not true."

He stopped and blinked in astonishment. "What's that got to do with it?"

Galton glanced helplessly at his grim-faced crew. "That's got everything to do with it," he explained to the boy. "Three guys, right? That's your story. There were three guys?"

"Yes."

"So what did they want? Did they want to kill people? Then why didn't they kill you both? That answer won't do. Did they just want to rape a girl? Then they'd mess you up to keep you from interfering. That's all right. But then they wouldn't kill the girl. They wouldn't do anything to her at all—outside of the rape, that is. She'd have gotten home alive."

"But she resisted! They hit her with the rock to subdue her!"

"Uh uh." Mike Galton shook his head. "One man, maybe. You, alone, might have to use a rock to have your way with her. But three men? What would they need a rock for? Two could hold her for the third so tight she couldn't move a muscle.'' The old man, studying the boy's face in the light, dropped the bitterness and said quietly, ''Forget the fancy tales, son. That girl's body is going to be examined very, very carefully for physical evidence.''

The boy's face crinkled suddenly and he started to sob.

CHARLES BOECKMAN

Blind Date

She was in the trunk of my car and she was dead.

I stood on the lonely stretch of country road in the middle of the night with the rain drumming down on me and splashing around my feet, and I stared at the body. My flashlight was frozen in my hand. I forgot about being wet and cold.

A sheet of lightning split the heavy black sky with a clap of thunder that shook the earth. For a second the macabre scene was lighted by an eerie, blue-white flash. The perimeter of my vision registered a water-filled ditch beside the road, a rusty barbed wire fence and muddy field beyond.

But the center of my vision was focused on the dead woman in the trunk of my car. In the flash of lightning her chalk-white features and staring eyes were in bold relief. The image lingered, ghostlike, in the retina of my eyes for moments after the lightning passed, revealing to me more detail than was illuminated by the sickly, yellow glow of my flashlight with its outdated batteries.

She was an attractive brunette in her early thirties. She was dressed in a suit of dark material and a light top coat that had fallen open. The cause of her death was apparent. There was a bullet hole in her forehead.

My numb mind struggled to sort facts out of the nightmare. She had undoubtedly ridden with me all the way from Kingsbury. I had not stopped once, even for gasoline, since I left there two hours ago. If highway construction had not forced me to take this detour where, in the darkness of the night, in a driving thunder storm, I'd hit a chuck-hole and blown a tire, she probably would have continued to be a passenger, unknown to me, for the remainder of my trip to New Orleans.

I realized I was standing in a frozen position like a statue, my left hand clutching the edge of the trunk lid.

My first reaction following the initial shock was one of instinctive self-preservation. I wanted to drag her out of there, change my tire, and put much distance between myself and this damned spot.

But logic warned me against acting so rashly. After all, she had not crawled into the trunk by herself. Someone had placed her there. This was a situation involving other people and matters I didn't know about. Running from this thing might have disastrous repercussions.

I bent closer, directing the feeble rays of my flashlight around the trunk's interior. The sickly glow touched briefly the spare tire, jack, and some odd rags stuffed in a corner, then returned to the dead woman.   I noticed a dark stain on the trunk mat caused by blood from the back of her head.

I forced myself to study her features more closely.   I had lived in Kingsbury for six months.   It was long enough to have seen at least once every person in a town that size.   But I was sure I had never laid eyes on this woman before I opened my trunk lid a few moments ago.

I noticed an object on the floor of the trunk near her feet.   Her purse.

I reached for it.   Then, temporarily, I closed the trunk lid and got back into the car out of the cold, driving rain.   I started the engine and turned on the heater, one of the few things that operated properly on my old heap.

The warmth crept into my chilled body.   I stopped shivering.   I switched on the dome light, opened the woman's purse, and spread the contents out on the front seat, hoping to find some identification.

The first thing that caught my eye was a bundle of letters, about a half dozen altogether.   They were held together by a rubber band.

I slipped the band off.   They all were addressed to the same person, Cora Miller, 1216 Mayberry Drive, Encinal.   That explained why I could not remember seeing her among the citizens of Kingsbury.   Encinal was another town roughly the same size, about thirty miles from Kingsbury.

Then, as I was staring at the handwritten address, I became aware of a striking familiarity about the writing.   Suddenly I felt the second shock of the evening. This was my handwriting!

Quickly, I opened one of the letters.   My gaze raced down the page to the signature, "Frank."   It was my first name.   It was my signature.

Blood pounded at my temples.   I started reading the letter.   By the time I was halfway down the page I was shivering again, but this time not from being wet. This was a love letter of the highly personal, intimate type, the kind that would cause a judge to clear the courtroom before it was read aloud to the jury.

It was brief but there was nothing vague about the message it contained.   The writer, who had the same name and handwriting as myself had committed himself on paper to being hopelessly in love with Cora Miller.   References were made to clandestine meetings and to Cora's husband, Thurman Miller.

With unsteady fingers I flipped through the other envelopes.   The postmarks covered the past two-month period and they had all been mailed from Kingsbury.

The most recent postmark was only two days ago.   I removed the letter from that envelope.   It was quite brief:

> My Dearest Cora,
>   I can hardly believe that in two days you will be mine completely.
> No more lies and slipping around for us.   I'm winding up things here.
> Quit my job this morning.   I'll pick you up at the corner of the bus
> station in Encinal at eight o'clock Friday night.   I have made reservations
> for us in New Orleans.
>
> Your lover, Frank

I stared at the page, blinking slowly.   The rain drummed steadily on the car top, splashed against the windshield, and leaked around the door.   Thunder rumbled and lightning flashed.   I had the eerie feeling of reality slipping from my grasp, of walking through a bad dream.

I *had* quit my job the morning the letter was written and mailed in Kingsbury. I *was* on my way to New Orleans where I had phoned ahead for reservations at a small hotel I knew.

But I had made reservations only for myself.   I had not known I would be taking along a blind date—Cora Miller.

I pawed through the objects from her purse, lipstick, bobby pins, keys, face tissues, the usual female junk.   Then I found her billfold.   In it was close to a hundred dollars in cash.   One of the compartments contained a driver's license and a number of credit cards all bearing the name, Mrs. Thurman Miller.   Plastic sleeves on a spiral binder held an assortment of small photographs.   There was a wallet-size snapshot of Cora Miller, and several of her with a beefy-faced man who I assumed was her husband, Thurman.   Other snapshots were relatives or friends perhaps, but all adults.   Apparently the Millers had no children.

I came to the final photo in the billfold.   The face on it leaped up to my startled eyes.   It was a snapshot of me.   Written in a corner, in my handwriting, were the words, "I love you, Cora Darling, Frank."

The human mechanism can absorb so much emotional shock, after which it becomes numb and dazed.   I had reached that point.

I sat half slumped against the wheel for several minutes.   The heater fan whirred. Cold drops of moisture trickled down my neck.   Finally I pulled myself together. I could not spend the rest of the night in this forsaken spot.   The normal processes of survival demanded that I do something.

I stuffed the objects back into the purse, and placed it on the rear seat among my suitcases and clothes.

Then I switched on my flashlight, turned up my collar, and again sloshed out into the rain.   I opened the trunk lid, hoping that some miracle would have caused Cora to dissolve.   But she was still very much there.   I swallowed a normal human aversion to dead people and pushed her out of the way of the spare tire.   When I did that I noticed, for the first time, her green overnight bag wedged in a far corner of the trunk atop one of my suitcases.

I went about the wet, muddy business of jacking up the car and changing the tire.

Then I was behind the wheel again.   I turned the car around.   In a few minutes I reached a small town a few miles back on the main highway, which I had remembered.

I got a handful of change from an all-night service station.   In a lighted street-corner phone booth I placed a call to the hotel in New Orleans.   When the clerk answered I said, "This is Frank Judson.   I want to check on a reservation I made."

"Yes, sir.   Hold on just a minute, please."

He was back almost at once.   "Yes, Mr. Judson.   We received your phone call and later the telegram."

"Telegram?" I asked blankly.

"Yes, sir.   The one asking us to change your reservation to a double because you'd have someone with you."

I stared at the water running in streams down the side of the phone booth. I suddenly found it difficult to breathe in the small enclosure.

"Did you wish to make any other changes, Mr. Judson?"

I wiped the back of my hand across my forehead where beads of perspiration were mingling with raindrops. "You might as well cancel the whole thing . . ."

I got back in the car. Cold perspiration was oozing out all over me. For a moment, reason gave way to wild fancy. I was a victim of amnesia. I'd had an affair with this woman. For some reason I had murdered her, and the shock of what I'd done had blanked out my memory.

Then I got a grip on myself. That was pure hogwash. I was turning into a hysterical fool. Somebody had murdered Cora all right, but it hadn't been me. An elaborate plan had been rigged to made it look as if I was eloping with Cora tonight, but had murdered her for some reason, perhaps because she was trying to back out at the last minute.

No doubt the police in New Orleans would be tipped off to check my car. If I hadn't accidentally had that blowout, I would have had no reason to look in the trunk before I reached New Orleans. They would have found Cora. I would have had some impossible explaining to do.

I mentally ran over the events of the past six months, trying to find a clue to this unpleasant mess.

I had driven into Kingsbury six months ago, broke and needing a job. I'd gone to work with the Kingsbury *Record*, a small daily newspaper.

The town and job had been pleasant, but, as usual, after six months I had the itchy feet to move on to greener pastures. I was twenty-six, no ties or responsibilities. I'd been out of the army four years now, and had spent that time seeing different parts of the country. There was still a lot I wanted to see before I settled down.

One thing had made leaving Kingsbury difficult—Emily Phillips. Every town had pretty girls. But only Kingsbury had Emily. I knew lately that she was falling pretty hard for me. What scared me was that I was starting to feel the same about her. I could hear wedding bells in the air. So I'd taken the only sensible course open to a guy with itchy feet. I'd quit my job and kissed Emily goodbye.

I hadn't known I'd be taking Cora Miller along as an uninvited guest.

I could get rid of Cora easily enough. There were plenty of muddy ditches along the highway. And I could burn the letters and my snapshot that was in her billfold. But there were probably other letters and snapshots planted at her home. And how would I explain to the police the matter of the double reservation at the New Orleans hotel? And the blood stains in my car trunk?

It boiled down to this, that I had to find out what Cora was doing in the trunk of my car, and who had put her there. And the answer was somewhere back in Encinal or Kingsbury.

Two hours later I pulled into the city limits of the town I'd left earlier this evening, Kingsbury. By then it was almost midnight. Except for all-night service stations on the highway, the town had rolled up the sidewalks.

I drove to the home of Buddy Gardner, my best friend in Kingsbury. Buddy was a deputy in the sheriff's department. Like myself, he was an avid chess player. We'd spent many long hours drinking beer and waging battles over a chess board at Pop Lassiter's beer joint.

If anybody could give me information about Thurman and Cora Miller it would be Buddy.

He lived with his parents in a big, old ramshackle house on the edge of town. When I turned my mud-splattered heap into their yard, I saw a light on in Buddy's room. He was my age and a bachelor. I knew he had a habit of reading paperback novels most of the night.

There was a private entrance to his room. I knocked. His door opened and the light in the room silhouetted his heavy, six-foot frame and his bushy head. He was naturally surprised to see me. Only a few hours ago we'd bid one another a fond farewell over a last chess game and a few beers at Pop's.

"Frank! What the heck? Thought you were long gone."

Buddy talked in a slow drawl even when he was surprised.

"I was," I said. "I had to come back."

He pushed open the screen door. "Come on in here. You look soaked."

I stepped inside, dripping water on the linoleum. He had a typical bachelor room. Deer horns and other hunting trophies adorned the walls along with hunting rifles. A book shelf, extending all the way to the ceiling, was filled with paperback novels. On one cluttered table was a portable TV set. A novel he had been reading was spread open on the rumpled bed. On the bedside table was a can of beer and his pipe.

"What happened?" he asked, peering at me curiously. "Have car trouble?"

"Something like that. I want you to help me with something, Buddy."

"Sure. How about a beer? Or maybe you'd better have a shot of bourbon. You look half drowned."

"The bourbon sounds fine," I nodded. My clothes felt clammy against my shivering body.

"You ought to get out of those wet clothes," he said, taking a bottle of whiskey out of a bureau drawer.

"Haven't got time. Thanks." I accepted the drink he handed me. I took it straight. I felt the warmth of the alcohol spreading into my bloodstream.

"Buddy," I said, "you've lived around these parts all your life. You ever hear of a guy named Thurman Miller?"

The bedsprings sighed as Buddy sat on the edge of the bed and picked up his can of beer. He was looking at me curiously. "Thurman Miller?" His brow wrinkled. "Do you mean the county auditor who lives in Encinal?"

"I guess I do. There wouldn't be two Thurman Millers in Encinal, would there?"

"Not that I know of." Then he chuckled. "I swear, Frank, if you ain't one for the books. This afternoon you and I were over at Pop's having a farewell beer together. Now here you are back at midnight, banging on my door, wanting to know about the county auditor in Encinal. What's up? You workin' on some kind of newspaper story?"

"Not exactly. Tell me about Thurman Miller."

Buddy shrugged. "What do you want to know? He's been county auditor over there a number of years. That's about all I know."

"Is he married?"

Buddy nodded. "Matter of fact, I think his wife's side of the family is from Kingsbury."

I took out one of Cora's wallet snapshots. "This Mr. and Mrs. Miller?"

Buddy studied the photo. "It looks like them," he said slowly, "though I wouldn't swear to it. I don't know them that well. The only times I see Thurman is when I run into him in the courthouse in Encinal when I'm over there."

"Do you think anybody in this town would know them?"

Buddy stared at me. "I swear you're acting mysterious. What's eating you anyway, Frank?"

"I'll tell you in a little while. The truth is, I'm in a kind of a jam. I thought maybe you could help me."

"Well, I'll sure try, Frank. I hope it ain't anything serious."

"It could be. Getting back to what I just asked you, do you think many people in Kingsbury know the Millers?"

Buddy massaged his jaw thoughtfully. "Oh, I guess quite a few people do. You know how folks in a small town are. And Mrs. Miller has relatives over here."

I swallowed the rest of the bourbon. I'd established who the Millers were, and that almost anyone in Kingsbury might know them.

But who, among my acquaintances, would be crooked enough or crazy enough to murder Cora Miller, and then try to make it look like I'd been having an affair with her over the past two months?

I paced around the room, trying to recall this afternoon in detail. If I could put my finger on the place where Cora's body was deposited in my car trunk I would be close to the truth.

I had packed my car late this afternoon. Cora had not been in the trunk of my car at that time because I had put a suitcase in it.

Then I'd driven to a service station to have the tank filled. But I had stood right beside the car. No one could have touched the trunk without my seeing them.

My next stop had been Pop Lassiter's, where I'd bid Buddy goodbye over our last beer together. Then I'd gotten in the car, and had driven steadily until I had the blowout.

The only time anyone could have tampered with my trunk was while I had my car parked back of Pop's place. That being the case, Pop Lassiter himself was the most logical suspect. He was a mean old devil, and an ex-con, and capable of anything. Furthermore, he knew all about my plans to quit and go to New Orleans.

"Buddy, will you come with me?" I asked. "You might say it's in the line of duty."

"Well, sure," he drawled. "I wish to heck you'd tell me why, though."

"Trust me," I said. It was a ticklish situation. Buddy was a good friend, and

I knew I could trust him to help me. But he was also a deputy sheriff. If I told him about having Cora in the trunk of my car, he'd be forced to act in an official capacity. I couldn't afford to be arrested at this point.

Buddy pulled on a pair of cowboy boots and took a rain slicker out of the closet. We sloshed out to my car.

"Man, this heap of yours leaks," he muttered after he'd gotten in and felt rain splash down the back of his neck.

"I need a new top," I said, turning on the switch.

"That ain't all it needs," he said, looking around.

I drove down to Pop's beer joint.

"What the heck are you doing here?" Buddy wanted to know. "You know Pop closes at midnight. It's past that now."

"I want to talk to Pop," I explained.

The old sinner lived in a room behind the beer joint. I walked around to his door and banged on it. Buddy was right behind me.

The door opened. Pop stood there in his long underwear. He looked mad. "What in blazes you want? I don't sell no booze after closin' time."

He tried to slam the door, but I stuck my foot in it. "Since when did you get so legal?" I asked. I pushed it further open and walked in. "You used to bootleg the stuff, didn't you?"

Pop looked even madder at this invasion of his privacy. "What's buggin' you, Frank?"

Buddy came in after me. Pop's glare switched to him. "This some kind of raid? You got a warrant?"

Buddy laughed. "Pop, I don't know no more 'n you do. Frank said he had to see you and asked me to come along. I'm just here as an interested citizen."

"You didn't answer my question about bootlegging," I said.

Pop shrugged. "What if I did? That was back in Prohibition. Thirty years ago."

"You've done time since then," I reminded him. "Once for manslaughter, and once for peddling marijuana under the counter."

He looked mad enough to shoot me. "All right, you smart aleck young newspaper jerk. What business you got comin' around here insulting me in the middle of the night?"

"I got a reason." I shoved the snapshot under his nose. "You know this couple?"

Grumbling and swearing, he put on a pair of gold-rimmed glasses. He glared briefly at the photo, then shoved it away. " 'Course I do. That's the Millers from over at Encinal."

"How come you know them so well?"

"Hell, why shouldn't I? Cora Miller comes from this town. She's one of Ed Shelby's girls. I've known the Shelbys all my life."

I grabbed myself a fistful of his dirty underwear just under his breastbone and twisted it until his eyes bulged. "You knew I was going to New Orleans, didn't you?"

"Well, sure!" he yelled angrily. "That's all you been yappin' about the last two months every time you been in my place—about how fed up you are with this town, and how you're headin' for New Orleans. Good riddance, if you ask me."

I shoved him up against a wall and gave his underwear another yank until he was dancing on his toes. "Tell me what kind of a deal you're in to tie me up with Cora Miller?"

His gold-rimmed glasses were dangling from one ear. His adam's apple danced in his stringy throat. "Buddy!" he yelled in a high-pitched, frightened voice. "He's a-killin' me."

Buddy placed a huge paw on my arm. "Take it easy now, Frank," he drawled soothingly. "Don't you think you'd better tell me what's got you so upset?"

I released Pop. "You'll know all about it pretty soon," I said. "When I get this old coot to talk. You already heard him admit he knows the Millers, and he knew all about me fixin' to leave for New Orleans."

Buddy looked perplexed. "I can't help you if you won't tell me what's got you so steamed up. You want to prefer some kind of charges against Pop here?"

I looked at him in hopeless frustration. I'd come here, driven by desperation, with no clear plan in mind. I'd hoped that the surprise of seeing me back might shake Pop up and, when I confronted him, he might break down and admit he had a part in putting Cora in my car. I might have known that a guy like Pop, who'd lived on the fringe of the law all his life, wouldn't come unglued that easily. He hadn't even looked surprised when I walked in.

Either he was putting up a good front, and with his criminal experience he'd be trained to do that, or I was totally wrong about his being involved.

We went back to my car. I drove out of town fast, headed toward Encinal. Again, I was motivated by fear and desperation, rather than any clear-cut plan. The only other person I could think of who might shed some light on this mess was Cora's husband, Thurman. If he proved to be a blind alley like Pop Lassiter, I was going to have to admit the whole thing to Buddy and let him arrest me, and hope the police would believe my side of the story—which was a pretty dim hope.

I thought about Cora getting stiff in the trunk of my car just a few feet behind us and I shivered.

Buddy could see he wasn't going to get any conversation out of me, so he patiently smoked his pipe and waited to see what I was going to do next.

When we arrived in Encinal, I drove arnound until I located Mayberry Drive. Then I found the address I'd seen on Cora's letters, 1216. It was a sprawling, ranch-style house worth at least thirty thousand dollars. That puzzled me. "A county auditor doesn't make much money, does he?"

"Not a heck of a lot, I don't think," Buddy said.

"Then how come Thurman Miller lives in a house like this?"

"He's well-fixed from some oil property his folks left him. That county auditor job is just local politics and prestige."

That explained Miller's obvious affluence.

"Come on," I muttered quietly.

We walked up to the house. I saw a light inside and I punched the doorbell.

Thurman Miller opened the door. I recognized him from the picture in my wallet. He stared at me through the screen door. Then his face turned pale. He uttered a cry and ran out of the house. The next thing I knew we were rolling on the ground, and he had me by the throat. He was a big guy, and might have choked me to death if Buddy hadn't dragged him off me.

We got him inside where he sank onto a couch and burst into sobs. I sat down too, shaken and weak-kneed from his unexpected, ferocious attack.

He raised his face from his hands and started cursing me. "What have you done with Cora?" he cried.

"Do you know Frank, Mr. Miller?" Buddy asked curiously.

Miller glared at me with hate-filled eyes. "I ought to. I've warned him to stay away from my wife. Tonight she eloped with him." He got up, walked heavily to a desk, took out a scrap of paper, and handed it to Buddy. "That's the farewell note she left me."

The nightmare had started all over again. I felt the hopeless, numb sensation creep through my body.

Buddy read the note, frowning. "Is this true, Frank? Did you take off with Mrs. Miller?"

"No," I said. But I said it without much conviction. I was ready to stop being sure of anything, including my own sanity. Those letters, the snapshot . . . now Thurman Miller recognizing me on sight. Did it mean my mind was playing tricks on me? Insanity takes many forms.

Was it possible that I had been running around with Cora Miller? Had I really murdered her in a fit of passion? Could a thing like that have been blanked from my memory by my sick, guilt-ridden mind?

My brain did feel feverish. My head throbbed. I pressed my fingers against my temples. For God's sake, what are the symptoms of madness? Is a mentally deranged person aware of his own illusions?

Dimly, I was aware of Thurman Miller demanding to know where his wife was. Buddy was staring at me intently, waiting for an answer.

What could I tell him? That I'd reached the point where I was no longer certain of reality?

"Buddy, come out here a minute," I said in a hollow voice. I felt wet and tired and scared. I dragged myself to my feet and started outside. Miller rose to go with us. "Make him stay here," I mumbled, stopping awkwardly.

Buddy shot a glance at Miller, who stared angrily at me, then shrugged and sank back down on the sofa.

I led Buddy out to the car. I gave him the keys. "Look in the trunk," I said. I sat in the car, listening to the rain drum on the roof. I stared straight ahead at nothing. I heard the trunk lid open. In a few moments it closed again. Buddy got in the car beside me. The springs creaked under his weight. His face mirrored the shock of what he'd just seen.

Slowly he let his breath out. "This is real bad, Frank," he said gravely. "Why didn't you tell me about it right away?"

"Because you would have been forced to arrest me, and I wanted to try and get at the truth first.   I hoped I could get Pop to admit he had put her in the trunk of my car.   When that didn't work, I came over here thinking Miller would be of some help to me.''   I made a useless gesture.

"But why Pop?"

"Because the only time her body could have been put in the trunk was while my car was parked behind Pop's beer joint earlier tonight, when you and I were having our farewell beer together.''

"Are you telling me you didn't put her there?"

"Buddy, I had a blowout on my way to New Orleans.   I got out to change the tire.   When I opened the trunk I found Cora Miller's body.   I swear that is the first time I ever saw her in my life.''   Then I admitted, "But I don't blame you if you don't believe me.   I'm not sure I believe myself any more.''

"What do you mean by that?"

I turned and dug Cora's billfold and the incriminating letters out from under my suitcase on the back seat.   "Look at these.''

He read them all carefully with the aid of a flashlight he'd brought along.   Then he took the picture of me out of Cora's wallet and studied it.

"Buddy, I haven't been running around with Cora Miller.   The only girl I've had anything to do with around here is Emily Phillips.   I was sure those letters were forged, that the whole thing was an elaborate scheme to frame me for her murder.   But when we knocked on Miller's door and he recognized me on sight— well, it's taken the wind out of my sails.''

"He could have recognized you from a picture.   Or somebody could have pointed you out to him on the street.''

I looked at Buddy curiously.   "You mean you think he's in on this scheme?''

"I don't think anything.   I'm just saying that his recognizing you doesn't prove anything, one way or the other.''

Suddenly, I felt better.   I realized I must be emotionally drained, or I wouldn't be giving away to wild emotions like I had been for a few minutes.

Buddy had relit his pipe.   He was puffing on it while he stared thoughtfully at my picture.   "This is a close-up front view.   You must have known when it was taken.''

I shook my head.   "I don't know how it was done.   Nobody has taken a picture of me since I've been in Kingsbury.   In fact, I don't remember having my picture taken since I was in the army.''

"Hmm.   This looks like a recent one, too.''   He puffed on his pipe and mumbled to himself, the way he did when he was analyzing a chess move.   "Looks like it was taken indoors by available light.''   He bent closer, squinting his eyes.   "Pretty grainy.   Could be blown up from part of a negative.''

He stared at it some more, turning it different ways under the flashlight, while puffing furiously on his pipe.   Then he said, "Listen, I don't want to break the news to Miller about his wife like this.   I'm going to tell him I'm taking you back to Kingsbury.   I'll phone him from over there after the coroner has a look at her, and we have her some place decent like a funeral home.''

He got out of the car.   Then he thrust his head back in.   "Frank, I have to tell you this. You're under arrest now, and anything you say can be held against you."

I nodded wearily. "Okay. I understand."

He went back into the house to talk to Thurman Miller. He was in there a few minutes, then came out and got behind the wheel of my car. He drove the car back to Kingsbury, which was fine with me. I was emotionally drained and physically exhausted.

When we reached Kingsbury, I expected Frank to take me straight to jail and phone the coroner from there. I was taken by complete surprise when he pulled up in back of Pop's beer joint instead.

"What's up?" I asked.

"Got a hunch. Come on."

For the second time that night, we banged on Pop's door. The old man jerked the door open. His disposition had not improved. "Now what?" he demanded.

This time he was dressed in shirt and trousers. "Going someplace, Pop?" Buddy asked.

"What makes you think that?" the old bar owner snapped.

Buddy shrugged. "Peculiar time of night for anybody to be dressed." Then he said, "Unlock your bar," his tone authoritative.

Pop stared at him as if he'd lost his mind. "At one o'clock in the morning?"

"Let's put it this way, it's an official request. But I can go wake up the J.P. and get a search warrant, if you want to put me to the trouble."

Swearing under his breath, Pop Lassiter got his keys, walked across the rain-drenched yard and opened his beer joint. He switched on the lights. It was still warm inside. Stale cigarette smoke lingered in the air from the night's business.

"Frank, sit over here at the bar," Buddy directed. He walked to a doorway leading to a room off the side of the bar. His voice came to me out of the dark room. "Glance this way. Can you see me?"

"No."

He emerged into the light. "That picture of you that you found in Cora's billfold—it was taken from this room."

I stared at him in amazement. "How did you figure that out?"

"The negative was blown up, and the background was cropped out, so your face and shoulders filled most of the print. But whoever did the enlargement left the rim of that clock, up there, on one corner of the print. I recognized it as the one on Pop's wall. All I had to do was figure what angle the picture was taken from in order to get your face in the foreground and that clock in the background and . . . well, I wound up in that room. A person could take your picture from in there and you'd never know it."

I felt myself growing excited. "Wouldn't I have seen the flash?"

"No flash was used. There's enough light here for fast film, and the right kind of processing. Isn't that right, Pop?" he asked, suddenly turning to the bar owner.

For the first time tonight the old man lost his composure. His face turned a dirty gray. "I—I don't know what you're talkin' about."

Buddy said, "Frank, earlier tonight you mentioned the things for which Pop has done time. Maybe you didn't know about this, but I did; he once served a stretch for forgery.''

Old Lassiter groped at the bar with a trembling hand. He licked his lips. "Now wait a minute . . .''

"Forging those letters in Frank's handwriting was a snap for you, Pop," Buddy said. "So was putting Cora's body in his car tonight. You knew he and I would have one last chess game here before he left. We'd talked about it in here the night before." Buddy moved toward him. "Why did you murder Cora Miller, Pop?''

All the wind out of his sails now, Pop collapsed against the bar. He held out one trembling palm as if to ward off Buddy. "You ain't hookin' me on no murder rap!'' he yelled in a quavering voice. "All right; I done the letters and the pictures. And I had a key made to fit the trunk of his car. That's all I had to do with it.''

"If you didn't kill her and put her in the trunk, who did?''

The old man took out a handkerchief and shakily mopped his forehead. "Her husband—Thurman," he said hoarsely.

Surprise rooted me to the spot.

Buddy and I were staring at Pop. "It's the truth," he croaked. "He's got him some young blonde on the string. He wants to marry her. Cora won't give him a divorce. He come to me a couple of months ago, offerin' me money if I'd knock Cora off. I'm not going to get myself in that kind of big trouble. But I told him I could figure a way he could do it, and come clean himself. I knew about Frank here. He'd been comin' in my place shootin' off his mouth about gettin' fed up with the town an' wantin' to move on. I've seen 'em like him all my life. Drifters. Transients. I could see just as soon as he got a few bucks ahead he was going to scat out of town.''

Pop Lassiter wiped his face with the handkerchief again. "Thurman paid me good money to set the thing up. I wrote those letters. He caught the mail before Cora got her hands on it. We waited until I heard you say you'd quit your job, and were leaving town tonight, Frank. Then I put in a call to Thurman. He shot Cora tonight, and brought her over here. He was parked back of my place in the dark, waiting for you to drive up and play that last chess game with Buddy. Then he put her in the trunk of your car, usin' that key I'd had made . . .''

Buddy took Pop down to the county jail, and phoned the coroner. Then, he drove over to Encinal to arrest Thurman Miller for the murder of his wife.

As for myself, I was chilled to the bone and close to nervous exhaustion. I drove back to the rooming house, woke my landlady, and got her to give me my old room. I took a hot bath, drank some more whiskey, fell into bed, and slept until about noon the next day.

When I woke, I phoned Buddy down at the sheriff's office. "Everything okay?''

"Fine," he boomed cheerfully. "Thurman gave us a complete statement. You're clear, Frank. 'Course you'll have to testify at the trial.''

"How about a chess game tonight?'' I asked.

"Well, sure," he said, with a tone of pleased surprise. "You mean you're not takin' off for New Orleans now that this mess is cleared up?''

I didn't explain it to him then, but I wasn't taking off for anywhere. I had come to the conclusion that not only does a rolling stone gather no moss, it also does not gather friends.   You have to stay in one place to do that.

I finished talking to Buddy.   I had two more important calls to make.   I had to phone my ex-boss at the newspaper to see if I could have my job back.   And then I was going to phone Emily and see if I could have my best girl back.

RODERICK WILKINSON

Pressure

Don't let anyone tell you that this Scotch boom is going to go on forever. *I* know it isn't. In fact nearly everybody in America who blends it, bottles it, or sells it knows that we simply can't go on importing millions of barrels of a liquor from a tiny island off the coast of Europe just because it can't be made anywhere else in the world.

Oh, yes, we make whisky in the U.S. Everybody knows that. It's darned good whisky, too. Don't try to tell me that a southern mash or a Kentucky single grain doesn't make life a lot easier for millions of fastidious Americans, but a Scotch malt whisky can't be made here. It simply can't be done. That's why—at a time when we're nearly colonizing the moon—it makes me mad to think that we have to get every single drop of the stuff from a country smaller than New York.

Don't ask me *why* this is. If anybody should know the answer, *I* should. I've been in the whisky business forty-odd years; I talk to whisky men all day in my New York office, at the bonding warehouses, at the brokers' places, in the U.S. grain distilleries, out in the field, in the bars, in saloons, at the dealers' places. I also discuss whisky with my gardener on Long Island, my barber, my travel agent, Joe at the country club, my wife, and anybody else who'll listen. Scotch is my business.

It's something to do with the water. Not even the water in the *lowlands* of Scotland will do. It *must* be water from a peaty, Highland river like the Spey or the Lochie or the Livet. It is also something to do with the barley they use—plump Aberdeen or Angus or Banff barley is taken up every year by the Scottish distillers, whole harvests at a time. All the rest has something to do with the peat-fire they use under the still, the aromatic juices in the hot stills which haven't been cleaned out in 150 years, the temperature, the humidity, the skill of the stillmen who know exactly when to "run off," as it's called in the industry.

If there's anything else it must be witchcraft and, believe me, *that* wouldn't surprise me about the Scots.

All I get is the product; and all I know is that I have to import barrels and barrels of the stuff to make a living for about two thousand of my employees who work three shifts getting it on the market.

I want to tell you about a day last March when a grey-haired man called Ogilvie from our Scottish supplier phoned me from Glasgow. The conversation went something like this:

"Mr. Sullivan?"

"Yes."

"This is Hector Ogilvie. From Glasgow."

"Hello, Hector."

"I'm phoning you because I don't want to put any of this in writing."

"Oh?"

"You know Andrew Lamont?"

"I don't think so."

"Yes, you do. You met him at our Tomintoul distillery last summer. He was the tall man, about thirty; wore a white coat; black hair—"

"He had a blonde wife, good-looking girl?"

"That's him. He's our chemical engineer based at Glasgow. He was at Tomintoul on a visit when you were there."

"What about him?"

I heard him breathe before he said, "He made ten gallons of Islay malt artificially last week."

It was a few seconds before I thought what to say. If it had been anyone but Hector Ogilvie on the other end of that phone four thousand miles away, I would have made polite noises and hung up. But this was a *whisky* man talking. Ogilvie had been managing one of Charlie McIntyre's distilleries at Glenasky for years. I said, "It went back to raw alcohol."

"It didn't."

"Then it didn't hold the flavor."

"It did."

"It won't mature."

"It will."

I found my voice a little thicker. "You're kidding."

"I am not. He's proved it out—many times."

"Who knows about it?"

"You. And me. And him."

"What about McIntyre?"

"He doesn't know. He wouldn't know what to do if he did. Lamont says the development's got to be done now in America. There isn't enough money here."

"What d'you want me to do?"

"Get Bailey and Green and Pudner lined up. I think I can bring Lamont over to New York next week for a test demonstration. He'll need a lab and three assistants."

"They'll take some convincing. So will I. We'll need to see long-term tests."

"You will also need a lot of money." Well, they came over. I got the other three whisky men together and by the time Lamont had worked on the fourth test I had a feeling we had kissed goodbye to four hundred years of the Scotch-whisky industry as we knew it. That meeting was supposed to last three hours and it lasted five days.   We almost slept in the place.   Lamont worked behind locked doors but he showed us all we wanted to know.   First he distilled a few pints from corn.   Then he went on to coarser grain like maize.   He finished up producing three gallons of the loveliest, peat-tanged, malt-flavored nectar we had ever tasted from a sack of Oklahoma potatoes.   He matured it by electronics.

I don't know if you realize what I'm saying here but, to get the picture straight in your mind, it was as if somebody from Vienna had brought over a computer and composed, scored, and played music that suddenly put everyone who made music all over the world out of business overnight—opera organizers, orchestra leaders, recording artists, singers and musicians—finished.

That was the size of the problem we had at 4 A.M. on the eighteenth floor of the Tallamady Building in New York, and it wasn't nice.   The next day we rushed in the specialists from the Midwest—men who *knew* whisky even better than we did—tasters, smellers, sniffers, blenders, who could tell precisely what kind of Orkney or Speyside would mix best with the sharp water of East San Francisco. They passed Andrew Lamont's product as one of the finest Glenlivets they had ever tasted.

The potato reached a dizzy height in the history of the liquor business that night, that's for sure.

At first everyone was too scared to talk money.   I just kept walking the carpet and horse-talking about "International consequences in the spirit trade . . . responsibilities far beyond the immediate profit incentives . . . a breakthrough in our industry as far-reaching as the atom bomb."

Ogilvie glared through his spectacles and said, "*Somebody's* got to get it started. The time to do it is here and now.   Let's get something drawn up."   He talked as if he were Lamont's theatrical agent.

Harold Bailey, a big whisky man from the West Coast, agreed with him. "To hell with this 'international consequences' jazz.   Is this the United Nations? Let's sign them up now, at least with a provisional contract."

The other two whisky men, James Green and O. B. Pudner, kept silent. They looked scared out of their wits with the Scotsman's discovery.   They knew this was the end of the Scotch trade.

All this time, Lamont just drew squiggles on a scratch pad and looked sad. Everybody knew what everybody else was thinking.   This was Survival Day, and the men who signed up Lamont would make a fortune.   Those who didn't were done.

We all started pushing Lamont at once—provisional rights for six months, guaranteed exclusives for the first three years, outright payments, royalties, stock-sharing—and the more we pushed the sadder Lamont looked.   I hoped he was just tired.

"Let's think about it," he said as he took off his white lab coat.   "We've plenty of time."

Bailey got panicky.   "Yeah, you do that, Andrew.   You think about it, and while you're doing that, somebody in Germany or Japan will get on to the method in a month and sell the world out in a year."

He started packing up his things. "They won't get on to it. It took me eight years working night and day. This is no do-it-yourself whisky-water. It's complicated." He smiled before he left. "I want to think about it." His mouth was tight.

We nearly went mad. Think about what? What was he trying to do, hike the price into billions? Had he no sense of decency? Think about it!

Bailey and I kept talking to him all the way back to his hotel. Then I went down to the airport and tried again. "Just tell me why you want to delay, Andrew."

He leaned against a stair railing. "I'll try. What *is* Scotland, anyway? The top part of a small volcanic hiccup off the coast of Europe; five million people. You could lose it in Los Angeles. We don't have much—a reputation for building ships, playing the bagpipes, and making tartan and whisky. That's about it, one way or another." He lit a cigarette. "Maybe we should keep the little we've got."

"Listen, Andrew, I know how you feel," I said, "but you can't keep back progress. You've found the way to mass-produce Scotch malt whisky anywhere in the world. This'll take money to develop, and a plant and men and materials. Let me develop it. I can raise the money—"

"Goodnight, Alex." He held out his hand.

I watched them walk to the runnway for his plane. Hector Ogilvie was waving his arms at him and, from where I stood, looked as if he were swearing continuously at the thickest, most stupid chemical engineer in the whisky business.

I think I'd better tell you something about myself at this stage, then you'll know why I went straight back to my New York office that evening and did some very clear thinking. I'm fifty-two years of age, although I don't look it. My father was an Irish immigrant and my mother came from Liverpool in England. You'll pardon my inverted snobbery if I tell you I came up the hard, hard way near the New York waterfront. And you'll pardon me if I leave out some of the years during prohibition; let's just say that's how I got into the liquor business. I married Kate Bergman in 1933, divorced her in 1939. I married again in 1942 and Lucy and I live on Long Island in a fine house with all the trimmings. Our boy Larry works with me in the business. He's sharp.

Don't press me for details; that's about the size and breadth of my life. Better people than you have tried to put a bite on me by digging up some early-Sullivan relics on that waterfront.

I sat in my office that night, and when all the anger and scare had left me I began to laugh. You know what this was, don't you? This was a Situation, and I hadn't had one of these in years. Business problems, yes; plenty of them. But something like this? Not since Ed Buccelli and I worked together had I got myself a Situation that had to be handled; managed; fixed.

I put together the facts. A young Scots chemical engineer had found a way of making Scotch malt whisky artificially from almost any kind of vegetable matter that would produce ethyl alcohol. If this development were launched anywhere in the world, Scotch whisky would no longer be a monopoly of the Scots. It could be produced in the Gobi Desert from sagebrush! It needed money to develop it.

I could get the money.   If I had that patent, or the rights, I could make a fortune and put every other Scotch importer in the world out of business.

So, I had to have that patent or the know-how.   That's me.   Why should I try to tell *you* otherwise?   D'you imagine I got to the top in the liquor business letting somebody *else* manipulate these things?

I picked up the telephone book and looked for "Buccelli."   Ed was a good starting point.

The man who came to see me later that night on Long Island looked like a lawyer. He was of medium height, had black, wavy hair, nice brown eyes, and a broad face that smiled easily.   His name was Daly, and he spoke with a Scottish accent.

I took him into the library and I poured drinks.   "That was quick."

"Mr. Buccelli said you were in a hurry, Mr. Sullivan."   He sat down in the big hide chair, and I noticed how well-cut was his dark-grey suit.

I sat on the sofa and hoped I looked younger than I felt with this thirty-odd-year-old, clean-cut, serene executive type.   "Did he tell you anything about what I want?"

"Only that you had an assignment you wanted to talk over."   He sat back.

I sipped my drink.   "Are you on your own or with an organization?"

He brought out a wallet and from it a card which he handed to me.   It read:

Gascoine Peterson, Inc.
328 44th Street
New York, N.Y.
U.S.A.

I had to use my reading glasses.   I said, "This doesn't tell me much."

"I'm not *selling* my company's services, Mr. Sullivan."   He picked up his glass.

"That doesn't give me much encouragement to buy them."

"I'm not encouraging you."   He took some whisky.

I sighed.   This was not going to be easy.   What was the world coming to? You ask for a pressure service and what do you get?   You get a crease-panted young so-and-so sitting back drinking your whisky, not giving a damn whether he wanted your work or not. In the old days—well, times have changed.   I said, "Let me tell you the story."

I told him about Lamont.

When I had finished he lit a cigarette, leaned forward and exhaled smoke slowly as he stared at the floor. "You want the know-how?"

"Legally or illegally."

"That means you want Lamont?"

"Right."

"You can raise the money?"

"Yes."

"How much?"

I shrugged and rose to refill our glasses.   How much!   I'd seen the day when anybody you hired to lean on somebody—well, I suppose these organizations operate differently now.   I said, "Half a million dollars."

"Is it worth that?"

"Every cent. I know."

He accepted the refill thoughtfully. "Is there a time factor?"

"Yes. Tomorrow."

He grinned. "Let's be realistic."

"That guy Lamont is on a plane tonight with enough power in his skull to blow my whisky business, and everyone else's in the world, to smithereens in a week. He'll be wandering around Scotland *asking* for something to happen to him. I want him and his know-how back here working for me within weeks. Is *that* realistic?"

"Maybe." He was making notes in a little pad. "He's married? Got children?"

I began to feel better about Daly. I smiled. "Mr. Daly, there's something I like about you and your outfit. You get to where people live."

We finished about 2 A.M. and by the end of our meeting I began to have a fresh respect for the modern approach of today's professional pressure business. There was no doubt about it, things had come a long way since Ed Buccelli and I made our first few thousand dollars unprohibiting on the New York riversides. Gascoine Peterson got my account that night.

My reckoning was that I had about six weeks, at the outside, to get Lamont's know-how into my business. I had no complaint when Daly visited me at my office in New York the following afternoon with a portfolio which he put on my desk in front of me. It was titled "Project 183". I grinned as he sat down in front of my desk. "I wonder what the other one hundred and eighty-two were."

"Successful." He lit a cigarette.

The twenty-two sheets of typewritten paper in the portfolio were laid out like a marketing plan or a new financial venture or a research report. In these later days of my business-running, I had seen hundreds like it. This one was exceptional; it planned only one thing—how to get me Andrew Lamont's process for making Scotch whisky artificially. Important giveaway words were coded. Whisky was called china-clay and Scotland was called Panama. Only Daly and I knew the code words.

I took three-quarters of an hour to read it, while Daly looked out the window and smoked cigarettes. When I had finished I asked, "How much?"

"Forty thousand dollars."

"You're crazy."

He came over to the desk, took the portfolio, and put it in his briefcase. He had put on his hat when I said, "I'll buy it." I had a feeling you didn't mess around with these people. Times had changed.

The first part of that plan involved me personally. The agreement was that if I succeeded and there was no need for further intervention by Gascoine Peterson, my outlay would be a token one of five thousand dollars. Naturally I wanted that part to succeed, although I didn't have much hope.

Helen Lamont was a good-looking woman. When she walked into the cocktail bar of the hotel in Glasgow, dressed in blue, I felt glad I had no stomach or double chin.

She smiled. "Mr. Sullivan?"

I rose. "Yes, Mrs. Lamont." We shook hands. "I'm glad you could come. Won't you sit down?"

She was shapely and had a clear pink complexion.

"Thanks for describing the color of your tie. It's distinctive, indeed."

"I met you once at a distillery opening in the Highlands, but I felt you wouldn't know me again. That's why I mentioned the tie."

"Did you have a pleasant flight?" For the wife of a Scots whisky chemist, she seemed very assured.

"Yes, thanks." I ordered drinks as she took off her white gloves. Yes, Mrs. Lamont *was* a good-looking woman. She had a very shapely neck and very clear blue eyes. "Did your husband enjoy his few days in New York?"

"Not very. He didn't say much about it to me, but I got the impression he was kept very busy. Of course, Andrew doesn't discuss business with me very much." She looked me straight between the eyes. "So I don't ask a great deal. He tells me what he wants to tell me. That suits me."

The waiter brought the drinks, and this gave me some time to think how I should approach her. "Mrs. Lamont, I think you know why I'm here today."

"I could make a guess."

"You know why your husband was in New York with Mr. Ogilvie."

"Yes." She smiled.

I lifted my glass and smiled. "That makes my job easier."

"Does it?"

"Do you want him to make a lot of money from his whisky process?"

"If that's what Andrew wants." She sipped her drink as if there were nothing more to say. It took me a few seconds to get used to it.

"You haven't told me what *you* want."

She nodded and put down her glass. "Mr. Sullivan, I think I know what you want. You would like me to try to influence my husband to sell you or lease you the rights of his process. You want to negotiate."

I offered her a cigarette which she accepted. "I admire your sense. Don't misunderstand me. I want to buy that process at a price which would make your head swim."

"My head doesn't swim easily. I think I know what it's worth, although I don't know anything about the process. I can tell you in a nutshell all *I* want. 1 want him to sell out so that he and I and the children can have all we've wanted for years. I want us to be rich."

I had a real job stemming my enthusiasm. "Then why in the world doesn't he sell it—to me?"

"Because he has scruples."

"Scruples about what?"

"You don't *have* to have scruples about anything, Mr. Sullivan. You just have to have them. Some people have a lot of them—like freckles, or hair on their heads. My husband is one of these." She sighed. "I know how he feels about this; he just doesn't want to be the means of ruining the Scotch whisky industry. He says it's like killing the French wine industry." She played with her glass. "Scotland means a great deal to him."

"Mrs. Lamont, listen to me—" It was the way she moved her eyes very slightly that made me turn around in my chair quickly. Andrew Lamont was standing right behind me. I felt terrible. Then I felt angry.

"Don't get up," he said, smiling. He moved around and sat in the vacant chair at our table. "You never give up, do you, Alex?"

I lit a cigarette. "No, I don't."

Mrs. Lamont appeared a little embarrassed. Frankly that's how I saw it, too. She said, "I told Andrew you'd asked to meet me here today. I don't keep secret appointments, Mr. Sullivan."

I tried to smile. "Look, let's face this right in the teeth. Andrew—"

"No, you face it right in the teeth, Alex," Lamont said. "I know what my wife wants because she's laid all her cards on the table to me; she wants the Lamont family to make a lot of money from this process. I know what I want; I want the process to be proved a success. And I know what *you* want; you just want your hands on that process so you can corner the artificial Scotch market and put everybody out of business in two years." He lit a cigarette. "There's just one snag. Nobody's going to *get* what he wants because I am not prepared to kill off a traditional industry that's been exclusive to this country for five hundred years."

Mrs. Lamont was looking at the water jug.

I sighed and swallowed some temper. "You really mean that?"

"That's exactly how I see it."

I got up because I couldn't just sit there and watch that jumped-up Scottish peasant lay down a statement like that which left me no room to move even an inch—no negotiation, no compromise, no nothing—so I pushed back my chair and said, "You're goin' to see this another way soon." I thought of the balance of payment to Daly and I felt angrier.

"I don't think so."

"But I *know* so. Don't you be crazy enough to imagine you can sit on something like this on your own terms and hold back progress of *this* size in the liquor industry, Lamont. If you don't have the brains to sell this process now to the industry, you'll have to be treated like an escaped lunatic and the responsibility taken out of your hands."

"And put into *yours*, Mr. Sullivan?" It was Helen Lamont who spoke.

"Yes. I have the money and the facilities to develop it, and I am going to use them."

Lamont took his wife's arm and she stood up as he said, "I wouldn't do a deal with you on this process if you were the last whisky man in the world, Sullivan. Goodbye."

I went out and straight to room 418 where Daly was waiting for me.

He laid down his newspaper as the door slammed. "No dice?"

"Pull the switch, Daly. Give them everything. You sold me pressure. I bought it. Now you apply it. And fast."

Nobody knows exactly how agencies like Gascoine Peterson work when they get going, but I did insist on knowing *what* they were doing in Scotland to the Lamonts.

They started on the children. First, they took the older boy to a country lane outside Glasgow, roughed him up and telephoned the parents where they would find him. Then they frightened the younger boy, ripped his clothing, and he scurried home screaming.

By Thursday of the following week I was beginning to feel back home on the New York waterfront with Buccelli.. On Monday they intended starting on Helen Lamont; I didn't like this—I always hated hearing about women being kicked—but Daly reckoned Lamont would be ready to crack by the end of that week.

I received no calls on Saturday or Sunday, and I got into my office early on Monday morning. Daly was looking out of the window of my office when I walked in. He didn't even turn around.

"Hello," I said as I put my hat on the rack.

He said nothing.

I walked behind my desk and sat down. I was about to talk to him again when I saw the package of papers, fastened with an elastic band and topped with a letter. I picked it up warily, as if I knew already it was something very important. The letter was multigraphed and it began "Dear . . ." then followed my name hand-written in ink.

"You'd better read it," Daly said in a flat voice.

I ripped off the elastic band, and the following is what I then read:

Dear Mr. Sullivan,

The enclosed papers, drawings, and chemical specifications will give you full details of a method for the production of Scotch malt whisky from any basic vegetable matter. The process has been scientifically proved at various periods under various conditions and at numerous locations over the past eight years.

Any further information you require about the process will be supplied to you free of charge on request from the writer. You should know that facsimile copies of the drawings and the specifications of the process have been mailed to every liquor-producing company in the world simultaneously. There are 1153 such companies in the mailing.

Yours faithfully,
Andrew Lamont

My hands were trembling. I dropped the package on my desk. "What the hell—is this?"

Daly turned around. "Mr. Lamont has delivered."

"This damn letter—it's—duplicated. He's sent it everywhere."

"That's what he says. He's sent it to every important manufacturer in the world." He sat down opposite my desk.

"Did you know it was here?"

He lit a cigarette. "I knew he was sending it. I came off the plane from Scotland this morning. Before I left he showed me a copy of it, and the drawings and specifications."·

I felt my voice bleating. "He's—but he's sent it everywhere."

"All over the world. The printing and mailing costs were eight hundred pounds sterling. He paid it himself."

"He's—nuts."

"It was his wife's idea. She's a clever woman. She organized it the day you left them in Glasgow."

"B-but what do I get out of this?"

"Nothing."

I felt the sweat on my upper lip. "Nothing!" I tried to laugh. "Well, well! You can't beat a public announcement, can you? You can't patent something everybody's got, can you?" I took out my handkerchief and patted my mouth. "This guy's fooled all of us. Or his wife has."

There was a silence. We looked at each other. Then I saw Daly smile and fetch a slip of paper from his pocket. He laid it on my desk. "May as well get it all over in one morning, Mr. Sullivan."

"What's this?"

"That's our bill."

"Bill? What for?" I picked up the paper. I don't remember what I said. All I can remember is my own babbling voice. I felt terrible but I couldn't stop. "Forty thousand dollars! This is crazy! You can't charge me for this. I know I said I wanted this process, but not like this. You must see that yourself. It's unreasonable. You can't push me to this. It's a lot of money. There were certain conditions. Be fair. What about a drink? Couldn't we talk this over? I didn't know it would turn out like this. Be reasonable."

I was still talking in a funny kind of high voice when Daly went to the door and opened it. Two large men came in quietly, and one of them took a rubber truncheon from his pocket. I tried to scream but no sound would come. I heard Daly say, "Leave his right arm intact. He'll need it for signing the check."

BILL PRONZINI

The Running Man

He had been walking under the blinding desert sun for two hours, following the straight, solid line of the railroad tracks, when he saw, first, the highway, and then the single building standing near it.

Having been put off the freight at a siding somewhere in the lower Arizona desert when he had been found hiding in a hot and dirty cattle car, he had wanted to rest in the shade of one of the buildings, but the man at the siding told him that the sheriff would be called if he stayed around there, and that he had better move on if he didn't want to spend time in the county jail.   He had asked for some water, because his mouth and throat were scorched from thirst, and he had been given a single cupful, nothing more.   Then he had begun to walk.

He had no idea where he was, except that he was in the desert, but he knew if he followed the tracks they would eventually lead him to a town.   It did not matter to him what town, not really, not any more.   They all looked alike.

Now he paused on the raised bank of the tracks, staring at the highway and along it, some five hundred yards, to where he could see the single building.   The highway came out of the west, diagonally toward the tracks, and then curved gradually to parallel them.   The building, standing back from the highway, was almost equidistant between it and the tracks.

He ran his tongue over dry, cracked lips and looked up into the red ball of the sun.   It had begun to sink now, slowly, moving down behind the long, thin, black ribbon of the highway.

He wondered about the building.   More than likely a gas station, he decided. That meant they would have water, and rest rooms where he could wash the smell of the cattle car from his body and change out of the sweat-soaked clothing he wore.

Taking a firmer grip on the small overnight bag he carried, he went down the sloped bank and began to walk through the mesquite and scrub brush to the highway, hurrying a little now, and wondering if they had food there at the building.   He felt the hunger in his stomach.   How long had it been since he'd eaten?   Last night—had it been almost twenty-four hours?

The highway was molten black glass, and he had to walk with his eyes cast downward to keep from being blinded by the sun-glare.   The building, he saw as he approached it, was old and wooden, a single-story, unpainted affair, fronted by a small, packed-dirt parking lot and two weathered gas pumps. To the right of the main building, and slightly behind it, was a smaller, squat building.

As he reached the dusty, unpaved access road leading off the highway, he saw a faded sign, the black-lettered words dulled by the hot desert winds, which read: *Charley's Oasis*.

He went down the access road, smelling the dry dust and tasting it in his mouth. When he came to the dirt lot, he could see a screen door under a wooden awning, and two windows, one on either side of the door. In one of the windows was a soft-drink sign; in the other was a colorful beer advertisement.

A sign on the front of the squat building to the right pointed to *Rest Rooms*, and he went there first. Inside, he peered into the small mirror over the lavatory. He saw a man named Jack Hennessy, a man who was thirty-one years old, and who looked forty. He saw pain lines etched at the corners. He saw close-cropped black hair that had already begun to lighten at the temples, making him look older. *I don't know this face anymore*, he thought.

He rubbed the beard stubble on his jaw. He hadn't shaved in two days. The desert sun had turned his skin a boiled pink color which looked incongruous against the blackness of the beard and the grime of the cattle car.

He wondered what Karen would say if she could see him like this. No. Not now. He didn't want to think about Karen.

He stripped off his sodden shirt and trousers and underwear. He turned on the tap and cupped his hands under the thin stream of water. He rinsed his mouth, resisting the urge to drink. The water tasted of chemicals. They would have fresh water inside.

From the overnight bag he took a thin bar of soap, washed his face and neck, then spilled water on the rest of his body. He took a towel from the bag and dried himself, then put on a thin blue shirt and his only other pair of shorts and a pair of wrinkled denim trousers. Looking in the mirror again, he debated shaving.

Oh, hell, he thought, *I'm not dressing to go out to dinner with Karen. I'm not . . . Oh, why do I have to keep thinking about her? How long will it go on? Aren't you ever able to forget?*

He put his soiled clothes in the bag, wet his hair and ran a comb through it, then stepped out onto the deserted sun-baked lot and walked to the main building.

It was warm inside, an overt stuffiness. A large ceiling fan whirred overhead, and there was an ice-cooler on a table in the rear, but they did little to appease the heat. He paused to let his eyes grow accustomed to the change in light, then went to a long, deserted lunch counter along the right-hand wall. The remainder of the room was taken up with wooden tables covered with red checked oilcloth, all of them empty now, and straight-backed chairs. On the wooden walls around the room were hung prospecting tools—picks, shovels, nugget pans and the like. In the rear, next to an old-fashioned wood stove, was a rocking cradle like the ones prospectors used.

Behind the lunch counter was a young blonde girl in a white uniform. She appeared to be about eighteen, was very pretty in a young, scrubbed sort of way. Her cheeks had a rosy glow, and she wore no makeup. As Jack sat down on one of the stools, he noticed she had blue eyes. *Karen had blue eyes, too. Karen, Karen, Karen . . .*

"May I help you, sir?" the girl said.

"A glass of water, please."

She took a large glass and filled it from a fountain tap. He tasted it—ice cold. Then drank thirstily, spilling some on his clean shirt, aware the girl was watching him.

"Would you like some more?" she asked.

"Yes, please." He drank another glass.

"I saw you come up," the girl said, indicating the window to the right of the door. "You weren't walking in that sun, were you?"

"My car broke down," he said, and then wondered why he had lied.

"We haven't got a mechanic here," she said.

"No, it's all right," Jack said. "I'm expecting a friend."

Another lie. Why? Why am I lying to this young girl?

"Would you care for something to eat?"

"Yes, all right. Something . . ."

She gave him a single card with the menu printed on it: *Hamburger, 50¢; Cheeseburger, 60¢; Grilled Ham and . . .* He put the card down and passed a hand across his face.

"Is something the matter, sir?" the girl asked.

"No, nothing."

"Have you decided?"

"Some eggs," he said. "Just some scrambled eggs and toast."

"Something cold to drink?"

"No," he said. "Coffee."

The girl turned to a square opening in the wall, said, "Poppa."

An old man with bright grey eyes and a long, thin nose, dressed in a white shirt and apron, appeared in the opening. "Two, scrambled," the girl said, and the old man nodded. The girl took a cup from a stack on the back counter, poured coffee into it from a glass pot on a two-burner there, and set the cup in front of Jack.

"You're not from around here, are you?" she said. "Back East someplace, I'll bet. I can tell by your accent. New York?"

"Boston," he said.

Still another lie. They seemed to flow from his lips without conscious thought. He did not know how many lies he had told in the past four months. He did not even know what reason he had for lying; not self-deception surely.

"Going to California?" the girl asked.

"Why do you ask that?"

"It seems like everybody is going to California these days," she said, and laughed.

"I'm going to Los Angeles."

"I was there once," the girl said. "It's awfully big. We're from Yuma."

"Is that near here?"

"About forty miles."

"Is that where the highway out there leads?"

"Yes, eventually."   The girl smiled at him.   "I'll be right back," she said.
"I have to chip up some fresh ice."

After she left, Jack took out his wallet and looked inside—two dollars.   He
looked in the coin pocket—a little more than a dollar in change.

That was the last of it.   Nothing left, then.   Karen would be frantic if she knew
he did not have any money.   The idea pleased him, but then she was undoubtedly
frantic as it was.

He wondered if she had the police looking for him.

Of course she would have the police looking for him.   It was four months since
he had left.   She might even have private detectives looking for him, too.   She
would do that, all right.   She would do anything to get what she wanted.   There
was no doubt about that, not any longer.   How could he have lived and slept and
eaten and laughed and talked with somebody for three long years and not have any
idea what she was really like.   How was that possible?

The girl came back behind the counter carrying a pan full of ice which she
dumped into a cooler filled with beer and soft drinks.

"The ice melts awfully fast in this heat," she told him.   "You have to keep
putting in fresh to keep things cold."

He nodded and lifted his cup.   He sipped some of the coffee, and burned his
tongue.

"Careful," the girl said.   "It's very hot."

"Yes," he said, and drank some ice water.

He wondered suddenly why he was running.   The thought came out of nowhere,
flashing into his mind, and he frowned.   Well, that was stupid.   It was very simple
why he was running.   He was running because he refused to work ten hours a day
drafting engineering designs to pay for his selfish wife's extravagance.   He was
running because there was a pain down deep inside him, the pain of a shattered
dream, and he wanted to forget that pain and the cause of that pain.   He was
running because he had been stripped of his pride, and left with nothing.   He was
running because . . .

Why am I running?   And where am I running to?   He sat rigidly erect, with
the coffee cup held halfway to his mouth.   *Come on, that's enough now.   You
thought it all out once, didn't you?   You decided this was the only way, didn't
you?   Come on, now.   Come on, you . . .*

He brought the cup clattering to the counter, spilling coffee.   He felt himself
sweating.   *It must have been the sun.   Yes, that was it.*

"Are you sure you're all right?" the girl asked.   She had been watching him
curiously.

"Fine," he said.   "I was just walking too long in the sun."

"Do you want some aspirin?"

"No, I'm fine now."

"Two, scrambled," the old man said from the kitchen.

The girl took the plate of eggs and a plate of toast from the sill and set them in front of Jack. He picked up his fork. He had an urge to lift the plate of eggs and scrape them into his mouth, but he forced himself to eat slowly, taking alternate bites of egg and toast, and then little sips of coffee. The girl watched him eat, not speaking.

He heard the car then, and turned slightly on his stool. Looking out one of the windows, he saw a dusty, dark green station wagon coming down the access road. It turned onto the lot and parked next to the building. Two men got out.

Jack could see that they were average-sized, dressed in sports shirts and slacks, and both wearing cotton jackets. In this heat? One had black hair and a neatly-trimmed moustache. The other was blond, had a wide forehead and a cupid's-bow mouth. Jack turned back to his eggs, but looked up again briefly when the door opened and the two men came inside. They stood just inside the door, as he had, to let the glare of the sun fade from their eyes. Then they went to one of the oilcloth-covered tables and sat down.

"Damn, it's hot," one of the men said, wiping his face with a handkerchief.

"A scorcher," the other man agreed.

The girl came around the counter and went to them, asked, "Can I help you, gentlemen?"

"Two beers, and I hope they're cold."

"Yes, sir," the girl said. "Ice cold."

"And bring a menu, will you?"

Jack finished his eggs, then spread jam thickly on his last piece of toast.

The girl took two beers from the cooler, opened them, put them on a tray with two of the menu cards and took them to the table where the two men were sitting.

They studied the menus. "What does the house recommend?" one of them asked.

"The ribs. They're charcoal-broiled, with our own special sauce."

"What do you say, Frank?"

"Sure, two orders of ribs. And bring two more beers."

"Yes, sir."

The girl came back and called the order into the kitchen. Jack said, "Miss, I'd like another cup of coffee, please."

"Certainly." She poured him another cup, and filled his water glass again.

He sipped his coffee, looking out the window and up to the shimmering asphalt highway. He wondered if he could get a ride. There didn't seem to be many cars on the road.

The girl opened another two bottles of beer and took them to the two men.

"Are you gentlemen going to California?" she asked.

"Are we going to California, Frank?"

"No," Frank said. "We're not going to California." He laughed.

"Are you salesmen?"

"Do we look like salesmen?"

"Well, we have a lot of salesmen stopping here."

"We're not salesmen," Frank said.

"We're hunters," the other man said, smiling.

"Oh, then you're going to Nevada. They say there's good hunting in Nevada."

"No, we're not going to Nevada," Frank said. "There's some good hunting right here."

The girl laughed. "No, you're wrong there. Unless you want to hunt jackrabbits. That's all we have around here."

"You're wrong there, missy."

"Ribs are ready," the old man called from the kitchen.

"Excuse me," the girl said to the men, and came around behind the counter to pick up the ribs.

Jack looked at his watch. It was after five o'clock. Maybe he could pick up a ride into the nearest town before it got to be too late; or maybe into Yuma. He would have to get a room for the night, and then in the morning he would have to find a job. Washing dishes was about all he could get, coming into a strange town. He'd washed a lot of dishes in the past four months.

He glanced at the tab the girl had put in front of him—fifty-seven cents. He found two quarters, a nickel and two pennies in the coin pocket of his wallet and put them on top of the tab. Then he stood, picked up his bag, and looked toward the two men.

He might be able to get a ride with them, but they had said they were hunters, were probably going into the mountains someplace.

Deciding he would try to catch a ride on the highway, he walked to the door.

"Hey, fellow, where you going in such a hurry?" one of the men sitting at the table asked.

Turning, Jack said, "I'm leaving."

"Why don't you sit down and have another cup of coffee?" the man invited.

"I don't want another cup of coffee."

"I think you better have one."

"Oh, hell," Jack said. Maybe they were drunk. He was glad he hadn't asked them for a ride. He turned for the door.

He had taken two steps when he heard the girl's muffled gasp behind him, and he came around again. Both of the men were standing, and each of them held a gun which they had taken from beneath their jackets.

Jack, staring at them, felt a cold knot in his stomach. "Hey," he said. "Hey, what is this? What's—"

"Sit down there," one of the men said, motioning with his gun.

"What kind of joke is this?"

"It's no joke. Sit down."

Jack sat down. Those were real guns. What was going on?

He saw the girl standing behind the counter, with one hand pressed to her mouth and her eyes wide like blue marbles. She stood absolutely motionless, as if she had been hypnotized.

Frank, the one with the black hair and moustache, said, "You, old man, come out here."

The old man stood behind the opening into the kitchen, but he did not move. He was frozen, like the girl.

"Didn't you hear me, old man?"

The old man moved then. He came around through the swing doors at the far end of the diner and stood next to the girl.

"There anybody else here?" Frank asked. "Dishwasher or a man on the pumps?"

"No."

"All right. Both of you come around and sit down next to your friend there."

The old man took the girl's arm and led her around to where Jack was sitting, and both of them sat down.

"Now," Frank said, "that's fine."

"What is this?" the old man asked loudly. "Is it a holdup?"

The two men laughed, and the blond one, Earl, said, "So you think it's a holdup?"

"We don't have any money," the old man said. "There's only twenty dollars in the register."

"Take it easy," Frank told him. "We don't want your money."

"What do you want then?"

"Just be quiet and you won't get hurt."

The girl, sitting next to Jack, began to cry. Instinctively, Jack put his arm around her, and she leaned against him, crying against his shoulder.

"That's nice," Frank said. "You take care of her."

Jack felt a sudden anger. "What the hell's the matter with you? What did you want to pull those guns for?"

"Maybe we like to pull guns," Earl said. "Maybe we do it all the time."

"You've got no right to scare people like this."

"If you don't shut up, I'm going to do more than scare you," Frank warned.

"What do you want here?" the old man asked.

"All right. So you want to know, do you? Earl, you tell him what we want here."

"We're here to kill a man."

"What!" Jack exploded.

"You heard me."

"You're crazy," the old man said, staring at them.

"We're not crazy," Frank denied.

"Who are you going to kill?"

"Maybe you," Earl said, and laughed.

"Shut up, Earl," Frank ordered.

"What do you mean by that?" the old man said.

"We're going to kill a man named Spikes," Earl told him.

"There's no one around here named Spikes."

"There will be."

"You're crazy," the old man said again.

"What time is it?" Frank asked Earl.

Earl looked at his watch, said, "Five-ten."

"Twenty minutes," Frank said.

"What happens in twenty minutes?" Jack asked.

"The train comes through."

"It's a freight," the old man said. "It doesn't stop anywhere around here."

"We know that," Earl said.

"Is the man you're going to kill on the five-thirty freight?"

"He'd better be."

"But it doesn't stop."

"It doesn't have to stop."

"The hell with all this," Frank said. "At five-thirty that freight is coming through here. There's a man named Spikes hiding in one of the boxcars, and when it passes by here he's going to jump off. Then he's going to come right here, because he thinks there's going to be a car waiting here for him, and a friend who's going to drive him to Mexico. But there isn't going to be any car and there isn't going to be any friend."

"Just us," Earl said.

"That's right, old man, just us."

"And you're going to kill him?"

"That's right, we're going to kill him."

"But why?"

"Let's just say he did something he shouldn't have done," Frank said.

No, Jack thought. *No, this is silly. This can't be happening. Things like this don't happen anymore.*

He felt the girl's body shaking beneath his arm. He looked at the two men, standing there very casually, holding the guns, and he felt the sweat, hot and slick, on his back and under his arms. It was very hot in the diner. A shaft of sunlight from the sinking red ball outside the window was splashed on the wooden floor, and dust motes danced inside. Jack's throat was parched.

It was very quiet. The only sounds were the whirring of the overhead fan, and the girl's crying. Finally, Earl said, "I'm going to finish my ribs."

"All right," Frank said. "You go ahead."

Earl sat down and began to eat noisily, smacking his lips.

"What are you going to do to us?" the old man asked. He was sitting stiffly, his back arched into a straight line, but he did not seem afraid.

"Nothing," Frank told him. "If you keep quiet and do just what we tell you, we're not going to do anything to you."

Jack knew he was lying. *They're going to kill us,* he thought. *After they kill this other man, this Spikes, then they're going to kill us too. Or maybe they'll just tie us up and leave us in the kitchen. But we can identify them. No, no, they're going to kill us.*

Then, for the first time since the men had taken out their guns, Jack began to feel fear.

Earl finished eating, and Frank was glancing around the room, his eyes moving slowly.

"What's back there?" he asked the old man, indicating the door at the rear of the diner.

"The storeroom."

"Is there a window in there?"

"Yes," the old man nodded.

"Earl, you go back there and watch for the train," Frank ordered. "Leave the door open so you can see in here." Earl drank the rest of his beer, then went into the storeroom, leaving the door open. Jack could see him standing beside the window, peering out at the desert. Through the window, in the distance, he could see the raised mound that was the railroad tracks.

They waited five minutes, ten, in silence. It seemed to grow hotter in the diner, as if all the desert heat had concentrated somehow inside the building. Jack was sweating freely now. Droplets of water rolled from his forehead down across his cheeks and fell on his shirt. His arm seemed to have gone to sleep around the girl's shoulders, but he made no move to take it away.

He felt protective somehow. Like a father with his daughter, that was how he felt. Yes, like a father to the child he'd wanted but never had. *Later*, Karen had said. *When we can afford it. Later, darling.*

Much, much later . . .

"Here comes the train," Earl called from the storeroom.

Jack could see the freight passing on the tracks outside; a long string of boxcars, a string of empty flats, two tankers, then a group of cattle cars and another set of boxes.

He could feel his heart pounding in his chest.

"Do you see him?" Frank called to Earl.

"No, not yet."

"Maybe he jumped on the other side."

The freight sped past.

"There he is!" Earl called, and Jack saw him then, standing in the half-open doorway of one of the boxcars near the end of the freight. He stood poised there for a moment, and then he jumped. He hit the sand at the side of the tracks, rolling, and then got to his feet slowly and stood there, brushing sand and dust from his clothing. The man looked in the direction of the building, then began to run toward them.

Earl came back inside the diner. "He'll come around to the parking lot, looking for the car," Frank said. "When he doesn't see it, he'll figure it's late. He'll have to come inside then. He can't stand out there in the sun."

Earl nodded, and moved to the window by the door, looking out.

"All right," Frank said, "the three of you come around and stand behind the counter. We don't want you catching any stray bullets, do we?"

The old man immediately went around behind the counter. Jack helped the girl up and around to where the old man stood.

"You just stand there and keep quiet," Frank said to them. "Don't move at all and don't make a sound, you understand?"

Jack realized the full impact of what was about to happen then. *They are going to kill a man. Oh, God, we are going to stand here and watch them murder a man and there is nothing we can do about it.*

"Put your head against my shoulder," Jack whispered to the girl.   "Don't look at this."

"Shut up, you," Frank said, moving the gun.

Jack looked at him and clamped his teeth tightly together.   As he brought his eyes back, he glanced at the old man.   He was standing just to the side of the two-burner, and his hand was resting on the back counter.   Jack saw the old man wet his lips, looking first to where Frank was and then down to where the glass coffee pot sat on the two-burner.

Jack knew instantly what the old man was thinking, and he felt a surge of hope. But just as quickly, the hope died.   No, it was crazy.   It wouldn't work.   There were two of them, and Earl was on the other side of the room, at the window. How could he—

The old man caught Jack's gaze then, and he moved his head slightly, rolling his eyes.   Jack, realizing he was trying to tell him something, followed the old man's eyes.   He was looking at the cash register.   No, no, he was looking to a small shelf beneath it, built into the counter; but there was nothing on the shelf except two empty mason jars, a cigar box that held cash register receipts, a roll of shelf paper, some rags . . .

He saw the gun then.

He saw the gun, and his heart gave a throbbing leap, moving up into his throat. It was wrapped in the rags on the shelf, so that only the tip of the barrel showed.

He kept looking at the gun, feeling a slight weakness in his legs, and listening to the pounding of his heart.   Then, realizing that Frank might be watching him, he tore his eyes away, looking up quickly.

Frank was staring at the window, to where Earl stood peering out.

Jack looked back to the old man, and saw the pleading question in the old man's eyes.   Would he try it?   Would he take the gamble?   It was Jack's choice. Neither of them could do it alone, but together they might be able to pull it off. Jack was nearer the gun, and the old man couldn't get to it without stepping around both Jack and the girl.   There was not enough time for that, not for him to do both.   It had to be the two of them, or nothing.

He didn't know if he could do it.   He hadn't fired a gun since the Army.   Ten years—he didn't know if he could shoot a man.   He didn't know if he could . . .

He felt the pressure of the girl's fingers on his arm.   He looked down at her. They would kill her, too; just a young girl, not even out of her teens—

He made up his mind, suddenly.

He met the old man's eyes, and the message passed between them silently, a mute understanding, and then they both looked away.

"I see him," Earl said from the window.

"Where is he?"

"Over by the rest rooms.   He sees the wagon."

"He knows that's not the car."

"He's just standing there."

"Give him time."

"He doesn't know what to do."

"He'll come inside," Frank said. "He doesn't have any choice."

"Wait," Earl said. "Here he comes."

Jack tensed the muscles in his back, standing stiffly. He made his mind a complete blank. He did not trust himself to think.

"He's coming to the door," Earl said softly, and backed away from the window, into the center of the room.

"Get set," Frank whispered.

The front door of the diner opened.

Everything that happened then seemed to happen simultaneously, jammed into a single, frozen second, so that when that second ended it was all over.

When Jack saw the front door starting to swing open, he yelled, breaking the heat-shrouded silence that hung in the room, "Look out, they've got guns! Don't come in!"

Immediately, the old man, his hand sweeping upward from the counter to the two-burner, and then outward in a single motion, threw the pot of hot coffee at Frank.

The pot struck him on the right shoulder, splashing the scalding liquid over his face and neck. He screamed, dropping his gun, his hands flying to his face.

Earl, on the opposite side of the room, fired a shot at the man in the doorway at the exact moment Frank screamed, but the sound of the scream jerked his arm and sent the shot thudding into the wall. The man in the doorway threw himself to the floor, tried to scuttle back outside on his hands and knees.

When the old man threw the pot of coffee, Jack had moved fast. He had jumped forward, with his warning yell and the sound of the gunshot ringing in his ears, and snatched the gun out of the rags, his finger automatically sliding off the safety the way he had been taught in the Army, and he brought the gun up in his right hand just as Earl swung around to the counter.

I'm going to kill a man, Jack thought, and pulled the trigger.

The bullet caught Earl high in the right shoulder. He staggered backward with the impact, his own gun flying from his hand, and toppled over one of the wooden tables, his head cracking on the solid wood floor. He lay very still.

Jack swung the gun, then, toward Frank, but he had fallen to the floor, his hands covering his scalded face. He was moaning. Jack lowered the gun.

The old man ran around to the front of the counter and picked up Frank's gun, holding it in both hands. The man from the train was still on the floor, half in and half out of the doorway, on his hands and knees. His face was the color of paste.

"They were going to kill you," the old man said to him. "They were going to kill you as soon as you walked in the door."

"Oh, my God," the man said. "Oh, my God."

The girl was crying hysterically. Jack looked down at the gun in his hand. It slipped from his fingers and clattered on the floor. His hands began to shake.

"I killed a man," he said.

The old man, standing above where Earl lay on the floor, said, "No, he's not dead. But he's out for a while."

"Get a doctor," Frank screamed from the floor. "Oh, get a doctor. My face is on fire."

Jack looked at him, and then at the girl. She was rocking on her feet, hugging herself. He went over to her. "Come on," he said. "Come on, it's all right. It's all over now."

At the sound of his voice she stopped crying and looked up at him. Her eyes said everything.

The old man was still holding Frank's gun with both hands. "Mandy," he said to the girl, "call the sheriff."

"Yes, Poppa," she said, and went to the phone on the rear wall.

The man in the doorway had scrambled to his feet. Then he turned and began to run.

"Hey!" the old man yelled. "Hey, you, come back here!"

The man, ignoring him, kept running toward the highway.

"What's the matter with him?" the old man complained.

"He's running away from something," Jack said. "He doesn't want to be here when the sheriff comes."

He's running away, Jack thought. *Yes, he's running away.*

He went to the door and stood there watching the man running up the dirt road.

That's me running, he thought with a sudden realization, and he wiped a hand across his eyes. *That's me running up there.*

We are very much alike, that man and me. Aren't we both frightened of what is behind us, and just as frightened of what lies ahead?

But I'm the lucky one. Oh, yes, I'm the lucky one because I don't have to run. I never had to run at all. I thought I was hurting Karen, but in reality the only person I had been hurting was myself.

Jack felt then as if a great and heavy burden had been lifted from his shoulders and from his mind. He felt a certain peace that he had not known for a long, long while, because on this single day, with all that had happened, he had learned more about himself than he had known in all his previous thirty-one years.

Turning from the doorway, he looked at the still figure of Earl lying on the floor, and at Frank holding his face in his hands and moaning. He looked at the girl just hanging up the telephone on the rear wall, and he looked at the old man, standing very straight and tall with the gun held in both hands.

The girl came to him and touched his arm, briefly, timidly.

The old man said simply, "Thanks, son."

Jack nodded slowly. There was nothing more to be said.

The sheriff arrived twenty minutes later with two deputies and an ambulance. After the two men were loaded into the ambulance, the sheriff asked the questions he was bound to ask and when he had finished, he tipped his hat and went outside to his car.

Jack picked up his bag, and solemnly shook hands with the old man. The girl kissed him on the cheek, like a daughter would kiss her father, and he smiled at her.   Then he went outside to where the sheriff was just starting his car.

"Can you give me a lift?" Jack asked.

"Be glad to," the sheriff said.   "Where you going?"

"Home," Jack said.   "I'm going home."

"Home?"

"Because I don't have to run, you see."

The sheriff just smiled, because he did not understand.

F. J. KELLY

The Vietnam Circle

Bars in Saigon are very functional. There are "bird-watching" bars, where the repressed tourist can sit and watch the local queens parade on the boulevard in their split-paneled, high-necked dresses over white-silk-trouser finery. There are "front parlor" bars to while away the time before going to the back parlor rooms or upstairs. And then there are out-and-out drinking bars, where you sit and drink, without distraction, without the loose-lip clichés of the once-in-a-lifetime tourist trying to convince everyone, particularly himself, that this slice of life is really old hat to him.

The Sugar Cane was a drinking bar. It was quiet, cool and dark. Waiters slid up to the table at the merest signal, quickly and efficiently replacing unwatered drinks. The proprietress was a slim, dainty doll with hardened good looks, a mass of piled-up black hair, slanting, black, snapping eyes, and dressed in the Vietnamese fashion. She sat perched near the cash register, playing solitaire. Intent on the cards, she nonetheless missed nothing going on in the small room. More and more frequently she flicked an eye toward the GI, sitting by himself near the door. Though she knew to the ounce how much he had drunk since his arrival two hours previously, she dismissed him as a man with a problem, drinking his way to a solution. He was quiet, he paid for each drink, he was no trouble. She shrugged and turned back to the cards.

The door opened. Two American soldiers of the Special Forces stood blinking to get their eyes accustomed to the dimness.

"There he is," said the smaller of the two.

"Hey, Robbie," asked the other, "what are you trying to do? Haven't we had enough trouble for one day?" The two newcomers stood staring at the soldier at the bar, who unhurriedly drained his glass and slowly turned in his chair. He looked at them. Despite the heat and their obvious haste, the green berets were perched nattily on their heads, the khaki uniforms were smartly crisp and unwrinkled, their paratroop boots reflected even the dim lighting of the bar.

"Beat it!" he snapped.

"Robbie, I figure we have just enough time to get to Tan Son Nhut and get on that chopper," pleaded the smaller trooper.

"Come on, Sarge," said the other, a corporal.

"Don't 'sarge' me!" The answer came with an oath.   "Just blow out of here and leave me alone!"

The two soldiers looked at each other, and as if by a prearranged signal, one grabbed Robbie's arms, the other snapped a jolting karate chop to Robbie's neck, and Robbie fell forward, unconscious.   They looked at the woman behind the register, got a slight negative shake of the head, gripped the slumped form under the arms, and hustled him through the door into a waiting jeep.

The H-2I was bouncing through the thermal layers, with its usual deafening roar. Private Munroe Robson sat staring out the rear door of the chopper, hardly seeing the gunner who blocked most of the view.   He rubbed his neck where the karate blow had landed.   He admitted ruefully to himself that whatever else he had done, he had gotten that part of the training across.   He judged from the changing terrain that the aircraft was only a few minutes away from their mountain camp in the highlands of South Vietnam.   The two troopers, Allen and Gentry, who had hauled him from the bar, sat opposite him, elaborately casual and completely unconcerned. Robson paused in his neck massage to notice the darker patch on his sleeve where the staff sergeant stripes had been.   Immediately the bitterness welled up.   At least these clowns had the sense not to put him on the same chopper with Barclay, he thought gratefully.

This led him off into further musings.   After six years with the Special Forces, he reflected, all I have to show for it is a dark patch on my sleeve.   Demolitions man, weapons man, intelligence operator, he had been climbing up through the ranks.   The Special Forces had been his life since the day he joined the Army. The unorthodox organization, the premium placed on independent and aggressive action, the brutal and dangerous life in the wildest terrain had appealed to his nature. He had long since mastered the art of living off the land.   He had a rare knack for getting along with complete strangers.   He could show anyone who could see, how to use a rifle, a sub-machine gun, a mortar, a plastic bomb.   He was good and he knew it.   He had been the top soldier in the detachment.   Until Barclay came along.

The chopper lurched as it started its descent.   Robson looked out at the clump of thatched huts built on poles, surrounded by a bamboo fence through which the sharpened spikes had been thrust.   A sharply banked moat encircled the area.   The moat was trapped at the bottom with ponjii spears, short, sharpened, pointed lengths of bamboo, firmly embedded in the floor of the moat.   One gate was provided at the east end of the compound.   As Robson looked, the first of the two choppers dipped into the compound.   The mountain people were running from all corners of the compound to greet them.   Then both choppers were on the ground, blades still whirling, anxious to depart for home station.

Lieutenant Higgs stood by the pad waiting for the men to alight.   He was new to this camp but not new to the job or the country.   He had been sent to take over the detachment when the former commander died in an ambush, a rugged, squat, bull-like man, quick to size up a friend or an opponent.   He was dressed in the camouflage suit, paratroop boots, and beret which was the working uniform in camp.

Robson saw Barclay jump from the chopper, and trot over to where the officer stood.   Barclay was a big man, knotty-shouldered, with a deep chest and big arms and hands.   Towering over the lieutenant, he saluted, answered quickly and tersely a few questions, saluted again, and moved off toward the detachment hut.   The lieutenant looked over toward Robson, started to shout, gave up as the helicopter motors began to roar, pointed for Robson to follow him, and strode off through the cloud of dust.

Robson climbed the rough ladder leading to the longhouse which served as office, communications room, warehouse, and sleeping quarters for the detachment.   It stood perched some six feet off the ground, supported by upright logs.   This perching provided a degree of protection against marauding animals, snakes, flooding from torrential rains, and crawling insects.   Though less protection was necessary because of the presence of the fence, the lifelong construction habits of the mountain people dictated this form of building.   The troopers lived in the rear half, with a partition of sorts separating the officers from the men.   Other reed partitions divided the remainder of the space functionally.

The office, into which Robson followed the lieutenant, consisted of a field desk, some folding chairs, and a crude map-board.   Robson stood rigidly at attention. "Sit down, Robson," the lieutenant invited, waving a hand at a chair.   He settled into a chair as Robson drew up a folding chair and sat stiffly before him.

"Well, what do we do now?" he asked.

"How do you mean, sir?"

"I mean about the remaining time you have here in the detachment, that's what I mean."

"Well, sir, I figured that since I have only twelve days to go, I'd continue as the weapons man until my replacement arrives."

"Robson," said the lieutenant, "I wasn't assigned here when this trouble began. All I know is what I learned from reading the reports and statements and the charge sheets."   He offered a pack of cigarettes to the soldier, was refused, and lit up.

"As I understand it," he resumed, "Barclay, as the senior NCO, put out an order that members of the detachment would not go out on operational patrols or raids trying to get prisoners or inflicting casualties.   Obviously, Barclay got that order from the captain; in fact, he told me so.   He surprised you and several of the Vietnamese soldiers coming back into the compound after a raiding patrol. You had gone without permission, without authority, and in direct disobedience to the order.   When Barclay called you on it, you got all worked up about it and read him off."

"He had no call to sound off in front of the Vietnamese," muttered Robson. "I just went out with them to keep an eye on them.   See how they operated at night."

"How come your rifle was fired?" the lieutenant countered.   "It was no secret you and that Vietnamese lead scout, Tuang, were hot to get yourselves some Viet Cong."

"I hate the VC," said Robson viciously.   "When you've been here longer, you'll see the villages burning, the rice crops destroyed, the men kidnapped, and the women and children killed.   You'll see—"

"I know what I'll see," interrupted Higgins.   "There's a reason to keep us out of these scrapes and you could have got us into a beaut!"

"Lieutenant," Robson's eyes were slits.   "I lived through a village raid by the Viet Cong.   They infiltrated at night, the villagers were slaughtered, and the captain caught a burst in the face.   Don't tell me about VC's."

"I'm not telling you about VC's," snapped the lieutenant, "I'm telling you how it will be here for the next twelve days.   You're the best weapons man we have.   But, as much as I need you, I don't want any more difficulties here.   I agreed to take you back after the court-martial because of your work and your record and your own request to come back.   But you'll be out of here in jig time if you don't behave.   And that includes Barclay, understand?"

"Yes, sir," replied Robson.   *I also understand how yellow Barclay is,* he thought.

"What will you do when you go back to the States?" asked the lieutenant, seeking to ease the tension.

"I'm not sure," Robson replied.   "I had intended to re-up, and get married.   That's all out the window now."

"Why do you say that?"

"Even if my girl would marry me, I'm not about to start a family as a buck private.   No, I had enough of that kind of hand-to-mouth living as a kid."

"Your girl won't care if you are a sergeant or not."

"No, Lieutenant, she wouldn't—but I do," cut in Robson, with chilling effect.

"Well, we'll see how it works out, Robson," said the lieutenant.   "Perhaps I can get you one stripe back before you leave, or at least write to your new outfit." Robson said nothing.

"When you look at it another way, Robson, you could have been creamed by that court.   After all, you got off with a fine and losing your stripes, when you could have drawn some time in jail."

Robson's mouth went taut.   "Yes, sir, I sure feel grateful.   All I was doing was out getting the enemy, and I lost my stripes and my marriage and my time in the Army."

The lieutenant stood up, signaling an end to the interview.   Robson stood quietly and alertly.

"O.K., Robson," he sighed.   "Perhaps this isn't the time to discuss it.   But I'm passing you the word.   I have enough trouble with Viet Cong outside the fence, without trouble between you and Barclay inside it.   Is that clear?"

"Perfectly," said Robson.   He saluted, about-faced, and left the hut.

The next few days passed calmly enough.   Barclay took pains to treat Robson in exactly the proper fashion.   An outsider would never have guessed the violent fury in Robson's thoughts as he went about his duties.   He took to spending more and more time at the firing ranges cut into the side of the hill about two hundred yards from the gate of the compound.   Tuang, the lead scout, found many occasions to drop by and polish up his meager English.   Tuang couldn't understand the extent of the trouble, but he knew all was not as before.   It was the day Tuang showed Robson his snares and traps set up along the edge of the rice field that the plan began to form in Robson's mind.

Several days later, during the morning operations briefing, Barclay announced the details for the next several days.   Robson's head snapped up at one announcement; Barclay and Robson, along with a squad of Vietnamese, would man the forward observation post two nights later, from dusk to dawn.   Barclay included the usual comment that personnel on the night shifts at the forward observation post would wear the black shirt usually worn by peasants to cut down the chances of being spotted.   Robson set off to his ranges as rapidly as he could.

After the morning firing, he walked into the surrounding jungle and searched the thicket until he found signs of animal passage.   He quickly set up a snare, restored the area to as close a natural setting as possible, and returned to the range.   Later that afternoon he found a small, fat rabbit caught in the snare.   He took the frightened animal, hurried to the farthest corner of the rice field, staked out the rabbit, and completed his preparations.   Skipping breakfast the following morning, he checked out the trap and found a contented, bulging, banded krait coiled around the remains of the rabbit.

He approached the trap gingerly.   The banded krait, though only about two feet long, is a deadly killer.   Generally nonaggressive, the krait is a vicious enemy when aroused or irritated.   The alternating bands of yellow and black are highly distinctive and easily spotted.   The krait, as with most poisonous snakes, usually moves and feeds by night, Robson knew.   Right now, this specimen was not too upset at being entrapped, though Robson knew he would be once the effects of the meal had worn off.

Robson circled him carefully, then gently but firmly placed a forked stick behind the head.   Even then, the krait barely wriggled.   Robson bent, seized the krait firmly behind the head, dropped the stick and, in one motion, dropped the snake into a cloth sack he carried, which he then firmly knotted.   He returned to the range area and hung the sack from a branch, out of sight of any chance visitors to the range.

Just before supper that night, when he knew Barclay would be busy with the Vietnamese NCO's, Robson casually strolled past Barclay's bunk.   After inspecting the area and observing no one in view, Robson picked up the black peasant shirt from Barclay's chair, walked back to his own bunk, and stuffed the shirt under his blanket.   Considerably cheered, he went off to supper.

The following morning, he looked up Tuang and asked to borrow a cooking pot, specifying he wanted one with a lid.   Tuang, a little surprised at such a strange request, delivered the pot, which was big enough to cook a good-sized chicken, to Robson at the firing range.

Robson set the pot on a large flat rock, then placed the black shirt inside it.   He retrieved the snake bag, and dumped the snake into the pot.   He had only a flash glimpse of the snake in the pot alongside the shirt before he slammed the lid into place.

Well, buster, he thought, *you'll be really cranked up about that shirt.* Robson's training and experience with snakes had taught him that poisonous snakes, if irritated, would blindly strike at whatever had been associated with the irritation. Robson knew that if the krait ever got near that shirt again, smelled the characteristic smell of that shirt, the snake would lash out in all its fury at the object which the snake associated with its torment.

During the afternoon, Robson returned to the pot, carefully upended it and gradually inched back the lid until the snake slid out into the bag.   He fastened the bag tightly and set it aside.   He removed the black shirt from the pot, folded the shirt inside his own, picked up the snake bag, and started back to camp.   He hid the snake bag on the trail near the outpost, and then hurried to the compound.

His timing was perfect.   Most of the detachment were already at supper.   He took the black shirt and draped it on a chair next to Barclay's bed.   Not too obvious, he thought, and walked out to the mess tent.

The forward observation post was really two lookout stations built on top of an earthen room.   The room was sunk into the ground for several feet, boards and packed earth constituted the ceiling.   Machine gun stations occupied a firing position in each wall.   A walkie-talkie radio provided contact with the main compound.   A ladder permitted ascent to a narrow trench passageway which led, in turn, to the two stations on top.   Each station resembled a cut-down phone booth. The booths reached nearly to a man's chest.   Lookouts had an open view on all four sides.   Standing as it did in the broiling sun, the observation post was always a sweat box, with the lookout stations perhaps the hottest part of all.

The squad assembled in the dim twilight outside the OP.

"When we are inside, I want no lights, no talking, no noise," said Barclay. The interpreter sing-songed this order to the squad.   Heads bobbed.

"If you see anything of the Viet Cong, tell Robson or me."   The interpreter rattled on.

"Once in position, nobody moves, nobody talks."   More sing-song, more heads bobbing.

"Robson and I will look together until night falls.   Viet Cong attack at any time.   Don't take chances—report everything," Barclay concluded. Though not fully comprehending, the squad moved into the bunker room.

"Come on, Robbie," said Barclay.   "I want to tell you something before we get up in the posts."

"I just want to finish this smoke," said Robson, not meeting his eyes.   "I'll be right along."

"All right," said Barclay, "but step on it.   We'll have trouble getting up the ladder in a few minutes."   Barclay went inside.   Robson heard him talking to the machine gunners, and heard ammo boxes being moved.

Robson sped down the trail to where he had cached the snake bag.   He was sure he was not seen in the diminishing light, especially dressed in his black peasant shirt.

He secured the bag, ran back to the door of the bunker, and called Barclay. The interpreter said softly that Barclay had gone up to the lookout station.

Robson climbed the ladder quickly, feeling the bag shake in his hand as the snake began to move.   He found his footing in the passageway and sidled down a step or two toward his station.

With his foot, he flipped over the grass cover closing off the ladder access to the stations.

The entire post settled down to watchful waiting.   He had two hours before a relief shift came up.   The lookout booth was stifling.   Even at night, the heat caused the sweat to pour.   He looked out at the countryside.   He looked, and counted to himself, and looked some more.   After an hour, he bent to his knees and carefully picked up the bundle of death.   He inched gently into the passageway for a foot or two, unwrapped the fastening fold, and upended the bag in the direction of Barclay's station.   He then edged back to his own station, balled up the bag, and flung it out into the blackness . . .

The compound was steeped in gloom.   The normally noisy, cheerfully grinning Vietnamese walked in tiptoe quiet as if to avoid offending the spirits of death. Peasants walked with eyes rooted on the ground, lifting their heads only to shoot a fearful glance at the longhouse where Barclay's body now lay.   The death of Barclay was the prime topic in every little cluster of Vietnamese.   They had looked on Barclay as a friend.   They were looking now to see what would be done.

Lieutenant Higgins had set a guard at each end of the longhouse.   The Special Forces troopers stood in stony silence.   Directly Barclay's body had been found, the lieutenant had radioed the base camp, and had received instructions to await the arrival of the deputy commander, Major Flynn.   He arrived in a light observation plane shortly after dawn, hurried to the longhouse, and was closeted with Lieutenant Higgins for almost an hour.   They both emerged to visit the outpost, and then returned to the office.   The parade of witnesses began, ending, finally, with Robson.   Robson stoically denied any knowledge of the death, and carefully and accurately provided all the details up to the time he and Barclay had assumed their posts in the lookout towers.

No, he hadn't heard an outcry.   No, he had not been aware of anyone on the ladder.   No, he had not talked to Barclay at all, once they ascended to the towers. No, he didn't know what Barclay intended to tell him, referring to Barclay's comment just before entering the outpost.   No, no, no.   Robson was excused.

Minutes later, both officers walked through the compound toward the little plane. The villagers watched.   After the plane took off, Robson was summoned to the detachment office.   When he walked in, he found the lieutenant pacing slowly behind the desk.   He reported, and stood at a brace.   Higgins waved him at ease.

"Robson, have I missed anything about this case?"

"I don't know what you mean, sir."

The lieutenant was silent a moment.   Finally, as if reaching a hard decision, he squared around, leaned on his knuckles on the desk, and looked at Robson bleakly.

"I have missed something, but I'm damned if I can put my finger on it.   There's something out of focus, but I can't lock on to it.   Well, that's neither here nor there.   The Major has decided to hold the formal inquiry at the Tan Son Nhut airbase tomorrow. He will want you there. A chopper will be here in the morning. You can be escort for Barclay to the airbase. His body is being returned to the States. Something wrong, Robson?'' he asked.

"No, sir, I just was surprised you picked me,'' Robson stammered.

"I didn't 'pick' you, Robson,'' the lieutenant continued. "I can't spare anyone here. Since you have to go to testify, you can be the escort. One other thing, take all your gear with you. Since you have only a few days, you are to be sent home after the investigation.''

Robson opened his mouth, started to say something, then shut it again.

"You will be ready to leave first thing in the morning. I'm going over to check on the coffin they are making for Barclay. Care to come along?''

"No, thank you,'' said Robson.

"O.K. then—move out,'' snapped Higgins.

When Robson left, he avoided the villagers standing near the longhouse. He hurried out to the range area and collected his few belongings there. He picked up the pot he had borrowed from Tuang and set out to return it to him. He found Tuang in the quarters area of the compound.

Tuang was obviously upset. Robson handed him the pot, some cigarettes, a handful of piasters, soap, and other odds and ends. Tuang, who normally would have been grinning from ear to ear at such a windfall, just looked morosely at his loot.

"What's wrong, Tuang?''

"Everything, everything. Barclay dead—snake spirit loose—all wrong, all wrong.'' Tuang dropped into the typical heel-squatting posture of the mountain man. He rocked slowly back and forth.

Robson looked at him in silence. He knew the Montagnards were animists, if indeed they had any religion at all. The spirits of the dead, the ancestors, were inextricably wound up in the living, the animal world, the symbolism of nature projected into the world beyond.

"Well, Tuang, I go tomorrow morning,'' said Robson. "The Major wants me to go with Barclay to Tan Son Nhut.''

"You come back?'' asked Tuang.

"No, I do not come back,'' said Robson.

Tuang rocked some more, groaning and grimacing.

The compound was alive all night. The rude coffin of boards, lashed together with native ropes, was finished. A rough bed of boughs and branches was placed in the box to cushion Barclay's remains. The body was installed, but Higgins ordered the lid to be left free until just before take-off. The villagers ranged the compound all night. Groups patrolled out into the surrounding jungle until dawn. Giant fires burned, drums tattooed without interruption. The Vietnamese women keened and moaned alternatively in sorrow for the dead soldier.

Robson spent the greater part of the night tossing and turning, while the minutes crept by. He was packed and ready to move out long before the dawn stole into the valley. He went outside and strained his eyes and ears into the morning stillness, as if trying to hurry the chopper.

The H-21 could be heard even before it was seen.   It settled down like a tired whale, blades swishing clouds of dust.   The two pilots and the crew chief were anxious to get off.

Lieutenant Higgins ordered the coffin to be brought to the chopper.   The villagers grouped around in a tight circle.   The lid was removed, and each trooper walked to the coffin to say his own farewell.   The Montagnards hung back.   The lid was replaced.   The coffin was lifted into the chopper and lashed to the floor of the cargo compartment.   A flurry of activity occurred near the compound gate, as Robson swung aboard the aircraft.

The tribal chief now walked forward carrying a small wooden case.   He walked to the door of the aircraft, presented the box to Robson, bowed formally, and backed away.   Robson was obviously pleased with the gift.   He stood in the door, smiling, while the chopper coughed to life, gathered itself and lurched into the air.   Those on the ground could see him fumbling with the box to open it.

"What was in that box, Tuang, and why did the chief give Robson a present?" asked Lieutenant Higgins.   The chopper was disappearing to the south.

"When a Montagnard dies, that which causes him to die must go with him," said Tuang, "or he has no peace in his grave.   We searched all night for the brother of Barclay's killer.   That is what was in the box."

"But Robson thought—" began Lieutenant Higgins.   He broke off to look up at the new sound in the air.

The helicopter was coming back.

ED MCBAIN

Sadie When She Died

"I'm very glad she's dead," the man said.

He wore a homburg, muffler, overcoat, and gloves. He stood near the night table, a tall man with a narrow face, and a well-groomed grey moustache that matched the greying hair at his temples. His eyes were clear and blue and distinctly free of pain or grief.

Detective Steve Carella wasn't sure he had heard the man correctly. "Sir," Carella said, "I'm sure I don't have to tell you—"

"That's right," the man said, "you don't have to tell me. It happens I'm a criminal lawyer and am well aware of my rghts. My wife was no good, and I'm delighted someone killed her."

Carella opened his pad. This was not what a bereaved husband was supposed to say when his wife lay disemboweled on the bedroom floor in a pool of her own blood.

"Your name is Gerald Fletcher."

"That's correct."

"Your wife's name, Mr. Fletcher?"

"Sarah. Sarah Fletcher."

"Want to tell me what happened?"

"I got home about fifteen minutes ago. I called to my wife from the front door, and got no answer. I came into the bedroom and found her dead on the floor. I immediately called the police."

"Was the room in this condition when you came in?"

"It was."

"Touch anything?"

"Nothing. I haven't moved from this spot since I placed the call."

"Anybody in here when you came in?"

"Not a soul. Except my wife, of course."

"Is that your suitcase in the entrance hallway?"

"It is. I was on the Coast for three days. An associate of mine needed advice on a brief he was preparing. What's your name?"

"Carella. Detective Steve Carella."

"I'll remember that."

While the police photographer was doing his macabre little jig around the body to make sure the lady looked good in the rushes, or as good as any lady *can* look in her condition, a laboratory assistant named Marshall Davies was in the kitchen of the apartment, waiting for the medical examiner to pronounce the lady dead, at which time Davies would go into the bedroom and with delicate care remove the knife protruding from the blood and slime of the lady, in an attempt to salvage some good latent prints from the handle of the murder weapon.

Davies was a new technician, but an observant one, and he noticed that the kitchen window was wide open, not exactly usual on a December night when the temperature outside hovered at twelve degrees. Leaning over the sink, he further noticed that the window opened onto a fire escape on the rear of the building. He could not resist speculating that perhaps someone had climbed up the fire escape and then into the kitchen.

Since there was a big muddy footprint in the kitchen sink, another one on the floor near the sink, and several others fading as they traveled across the waxed kitchen floor to the living room, Davies surmised that he was onto something hot. Wasn't it possible that an intruder *had* climbed over the window sill, into the sink, and walked across the room, bearing the switchblade knife that had later been pulled viciously across the lady's abdomen from left to right? If the M.E. ever got through with the damn body, the boys of the 87th would be halfway home, thanks to Marshall Davies. He felt pretty good.

The three points of the triangle were Detective-Lieutenant Byrnes, and Detectives Meyer Meyer and Steve Carella. Fletcher sat in a chair, still wearing homburg, muffler, overcoat, and gloves as if he expected to be called outdoors at any moment. The interrogation was being conducted in a windowless cubicle labeled Interrogation Room.

The cops standing in their loose triangle around Gerald Fletcher were amazed but not too terribly amused by his brutal frankness.

"I hated her guts," he said.

"Mr. Fletcher," Lieutenant Byrnes said, "I *still* feel I must warn you that a woman has been murdered—"

"Yes. My dear, wonderful wife," Fletcher said sarcastically.

". . . which is a serious crime . . ." Byrnes felt tongue-tied in Fletcher's presence. Bullet-headed, hair turning from iron-grey to ice-white, blue-eyed, built like a compact linebacker, Byrnes looked to his colleagues for support. Both Meyer and Carella were watching their shoelaces.

"You have warned me repeatedly," Fletcher said. "I can't imagine why. My wife is dead—someone killed her—but it was not I."

"Well, it's nice to have your assurance of that, Mr. Fletcher, but this alone doesn't necessarily still our doubts," Carella said, hearing the words and wondering where the hell they were coming from. He was, he realized, trying to impress Fletcher. He continued, "How do we know it *wasn't* you who stabbed her?"

"To begin with," Fletcher said, "there were signs of forcible entry in the kitchen

and hasty departure in the bedroom, witness the wide-open window in the afore-
mentioned room and the shattered window in the latter.   The drawers in the dining-
room sideboard were open—"

"You're very observant," Meyer said suddenly.   "Did you notice all this in
the four minutes it took you to enter the apartment and call the police?"

"It's my *job* to be observant," Fletcher said.   "But to answer your question,
no.   I noticed all this *after* I had spoken to Detective Carella here."

Wearily, Byrnes dismissed Fletcher, who then left the room.

"What do you think?" Byrnes said.

"I think he did it," Carella said.

"Even with all those signs of a burglary?"

"*Especially* with those signs.   He could have come home, found his wife stabbed—
but not fatally—and finished her off by yanking the knife across her belly.   Fletcher
had four minutes, when all he needed was maybe four seconds."

"It's possible," Meyer said.

"Or maybe I just don't like the guy," Carella said.

"Let's see what the lab comes up with," Byrnes said.

The laboratory came up with good fingerprints on the kitchen window sash and
on the silver drawer of the dining-room sideboard.   There were good prints on
some of the pieces of silver scattered on the floor near the smashed bedroom window.
Most important, there were good prints on the handle of the switchblade knife.
The prints matched; they had all been left by the same person.

Gerald Fletcher graciously allowed the police to take *his* fingerprints, which were
then compared with those Marshall Davies had sent over from the police laboratory.
The fingerprints on the window sash, the drawer, the silverware, and the knife did
not match Gerald Fletcher's.

Which didn't mean a damn thing if he had been wearing his gloves when he'd
finished her off.

On Monday morning, in the second-floor rear apartment of 721 Silvermine Oval,
a chalked outline on the bedroom floor was the only evidence that a woman had
lain there in death the night before.   Carella sidestepped the outline and looked
out the shattered window at the narrow alleyway below.   There was a distance of
perhaps twelve feet between this building and the one across from it.

Conceivably, the intruder could have leaped across the shaftway, but this would
have required premeditation and calculation.   The more probable likelihood was
that the intruder had fallen to the pavement below.

"That's quite a long drop," Detective Bert Kling said, peering over Carella's
shoulder.

"How far do you figure?" Carella asked.

"Thirty feet.   At least."

"Got to break a leg taking a fall like that.   You think he went through the
window headfirst?"

"How else?"

"He might have broken the glass out first, then gone through," Carella suggested.

"If he was about to go to all that trouble, why didn't he just *open* the damn thing?"

"Well, let's take a look," Carella said.

They examined the latch and the sash.   Kling grabbed both handles on the window frame and pulled up on them.   "Stuck."

"Probably painted shut," Carella said.

"Maybe he did try to open it.   Maybe he smashed it only when he realized it was stuck."

"Yeah," Carella said.   "And in a big hurry, too.   Fletcher was opening the front door, maybe already in the apartment by then."

"The guy probably had a bag or something with him, to put the loot in.   He must have taken a wild swing with the bag when he realized the window was stuck, and maybe some of the stuff fell out, which would explain the silverware on the floor.   Then he probably climbed through the hole and dropped down feet first.   In fact, what he could've done, Steve, was drop the bag down first, and *then* climbed out and hung from the sill before he jumped, to make it a shorter distance."

"I don't know if he had all that much time, Bert.   He must have heard that front door opening, and Fletcher coming in and calling to his wife.   Otherwise, he'd have taken his good, sweet time and gone out the kitchen window and down the fire escape, the way he'd come in."

Kling nodded reflectively.   "Let's take a look at that alley," Carella said.

In the alleyway outside, Carella and Kling studied the concrete pavement, and then looked up at the shattered second-floor window of the Fletcher apartment.

"Where do you suppose he'd have landed?" Kling said.

"Right about where we're standing."   Carella looked at the ground.   "I don't know, Bert.   A guy drops twenty feet to a concrete pavement, doesn't break anything, gets up, dusts himself off, and runs the fifty-yard dash, right?"   Carella shook his head.   "My guess is he stayed right where he was to catch his breath, giving Fletcher time to look out the window, which would be the natural thing to do, but which Fletcher didn't."

"He was anxious to call the police."

"I still think he did it."

"Steve, be reasonable.   If a guy's fingerprints are on the handle of a knife, and the knife is still in the victim—"

"*And* if the victim's husband realizes what a sweet setup he's stumbled into, wife lying on the floor with a knife in her, place broken into and burglarized, why *not* finish the job and hope the burglar will be blamed?"

"Sure," Kling said.   "Prove it."

"I can't," Carella said.   "Not until we catch the burglar."

While Carella and Kling went through the tedious routine of retracing the burglar's footsteps, Marshall Davies called the 87th Precinct and got Detective Meyer.

"I think I've got some fairly interesting information about the suspect," Davies said.   "He left latent fingerprints all over the apartment and footprints in the kitchen.   A very good one in the sink, when he climbed in through the window, and some middling-fair ones tracking across the kitchen floor to the dining room. I got some excellent pictures and some good blowups of the heel.''

''Good,'' Meyer said.

''But more important,'' Davies went on, ''I got a good walking picture from the footprints on the floor.   If a man is walking slowly, the distance between his footprints is usually about twenty-seven inches.   Forty for running, thirty-five for fast walking.   These were thirty-two inches.   So we have a man's usual gait, moving quickly, but not in a desperate hurry, with the walking line normal and not broken.''

''What does that mean?''

''Well, a walking line should normally run along the inner edge of a man's heelprints.   Incidentally, the size and type of shoe and angle of the foot clearly indicate that this *was* a man.''

''O.K., fine,'' Meyer said.   He did not thus far consider Davies' information valuable nor even terribly important.

''Anyway, none of this is valuable nor even terribly important,'' Davies said, ''until we consider the rest of the data.   The bedroom window was smashed, and the Homicide men were speculating that the suspect had jumped through the window into the alley below.   I went down to get some meaningful pictures, and got some pictures of where he must have landed—on both feet, incidentally—and I got another walking picture and direction line.   He moved toward the basement door and into the basement.   But the important thing is that our man is injured, and I think badly.''

''How do you know?''   Meyer asked.

''The walking picture downstairs is entirely different from the one in the kitchen. When he got downstairs he was leaning heavily on the left leg and dragging the right.   I would suggest that whoever's handling the case put out a physicians' bulletin.   If this guy hasn't got a broken leg, I'll eat the pictures I took.''

A girl in a green coat was waiting in the apartment lobby when Carella and Kling came back in, still retracing footsteps, or trying to.   The girl said, ''Excuse me, are you the detectives?''

''Yes,'' Carella said.

''The super told me you were in the building,'' the girl said.   ''You're investigating the Fletcher murder, aren't you?''   She was quite soft-spoken.

''How can we help you, miss?'' Carella asked.

''I saw somebody in the basement last night, with blood on his clothes.''

Carella glanced at Kling and immediately said, ''What time was this?''

''About a quarter to eleven,'' the girl said.

''What were you doing in the basement?''

The girl looked surprised.

''That's where the washing machines are.   I'm sorry, my name is Selma Bernstein.   I live here in the building.''

''Tell us what happened, will you?'' Carella said.

''I was sitting by the machine, watching the clothes tumble, which is simply *fascinating,* you know, when the door leading to the back yard opened—the door to the alley.   This man came down the stairs, and I don't even think he saw me. He went straight for the stairs at the other end, the ones that go up into the street. I never saw him before last night.''

''Can you describe him?'' Carella asked.

''Sure.   He was about twenty-one or twenty-two, your height and weight, well, maybe a little bit shorter, five ten or eleven, brown hair.''

Kling was already writing.   The man was white, wore dark trousers, high-topped sneakers, and a poplin jacket with blood on the right sleeve and on the front.   He carried a small red bag, ''like one of those bags the airlines give you.''

Selma didn't know if he had any scars.   ''He went by in pretty much of a hurry, considering he was dragging his right leg.   I think he was hurt pretty badly.''

What they had in mind, of course, was identification from a mug shot, but the I.S. reported that none of the fingerprints in their file matched the ones found in the apartment.   So the detectives figured it was going to be a tough one, and they sent out a bulletin to all of the city's doctors just to prove it.

Just to prove that cops can be as wrong as anyone else, it turned out to be a nice easy one after all.

The call came from a physician in Riverhead at 4:37 that afternoon, just as Carella was ready to go home.

''This is Dr. Mendelsohn,'' he said.   ''I have your bulletin here, and I want to report treating a man early this morning who fits your description—a Ralph Corwin of 894 Woodside in Riverhead.   He had a bad ankle sprain.''

''Thank you, Dr. Mendelsohn,'' Carella said.

Carella pulled the Riverhead directory from the top drawer of his desk and quickly flipped to the C's.   He did not expect to find a listing for Ralph Corwin.   A man would have to be a rank amateur to burglarize an apartment without wearing gloves, then stab a woman to death, and then give his name when seeking treatment for an injury sustained in escaping from the murder apartment.

Ralph Corwin was apparently a rank amateur.   His name was in the phone book, and he'd given the doctor his correct address.

Carella and Kling kicked in the door without warning, fanning into the room, guns drawn.   The man on the bed was wearing only undershorts.   His right ankle was taped.

''Are you Ralph Corwin?'' Carella asked.

''Yes,'' the man said.   His face was drawn, the eyes in pain.

''Get dressed, Corwin.   We want to ask you some questions.''

''There's nothing to ask,'' he said and turned his head into the pillow.   ''I killed her.''

Ralph Corwin made his confession in the presence of two detectives of the 87th, a police stenographer, an assistant district attorney, and a lawyer appointed by the Legal Aid Society.

Corwin was the burglar.   He'd entered 721 Silvermine Oval on Sunday night, December twelfth, down the steps from the street where the garbage cans were. He went through the basement, up the steps at the other end, into the back yard, and climbed the fire escape, all at about ten o'clock in the evening.   Corwin entered the Fletcher apartment because it was the first one he saw without lights.   He figured there was nobody home.   The kitchen window was open a tiny crack; Corwin squeezed his fingers under the bottom and opened it all the way.   He was pretty desperate at the time because he was a junkie in need of cash.   He swore that he'd never done anything like this before.

The man from the D.A.'s office was conducting the Q. and A. and asked Corwin if he hadn't been afraid of fingerprints, not wearing gloves.   Corwin figured that was done only in the movies, and anyway, he said, he didn't own gloves.

Corwin used a tiny flashlight to guide him as he stepped into the sink and down to the floor.   He made his way to the dining room, emptied the drawer of silverware into his airline bag.   Then he looked for the bedroom, scouting for watches and rings, whatever he could take in the way of jewelry.   "I'm not a pro," he said. "I was just hung up real bad and needed some bread to tide me over."

Now came the important part.   The D.A.'s assistant asked Corwin what happened in the bedroom.

A.   There was a lady in bed.   This was only like close to ten-thirty, you don't expect nobody to be asleep so early.

Q.   But there was a woman in bed.

A.   Yeah.   She turned on the light the minute I stepped in the room.

Q.   What did you do?

A.   I had a knife in my pocket.   I pulled it out to scare her.   It was almost comical.   She looks at me and says, "What are you doing here?"

Q.   Did you say anything to her?

A.   I told her to keep quiet, that I wasn't going to hurt her.   But she got out of bed and I saw she was reaching for the phone.   That's got to be crazy, right? A guy is standing there in your bedroom with a knife in his hand, so she reaches for the phone.

Q.   What did you do?

A.   I grabbed her hand before she could get it.   I pulled her off the bed, away from the phone, you know?   And I told her again that nobody was going to hurt her, that I was getting out of there right away, to just please calm down.

Q.   What happened next?

A.   She started to scream.   I told her to stop.   I was beginning to panic.   I mean she was really yelling.

Q.   Did she stop?

A.   No.

Q.   What did you do?

A.   I stabbed her.

Q.   Where did you stab her?

A.   I don't know.   It was a reflex.   She was yelling, I was afraid the whole building would come down.   I just . . . I just stuck the knife in her.   I was very scared.   I stabbed her in the belly.   Someplace in the belly.

Q.   How many times did you stab her?

A.   Once.   She . . . she backed away from me.   I'll never forget the look on her face.   And she . . . she fell on the floor.

Q.   Would you look at this photograph, please?

A.   Oh, no . . .

Q.   Is that the woman you stabbed?

A.   Oh, no . . . I didn't think . . . Oh, no!

A moment after he stabbed Sarah Fletcher, Corwin heard the door opening and someone coming in.   The man yelled, "Sarah, it's me, I'm home."   Corwin ran past Sarah's body on the floor, and tried to open the window, but it was stuck. He smashed it with his airline bag, threw the bag out first to save the swag because, no matter what, he knew he'd need another fix, and he climbed through the broken window, cutting his hand on a piece of glass.   He hung from the sill, and finally let go, dropping to the ground.   He tried to get up, and fell down again.   His ankle was killing him, his hand bleeding.   He stayed in the alley nearly fifteen minutes, then finally escaped via the route Selma Bernstein had described to Carella and Kling.   He took the train to Riverhead and got to Dr. Mendelsohn at about nine in the morning.   He read of Sarah Fletcher's murder in the newspaper on the way back from the doctor.

On Tuesday, December 14, which was the first of Carella's two days off that week, he received a call at home from Gerald Fletcher.   Fletcher told the puzzled Carella that he'd gotten his number from a friend in the D.A.'s office, complimented Carella and the boys of the 87th on their snappy detective work, and invited Carella to lunch at the Golden Lion at one o'clock.   Carella wasn't happy about interrupting his Christmas shopping, but this was an unusual opportunity, and he accepted.

Most policemen in the city for which Carella worked did not eat very often in restaurants like the Golden Lion.   Carella had never been inside.   A look at the menu posted on the window outside would have frightened him out of six months' pay.   The place was a faithful replica of the dining room of an English coach house, circa 1627: huge oaken beams, immaculate white cloths, heavy silver.

Gerald Fletcher's table was in a secluded corner of the restaurant.   He rose as Carella approached, extended his hand, and said, "Glad you could make it.   Sit down, won't you?"

Carella shook Fletcher's hand, and then sat.   He felt extremely uncomfortable, but he couldn't tell whether his discomfort was caused by the room or by the man with whom he was dining.

"Would you care for a drink?" Fletcher asked.

"Well, are you having one?" Carella asked.

"Yes, I am."

"I'll have a Scotch and soda," Carella said.   He was not used to drinking at lunch.

Fletcher signaled the waiter and ordered the drinks, making his another whiskey sour.

When the drinks came, Fletcher raised his glass. "Here's to a conviction," he said.

Carella lifted his own glass. "I don't expect there'll be any trouble," he said. "It looks airtight to me."

Both men drank. Fletcher dabbed his lips with a napkin and said, "You never can tell these days. I hope you're right, though." He sipped at the drink. "I must admit I feel a certain amount of sympathy for him."

"Do you?"

"Yes. If he's an addict, he's automatically entitled to pity. And when one considers that the woman he murdered was nothing but a—"

"Mr. Fletcher . . ."

"Gerry, please. And I know: it isn't very kind of me to malign the dead. I'm afraid you didn't know my wife, though, Mr. Carella. May I call you Steve?"

"Sure."

"My enmity might be a bit more understandable if you had. Still, I shall take your advice. She's dead, and no longer capable of hurting me, so why be bitter. Shall we order, Steve?"

Fletcher suggested that Carella try either the trout *au meuniere* or the beef and kidney pie, both of which were excellent. Carella ordered prime ribs, medium rare, and a mug of beer.

As the men ate and talked, something began happening, or at least Carella *thought* something was happening; he might never be quite sure. The conversation with Fletcher seemed on the surface to be routine chatter, but rushing through this inane, polite discussion was an undercurrent that caused excitement, fear, and apprehension. As they spoke, Carella knew with renewed certainty that Gerald Fletcher had killed his wife. Without ever being told so, he knew it. *This* was why Fletcher had called this morning; *this* was why Fletcher had invited him to lunch; *this* was why he prattled on endlessly while every contradictory move of his body signaled on an almost extrasensory level that he *knew* Carella suspected him of murder, and was here to *tell* Carella (*without* telling him) that, "Yes, you stupid cop, I killed my wife. However much the evidence may point to another man, however many confessions you get, I killed her and I'm glad I killed her. And there isn't a damn thing you can do about it."

Ralph Corwin was being held before trial in the city's oldest prison, known to law enforcers and lawbreakers alike as Calcutta. Neither Corwin's lawyer nor the district attorney's office felt that allowing Carella to talk to the prisoner would be harmful to the case.

Corwin was expecting him. "What did you want to see me about?"

"I wanted to ask you some questions."

"My lawyer says I'm not supposed to add anything to what I already said. I don't even *like* that guy."

"Why don't you ask for another lawyer? Ask one of the officers here to call the Legal Aid Society.   Or simply tell him.   I'm sure he'd have no objection to dropping out.''

Corwin shrugged.   "I don't want to hurt his feelings.   He's a little cockroach, but what the hell.''

"You've got a lot at stake here, Corwin.''

"But I killed her, so what does it matter *who* the lawyer is?   You got it all in black and white.''

"You feel like answering some questions?'' Carella said.

"I feel like dropping dead, is what I feel like.   Cold turkey's never good, and it's worse when you can't yell.''

"If you'd rather I came back another time . . .''

"No, no, go ahead.   What do you want to know?''

"I want to know exactly how you stabbed Sarah Fletcher.''

"How do you *think* you stab somebody?   You stick a knife in her.''

"Where?''

"In the belly.''

"Left-hand side of the body?''

"Yeah.   I guess so.''

"Where was the knife when she fell?''

"I don't know what you mean.''

"Was the knife on the *right*-hand side of her body or the *left?*''

"I don't know.   That was when I heard the front door opening and all I could think of was getting out of there.''

"When you stabbed her, did she *twist* away from you?''

"No, she backed away, straight back, as if she couldn't believe what I done, and . . . and just wanted to get *away* from me.''

"And then she fell?''

"Yes.   She . . . her knees sort of gave way and she grabbed for her belly, and her hands sort of—it was terrible—they just . . . they were grabbing *air,* you know? And she fell.''

"In what position?''

"On her side.''

"*Which* side?''

"I could still see the knife, so it must've been the opposite side.   The side opposite from where I stabbed her.''

"One last question, Ralph.   Was she dead when you went through that window?''

"I don't know.   She was bleeding and . . . she was very quiet.   I . . . guess she was dead.   I don't know.   I guess so.''

Among Sarah Fletcher's personal effects that were considered of interest to the police before they arrested Ralph Corwin, was an address book found in the dead woman's handbag on the bedroom dresser.   In the Thursday afternoon stillness of the squad room, Carella examined the book.

There was nothing terribly fascinating about the alphabetical listings.   Sarah

Fletcher had possessed a good handwriting, and most of the listings were obviously married couples (Chuck and Nancy Benton, Harold and Marie Spander, and so on), some were girlfriends, local merchants, hairdresser, dentist, doctors, restaurants in town or across the river.   A thoroughly uninspiring address book—until Carella came to a page at the end of the book, with the printed word MEMORANDA at its top.

Under the word, there were five names, addresses and telephone numbers written in Sarah's meticulous hand.   They were all men's names, obviously entered at different times because some were in pencil and others in ink.   The parenthetical initials following each entry were all noted in felt marking pens of various colors:

Andrew Hart, 1120 Hall Avenue, 622-8400 (PB&G) (TG)

Michael Thornton, 371 South Lindner, 881-9371 (TS)

Lou Kantor, 434 North 16 Street, FR 7-2346 (TPC) (TG)

Sal Decotto, 831 Grover Avenue, FR 5-3287 (F) (TG)

Richard Fenner, 110 Henderson, 593-6648 (QR) (TG)

If there was one thing Carella loved, it was a code.   He loved a code almost as much as he loved German measles.   He flipped through the phone book and the address for Andrew Hart matched the one in Sarah's handwriting.   He found an address for Michael Thornton.   It, too, was identical to the one in her book.   He kept turning pages in the directory, checking names and addresses.   He verified all five.

At a little past eight the next morning, Carella got going on them.   He called Andrew Hart at the number listed in Sarah's address book.   Hart answered, and was not happy.   "I'm in the middle of shaving," he said.   "I've got to leave for the office in a little while.   What's this about?"

"We're investigating a homicide, Mr. Hart."

"A *what?*   A homicide?   Who's been killed?"

"A woman named Sarah Fletcher."

"I don't know anyone named Sarah Fletcher," he said.

"She seems to have known you, Mr. Hart."

"Sarah *who?*   Fletcher, did you say?"   Hart's annoyance increased.

"That's right."

"I don't know anybody by that name.   Who says she knew me?   I never heard of her in my life."

"Your name's in her address book."

"*My* name?   That's impossible."

Nevertheless, Hart agreed to see Carella and Meyer Meyer at the office of Hart and Widderman, 480 Reed Street, sixth floor, at ten o'clock that morning.

At ten, Meyer and Carella parked the car and went into the building at 480 Reed, and up the elevator to the sixth floor.   Hart and Widderman manufactured watchbands.   A huge advertising display near the receptionist's desk in the lobby proudly proclaimed "H&W Beats the Band!" and then backed the slogan with more discreet copy that explained how Hart and Widderman had solved the difficult engineering problems of the expansion watch bracelet.

"Mr. Hart, please," Carella said.

"Who's calling?" the receptionist asked.   She sounded as if she were chewing gum, even though she was not.

"Detectives Carella and Meyer."

"Just a minute, please," she said, and lifted her phone, pushing a button· in the base.   "Mr. Hart," she said, "there are some cops here to see you."   She listened for a moment and then said, "Yes, sir."   She replaced the receiver on its cradle, gestured toward the inside corridor with a nod of her golden tresses, said, "Go right in, please.   Door at the end of the hall," and then went back to her magazine.

The grey skies had apparently infected Andrew Hart.   "You didn't have to broadcast to the world that the police department was here," he said immediately.

"We merely announced ourselves," Carella said.

"Well, O.K., now you're here," Hart said, "let's get it over with."   He was a big man in his middle fifties, with iron-grey hair and black-rimmed eyeglasses.   "I told you I don't know Sarah Fletcher and I don't."

"Here's her book, Mr. Hart," Carella said.   "That's your name, isn't it?"

"Yeah," Hart said, and shook his head.   "But how it got there is beyond me."

"Is it possible she's someone you met at a party, someone you exchanged numbers with?"

"No."

"Are you married, Mr. Hart?"

"No."

"We've got a picture of Mrs. Fletcher.   I wonder—"

"Don't go showing me any pictures of a corpse," Hart said.

"This was taken when she was still very much alive, Mr. Hart."

Meyer handed Carella a manila envelope.   He opened the flap and removed from the envelope a framed picture of Sarah Fletcher which he handed to Hart. Hart looked at the photograph, and then immediately looked up at Carella.

"What is this?" he said.   He looked at the photograph again, shook his head, and said, "Somebody killed her, huh?"

"Yes, somebody did," Carella answered.   "Did you know her?"

"I knew her."

"I thought you said you didn't."

"I didn't know Sarah Fletcher, if that's who you think she was.   But I knew this broad, all right."

"Who'd you think she was?" Meyer asked.

"Just who she told me she was.   Sadie Collins.   She introduced herself as Sadie Collins, and that's who I knew her as.   Sadie Collins."

"Where was this, Mr. Hart?   Where'd you meet her?"

"A singles bar.   The city's full of them."

"Would you remember when?"

"At least a year ago."

"Ever go out with her?"

"I used to see her once or twice a week."

"When did you stop seeing her?"

"Last summer."

"Did you know she was married?"

"Who, Sadie? You're kidding."

"She never told you she was married?"

"Never."

Meyer asked, "When you were going out, where'd you pick her up? At her apartment?"

"No. She used to come to my place."

"Where'd you call her when you wanted to reach her?"

"I didn't. She used to call me."

"Where'd you go, Mr. Hart? When you went out?"

"We didn't go out too much."

"What *did* you do?"

"She used to come to my place. The truth is, we never went out. She didn't want to go out much."

"Didn't you think that was strange?"

"No," Hart shrugged. "I figured she liked to stay home."

"Why'd you stop seeing her, Mr. Hart?"

"I met somebody else. A nice girl. I'm very serious about her."

"Was there something wrong with Sadie?"

"No, no. She was a beautiful woman, beautiful."

"Then why would you be ashamed—"

"Ashamed? Who said anything about being ashamed?"

"I gathered you wouldn't want your girl friend—"

"Listen, what *is* this? I stopped seeing Sadie six months ago. I wouldn't even talk to her on the phone after that. If the crazy babe got herself killed—"

"Crazy?"

Hart suddenly wiped his hand over his face, wet his lips, and walked behind his desk. "I don't think I have anything more to say to you gentlemen."

"What did you mean by crazy?" Carella asked.

"Good day, gentlemen," Hart said.

Carella went to see Lieutenant Byrnes. In the lieutenant's corner office, Byrnes and Carella sat down over coffee. Byrnes frowned at Carella's request.

"Oh, come on, Pete!" Carella said. "If Fletcher *did* it—"

"That's only *your* allegation. Suppose he *didn't* do it, and suppose *you* do something to screw up the D.A.'s case?"

"Like what?"

"I don't know like what. The way things are going these days, if you spit on the sidewalk, that's enough to get a case thrown out of court."

"Fletcher hated his wife," Carella said calmly.

"Lots of men hate their wives. Half the men in this city hate their wives."

"But her little fling gives Fletcher a good reason for . . . Look, Pete, he had a motive; he had the opportunity, a golden one, in fact; and he had the means—another man's knife sticking in Sarah's belly. What more do you want?"

"Proof. There's a funny little system we've got here—it requires proof before we can arrest a man and charge him with murder."

"Right.   And all I'm asking is the opportunity to *try* for it."

"Sure, by putting a tail on Fletcher.   Suppose he sues the city?"

"Yes or no, Pete?   I want permission to conduct a round-the-clock surveillance of Gerald Fletcher, starting Sunday morning.   Yes or no?"

"I must be out of my mind," Byrnes said, and sighed.

Michael Thornton lived in an apartment building several blocks from the Quarter, close enough to absorb some of its artistic flavor, distant enough to escape its high rents.   A blond man in his apartment, Paul Wendling, told Kling and Meyer that Mike was in his jewelry shop.

In the shop, Thornton was wearing a blue work smock, but the contours of the garment did nothing to hide his powerful build.   His eyes were blue, his hair black.   A small scar showed white in the thick eyebrow over his left eye.

"We understand you're working," Meyer said.   "Sorry to break in on you this way."

"That's O.K.," Thornton said.   "What's up?"

"You know a woman named Sarah Fletcher?"

"No," Thornton said.

"You know a woman named Sadie Collins?"

Thornton hesitated.   "Yes," he said.

"What was your relationship with her?" Kling asked.

Thornton shrugged.   "Why? Is she in trouble?"

"When's the last time you saw her?"

"You didn't answer my question," Thornton said.

"Well, you didn't answer ours either,"   Meyer said, and smiled.   "What was your relationship with her, and when did you see her last?"

"I met her in July, in a joint called The Saloon, right around the corner.   It's a bar, but they also serve sandwiches and soup.   It gets a big crowd on weekends, singles, a couple of odd ones for spice—but not a gay bar.   I saw her last in August, a brief, hot thing, and then goodbye."

"Did you realize she was married?" Kling said.

"No.   Is she?"

"Yes," Meyer said.   Neither of the detectives had yet informed Thornton that the lady in question was now unfortunately deceased.   They were saving that for last, like dessert.

"Gee, I didn't know she was married."   Thornton seemed truly surprised.   "Otherwise, nothing would've happened."

"What *did* happen?"

"I bought her a few drinks and then I took her home with me.   Later, I put her in a cab."

"When did you see her next?"

"The following day.   It was goofy.   She called me in the morning, said she was on her way downtown.   I was still in bed.   I said, 'So come on down, baby.' And she did.   *Believe* me, she did."

"Did you see her again after that?" Kling asked.

"Two or three times a week."

"Where'd you go?"

"To my pad on South Lindner."

"Never went anyplace but there?"

"Never."

"Why'd you quit seeing her?"

"I went out of town for a while. When I got back, I just didn't hear from her again. She never gave me her number, and she wasn't in the directory, so I couldn't reach her."

"What do you make of this?" Kling asked, handing Thornton the address book.

Thornton studied it and said, "Yes, what about it? She wrote this down the night we met—we were in bed, and she asked my address."

"Did she write those initials at the same time, the ones in parentheses under your phone number?"

"I didn't actually see the page itself, I only saw her writing in the book."

"Got any idea what the initials mean?"

"None at all." Suddenly he looked thoughtful. "She *was* kind of special, I have to admit it." He grinned. "She'll call again, I'm sure of it."

"I wouldn't count on it," Meyer said. "She's dead."

His face did not crumble or express grief or shock. The only thing it expressed was sudden anger. "The stupid . . ." Thornton said. "That's all she ever was, a stupid, crazy . . ."

On Sunday morning, Carella was ready to become a surveillant, but Gerald Fletcher was nowhere in sight. A call to his apartment from a nearby phone booth revealed that he was not in his digs. He parked in front of Fletcher's apartment building until five P.M. when he was relieved by Detective Arthur Brown. Carella went home to read his son's latest note to Santa Claus, had dinner with his family, and was settling down in the living room with a novel he had bought a week ago and not yet cracked, when the telephone rang.

"Hello?" Carella said into the mouthpiece.

"Hello, Steve? This is Gerry. Gerry Fletcher."

Carella almost dropped the receiver. "How are you?"

"Fine, thanks. I was away for the weekend, just got back a little while ago, in fact. Frankly I find this apartment depressing as hell. I was wondering if you'd like to join me for a drink."

"Well," Carella said. "It's Sunday night, and it's late . . ."

"Nonsense, it's only eight o'clock. We'll do a little old-fashioned pub crawling."

It suddenly occurred to Carella that Gerald Fletcher had already had a few drinks before placing his call. It further occurred to him that if he played this *too* cozily, Fletcher might rescind his generous offer.

"Okay. I'll see you at eight-thirty, provided I can square it with my wife."

"Good," Fletcher said. "See you."

Paddy's Bar & Grill was on the Stem, adjacent to the city's theater district. Carella and Fletcher got there at about nine o'clock while the place was still relatively quiet. The action began a little later, Fletcher explained.

Fletcher lifted his glass in a silent toast.   "What kind of person would you say comes to a place like this?"

"I would say we've got a nice lower-middle-class clientele bent on making contact with members of the opposite sex."

"What would you say if I told you the blonde in the clinging jersey is a working prostitute?"

Carella looked at the woman.   "I don't think I'd believe you.   She's a bit old for the young competition, and she's not *selling* anything.   She's waiting for one of those two or three older guys to make their move.   Hookers don't wait, Gerry. *Is* she a working prostitute?"

"I haven't the faintest idea," Fletcher said.   "I was merely trying to indicate that appearances can sometimes be misleading.   Drink up, there are a few more places I'd like to show you."

He knew Fletcher well enough by now to realize that the man was trying to tell him something.   At lunch last Tuesday, Fletcher had transmitted a message and a challenge: *I killed my wife, what can you do about it?*   Tonight, in a similar manner, he was attempting to indicate something else, but Carella could not fathom exactly what.

Fanny's was only twenty blocks away from Paddy's Bar and Grill, but as far removed from it as the moon.   Whereas the first bar seemed to cater to a quiet crowd peacefully pursuing its romantic inclinations, Fanny's was noisy and raucous, jammed to the rafters with men and women of all ages, wearing plastic hippie gear purchased in head shops up and down Jackson Avenue.

Fletcher lifted his glass.   "I hope you don't mind if I drink myself into a stupor," he said.   "Merely pour me into the car at the end of the night."   Fletcher drank. "I don't usually consume this much alcohol, but I'm very troubled about that boy."

"What boy?" Carella asked.

"Ralph Corwin," Fletcher said.   "I understand he's having some difficulty with his lawyer and, well, I'd like to help him somehow."

"*Help* him?"

"Yes.   Do you think the D.A.'s office would consider it strange if I suggested a good defense lawyer for the boy?"

"I think they might consider it passing strange, yes."

"Do I detect a note of sarcasm in your voice?"

"Not at all."

Fletcher squired Carella from Fanny's to, in geographical order, The Purple Chairs and Quigley's Rest.   Each place was rougher, in its way, than the last. The Purple Chairs catered to a brazenly gay crowd, and Quigley's Rest was a dive, where Fletcher's liquor caught up with him, and the evening ended suddenly in a brawl.   Carella was shaken by the experience, and still couldn't piece out Fletcher's reasons.

Carella received a further shock when he continued to pursue Sarah Fletcher's address book.   Lou Kantor was simply the third name in a now wearying list of Sarah's bedmates, until she turned out to be a tough and striking woman.   She confirmed Carella's suspicions immediately.

"I only knew her a short while," she said.   "I met her in September, I believe. Saw her three or four times after that."

"Where'd you meet her?"

"In a bar called The Purple Chairs.   That's right," she added quickly.   "That's what I am."

"Nobody asked," Carella said.   "What about Sadie Collins?"

"Spell it out, Officer, I'm not going to help you.   I don't like being hassled."

"Nobody's hassling you, Miss Kantor.   You practice your religion and I'll practice mine.   We're here to talk about a dead woman."

"Then talk about her, spit it out.   What do you want to know?   Was she straight? Everybody's straight until they're *not* straight anymore, isn't that right?   She was willing to learn.   I taught her."

"Did you know she was married?"

"She told me.   So what?   Broke down in tears one night, and spent the rest of the night crying.   I knew she was married."

"What'd she say about her husband?"

"Nothing that surprised me.   She said he had another woman.   Said he ran off to see her every weekend, told little Sadie he had out-of-town business.   *Every* weekend, can you imagine that?"

"What do you make of this?" Carella said, and handed her Sarah's address book, opened to the MEMORANDA page.

"I don't know any of these people," Lou said.

"The initials under your name," Carella said.   "TPC and then TG.   Got any ideas?"

"Well, the TPC is obvious, isn't it?   I met her at The Purple Chairs.   What else could it mean?"

Carella suddenly felt very stupid.   "Of course.   What else could it mean?" He took back the book.   "I'm finished," he said.   "Thank you very much."

"I miss her," Lou said suddenly.   "She was a wild one."

Cracking a code is like learning to roller-skate; once you know how to do it, it's easy.   With a little help from Gerald Fletcher, who had provided a guided tour the night before, and a lot of help from Lou Kantor, who had generously provided the key, Carella was able to crack the code wide open—well, almost.   Last night, he'd gone with Fletcher to Paddy's Bar and Grill, or PB&G under Andrew Hart's name; Fanny's, F under Sal Decotto; The Purple Chairs, Lou Kantor's TPC; and Quigley's Rest, QR for Richard Fenner on the list.   Probably because of the fight, he hadn't taken Carella to The Saloon, TS under Michael Thornton's name—the place where Thornton had admitted first meeting Sarah.

Except, what the hell did TG mean, under all the names but Thornton's?

By Carella's own modest estimate, he had been in more bars in the past twenty-four hours than he had in the past twenty-four years. He decided, nevertheless, to hit The Saloon that night.

The Saloon was just that. A cigarette-scarred bar behind which ran a mottled, flaking mirror; wooden booths with patched, fake leather seat cushions; bowls of pretzels and potato chips; jukebox gurgling; steamy bodies.

"They come in here," the bartender said, "at all hours of the night. Take yourself. You're here to meet a girl, am I right?"

"There *was* someone I was hoping to see. A girl named Sadie Collins. Do you know her?"

"Yeah. She used to come in a lot, but I ain't seen her in months. What do you want to fool around with her for?"

"Why? What's the matter with her?"

"You want to know something?" the bartender said. "I thought she was a hooker at first. Aggressive. You know what that word means? Aggressive? She used to come dressed down to here and up to there, ready for action, selling everything she had, you understand? She'd come in here, pick out a guy she wanted, and go after him like the world was gonna end at midnight. And always the same type. Big guys. You wouldn't stand a chance with her, not that you ain't big, don't misunderstand me. But Sadie liked them gigantic, and mean. You know something?"

"What?"

"I'm glad she don't come in here anymore. There was something about her— like she was compulsive. You know what that word means, compulsive?"

Tuesday afternoon, Arthur Brown handed in his surveillance report on Gerald Fletcher. Much of it was not at all illuminating. From 4:55 P.M. to 8:45 P.M. Fletcher had driven home, and then to 812 North Crane and parked. The report *did* become somewhat illuminating when, at 8:46 P.M., Fletcher emerged from that building with a redheaded woman wearing a black fur coat over a green dress. They went to Rudolph's restaurant, ate, and drove back to 812 Crane, arrived at 10:35 P.M. and went inside. Arthur Brown had checked the lobby mailboxes, which showed eight apartments on the eleventh floor, which was where the elevator indicator had stopped. Brown went outside to wait again, and Fletcher emerged alone at 11:40 P.M. and drove home. Detective O'Brien relieved Detective Brown at 12:15 A.M.

Byrnes said, "This woman could be important."

"That's just what I think," Brown answered.

Carella had not yet spoken to either Sal Decotto or Richard Fenner, the two remaining people listed in Sarah's book, but saw no reason to pursue that trail any further. If the place listings in her book had been chronological, she'd gone from bad to worse in her search for partners.

Why? To give it back to her husband in spades? Carella tossed Sarah's little black book into the manila folder bearing the various reports on the case, and turned his attention to the information Artie Brown had brought in last night. The red-headed woman's presence might be important, but Carella was still puzzling over Fletcher's behavior.   Sarah's blatant infidelity provided Fletcher with a strong motive, so why take Carella to his wife's unhappy haunts, why *show* Carella that he had good and sufficient reason to kill her?   Furthermore, why the offer to get a good defense attorney for the boy who had already been indicted for the slaying?

Sometimes Carella wondered who was doing what to whom.

At five o'clock that evening, Carella relieved Detective Hal Willis outside Fletcher's office building downtown, and then followed Fletcher to a department store in midtown Isola.   Carella was wearing a false moustache stuck to his upper lip, a wig with hair longer than his own and of a different color, and a pair of sunglasses.

In the department store, he tracked Fletcher to the Intimate Apparel department. Carella walked into the next aisle, pausing to look at women's robes and kimonos, keeping one eye on Fletcher, who was in conversation with the lingerie salesgirl.

"May I help you, sir?" a voice said, and Carella turned to find a stocky woman at his elbow, with grey hair, black-rimmed spectacles, wearing Army shoes and a black dress.   Her suspicious smile accused him of being a junkie shoplifter or worse.

"Thank you, no," Carella said.   "I'm just looking."

Fletcher made his selections from the gossamer undergarments which the salesgirl had spread out on the counter, pointing first to one garment, then to another.   The salesgirl wrote up the order and Fletcher reached into his wallet to give her either cash or a credit card; it was difficult to tell from an aisle away.   He chatted with the girl a moment longer, and then walked off toward the elevator bank.

"Are you *sure* I can't assist you?" the woman in the Army shoes said, and Carella answered, "I'm positive," and moved swiftly toward the lingerie counter. Fletcher had left the counter without a package in his arms, which meant he was *sending* his purchases.   The salesgirl was gathering up Fletcher's selections and looked up when Carella reached the counter.

"Yes, sir," she said.   "May I help you?"

Carella opened his wallet and produced his shield.   "Police officer," he said. "I'm interested in the order you just wrote up."

The girl was perhaps nineteen years old, a college girl working in the store during the Christmas rush.   Speechlessly, she studied the shield, eyes bugging.

"Are these items being sent?" Carella asked.

"Yes, *sir*," the girl said. Her eyes were still wide.   She wet her lips and stood up a little straighter, prepared to be a perfect witness.

"Can you tell me where?" Carella asked.

"Yes, *sir*," she said, and turned the sales slip toward him.   "He wanted them wrapped separately, but they're all going to same address.   Miss Arlene Orton, 812 North Crane Street, right here in the city, and I'd guess it's a swell—"

"Thank you very much," Carella said.

It felt like Christmas day already.

The man who picked the lock on Arlene Orton's front door, ten minutes after she left her apartment on Wednesday morning, was better at it than any burglar in the city, and he happened to work for the Police Department.   It took the technician longer to set up his equipment, but the telephone was the easiest of his jobs.   The tap would become operative when the telephone company supplied the police with a list of so-called bridging points that located the pairs and cables for Arlene Orton's phone.   The monitoring equipment would be hooked into these and whenever a call went out of or came into the apartment, a recorder would automatically tape both ends of the conversation.   In addition, whenever a call was made from the apartment, a dial indicator would ink out a series of dots that signified the number being called.

The technician placed his bug in the bookcase on the opposite side of the room. The bug was a small FM transmitter with a battery-powered mike that needed to be changed every twenty-four hours.   The technician would have preferred running his own wires, but he dared not ask the building superintendent for an empty closet or workroom in which to hide his listener.   A blabbermouth superintendent can kill an investigation more quickly than a squad of gangland goons.

In the rear of a panel truck parked at the curb some twelve feet south of the entrance to 812 North Crane, Steve Carella sat behind the recording equipment that was locked into the frequency of the bug.   He sat hopefully, with a tuna sandwich and a bottle of beer, prepared to hear and record any sounds that emanated from Arlene's apartment.

At the bridging point seven blocks away and thirty minutes later, Arthur Brown sat behind equipment that was hooked into the telephone mike, and waited for Arlene Orton's phone to ring.   He was in radio contact with Carella.

The first call came at 12:17 P.M.   The equipment tripped in automatically and the spools of tape began recording the conversation, while Brown simultaneously monitored it through his headphone.

"Hello?"

"Hello, Arlene?"

"Yes, who's this?"

"Nan."

"Nan?   You sound so different.   Do you have a cold or something?"

"Every year at this time.   Just before the holidays.   Arlene, I'm terribly rushed, I'll make this short.   Do you know Beth's dress size?"

The conversation went on in that vein, and Arlene Orton spoke to three more girl friends in succession.   She then called the local supermarket to order the week's groceries.   She had a fine voice, deep and forceful, punctuated every so often (when she was talking to her girl friends) with a delightful giggle.

At four P.M., the telephone in Arlene's apartment rang again.

"Hello?"

"Arlene, this is Gerry."

"Hello, darling."

"I'm leaving here a little early.   I thought I'd come right over."

"Good."

"I'll be there in, oh, half an hour, forty minutes."

"Hurry."

On Thursday morning, two days before Christmas, Carella sat at his desk in the squad room and looked over the transcripts of the five reels from the night before. The reel that interested him most was the second one.   The conversation on that reel had at one point changed abruptly in tone and content.   Carella thought he knew why, but he wanted to confirm his suspicion.

Fletcher: I meant after the *holidays*, not the trial.

Miss Orton: I may be able to get away, I'm not sure.   I'll have to check with my shrink.

Fletcher: What's he got to do with it?

Miss Orton: Well, I have to pay whether I'm there or not, you know.

Fletcher: Is he taking a vacation?

Miss Orton: I'll ask him.

Fletcher: Yes, ask him.   Because I'd really like to get away.

Miss Orton: Ummm.   When do you think the case (inaudible).

Fletcher: In March sometime.   No sooner than that.   He's got a new lawyer, you know.

Miss Orton: What does that mean, a new lawyer?

Fletcher: Nothing.   He'll be convicted anyway.

Miss Orton: (Inaudible).

Fletcher: Because the trial's going to take a lot out of me.

Miss Orton: How soon after the trial . . .

Fletcher: I don't know.

Miss Orton: She's dead, Gerry, I don't see . . .

Fletcher: Yes, but . . .

Miss Orton: I don't see why we have to wait, do you?

Fletcher: Have you read this?

Miss Orton: No, not yet.   Gerry, I think we ought to set a date now.   A provisional date, depending on when the trial is.   Gerry?

Fletcher: Mmmm?

Miss Orton: Do you think it'll be a terribly long, drawn-out trial?

Fletcher: What?

Miss Orton: Gerry?

Fletcher: Yes?

Miss Orton: Where are you?

Fletcher: I was just looking over some of these books.

Miss Orton: Do you think you can tear yourself away?

Fletcher: Forgive me, darling.

Miss Orton: If the trial starts in March, and we planned on April for it . . .

Fletcher: Unless they come up with something unexpected, of course.

Miss Orton: Like what?

Fletcher: Oh, I don't know.   They've got some pretty sharp people investigating this case.

Miss Orton: What's there to investigate?

Fletcher: There's always the possibility he didn't do it.

Miss Orton: (Inaudible) a signed confession?

Fletcher: One of the cops thinks I killed her.

Miss Orton: You're not serious.   Who?

Fletcher: A detective named Carella.   He probably knows about us by now. He's a very thorough cop.   I have a great deal of admiration for him.   I wonder if he realizes that.

Miss Orton: Where'd he even get such an idea?

Fletcher: Well, I told him I hated her.

Miss Orton: What?   Gerry, why the hell did you do that?

Fletcher: He'd have found out anyway.   He probably knows by now that Sarah was sleeping around with half the men in this city.   And he probably knows I knew it too.

Miss Orton: Who cares what he found out?   Corwin's already confessed.

Fletcher: I can understand his reasoning.   I'm just not sure he can understand mine.

Miss Orton: Some reasoning.   If you were going to kill her, you'd have done it ages ago, when she refused to sign the separation papers.   So let him investigate, who cares?   Wishing your wife dead isn't the same thing as killing her.   Tell that to Detective Copolla.

Fletcher: Carella.   (Laughs).   I'll tell him, darling.

According to the technician who had wired the Orton apartment, the living room bug was in the bookcase on the wall opposite the bar.   Carella was interested in the tape from the time Fletcher had asked Arlene about a book—"Have you read this?"—and then seemed preoccupied.   It was Carella's guess that Fletcher had discovered the bookcase bug.   What interested Carella more, however, was what Fletcher had said *after* he knew the place was wired.   Certain of an audience now, Fletcher had:

(1) Suggested the possibility that Corwin was not guilty.

(2) Flatly stated that a cop named Carella suspected him.

(3) Expressed admiration for Carella, while wondering if Carella was aware of it.

(4) Speculated that Carella had already doped out the purpose of the bar-crawling last Sunday night, was cognizant of Sarah's promiscuity, and knew Fletcher was aware of it.

(5) Made a little joke about "telling" Carella.

Carella felt as eerie as he had when lunching with Fletcher and later when drinking with him.   Now he'd spoken, through the bug, directly to Carella.   But what was he trying to say?   And why?

Carella wanted very much to hear what Fletcher would say when he *didn't* know he was being overheard.   He asked Lieutenant Byrnes for permission to request a court order to put a bug in Fletcher's automobile.   Byrnes granted permission, and the court issued the order.

Fletcher made a date with Arlene Orton to go to The Chandeliers across the river, and the bug was installed in Fletcher's 1972 car.   If Fletcher left the city, the effective range of the transmitter on the open road would be about a quarter of a mile.   The listener-pursuer had his work cut out for him.

By ten minutes to ten that night, Carella was drowsy and discouraged.   On the way out to The Chandeliers, Fletcher and Arlene had not once mentioned Sarah nor the plans for their impending marriage.   Carella was anxious to put them both to bed and get home to his family.   When they finally came out of the restaurant and began walking toward Fletcher's automobile, Carella actually uttered an audible, "At *last*," and started his car.

They proceeded east on Route 701, heading for the bridge, and said nothing. Carella thought at first that something was wrong with the equipment, then finally Arlene spoke and Carella knew just what had happened.   The pair had argued in the restaurant, and Arlene had been smoldering until this moment.

"Maybe you don't want to marry me at all," she shouted.

"That's ridiculous," Fletcher said.

"Then why won't you set a date?"

"I have set a date."

"You haven't set a date.   All you've done is say after the trial.   *When*, after the trial?   Maybe this whole damn thing has been a stall.   Maybe you *never* planned to marry me."

"You know that isn't true, Arlene."

"How do I know there really *were* separation papers?"

"There were.   I told you there were."

"Then why wouldn't she sign them?"

"Because she loved me."

"If she loved you, then why did she do those horrible things?"

"To make me pay, I think."

"Is that why she showed you her little black book?"

"Yes, to make me pay."

"No.   Because she was a slut."

"I guess.   I guess that's what she became."

"Putting a little TG in her book every time she told you about a new one.   *Told Gerry*, and marked a little TG in her book."

"Yes, to make me pay."

"A slut.   You should have gone after her with detectives.   Gotten pictures, threatened her, forced her to sign—"

"No, I couldn't have done that.   It would have ruined me, Arl."

"Your precious career."

"Yes, my precious career."

They both fell silent again.   They were approaching the bridge now.   Carella tried to stay close behind them, but on occasion the distance between the two cars lengthened and he lost some words in the conversation.

"She wouldn't sign the papers and I (   ) adultery because (   ) have come out."

"And I thought (   )."

"I did everything I possibly could."

"Yes, Gerry, but now she's dead.   So what's your excuse now?"

"I'm suspected of having *killed* her, damn it!"

Fletcher was making a left turn, off the highway. Carella stepped on the accelerator, not wanting to lose voice contact now.

"What difference does that make?" Arlene asked.

"None at all, I'm sure," Fletcher said. "I'm sure you wouldn't mind at all being married to a convicted murderer."

"What are you talking about?"

"I'm talking about the possibility . . . Never mind."

"Let me hear it."

"All right, Arlene. I'm talking about the possibility of someone accusing me of the murder. And of my having to stand trial for it."

"That's the most paranoid—"

"It's not paranoid."

"Then what is it? They've caught the murderer, they—"

"I'm only saying suppose. How could we get married if I killed her, if someone says I killed her?"

"No one has said that, Gerry."

"Well, *if* someone should."

Silence. Carella was dangerously close to Fletcher's car now, and risking discovery.

Carella held his breath and stayed glued to the car ahead.

"Gerry, I don't understand this," Arlene said, her voice low.

"Someone could make a good case for it."

"Why would anyone do that? They know that Corwin—"

"They could say I came into the apartment and . . . They could say she was still alive when I came into the apartment. They could say the knife was still in her and I . . . I came in and found her that way and . . . finished her off."

"Why would you do that?"

"To end it."

"You wouldn't kill anyone, Gerry."

"No."

"Then why are you even suggesting such a terrible thing?"

"If she wanted it . . . If someone accused me . . . If someone said I'd done it . . . that I'd finished the job, pulled the knife across her belly, they could claim she *asked* me to do it."

"What are you saying, Gerry?"

"I'm trying to explain that Sarah might have—"

"Gerry, I don't think I want to know."

"I'm only trying to tell you—"

"No, I don't want to know. Please, Gerry, you're frightening me."

"*Listen* to me, damn it! I'm trying to explain what *might* have happened. Is that so hard to accept? That she might have *asked* me to kill her?"

"Gerry, please, I—"

"I *wanted* to call the hospital, I was *ready* to call the hospital, don't you think I could *see* she wasn't fatally stabbed?"

"Gerry, please."

"She begged me to kill her, Arlene, she begged me to end it for her, she . . . Damn it, can't *either* of you understand that?   I tried to show him, I took him to all the places, I thought he was a man who'd understand.   Is it that difficult?"

"Oh, my God, *did* you kill her?   *Did* you kill Sarah?"

"No.   Not Sarah.   Only the woman she'd become, the slut I'd forced her to become.   She was Sadie, you see, when I killed her—when she died."

"Oh, my God," Arlene said, and Carella nodded in weary acceptance.

Carella felt neither elated nor triumphant.   As he followed Fletcher's car into the curb in front of Arlene's building, he experienced only a familiar nagging sense of repetition and despair.   Fletcher was coming out of his car now, walking around to the curb side, opening the door for Arlene, who took his hand and stepped onto the sidewalk, weeping.   Carella intercepted them before they reached the front door of the building.

Quietly, he charged Fletcher with the murder of his wife, and made the arrest without resistance.

Fletcher did not seem at all surprised.

So it was finished, or at least Carella thought it was.

In the silence of his living room, the telephone rang at a quarter past one.

He caught the phone on the third ring.

"Hello?"

"Steve," Lieutenant Byrnes said.   "I just got a call from Calcutta.   Ralph Corwin hanged himself in his cell, just after midnight.   Must have done it while we were still taking Fletcher's confession in the squad room."

Carella was silent.

"Steve?" Byrnes said.

"Yeah, Pete."

"Nothing," Byrnes said, and hung up.

Carella stood with the dead phone in his hands for several seconds and then replaced it on the hook.   He looked into the living room, where the lights of the tree glowed warmly, and thought of a despairing junkie in a prison cell, who had taken his own life without ever having known he had not taken the life of another.

It was Christmas day.

Sometimes none of it made any sense at all.

GILBERT RALSTON

A Very Cautious Boy

Rosetti's Restaurant is tucked away in a remodeled brownstone on New York's 46th Street, close enough to Park Avenue to be considered a good address. Once, in the days of the Charleston and the blind pig, it was one of the town's plushier speakeasies. Now it has become one of the string of expensive character restaurants which dot the East Side.

Lee Costa took a moment to remember it as it was in the old days when Fat Joe Waxman owned it, keeping a fatherly eye out for the welfare of the young tenement boys who ran his less dubious errands, with particular solicitude for the developing skills of the brightest of these, one of whom was Costa.

His faith was not misplaced. Lee Costa had turned out well. Fat Joe would have been proud of him on this August night as he stood, a compact, ruggedly powerful man, amusing himself with nostalgic thoughts, quietly watching a group of opulent-looking customers enter the refurbished establishment.

Costa took another moment to look it over after he made his way past the door. The layout of the place was as he remembered it: a long bar running the length of one wall opposite a row of booths, a dining area, a check room at his right.

He stood for a moment in the entranceway near the reservation desk, pausing while a headwaiter made his way out of the gloom.

"I'm looking for Joe Rosetti," Costa said.

"Who shall I say is calling?"

"Tell him the insurance man is here."

"No name?"

"Just tell him. He'll know."

"You may wait in the bar, if you wish."

Costa crossed to the check room to leave his coat. As he turned to go toward the bar, he found his way blocked by the hulking form of one of the waiters. "C'mon," he said. "I'll take you up." He jerked a thumb at an ancient elevator in the corner of the room.

The Rosetti apartment was the only one on the fourth floor, the lock on the door opening with a muted buzz after the guide had pressed the doorbell. They entered a living room which spread across a large part of the side of the building, furnished simply and well, a group of heavy antiques giving it a comfortable feeling of old-fashioned luxury.

A rotund little man stood in the doorway of the room, examining Costa with a quizzical eye. "I'm Joe Rosetti," he said, his accent betraying his Italian parentage. He made no move to take Costa's hand, simply stood and looked at him, his head cocked a little to one side, a tiny frown of concentration on his forehead.

"You're smaller than I thought you'd be," he said. "Come in. Sit. You too, Ziggy." He held the door of the interior room open as Costa and his guide passed through. "Meet Lee Costa, Mama," he said. Across the room a tiny, dark woman raised her head, holding Costa's eyes with her own, searching his face. She sighed, the sound making a little explosive punctuation in the still room. "This is him?" she said.

Rosetti nodded his head.

She stared at Costa as she gathered up her knitting. "Take care of your business, Papa. After, we will eat." She left the room.

Ziggy stood up, looking down at Costa. "This guy bringing you some trouble?" he asked Rosetti.

Rosetti shook his head.

Costa's cold blue eyes were suddenly alert. "If I was bringing trouble, what would you do?"

"Throw you away somewhere," the big man said, taking a step toward him.

Costa turned to Rosetti. "Better chain up your ape." He turned a bland face to the standing man. "Back off, fat boy," he said calmly.

The man started for him, hands reaching for his lapels. As he bent over, Costa's foot shot out, catching him squarely in the midriff. He doubled over with an agonized gasp. Costa went to him, flipping him to the floor with a crash. "Sorry, Mr. Rosetti," Costa said. "He asked for it."

Rosetti leaned across his desk to look at the prone man writhing on the floor. "So fast," he said. "Like a snake."

"You're good at your job, Mr. Rosetti, I'm good at mine."

"He'll kill you," Rosetti said.

Costa shook his head. "No, he won't, Mr. Rosetti. He'll go downstairs and take care of the drunks. Won't you, Ziggy?"

On the floor, the man gasped for breath, turning his head like a wounded turtle. His eyes went to Costa's smiling face.

"Next time," Costa said, "I won't treat you so gently."

With an inarticulate grunt, the man staggered to his feet and out of the room.

"Why was Ziggy here, Mr. Rosetti?" Costa asked.

"I was afraid."

"Of me? You don't have to be. I'm a professional. I do what I'm paid for, nothing more."

Rosetti settled back in his chair, nervously.

"Go ahead, tell me about it," Costa said. "Our mutual friend said you had a problem."

"I have a problem. That's why I sent for you."

"Tell me the name of the problem, Mr. Rosetti."

"His name is Baxter. Roy Baxter."

"No other way to handle it?"

"I could pay."

"That doesn't usually work with a blackmailer," Costa said.

"You know about it?"

"Only what our friend told me.   He said that someone was trying to shake you down."

Rosetti hesitated.

"Go ahead, Mr. Rosetti.   You can trust me."

Rosetti looked away, his face working.   "It was a long time ago.   I killed a man.   Baxter found out about it.   He wants money.   I know him.   He won't stop.   He'll never stop, if I pay.   So I called our friend.   I did him a favor once. A big one.   Now he pays me back.   With you."

"Have you told your wife?"

"She knows.   But she don't talk."

"Anybody else know about me?"

"No.   Just me, Mama and our friend."   Rosetti reached into the drawer of his desk.   "Here's the addresses for Baxter.   His house.   His business.   A picture."

Costa glanced at the addresses.   "What's his business?"

"He's a lawyer.   Or says he is.   I don't know how he makes his money.   He's supposed to have some."

"Why does he want yours, then?"

"I don't know.   Maybe he's got expenses."

"Expenses.   I have them too," Costa said.

"I know.   I can pay."

"Our friend said to give you the wholesale rate."   Costa smiled at him again. "Could you afford five thousand?"

"Yes.   What Baxter wants makes that sound like a bargain."

"How much time did he give you?"

"He said he would give me two weeks to raise twenty-five-thousand dollars. Then he goes to the police."

Costa stood, carefully tucking the papers into his pocket.   "I'll look the situation over.   Let you know."

Rosetti looked at him, his hands working.   "Please," he said.

"I'm a very cautious boy, Mr. Rosetti.   I'll check it out.   Let you know." Costa let his eyes wander to the mounted tarpon over the mantel.   "You're jumpy," he said.   "Why don't you go fishing for a few days?"

Rosetti made a little wry grimace.   "Me?" he said.   "Every weekend I fish. All summer.   Mama and I.   Every weekend.   We have a little boat.   We live quiet.   Run the restaurant.   Fish.   All of a sudden, I get a call from that Baxter. I don't fish.   I don't run the restaurant.   Just worry."

"I'll do what I can, Mr. Rosetti.   Maybe you'll be fishing again soon."

Costa left the room, nodding pleasantly to Mama Rosetti as he passed her in the living room.   She looked up, her sad little face following him.   "You have your dinner?" she asked.

"Not yet."

"Come downstairs. We'll eat." She crossed to the door. "Coming, Papa?''
He appeared in the doorway. "Go eat," he said. "While I sleep."
"Cover up good, Papa," she said.

They sat in one of the booths in the restaurant, the little woman saying only a
few words while they ate. Finally, after the coffee was served, she looked up at
him.
"It is a sad thing," she said. "Papa is so afraid."
"Are you?" Costa asked.
"Me? No, I am not afraid. What must be done, must be done. There is no
other way. Always must a person fight. All his life. I know this."
"Don't worry about it. I will be very careful."
"Careful. Yes. I too am careful. You must be very sure."
"Don't worry, Mama Rosetti."
He rose to leave.
"You have a coat?"
"Yes. In the check room."
"Wrap up good," she said. "Don't catch cold."
Her black eyes followed him as he left the restaurant.

He made a routine check of the job the next morning. Baxter's office was on
the West Side in a building on 56th Street. Costa arrived there a little before nine
o'clock, losing himself in the crowd of incoming office employees, waiting at the
end of the hall on the eleventh floor where he could see the entrance to Baxter's
office. He was not pleased with the area. It was awkwardly arranged for a
killing, with its manned elevators, people coming and going and too many late-
hour businesses.
Baxter entered his office at nine-thirty, a dapper, squat individual, with the stub
of a cigar clamped in his jaws. Costa waited another fifteen minutes in the hall,
then entered the office, handing Baxter's secretary a card showing him to be the
salesman for an office-supply company. He politely accepted the secretary's statement that Mr. Baxter was happy with his present supplier, and left, after a pho-
tographic glance at the interior of the office. He shook his head in dissatisfaction
as he rode down in the elevator.

That afternoon he drove to Connecticut in a rented car, stopping at a real-estate
agent's office close to the second address that Rosetti had given him for Baxter.
The agent obligingly drove him through the area, rattling off the virtues of life in
Connecticut as she did so. His examination of the Baxter house was made easier
by the presence of a vacant house a few doors away, in which he indicated great
interest. At his request, the agent drove him down the street while he examined
the homes of his potential neighbors. Baxter's house was the last one in a group
of six, an ostentatious modern facing the Sound, enclosed by a high brick wall.
Costa stopped for a moment to study it. The entrance was barred by an ornamental

iron gate, a large "Beware of the Dog" sign across the corner of it. In the yard beyond the gate, a large boxer set up a frantic clamor at their approach.

Costa spent the rest of the afternoon as a prospective customer, thoroughly convincing the receptive agent that he was a transplanted executive named Zweller from a small business in Ohio, that his wife would arrive shortly, and that he would be back with her to buy a house. In the process, he was given a gratuitous rundown on the goings and comings of the local homeowners, including Baxter, who was known as a widower of quiet habits, currently living alone, cared for by a Swedish couple who slept in town.

At six o'clock he was back at the Rosettis', seated in their living room. Rosetti was planted in the chair behind his desk, Mama Rosetti across the room with her knitting.

Costa looked at the woman, then back to Rosetti. "I wanted to talk to you together," he said. "The job is possible. Only one thing about it I don't like."

"What don't you like?"

"I need a little insurance," Costa said.

Rosetti leaned toward him. "You mean you won't do it?"

"I mean I won't do it without help. I'll need you both."

Mama Rosetti folded her hands into her lap. "Make me understand," she said.

"I don't like his office for the job. Too busy. It'll have to be the house. And I won't drive to it."

He paused.

"So?" Rosetti said.

"So we go fishing this weekend. All three of us. I'll take care of the assignment while we're there. That will make you both accessories before and after the fact. Makes for a nice silent relationship in the future."

Rosetti turned to the woman. "Mama?" he said.

She looked at Costa for a long moment. Then she sighed, nodding her head slowly. "I think it is all right, Papa," she said. "It is a thing we have to do. I do not blame him for his caution."

Rosetti turned to Costa. "We will do it," he said. "We have no choice."

"We have a deal," Lee Costa said.

"What must we do?" Rosetti asked.

"Pick me up Saturday morning at the gas dock at City Island. Gas the boat. I'll come aboard while the attendant's busy." Costa rose to leave. "After that, I'll tell you where to go. Leave the rest to me."

"Wrap up good," Mama Rosetti said. "Don't catch cold."

Lost in a crowd of yachtsmen and guests, Costa was an unobtrusive figure as he waited on the public dock the following Saturday. He watched quietly while the Rosettis arrived on a small cruiser, edging to the dock. Then he worked his way through a crowd of noisy fishermen and stepped aboard, moving into the cabin while Rosetti kept the harassed attendant busy. Minutes later they were moving toward the Connecticut shore, Rosetti at the wheel, Costa beside him, Mama Rosetti at her endless knitting in a wicker chair.

Early in the afternoon, they anchored the boat in the sheltered area around the point of the peninsula on which the Baxter house rested.

"What now?" Rosetti asked nervously.

"Eat. Fish. Be a playboy," Costa said.

"You hungry?" Mama Rosetti asked.

"A little."

"All right, I make dinner. Now, you fish with Papa."

At six o'clock she called to them from the cabin door. "Come downstairs," she called. "We'll eat."

"Below, Mama," Rosetti said. "Not downstairs."

"Downstairs," she said. "You're the sailor. I'm the cook."

It was a tense meal, Rosetti stopping to look nervously at Costa, Mama Rosetti silent and occupied with serving them from the galley stove.

Costa rested on one of the bunks for half an hour afterwards, arising to find the questioning eyes of the Rosettis on him again. "I'm going for a little swim," he said.

Mama Rosetti reached out a small brown hand, patted his arm. "Be careful," she said.

He smiled down at her. "I'm always careful," he said. "I'm a very cautious boy."

He disappeared into the cabin, appearing a few minutes later in swimming trunks and the top half of a skindiver's wet suit. He stood for a moment near the stern, placed a black rubber hood on his head, flippers on his feet, worked mask and snorkel into place and dropped softly into the water. He checked the collar of his wet suit to be sure that the small plastic bag he had tucked there was still in place, felt for the rubber gloves attached to his belt and swam slowly toward the shore, slipping smoothly through the black water, the rubber suit and flippers giving him enough buoyancy to conserve his strength.

A half-hour later, he stopped a few feet away from the end of the Baxter dock, then drifted in until he could rest his weight on the bottom. He reached again under the collar of his suit, pulled out the bag, opened it, carefully keeping the piece of meat it contained out of the water. He gave a low whistle, waiting while the dog's feet made a rhythmic thumping on the dock. He threw the meat almost at the feet of the dog, whose barking echoed along the quiet beach. Then he slipped back to deep water again, floating, head low in the water, breathing through his snorkel, head down, virtually invisible from the shore. The barking grew louder.

A moment later, the robed figure of Baxter came out onto the upstairs porch, flashlight in hand. After a careful examination of the yard, he called down to silence the dog. Costa waited.

After Baxter returned to his room, the dog nosed around the end of the dock restlessly, then turned to give his attention to the meat. Costa could see the outline of the animal as he nuzzled it, hear the ugly little sounds as he gulped it down. He waited while an agonized whine came from the dog, his frantic feet drumming on the dock. When the sound stopped, Costa floated in again, gave another low whistle. There was no reaction from the dog. Costa stuck his head up cautiously. The animal was lying near the edge of the dock. Costa pulled off the mask and flippers, then pulled the body of the dog into the shadow cast by the boathouse. A tiny portion of the meat was still on the wooden floor of the dock. Carefully, he picked it up and threw it into the sea, returning to the shadowed area to wait patiently for a long half-hour, pleased when the servants appeared at the back door on schedule to climb into a station wagon. They drove away, the gate closing automatically after them.

Costa let the sound of the disappearing car die out before he got out of his swimming gear and moved to the balustrade of the porch. Slowly, he snaked up it, slipping over the edge of the upstairs rail soundlessly, lying on the floor of the porch a good ten minutes before he moved again. On his belly, he slipped the gloves on his hands, after which he wormed his way to the edge of the French windows. They were open. Two minutes later, he was standing over the sleeping form of Roy Baxter. Costa braced his feet. His hands fastened to the throat of the sleeping man. Costa held on for a long time, then stripped the glove from his right hand to check the pulse of the body in the bed. Satisfied that Baxter was dead, he placed the glove on his hand again and left the way he had come.

At the dock, he replaced the swimming gear, pulled the dog's body to the edge of the dock and dropped with it into the water. He stopped to estimate the direction of the Rosetti boat before he towed the dog's body well out into the Sound, releasing it where the outgoing tide would carry it away. He worked his way slowly and easily back to the boat, letting the tide aid him in the long swim. As he approached it, he could see the Rosettis sitting in the stern cockpit.

"Costa?" Rosetti called.

"Coming in," Costa said. He handed them the flippers and the mask, climbing over the edge of the cockpit almost at the feet of the Rosettis. "It's done," he said.

Mama Rosetti looked at him, her black eyes inscrutable in the soft light.

"No trouble."

"No trouble."

"Take off those wet clothes. You'll freeze to death."

Costa went into the cabin, peeled out of the rubber jacket, dried his head, put on slacks and a sweater and returned to the Rosettis.

Mama Rosetti was back in her wicker chair, her hands busy again with the knitting. From somewhere Papa Rosetti had pulled out a bottle of wine.

"Here," he said to Costa. "Drink." He poured three glasses.

They drank. For a long time Mama Rosetti studied Costa's face. "Everything all right, huh?" she said.

"Worked fine," Lee Costa said. "Nobody saw me. Nobody knows I'm here. Nobody knows what happened. Except you and me."

"You shoot him?" Rosetti asked.

"I don't use guns," Costa said. "These are good enough." He held up a hard hand, pointed to the rim of calluses on the edge of his palm.

Rosetti stood and went to the cabin door. "I'm tired, Mama."

She looked over at him, her face warm with concern. "Cover up good, Papa. Sleep well." She turned to Costa. "You too, Mr. Costa. You need to go to bed."

Costa rose, standing on the deck of the boat to stretch. "Nice night, isn't it?" he said, smiling down at her.

"Yes," she said, pulling an ugly little automatic out from under her knitting. "A very nice night." She shot him, twice, over the heart. Costa's body was thrown backwards, hitting the water with a soft splash. Mama Rosetti leaned over the rail of the boat, the pistol in her hand, while she watched the body sink, as it slowly moved away with the tide.

"What now, Mama?" Rosetti's head was sticking out of the cabin door.

She turned to him gravely. "Nothing more." She threw the pistol over the side.

"Cover up good, Papa. Don't catch cold."

A Try for the Big Prize

Blake was a cop. He had been a cop for a very long time. He had forgotten how to quit being a cop and so he worked at the job twenty-four hours of every day. Even now, relaxed in front of the TV set on his day off, a glass of beer at his side, somewhere far back under his conscious mind a desk sergeant toiled, a mug man flipped pictures, a traffic cop ticked off license plates. So Blake recognized the man on the TV screen.

Blake had felt himself lucky that the pro championship game was coming on his day off—and that it was being televised at all, instead of blacked out locally. He had missed a lot of the football games, of course, and he had half-expected to miss this one. But he hadn't known just how lucky he was going to be.

It had been a good game, tight all the way, with the kind of thumping line play that Blake particularly liked to watch. The lead had changed hands a couple of times and now it was all tied up again. The camera swung down over the crowd and the announcer said, "And here's part of the vast turn-out for this great game." It was then that Blake saw him.

Blake was a big man, cop-size, with a shambling walk and bulky shoulders. He had played football himself, in high school, though he hadn't been able to go on to college like he had wanted to. There weren't as many football scholarships in those days. He had always thought of going on to college and then into the pros, where the real football playing took place, where you had to be a man to stay in that line. But it hadn't worked out that way; Blake had become a cop instead.

He had been a good cop. He had started out on the traffic detail. In those days, he had made a habit of scanning the lists of stolen cars—their makes, models and license number—each morning before reporting for duty. In his rookie year, he had spotted and turned in more stolen cars than any other man on the force.

He had a trick memory for names, numbers and faces. He still remembered the telephone number of the first girl he had ever dated, his serial number during the war, the face of the first criminal he had ever arrested. Later, after he was off traffic, he began spending time in the mug room, looking at pictures. As he had worked his way up the ladder of promotion, as the years slowly bruised his big frame, as the old dream of football glory faded into an avid spectator-interest in the sport, he had several times a year spotted a wanted man—on the street, in a crowd, on a circus lot, serving hot dogs, running an elevator.   He had never been wrong; and so this time he was also sure.

Blake was a gray man with a heavy pale-gray face.   He had never married; he had always lived alone.   And his associates had for a long time been wary and respectful of his self-contained silences, of his fabled memory for the face of a criminal, of the man himself in all his totality.   For years now he had been a full detective, having gone as far as a man with his education and attainments could hope to go.

Blake stood up out of the chair.   Automatically his mind had noted the exit ramp near the man he had seen, so that he would know where he was seated in the stands.   FF.   Out of the hole into the football sunshine, turn to the left, and there he would be—if he was still there—if the game was not already over.

The game was coming close to an end now.   As he put on his shoes and stood up, strapping on his shoulder holster, Blake considered the problem.   He couldn't possibly make it to the stadium if the game ended on schedule.   There would have to be a tie and a sudden death play-off to give him a chance at all.   His best bet would be to call the precinct, report the presence of the wanted man, let them stake out the stadium and pick him up.

His lips tightened.   Blake knew the man, knew his whole history, though he had seen only a snapshot taken through a telephoto lens.   He would take a chance on the sudden death playoff.   This one was for Blake, not for the force.   Blake had always been a loner and he would play this one alone.   If the game ended and the man was gone . . .   He shrugged his shoulders.   It was a chance he would have to take—and he would know to keep looking for him, know he was still in town.

He was going out of the door of his two-room apartment by the time the thinking was ending, leaving the television set on behind him.   He went down and got into his car, immediately switching the radio to the ball game.   He backed out into the street and headed across town toward the football stadium.   He fought the traffic with a steady remorseless determination to arrive before the game ended.   The plan of the city was firm in his mind, too, and he worked his way through the fastest routes, the least traffic, that he could find.

On the radio, the game was going on, drawing towards its close, and it was still tied.   The sound of the crowd in the speaker was tense and thrilling and Blake wondered if the man was yelling with them.   Or had he felt panic, with the deep criminal instinct of his kind, had he already left the game?   No, he would not want to leave except in the cloaking of the crowd.   And, besides, he must be a good fan himself.

Blake was caught by a traffic light, eased to a stop.   He heard the roar of the crowd, the excited voice of the announcer.   A long pass had been thrown, a football hero had galloped with the ball to a touchdown, and one of the teams was leading. Not Blake's team—the other.   Blake gritted his teeth.   Come on, boys, he said in his mind.   Get it back.   Tie it up.   Put it into overtime.

He lurched into speed as the light changed, listening to the crowd, listening to the chanting of the announcer.   There was the kickoff and he leaned forward, praying for a long runback. But the man was smeared on the fifteen-yard line as he fumbled the ball and then fell on it. Blake cursed. There was only a minute left in the game and he was not going to be in time.

The minute ticked on. There was an incomplete pass, a time out, another incomplete pass. Then the quarterback completed a pass and the receiver stepped out of bounds, stopping the clock. Time for one more play, two at the most. Blake gripped his hands on the steering wheel.

He should have phoned in, instead of taking it on himself. He slid through an amber light just before it changed to red, felt the caress of luck in his mind. Then the quarterback was fading, they were after him, they were red-dogging him. He almost fell down, he ran out of the pocket, he threw long . . . long . . . he'd got it . . . he was over for a touchdown! The extra-point kick and then the whistle blew, ending the game.

Blake leaned back, pursing his lips and whistling through them. It was his now. Just as he had felt in the instant of seeing the man's face he had seen only once before, in a telephoto snapshot—this one belonged to Blake.

He relaxed, driving on to the stadium. There was time now. A few minutes before the play-off started. He could think beyond arriving, beyond spotting the man in the flesh. The whole eastern seaboard, if not the whole country, had been looking for him for six weeks, with only a telephoto snapshot to go on. No wonder he had been cool enough, sure enough, to take his pleasure at a championship football game. Blake, the first time he had studied the single blurred picture, had known that this man was not in any mug book he had ever studied. He was the hardest of all to catch, a freelance criminal who had never fallen, never served time, never been mugged and fingerprinted. He had either been very, very lucky or he had planned the one big caper for his first and last venture.

Blake had had to admire the operation. The kidnap victim had been a man with plenty of money, who would not be likely to cooperate with the police, a man who wouldn't want the police or the FBI prying too closely into his own affairs. Not a wanted man, only a dubious man who operated close to the fringe of the law. The pickup had been executed smoothly, the ransom arranged quickly, the victim released even before the ransom was paid, turned loose in a wooded countryside miles from any communication. The kidnaper had gotten his money and made a clean getaway. The only thing the police had on him was the telephoto shot taken at the moment of payoff. Blake had a taste for neat, clean operations and this was one of the finest of its type. He had gotten away with it. The case was dying now, six weeks after the payoff and not a sign of the kidnaper, nothing for the police to go on. But the kidnaper had not figured on Blake's memory for names and figures and faces.

Blake stopped the car in the stadium parking lot, got out, and hurried to the exit. He flashed his badge and went inside, trudging up the long ramp to entrance FF. He did not even glance at the uniformed policeman on duty at the entrance of the ramp. He was breathing hard by the time he reached the tunnel opening and the sights and sounds of football smote on his ears like a blow. They were playing again and the crowd was standing on its feet, wild with excitement.

Blake waited until a couple of vendors exited from the tunnel; then he followed them out.   He turned to the left, climbed the stairs a step or two, stopped and looked at the field.   There were no empty seats, so he stood close to a row of seats to blend with the crowd.   A player was running with the football.   Then he was tackled, swarmed over as he tried to get around the end.

Blake turned his head, looking for the man.   The sight of him was a shock, even to Blake's hardened nerves.   Blake let his eyes drift on over him, before he looked again at the football field.   Now he knew the man, in every detail.

He was young, not over thirty-five.   He had a compact, muscular body, a face that was very ordinary, a good kind of face for a criminal to own.   He was wearing a blue overcoat, in the medium price range, and under it a blue suit. Blake suspected there was a gun in the armpit, though he couldn't be sure because of the overcoat.   The man had tan gloves on his hands and he was very excited with the ball game.   He looked as though he had once played football himself.

The game went on in the sudden death play-off.   But Blake had lost interest. He only wanted it to end now.   He was engaged in a greater game than even football could be.   He was surprised to find that feeling inside himself.   He had never before felt that way.   But now, suddenly, he did, and he knew why. There was a great deep calmness inside him, a sureness of the chances.

There was a long surging roar as a man sprinted for the goal line, breaking out of the ruck of blocking and tackling with an almost miraculous ease, and the game was over.   The crowd whooped and yelled and threw things onto the field.   Out of the corner of his eye, Blake saw his man begin edging toward the exit.

Blake went down the steps, got into the exit ahead of him.   He went on down the ramp in the first jostling fringe of the throng without looking over his shoulder, knowing there was no other way out, and got outside the gate.   He found his car quickly; then he turned his head, scanning the crowd, watching for his man. There he was, walking quickly into the parking area.   Blake leaned over his wheel and started the motor.   This was going to be the difficult part, with the crowd and the traffic.   If he could keep from losing him here . . .

The man got into a compact car and pulled out into the exit lane just in front of Blake.   That was lucky.   There was nothing between them.   Blake was riding his luck today; it was deep and calm and certain inside him.   For the first time in his life, he felt absolutely and completely right.

It had been so long in coming.   First there had been football, the tedious and painful learning and then the sudden ending of playing the game after high school. He had started all over again on the police force, the slow and tedious learning, the grinding single-minded application, the slow, slow climb toward the top with the years moving just as slowly over him.   He had reached the limit on the force also without reaching the peak, and now the years were ending on him.   He had known for a long time that he had gone as far as he could go, just as he had known it about football.   It was only three months until mandatory retirement age.

He was swinging smoothly behind the compact car as it threaded into the city. The man was driving sedately.   He was a loner, as Blake was a loner.   Loner pitted against loner.   The payoff would be . . .?

It was a nice, quiet residential area where the man stopped the car.   This was intelligent too.   The man obviously didn't associate on the criminal level.   That was why he had never been mugged, why his caper had been so spectacularly successful.   He had not tried to skip after the ransom payoff, but had stayed quietly in his snug deceptive covering.

The man stopped the car before a medium-sized apartment house.   Blake parked down the street from him, got out, and began walking toward the man, looking at the fronts of the apartment houses as though searching for a number.   The man was locking his car carefully, meticulously, checking the windows to be sure they were all up.   Blake was opposite him as the man came around to the sidewalk.

Blake, in a sudden movement, crowded him against the side of the car.   "All right," he said.   "You're under arrest."

The man tried to whirl away, but Blake jabbed the gun into his ribs, gripped his arm with the other hand.

"Hold it," he said.   "Or I'll splatter you all over the sidewalk."

The man was pale.   Blake looked around quickly.   Their little flurry had not been noted on the quiet street.

"Quick," Blake said.   "Into the building."

They walked quickly into the lobby, Blake holding the man's arm tightly in his big hand.

"Which floor do you live on?"

"Fifth," the man said.

They got into the self-service elevator and Blake punched the fifth-floor button. The door slid closed and the elevator whined slightly as it began to rise.   Blake crowded the man against the elevator wall, slipped his hand inside the man's coat. He took out the thirty-two, looked at it, put it into his overcoat pocket. The man leaned against the elevator wall.   Their breathing was loud in the quietness.

"Are you a cop?" the man said.

"Yes," Blake said.   "I'm a cop."

The elevator door slid open and they stepped out into the hall.

"Which door?"

"Number seven."

They went down the carpeted hall.   The building murmured with people, but the hall was empty.   They stopped in front of number seven.

"Anybody in there?" Blake said.

The man shook his head.

"If there is, you're dead," Blake said.   "Remember that.   Now I'll ask you again."

"I live alone," the man said.   "The place's empty."

"Open it."

The man reached slowly into his pocket for the key, opened the door, and they went inside.   The man tried to swing the door against Blake and Blake slugged him, sending him to the floor.   The man rolled, moaning, then sat up.

"Say, what is this?" he said.

Blake ignored him. "Get the coat off."

The man struggled out of the overcoat and Blake kicked it to one side. He leaned down, lifted the man, and shook him down thoroughly. He took out the handcuffs, snapped them on. Then he stepped back, looking the man full in the face.

"Where's the money?" Blake said.

"Look," the man said, his voice rising, "you're not acting like any cop I ever heard of. Are you—?"

"Yes," Blake said calmly. "I am. I've been a cop for thirty years. But I'm not taking you in."

Blake was as startled by his words as the other man was. They had sprung out of his depths, where they had been building slowly, inevitably, from the moment he had recognized the man on television.

Blake stood still, examining what he had said, and he knew that it was the truth. All of his life he had been looking for the big one. First, he had thought to find it in football. Then he had thought to find it, somehow, on the force. But over the years, the thought and the desire had submerged itself in the day-to-day routine, in the pride of being a good cop, in his own special talent for recognition and remembering. But all the time it had been there.

A man can surprise himself any day of his life. Blake had thought the old ambition was gone, bruised out of him by event and circumstance, sublimated as his desire to play championship football had been sublimated. Just as he liked to watch football, so too did he like to read about the big scores: the baseball player getting the top salary for the year, the financier cleaning up through a control fight for a big company. For days, weeks, he had been as excited by the Brinks robbery as another man might be by a woman.

The man drew a long ragged breath. His face had changed, his whole posture. "I see," he said slowly. "I see." They were no longer facing each other as cop and criminal; there was a sudden subtle alteration in their relationship, so that they were man and man, equal in their common hunger.

Blake smiled. "That was a pretty cute operation you pulled," he said. "Waited a long time for it, didn't you? Worked it out as careful as a football play. No known criminal record—striking for the top money the first time, instead of starting out on peanuts like most guys do. I've got to admire you."

"Thanks," the man said drily.

"Now I want the money."

There was no doubt of it. There had not been any doubt of it since he had strapped on his gun and started out of the apartment. Mentally, Blake stood back and admired himself. He felt, suddenly, twenty years younger, bigger than himself. He had thought that the old lust had ebbed out of him. But he was not finished yet, as they all thought he was finished. When he retired in three months, he would retire full of the secret knowledge of his victory over them all, over all the years, all the disappointments, all the men who had climbed past him to greater heights.

The man shook his head. Blake slapped him in the face with his hard, jarring palm.

"Don't talk back to me, son," he said in a low, hard voice. "I've waited a long time too. Longer than you have."

"What kind of cop are you, anyway?"

"I'm a good cop," Blake said. "I've been a good cop ever since I've been on the force. I've kept clean. I've never taken a bribe. I've never looked the other way. I've gone through more investigations and shake-ups than you can dream of, and they've never had a chance to lay a finger on me."

The man nodded. "Now you're going for the big one."

Blake nodded too. "Just like you, buddy-boy," he said. "I'm going for the two hundred thousand you took Johnny Roth for."

"Look," the man said. "I worked for the money. Five years I planned and watched. When Johnny Roth got into that congressional investigation bind so he couldn't kick too much, I went after him. I earned that money."

"I've waited too," Blake said. "Waited longer than you can even think of. I've put in the time. I've turned down a thousand small chances, waiting for the big one. We're just alike, buddy-boy. Except I've got the handcuffs on you, now, like you had them on Johnny Roth. Where's the money?"

The man shook his head. Blake pushed him down into a chair, leaned over him. "What's your name?"

The man glared up at him. Blake caught his coat, looked inside at the label. Then he picked up the overcoat, looked at it. He prowled the apartment, found a desk, opened it and picked up an address book, looking inside the cover. Then he looked at the man.

"Ronald O'Steen," he said. "Say, didn't you play football?"

O'Steen didn't move.

"Sure," Blake said. "You played left half for Midwestern a few years ago. Did pretty good too." He stopped looking at O'Steen. "I played a little football in my time."

O'Steen looked up at him. He shrugged his shoulders. "Sure," he said. "I played out there."

Blake studied him. "Didn't football pay off for you, either?" he said. "You did better than I did. I didn't even get to college."

O'Steen's mouth twisted. "I was too light for the pros," he said. "I tried out, the year I finished, but they dropped me."

"So you went for the big one."

"Yes. I went for the big one."

"Where is it?"

"I'm not going to tell you."

"Yes," Blake said quietly. "You're going to tell me. Is it here in the apartment?"

O'Steen did not answer. Blake waited.

"All right," he said. "I'm going to try to make it light on you. If I can find it by myself, okay.   If I can't, I'm going to lean on you until you tell me where it is.''

He unlocked one of the handcuffs, pulled O'Steen to his feet.   He led him to the bed, pushed him over backward, and snapped the handcuff around the bedpost. He left him there and began methodically tearing up the apartment.

He worked silently for a long time, with O'Steen watching him.   When he was through, the apartment was a shambles.   But he hadn't uncovered the money.   He pulled O'Steen off the bed and took that apart, too, before he stopped, panting.

"All right," he said at last.   "I guess it's going to be the hard way."   O'Steen looked up at him, his face flinching.   "Don't think you can hold out," Blake said. "I'm an expert, O'Steen.   And I'll kill you with my bare hands for that money. You know that.   Because you'd kill me for it."

"Look," O'Steen said.   "Why don't you just be a hero and take me in?   That ought to be enough for you."

Blake shook his head.   "Not any more," he said.   "I'm too old now.   I'm coming up for mandatory retirement in three months.   If I was a younger man . . . but I'm not."   He advanced on O'Steen.   "All right," he said.   "Here we go."

He worked as diligently as he had worked in tearing up the apartment.   O'Steen whimpered and grunted with the pain, his teeth tightly clenched.   Blake remembered that he might have to take O'Steen out of the apartment to get the money, so he stayed away from the face.   He stopped when O'Steen passed out.   He went into the bathroom.   He drank a glass of water, brought back a full glass and threw it into O'Steen's face.   O'Steen moaned, coming out of it.

Blake stared down at him.   O'Steen was a tough one, all right.   Blake had not seen many men who could take what Blake had just given him.

"You're a pretty good boy," Blake said.

O'Steen's mouth twisted wryly.   "Thanks a lot."

"What are you holding out for?" Blake said.   "You know I can keep this up all night if necessary."

O'Steen began levering himself up off the floor, his face wincing with the pain of his body.   He sat down in the chair and looked at Blake across the two feet of space that separated them.

"I'm not going to give it all up," he said.   "You can kill me before I'll give it all up.   I worked too hard.   I wanted it too much . . .''

Blake recognized the truth in this.   "All right," he said, "I'll split it with you. One hundred thousand for each of us.   Half is enough for me, if it's enough for you."

They stared at each other.   Their relationship was changing again.   It had shifted subtly, constantly, since the moment of their meeting.   First, briefly, it had been cop and criminal; then it had been man and man; then torturer and tortured.   Now it was becoming something neither of them could immediately define.

Blake saw the sudden decision come into O'Steen's face.

"All right," O'Steen said.   "I know when to cut the take.   We'll split it fifty-fifty."   He tried to smile again, but it was not much of a smile.   "I just wish you'd made your proposition before working me over."

"I had to see whether you'd hold together or not," Blake said coldly. "Just like you had to see whether I'd hold together for it too. We couldn't have made the deal before."

O'Steen nodded his head. They understood each other. All the way through, all the way down.

"Where is it?" Blake said.

"In a safety deposit box."

"Where's the key? I was looking for a key."

O'Steen smiled. "It's in the envelope," he said. "In my mail slot downstairs."

"Then we can't get the money until tomorrow," Blake said. "The bank's closed now."

"That's right."

"We'll wait."

"Can you stay awake all night?" O'Steen said. "I'll kill you if I get a chance. You know that."

"I can stay awake," Blake said stolidly.

The long night passed slowly in the ripped-apart apartment. Blake sat in a chair, watching O'Steen in the other chair. For a while, desultorily, they talked, and O'Steen told how he had planned to wait six months, then take a Far Eastern cruise on a tourist ship. In the Far East, it would be easy to make a deal on the hot money.

"You can still do that," Blake said. "With your half."

"If you let me," O'Steen said wearily.

"I don't care what you do afterward," Blake said. "In fact, I'll help you when it's time to go. I don't want you caught, either."

Blake did not call in the next morning, though he was on duty for the day. The captain was used to Blake failing to call in or come in, occasionally; he would assume that Blake had a live one. The captain had implicit faith in Blake and his abilities, though he had never understood him.

When it was time to go, Blake took the handcuffs off, waited while O'Steen put on his overcoat.

"Remember," Blake said, "if you make a break, I'll shoot you down. I can always claim I was making an arrest. You don't have an out, except dividing the money."

"I know that," O'Steen said. He looked at Blake. "I'd just like to know how you caught me."

Blake smiled. "I've got a talent," he said. "I never forget a face. They got a snap of you on the payoff. I was watching television yesterday and I saw you in the crowd."

O'Steen took a deep breath. "A long chance like that," he said. "I lost on a chance like that."

"If you hadn't been a fool about football, I wouldn't have caught you," Blake said. "If I hadn't been a fool about football too."

O'Steen shrugged. "I should have got you on the operation from the start," he said. "We'd operate well together."

"Yes," Blake said. "Too bad it didn't work out that way."

They went out the door, down the elevator, and got into Blake's car. Blake made O'Steen drive the short way to the bank. They went inside the bank, shoulder to shoulder, and Blake watched O'Steen sign the register. They went together into the vault and Blake waited while O'Steen and the bank clerk unlocked the box. Then the bank clerk went away and O'Steen pulled the deep box out. Blake watched hungrily as he reached inside and pulled out the thick pad of bills. O'Steen handed them to Blake who put them into an airline satchel they had brought along from the apartment. It was the same satchel that had shown in the photograph of O'Steen taking the payoff.

Then they locked the safety deposit box, went side by side out of the bank and sat in the car. It had gone as smoothly as a well-executed draw play and Blake wondered why both of them were sweating so hard.

"Back to the apartment," he said.

They returned by another route, at circumspect speed, and parked the car. They got out and went upstairs, both of them breathing with relief as the door closed behind them. They felt almost partners in danger, instead of antagonists.

"Well, we made it," O'Steen said. "You still going to split with me?"

"Sure," Blake said.

He put the satchel on the chair, unzipped the zipper. He stared at the money, his breath caught. It was the big payoff he had been looking for all his life. Only now, in the last days of his long police service, had it come to him. It had been a sudden death play-off for sure.

He caught a flicker of movement out of the corner of his eye. He whirled, but it was too late. O'Steen had tackled him low and hard. The gun flew out of Blake's hand and he crashed to the floor, O'Steen on top of him. Blake slugged at O'Steen with one hand, whirled him over on the bottom. O'Steen was too light to resist the bulk and weight of Blake. He hit O'Steen again, felt O'Steen's fist smash into his face. He bore down with his greater weight as O'Steen's body surged against him, leaning on his struggling violence, and the thinking was clear and sharp in his mind, as though he were talking to O'Steen aloud.

I was going to kill you when we got the money. Then I decided not to. Because you're me, and I'm you. But now I know I've got to kill you. For that same reason. Because you're me. You'd come after me and the money.

It was clear and loud and hard in his mind and he turned his head so he wouldn't see what his hands were doing. He stood up at last from the limp body and his breath was a long hard sob of sound when it caught again. He was weeping. Blake had never wept in his adult life; not since he had broken his collarbone in a football game.

He looked dully at the money, knowing it was all his. He took a long slow step towards it, reaching for it with both hands.

There was a burst of sound at the door and he whirled around. The door was splintering off its hinges as men's shoulders slammed against it and Blake reached for the gun that wasn't there. Then he recognized the men. They were precinct men, and behind them was the captain. Blake stood still, watching them as they swarmed into the room.

"We heard you fighting," the captain told Blake. "We got in here as soon as we could. Why didn't you tell me you had a lead on this case?"

"Heard us fighting?" Blake said dully. His mind moved sluggishly, frozenly. "You had the place staked out all the time?"

The captain laughed. "The FBI got us onto him. They did it the hard way. They decided he looked like an athlete, so they started checking newspaper pictures for boxers and football players about the time he would've been playing. We just started the stake-out yesterday, hoping he'd lead us to the money. Looks like we'd have had a long wait without you."

Blake watched the young dapper stranger, who surely was the FBI agent, examine the money satchel. The FBI agent gestured to one of the policemen. "Take charge of this money," he said. He turned, looked at Blake. He had cold, suspicious eyes. "It was quite a surprise when you checked into the apartment with him," he said. "But the captain insisted you had to have a chance to make your play."

Blake looked at the money the FBI man was holding in the zipper bag. He put his hand into his coat and then he remembered that the gun was on the floor.

The captain chuckled. "You played it smart," he said. "You made him think you were just after the money. You let him think it was a heist instead of an arrest. Smart, Blake, damned smart."

Blake stared at him, not understanding the words.

The captain jerked a thumb at the agent. "This FBI guy here thought you were serious about the money," he said. "He wanted to come on in, but I wouldn't let him. Hell, I knew you knew what you were doing. He'd never have told where the money was otherwise. He was too tough. I told this guy we could depend on you."

Blake stood stunned in the middle of the room. The precinct men swarmed around him, busy with their duties of tidying up the case, nailing it down.

"We tailed you to the bank this morning," the FBI agent said. His eyes were still cold, hard, intent. "When we saw you didn't head for the precinct station straight from the bank, we couldn't figure it. But your captain just kept on waiting for you. Why did you come back here, anyway?"

Blake was too stunned to grasp the danger. He merely shook his head, mumbling the words. "I had to make sure of the money," he said. "I had to be sure it was all there." He turned his head, looked at the dead man. "I didn't want to kill him."

The captain slapped him on the shoulder. "Always tying down the details," he said. "Take-no-chances-Blake, that's you. Snap out of it, man. Too bad you had to kill him when he went for you. Why, you'll be a hero now. There'll be newspaper guys at the precinct, photographers, the whole works. Why, it's your greatest case, Blake. That's why I let you take the play all the way, so you wouldn't lose any of the glory. How does it feel to be a hero?"

"Great," Blake said. "Just great." He looked at the FBI agent, recognized the residual suspicion. But there was no danger there. It was only a suspicion and the agent could never make more of it than that in the midst of the captain's faith. Blake smiled a weak smile. "When I retire," he said, "I can sit and read all my clippings. Over and over and over again."

He went on out of the apartment. He would go home now, and sleep. He needed sleep. Tomorrow there would be reporters and excitement at the precinct station and he would have to live through it all. But now he only wanted sleep. He was an old man and he needed all the sleep that he had missed.

ROBERT COLBY

Voice in the Night

For two nights there had been thundershowers and since it never seemed to work very well when it rained, he had been moody and tense, violently caged within himself and the empty house. Perched atop a hill in the isolation of three high-walled acres, the house was an elegant straggle of stone and wood hunched down in a cloister of giant trees.

Broodingly confined to it, he lounged about in one room or another, reading and watching television (a set in every room), or occasionally took a swim in the regulated, tepid water of the glass-sheltered pool. Despite the frigid breath of central air-conditioning at work to dispel the dense humidity of late summer, during the night he lay in a damp huddle of sleeplessness. The urge had come upon him again and now it consumed even his sleep.

Monday evening came with a pure sky after a day of searing sun. Monday was a good time. People settled down after the weekend and seldom made plans for a Monday night. He fixed an early dinner of leftovers from the refrigerator, then barely touched a morsel. At six-thirty he went to the study, seated himself behind the desk and rubbed his hands together gleefully.

He placed the heavy phone book before him and opened it at random. His finger idly roved a column, paused, continued slowly: *Landrith, Landruf—Landrum!* A good, solid name, Landrum. There were Landrums, *Albert, Bruce, Dewey, Edward* . . . Ed Landrum? Fine. Just right! He printed the name boldly on a sheet of paper, closed the phone book, once more opened it carelessly.

His finger came to rest on the name Henderson. There were dozens of Hendersons, nearly three columns. When in doubt, begin at the beginning. Skip *Henderson Adrian C.,* forget *Henderson Agnes B. Mrs.* How about *Henderson Alice?* Let's see if we can get a winner with Alice.

He wrote the number down and then dialed it.

A woman answered. She sounded eighty, going on ninety. The grandmother? "Hello there! May I speak with Alice, please?"

"What's that?"

This one forgot the ear trumpet! "Alice. Alice Henderson!"

"This here is Alice speakin'."

"Sorry, wrong Alice." He dropped the receiver. A real dud. Well, you couldn't expect to make it on the first try. He never had. Anyway, with every failure the excitement mounted.   The first thrill came with the hunt.   Now he dialed an Arline Henderson.   A man growled at him and he erased the connection.

Barbara Henderson wasn't home.   Lucky Barbara!   He dialed Beatrice.   After a while she came on like one foot out the door.   She had a hard pushy voice.

"Bea?   Is that you, Bea?"

"Yeah, this is Bea.   Who's this?"

"Bet you'll never guess."

"You wanna play games, try solitaire!"

"Well, it's been a long time, Bea.   I'm being cute, I just wanted to see if you still—"

"I shoulda known," she cut in.   "It's Bernie!   Right?"

He chuckled.   "Okay, I confess.   It's Bernie.   I realize it's short notice, Bea, but I thought maybe you might—"

"Listen, Bernie," she said in a muted, deadly voice, "know what you are? You're a creep.   I don't go out with creeps.   Where you staying this time, Bernie? At the zoo?   What's your cage number in case I change my mind?"

He snorted.   "You got a great sense of humor, Bea.   Too bad we can't get together.   I had a big night planned for us."   He turned her off with a thumb on the cross-bar.

The Bea Henderson types were poison.   For this you had to snare one that was soft and pliable and not very bright.   In one way or another the rest fizzled, but he stuck with the Hendersons until he got to Victoria.

"Vicky?   Is that you, Vicky?'

"Yes—this is Vicky."   This was a young one, late twenties or first thirties, maybe.

"It's been a long time, Vicky."

"Well, who is this?"   she said, "I—I can't seem to place you."

"Can't place me?   And to think that only a few years back you placed me first, Vicky."

"Heavens!"   Nervous giggle.   "You're putting me on the spot."

"Kinda fun though, isn't it?"

"For you, maybe.   Have a heart.   Who *are* you?"

Man, this one was a dilly!   Made to order.   "Ah, c'mon, give it a whirl.   You always were a good sport, Vicky.   I'll give you a clue.   I'm either Bill, Joe, or Dave.   Check one out of three."   He didn't care.   If that didn't work he'd bang the phone and spin the dial for a live one.   Sooner or later . . .

"You serious?   Bill, Joe, or Dave?"

"Dead serious."

"Mmm, let's see.   I know a couple of Bills, but they're pretty recent."   Pause. "Hey, you're not Walter Buckley, are you?"

Wow, a real brain!   "Honey, you can't find a Walter in Bill, Joe, or Dave."

"Of course not!"   Peevishly.   "He just came into my mind, that's all."

"Well, I'll admit you're getting close.   Say, whatever happened to Walt?"

"Walter?   Last I heard he was working for some law firm and going around with that tacky Jane Vogel."

"You're kidding!   Jane Vogel, huh?   I never could stand her type."

"You and me, ditto.   I hope they got married, they deserve each other.   Are you married?"

"Would I be calling?"

"Mm.   Were you *ever* married?"

"Was.   Got a divorce."

"Well, join the club!"   Long pause.   "I don't know any Joes and I only know one— Ahh, *now* I've got you.   You're Dave Mosby!"

"At last!   And for shame.   How could you forget?"

"Dave!   Is it really you, Dave?"

"Yours truly, Dave Mosby."

"After all this time!"

"Lotta water, Vicky."

"How long is it—five years?"

"More like six, I'd say."

"You and Betty got divorced?"

"Yeah, can you beat it?   Well, that's the way it goes."

"Did you know that I had divorced Clint?"

"Heard a rumor.   That's why I called."

"How sweet!"

Careful with this one, baby; it's loaded.   "So what happened after you said bye-bye to Clint?   Move in with a girlfriend?"

"Nope.   Rented my own little apartment and went back to work.   That's how much Clint is doing for me.   You still selling insurance for—what's the name of that outfit?"

Think fast!   "Got my own agency now, Vicky.   I'm part of it, anyway.   Big agency."   He pulled the sheet of paper toward him.   "This friend of mine, Ed Landrum, a guy with trunkloads of dough, took me in with him."

"Marvelous."

"Want you to meet Ed.   His wife and kids too."

"That would be nice."

"I'm staying with Ed.   He has this big house, really a showplace."

"My!   What part of town would that be, Dave?" she questioned.

When they asked, he couldn't avoid the truth.   They rarely asked and anyway, especially when they lived alone, it didn't matter.   "Crestview Gardens," he said.

"Really?   Oh, that's the living end.   I'll bet you couldn't get a house there for under seventy-five thousand."

"A hundred and up; mostly up."

"And you're staying there in Swankville?"

"Just for the time being.   Recovering from an accident."

"Oh, dear!"

"Cost me a fractured leg—in three places."

"How terrible for you."

"Not really.   It's healing great, but I can't get out for a while longer.   Pretty dull.   Lonely too.   Will you come visit me, Vicky?   Meet the Landrums, see how the other half lives?"

"I'd love to!"

"Come tonight, then.   Ed's still down at the office with some paper work and I could ask him to pick you up."

"Tonight?   Well, I don't know.   Working gals have to get their beauty sleep."

"Just for an hour or two.   Whatta you say, Vicky?   Old time's sake?"

"Honestly, Dave, what a rush job!   I feel as if I don't quite know you anymore.   You seem different somehow.   More mature . . . older."

"We don't get any younger, Vicky."

"How old *are* you now?   Let's see, you were—"

"I stopped counting.   How old are *you* now, Vicky?"

"Just add five or six years."

"Oh, you are a coy one.   Well, let me ring Ed, see if he can drive you up here. Get right back to you, okay?"

"You don't think he'll mind?"

"Ed?   My best friend!   Just give me a minute to arrange something."

He rang off and then waited three minutes.   "Ed says it's a deal," he reported. "But would you mind meeting him in the lobby of the Winston Plaza?   It's close by the office.   He'll send a cab to your apartment at eight sharp."

"Well—"

"Sit near the desk in the lobby."

"How will he recognize me?"

"I painted a nice picture for him, but better tell me what you'll be wearing so I can pass it on to him."

"Nothing fancy?"

"As you are, Vicky."

"I'll be wearing a green silk dress with a gold chain belt."

"Cab'll fetch you at eight, then.   And listen, I can't wait to see you again, Vicky!"

The instant he put down the phone he began to snicker.

At five minutes to eight he was waiting in an obscure corner, where there was a view of the entrance and the desk.   It was a crazy gamble.   Sometimes he caught a real dog, in which case, being as yet uncommitted, he could leave the dope squirming on the hook and spin the dial another night.

He never went in person to pick them up, never used the same meeting place twice, and always sent the cab by phone.   Still, there was an element of risk which gave him an exquisite sense of excitement.

Vicky Henderson, in the green dress with the gold chain belt, arrived at ten past eight.   She stood near the desk a moment but after a quick glance about sat down primly and then began a fussy examination of her makeup, head cocked as she viewed herself in the mirror of her compact.

Her voice hadn't lied about her age.   She was looking back on her twenties from no great distance, but in all other aspects she failed to match his vague conception.   He had imagined her to be tall and blonde, while she was short and dark-haired.   She had tiny features.   A receding chin gave her face a look of incompletion.   Her eyes were wide and solemn, with long, fake lashes.   She had a cute little mouth, however, and for one so petite, an astonishingly good figure.

He was pleased. She was better than most. She would do very well.

He went right up to her then, stood peering down at her with his odd little smile as she let the compact fall back into her purse and looked up.

"Hello there," he said. "You must be Vicky, and I'm Ed Landrum."

Though she quickly recovered and offered him a flickering smile, she had been startled. They always were because, while one side of his face was quite handsome, the other somehow just missed the boat as a perfect match. It was almost as if he were two people in one face. Few things gave him such a kick as to let it come as a shock, watching them coil inside, as if ready to run. Perhaps they would, too, if not for his polite manner, the expensively tailored suit, and the Dave Mosbys waiting.

"I'm so happy to meet you, Ed," Vicky cooed, overdoing it to reimburse for her initial reaction. Standing, she bravely delivered her hand to his own. "So nice of you to go to so much trouble."

"Not at all. Anything for old Dave. He's my closest friend. Shall we go?"

With a gentle pressure against her elbow, he guided her rapidly from the lobby and into the street, now becoming dusky as the last light seeped from the sky. She was so short she had to doubletime to keep up with him.

The car was a gleaming, pearl-gray Bentley. While she drooled over it, he started the motor, closed the windows and adjusted the air-conditioning. They slid away.

"It's such a hot night," she said in a minute. "How good to ride in such a lovely, cool automobile."

He smiled from one side of his face, accelerated and needled swiftly through the traffic. She kept yanking nervously at her skirt and poking at her hair.

"Have you known Dave long?"

"It seems like I've known him all my life. Actually, it's been only a couple of years." Tell them anything. The idiots are dying to believe.

"You met Betty, of course."

"Yes. Oh, yes! Too bad. I was fond of Betty. So was Joyce."

"Joyce?"

"My wife. You'll meet her presently."

"Dave said you have children."

"Bobby, he's seven, and Gloria, she's nine."

"Seven and nine," she mused. "Kids are cute at that age."

"Delightful." He offered her a cigarette but she refused with a shake of her head. He plugged the dashboard lighter.

"I lost complete track of Dave. Did he and Betty have kids?"

"No."

"I'm glad."

"Are you?" He turned onto the parkway and settled comfortably in his seat. He had it made.

"Well, I mean, if two people don't get along, it's always lucky when they don't have kids."

"How true," he said, and brushed a cigarette ash from his trousers. "I never thought of that." He almost laughed.

She leaned against the door and studied him, with her chin cupped in her palm. "You seem like such a nice person, Ed."

"Think so?"

"Mind if I ask how—how it happened?"

"How what happened?"

"You know, your face."

"Most people don't mention it."

"Oh, now, did I offend you?"

"No, I like girls with enough guts to come right out with it."

"Tell me, then."

"Viet Nam. I was a captain, infantry. A shell fragment blasted a chunk out of my head and pulverized one side of my face."

"Did they use plastic surgery to—"

"Sure, but they didn't have much left to work with. Since then I haven't been very popular." He laughed bitterly. "Especially with the girls—until I met Joyce."

"Oh, now, I don't really think it's so bad as all—"

"Don't hand me that, you hear! I hate liars and phonies! Why don't you just say I look like a damn freak or keep your silly mouth shut!"

She gasped. "Well—I—I didn't mean—I was just trying to be—"

"That's it, you were just trying to be—but you didn't make it, did you?" He stared at her briefly. The skin under one eye dropped, giving it a look of baleful malevolence.

"Maybe you'd better take me back home, Ed. Just tell Dave some other time. Okay?"

He didn't answer; not until he swerved from the parkway and began to climb into the hills of Crestview Gardens.

"I'm sorry," he said. "I come unglued now and then but it doesn't mean anything. Nothing personal. You understand?"

"Of course," she replied stiffly. Then, warming after a moment, "It's not your fault, it's mine. I'm just plain dumb, that's all."

"Yeah, sure." You're dumb all right, baby, he told her in his mind.

They wound up and up and came to a high, redwood gate. There was a gadget on a post. He stuck a square of plastic into its mouth and the gate swung open, closing behind them.

"How clever," she said.

From here the ground rose gently in a vast carpet of lawn and shrubs and ancient, towering trees, all shrouded in darkness. Out of this darkness, at the crest of the slope, loomed the long silhouette of the house. Its dim, curtained lights winking distantly through the trees, it had somewhat the appearance of a ship in the night.

"Oh, my!" exclaimed Vicky. "What a fantastic place! So beautiful and yet so—I can't find the right word—lonely, I guess. It's like when you pass through that gate, you enter another world."

He was listening to the cry of his thoughts and heard her distantly, as if from a faraway station, badly tuned. He hurled the big car up the drive, brought it around in front of the house and pulled up sharply, dousing the lights and killing the motor.

"C'mon," he said, "Dave'll be waiting." Moving ahead of her, he eyed the big door and stood poised on the threshold until she had passed inside. Then he closed the door.

The splendid, cavernous living room, bleakly lighted, was cool as a deep cellar. Heavy drapes had been pulled across sealed windows. A silence like some guarded secret clung to the place.

He listened. "They must be down in the playroom with the kids," he said. "Watching TV, I expect. Let's go and see."

Vicky smiled unevenly, then followed him toward the rear of the house, through an enormous kitchen to a door which stood open. Light sprang from below, casting a pale radiance over wide, carpeted stairs which curved down to a cheerfully paneled basement.

"How very pleasant," she said as they descended. "It's not at all like those damp, gloomy cellars you find in most houses."

"Joyce won't allow the kids to romp and scream all over the house," he explained, "so I had this soundproof playroom constructed and stocked it with the sort of sturdy junk that can't be soiled or damaged very much."

"How does Dave manage these stairs with a broken leg?" she asked, glancing back over her shoulder.

"He doesn't. There's a lift, an elevator; runs top to bottom."

"How lucky for him."

"But I thought you could handle one little flight." (See? I have all the answers, lover.) Chuckling, he moved off down the corridor, pausing at a door, which he opened casually. Light fell from the room and the strident sound of a television was sending voices above a moody underline of background music.

He stood aside and she stepped in. The door closed behind them with a click.

Gay tiles covered the floor. The walls and ceiling were ornamented with juvenile designs in gaudy colors. The empty, windowless room contained a daybed with a corduroy cover, two leather chairs and a couple of standing lamps. The portable television, in full swing, eyed the room from a corner shelf.

As she glanced about, Vicky's mouth parted slightly and in her saucer eyes with the long, fakey lashes, there was the first shadow of fear.

"Why, there's no one here," she declared. "Where is everybody? Where's Dave?" She turned. "Ed? Why don't you answer me? Is this some sort of— Listen, what *is* this?"

He leaned back against the door and smiled his odd little smile in which only half of his face seemed to take part, and Vicky screamed.

Shortly after seven the next evening, Detectives Linwood and Mallick were seated in the apartment of Miss Rena Whalen, who lived on the floor above Vicky Henderson.

"Now," said Linwood, "let's take it right from the beginning, Miss Whalen. How long have you known Vicky Henderson?"

"Going on three years," said Rena Whalen, a heavyset blonde with a round, fleshy face and pouty lips. "We work in the same office and I found Vicky an apartment here after she got her divorce."

"And you drove her to work every morning and brought her back every evening, right?" inquired Mallick, who was taking notes.

"Yes, that's right. She doesn't have a car and we split the gas, the expense, that is. This morning I went down at the usual time and banged her door, but she didn't answer. So then I went back up and called her on the phone. I figured, you know, maybe she was in the shower or something. But I couldn't reach her on the phone either, and I went on to the office.

"I kept calling her all day long and then late this afternoon I got the manager to open up and see if she was sick or something. Everything was nice and neat, but no Vicky. Her bed hadn't even been slept in."

"Is it unusual for her to be away all night?" Linwood asked.

"Very unusual. I mean, it just never happened before in the time I've known her. She's not at all that sort of girl. Decent and reliable, you know."

"But," said Mallick, "you knew she had gone out with this, uh, Dave—"

"Mosby," Rena supplied. "She wasn't exactly going out with him, she was just visiting him. He couldn't leave the house because he had a broken leg from an accident. Vicky said he was staying with some rich friend, in Crestview Gardens."

"And how did Vicky happen to tell you this?" asked Linwood.

"Well, I dropped in on her about—oh, sometime before eight, it was—and she told me. She was all excited. This Dave was an old flame and he just phoned right out of the blue. She hadn't heard from him in five, six years."

Linwood said, "And what was the name of the man this Mosby was supposed to be staying with?"

"Landrum. Ed Landrum. I didn't remember the name but Vicky had written it across the top of a magazine by the phone. So I looked it up in the book and sure enough there's an Ed Landrum and I call him and I ask him, so where's Vicky? 'What Vicky?' he says, real dumb, you know. He never even heard of Vicky Henderson. What's more he doesn't live in any Crestview Gardens; he lives out southside in Dumpville."

The two detectives exchanged glances and Mallick said, "Well, we'll go over and have a little talk with Mr. Ed Landrum. And meanwhile, I'll have them check on this Dave Mosby." He stood. "We'll get back to you in the morning, Miss Whalen."

Rena nodded. "So whatta you think, officer?"

"I think," said Mallick, "that it's very much like a case we had last summer; and who knows how many others, where there wasn't someone like you around to furnish a clue."

Rena moistened her puffy lips. "So what happened in that other case?"

"In a nut," said Mallick, "the girl made a date with some guy on the phone. She went out to meet him and never came back."

He was in the study, furiously dialing. As a rule he would let a week or two pass, but it was to be the last night and so far he had called dozens without success, skipping all over the book at random. Presently, he was dialing a Mildred Perry. She came on with a rich, eager voice.

"Millie? Is that you, Millie?"

"It certainly is!"

"Guess who? Millie, after all this time you'll never believe it . . ."

Shortly before nine the two detectives were down at headquarters discussing the case. "This is a beaut," said Mallick, who had just completed a call to Chicago. "A stone-wall deadend, just like the one last summer. Mosby can't be lying, he and the wife have been in Chicago a year and a half. Landrum and the missus had guests to the house last night for bridge, they tell us. And you can bet your bottom buck the guests will clear him. So where does that leave us?"

"Somewhere in Crestview Gardens," said Linwood.

"Ahh, c'mon now, Harry. The kinda people who live up in Crestview Gardens don't play deadly phone games with lonely women. That was just part of the gag, a little sugar on the bait. He pulled that one right outa his hat."

"Well, maybe," said Linwood, "although money doesn't buy sanity if you're a kook. Still, I don't dig that Crestview bit myself. No sense at all. This guy is a weirdo, probably operates from a booth."

"If he kept at it all year 'round," said Mallick, "we might have a chance to grab him. But evidently he hangs it up until summer. Does that tell us anything?"

"Sure," said Linwood. "In winter he goes south with the rest of the cuckoo birds."

While the detectives argued the question, the subject of their conversation stood with Mildred Perry at the edge of that hushed living room in Crestview Gardens.

"Quiet as a tomb," he said. "Guess they went down to the playroom with the kids. Well, then, Millie, let's go have a look . . ."

Just after dawn he tidied up the house, then went down to the playroom. After he mopped the linoleum floor and wiped every surface clean, he made a thorough search, inspecting corners, peering around and under the skimpy furniture. A good thing, too, because beneath the daybed he found Vicky Henderson's gold compact. It had broken open and there was a smear of powder on the floor. He erased it with a damp cloth and put the compact into his pocket.

He went outside and began to hike over the sloping expanse of lawn, which had recently been manicured by a team of gardeners under his supervision. Far to the rear of the house he came in time to a dense stand of trees, an unspoiled woodland, left for its scenic value. He entered these woods, crossed a rustic bridge over a stream and walked on until he came to a spot so thickly populated with tangles of tall trees that, even under a summer sun, it was a place of twilight and shadow.

He began to hunt about the area until he spied a rock to guide him. Some twenty paces beyond the rock he paused and, after a squinting scrutiny of the ground, kicked aside some leaves and brought a trowel from his pocket. With a perverse sense of order, he buried the compact in the precise location.

Restoring the leaves, he straightened and dropped the trowel into his pocket. "There you go, Vicky," he murmured, "just in case your little nose gets shiny."

As he returned from the woods, the sun had taken a firm hold on the rim of the sky.   Moving in another direction, he came at last to the tiny caretaker's cottage close by the gate.   In the cottage he shaved the left half of his face, took a leisurely shower and fixed his breakfast.   Soon, after a glance at his watch, he donned an immaculate gray uniform, adjusted the visored cap in the mirror, offered himself a twisted half-smile of disapproval, and went out.

He strolled up the hill to the four-car garage and rolled out the long, deep-blue limousine.   Part-time caretaker and full-time chauffeur; well, it was a job, and in the summer, when the "family," complete with its entourage of servants, embarked for Europe and the house on the French Riviera, there were certain fringe benefits. Now the summer was gone, in a couple of hours they would return, and the routine would begin again.

Down at the gate he braked and gazed back toward the woods.   For a space, welling up like bitter champagne, there was in him a curious, bubbling triumph; but as he drove away, a voice in some long disconnected part of him began a scream in his head.

I hope they catch me, cried the voice.   *Oh, God, I hope they catch me!*

RON GOULART

Undertaker, Please Drive Slow

He kept telling me she wasn't dead. I listened, nodding, smoking a menthol cigarette, watching the autumn wind shuffle the dead leaves in the big flagstone back yard outside his den windows.

George Oland's breathing had been getting more raspy as he talked and he stopped now and pointed a big freckled hand at my cigarette. "Maybe you ought to put it out."

Twisting the butt in a seashell ashtray I aimed an elbow at the window with the sliced screen. "Why should your daughter want to burgle the house?" I probed.

"I don't know if she did, Mr. Lowe. I don't know what the poor kid is up to." He rested his palms on the coffee table in front of him, then picked up the letters again. "It's been two and a half years—two years, seven months—but I always knew she hadn't drowned. I knew she'd come back."

Two years and seven months ago, according to the clippings he'd shown me, Nancy Oland had jumped over the side of a yacht at a spot down the coast from San Pedro. She'd left no note. Her body had never been found. Apparently she had jumped sometime before dawn and no one had missed her for several hours. The police decided none of the other people on the yacht were involved.

Then, five days before he'd called me, Nancy's father had received a letter from her, telling him to register at a motel out near Palm Springs the next day and wait for her. Oland, who'd never once left his house since his daughter disappeared, took a bus out to the desert. He waited two and a half days and the girl never showed. The motel people had never heard of her. Reluctantly he came back home to Glendale, where he found his house had been broken into and that someone had gone through Nancy's old room, a room he kept just as she'd left it.

I'd told Oland the obvious. Someone wanted him out of his house and had used the one sure lure. He said no, he knew Nancy was alive somewhere; alive, confused and needing help. He wouldn't go to the police about the break-in, but called in a private detective agency.

He handed me the new letter, mailed in Glendale, the one that had pulled him out into the desert, and one of the letters his daughter had written him the semester she was away at UC in Berkeley. "You can see it's the same writing," he told me again.

I held the two letters, not looking at them. The writing had seemed similar the first time he'd shown me, but I wasn't a handwriting specialist.   Usually I worked on skip tracing, divorce stuff, bugging and debugging, but every once in a while, and a lot of times it was in the fall when the Santa Ana wind was blowing and the canyons above Los Angeles were burning, a client would show up with an odd one—like Oland's daughter who had come back to life.   "Let me take these to a handwriting man," I said.

"No," he said, grabbing both letters.   "It's the first word I've had."   He fingered the new letter.   "She's a sensitive kid.   She's afraid, after all the fuss made when she went away.   I know she wants to see me."

"Jumping into the Pacific Ocean isn't like taking a two-week vacation."   It was a bright, harsh afternoon but in here there was a twilight feeling.

Oland was big, heavy, had thick white hair and a sheriff's moustache.   He straightened up in his wicker chair.   "I don't know if I care for your flippancy, Lowe."

I cocked my head.   "Okay.   For fifty bucks a day you can find a lot of guys who'll humor you."   I stretched out of my chair.

"I don't want to be humored," he said, rising and blocking me.   "I know your agency.   They did work for my company when I was still active.   I want you to handle this.   It's just that I don't want you to mock me, Lowe.   I know Nancy's alive.   Please find her."

"What was taken from here?" I asked him.

His big head shook.   "Nothing.   Nothing I can tell."

He'd shown me the room upstairs, a pink and white young college girl's room. It was obvious someone had carefully searched it.   There was a subtle disorder. "Now," I said, moving a few steps back, "you know what I feel.   We're not going to find her."

"We have to look," Oland said, and sank back into his chair.   "Somehow we have to look."   He covered half his face with his spread fingers, began crying.

I turned, went to his desk and picked up the photos of Nancy Oland he'd shown me.   She had been a tall girl, nearly five-ten.   Pretty in a strong, outdoors way, a brunette, she was twenty-three when she disappeared.   "I'll take one or two of these," I told him.

"Don't take the one of her in the navy blue suit.   It's the only copy I have."

It didn't make any difference which ones I took, since I didn't think the girl was alive.   "How about friends of your daughter's?   People she might have been in touch with."

Oland took out a handkerchief, wiped his eyes.   "Nancy was a quiet girl.   There was no regular man friend in her life.   I can give you names and addresses of a few of her close friends.   The last year before she went away she lived in Hollywood with a girl named Beth Eisner.   Then there's Carrie Milligan, she's been a friend since high school."   He told me how to find them and a few others.

The wind scattered brown and yellow leaves against the glass.   "I'll ask some questions.   Probably drive out to Palm Springs and talk to the motel people."   A gray cat, fat and dusty, had come into the room and was watching us from under the heavy desk.

"She's going to be coming back," Oland said to the cat.   Up again, he led me into the hall.   He held out his hand and I shook it.   I couldn't think of anything more to say to him.

Oland's big brown shingle house was on a wide street, tree lined.   Most of it looked like Southern California in the Thirties, pleasant with a porched, Midwest feeling.   The present, though, was infiltrating.   Nearby were a liquor store, a coin laundry, and, directly across, a pizza place—the World Pizzeria, featuring Pizza of All Nations.

I went over and wandered in.   It was two-thirty in the afternoon so I was ahead of the school letout crowd.   The tables were empty.   An old woman in slacks, with blue-tinted hair, was resting against the counter eating the house specialty, a pizza dog.   Behind the counter a small man in a buff jumpsuit was talking on a wall phone.

I rested my left elbow on the formica and waited.   The man made a just-a-minute gesture at me, spoke into the phone, his head bobbing.   He hung up and hurried over.   "I always call my mother this time of day.   She's past seventy and I share a two-room apartment with her in Pasadena.   She broke her hip last April and her life is pretty circumscribed."

I added the information to my store of countermen's autobiographies and said, "Coffee."

The old woman down-counter said, "More people should call their mothers."

When my coffee came I asked the guy, "You here most days?"

"Except Sunday," he answered.   "Sundays I push Mother around Forest Lawn. She likes the pageantry."

"More boys should push their mothers' wheelchairs," the blue-haired woman said.   "Another hot dog, Don."

I got Don back in front of me in a few minutes.   "From here you can get a fair view of the brown shingle house across the street.   Right?"

He admitted it.   "A retired gentleman lives there, as I understand.   Never leaves the indoors, though he did last—let me see—last Tuesday."

"Notice anyone prowling around over there?"

"No."   He put his tomato-stained thumb against his small nose.   "But last Wednesday, and then again this past Monday and Tuesday, there was a girl in here—dark-haired girl, tall, very attractive.   I often say to my mother it's darned hard to get to know girls in this town.   Attractive ones do come in here, and certainly I kid around with them.   I mean, I have a fair sense of humor, but it never seems to lead to anything."

"If I had a daughter," said the hot dog woman, "I'd drag her in here and introduce her to you, Don.   You're a gentleman."

"What about this brunette?" I put in.

"She asked me if I knew the fellow who lived there.   Asked me if I ever saw him leave his home.   I had to tell her the story in the neighborhood is he never goes out at all, due to a personal tragedy.   Usually I don't incline toward gossip. I always hope if I'm nice to a girl it will lead to something."

"This girl came in more than once then?"

"Wednesday. Then again Monday and Tuesday, as I said. Sat there at table three, right near the window. Usually spent nearly a couple of hours. I was flattered and assumed she might be dropping in to chat. After the first encounter, however, she rarely spoke. Very attractive girl, sports car lover."

"What?"

"She likes sports cars. Drives a little red one. I saw her park it out in front."

I drew out one of the studio portraits of Nancy Oland. "Know this girl?"

Don took a pair of rimless glasses from the breast pocket of his World Pizza uniform. After moving the photo as though it were a stereoscope slide, he said, "No. She's not the one. Are you a police officer?"

"Nope," I said.

"What about all this police brutality we hear about?" asked the old woman.

I smiled at her. "Not a word of truth to it."

"The girl in here was smaller than that," said Don. "I have a little hunch she'll come in again. My mother tells me any girl who likes pizza wouldn't make a good wife. I don't agree."

"My uncle married a woman who lived for three years on nothing but pizza," I said, taking the picture back.

Outside, the afternoon street was filling up with transistor-eared high school kids. I looked at the bell-bottomed girls and felt obsolete. You do sometimes at thirty-six.

Carrie Milligan wasn't home at the Beau Geste Apartments in Hollywood. The manager of the building was doing handstands beside the pool, a thick bronze guy about my age. He told me Carrie worked the cocktail hour shift at the Great Depression, a bar down on Santa Monica Boulevard. Two airline stewardesses came home from a flight while I was talking to him. They waved and called, "Hi, Sonny," walking along the catwalk stairs to their apartment. Sonny's portable phonograph changed records and a lot of Tijuana Brass came out. A blonde in a scarlet bikini ran out of a ground-floor apartment and did a fair jackknife into the pool. "We're like those coffee shops down the street," Sonny said. "Open twenty-four hours. One continual round of fun and games. The basic rent is only $150 a month and no lease required."

I told him I was studying for the ministry and liked quiet nights. I drove my secondhand car to the Great Depression and bumped up into the customer lot. The hot wind was carrying the smell of the burning hills. Walking toward the back entrance to the low black building, I noticed a dusty red sports car parked next to the garbage cans. The registration was taped to the windshield. The car was Carrie Milligan's, an interesting coincidence.

The Great Depression was chill and dark. All the walls were covered with a collage of trivia: candy wrappers, comic-book pages, stills from Bogart movies, newspaper photos of FDR, Thomas Hart Benton prints, Rockwell covers, Krazy Kat, Amelia Earhart.

The two waitresses weren't from the Thirties. They were Carnaby style, striped pants, boots, caps.   One, a brunette with wide-set smoky eyes, was leaning, hands locked behind her, against a post.

I sat at the black bar and ordered an Olympia.   When the bartender brought it I asked, "Carrie Milligan works here, I believe?"

He had a fluffy moustache and he touched both ends of it before he answered. "Yes, that's so.   Why, pal?"

From my coat I took a card an insurance man had left under my apartment door the week before.   "I'm Ralph E. Minton, with Los Angeles Provident.   We're trying to locate a missing beneficiary.   I wonder if I might speak with Miss Milligan."

He felt his moustache again, seemed to want to find a resemblance between me and the typeface on the card.   "That's her holding up the pillar.   Tell her Rick said you could talk a few minutes in one of the empty booths.   She going to get some money?"

"It's difficult to say at this stage.   There is surely cause for anticipation."

Only the dark girl's eyes moved when I spoke to her.   "My name is Lowe," I said.   "Nancy Oland's father says you were a friend of hers.   I'd like to talk to you."

Her long hands moved and came to rest on her legs.   "Check with Rick."

"I got his permission."

She detached herself from the post and walked to an empty rear booth.   "What does Mr. Oland want?" she asked when she was seated.

"He got a letter from somebody claiming to be Nancy," I said, across from her. "Know anything about it?"

"Nancy's dead," she said.   Her voice was soft, far off.   "She killed herself. Mr. Oland won't believe that."   Swinging her long legs up onto her bench, she cupped her hands on her knees.   "You know that spiritual?   'Undertaker, please drive slow, because the lady that you're taking, I hate to see her go.'   That's Nancy's father.   He hates to see her go and he's trying to make it as slow as he can.   She's been dead for nearly three years."

"Been out there lately, to the Oland home?"   I'd brought my beer with me. I drank, watching her thin, sad face.   She was pretty in a forlorn sort of way.

"No.   I wasn't very close to Nancy the last year or so.   I've never been near her father since she died.   He called me a few times.   I haven't seen him."

"You and your red car weren't out there the beginning of this week?"

Carrie smiled faintly, shaking her head.   She touched the visor of her cap.

"Couldn't have.   My car was in the garage Monday and Tuesday."

"What for?"

Her hands massaged her knees.   "If it makes any difference, I took it in Monday before work here and picked it up Tuesday noon.   I had it lubricated, and the oil changed.   Okay?"

"Think of any reason why somebody would want to hurt Oland this way?   With a fake letter?"

"Oh, come on," she said, swinging her legs down.   "It's a mean old world.

Lots of people get hurt, a lot worse than Mr. Oland.   All he has to do is sit around that big house and hide from the daylight and pretend Nancy didn't jump.   There are worse lives to live.''   She left me, adjusting her cap with a flourish.

In the parking lot I stood by her car for a moment, lit another cigarette and decided they weren't any easier on my respiratory system than the non-menthol kind.   The only garage sticker I could find anywhere on her car indicated it hadn't been lubricated since November of the year before, seven thousand miles ago. Thinking, I got into my old car and fought for a place in the confusion of traffic.

Beth Eisner was a rangy brunette too, a year or so older than Carrie, not quite as sad.   She had a three-room cottage up in Beverly Glenn, a ten-minute climb above Sunset Boulevard where, she told me later, she worked as a secretary.   After I'd identified myself she released the chain lock and let me into a big sparse living room.   The furniture was simple, quiet.   A bad oil painting of Beth was hanging over the full bookcase.

"I keep thinking this whole block is going to burn down.   I sleep pretty well. One thing I always come bolt awake for is a fire engine.   I think I can hear them as far away as Oxnard.''   She took a perch on a low sofa and let me pick my own.

From a canvas chair I asked, "Who would try to make Nancy Oland's father think she's alive?''

She bit her lower lip.   "That's what it is?''

"He got a letter, supposed to be from her, telling him to meet her at a certain time out in Palm Springs.   He went, waited.   When he finally came home he found he'd been robbed.''

"Poor Mr. Oland.   He wants to believe she's alive.''

"You drive a compact?''

"Yes, that's it out in front.''

I'd checked.   "When's the last time you saw Nancy's father?''

"Something like a year ago,'' she said.   She was wearing a dark pullover and tan corduroy pants.   "I used to go out there to visit him.   I had to stop.   I like Mr. Oland, but all he'd want to talk about was the possibility Nancy would turn up alive.   He didn't really know Nancy at all, not even when she lived with him.''

"Was it here that she lived with you?''

"No, an apartment down in Hollywood, one of those fake Moorish ones.   Six months, at least, before she died she had a place by herself.   Her father doesn't know that.''

"What about guys?''

"I'm pretty sure Mr. Oland told you Nancy wasn't much interested in men.''

"He said something like that.''

"Well,'' Beth said, "that isn't really quite the story.   Nancy knew several men, quite an assortment of people; people Mr. Oland probably wouldn't admit existed. You know, Nancy's mother died back around 1950 and her father started turning off that long ago.''

"You've never told him any of this?''

"No, and you shouldn't.   He's not going to believe anyway,'' she said.   "Nancy was nervous, high key.   She was never quite sure what she was up to.   She'd tried a couple of colleges.   She was always drifting, looking for some kind of edge, a handle to things.''   Her eyes closed for a second.   ''I think the last few months of her life she was addicted someway, to something.   Maybe that's why she killed herself.''

''I've seen Oland's clippings on the suicide.   There didn't seem to be anything suspicious about the others involved.''

''On the boat?   No, they were straight.   Nancy had friends on two or three levels.''

''What about Carrie Milligan?''

Beth shook her head.   ''I guess she's like Nancy, like Nancy several ways, but a little more in control.''

''What do you know for sure about Nancy being hooked?''

''I'm not certain,'' said the girl.   Her face had grown paler.   ''I began to get odd feelings about her, the way she was acting, so I moved out.   I did offer to help, in my dumb pigeon-toed way.   I maybe should have stuck.   I don't know. I didn't like Carrie—or Tamerlane.''

''Who?''

''Jack Tamerlane,'' she said.   ''He was the one Nancy saw most.   I think he also saw Carrie a lot.   They were a kind of trio.   Tamerlane's a big tall guy, a skinny cowboy-looking guy.   He even did do extra work in Westerns now and then, Nancy told me.''

''And how straight was Tamerlane?''

She let out her breath.   ''He was sent up for possession of narcotics, went away a while before Nancy killed herself.   Maybe that was the reason.''   She shrugged. ''Maybe anything was a reason.   I keep trying to figure.''

''I'll check into Tamerlane,'' I said.

''He's out of prison.''   She leaned back, frowning.   ''I heard from a friend, someone who knew us both, Nancy and me.   Tamerlane's been out nearly a month.''

That would fit.   I shook out a cigarette, looked at it, let it slide away.   ''Yeah,'' I said.

''You're wondering what to tell Mr. Oland.   I'm sorry.   I should have kept quiet.''   She spread her hands.   ''I still wonder about Nancy, and worry.   I suppose I feel she's still alive too.''

I pushed up to my feet.   ''Thanks,'' I said.

The day was fading, night was coming.   You wouldn't be able to see any stars.

I phoned a couple of cops.   Jack Tamerlane, age twenty-eight, had been free for nearly four weeks.   He had a moderate-sized narcotics record.   He lived now and worked at a place called The Birks' Works Farms, a tourist attraction run by a remote relative of his, out on the road to Disneyland.   They sold country-style lunches and souvenirs to fifteen hundred smog-dulled people a day.

I figured I could get there by freeway in under an hour, talk to Tamerlane before bedtime.   If he wasn't there, I could still look around, ask questions, buy a souvenir.

A private cop stood at the redwood gate to Birks' Works Farms.

"I'm Ferguson with the Urban Parole Authority," I said.   "Jack Tamerlane around?"

"Employees live in the rustic auto court half a mile down-road.   Gate eleven. He's in cottage fifteen.   Why you want Jack?"

"Routine," I said, a reason that usually works to avoid questions.

The guard nodded.

I drove on down and turned in at gate eleven.   In among some trees were three dozen cottages.   I parked next to what I thought might be a willow tree and started to search for cottage fifteen.   It wasn't hard to find.   A dusty red sports car was resting in the slot next to it.   Lights were on in the front room of the shingle cottage, which was a miniature version of the Oland house.   Putting my guerilla knowledge to work, I skulked around the back of Tamerlane's and came up in the dry brush under his side windows.

A television set was murmuring and above it I could make out Carrie's voice, not soft now.

"Well, you have to put some faith in me too.   I know whether somebody followed me out or not."

"Swell, swell," said Tamerlane.   "Stop yelling."

"Come on now," the girl said.   "Did you find the stuff?"

"Why sure," he answered.   "Taped under her bureau drawer in a plastic bag."

"What's it worth?"

"Oh," said Tamerlane in his slow, careful voice, "it was worth fifty thousand when I gave it to Nancy to hold.   Probably sixty, sixty-five now."

"I still say you'll get hurt for sidetracking it."

"Not this late," said Tamerlane.

"You've got old Oland really thinking she's alive."

"So?   It got him away from where I'd told Nancy to stow it.   I always got good penmanship marks in school.   Miss Cooper always said that was the only thing I did good."

I felt up under my arm, touching the holster of my .38.   Quietly I moved around to the front, climbed the small porch and knocked on the door.

When Tamerlane looked out a six-inch opening I said, "I'd like to talk to you about Nancy Oland."

"It's him," Carrie said.

Tamerlane lost his slowness.   The door slammed shut.   There was running inside and then the back door sounded.   I cut around to the car side of the cottage. Tamerlane was half into the red car.   He saw my gun coming out, ducked.   He popped up and a tire iron came sailing at me.   I dodged, and he started running out from behind the car, around the next house.

From the next parking slot I spotted him running through the dark trees, heading for the tourist buildings.   I went after him.   Once through the woods, Tamerlane scaled a wood fence and I heard him go rattling down a board street.   Then it got quiet.

The fence was spotted with lettering, ornate announcements that beyond the fence there was an authentic ghost town.   The fence creaked and swayed as the sharp hot wind brushed it.   Cutting around, I found the back gate to the town, picked the old padlock and let myself in.

There was one street, two rows of badly imagined frontier buildings, a saloon, a jail, a hotel, a souvenir shop.   It was silent, dark, with wax figures leaning against hitching posts, lined up at a long bar, sitting in the hotel lobby.   In a buckboard parked outside the livery stable one of the men on the seat was breathing a little.   From ten feet away I called with my gun loosely ready, "Jump on down, Tamerlane."

He didn't move for nearly a minute.   Then he stood.   "I don't have a gun."

"Over here."

"Why don't you toss yours aside and take me on, man to man?"   He hopped to the dusty street.

I grinned.   "You're letting the setting overwhelm you."

"I'll take you on if you're not scared."   He started to run at me.

I shot him in the leg.

A sticky hot rain was falling.   George Oland took back the pictures of his daughter.   "The whole story doesn't ring true, doesn't make a bit of sense," he protested.

I had told him most of what I'd found out, about how Tamerlane had highjacked a shipment of heroin coming in from Mexico, given it to Nancy to hide in a safe place for a while, a safe place like her old room at home.   Before Tamerlane had had a chance to do anything he'd been caught on another deal and locked up.   As soon as he got out he set about figuring a way to retrieve the stuff.   Since Oland never left the place, he and Carrie, who knew Oland believed Nancy was still alive, came up with a way to get him out of the house.   When I'd said it all I added, echoing Beth Eisner, "I'm sorry."

"If you knew Nancy you'd know how false it all is."

I left my chair.   "I'll get going."

"You haven't found her," said Oland.   "You didn't even go out to Palm Springs and check."

"Tamerlane admits writing the letter to get you out of here for a day so he could dig around."   I stepped around him into the dim hallway.   "There's nothing else to find out."

"I want you to stay on the case and find Nancy."

"No," I said.   I got to the front door and opened it.

Oland caught my arm as I hit the porch, kept telling me she wasn't dead.

DONALD E. WESTLAKE

Never Shake a Family Tree

Actually, I have never been so shocked in all my born days, and I seventy-three my last birthday and eleven times a grandmother and twice a great-grandmother. But never in all my born days did I see the like, and that's the truth.

Actually, it all began with my interest in genealogy, which I got from Mrs. Ernestine Simpson, a lady I met at Bay Arbor, in Florida, when I went there three summers ago. I certainly didn't like Florida—far too expensive, if you ask me, and far too bright, and with just too many mosquitoes and other insects to be believed—but I wouldn't say the trip was a total loss, since it did interest me in genealogical research, which is certainly a wonderful hobby, as well as being very valuable, what with one thing and another.

Actually, my genealogical researches had been valuable in more ways than one, since they have also been instrumental in my meeting some very pleasant ladies and gentlemen, although some of them only by postal, and of course it was through this hobby that I met Mr. Gerald Fowlkes in the first place.

But I'm getting far ahead of my story, and ought to begin at the beginning, except that I'm blessed if I know where the beginning actually is. In one way of looking at things, the beginning is my introduction to genealogy through Mrs. Ernestine Simpson, who has since passed on, but in another way the beginning is really almost two hundred years ago, and in still another way the story doesn't really begin until the first time I came across the name of Euphemia Barber.

Well. Actually, I suppose, I really ought to begin by explaining just what genealogical research is. It is the study of one's family tree. One checks marriage and birth and death records, searches old family Bibles and talks to various members of one's family, and one gradually builds up a family tree, showing who fathered whom and what year, and when so-and-so died, and so on. It's really a fascinating work, and there are any number of amateur genealogical societies throughout the country, and when one has one's family tree built up for as far as one wants—seven generations, or nine generations, or however long one wants—then it is possible to write this all up in a folder and bequeath it to the local library, and then there is a *record* of one's family for all time to come, and I for one think that's important and valuable to have even if my youngest boy Tom does laugh at it and say it's just a silly hobby. Well, it *isn't* a silly hobby. After all, I found evidence of murder that way, didn't I?

So, actually, I suppose the whole thing really begins when I first came across the name of Euphemia Barber. Euphemia Barber was John Anderson's second wife. John Anderson was born in Goochland County, Virginia, in 1754. He married Ethel Rita Mary Rayborn in 1777, just around the time of the Revolution, and they had seven children, which wasn't at all strange for that time, though large families have, I notice, gone out of style today, and I for one think it's a shame.

At any rate, it was John and Ethel Anderson's third child, a girl named Prudence, who is in my direct line on my mother's father's side, so of course I had them in my family tree. But then, in going through Appomattox County records—Goochland County being now a part of Appomattox, and no longer a separate county of its own—I came across the name of Euphemia Barber. It seems that Ethel Anderson died in 1793, in giving birth to her eighth child—who also died—and three years later, 1796, John Anderson remarried, this time marrying a widow named Euphemia Barber. At that time, he was forty-two years of age, and her age was given as thirty-nine.

Of course, Euphemia Barber was not at all in my direct line, being John Anderson's second wife, but I was interested to some extent in her pedigree as well, wanting to add her parents' names and her place of birth to my family chart, and also because there were some Barbers fairly distantly related on my father's mother's side, and I was wondering if this Euphemia might be kin to them. But the records were very incomplete, and all I could learn was that Euphemia Barber was not a native of Virginia, and had apparently only been in the area for a year or two when she had married John Anderson. Shortly after John's death in 1798, two years after their marriage, she had sold the Anderson farm, which was apparently a somewhat prosperous location, and had moved away again. So that I had neither birth nor death records on her, nor any record of her first husband, whose last name had apparently been Barber, but only the one lone record of her marriage to my great-great-great-great-great-grandfather on my mother's father's side.

Actually, there was no reason for me to pursue the question further, since Euphemia Barber wasn't in my direct line anyway, but I had worked diligently and. I think, well, on my family tree, and had it almost complete back nine generations, and there was really very little left to do with it, so I was glad to do some tracking down.

Which is why I included Euphemia Barber in my next entry in the Genealogical Exchange. Now, I suppose I ought to explain what the Genealogical Exchange is. There are any number of people throughout the country who are amateur genealogists, concerned primarily with their own family trees, but of course family trees do interlock, and any one of these people is liable to know about just the one record which has been eluding some other searcher for months. And so there are magazines devoted to the exchanging of some information, for nominal fees. In the last few years, I had picked up all sorts of valuable leads in this way. And so my entry in the summer issue of the Genealogical Exchange read:

BUCKLEY, Mrs. Henrietta Rhodes, 119A Newbury St., Boston, Mass. Xch data on *Rhodes, Anderson, Richards, Pryor, Marshall, Lord.* Want any info Euphemia *Barber,* m. John Anderson, Va. 1796.

Well. The Genealogical Exchange had been helpful to me in the past, but I never received anywhere near the response caused by Euphemia Barber. And the first response of all came from Mr. Gerald Fowlkes.

It was a scant two days after I received my own copy of the summer issue of the Exchange. I was still poring over it myself, looking for people who might be linked to various branches of my family tree, when the telephone rang. Actually, I suppose I was somewhat irked at being taken from my studies, and perhaps I sounded a bit impatient when I answered.

If so, the gentleman at the other end gave no sign of it. His voice was most pleasant, quite deep and masculine, and he said, "May I speak, please, with Mrs. Henrietta Buckley?"

"This is Mrs. Buckley," I told him.

"Ah," he said. "Forgive my telephoning, please, Mrs. Buckley. We have never met. But I noticed your entry in the current issue of the Genealogical Exchange—"

"Oh?"

I was immediately excited, all thought of impatience gone. This was surely the fastest reply I'd ever had to date!

"Yes," he said. "I noticed the reference to Euphemia Barber. I do believe that may be the Euphemia Stover who married Jason Barber in Savannah, Georgia, in 1791. Jason Barber is in my direct line, on my mother's side. Jason and Euphemia had only the one child, Abner, and I am descended from him."

"Well," I said. "You certainly do seem to have complete information."

"Oh, yes," he said. "My own family chart is almost complete. For twelve generations, that is. I'm not sure whether I'll try to go back farther than that or not. The English records before 1600 are so incomplete, you know."

"Yes, of course," I said. I was, I admit, taken aback. Twelve generations! Surely that was the most ambitious family tree I had ever heard of, though I had read sometimes of people who had carried particular branches back as many as fifteen generations. But to actually be speaking to a person who had traced his entire family back twelve generations!

"Perhaps," he said, "it would be possible for us to meet, and I could give you the information I have on Euphemia Barber. There are also some Marshalls in one branch of my family; perhaps I can be of help to you there, as well." He laughed, a deep and pleasant sound, which reminded me of my late husband, Edward, when he was most particularly pleased. "And, of course," he said, "there is always the chance that you may have some information on the Marshalls which can help me."

"I think that would be very nice," I said, and so I invited him to come to the apartment the very next afternoon.

At one point the next day, perhaps half an hour before Gerald Fowlkes was to arrive, I stopped my fluttering around to take stock of myself and to realize that if ever there were an indication of second childhood taking over, my thoughts and actions preparatory to Mr. Fowlkes' arrival were certainly it. I had been rushing hither and thither, dusting, rearranging, polishing, pausing incessantly to look in the mirror and touch my hair with fluttering fingers, all as though I were a flighty teen-ager before her very first date. "Henrietta," I told myself sharply, "you are seventy-three years old, and all that nonsense is well behind you now. Eleven times a grandmother, and just look at how you carry on!"

But poor Edward had been dead and gone these past nine years, my brothers and sisters were all in their graves, and as for my children, all but Tom, the youngest, were thousands of miles away, living their own lives—as of course they should— and only occasionally remembering to write a duty letter to Mother. And I am much too aware of the dangers of the clinging mother to force my presence too often upon Tom and his family. So I am very much alone, except of course for my friends in the various church activities and for those I have met, albeit only by postal, through my genealogical research.

So it *was* pleasant to be visited by a charming gentleman caller, and particularly so when that gentleman shared my own particular interests.

And Mr. Gerald Fowlkes, on his arrival, was surely no disappointment. He looked to be no more than fifty-five years of age, though he swore to sixty-two, and had a fine shock of gray hair above a strong and kindly face. He dressed very well, with that combination of expense and breeding so little found these days, when the well-bred seem invariably to be poor and the well-to-do seem invariably to be horribly plebeian. His manner was refined and gentlemanly, what we used to call courtly, and he had some very nice things to say about the appearance of my living room.

Actually, I make no unusual claims as a housekeeper. Living alone, and with quite a comfortable income having been left me by Edward, it is no problem at all to choose tasteful furnishings and keep them neat. (Besides, I had scrubbed the apartment from top to bottom in preparation for Mr. Fowlkes' visit.)

He had brought his pedigree along, and what a really beautiful job he had done. Pedigree charts, photostats of all sorts of records, a running history typed very neatly on bond paper and inserted in a loose-leaf notebook—all in all, the kind of careful, planned, well-thought-out perfection so unsuccessfully striven for by all amateur genealogists.

From Mr. Fowlkes, I got the missing information on Euphemia Barber. She was born in 1765, in Salem, Massachusetts, the fourth child of seven born to John and Alicia Stover. She married Jason Barber in Savannah in 1791. Jason, a well-to-do merchant, passed on in 1794, shortly after the birth of their first child, Abner. Abner was brought up by his paternal grandparents, and Euphemia moved away from Savannah. As I already knew, she had then gone to Virginia, where she had married John Anderson. After that, Mr. Fowlkes had no record of her, until her death in Cincinnati, Ohio, in 1852. She was buried as Euphemia Stover Barber, apparently not having used the Anderson name after John Anderson's death.

This done, we went on to compare family histories and discover an Alan Marshall of Liverpool, England, around 1680, common to both trees. I was able to give Mr. Fowlkes Alan Marshall's birth date. And then the specific purpose of our meeting was finished. I offered tea and cakes, it then being four-thirty in the afternoon, and Mr. Fowlkes graciously accepted my offering.

And so began the strangest three months of my entire life. Before leaving, Mr. Fowlkes asked me to accompany him to a concert on Friday evening, and I very readily agreed. Then, and afterward, he was a perfect gentleman.

It didn't take me long to realize that I was being courted. Actually, I couldn't believe it at first. After all, at *my* age! But I myself did know some very nice couples who had married late in life—a widow and a widower, both lonely, sharing interests, and deciding to lighten their remaining years together—and looked at in that light it wasn't at all as ridiculous as it might appear at first.

Actually, I had expected my son Tom to laugh at the idea, and to dislike Mr. Fowlkes instantly upon meeting him. I suppose various fictional works that I have read had given me this expectation. So I was most pleasantly surprised when Tom and Mr. Fowlkes got along famously together from their very first meeting, and even more surprised when Tom came to me and told me Mr. Fowlkes had asked him if he would have any objection to his, Mr. Fowlkes', asking for my hand in matrimony. Tom said he had no objection at all, but actually thought it a wonderful idea, for he knew that both Mr. Fowlkes and myself were rather lonely, with nothing but our genealogical hobbies to occupy our minds.

As to Mr. Fowlkes' background, he very early gave me his entire history. He came from a fairly well-to-do family in upstate New York, and was himself now retired from his business, which had been a stock brokerage in Albany. He was a widower these last six years, and his first marriage had not been blessed with any children, so that he was completely alone in the world.

The next three months were certainly active ones. Mr. Fowlkes—Gerald—squired me everywhere, to concerts and to museums and even, after we had come to know one another well enough, to the theater. He was at all times most polite and thoughtful, and there was scarcely a day went by but what we were together.

During this entire time, of course, my own genealogical researches came to an absolute standstill. I was much too busy, and my mind was much too full of Gerald, for me to concern myself with family members who were long since gone to their rewards. Promising leads from the Genealogical Exchange were not followed up, for I didn't write a single letter. And though I did receive many in the Exchange, they all went unopened into a cubbyhole in my desk. And so the matter stayed, while the courtship progressed.

After three months, Gerald at last proposed. "I am not a young man, Henrietta," he said. "Nor a particularly handsome man—" though he most certainly was very handsome, indeed "—nor even a very rich man, although I do have sufficient for my declining years. And I have little to offer you, Henrietta, save my own self, whatever poor companionship I can give you, and the assurance that I will be ever at your side."

What a beautiful proposal! After being nine years a widow, and never expecting even in fanciful daydreams to be once more a wife, what a beautiful proposal and from what a charming gentleman!

I agreed at once, of course, and telephoned Tom the good news that very minute. Tom and his wife, Estelle, had a dinner party for us, and then we made our plans. We would be married three weeks hence. A short time? Yes, of course, it was, but there was really no reason to wait.   And we would honeymoon in Washington, D.C., where my oldest boy, Roger, has quite a responsible position with the State Department.   After which, we would return to Boston and take up our residence in a lovely old home on Beacon Hill, which was then for sale and which we would jointly purchase.

Ah, the plans!   The preparations!   How newly filled were my so-recently empty days!

I spent most of the last week closing my apartment on Newbury Street.   The furnishings would be moved to our new home by Tom, while Gerald and I were in Washington.   But, of course, there was ever so much packing to be done, and I got at it with a will.

And so at last I came to my desk, and my genealogical researches lying as I had left them.   I sat down at the desk, somewhat weary, for it was late afternoon and I had been hard at work since sun-up, and I decided to spend a short while getting my papers into order before packing them away.   And so I opened the mail which had accumulated over the last three months.

There were twenty-three letters.   Twelve asked for information on various family names mentioned in my entry in the Exchange, five offered to give me information, and six concerned Euphemia Barber.   It was, after all, Euphemia Barber who had brought Gerald and I together in the first place, and so I took time out to read these letters.

And so came the shock.   I read the six letters, and then I simply sat limp at the desk, staring into space, and watched the monstrous pattern as it grew in my mind. For there was no question of the truth, no question at all.

Consider: Before starting the letters, this is what I knew of Euphemia Barber: She had been born Euphemia Stover in Salem, Massachusetts, in 1765.   In 1791, she married Jason Barber, a widower of Savannah, Georgia.   Jason died two years later, in 1793, of a stomach upset.   Three years later, Euphemia appeared in Virginia and married John Anderson, also a widower.   John died two years thereafter, in 1798, of stomach upset.   In both cases, Euphemia sold her late husband's property and moved on.

And here is what the letters added to that, in chronological order:

From Mrs. Winnie Mae Cuthbert, Dallas, Texas: Euphemia Barber, in 1800, two years after John Anderson's death, appeared in Harrisburg, Pennsylvania, and married one Andrew Cuthbert, a widower and a prosperous feed merchant.   Andrew died in 1801, of a stomach upset.   The widow sold his store, and moved on.

From Miss Ethel Sutton, Louisville, Kentucky: Euphemia Barber, in 1804, married Samuel Nicholson of Louisville, a widower and a well-to-do tobacco farmer. Samuel Nicholson passed on in 1807, of a stomach upset.   The widow sold his farm, and moved on.

From Mrs. Isabelle Padgett, Concord, California: in 1808, Euphemia Barber married Thomas Norton, then Mayor of Dover, New Jersey, and a widower.   In 1809, Thomas Norton died of a stomach upset.

From Mrs. Luella Miller, Bicknell, Utah: Euphemia Barber married Jonas Miller, a wealthy shipowner of Portsmouth, New Hampshire, a widower, in 1811.   The same year, Jonas Miller died of a stomach upset.   The widow sold his property and moved on.

From Mrs. Lola Hopkins, Vancouver, Washington: In 1813, in southern Indiana, Euphemia Barber married Edward Hopkins, a widower and a farmer.   Edward Hopkins died in 1816, of a stomach upset.   The widow sold the farm, and moved on.

From Mr. Roy Cumbie, Kansas City, Missouri: In 1819, Euphemia Barber married Stanley Thatcher of Kansas City, Missouri, a river barge owner and a widower.   Stanley Thatcher died, of a stomach upset, in 1821.   The widow sold his property, and moved on.

The evidence was clear, and complete.   The intervals of time without dates could mean that there had been other widowers who had succumbed to Euphemia Barber's fatal charms, and whose descendants did not number among themselves an amateur genealogist.   Who could tell just how many husbands Euphemia had murdered?   For murder it quite clearly was, brutal murder, for profit.   I had evidence of eight murders, and who knew but what there were eight more, or eighteen more?   Who could tell, at this late date, just how many times Euphemia Barber had murdered for profit, and had never been caught?

Such a woman is inconceivable.   Her husbands were always widowers, sure to be lonely, sure to be susceptible to a wily woman.   She preyed on widowers, and left them all a widow.

Gerald.

The thought came to me, and I pushed it firmly away.   It couldn't possibly be true; it couldn't possibly have a single grain of truth.

But what did I know of Gerald Fowlkes, other than what he had told me?   And wasn't I a widow, lonely and susceptible?   And wasn't I financially well off?

Like father, like son, they say.   Could it be also, like great-great-great-great-great-grandmother, like great-great-great-great-great-grandson?

What a thought!   It came to me that there must be any number of widows in the country, like myself, who were interested in tracing their family trees.   Women who had a bit of money and leisure, whose children were grown and gone out into the world to live their own lives, and who filled some of the empty hours with the hobby of genealogy.   An unscrupulous man, preying on well-to-do widows, could find no better introduction than a common interest in genealogy.

What a terrible thought to have about Gerald!   And yet, I couldn't push it from my mind, and at last I decided that the only thing I could possibly do was try to substantiate the autobiography he had given me, for if he had told the truth about himself, then he could surely not be a beast of the type I was imagining.

A stockbroker, he had claimed to have been, in Albany, New York.   I at once telephoned an old friend of my first husband's, who was himself a Boston stockbroker, and asked him if it would be possible for him to find out if there had been, at any time in the last fifteen or twenty years, an Albany stockbroker named Gerald Fowlkes.   He said he could do so with ease, using some sort of directory he had, and would call me back.   He did so, with the shattering news that no such individual was listed!

Still I refused to believe.   Donning my coat and hat, I left the apartment at once and went directly to the telephone company, where, after an incredible number of white lies concerning genealogical research, I at last persuaded someone to search for an old Albany, New York telephone book.   I knew that the main office of the company kept books for other major cities, as a convenience for the public, but I wasn't sure they would have any from past years.   Nor was the clerk I talked to, but at last she did go and search, and came back finally with the 1946 telephone book from Albany, dusty and somewhat ripped, but still intact, with both the normal listings and the yellow pages.

No Gerald Fowlkes was listed in the white pages, or in the yellow pages under Stocks & Bonds.

So.   It was true.   And I could see exactly what Gerald's method was.   Whenever he was ready to find another victim, he searched one or another of the genealogical magazines until he found someone who shared one of his own past relations.   He then proceeded to effect a meeting with that person, found out quickly enough whether or not the intended victim was a widow, of the proper age range, and with the properly large bank account, and then the courtship began.

I imagined that this was the first time he had made the mistake of using Euphemia Barber as the go-between.   And I doubted that he even realized he was following in Euphemia's footsteps.   Certainly, none of the six people who had written to me about Euphemia could possibly guess, knowing only of one marriage and death, what Euphemia's role in life had actually been.

And what was I to do now?   In the taxi, on the way back to my apartment, I sat huddled in a corner, and tried to think.

For this *was* a severe shock, and a terrible disappointment.   And could I face Tom, or my other children, or any one of my friends, to whom I had already written the glad news of my impending marriage?   And how could I return to the drabness of my days before Gerald had come to bring gaiety and companionship and courtly grace to my days?

Could I even call the police?   I was sufficiently convinced myself, but could I possibly convince anyone else?

All at once, I made my decision.   And, having made it, I immediately felt ten years younger, ten pounds lighter, and quite a bit less foolish.   For, I might as well admit, in addition to everything else, this had been a terrible blow to my pride.

But the decision was made, and I returned to my apartment cheerful and happy.

And so we were married.

Married?   Of course.   Why not?

Because he will try to murder me?   Well, of course, he *will* try to murder me. As a matter of fact, he has already tried, half a dozen times.

But Gerald is working at a terrible disadvantage.   For he cannot murder me in any way that looks like murder.   It must appear to be a natural death, or, at the very worst, an accident.   Which means that he must be devious, and he must plot and plan, and never come at me openly to do me in.

And there is the source of his disadvantage.   For I am forewarned, and forewarned is forearmed.

But what, really, do I have to lose?   At seventy-three, how many days on this earth do I have left?   And how *rich* life is these days!   How rich compared to my life before Gerald came into it!   Spiced with the thrill of danger, the excitement of cat and mouse, the intricate moves and countermoves of the most fascinating game of all.

And, of course, a pleasant and charming husband.   Gerald *has* to be pleasant and charming.   He can never disagree with me, at least not very forcefully, for he can't afford the danger of my leaving him.   Nor can he afford to believe that I suspect him.   I have never spoken of the matter to him, and so far as he is concerned I know nothing.   We go to concerts and museums and the theater together.   Gerald is attentive and gentlemanly, quite the best sort of companion at all times.

Of course, I can't allow him to feed me breakfast in bed, as he would so love to do.   No, I told him I was an old-fashioned woman, and believed that cooking was a woman's job, and so I won't let him near the kitchen.   Poor Gerald!

And we don't take trips, no matter how much he suggests them.

And we've closed off the second story of our home, since I pointed out that the first floor was certainly spacious enough for just the two of us, and I felt I was getting a little old for climbing stairs.   He could do nothing, of course, but agree.

And, in the meantime, I have found another hobby, though of course Gerald knows nothing of it.   Through discreet inquiries, and careful perusal of past issues of the various genealogical magazines, the use of the family names in Gerald's family tree, I am gradually compiling another sort of tree.   Not a family tree, no. One might facetiously call it a hanging tree.   It is a list of Gerald's wives.   It is in with my genealogical files, which I have willed to the Boston library.   Should Gerald manage to catch me after all, what a surprise is in store for the librarian who sorts out those files of mine!   Not as big a surprise as the one in store for Gerald, of course.

Ah, here comes Gerald now, in the automobile he bought last week.   He's going to ask me again to go for a ride with him.

But I shan't go.

BILL PRONZINI

Here Lies Another Blackmailer

My Uncle Walter studied me across the massive oak desk in his library, looking at once irascible, anxious and a little fearful. "I have some questions to ask you, Harold," he said at length, "and I want truthful answers, do you understand?"

"I am not in the habit of lying," I lied stiffly.

"No? To my mind your behavior has always left much to be desired, and has been downright suspect at times. But that is not the issue at hand, except indirectly. The issue at hand is this: where were you at eleven-forty last evening?"

"At eleven-forty? I was in bed, of course."

"You were not," my uncle said sharply. "Elsie saw you going downstairs at five minutes of eleven, fully dressed; she told me about it when I questioned her this morning."

Elsie was the family maid, and much too nosy for her own good. She was also the only person who lived on this small estate except for myself, Uncle Walter, and Aunt Pearl. I frowned and said, "I remember now. I went for a walk."

"At eleven P.M.?"

"I couldn't sleep and I thought the fresh air might help."

"Where did you go on this walk?"

"Oh, here and there. Just walking, you know."

"Did you leave the grounds?"

"Not that I recall."

"Did you go out by the old carriage house?"

"No," I lied.

My uncle was making an obvious effort to conceal his impatience. "You *were* out by the old carriage house, weren't you?"

"I've already said I wasn't."

"I saw you there, Harold. At least, I'm fairly certain I did. You were lurking in the oleander bushes."

"I do not lurk in bushes," I lied.

"*Somebody* was lurking in the bushes, and it couldn't possibly have been anyone but you. Elsie and Aunt Pearl were both here in the house."

"May I ask a question?"

"What is it?"

"What were *you* doing out by the old carriage house at eleven-forty last night?"

Uncle Walter's face had begun to take on the unpleasant color of raw calf's liver. "What I was doing there is of no consequence. I want to know why you were there, and what you might have seen and heard."

"Was there something to see and hear, Uncle?"

"No, of course not. I just want to know—Look here, Harold, what did you see and hear from those bushes?"

"I wasn't *in* them in the first place, so I couldn't have seen or heard anything, could I?"

Uncle Walter stood abruptly and began to pace the room, his hands folded behind his back. He looked like a pompous old lawyer, which is precisely what he was. Finally he came over to stand in front of my chair, glaring down at me. "You were not out by the carriage house at eleven-forty last night? You did not see anything and you did not hear anything at any time during your alleged walk?"

"No," I lied.

"I have no recourse but to accept your word, then. Actually it doesn't matter whether you were there or not, in one sense, because you refuse to admit it. I trust you will continue to refuse to admit it, to me and to anyone else."

"I don't believe I follow that, Uncle."

"You don't have to follow it. Very well, Harold, that's all."

I stood up and left the library and went out to the sun porch at the rear of the house. When I was certain neither Elsie nor Aunt Pearl was about, and that my uncle had not chosen to pursue me surreptitiously, I slipped out and hurried through the landscaped grounds to the old carriage house. The oleander bushes, where I had been lurking at eleven-forty the previous night after following Uncle Walter from the house—I *had* gone for a short walk, and had noticed him sneaking out— were located along the southern wall of the building. I passed along parallel to them and around to the back, to the approximate spot where my uncle had stood talking to the man whom he had met there. They had spoken in low tones, of course, but in the late-evening summer stillness I had been able to hear every word. I had also been able to hear the muffled report which had abruptly terminated their conversation.

Now, what, I wondered, glancing around, *did Uncle Walter do with the body?*

The gunshot had startled me somewhat, and I had involuntarily rustled the bushes and therefore been forced to run when my uncle came quickly to investigate. I had then hidden behind one of the privet hedges until I was certain he did not intend to search for me. Minutes later I slipped around by the carriage house again; but I had not been able to locate my uncle and I had not wanted to chance discovery by prowling through the darkness. So I returned to the privet hedge and waited, and twenty-five minutes later Uncle Walter had appeared and gone directly back to the house.

A half hour or so is really not very much time in which to hide a dead man, so I found the body quite easily. It was haphazardly concealed among several tall eucalyptus trees some sixty yards from the carriage house, covered with leaves and strips of aromatic bark which regularly peels from the trees. A rather unimaginative hiding place, to be sure, although it was no doubt intended to be temporary. Uncle Walter had obviously given no prior consideration to body disposal, and had therefore hidden the corpse here until he could think of something more permanent to do with it. If he arrived at a decision by this evening, he would then, I reasoned, return here for the purpose of removal and ultimate secretion.

I uncovered the dead man and studied him for a moment. He was small and slender, with sharp features and close-set eyes. In the same way my uncle looked exactly like what he was, so did this person look like what *he* was, or had been—a criminal, naturally. In his case, a blackmailer—and not at all a clever or cautious one, to have allowed Uncle Walter to talk him into the time and place of last night's rendezvous. What excuse had my uncle given him for the unconventionality of it all? Well, no matter. The man really had been quite stupid to have accepted such terms under any circumstances, and was now quite dead as a result.

Yet Uncle Walter was equally as stupid: first, to have put himself in a position where he could be blackmailed; and second, to have perpetrated a carelessly planned and executed homicide on his own property. My uncle, however, was impulsive, and much less bright than he seemed to most people. He also apparently had a predilection for beautiful blonde show girls, about which my Aunt Pearl knew nothing, and about which I also had known nothing until overhearing last evening's conversation. This was the reason he had been blackmailed. He had committed murder because the extortionist wanted considerably more money than he had been getting for his continued silence—and Uncle Walter was a notoriously tightfisted man.

It took me the better part of two hours to move the body. I am not particularly strong, and even though the dead man was small and relatively light, it was a physical struggle to which I am not accustomed. At last, however, I had secreted the blackmailer's remains in what I considered to be quite a clever hiding place—one that was not even on my uncle's property.

Across the dry creek which formed the rear boundary line was a grove of densely-grown trees, and well into them I found a large decaying log, all that was left of a long-dead tree felled by insects or disease. At first glance it seemed to be solid, but upon careful inspection I discovered that it was for the most part hollow. I dragged the body to the log and managed to stuff it inside; then I carefully covered all traces of the entombment. No one venturing into this grove, including my unimaginative uncle, would think of investigating a seemingly solid log.

Satisfied, I returned unobserved to the house, had a bath, and spent the remainder of the day reading in my room.

Uncle Walter was apoplectic. "What did you do with it?" he shouted at me. "What did you *do* with it?"

I looked at him innocently across his desk. It was shortly past eight the following morning, and he had summoned me from my room with furious poundings on the door. I was still in my robe and slippers.

"What did I do with what?" I asked.

"You know what!"

"I'm afraid I don't, Uncle."

"I know it was you, Harold, just as I knew all along it was you in the oleander bushes two nights ago.   So you heard and saw everything, did you?   Well, go ahead—admit it."

"I have nothing to admit."

He slapped the desk top angrily with the palm of one hand.   "*Why* did you move it?   That's what I fail to comprehend.   Why, Harold?   Why did you move it?"

"The conversation seems to be going around in circles," I said.   "I really don't know what you're talking about, Uncle."

"Of course you know what I'm talking about!   Harold—what did you do with it?"

"With what?"

"You know—" He caught himself, and his face was an interesting color bordering on mauve.   "Why do you persist in lying to me?   What are you up to?"

"I'm not up to anything," I lied.

"Harold . . ."

"If you're finished with me, I would like to get dressed.   This may be the middle of summer, but it's rather chilly in here."

"Yes, get dressed.   And then you're coming with me."

"Where are we going?"

"Out to look for it.   I want you along."

"What are we going to look for?"

He glared at me malevolently.   "I'll find it," he said.   "You can't have moved it far.   I *will* find it, Harold!"

Of course he didn't.

I knocked on the library door late that evening and stepped inside.   Uncle Walter was sitting at his desk, holding his head as if it pained him greatly; his face was gray, and I saw that there were heavy pouches under his eyes.   The time, it seemed, was exactly right.

When he saw me, the gray pallor modulated into crimson.   He certainly did change color often, like a chameleon.   "You," he said.   "You!"

"Are you feeling all right, Uncle?   You don't look very well at all."

"If you weren't a relative of mine, if you weren't— Oh, what's the use?   Harold, look, just tell me what you did with it.   I just want to know that it's . . . safe.   Do you understand?"

"Not really," I said.   I looked at him steadily.   "But I seem to have the feeling that whatever it is you were looking for today *is* safe."

He brightened.   "Are you sure?"

"One can never be sure about anything, can one?"

"What does that mean?"

I sat down and said seriously, "You know, Uncle, I've been thinking.   My monthly allowance is really rather small, and I wonder if you could see your way clear to raising it."

His hands gripped the edge of his desk. "So that's it."

"What's it?"

"What you're up to, why you keep lying to me and why you moved the . . . *it*. All I've done is trade one blackmailer for another, and my own nephew at that!"

"Blackmailer?" I managed to look shocked. "What a terrible thing to say, Uncle. I'm only asking politely for an increase in my monthly allowance. That's not the same thing at all, is it?"

His face took on a thoughtful expression, and he calmed down considerably. "No," he said. "No, it isn't. Of course not. Very well, then, you shall have your increase. Now, where is it?"

"Where is what?" I asked.

"Now look here—"

"I still don't know what it is you're talking about," I said. "But then, if I weren't to get my increase—or if I were to get it and it should suddenly be revoked— I suppose I could find out easily enough what is going on. I could talk to Aunt Pearl, or even to the police . . .''

My uncle sighed resignedly. "You've made your point, Harold. I suppose the only important thing is that . . . *it* is safe, and you've already told me that much, haven't you? Well, how much of an increase do you want?"

"Triple the present sum, I think."

"One hundred and fifty dollars a month?"

"Yes."

"What are you going to do with that much money? You're only eleven years old!"

"I'll think of something, Uncle. I'm very clever, you know."

He closed his eyes. "All right, consider your allowance tripled, but you're never to request a single penny more. Not a single penny, Harold."

"Oh, I won't—not a single penny," I lied, and smiled inwardly. Unlike most everyone else of my age, I knew just exactly what I was going to be when I grew up . . .

LAWRENCE TREAT

Dead Duck

The squad car stopped in front of the Brooklyn precinct-house and Perinsky, the big, reckless-looking detective, got out first, then Burson, the man he was bringing in. They went up the steps together.

Burson felt his stomach muscles twitch, contract. He sniffed at the air. He was a dark, slender young man, high-nosed, with serious, grey-green eyes. His mouth quivered slightly, and he compressed his lips. You weren't there, he told himself. Remember that, and stick to it. They can't prove otherwise. Even if the pair on the stoop speak up, they only saw you briefly; they can't be sure.

Burson was aware that the next half hour would be crucial. Convince them he hadn't seen Karen in almost a year, and he was safe. But one misstep, and he was a dead duck.

It had been only twenty minutes since Perinsky walked into Burson's commercial-art studio and identified himself.

"Mr. Clyde Burson?" he had said. He kept slapping his teeth down on a wad of gum, as if he had to use up some of his surplus energy. "We'd like to talk to you, over in Brooklyn."

"What about?"

"You know your wife's dead, don't you?"

Burson's head lifted with a jerk. "Karen—dead? What happened to her?"

"You tell us."

But Burson had read enough books to be familiar with the way the police worked. They took the offensive; they acted as if they knew everything; they tried to throw you off balance and make you slip up. So Perinsky's approach and his refusal to give out information during the ride to Brooklyn was orthodox procedure. No worry on that account. In fact, Burson derived a kind of strength from the detective's ample self-confidence and felt, illogically, that Perinsky was on his side.

Perinsky's hand touched Burson's arm now, protectively, and steered him towards a door. "This way, Buster," Perinsky said amiably. He knocked and entered a cheerless room of cracked walls, hardwood chairs and metal filing cabinets. "Lieutenant," he said. "Here's Clyde Burson."

Burson stiffened at the sight of the stocky, sandy-haired man seated at the desk. To Burson, the blue eyes looked cold and mean, the mouth a thin, ominous slash.

"Sit down, Mr. Burson," the police officer said. To Burson's astonishment, the voice was pleasant, soothing, almost gentle.   "I'm Lieutenant Malliner.   You know why you're here, don't you?"

Burson sat down uneasily.   "Not exactly," he said, picking his words carefully.   "Mr. Perinsky said Karen, my wife—she's dead."

"When was the last time you saw her?"   Malliner asked.

"Close to a year ago, I guess."

"What did you bust up about?"

"We didn't get along, and so we parted by mutual agreement.   Perfectly friendly."

"Expecting to get a divorce?"

Burson nodded.   "We were negotiating."

That much was true.   And on record, although it didn't hint at Karen's vindictiveness and her obstinate, spiteful refusal.   He thought of the hysteria with which she'd screamed out, "Never, never, never!   You'll have to kill me first!"

Malliner said bitingly, "You forgot to ask how she died."

"I didn't get the chance.   Tell me, please."

Malliner handed Burson a sheet of blank paper.   "Would you write your name on this?"

Burson took it, frowned.   "Oh.   I guess you want my fingerprints."

"That's right," Malliner said crisply.   "And we got them."   He snatched the paper and gave it to Perinsky.   "Okay, Lou."

Burson cleared his throat.   He shouldn't have said that.   It marked him as a wise guy, prepared to withhold, deny, evade.   Regretfully, he watched Perinsky walk past him.   The door closed with an echoless bang, and Malliner ruffled his hands together.

"Where were you yesterday afternoon?" he asked.

"I went to a movie at Radio City.   I had to wait on line quite awhile."

"What time were you there?"

"Well, from three to six, at least."

"Then how come two people saw you go into Mrs. Burson's house in Brooklyn at five o'clock, and come out at five-thirty?"

Burson betrayed no emotion.   "They were mistaken," he said flatly.

"When you came out, you were upset.   You stumbled on the steps and almost fell.   They thought you were drunk."

The red-headed guy, Burson told himself, and the woman who looked like a janitress.   She'd probably discovered the body and notified the police, but in any case she must have been on the premises this morning and have been questioned immediately.   As for the identification of Burson, it could have been made from the dozens of pictures of him in Karen's album.

"Well?" said Malliner.   "Did you expect to get away with your movie story?   We run into that one every day in the week.   No trouble cracking it."

Burson's hands balled up into fists.   He lowered them and dug the knuckles against his thighs.   "Lieutenant," he said.   "What happened to Karen?"

"Homicide," Malliner said, staring intently.   "She was stabbed, with a kitchen knife."

"Oh."   Burson licked his lips.   A green-handled kitchen knife, imbedded deep in her chest. She'd fallen near the window, and her eyes had been wide and staring. Her dress had been rumpled and he'd smoothed it down and tucked it under her legs.

"Got a girl friend?" Malliner asked.

Elise, small and soft and dreamy, and willing to go to the ends of the earth with him. "Clyde," she'd whispered, "if only we were free to be together, for always. We could be so happy."

Burson wiped the sweat from his forehead. "I don't want to bring anyone else into this."

"Who is she?" Malliner demanded. "Do you think we're so dumb we can't locate her?"

Burson shook his head. They wouldn't have to look for her. She'd come running to him as soon as she found out where he was.

"Elise Vandyke," he said in a low voice. "295 East 73rd."

Malliner jotted down the address, pressed a button, handed the paper to a uniformed cop who had come in, and whispered something. The cop went out. Perinsky strode in and gave Malliner a note. The lieutenant read it, crumpled it up.

"Still claim you weren't there?" he asked Burson. "And that you hadn't seen her in a year?"

Burson nodded. "Of course."

"Then how did your fingerprints get on her bureau?"

"Her bureau?" said Burson. He'd wiped his prints; he'd been careful about that. Had he missed up on the bureau, or was Malliner trying to put something over on him?

"You think I'm bluffing, don't you?" Malliner said. "Well, I'm going to give you a little advice. You sit down with yourself and come out of your dream world. Would I risk bluffing about fingerprints and get a confession based on fraud, so I can get blasted in court and maybe lose my job? You're an intelligent man, and you got sense enough to see I'm laying it on the line."

"But I didn't kill Karen. I couldn't kill anybody."

Malliner shot forward and hammered out his words like the thuds of a battering ram. "You don't have a chance," he roared. "I'll find out everything you did. I'll know every damn thought you had in your head. I'll lay you wide open, Burson. Because I hate killers."

Then he eased up. And after a moment or two, he forced a grin, baring his strong, even teeth.

"She told everybody," he said, "that she'd never give you a divorce. So there's your motive. I wish every case was as easy as this one. That's all for now."

Perinsky tapped Burson on the shoulder and led him out of the room.

"Look, Buster," the big detective said, as they went down the corridor, "get wise to yourself. Your best bet is to admit it, because you can't buck the Lieutenant. Not you."

Burson shook his head. "Find out who really killed her," he said in a tight voice. "You have the wrong man."

Perinsky shrugged and led him to a side room. There, under the jaundiced eye of a bored-looking cop, Burson sat down dejectedly.

Was he being smart? It had taken Malliner just about ten minutes to accuse him of murder. And while he waited here, twenty cops, or maybe fifty or a hundred of them, were piling up the evidence. Detectives knocking on doors and showing his picture and saying, "Know him? Then tell us—"

Tell us about the scraps he used to have with his wife, before he left her. Tell us how she created scenes, stirring him up to an anger he could hardly control. Tell us how she used to shriek at him, "You hate me! You want to get rid of me! You want to kill me!" Until finally, in rage and exasperation, he'd almost agree.

Tell us how he and Elise yearned for each other and could do nothing about it, and how he'd made the appointment with Karen for yesterday afternoon. "Don't worry, darling," he'd said to Elise. "I won't be soft this time. By Sunday night, we can plan on getting married. I promise it."

Would they get that statement out of Elise? Would they?

He thought of lab men with cameras and microscopes, analyzing the evidence in Karen's apartment and tracing his actions step by step. They'd recreate his frantic search of her desk. He'd pulled out every paper and ransacked every drawer. How could he explain that?

He held his face in his hands and groaned. Knowing Karen, he was certain she'd had a lover, and must have whipped him into a frenzy and screamed at him the same way she used to scream at her husband. "Kill me—that's what you want—go ahead and do it!"

Sure. Tell that to Malliner, and the lieutenant would have one more link in his chain of evidence. Admit she'd answered her bell when he had rung it, and it would prove she'd been alive when he got there. Every word of truth that he could utter would merely bolster the case against him. Malliner had his fall guy; he had Clyde Burson.

At three P.M., Perinsky brought Burson back to the lieutenant's office. A couple of other men sat at the far side of the room, but they didn't count. This was between Malliner and Burson, and it was personal.

"Well?" Malliner began. "Ready to talk?"

"If you'd investigate," Burson said shakily, "instead of trying to railroad me, you'd find out who did it."

"I've investigated," Malliner said drily. "You had an appointment with your wife yesterday afternoon. You'd decided to get tough with her, and so you stopped at the corner bar for a couple of quick ones. You were drunk, Burson. Even the bartender noticed."

A double scotch, Burson told himself. But he hadn't been drunk. Merely upset, trying to steel himself for the ordeal.

"At five P.M., you went up the steps to her house. The janitress, Mrs. Kurtz, and a tenant named Rayburn saw you go into the vestibule and lean down to ring her bell.''

That was right.   Still blinking from the sunlight, he had bent down to examine the name-plates.   You had to ring the apartment you wanted, so that they could press the buzzer that released the lock of the downstairs door.

"She answered your ring," Malliner said, "and you went up and stayed for a half hour.   You had a violent argument, and you stabbed her with a kitchen knife. Then you went through her desk.   You grabbed every paper and every letter. What were you looking for?''

"Nothing," Burson said.   "I wasn't there."

"You came out at five-thirty, looking sick.   Green in the face, is the way Rayburn described you.''

And why not?   Burson thought.   When you find the body of your estranged wife—she's just been killed and you realize the jam you're in—who wouldn't look green?

"At quarter of six," Malliner said evenly, "you called Miss Vandyke and canceled your evening date.   You told her you hadn't seen your wife, that you just couldn't face her.   But you lied, Burson.''

Sure I lied, Burson thought.   I wasn't going to drag Elise into it; I didn't want to make her part of the horror.   But I failed there, too.

"Why don't you try to find out who saw Karen yesterday?''   Burson demanded jerkily.   "Why pick on me?   There were other people in the building.   What about them?''

"Ten apartments," Malliner said.   "Five of them empty, tenants were in the country for the weekend and can prove it.   Then there's a little old lady about eighty-five years old, who hardly has the strength to lift a knife.   Two couples were home, with company, and we checked them out.   Then there's the girl on the second floor, her boy friend was with her and they were looking at television, and finally there's this guy Rayburn, who saw you.''

"Rayburn," Burson exclaimed.   "What about him?   What's *he* like?   How do you know *he* didn't kill her?''

"Because he was on the stoop talking to the janitress, and the pair of them saw you go in.   Look, Burson, we know our business, we been at it a long time.   We looked at every possibility and there's only one answer.   You.''

"But I wasn't there."

"Your fingerprints were."

It went on like that for hours, while Malliner demolished him piece by piece: Fingerprints, with blown-up photographs that he couldn't argue himself out of. Traces of blood on the shoes he'd worn yesterday.   Threads from his jacket caught on the splintered edge of Karen's desk.   Proof, crushing and overwhelming.

Malliner hammered at him; Perinsky pleaded with him; the others took turns sniping at him.   But it always came back to Malliner, who went at Burson with the single-minded malice of a deep grudge.   No reason for it.   Just two men who'd disliked each other on first sight.

Burson fought them off and shook his head haggardly, but gradually the hope and the will drained out of him. His mind would go blank, and he'd glance at Perinsky, who'd nod encouragement.

"Go ahead, Buster. We know you were there, so why not admit it?"

Why not? What difference could it make? Then they'd let up; they'd stop badgering him; he could rest. And he was tired, tired. He couldn't hold out against the weight of facts. Why kid himself? He wasn't even a good liar; he believed in truth and justice and the good will of men. And where was he getting, this way?

He rubbed his forehead and leaned back. He tried to speak, but his voice choked up and his words stuck. His hands trembled and his stomach rumbled and he had trouble breathing.

"I was there," he sobbed out. Strangely, he felt relief, almost a sense of peace. The problem was out of his hands now. He'd done his best, and he'd lost.

"I did go there," he said, "to her apartment. And I found her lying on the floor. Dead. It must have happened just a little while before I got there. I picked up the phone and I was going to call the police and then I was afraid you'd accuse me. It looked bad, and so I put the phone down and I began looking around. I lost my head. I can hardly remember what I did. After a while I realized I was acting like a fool, so I wiped off some prints and then I went downstairs and took the subway home."

"Who let you into her apartment?" Malliner asked crisply.

"Nobody. The door was unlocked. She was always careless that way; she'd unlatch the door and then forget about it."

"Did you lock it when you left?"

"No. I just went out."

"It was locked in the morning, when Mrs. Kurtz found her."

"Then somebody locked it," Burson said.

"How did you get into the building?"

"I rang her bell."

"If she was dead," said Malliner, "how could she let you in?"

"That's just it," Burson said excitedly. "That's what I've been racking my brains about. The killer must have been there when I rang. Somebody who knew I was coming and counted on it."

"Meet anybody on the stairs?"

"No. He must have escaped. Through the skylight to the roof, or else down the fire escape."

"The fire escape had wet paint, and nobody went down it. And the ladder to the skylight was jammed. It had dust on it that hadn't been touched in weeks."

"Then where did he go?"

"Yeah," Malliner said. "Where did he?"

"There was somebody," Burson said slowly. "There had to be."

Malliner leaned forward and said slyly, as if he hoped Burson would fall into some kind of a trap, "Maybe you rang the wrong bell, huh?"

Burson lifted his head. "Lieutenant, I'm telling you the truth, every word of it. I could say sure, I rang the wrong bell, but I didn't. I examined the name plates and I rang hers, and I remember it because she was still using one of my visiting cards and she'd written *Mrs.* in front of my name, in red ink.''

"That's right," Malliner said. He smiled broadly, and Burson sucked in his lips. He'd been tricked. He'd had his chance and flubbed it.

Malliner stood up. "Lou," he said to Perinsky, "let's take a trip over to Mrs. Burson's place and he can show us exactly what he did. Including where he got the knife from, and how he killed her." Malliner grinned. "This is going to look good, Lou. We'll have it all wrapped up before homicide or the big brass know what we're doing."

They went out a side entrance. Burson sat in back between Perinsky and the lieutenant. A pair of detectives got in the front, and the car rolled out to the street, turned, and sped west.

"I know what must have happened," Burson said. "The killer knew I was coming, so he waited for me to ring and then he pushed the buzzer and hid while I came upstairs."

"You show me where he hid," the lieutenant said. "No closets, no bathrooms, no nothing."

"Then he went into another apartment," Burson said hoarsely. "Rayburn lives there, he must have killed her."

"He was out on the street when you rang, and he's got *you* to prove it."

Burson sank back. He had the growing conviction that Rayburn had killed her, that Karen had driven him to it in one of her hysterical outbursts. But how show it? There was no breaking through the circle of evidence. Either Burson's mind was too weary, or else there were no weak spots. He wondered for a moment whether he really could have killed her.

"No," he said in a loud, stubborn voice.

Perinsky's big, warm hand patted Burson's knee. "Take it easy," the big detective said. "You got a long ways to go."

Only a few people noticed them as they stepped out of the car. Burson and Perinsky led the procession, with Malliner a step behind and then the pair of detectives. Perinsky loomed over Burson as he opened the glass door of the vestibule and Burson stepped inside. He continued to hold the door open for the others.

"The sun was shining," Burson said, "and I waited here a few seconds. I had trouble adjusting my eyes. Then I recognized my visiting card and I pressed the button. Like this." He bent down and pushed the second bell from the end.

Malliner said, "What are you trying to pull? That's not her bell. That's Mrs. Henshaw's, the old lady's."

"It's the one I rang," Burson said.

"You told us you recognized your own visiting card, with *Mrs.* written in red. Remember?"

"Yes, but—"

"Well, look at it."

Burson glanced down and saw his mistake. Then a buzzer sounded, and he turned and pushed the door. An idea began to form hazily, but he couldn't think straight.

"Show us where a guy could have hid," Malliner said.

Burson scanned the corridor. No closets on this floor. And undoubtedly none anywhere, else Malliner wouldn't have been so sure. And yet—

Burson's legs were weak; he felt out of breath before he was halfway up the first flight. The staircase was narrow and he seemed to be dragging Perinsky, who held Burson's arm and was squeezed between him and the wall.

Burson said, frowning, "You want me to do exactly what I did on Sunday, don't you?"

"Yes."

He mounted uncertainly. No closets on the second floor, no possible hiding place here. Merely two doors to two apartments, and a brass knocker on each. He turned, started up the next flight. The detectives, alert, ready to jump him if he tried to break free, hemmed him in. He could hear voices talking from somewhere above.

"Somebody's up there," he said.

Malliner answered. "Sounds like Inspector O'Shea's voice," he said. "He's going to see us wrap it up, huh, Lou?"

Perinsky grunted, and Burson began the ascent of the next flight. At the third floor landing, he stopped.

"I misread her apartment number," he said. "I thought it was 3A instead of 5A." With Perinsky watching him alertly, Burson marched to the rear door. He rapped sharply with the knocker. "I went in here, and she told me where I could find Karen's apartment."

Malliner started to object, and then the door opened and a small, white-haired old lady smiled up at him.

"I rang your bell," Burson said, hoping she'd recognize him.

"Oh, did you? What do you want?"

"Remember last Sunday?"

"Of course I do." Her eyes beamed happily. "It was such a beautiful day."

"Remember me? I was looking for Mrs. Burson."

She frowned. "Mrs. Burson? Why, she's the one that—" The little old lady's lips quivered, and she backed away in fright.

Malliner said to her, "Ever see this man before?"

She shook her head. "No. Should I know you, young man?" She hovered expectantly. When nobody answered her, she withdrew shyly and closed her door.

Malliner swung Burson around. "Come on," he said. "Whatever you were trying to pull, it didn't work."

"She's mixed up," Burson said. "Don't you see that she's half senile and can't remember anything?"

"She said she'd never seen you before, didn't she? And that means she didn't see you Sunday."

Burson felt himself droop. He'd almost broken through the circle, but it was closed again, tighter than ever. And his idea was still vague, amorphous. Suppose the old lady had recognized him, then what? Then—nothing.

When Burson reached the fourth floor, he had to slow up and lean against the bannister. He was all in; he didn't want to go any further. He listened to the voices upstairs. They were louder now, and yet blurred, as if they came from Karen's apartment.

"Did you wait here?" Malliner said. And when Burson made no reply, Malliner added gruffly, "Come on, get going. The sooner you show us, the sooner you'll get this over with."

Burson didn't move. Malliner seized Burson's arm and gave it a sharp wrench. The pain, like a sharp slap, cleared Burson's mind. Almost immediately, it went blank again. He trudged forward on heavy, dragging feet. On the fourth floor, he saw a name on the front apartment. Richard Rayburn.

Burson glanced up at Perinsky. The big detective eyed him queerly, as if sensing Burson's inner excitement, and then dropped an admonishing hand on Burson's shoulder. Burson felt a solid, healthy strength flow through him. Something in his mind seemed to bump down, then lift and leave a strange, lucid clarity. He said in a loud voice, "I know—I know—I have it!"

Perinsky muttered under his breath and Malliner began swearing, and Burson yelled out in a high, piercing voice that drowned out both of them.

"Rayburn!" he shouted. "It had to be somebody in the building. Rayburn— he switched the name plates downstairs, Karen's and the little old lady's. I rang the old lady's bell on Sunday, 3A, the second from the end, and *she* answered. But I didn't make a mistake, because yesterday, Sunday, Karen's name was second from the end."

Burson heard someone coming down the stairs and he saw the shape of the inspector who was listening intently. Burson went on in the same shrill, excited voice. "Don't you see? Rayburn killed her before I came, and later on that night he put the name-plates back the way they belonged, and so the proof is right there, waiting. Rayburn's fingerprints are on the back of the two name cards. On the backs—"

Rayburn's door shot open and a burly, red-headed man charged out and made a wild dash for the staircase leading down. The two detectives grabbed him and held him fast. He yelled, "Let me go, let me go!" But his eyes, lost and scared, betrayed him.

The inspector snapped out, "Malliner, what the hell were you trying to pull?"

Burson let out a loud guffaw, then he relaxed and sighed deeply. "Thanks for your help," he said. "Buster." And he smiled.

He'd see Elise this evening. Their troubles were over.

JOHN LUTZ

Games for Adults

It was seven P.M., and a fine, cool drizzle was settling outside the cozy Twelfth Avenue apartment building, when the Darsts' telephone rang. Bill Darst got up from where he'd been half-reclining on the sofa reading the paper and moved to answer the ring. His wife Della had been in the kitchenette preparing supper, and he beat her to the phone in the hall by three steps. A medium-size, pretty brunette, she smiled at her husband and stood gracefully with a serving fork in her hand, waiting to see if the call was for her.

Apparently it wasn't, but she stood listening anyway.

Bill watched her at a slightly sideways angle as he talked. "Oh, yes, sure I do. Yes," he said. " . . . Well, sort of short notice, but I'll see." He held the receiver away from his face and spoke to Della.

"Is supper so far along you can't hold it up? We have an invitation for this evening from the Tinkys."

"The what?"

"He's on the phone," Bill said impatiently. "Quick, yes or no." He smiled knowingly, aware that she hated to cook and seldom turned down an opportunity to escape the chore.

"Sure," she said, shrugging. "Why not?"

As Bill accepted the invitation and hung up, he watched her walk back into the kitchen, untying the apron strings from around her slender waist. They had been married only two years, and he still sometimes experienced that feeling of possessive wonderment at what he considered his incomprehensible and undeserving luck.

"They'll pick us up here in about twenty minutes," he called after Della. "Said the directions were too complicated to understand over the phone."

"Fine." Her voice came from the bedroom now, where she was changing clothes.

Della appeared shortly, wearing the form-fitting but modest green dress that he liked on her. "Now, just where are we going?" she asked. "Who on earth are the Tinkys?"

Bill grinned at her. "Cal and Emma Tinky," he said. "Remember, we met them in that lounge on Fourteenth Street when we went there to escape the rain last week."

Recognition widened her eyes.   "The toy manufacturer and his wife!   I'd forgotten about them completely."

"Well, they didn't forget about us.   Cal Tinky said something at the bar about inviting us for dinner and games some night, and I guess he meant it.   I don't see any harm in us taking him up on a free meal."

"Games?" Della asked, raising an artistically penciled eyebrow.

"Tinky's the president and owner of Master Games, Incorporated," Bill reminded her, "and they're not toy manufacturers.   They make games, mostly for adults. You know, three-dimensional checkers, word games, party games.   They're the ones who make crossword roulette."

"We played that once," Della said, "at the Grahams'."

"Right," Bill said.   "Anyway, the Tinkys live outside of town and Cal Tinky happened to be in this neighborhood, so he invited us out to his place."

"I hope his wife knows about it."

"He said she does."   Bill picked up the paper again and began idly going over the football scores that he'd read before, but he didn't really concentrate on them. He thought back on the evening he and Della had met the Tinkys.   Both couples had gone into the tiny lounge to escape the sudden deluge of rain, and they had naturally fallen into an easy conversation that had lasted as long as the rain, well over an hour.   Cal Tinky was a large-boned, beefy man with a ruddy complexion and a wide, toothy smile.   His wife, Emma, was a stout woman in her early forties. While friendly, she seemed to be rather withdrawn at times, the line of her mouth arcing downward beneath the suggestion of a fine moustache.

Only fifteen minutes had passed since the phone call when the doorbell rang and Bill went to answer it.

Cal Tinky stood in the hall, wearing a wide, amiable grin and a tweed sport coat and red tie that brought out the floridness of his complexion.   "You folks ready? Emma's waiting down in the car."

Sure," Bill said.   "Come on in a minute and we can go."

"Evening, Mrs. Darst," Tinky said as he stepped inside.

Della said hello and they chatted while Bill went into the bedroom and put on a coat and tie.   He could hear Della's laughter and Tinky's booming, enthusiastic voice as he stood before the mirror and ran a brush over his thick dark hair.   He noted his regular-featured, commonplace appearance marred by a slightly large, slightly crooked nose and again counted his good fortune for having Della.

"We'll just take my car," Tinky said as Bill crossed the living room and got the coats from the hall closet.   "You're apt to lose me in the fog, and it's not so far I can't drive you back later on."

"You don't have to go to all that trouble, Mr. Tinky," Della said, backing into the raincoat that Bill held for her.

"No trouble," Tinky said reassuringly.   "And call me Cal—never did like that name Tinky."

Bill put on his topcoat and they left and took the elevator to the lobby, then crossed the street to where Emma Tinky was waiting in a rain-glistening gray sedan.

The ride to the Tinkys' home took almost an hour through the misting, foggy night. They wound for miles on a series of smooth blacktop roads surrounded by woods, listening to the steady, muffled rhythm of the sweeping wiper blades. Cal Tinky kept up an easy conversation of good-natured little stories as he drove, while Emma sat silently, gazing out the side window at the cold rain.

"I hope you won't go to too much trouble," Della said from the rear seat.

Bill watched Emma Tinky start from her silent thoughts, and smile. "Oh, no, I put a roast in the oven before we came into the city. It's cooking now."

The big car took another turn, this time onto a steep gravel road. Bill caught a glimpse through the trees of the distant city lights far below them. He hadn't realized they'd driven so far into the hills.

"I don't suppose you have much in the way of neighbors," he said, "living way up here."

"You're right there, Bill," Cal Tinky said. "Nearest is over two miles. Folks up here value their privacy. You know how it is when you work hard half your life and manage to become moderately wealthy—always somebody wanting to take it away from you. Up here we're not pestered by people like that."

By the looks of the Tinkys' home they were more than moderately wealthy. As the car turned into the long driveway bordered by woods, Bill gazed through the rain-streaked windshield at a huge house that seemed in the dark to be built something like a horizontal wheel. Its rounded brick walls curved away into the night in perfect symmetry on either side of the ornate lighted entrance. Off to the left of the car Bill saw a small beach house beside a swimming pool.

"Like it?" Cal Tinky asked. "I can tell you it cost more than a pretty penny, but we sure enjoy it, Emma and I."

"What I can see of it looks great," Bill said.

"You shouldn't brag," Emma said to her husband.

"Just giving them the facts," Tinky said heartily as he neared the house and a basement garage door opened automatically.

For just a moment the sound of the car's engine was loud and echoing in the spacious garage, then Cal Tinky turned the key and they sat in silence. Bill saw a small red foreign convertible parked near some stacks of large cartons.

"No fun sitting here," Cal Tinky said. "Let's go upstairs."

They got out of the car and the Tinkys led them up some stairs to a large utility room of some sort. After passing through that room they entered a large room containing some chairs, a sofa and a grand piano.

"Come on in here," Cal Tinky said, "into our recreation room."

Bill thought the recreation room was fantastic.

It was a spacious room, about thirty feet square, with a red and white checkerboard tiled floor and walls hung with large, decorative dominoes and ornate numerals. At strategic spots on the gleaming tile, four-foot-tall wood chessmen stood on some of the large red squares. Several tables were in the room, with various games spread out on them; chess, dominoes, and several complex games that were manufactured by Master Games, Incorporated. A smoldering fire glowed in the fireplace over which hung a huge dart board.

"Let's sit down," Cal Tinky invited. "Dinner'll be ready soon."

Bill removed his coat and crossed an area rug designed to resemble the six-dotted plane of a huge die.   He sat down next to Cal Tinky on a sofa embroidered with tick-tack-toe symbols.

"Is there anything I can do to help?"   Della asked Emma Tinky as the heavyset woman took her coat.

"No, no," Emma said, "you are a guest."

Bill watched Emma remove her own bulky coat and saw that she was wearing slacks and a black sweater covered with a heavy corduroy vest.   There was something that suggested hidden physical power in her walk as she left the recreation room to hang up the coats and prepare dinner.

Della sat opposite Bill and Cal Tinky on a chair that matched the sofa.   "Quite a decorating job."

Cal Tinky beamed.   "Thanks.   Designed most of it ourselves.   After we eat we can make use of it."

"A house this big," Bill said, "do you have any servants?"

Cal Tinky stood and walked to an L-shaped bar in a corner.   "No," he said, "we mostly take care of it all ourselves, fifteen rooms.   Had servants, but they stole on us.   Now we have someone come in from the city twice a week to clean.   Course, most of the rooms we don't even use."   He reached for a top-brand bottle of Scotch and held it up.   "Good enough?"

Bill nodded.

"Make mine with water," Della said.

Cal Tinky mixed the drinks expertly.   When he'd given the Darsts their glasses he settled down on the couch and took a long sip of his straight Scotch.

Emma Tinky came back into the room then, picked up the drink that her husband had left for her on the bar and sat in a chair near the sofa.

"You certainly must be fond of games," Bill said, looking around him again in something like awe at the recreation room.

Cal Tinky smiled.   "Games are our life.   Life is a game."

"I agree with that last part," Bill said, raising the excellent Scotch to his lips.

"There are winners and losers," Emma said, smiling at Della.

They sat for a moment in that awkwardness of silence that sometimes descends on people who don't really know one another.   Bill heard a faint clicking that he'd noticed in the car earlier.   He saw that Emma was holding in her left hand one of those twisted metal two-part puzzles that separate and lock together only a certain way.   With surprisingly nimble fingers she was absently separating and rejoining the two pieces expertly.

"Winners and losers," Della said to fill the void. "I suppose that's true."

"The basis of life," Cal Tinky said.   "Have you folks ever stopped to think that our whole lives are spent trying to figure out bigger and better ways to amuse ourselves, bigger and better challenges?   From the time we are infants we want to play the 'grown-up' games."

Bill didn't say anything.   It was something about which he had never thought much.

"And business!" Cal Tinky laughed his booming laugh. "Why, business is nothing but a game!"

Now Bill laughed. "You appear to be a winner at that game." He motioned with his hand to take in the surroundings.

Emma joined in the laughter. She had a high, piercing laugh, long and lilting with a touch of . . . Of what? "Yes," she said then in a suddenly solemn voice though a smile still played about her lips. "Material possessions are some of the prizes."

"Enough talk of games," Cal Tinky said. "I'm hungry."

Emma put the twisted pieces of shining metal into her vest pocket. "We can eat any time," she said, "unless you'd like another drink."

"No," Bill said, "not unless the food's so bad you don't want me to taste it."

Again came her high, lilting laugh, backgrounded by her husband's booming laughter.

At least she has a sense of humor, Bill thought, as they all rose and went into the large and well-furnished dining room.

The meal was simple but delicious; a well-done roast served with potatoes and carrots, a gelatin dessert with coffee, topped by an excellent brandy.

Throughout the meal they had kept up a running conversation, usually led by Cal Tinky, on the importance and celestial nature of games in general. Emma would join in now and then with a shrewd comment, a high and piercing laugh, and once, over the lime gelatin, Bill had seen her staring at Della with a strange intensity. Then she had looked away, spooning the quivering dessert into her mouth, and Bill heard again the soft, metallic, clicking sound.

After the brandy Cal Tinky suggested they go back into the recreation room for some drinks and relaxation. For a short time the Tinkys stayed in the dining room as Cal helped Emma put away some perishables, and Bill and Della were alone.

Della nudged Bill playfully in the ribs and moved close to him. "These people are weird," she whispered.

Bill grinned down at her. "Just a little eccentric, darling. Maybe we'd be, too, if we had their money."

"I hope we find out someday," Della said with a giggle. She quickly hushed as the Tinkys came into the room.

Cal Tinky was carrying a fresh bottle of Scotch. "The first order is more drinks," he proclaimed in his loud voice.

He mixed the drinks at the bar and served them, then he looked around at the many games and entertainment devices. "Anything for your amusement," he said with his wide grin.

Bill smiled and shrugged his shoulders. "You're the game expert, Cal."

Cal Tinky looked thoughtful and rubbed his square jaw.

"Make it something simple, if you will," Della said. "I don't feel very clever tonight."

"How about Bank Vault?" Cal asked. "It's a simple game, but it's fun for four people."

He walked to a shelf and took down the game.   Bill and Della followed him to a round, shaggy rug, where he opened the box and spread out the game board. Emma spread four cushions for them to sit on.

When they were seated with fresh drinks, Cal Tinky proceeded to explain the rules.

It was an easy game to learn, uncomplicated, based like so many games on the advance of your marker according to the number you rolled on a pair of dice.   The board was marked in a concentric series of squares, divided into boxes, some of which had lettering inside them: 'Advance six squares', 'Go back two', 'Return to home area'.   Occasionally there were shortcuts marked on the board, where you had your choice of direction while advancing.   Each player had a small wooden marker of a different color, and if the number he rolled happened to land his block on the same square as an opponent, the opponent had to return to the home area and start over.   Whoever reached the bank vault first was the winner.

They rolled the dice to determine in what order they'd play, then settled down on the soft cushions to enjoy themselves.

Cal and Emma Tinky played seriously and with complete absorption.   Cal would roll his number and move his red block solemnly while his eyes measured the distance his opponents were behind him.   Emma would move her yellow block in short, firm steps, counting the number of squares as she moved it.

The game lasted through two drinks.   Bill had rolled consecutive high numbers, and his green block was ahead until near the end of the game.   Then he had landed on a 'Go back ten' square and Cal had overtaken him to win.   Emma was second, only three squares ahead of Bill, and Della's blue block brought up the rear after an unfortunate 'Return to home area' roll.

"Say, I have another game similar to this only a little more interesting," Cal said, picking up the board.   "Let's try it."

Bill reached to help him put the game away and found that his fingers missed the block he'd tried to pick up by half an inch.   He decided to go easier on the Scotch.

Cal returned with the new game and spread it out on the soft rug to explain it to them.   It was almost exactly like the first game.   This time the board was laid out in a circle divided into compartments.   The compartments were marked as rooms and the idea was to get back first to the room in which you started.   This time the obstacles and detours were a little more numerous.

"Does your company manufacture this game?" Bill asked.

"Not yet," Cal Tinky said with his expansive grin, "but we're thinking about it.   It's not the sort of game with mass appeal."

They rolled the dice in the same order.   Bill rolled a twelve and moved well out ahead, but on his second roll he came up with a seven, landing him in the dining room where the lettered message instructed him to skip his next turn for a snack.   Della moved out ahead of him then, landing in the den.   Emma rolled a three, but landed in the utility room where she was instructed to advance ten squares. This brought her yellow block only two squares behind Della's and she emitted her high, strange laughter. Cal rolled snake eyes, allowing him a free roll, and he came up with a twelve. His red block landed on the den, and he placed it directly atop Della's blue block.

"Does that mean I go back to the entrance hall?" Della asked, smiling like a sport but feeling disappointed.

"In a manner of speaking," Cal Tinky said. He drew from beneath his sport jacket a large revolver and shot Della.

The slam of the huge caliber bullet smashing into her chest sounded almost before the shot. Della flopped backward, still smiling, her legs still crossed. A soft sigh escaped her body and her eyes rolled back.

"*Della . . .*" Bill whispered her name once, staring at her, wanting to help her, knowing she was dead, finally and forever. A joke, a mistake, a horrible, unbelievable mistake! He turned toward the Tinkys. Cal Tinky was smiling. They were both smiling.

Words welled up in Bill's throat that would not escape—anger that paralyzed him. He stood unsteadily, the room whirling at first, and began to move toward Cal Tinky. The long revolver raised and the hammer clicked back into place. Bill stood trembling, grief-stricken, enraged and afraid. Cal Tinky held the revolver and the smile steady as the fear grew, cold and pulsating, deep in the pit of Bill's stomach. The floor seemed to tilt and Bill screamed, a hoarse, sobbing scream. He turned awkwardly and ran in panic from the room, from death.

He stumbled through the dining room, struggling to keep his balance. On the edge of his mind he was aware that Cal had put something in the drinks, something that had destroyed his perception, sapped his strength, and he tried to fight it off as he ran to a window. The window was small and high, and as he flung aside the curtains he saw that it was covered with a steel grill. With a moan, he ran awkwardly into the next room, to the next window. It, too, was barred. All the rooms that had windows were inescapable, and all the outside doors were locked. He ran, pounding against thick, barred windows that wouldn't break or open, flinging himself against doors that wouldn't give, until finally, exhausted and broken, he found himself in the kitchen and dragged his heaving body into a small alcove lined with shelves of canned goods, where he tried to hide, to think, to think . . .

In the recreation room, Cal Tinky looked at his wife over the game board. "I think he's had enough time," he said. "It never takes them more than a few minutes to run to cover."

Emma Tinky nodded and picked up the dice. With a quick, expert motion of her hand she rolled a nine.

Cal rolled a six. "Your shot," he said.

Emma rolled the dice again, a seven. She leaned over the board and, counting under her breath, moved her yellow block forward in short, tapping jerks.

"The kitchen," she said. "Damn! They never hide in the kitchen."

"No need to get upset," Cal Tinky said. "You'll probably get another roll."

Emma drew a long revolver exactly like her husband's from beneath her corduroy vest and stood. Stepping over Della, she walked from the recreation room toward the kitchen. Her husband picked up the game and followed, careful to hold the board absolutely level so that the dice and the colored blocks wouldn't be disturbed.

The sound of the shot that came from the kitchen a few minutes later wasn't very loud, like the hard slap of an open hand on a solid tabletop—but Emma Tinky's high, long laugh might have been heard throughout the house.

JAMES MICHAEL ULLMAN

Night of the Twisters

All afternoon the air had been humid and oddly still, with the temperature hovering in the nineties. Old-timers, wiping their brows and gazing at dark thunderheads gathering in the southwestern sky, knew they were in for trouble.

At dusk, as thunder cracked and rain pelted down in blinding sheets, the trouble came in the form of whirling, funnel-shaped clouds.

One tornado ripped through a mobile-home court, killing five people. Another flattened every structure in a whistle-stop on the St. Louis-San Francisco Railway, and a third blew a sedan off a county road, fatally injuring its occupant.

At least a dozen funnel clouds had been sighted by 9:08 P.M., at which time a tall, dark-haired woman walked from the kitchen of a remote farmhouse into the parlor. She thought she'd heard a car in the front yard. Her imagination, probably. Nobody in his right mind would be out driving on a wild night like this.

She started toward a window, but never made it.

Someone kicked the front door open, springing the lock, and two men stumbled in. Both carried pistols.

The taller and older of the two swung the bore of his weapon toward the young woman's midsection and said, "Freeze, lady. Anyone else in this house?"

Wordlessly, she shook her head.

"Okay. You can sit down now. But be nice and quiet, and keep your hands at your sides."

Slowly, she eased into a chair.

The room's only light came from kerosene lamps. The power had gone out long ago. From the kitchen, music wafted faintly from a transistor radio.

The two intruders, bareheaded, with crew cuts, were dressed in soaking wet blue denim uniforms.

"Jerry, close that door," the older man ordered. "Then see if there's anyone else here. She might be lying."

Jerry, a thin, short youth of about twenty, hesitated a moment to stare at the young woman. Her features were plain but she was well-built, with a robust figure quite clearly defined under a sleeveless blouse and fashionably brief shorts. Then he slammed the front door, braced it with a table and took off to search the house.

The other man walked around behind the woman. He had broad shoulders, a flat belly, a hawklike profile and dark rings under eyes that burned with an abnormal intensity. His age could have been anywhere between thirty-five and fifty.

Placing the pistol's muzzle to the woman's head, he asked, "What's your name?"

"Karen." Terrified, she worked hard at keeping her voice steady. Her intuition told her that any display of panic might trigger violence against her person. "Karen Smallwood."

"Who lives here with you?"

"I don't live here. My parents do, but they're away. I'm a teacher—I live in town. I came out to straighten up for them but got caught by the storm."

"We're lost. We were on County B, headed for Hanksville and the Interstate, when we hit a washout. We had to detour onto the cowpath that took us here. Where's it go?"

"Same place as County B—to Hanksville—only it takes a few minutes longer to get there."

"Any bridges in between?"

"No, there'll be no more washouts."

"Driving to this farm, we were going up a hill. What's on the other side? Another farm?"

"Not right away. Nobody lives within three miles of here."

"If you been listening to that radio, you must know who we are. Except for the tornadoes, we been the big story on every newscast."

"Yes," she said. "I know. I don't remember your name . . ."

"Garth," he said pleasantly. "Ben Garth."

"You and your friend broke out of prison yesterday. The police in half the country are looking for you."

She didn't bother adding what they both knew very well: that Garth had been serving a sentence for murder, Jerry for rape; that since breaking out, they had shot and killed a motorist whose car they had stolen, and then beaten a waitress to death in a roadside diner. The newscaster had termed it a "senseless killing spree."

Jerry came back. "There's nobody else," he reported, "but I found this."

He held a faded photograph of Karen, then a leggy teen-ager, and a middle-aged couple. The man in the picture wore a state police uniform.

"The cop your father?" Garth asked.

"Yes," she admitted. "But he isn't a trooper anymore. He was hurt chasing a speeder, so they pensioned him off."

"Where are your folks now?"

"A flea market in Canton, Texas. They won't be back until next week."

"A what?"

"Flea market," she repeated. "A place where anyone can go and sell anything. My folks barely make out on my father's pension. As a sideline, they sell antiques. Just look around . . ."

Garth scrutinized the home's interior more closely. She was right. The parlor and dining room looked more like an antique store than a farmhouse. Pictures in Victorian frames hung from the walls; shelves and cupboards were filled with china and glassware; and the floor areas were jammed with heavy old chairs and tables.

"You're pretty cool about all this," Garth said. "I admire women who don't lose their heads and start hollerin', like the one in the diner this mornin'—the one we had to shut up . . ."

He didn't admire her. He was probing, wondering how much she could take.

"There's no point in screaming," Karen said as casually as she could, "if nobody but you two would hear."

"Smart girl. Just in case the storm gets worse, you got a storm cellar in this place?"

"The door's in the kitchen floor."

Jerry went to the kitchen, lifted the door and swung a kerosene lantern down for a better look. "It's no fancy hotel," he called back, "but we could sweat it out if we had to."

"Any guns in this house?" Garth went on. "If your old man was a cop, he must have some guns."

"Two hunting rifles, a shotgun and two revolvers," she replied without hesitation. "They're locked in a case upstairs. My father has the key, but if you want them you can just break the glass."

"We'll take 'em when we leave."

"You were wise," Karen said, "ditching your car to find shelter. A car's the worst place to be if a twister hits."

She said that to get Garth's mind off guns. She didn't want him thinking about guns because there was one she hadn't mentioned, an ancient, double-barreled shotgun hanging in plain sight on the wall over the mantel in the dining room.

Apparently, it was now nothing more than a decorative but useless antique; it hung so high that to get it, she'd have to climb up on a chair to lift it off its brackets.

While it was antique it was not useless, however. Despite its age it was loaded and in perfect working condition. That old shotgun, her father had said, would be his ace in the hole. He hoped he'd never need it, but as a former law officer living far out in the country, and knowing some men held grudges against him, he wanted an emergency weapon.

At the moment, though, it seemed the shotgun would not do Karen much good. It was difficult to imagine the circumstances under which Garth would allow her to climb the chair, reach up and turn the weapon on her captors . . .

Garth took the pistol away from Karen's head and jammed it under his belt. "Okay," he drawled, "we ain't ate since mornin' and I never been fed by a lawman's daughter before. So you just haul into that kitchen and fix us somethin'—fast."

The men drank beer and watched her every move as she prepared a quick supper of frankfurters and canned beans. As they ate, they made her sit across the dining-room table from them—the shotgun on the wall behind them.

When they were through, Karen cleared the table and brought more beer. On the radio, the announcer reported the sighting of more funnel clouds.

"I don't suppose," Karen said, settling back in her chair, "either of you has ever seen a tornado."

"No, I ain't," Garth said. "And I don't hanker to."

Jerry asked, "Have you?"

"Yes."

"What's it like?"

She thought back to that terrifying afternoon so many years ago. "It's a black, whirling piece of hell, that's what. They say the funnel's wind moves so fast it can drive a splinter of wood into your brain like a highpowered bullet. And pieces of glass—God help you if you're near a window. You'll be cut to ribbons."

Uneasily, Jerry glanced at the broad expanse of windows in the dining room. "Then it's dangerous just sitting here. We should be down in the cellar, like the radio said."

"It's a little dangerous," Karen conceded. "If a twister dipped down from the sky to exactly this spot, we'd be finished. But if it's already on the ground and moving toward you, you'll probably know it and have warning. Even if it's night and you can't see the twister, you can hear it."

"I read about that," Jerry told her. "They make a noise."

"Yes. Like a freight train. The time I heard that sound I was in open country. I looked up and there it was, bearing down on me. There was a ditch nearby and I had enough sense to climb into a culvert. Even so, it's a miracle I lived through it. You know what happens sometimes? The funnels pick people up and pull them so high into the sky that when they drop down, they're frozen solid. And then at other times they simply—"

"That's enough." Garth frowned. "I don't wanna hear no more about it."

Again, he looked around the house. This time his perusal was slower and more thorough. His gaze even paused briefly at the ancient shotgun before moving on.

He asked, "Any money around here?"

"Only the few dollars in my purse. My father never leaves cash in the house when he's going out of town."

"Uh-huh." Garth turned to Jerry. "Get it. Then go through the rest of this place. See if there's more stashed away."

Rummaging through Karen's purse, Jerry came up with a few bills and coins. "Four dollars and thirty-five cents," he said in disgust. "That won't take us far . . ."

He shoved the money into his pocket and began ransacking the house, sweeping shelves clean and pulling out drawers and dumping their contents onto the floor. It was part search and part pure vandalism, random destruction for its own sake. Karen compressed her lips to keep from crying out as the boy smashed the collections of porcelain, glassware and other fragile artifacts her parents had spent so much of their time assembling.

When Jerry was through on the ground floor he went upstairs. They could hear him tramping around, smashing more things.

Watching Karen while sipping from still another can of beer, Garth smiled humorlessly. Even the modest amount of alcohol in the beer seemed to be having a bad effect on his mood. Clearly she was dealing with a highly unstable psychopath likely to go berserk upon little or no provocation.

Jerry returned with only a few more coins for his efforts.

"I told you," Karen said patiently, "my father didn't keep money here."

"Yeah." Garth was looking at her in an odd way. "Too bad. If he had, we'd be more friendly-inclined. We need money to get out of the country."

"I'm sorry."

"Teacher, you just *think* you're sorry. But before we're through with you, you'll *really* be sorry."

He was tormenting her verbally before getting around to the real thing. She had to stall him as long as possible.

"Why would you want to hurt me?" She tried to sound friendly and reasonable. "I haven't made any trouble. I've done everything you asked."

"Maybe just because you're a lawman's daughter. We got an abiding dislike for lawmen and anyone connected with 'em. Matter of fact, we don't much like teachers either. Do we, Jerry?"

The boy grinned at her vacuously. She'd get no help from that quarter.

"It wouldn't make sense anyhow," Garth went on, "leavin' you here alive. The police think we're a couple hundred miles north of here. But the first thing you'd do after we left would be to put 'em straight."

"You could lock me in the storm cellar. That'd give you plenty of time for a head start."

"Nope. Can't take chances. We'll lock you in the storm cellar, all right, but when we do you won't be in no condition to climb out. Not ever. That way, we *know* we'll have a head start. It might be a long time before anyone gets curious enough to bust in, to see why you ain't been around lately."

Despite the fear tearing at her insides, Karen managed a smile. "You're just trying to frighten me. You're playing games. Well, sure I'm scared. What girl wouldn't be? But you know you don't have to kill me, Garth. If you don't want to leave me, take me along. I won't try anything stupid. I'll . . ." She paused. "Just a minute. You hear that?"

Garth stood up. "Hear what?"

"Shut up," Jerry broke in, his grin gone. "I think I hear it, too."

Then there was no doubt. They all heard it, far off but coming closer, a growing clatter and roar suggestive of an approaching freight train . . .

Karen rose. "I don't know about you," she announced, "but while there's still time, I'm going into that storm cellar!"

She took a step forward but Jerry lunged ahead, shoving her aside. Garth hesitated a moment and then, as the sound mounted in intensity, he plunged after Jerry.

As they scrambled for the door in the kitchen floor, Karen climbed up on the chair. She lifted the shotgun from its rack, stepped down, cocked the piece, aimed it while shoving the stock tight against her shoulder, and braced herself against the wall.

As Garth looked up and clawed for his pistol, she squeezed one trigger and then the other.

At dawn, her face expressionless, Karen watched from a parlor window as Garth's body was loaded into a hearse. The blasts had killed him almost instantly. Jerry had been seriously wounded but would live.

Standing beside Karen, a state police detective said, "I know how you feel. No matter how justified, it's terrible to kill someone. But you had no choice. If you hadn't stopped them, they'd almost surely have killed you and others."

"I know. Thinking about that is the only way I'll be able to live with this."

"Anyhow, either you were mighty lucky or they were mighty careless, allowing you to get your hands on the gun."

"Oh, that." She smiled faintly. "At the time, they were trying to get into the storm cellar. I'd told them how a tornado sounded like a fast freight train." Her gaze strayed beyond the yard to the other side of the hill and the main line of the St. Louis-San Francisco Railway. "So when the night freight came high-balling by a little before ten, like it always does, I made out like it was a twister."

PATRICIA HIGHSMITH

Variations on a Game

It was an impossible situation. Penn Knowlton had realized that as soon as he realized he was in love with Ginnie Ostrander—Mrs. David Ostrander. Penn couldn't see himself in the role of a marriage-breaker, even though Ginnie said she had wanted to divorce David long before she met him. David wouldn't give her a divorce, that was the point. The only decent thing to do, Penn had decided, was to clear out, leave before David suspected anything. Not that he considered himself noble, but there were some situations . . .

Penn went to Ginnie's room on the second floor of the house and knocked.

Her rather high, cheerful voice called, "You, Penn? Come in!"

She was lying on the sunlit chaise longue, wearing black, close-fitting slacks and a yellow blouse, and she was sewing a button on one of David's shirts.

"Don't I look domestic?" she asked, pushing her yellow hair back from her forehead. "Need any buttons sewed on, darling?" Sometimes she called him darling when David was around, too.

"No," he said, smiling, and sat down on a hassock.

She glanced at the door as if to make sure no one was about, then pursed her lips and kissed the empty air between them. "I'll miss you this weekend. What time are you leaving tomorrow?"

"David wants to leave just after lunch. It's my last assignment, Ginnie. David's last book with me. I'm quitting."

"Quitting?" She let her sewing fall into her lap. "You've told David, too?"

"No. I'll tell him tomorrow. I don't know why you're surprised. You're the reason, Ginnie. I don't think I have to make any speeches."

"I understand, Penn. You know I've asked for a divorce. But I'll keep on asking. I'll work something out and then—" She was on her knees suddenly in front of him, crying, her head down on her hands that gripped his hands.

He turned his eyes away and slowly stood up, drawing her up with him. "I'll be around another two weeks, probably; long enough for David to finish this book, if he wants me around that long. And you needn't worry. I won't tell him why I'm quitting." His voice had sunk to a whisper, though David was downstairs in his soundproofed study, and the maid, Penn thought, was in the basement.

"I wouldn't care if you told him," she said with quiet defiance.

"It's a wonder he doesn't know."

"Will you be around, say in three months, if I can get a divorce?" she asked.

He nodded, then feeling his own eyes start to burn, he smiled. "I'll be around an awful long time. I'm just not so sure you want a divorce."

Her eyebrows drew down, stubborn and serious. "You'll see. I don't want to make David angry. I'm afraid of his temper, I've told you that. But maybe I'll have to stop being afraid." Her blue eyes looked straight into his. "Remember that dream you told us, about the man you were walking with on the country road, who disappeared? And you kept calling him and you couldn't find him?"

"Yes," he said, smiling.

"I wish it would happen to you—with David. I wish David would just disappear suddenly, this weekend, and be out of my life forever, so I could be with you."

Her words did strange and terrible things to him. He released her arm. "People don't just disappear. There're other ways." He was going to add, "Such as divorce," but he didn't.

"Such as?"

"I'd better get back to my typewriter. I've got another half-hour tape to do."

David and Penn left in the black convertible the next afternoon with a small suitcase apiece, one typewriter, the tape recorder, and an iced carton of steaks and beer and a few other items of food. David was in a good mood, talking about an idea that had come to him during the night for a new book. David Ostrander wrote science fiction so prolifically that he used half a dozen pen names. He seldom took longer than a month to write a book, and he worked every month of the year. More ideas came to him than he could use, and he was in the habit of passing them on to other writers at his Wednesday night Guild meetings.

David Ostrander was forty-three, lean and wiry, with a thin, dry-skinned face thatched with fine, intersecting wrinkles—the only part of him that showed his age at all and exaggerated it at that—wrinkles that looked as if he had spent all his forty-three years in the dry, sterile winds of the fantastic planets about which he wrote.

Ginnie was only twenty-four, Penn remembered, two years younger than himself. Her skin was pliant and smooth, her lips like a poppy's petals. He stopped thinking about her. It irked him to think of David's lips kissing hers. How could she have married him? Or why? Or was there something about David's intellect, his bitter humor, his energy, that a woman would find attractive? Of course David had money, a comfortable income plus the profits of his writing, but what did Ginnie do with it? Nice clothes, yes, but did David ever take her out? They hardly ever entertained. As far as Penn had been able to learn, they had never traveled anywhere.

"Eh? What do you think of that, Penn? The poison gas emanating from the blue vegetation and conquering the green until the whole earth perishes! Say, where are you today?"

"I got it," Penn said without taking his eyes from the road. "Shall I put it down in the notebook?"

"Yes. No. I'll think about it a little more today." David lit another cigarette. "Something's on your mind, Penn, my boy. What is it?"

Penn's hands tightened on the wheel. Well, no other moment was going to be any better, was it? A couple of Scotches this evening wouldn't help, just be a little more cowardly, Penn decided. "David, I think after this book is over, I'll be leaving you."

"Oh," said David, not manifesting any surprise. He puffed on his cigarette. "Any particular reason?"

"Well, as I've told you, I have a book of my own to write. The Coast Guard thing." Penn had spent the last four years in the Coast Guard, which was the main reason David had hired him as a secretary. David had advertised for a secretary "preferably with a firsthand knowledge of Navy life." The first book he had worked on with David had a Navy background—Navy life in 2800 A.D., when the whole globe had been made radioactive. Penn's book would have to do with real life, and it had an orthodox plot, ending on a note of hope. It seemed at that moment a frail and hopeless thing compared to a book by the great David Ostrander.

"I'll miss you," David said finally. "So'll Ginnie. She's very fond of you, you know."

From any other man it might have been a snide comment, but not from David, who positively encouraged him to spend time with Ginnie, to take walks in the woods around the estate with her, to play tennis on the clay court behind the summerhouse. "I'll miss you both, too," Penn said. "And who wouldn't prefer the environment to an apartment in New York?"

"Don't make any speeches, Penn. We know each other too well." David rubbed the side of his nose with a nicotine-stained forefinger. "What if I put you on a part-time basis and gave you most of the day for your own work? You could have a whole wing of the house to yourself."

Penn declined it politely. He wanted to get away by himself for a while.

"Ginnie's going to sulk," David said, as if to himself.

They reached the lodge at sundown. It was a substantial one-story affair made of unhewn logs, with a stone chimney at one end. White birches and huge pine trees swayed in the autumn breeze. By the time they unpacked and got a fire going for the steak, it was seven o'clock. David said little, but he seemed cheerful, as if their conversation about Penn's quitting had never taken place. They had two drinks each before dinner, two being David's limit for himself on the nights he worked and also those on which he did not work, which were rare.

David looked at him across the wooden table. "Did you tell Ginnie you were leaving?"

Penn nodded, and swallowed with an effort. "I told her yesterday." Then he wished he hadn't admitted it. Wasn't it more logical to tell one's employer first?

David's eyes seemed to be asking the same question. "And how did she take it?"

"Said she'd be sorry to see me go," Penn said casually, and cut another bite of steak.

"Oh. Like that. I'm sure she'll be devastated."

Penn jumped as if a knife had been stuck into him.

"I'm not blind, you know, Penn. I know you two think you're in love with each other."

"Now listen, David, just a minute. If you possibly imagine—"

"I know what I know, that's all. I know what's going on behind my back when I'm in my study or when I'm in town Wednesday nights at the Guild meeting!" David's eyes shone with blue fire, like the cold lights of his lunar landscapes.

"David, there's nothing going on behind your back," Penn said evenly. "If you doubt me, ask Ginnie."

"Hah!"

"But I think you'll understand why it's better that I leave. I should think you'd approve of it, in fact."

"I do." David lit a cigarette.

"I'm sorry this happened," Penn added. "Ginnie's very young. I also think she's bored—with her life, not necessarily with you."

"Thanks!" David said like a pistol shot.

Penn lit a cigarette, too. They were both on their feet now. The half-eaten meal was over. Penn watched David moving about as he might have watched an armed man who at any minute might pull a gun or a knife. He didn't trust David, couldn't predict him. The last thing he would have predicted was David's burst of temper tonight, the first Penn had seen. "Okay, David. I'll say again that I'm sorry. But you've no reason to hold a grudge against me."

"That's enough of your words! I know a heel when I see one!"

"If you were my weight, I'd break your jaw for that!" Penn yelled, advancing on him with his fists clenched. "I've had enough of your words tonight, too. I suppose you'll go home and throw your bilge at Ginnie. Well, where do *you* get off, shoving a bored, good-looking girl at your male secretary, telling us to go off on picnic lunches together? Can you blame either of us?"

David muttered something unintelligible in the direction of the fireplace. Then he turned and said, "I'm going for a walk." He went out and slammed the thick door so hard that the floor shook.

Automatically, Penn began clearing the dishes away, the untouched salad. They had started the refrigerator, and Penn carefully put the butter away on a shelf. The thought of spending the night here with David was ghastly, yet where else could he go? They were six miles from the nearest town, and there was only one car.

The door suddenly opened, and Penn nearly dropped the coffeepot.

"Come out for a walk with me," David said. "Maybe it'll do us both good." He was not smiling.

Penn set the coffeepot back on the stove. A walk with David was the last thing he wanted, but he was afraid to refuse. "Have you got the flashlight?"

"No, but we don't need it. There's moonlight."

They walked from the lodge door to the car, then turned left onto the dirt road that went on for two miles through the woods to the highway.

"This is a half moon," David said. "Mind if I try a little experiment? Walk on ahead of me, here where it's pretty clear, and let me see how much of you I can make out at thirty yards.   Take big strides and count off thirty.   You know, it's for that business about Faro.''

Penn nodded.   He knew.   They were back on the book again, and they'd probably work a couple of hours tonight when they went back to the lodge.   Penn started counting, taking big strides.

"Fine, keep going!''   David called.

Twenty-eight . . . twenty-nine . . . thirty.   Penn stopped and stood still.   He turned around.   He couldn't see David.   "Hey!   Where are you?''

No answer.

Penn smiled wryly, and stuffed his hands into his pockets.   "Can you see me, David?''

Silence.   Penn started slowly back to where he had left David.   A little joke, he supposed, a mildly insulting joke, but he resolved to take no offense.

He walked on toward the lodge, where he was sure he would find David thoughtfully pacing the floor as he pondered his work, perhaps dictating already into the tape recorder; but the main room was empty.   There was no sound from the corner room where they worked, nor from the closed room where David slept. Penn lit a cigarette, picked up the newspaper and sat down in the single armchair. He read with deliberate concentration, finished his cigarette and lit another.   The second cigarette was gone when he got up, and he felt angry and a little scared at the same time.

He went to the lodge door and called, "David!'' a couple of times, loudly. He walked toward the car, got close enough to see that there was no one sitting in it.   Then he returned to the lodge and methodically searched it, looking even under the bunks.

What was David going to do, come back in the middle of the night and kill him in his sleep?   No, that was crazy, as crazy as one of David's story ideas.   Penn suddenly thought of his dream, remembered David's brief but intense interest in it the night he had told it at the dinner table.   "Who was the man with you?''   David had asked.   But in the dream, Penn hadn't been able to identify him.   He was just a shadowy companion on a walk.   "Maybe it was me,'' David had said, his blue eyes shining.   "Maybe you'd like *me* to disappear, Penn.''   Neither Ginnie nor he had made a comment, Penn recalled, nor had they discussed David's remark when they were alone.   It had been so long ago, over two months ago.

Penn put that out of his mind.   David had probably wandered down to the lake to be alone for a while, and hadn't been courteous enough to tell him.   Penn did the dishes, took a shower and crawled into his bunk.   It was 12:10.   He had thought he wouldn't be able to sleep, but he was asleep in less than two minutes.

The raucous cries of ducks on the wing awakened him at 6:30.   He put on his robe and went into the bathroom, noting that David's towel, which he had stuck hastily over the rack last night, had not been touched.   Penn went to David's room and knocked.   Then he opened the door a crack.   The two bunks, one above the other, were still made up.   Penn washed hurriedly, dressed, and went out.

He looked over the ground on both sides of the road where he had last seen David, looking for shoeprints in the moist pine needles. He walked to the lake and looked around its marshy edge; not a footprint, not a cigarette butt.

He yelled David's name, three times, and gave it up.

By 7:30 A.M. Penn was in the town of Croydon. He saw a small rectangular sign between a barber's shop and a paint store that said POLICE. He parked the car, went into the station, and told his story. As Penn had thought, the police wanted to look over the lodge. Penn led them back in David's car.

The two policemen had heard of David Ostrander, not as a writer, apparently, but as one of the few people who had a lodge in the area. Penn showed them where he had last seen David, and told them that Mr. Ostrander had been experimenting to see how well he could see him at thirty yards.

"How long have you been working for Mr. Ostrander?"

"Four months. Three months and three weeks to be exact."

"Had he been drinking?"

"Two Scotches. His usual amount. I had the same."

Then they walked to the lake and looked around.

"Mr. Ostrander have a wife?" one of the men asked.

"Yes. She's at the house in Stonebridge, New York."

"We'd better notify her."

There was no telephone at the lodge. Penn wanted to stay on in case David turned up, but the police asked him to come with them back to the station, and Penn did not argue. At least he would be there when they talked with Ginnie, and he'd be able to speak with her himself. Maybe David had decided to go back to Stonebridge and was already home. The highway was only two miles from the lodge, and David could have flagged a bus or picked up a ride from someone, but Penn couldn't really imagine David Ostrander doing anything that simple or obvious.

"Listen," Penn said to the policemen before he got into David's convertible, "I think I ought to tell you that Mr. Ostrander is kind of an odd one. He writes science fiction. I don't know what his objective is, but I think he deliberately disappeared last night. I don't think he was kidnapped or attacked by a bear or anything like that."

The policemen looked at him thoughtfully.

"Okay, Mr. Knowlton," one of them said. "Now you drive on ahead of us, will you?

Back at the station in Croydon, they called the number Penn gave them. Hanna, the maid, answered. Penn, six feet from the telephone, could hear her shrill, German-accented voice; then Ginnie came on. The officer reported that David Ostrander was missing since 10 o'clock last night, and asked her if she'd had any word from him. Ginnie's voice, after the first exclamation which Penn had heard, sounded alarmed. The officer watched Penn as he listened to her.

"Yes . . . What's that again? . . . No, no blood or anything. Not a clue so far. That's why we're calling you." A long pause. The officer's pencil tapped but did not write. "I see . . . I see . . . We'll call you, Mrs. Ostrander."

"May I speak to her?" Penn reached for the telephone.

The captain hesitated, then said, "Good-bye, Mrs. Ostrander," and put the telephone down. "Well, Mr. Knowlton, are you prepared to swear that the story you told us is true?"

"Absolutely."

"Because I've just heard a motive if I ever heard one. A motive for getting Mr. Ostrander out of the way. Now, just what did you do to him—or maybe *say* to him?" The officer leaned forward, palms on his desk.

"What did she just tell you?"

"That you're in love with her and you might have wanted her husband out of the picture."

Penn tried to keep calm. "I was quitting my job to get *away* from the situation! I told Mr. Ostrander yesterday that I was going to quit, and I told his wife the day before."

"So you admit there was a situation."

The police, four of them now, looked at him with frank disbelief.

"Mrs. Ostrander's upset," Penn said. "She doesn't know what she's saying. Can I talk to her, please? Now?"

"You'll see her when she gets here." The officer sat down and picked up a pen. "Knowlton, we're booking you on suspicion. Sorry."

They questioned him until 1 P.M., then gave him a hamburger and a paper container of weak coffee. They kept asking him if there hadn't been a gun at the lodge—there hadn't been—and if he hadn't weighted David's body and thrown it in the lake along with the gun.

"We walked half around the lake this morning," Penn said. "Did you notice any footprints anywhere?"

By that time, he had told them about his dream and suggested that David Ostrander was trying to enact it, an idea that brought incredulous smiles, and he had laid bare his heart in regard to Ginnie, and also his intentions with her, which were nil. Penn didn't say that Ginnie had said she was in love with him, too. He couldn't bear to tell them that, in view of what she had said about him.

They went into his past. No police record. Born in Raleigh, Virginia, graduated from the state university, a major in journalism, worked on a Baltimore paper for a year, then four years in the Coast Guard. A clean slate everywhere, and this the police seemed to believe. It was, specifically, the cleanliness of his slate with the Ostranders that they doubted. He was in love with Mrs. Ostrander and yet he was really going to quit his job and leave? Hadn't he any plans about her?

"Ask her," Penn said tiredly.

"We'll do that," replied the officer who was called Mac.

"She knows about the dream I had, too, and the questions her husband asked me about it," Penn said. "Ask her in privacy, if you doubt me."

"Get this, Knowlton," Mac said. "We don't fool around with dreams. We want facts."

Ginnie arrived a little after three P.M. Catching a glimpse of her through the bars of the cell they had put him in, Penn sighed with relief. She looked calm, perfectly in command of herself.   The police took her to another room for ten minutes or so, and then they came and unlocked Penn's cell door.   As he approached Ginnie, she looked at him with a hostility or fear that was like a kick in the pit of his stomach.   It checked the "Hello, Ginnie" that he wanted to say.

"Will you repeat to him what he said to you day before yesterday, Mrs. Ostrander?'' asked Mac.

"Yes.   He said, 'I wish David would disappear the way he did in my dream. I wish he were out of your life so I could be alone with you.' ''

Penn stared at her.   "Ginnie, *you* said that!''

"I think what we want to know from you, Knowlton, is what you did with her husband,'' said Mac.

"Ginnie,'' Penn said desperately, "I don't know why you're saying that.   I can repeat every word of the conversation we had that afternoon, beginning with me saying I wanted to quit.   That much you'll agree with, won't you?''

"Why, my husband had *fired* him—because of his attentions to *me!*''   Ginnie glared at Penn and at the men around her.

Penn felt a panic, a nausea rising.   Ginnie looked insane—or like a woman who was positive she was looking at her husband's murderer.   There flashed to his mind her amazing coolness the moment after the one time he had kissed her, when David, by an unhappy stroke of luck, had tapped on her door and walked in. Ginnie hadn't turned a hair.   She was an actress by nature, apparently, and she was acting now.   "That's a lie and you know it,'' Penn said.

"And it's a lie what you said to her about wanting to get rid of her husband?'' Mac asked.

"Mrs. Ostrander said that, I didn't,'' Penn replied, feeling suddenly weak in the knees.   "That's why I was quitting.   I didn't want to interfere with a marriage that—''

The listening policemen smiled.

"My husband and I were devoted.''

Then Ginnie bent her head and gave in, it appeared, to the most genuine tears in the world.

Penn turned to the desk.   "All right, lock me up.   I'll be glad to stay here till David Ostrander turns up—because I'll bet my life he's not dead.''

Penn pressed his palms against the cool wall of the cell.   He was aware that Ginnie had left the station, but that was the only external circumstance of which he was aware.

A funny girl, Ginnie.   She was mad about David, after all.   She must worship David for his talent, for his discipline, and for his liking her.   What was she, after all?   A good-looking girl who hadn't succeeded as an actress (until now), who hadn't enough inner resources to amuse herself while her husband worked twelve hours a day, so she had started flirting with her husband's secretary.   Penn remembered that Ginnie had said their chauffeur had quit five months ago.   They hadn't hired another.   Penn wondered if the chauffeur had quit for the same reason he had been going to leave?   Or had David fired him?   Penn didn't dare believe anything, now, that Ginnie had ever said to him.

A more nightmarish thought crossed his mind: suppose Ginnie really didn't love David, and had stopped on her way to Croydon and found David in the lodge and had shot him?   Or if she had found him on the grounds, in the woods, had she shot him and left him to be discovered later, so that he would get the blame?   So that she would be free of David and free of him, too?   Or was there even a gun in Stonebridge that Ginnie could have taken?

Did Ginnie hate David or love him?   On that incredible question his own future might hang, because if Ginnie had killed him herself . . .   But how did it explain David's voluntarily disappearing last night?

Penn heard footsteps and stood up.

Mac stopped in front of his cell.   "You're telling the truth, Knowlton?" he asked a little dubiously.

"Yes."

"So, the worst that can happen is, you'll sit a couple of days till Ostrander turns up."

"I hope you're looking for him."

"That we are, all over the state and farther if we have to."   He started to go, then turned back.

"Thought I'd bring you a stronger light bulb and something to read, if you're in any mood for reading."

There was no news the next morning.

Then, around four P.M., a policeman came and unlocked Penn's cell.

"What's up?" Penn asked.

"Ostrander turned up at his house in Stonebridge," the man said with a trace of a smile.

Penn smiled, too, slightly.   He followed him out to the front desk.

Mac gave Penn a nod of greeting.   "We just called Mr. Ostrander's house.   He came home half an hour ago.   Said he'd taken a walk to do some thinking, and he can't understand what all the fuss is about."

Penn's hand shook as he signed his own release paper.   He was dreading the return to the lodge to get his possessions, the inevitable few minutes at the Stonebridge house while he packed up the rest of his things.

David's convertible was at the curb where Penn had left it yesterday.   He got in and headed for the lodge.   There, he packed first his own things and closed his suitcase, then started to carry it and the tape recorder to the car, but on second thought decided to leave the tape recorder.   How was he supposed to know what David wanted done with his stuff?

As he drove south toward Stonebridge, Penn realized that he didn't know what he felt or how he ought to behave.   Ginnie: it wasn't worthwhile to say anything to her, either in anger or by way of asking her why.   David: it was going to be hard to resist saying, "I hope you enjoyed your little joke.   Are you trying to get a plot out of it?"   Penn's foot pressed the accelerator, but he checked his speed abruptly.   *Don't lose your temper,* he told himself.   *Just get your stuff quietly and get out.*

Lights were on in the living room, and also in Ginnie's room upstairs.   It was around nine o'clock.   They'd have dined, and sometimes they sat awhile in the living room over coffee, but usually David went into his study to work.   Penn couldn't see David's study window.   He rang the bell.

Hanna opened the door.   "Mister Knowlton!" she exclaimed.   "They told me you'd gone away for good!"

"I have," Penn said.   "Just came by to pick up my things."

"Come right in, sir!   Mister and Missus are in the living room.   I'll tell them you're here."   She went trotting off before he could stop her.

Penn followed her across the broad foyer.   He wanted a look at David, just a look.   Penn stopped a little short of the door.   David and Ginnie were sitting close together on the sofa, facing him, David's arm on the back of the sofa, and as Hanna told them he was here, David dropped his arm so that it circled Ginnie's waist.   Ginnie did not show any reaction, only took a puff on her cigarette.

"Come on in, Penn!" David called, smiling.   "What're you so shy about?"

"Nothing at all."   Penn stopped at the threshold now.   "I came to get my things, if I may."

"If you may!" David mocked.   "Why, of course, Penn!"   He stood up, holding Ginnie's hand now, as if he wanted to flaunt before Penn how affectionate they had become.

"Tell him to get his things and go," Ginnie said, smashing her cigarette in the ash tray.   Her tone wasn't angry, in fact it was gentle, but she'd had a few drinks.

David came toward Penn, his lean, wrinkled face smiling.   "I'll come with you.   Maybe I can help."

Penn turned stiffly and walked to his room which was down the hall.   He went in, dragged a large suitcase out of the bottom of a closet, and began with a bureau drawer, lifting out socks and pajamas.   He was conscious of David watching him with an amused smile.   The smile was like an animal's claws in Penn's back. "Where'd you hide that night, David?"

"Hide?   Nowhere!" David chuckled.   "Just took a little walk and didn't answer you.   I was interested to see what would happen.   Rather I *knew* what would happen.   Everything was just as I'd predicted."

"What do you mean?"   Penn's hands trembled as he slid open his top drawer.

"With Ginnie," David said.   "I knew she'd turn against you and turn to me. It's happened before, you see.   You were a fool to think if you waited for her she'd divorce me and come to you.   An absolute fool!"

Penn whirled around, his hands full of folded shirts.   "Listen, David, I wasn't waiting for Ginnie.   I was clearing out of this——"

"Don't give me that, you sneak!   Carrying on behind your employer's back!"

Penn flung the shirts into his suitcase.   "What do you mean, it's happened before?"

"With our last chauffeur.   And my last secretary, too.   I'd get a girl secretary, you see, but Ginnie likes these little dramas.   They serve to draw us together and they keep her from getting bored.   Your dream gave me a splendid idea for this one.   You see how affectionate Ginnie is with me now?   And she thinks you're a prize-winning sucker."   David laughed and lifted his cigarette to his lips.

A second later, Penn landed the hardest blow he had ever struck, on David's jaw.   David's feet flew up in the wake of his body, and his head hit a wall six feet away.

Penn threw the rest of his things into his suitcase and crushed the lid down as furiously as if he were still fighting David.   He pulled the suitcase off the bed and turned to the door.

Ginnie blocked his way.   "What've you *done* to him?"

"Not as much as I'd like to do."

Ginnie rushed past him to David, and Penn went out the door.

Hanna was hurrying down the hall.   "Something the matter, Mr. Knowlton?"

"Nothing serious.   Goodbye, Hanna," Penn said, trying to control his hoarse voice.   "And thanks," he added, and went on toward the front door.

"He's *dead!*" Ginnie cried wailingly.

Hanna was running to the room.   Penn hesitated, then went on toward the door.   The little liar!   Anything for a dramatic kick!

"Stop him!" Ginnie yelled.   "Hanna, he's trying to get away!"

Penn set his suitcase down and went back.   He'd yank David up and douse his head in water.   "He's not dead," Penn said as he strode into the room.

Hanna was standing beside David with a twisted face, ready for tears.   "Yes—he is, Mr. Knowlton."

Penn bent to pull David up, but his hand stopped before it touched him.   Something shiny was sticking out of David's throat, and Penn recognized it—the haft of his own paper knife that he'd neglected to pack.

A long, crazy laugh—or maybe it was a wailing sob—came from Ginnie behind him.   "You *monster!*   I suppose you wiped your fingerprints off it!   But it won't do you any good, Penn!   Hanna, call the police at once.   Tell them we've got a murderer here!"

Hanna looked at her with horror.   "I'll call them, ma'am.   But it was you that wiped the handle.   You were wiping it with your skirt when I came in the door."

Penn stared at Ginnie.   He and she were not finished with each other yet.

WILLIAM LINK and RICHARD LEVINSON

Child's Play

Camp Summit drowsed in the two o'clock heat. In the cedar cabins little boys lay in their bunks, staring out through screened doors at the lawns and sleeping tennis courts. Breezes stirred in the pines, but moved off toward the tent row and the lake. The boys, dreaming of afternoon triumphs, turned over and over in their bunks, waiting for rest period to end.

Arnold came slowly up the path from the lakefront. He wore khaki shorts and a T-shirt, and his socks and sneakers were dripping wet. His round solemn face, in the open sun, was curiously white.

He entered cabin 12 and sat down on the bunk next to the door. A boy in the back glanced up from his comic book, but said nothing. Another boy, stretched out on his bed, picked up a tennis ball and stared at the newcomer. He watched Arnold kick off his sneakers and socks and change into a new pair of loafers. "You're lucky Uncle Jack isn't here," said the boy with the tennis ball. "You'd catch it for sure if he found out you just came in. You're supposed to stay in the bunk during rest period."

Arnold switched on the Hallicrafter radio set next to his bed and moved the selector band. He slid a pair of earphones over his large ears.

"Where have you been, Arnold?" asked the boy.

Arnold moved the selector band again.

"You can hear me. Those earphones aren't *that* thick. Arnold!" He threw the tennis ball at the little boy, but it hit the bunk ledge and rolled to a stop.

"Shut up," said Arnold.

"Where have you been? On another of your expeditions?"

Arnold adjusted the earphones.

The boy who had thrown the ball rolled over on his back and stared up at the raftered ceiling. "You don't know everything," he said abruptly. "There's a *lot* you don't know. There's a kid in bunk 7 that knows three times as much as you do. And *his* father works up at Princeton. Arnold?" He looked over at the bed. "What are you listening to?"

Arnold cupped his small hands over the earphones.

"Arnold? What are you listening to?" The boy stared at Arnold for a few more minutes and then lost interest and took a comic book from his trunk. He turned away against the wall.

Arnold switched off the set and put the earphones down.   He removed a key from his pocket and opened the trunk at the foot of his bed.   It was a green trunk, new and unmarred by labels.   Inside was a jumble of crumpled T-shirts and dirty pants; at the bottom, under some luminous white stones and the mechanism of a clock, was a sheaf of stationery.   Arnold took out a piece and closed the trunk, locking it carefully.   He removed a handful of pencils from his pocket and selected one with a point.   Then, using the steel surface of the trunk top, he began to write in a clear, firm hand.

> Dear Mother: This is the third time I have written to you this
> week (and today is only Tuesday).   I want to come home.   You
> know that.   In your last letter (which I received last Friday) you
> did not even refer to this subject, even though I told you about
> it in my last four letters and two postcards.   You know why I want
> to leave here.   Father can send Walter up with the car, it is only
> a five hour drive (I checked).   I am quite sure that Mr. Whiteman
> will refund most of what you paid.   Don't bother sending him a
> letter to find out, as that will waste too much time and complicate
> things.   I want to come home.
>
> > (signed) Arnold

He was folding the letter when a bugle call sounded.   There was an immediate yelling and shouting, the sound of feet pounding on the lawns.   Youngsters raced by outside the cabin, their white shirts flashing against the summer dazzle of the lake.   The bugle stopped abruptly, and there remained only the sound of boys' voices raised in the warm wonder of afternoon.

Arnold was left alone in the cabin.   He addressed an envelope, slipped the letter inside, and placed it in his back pocket.   Then he turned on the Hallicrafter and adjusted the earphones.   He watched a group of boys in bathing suits walking down toward the beach.

"Arnold."   A man stood in the doorway.   He was short and balding, with a pleasant, tanned face.   A whistle dangled at the end of a blue lanyard around his neck.   "Arnold.   Come on."

Arnold turned the selector band.

"It's activities period," the man said.   He came in and stood looking down at the little boy.   "Come on, Arnold."

"I don't feel like going."

"You have to.   Look, you know what will happen if I tell Mr. Whiteman. He'll dock you your free period.   You don't want that to happen, do you?"

"You don't *have* to tell him."

"Yes I do.   I let you get away with this before, but I can't this time.   Now come on.   You've got riflery, and Uncle Paul will be checking on you if you don't show.   Arnold?"

The boy hunched his thin shoulders.

"Take those earphones off.   You can't hear me."

"Yes I can."

The man wiped his sweaty neck with the front of his shirt.   His nose was peeling.
He sat down next to the boy on the bunk and tried a different approach.

"What are you listening to on that thing?"

"Radio Moscow."

"Is that so?   What are they saying?"

"Lots of things."

"Like what, for example?"

"They claim we're going to have a depression."

"Do you think they're right?"

Arnold frowned and touched his smooth white cheek.   "No.   There are a lot
of reasons why we won't.   One is that—"

The man put his hand on his shoulder.   "Arnold, will you come with me?   If
you don't I'll have to tell Mr. Whiteman.   Now I mean that.   I'm not kidding."

Arnold thought for a moment and then removed the earphones.   The cabin was
quiet except for the sounds of shouting and splashing from the lake.

"Okay, Uncle Jack," Arnold said to the man.   He fingered the letter in his
back pocket.   "I'll go if you won't tell Mr. Whiteman . . . "

It was cool in the pine forest and the air smelled of summer leaves.   A group
of campers, with .22 rifles, lay stomach-down on a strip of canvas matting.   Their
firing sounded flat and ineffectual in the dim grove.   After each round a young
counselor would walk back to remove the little black and white paper targets from
the rack.

Arnold sat in the shadow of a dwarf evergreen, waiting his turn with the second
group of boys.   He was drawing numbers with a stick in the soft earth.

"Okay.   The rest of you guys."   The counselor turned a red, critical face to
the new group and watched them tumble down on the matting.   "And cut out the
talk.   You can't get a decent score unless you concentrate."

Arnold pressed the heavy rifle to his shoulder.   The counselor stood beside him,
his black moccasins almost touching the little boy's legs.

"Now concentrate."

The others began firing.   Arnold yawned, closed his left eye, and pulled the
trigger.   He loaded and fired six times, and each bullet sang off into the dark
underbrush.

"What are you doing?" cried the counselor.   His foot pinned Arnold's rifle to
the matting.   "What's wrong with you?   You didn't even have your barrel pointing
at the target."

Arnold said nothing.   He leaned his head on his elbow.   The other boys stared
at him.

"Didn't I teach you how to fire?" asked the counselor.   "You squeeze the
trigger.   Sque-e-eze it.   And you hold your breath.   Didn't I teach you that?"

Arnold watched an ant cross a long gully in the matting.

"What's your name?"   He waited for an answer.

"His name's Arnold," said one of the boys.

"Can't he talk for himself?"

"Can he talk?" said another boy. "You should hear him sometimes." The little boys snickered. A few threw stones into the bright sky.

The counselor bent down and tried to get Arnold's attention. "So *you're* Arnold. Well I've been told about you."

Arnold lowered his eyes and puckered his lips as if to whistle.

"You've got the idea that you can do whatever you want around here. Well, not with me. Pick up that rifle."

Arnold watched the ant. The other boys were silent.

"I told you to pick it up," said the counselor.

Arnold looked at him. "I'm through using the rifle," he said.

"You're *what?*"

"Through using the rifle."

The other boys giggled.

"You're getting out of this period," said the counselor. "Right now. You go find Mr. Whiteman and tell him that I don't want you here with the rest of us. Tell him he'll have to reassign you to volleyball or arts and crafts. I'm certainly not going to bother with you."

Arnold got up.

"Do you hear me? Go tell Mr. Whiteman that. I'll check with him tonight to make sure you did."

Arnold turned his back and walked out of the clearing. He was on the path before the others began to talk. Then the rifles sounded again and frightened birds fluttered in the underbrush. He walked very slowly with his chin pressed down on his chest, his body swaying.

Soon he was out of the forest and standing on a grassy hill that overlooked the shining ring of beach and lake. There was a group of campers already there, including two of Arnold's bunkmates.

"Arnold!" called one of the campers.

The small boy came over.

"You're supposed to know everything," said the camper. "What's going on down there?"

Arnold looked. There were three automobiles and an ambulance parked in the shimmering sand. A few state policemen were walking out near the dock, and Mr. Whiteman was talking to another on the deserted beach.

"They won't let anybody down there," said the camper.

"They say we all have to go back to our bunks," cried a boy with glasses. "I think somebody was hurt."

"Did *you* hear anything?" asked the camper.

"No," said Arnold. He stood silently watching the activity on the beach and then turned abruptly in the direction of his bunk.

When he entered, the boys were waiting in line to take showers in the cramped bathroom. Uncle Jack wasn't around. Arnold opened his trunk, took out a book, and began reading. The campers were talking excitedly in the showers, and steam poured through the canvas doorway.   When they were finished they came out, wrapped in towels, and padded over to the front porch.   They stood there in dripping groups, staring off through the clearing at the lake.   Arnold continued to read.

Before dinner the campers usually gathered by the administration building for the lowering of the flag.   Mr. Whiteman would tell them the evening's activities and read any necessary announcements.   Tonight the ceremony had been called off, and the boys went directly to the dining hall from their bunks.   Arnold had changed his clothes, and he strolled along the gravel path behind the others.   On the steps of the old building he noticed a stone that gleamed in the fading sunlight. He picked it up and placed it in his pocket.

When he got inside he went slowly over to the mail table, where all late afternoon mail was stacked according to bunks.   He shuffled through the Bunk 12 pile, but there were no letters for him.   Angrily, he swept the other envelopes to the floor and went over to his table.   Uncle Jack was sitting at its head, his peeling face disturbed.   He still wore the same sportshirt, and there were dark perspiration stains at the armpits.

"Sit down, Arnold, you're late," he said.

Arnold took his seat.   He glanced at Mr. Whiteman's table across the crowded, noisy room.   The camp owner sat with three other men, and they were talking quietly.   Arnold looked down at his grapefruit and attacked it with his spoon.

One of the little boys, who had been lost in thought at the other end of the table, suddenly said in a loud clear voice, "Uncle Jack.   What happened to Bobby Thompson?   He drowned, didn't he?"

The large room was suddenly still.   Mr. Whiteman and the three men glanced up.   Uncle Jack frowned and waited for the rumble of conversation to begin again before he answered.   "Keep your voice down, Teddy.   I can hear you."

"But what happened, Uncle Jack?   He's not here for dinner tonight, and one of the guys in his bunk told me—"

The counselor interrupted him.   "Bobby Thompson had an accident, that's all. Mr. Whiteman will tell you all about it in the morning."

"I'll bet he's dead," said another boy, heaping sugar on his grapefruit.   "I heard they found him after rest period underneath the old docks up the lake."

"Now where did you hear a thing like that?"   Uncle Jack tried a tentative smile. "The way foolish rumors spread around here.   You boys dream up the wildest stories."

"It is *not* a wild story," said the boy stoutly.   "Why would the cops be up here if something wasn't wrong?   He's dead, all right."

"Maybe he was killed or something," another camper volunteered timidly.

"It was an accident," said Uncle Jack.   "A simple accident.   The police always come when there's an accident.   Now I don't want to hear any more about it."

"Bobby was in Bunk 9, wasn't he?" somebody whispered to Arnold.   "Uncle Paul's the head of that bunk, maybe he did it.   Nobody likes Uncle Paul anyway. I wish they'd put him in jail."

Arnold shrugged and buttered a piece of bread.

Dinner progressed and the big room throbbed with high, young voices and the crash of silverware. A waiter dropped his tray and it rattled like a coin on the floor. His tables laughed and applauded. Someone near the windows began to sing, *"Oh, the Deacon went down . . ."* The song caught on, moving from table to table across the warm room. But the old verses failed to bring the usual enthusiasm, and the song died before it reached the head counselors' table. Mr. Whiteman got up, his eyes lowered, and left the room.

Arnold ate slowly, finishing a second plate of ice cream after most of his bunk-mates had been excused. Uncle Paul came over and stopped beside the table.

"Hello, Paul," said Uncle Jack, mopping his mouth with a napkin. "What's up?"

The counselor frowned. "I had a little difficulty with this boy here on the rifle range today," he said, indicating Arnold. "He was causing trouble."

"Is that true, Arnold?" asked Uncle Jack.

Arnold licked his spoon carefully.

Uncle Paul shook his head. "His attitude is uncooperative. I sent him down to talk to Whiteman. Did he go?"

"Did you, Arnold?"

"No," said the little boy.

"Why not?" snapped Uncle Paul. "I *told* you to see him."

"I don't want to talk to him," said Arnold slowly.

"You're going to have to learn, fella, that you don't always do what you want."

Uncle Jack's face grew stern. "Arnold, go over to the office and see Mr. Whiteman right now. You'll probably catch him in. Then report to me after you see him."

"I don't want to talk to him. I already told you that."

"Maybe he'd better not, at least not tonight," said Uncle Paul. "Whiteman's got enough on his mind since this afternoon. Arnold can see him tomorrow."

"No, I want him to go tonight. Whiteman wants to see him sometime this week anyway. Now you go ahead, Arnold, and no back talk."

Arnold started to say something, but the two men did not seem in the mood for arguments. He slid back his chair. "Okay," he said. "But if any Special Delivery mail comes for me tonight, let me know about it." He got up and walked over to the door.

A light burned in the office of the administration building as Arnold came up the path. The place was constructed of white wood with mildewed window flaps that could be lowered in case of rain. It sat back near the clearing at the edge of the rippled lake, and Arnold could hear the cold waters sucking against the sides of discarded rowboats. He shivered a little as the night wind whipped along the path and pressed at his thin jacket. Off in the distance, orange lights went on in the recreation hall.

Arnold pushed quietly through the screen door and stood still in the room's mild darkness. Mr. Whiteman sat behind a desk, talking on the telephone. Arnold went over to a high bookcase near a row of filing cabinets and scanned the titles. He slid out one of the books and began paging through it.

Mr. Whiteman hung up the phone and swung around in his chair. "Oh, hello, Arnold," he said. "I didn't hear you come in." He was a tall, heavy man, with a brown face and short white hair.

Arnold put the book back and approached the circle of light on the desk.

"What were you reading, son?"

"*The Psychology of Children,* by Klarmann," said the boy.

"Oh, yes. That thing's been kicking around this office for years."

"It's a new book," said Arnold. "You probably just got it this season."

Mr. Whiteman tilted back in his chair and looked at the boy. He took a pipe from a desk rack and tapped it on his palm.

"Well sit down, son. You want a Coke or something? Some soda?"

Arnold shook his head. "I just ate a little while ago."

Mr. Whiteman packed the pipe from a small pouch and lit it. He puffed vigorously for a moment, then settled back even further in his chair. "What's the problem, Arnold? What can I do for you?"

"Uncle Paul and Uncle Jack told me to see you. Uncle Paul is mad at me because I didn't listen to him on the rifle range this afternoon."

"Well why didn't you, son? After all, he's your instructor."

"He doesn't like me."

Mr. Whiteman laughed comfortably. "Of *course* he likes you. Why that's downright silly, Arnold. Uncle Paul likes all of the campers."

The little boy was silent.

"Now come on, Arnold. You don't actually believe that any of the counselors has anything against you. Do you?"

Arnold looked up, his small eyes momentarily alive in the glow of the desk lamp. "My mother's been writing you, hasn't she?"

"What's that?"

"She won't answer my letters because she wants to keep me here. But she's been writing to you."

Mr. Whiteman expelled a long sigh. He pressed his finger tips against the edge of the desk. "Maybe we'd better have a real talk, eh, son? Now I'm going to level with you, and I expect you to be honest with me. Your mother *has* written to me. She said you're unhappy here. Is that true?"

"Yes."

"Well why, Arnold? You're here for a vacation, to have a good time. Why don't you like it?"

Arnold compressed his lips and remained silent.

"Is it because the other boys don't understand you? Is that it? Frankly, son, we would have put you into an advanced bunk, but we didn't think you'd enjoy yourself there."

Arnold toyed with the zipper on his jacket, sliding it up and down.

"I'm not going to lie to you, Arnold. I've been checking with your counselor and some of the campers. I understand that you're being given a rough time. I heard that somebody cut all the strings off your tennis racket." Arnold nodded. "And I also know that somebody stole a tube from your radio set."

"I got it back." The boy's thin fingers snapped the zipper along its grooved track.

"That's not the point. If you're being bothered, I want to know about it. You should have come and told me these things." Mr. Whiteman's pipe had gone out and he relit it impatiently. "Now who's behind this, Arnold? Are they boys in your bunk?"

"No."

"How many are there? I can dock them their free period if they give you any more trouble."

"Only one boy's been bothering me, and you don't have to do anything."

"Look, Arnold," said Mr. Whiteman earnestly, "I'm not asking you to tell tales or anything. I just want to make things better for you. Your mother's been very concerned about your welfare, and I want to be able to tell her that you're getting along."

"Can I have a Coke now?" asked Arnold.

Mr. Whiteman frowned and went over to a small refrigerator. He removed a bottle, opened it, and handed it to Arnold. Then he sat down, rather wearily. "Now I'd like to know the name of the boy who's been picking on you. Arnold?" Arnold wiped off the top of the bottle and drank the Coke slowly. "Tell me, Arnold."

Arnold rolled the bottle between his hands. "It's not important now."

"Tell me."

"Okay. It was Bobby Thompson."

Mr. Whiteman paled. "Did you . . . say Bobby Thompson was the boy who was giving you trouble?"

"Yes."

Mr. Whiteman stood up very carefully and moved around the desk. He pulled on his coat. "I want you to stay here for a few minutes, Arnold." His voice was uneven. "I want you to stay right here. Promise me that. I just have to see somebody for a minute."

Arnold put the bottle on the floor. "Okay," he said.

"Read that book you were looking at. I'll be right back. All right?" He went over to the door and looked back at the boy. Then he left. Arnold heard him begin to run as soon as he reached the gravel path.

The little boy stood up. He wandered around the room, his hands in his pockets, then went over to the desk. He sat down in Mr. Whiteman's chair, opened a drawer, and took out some stationery. He uncapped a fountain pen and began to write on the creamy paper.

Dear Mother:

This is the last time I'm going to write unless I hear from you. I want to come home . . .

RICHARD STARK

Just a Little Impractical Joke

Harry Chesterton, murderer, surveyed the scene of carnage. Everything was in place, everything was right. Miriam lay sprawled on her tummy on the bathroom floor, her head under the sink. The bathmat, the towel, the soap and washcloth and loofah, all were in position. The red-stained scissors lay on the floor near Miriam's right elbow. The bread knife was clutched in Miriam's right hand.

Perfect. Everything was perfect.

Harry nodded in satisfaction and stepped out of the bathroom, closing the door behind him. He walked down the hall to the master bedroom, removed his clothing, donned his terrycloth robe, and whistled his way back to the bathroom. He turned his face toward the kitchen. "Don't run water for a few minutes, Miriam!" he shouted, loud enough to be heard by any neighbor in a backyard or next to an open window. "I'm going to take a shower now!"

He nodded again, whistled some more, and went into the bathroom, closing the door behind him again. He stepped over Miriam, who was in the same position, bleeding quietly on the floor, and removed his robe. He turned on the shower, adjusted the flow to the force and temperature he wanted, and stepped into the tub, pulling the shower curtain closed behind him. He lathered briskly, and burst into song.

He was happy, deliriously happy. After three years of careful planning, of working on and rejecting scheme after scheme after scheme, Harry Chesterton had finally found the one absolutely foolproof way to murder his wife.

Foolproof, it was foolproof. And now Miriam was dead. After a decent interval of mourning—a safe interval—he would marry dear sweet Cathy, who would never, never, never turn into the shrill nag that Miriam had become in seven years of marriage. "When are you going to settle down, Harry? When are you going to give up these get-rich-quick schemes of yours and find a decent job, Harry? The department store called again about the payments on the furniture, Harry; they say they're going to take it away. What are you going to do about *that*, Harry? You're just lucky your schemes haven't landed you in jail, Harry, lucky, that's all *I* have to say."

How accurate. That was all she had to say. Over and over and over again, that was all Miriam had to say. Nag, nag, nag. How could a man concentrate on his ambitions and plans and prospects with a nagging wife hounding him all the time?

He couldn't, that was all, he just couldn't.

It would be different with Cathy. Cathy believed in him, that was the important thing. Cathy would stand behind him, help him in countless ways. Why, the very fact that she was the daughter of a man who owned thirty-seven percent of National Atronics and was chairman of that company's board of directors was helpful. That very fact alone.

Harry wielded the loofah and sang lustily of moon and June, while dreaming of Long Island estates, vacations on the Riviera, Porsches, and Mercedes-Benzes . . .

His leisurely shower done, Harry shut the water off and stepped from the tub. He was a tall, lithe, well-muscled young man of thirty-two, who didn't look a day over thirty-one. He now sat down next to the sink and surveyed the three clipped toenails on his right foot. He had cut those earlier in the day, since the scissors would not be available for use at this stage of the proceedings.

Planning, that was all it took. Careful planning.

All at once, he shouted, *"Miriam!"* at the top of his voice, and thumped both bare feet against the floor. Then he stood, left the bathroom, and lay down on his stomach on the hall rug. He did twelve fast push-ups and, completely out of breath, got to his feet again and staggered nude to the living room. He grabbed for the phone, and dialed the operator. "Operator!" he cried, gasping a bit. "An ambulance! The police! I—I've killed my wife!"

The house was absolutely full of people. There were people with cameras and pieces of chalk and black bags crammed into the bathroom. There were uniformed policemen by the front door, and more uniformed policemen in the living room. There were two detectives in civilian clothing in the kitchen, talking to Mr. and Mrs. Anderson from downstairs. There were reporters all over the sidewalk and front lawn and first floor porch, kept by firm silent policemen from rushing up to the second-floor flat, where the terrible accident had taken place.

And there was a detective named Hotchkiss in the bedroom, listening to the rattled, grief-stricken, and totally inconsolable husband tell his story for the seventh time.

"It was just a joke," Harry was saying. He lit a new cigarette from the butt of the old and nervously stubbed the butt into an ashtray. He was sitting distractedly on the edge of the bed, dressed again in the terrycloth robe, his black hair now dry, but terribly uncombed. He had made the phone call at just a few minutes after four, and now it was well after eight. Over four hours, and he was still telling his story.

"A joke," echoed Detective Hotchkiss. He was short and stocky, with a roundish heavy-jowled face and sad beagle eyes. His suit was gray and rumpled, his shoes black and scuffed, his tie blue and wrinkled. He wasn't a very prepossessing figure.

"I'm sure it was," said Harry emotionally. He dragged on the cigarette. "I can't believe she really *meant* to . . ." He let the sentence trail away, and shook his head in apparent agitation.

"You saw this movie last night, is that right?" asked Detective Hotchkiss.

"Yes. Like I've told you, it was all about a homicidal maniac, and a woman was brutally stabbed to death in a shower. We talked about it on the way home last night, joking about how neither of us would dare take a shower for months. We—it was just last night, and we were laughing together, we—"

"All right, Mr. Chesterton," said Hotchkiss. "Take it easy."

"Yes," said Harry. "Thank you. Yes. Anyway, today, when I told Miriam I was going to take a shower, she joked about it again, she—she said she couldn't see how I had the nerve."

"Those were her exact words?"

"I—-yes, I—I'm not sure. She said something about that, she—" Harry pressed a trembling hand to his forehead. "I'm no longer sure of anything," he said brokenly.

"Yes. I understand." Detective Hotchkiss, behind a perfunctory sympathy, was watchful and expressionless. "What happened next?" he asked.

"Well, I showered, and then I was sitting clipping my toenails, when she came in, wi-with the knife. Brandishing the knife. It was—it was just like in the movie last night."

"A practical joke, is that it?" said Hotchkiss.

"It *must* have been. But then—at the time—it was so sudden, and so startling—"

"You reacted instinctively, is that it?"

"Yes, that's it. I jumped to my feet and—-well, I was holding the scissors, and—"

"You stabbed her," said Hotchkiss unemotionally.

Harry winced. "Yes. I stabbed her."

"I see." Hotchkiss solemnly surveyed the lack of crease in his right trouser leg. "Did your wife go in for practical jokes often, Mr. Chesterton?"

Harry was ready for that question. The obvious answer was to say yes, that she did such things all the time. But that would have given the whole thing away. In the first place, the police would have reasoned that Harry might have expected some such stunt from his wife, and a murderous shock reaction would be inexplicable. In the second place, it wouldn't take much questioning of friends and relatives to determine that Miriam was anything but a jester. A more sour, stolid, down-to-earth type couldn't be imagined.

So he said, "No, not really. That was what made it so startling. Oh, once in a while, I suppose. We've both kidded with one another from time to time."

"I see," said Hotchkiss. "One more thing. The scissors. They weren't the usual nail-clipping style of scissors, they were much larger than that. If they'd been nail-clipping scissors—"

"Yes, I know," said Harry sorrowfully, nodding his head. "Miriam would still be alive. But my wife—well, you know how women are about tools, never using the right tools for the right job. Miriam—well, she was that way. She's used scissors for screwdrivers, pliers, hammers, all sorts of jobs for which they weren't intended. That pair of scissors is the last in the house, that's why I was using them.''

That part was the truth. That had been another of Miriam's irritating habits— a minor irritation, compared to the rest, but an irritation nonetheless, like her insistence upon squeezing the middle of the toothpaste tube—and practically all of the tools in his basement workshop bore the scars of her usage.

There was a bump-bump from the hall, and Harry dropped the cigarette in alarm. Stooping to pick it up before it could burn the unpaid-for rug, he said, ''What's that?''

''I imagine they're taking your wife away,'' said Hotchkiss.

''Oh.''

Harry fumblingly lit a new cigarette. His nervousness was only partially an act. It was one thing to plan something like this, work out the details as Harry had worked them out. It was something else entirely to be actually in the middle of the plan, the Rubicon having been crossed, the die having been cast, the wife having been launched into eternity and the house being full of policemen. Something else entirely. No matter how sure he was of his plan, its execution was still nerve-wracking.

But the plan was foolproof, no matter how watchful this detective was. Why shouldn't it be? It had the impromptu idiocy of truth. Who would expect a man to murder his wife in cold blood, with such a completely inane cover-up story? The inanity of the thing was what saved it.

Hotchkiss got to his feet. ''I guess that's it for tonight,'' he said. ''I know you're still upset. But I'd like you to come in tomorrow and dictate a statement. Do you know where headquarters is?''

''I think so,'' said Harry. ''Across the street from the Strand Theater, isn't it?''

''Right. Is there anyone you'd like us to call? To stay with you?''

''No,'' said Harry. ''That's all right. I'll take a pill, I guess. I think I'd just rather be alone for a while.''

''All right, then,'' said Hotchkiss. ''And you come on down to the station tomorrow, and dictate a statement. Ask for me at the desk—Hotchkiss.''

''I'll do that,'' Harry promised.

Hotchkiss paused in the doorway. ''Don't plan any extended trips for a while,'' he said.

''Of course not,'' said Harry.

It was a lovely morning. Spring it was, dripping with sunshine, the grass all about as green as an Irishman on March seventeenth. Birds were singing, too. All in all, a lovely morning.

Harry got up at nine-thirty. He wouldn't have awakened then, except the boss called to make inquiry as to his whereabouts. For the last couple of months, while waiting for various really big prospects to break one way or the other, Harry had worked for Smiling Stanley's Guaranteed Used Cars, as a commission salesman. And Smiling Stanley now called at nine-thirty in the morning, wondering just where in hell Harry was.

"I'm in bed," Harry told him.

And precisely what, Smiling Stanley wanted to know, did he think he was doing in bed?

"Sleeping," Harry told him.

And did Harry know, Smiling Stanley snarled, just what time it was?

Harry checked the alarm clock. "Nine-thirty," he said.

Then just why, roared Smiling Stanley, wasn't Harry at work?

"Because," Harry told him evenly, "my wife passed away last night. Don't you ever read the papers?"

Smiling Stanley didn't say a word.

Harry said, "Hello?"

Smiling Stanley sort of choked.

"All right, then," said Harry, and he returned the phone to its cradle. He smiled a bit at the telephone, looked at the emptiness in the bed beside him and smiled, looked out the window at the green and sunny spring, and smiled.

What a lovely morning!

He scrunched down beneath the covers. The whole bed to himself! He closed his eyes and composed himself for sleep.

But he couldn't get back to sleep. No matter how lovely the morning, no matter how delicious it was to have the whole bed to himself, no matter how charming the notion that no nagging harridan was going to come bursting in from the kitchen wanting to know when he was going to drag his lazy self out of bed and go earn an honest dollar, no matter how delightful all of life had suddenly become, Harry couldn't go to sleep.

He couldn't go to sleep, because the morning paper was on the front porch.

He just had to get up and read his press notices, right away.

He quit the bed at last, and donned his robe, glancing at himself in the full-length mirror on the closet door. Yes sir, he was a fine figure of a man. A fine *happy* figure of a man. He beamed at himself, sparkle-toothed.

"Cathy," he whispered, "you are a lucky little girl."

Should he call her? No, not yet, wait a few days anyway. No sense doing something stupid at this point in the game, exciting anyone's suspicions.

Harry walked through the house to the front door, and down the stairs to the porch. The newspaper was there, and so were two full quarts of milk, homogenized grade A. The newspaper had been folded by the delivery boy, for better throwing, and Harry tucked it under his arm still folded, putting off the lovely moment when he would read about himself, with all the gory details. He picked up the milk bottles, closed the front door, and went scuffing back upstairs in his old slippers.

The milk in the refrigerator, a cup of steaming coffee on the kitchen table, Harry at last sat down and opened the paper.

He wasn't on the first page, or the second page, or the third. He was frowning, just about convinced that he hadn't made the paper at all, when finally he found the headline, on the first page of the second section.   Of course.   Naturally.   The first section was international news—FAR EAST CRISIS—and the second section was local news.

WOMAN SLAIN
IN PRACTICAL JOKE

Mrs. Miriam Chesterton, of 148 Coleridge Drive, was reported slain yesterday afternoon, the bizarre climax of a bizarre practical joke.   According to her husband, Harry Chesterton, the good-looking Mrs. Chesterton played an unfortunate practical joke, the result of a motion picture she had seen only the night before, a joke which ended in her tragic death.

According to the grieving husband, stunned by this fantastic turn of events . . .

It was absolutely the most amusing thing Harry had ever read in his entire life. He read the item three times, all the way through, and then he went to get a pair of scissors to clip it out of the paper.   I'll start a scrapbook, he thought to himself.

After five minutes of fruitless search, he suddenly remembered that the last pair of scissors in the house had gone out the night before, embedded in Miriam.

He was in the process of carefully sawing the article free with a razor blade when the urge to call Cathy came over him once again.

But that would be idiocy.   In the first place, he had, of course, never told her about his plan.   No matter how much she loved him, he didn't want to test her feelings quite that far.   She might, if she knew the truth, be somewhat loath to pledge her troth with him.   No woman could feel completely at ease with her husband, if she knew for a fact that he had hastened her predecessor's journey to the desk of Saint Peter.

Besides which, Cathy, when all was said and done, just wasn't very bright.   She wasn't exactly the type who could be trusted with a secret of such import.   No, she just wasn't the smartest girl in the world.

But, oh, was she rich!   Or, at least, she was going to be rich, when her old man kicked the bucket.

In a year or two, given the right circumstances, perhaps he could figure out a little something for the old man, too.   The thought had never occurred to him before, but now it did, and he rather liked it.   What was real creativity on his part, Miriam always called schemes.   And he did seem to have a special knack for murder.

In the meantime, of course, Cathy had to be kept completely out of the picture, as she had been up till now.   Detective Hotchkiss could entertain vague suspicions, but until he was given some item of proof or of motive, that was all he could do.

Cathy would be kept out of sight until all this blew over and was forgotten. And then—marriage.

This thought through, Harry finished sawing out the clipping and went whistling toward the bedroom.   He suddenly stopped whistling when he remembered the

Andersons, downstairs.   Lord knew if they could hear whistling from upstairs, but just to be on the safe side he should content himself with silent smiles while at home.

Well, it wouldn't be for much longer.   Soon, he would say farewell forever to this cheap, grubby kind of life.   No more living in two-family houses, no more having to take the bus downtown, no more having to con suspicious yokels into buying junky automobiles.   And Harry knew that at Smiling Stanley's, the bribe paid to obtain the state inspection tag was a normal part of the overhead.

But that was all behind him now—or almost behind him.   Ahead of him awaited yachts, and private estates, and maybe even a cute French upstairs maid . . .

Reflecting on these happy thoughts, Harry entered the bedroom and laid the clipping lovingly on the dresser.   This afternoon, he decided, while he was downtown, he would have to buy a scrapbook.

He went back to the kitchen, found the remains of his coffee stone cold, and decided to make himself a new cup.   Then he thought it might be a nice idea to have an entire meal—five or six eggs and lots of bacon and piece after piece of toast—because it was the kind of day that deserved a good breakfast.

It was a *lovely* day.

He got to the police station shortly after noon, and it was a breeze.   The only troublesome part was the waiting.   He kept having to wait for people, and then someone would come along and explain some legal point to him or some such thing, and he would nod, and then he would wait some more.   But, finally, a male stenographer appeared, pencil and notebook at the ready, and took down in shorthand Harry's story of the killing.   Then there was some more waiting, while the statement was typed—with millions of carbons—and then he signed all the copies of the statement and left the police station, with writer's cramp.

It was almost five o'clock, he discovered, and the bus stop was crowded with people waiting to go home.   Every bus left the corner groaning with its overload of standees.   The sidewalks were jammed with rushing humanity, most of it female and most of it vicious.

To be buffeted about by this rush-hour crowd, Harry felt, was just too much. Here he was on the verge of a life of leisure, and he was going to have to stand up all the way home on a bus.

No, he wasn't, either.   He'd just stay downtown until the rush hour was over. He wanted to buy a scrapbook, anyway.

Harry headed for the five-and-dime at once.   He bought his scrapbook there— a lovely thing, blood red, with "Memories" engraved on the cover in sentimental script—and left with it beneath his arm.

He deserved a drink, he told himself.   He hadn't had a thing to drink since yesterday.

He *deserved* a drink.

At the same time, he wondered if it would look good for the so-recently-bereaved husband to be tilting a few at the bar?   Some people might give him the benefit of the doubt, say it was simply a case of a grieving husband drowning his sorrows, but others, of a coarser nature, might get the idea it was a not-so-grief-stricken husband tasting feedom.

So Harry compromised.   He went for a drink, but he went into a bar that had never seen his face before, one way down by the railroad depot, and with a filthy window and a surly bartender and a bar half-full of sozzled regulars who probably hadn't seen a newspaper since V-J Day.

There was a certain ironic sweetness in being in this particular bar.   Here were the dregs of humanity, in their natural habitat.   And here was Harry Chesterton, on his way fom middle-class insecurity to upper-class wealth, stopping off in this lower-class dump to hoist a few before moving on.   It kind of gave him a sense of history.

Sense of history or no, he wasn't prepared to stand cheek-by jowl with the bums at the bar.   He got a bottle of beer and a not-too-clean glass from the surly bartender, and sat down in the last booth to the back, on the side wall across fom the bar. He drank out of the bottle, leaving the not-too-clean glass alone.

He sat facing the back wall, the high top of the booth shielding him from the view of anyone in the street and all but one of the loungers at the bar.   That one lounger was leaning against the wall at the end-curve of the bar.   Harry glanced at him, recognized the man's type, and looked immediately away.

He didn't like the type.   A stocky, large-faced, ham-handed individual in work pants and flannel shirt and brown leather truck-driver's jacket.   He was the only one in the bar making any noise at all.   He was bellowing a joke of some sort at the surly bartender, who was ignoring him.   It wasn't that he was drunk; in fact, he seemed to be nearly sober.   He was just one of the loud, crass braggarts and bullies of this world.

Harry knew the type.   Braggarts and bullies.   It reminded him of grammar school, when people like that yowling Neanderthal over there used to beat him up and make fun of him because he always managed to get good grades and always tried to get in good with the teachers.

It was the loud vicious type who had made his childhood difficult, and had later worsened his lot during his compulsory two years of goldbricking in the Army. On various jobs, he had run into loud oafs like this one, who thought their strength of arm made them superior to their intellectual peers.

The bully in question came to the end of his joke at last, and silence descended on the bar.   Blessed silence.   Harry glanced up again, and looked quickly away.

The man was looking at him.   Staring at him.   Studying him.

Oh no, thought Harry, oh no.   He sees the clothing I'm wearing, he sees my face, he knows me for the bullyable type.   If only he'll leave me alone.

Memories òf childhood, of the Army, flashed through Harry's mind.   He drank from the beer bottle, and chanced another look.

The man was still studying him, frowning in ludicrous concentration.   All at once, he snapped his fingers, and cried, "Ah hah!"

Harry, baffled and frightened, looked quickly away again.

But the man was not to be put off.   He left his bar-stool and came striding over to the table.   And, of course, none of the other people in the bar paid him the slightest attention.   Not that any of them would come to Harry's aid, anyway.

The man loomed over Harry and growled, "Ain't you the two-bit chiseler works for Smiling Stanley?"

Harry looked up in surprise, and all at once recognized the man.   Of course, he remembered him now.   A railroad worker.   Harry, three or four weeks ago, had sold him a little old junkheap that practically ran on rubber bands.

Harry replied unhesitatingly, "No, I'm not."

"Yes, you are," insisted the man.   "You're the chiseler works for Smiling Stanley."

"No, I'm not," said Harry again.

"You calling me a liar," said the man.   He reached fumblingly into his pocket. "I've got you *now,* you so-and-so!" he yelled, and withdrew from his pocket a small gun, which he pointed directly at Harry's left eye.

Detective Hotchkiss was being patient.   "Twice in a row, Mister Chesterton?" he said, and his whole tone implied that twice in a row was rather too much.

They were at a different booth in the same bar.   Harry, absolutely panic-stricken, babbled, "How did I know?   He pointed the gun at me—"

"And you slammed him with the beer bottle," said Detective Hotchkiss.

"How'd I know it was just a joke?   He didn't *act* as though it was just a joke."

Two men carrying a large wicker basket went by, and the basket bumped the table.   Harry looked at it in terror.   Then it went on by and out the front door, and Harry looked back at Detective Hotchkiss.   Detective Hotchkiss had the gun in his hand.   He pulled the trigger.   A little section in the top of the gun snapped open, and flame came out.

It was a cigarette lighter.

Detective Hotchkiss released the trigger, which closed the section in the top and snuffed out the flame.   He put the lighter down on the table between them, and studied it.

"Does that thing *look* like a real gun, Mister Chesterton?"

"It all happened so *fast,*" wailed Harry.   "Ask the other people in here, ask them if he didn't—"

Detective Hotchkiss shook his head.   "None of them were paying any attention at all," he said.

"But that's the way it *happened!*" cried Harry.

Detective Hotchkiss sighed.   "Twice in a row," he said.   "Who was he, Chesterton?"

"Just a man I'd sold a car to," said Harry.   "He acted as though he was mad at me because of the car."

"Of course," said Detective Hotchkiss.   "Of course, Chesterton.   And did this gentleman——what was his name, by the way?"

"I don't know," said Harry.   "I don't remember."

"I see.   At any rate, did he by any chance know your wife?   Your *late* wife, I mean."

"Know my *wife?*"   Great heavens, what was the man thinking?   "Of course not!   How could he know my wife?"

Detective Hotchkiss shook his head.   "I don't know," he said thoughtfully.   "This changes the picture.   Now, if there were any reason why you might have wanted this gentleman dead, or if there were any reason why you might have wanted your wife dead—"

"He came at me so *fast!*" wailed Harry.

"Yes, yes, of course.   But if there were, perhaps, a motive of some sort, something you haven't as yet told us—"

"There's nothing!" cried Harry.   "Nothing!"

Detective Hotchkiss got to his feet.   "Perhaps," he said, "you ought to come on back to the station with me.   I think we have to talk."

They talked for fourteen hours before Harry mentioned Cathy.

JEAN POTTS

Murderer #2

It would never have occurred to Rolfe Jackson to kill his mother if it had not been absolutely necessary.

He was not a criminal. He was an artist. (True, there were those who held that the pictures Rolfe painted were crimes of a particularly brutal sort. They were fools, of course; he had not yet found himself, that was all.)

Besides, he was really quite fond of the old girl. He had her to thank for his name, for instance. She might so easily have called him Henry or Albert, both of which were traditional family names. Henry Jackson. Albert Jackson. Why, with such a name he might never have had the heart to embark on his artistic career at all! Certainly the identity he had created for himself as Rolfe J.—which was the way he chose to sign his pictures—would have been inconceivable.

He was quite a character, this Rolfe J. who had been built up with such care and who would someday come into his own. Hard-boiled. Dedicated. A Hemingway among painters. There was his stubby beard to prove it, and his lumberjack taste in clothes. Without them, he would have looked what he was—short and pudgy. With them he was impressively burly. Rolfe J. talked tough. He had choice unprintable phrases for the critics and for the work of other artists. He sneered at creature comforts. Publicly, that is. Very few people ever saw the inside of his apartment, and so very few people knew how much he loved luxury.

None of it—his whole beloved, outwardly rough-hewn, secretly luxurious life—would have been possible without Mother. Because it was Mother's father who had set up the trust fund, and the trust fund saved Rolfe J. from having to make a living.

Yet it was also the trust fund that made it absolutely necessary for him to kill Mother. The realization hit him, like a blow from a fist, while he and Mr. Webb were having their little talk. Mr. Webb was Mother's attorney, and a friend of many years' standing; he lived in an apartment just across the hall from hers. Rolfe was instantly wary when one night Mr. Webb asked him to come in. His own relations with the man had always been notable for their lack of cordiality. No open quarrels. Just a mutual case of low estimation. Mr. Webb looked like a Yankee farmer—stringy, lantern-jawed, granite-eyed. His study was just what you would expect. Rolfe had never in his life sat on a more uncomfortable chair.

"I've been meaning to have a little talk with you for some time," Mr. Webb began. "Ever since your mother had this stroke. How are things going with the nurse?"

Mr. Webb had found the nurse for Mother. An ugly, devoted woman named Stella, who came in every day. By now Mother could manage alone, at night. But she was never going to get beyond the wheelchair stage. Poor old girl. What a change after all the bustle and pressure of the job she had had for years with one of the ladies' magazines . . .

"Stella? She's a paragon," said Rolfe. He felt, as usual, an impulse to shock Mr. Webb, jolt him out of his flinty composure. "If she wasn't god-awful ugly I'd marry her, to save her salary."

Mr. Webb just looked at him. He had a talent for the unsettling silence. Finally he said, "That's what your mother's worried about. Money. She shouldn't be. But she is. So I thought we ought to get the whole thing straightened out."

"What's to straighten out? She's got the pension from her office—"

"Peanuts," said Mr. Webb curtly. "Hardly pays the rent. That's why she's worried. She knows she's going to have to dip into your trust fund to pay the nurse and the doctors' bills." He opened his brief case and spread some papers out on the desk in front of him. "I don't know how familiar you are with the terms of your grandfather's will. It might be well to review them. He left his money in trust for you, with the proviso that your mother may draw on it, in case of emergency. Now I don't believe anyone would question the fact that your mother's illness constitutes an emergency."

"Who's questioning it?" said Rolfe irritably. "Not me."

"I'm glad of that. It's only fair to warn you that the drain on your trust fund will be considerable. Very likely you will find it necessary to curtail your present and future expenses." Mr. Webb said this with relish. "Your living arrangements, for example, aren't exactly economical. My own suggestion would be that you move in with your mother. Why not? You're already living in the same apartment house. It would simply mean paying rent on one apartment, instead of two. As far as Stella's salary, and her appearance, are concerned"—he produced a wintry smile—"it's not necessary for you to marry her. Since you don't go out to work anyway, I don't see why you shouldn't take over some of the care of your mother. Combine art and nursing, say, two or three days a week. It would mean quite a saving."

It was Rolfe's turn to just look at Mr. Webb. For once in his life he had nothing whatever to say. Mr. Webb did not seem to notice. Having curtailed living expenses to his Yankee heart's content, he was now proceeding to "go over the figures."

They appalled Rolfe. He had not realized their true nature until now; it was like the moment when the dentist's drill touches a live nerve, sending out shoots of excruciating pain. He sat bolt upright (there was no other way to sit in that contemptible chair of Mr. Webb's), his eyes riveted on Mr. Webb's bony face, while he watched his beautiful trust fund trickle away day after day, year after

year.   The doctor had said Mother might live for years.   Fifteen, even twenty.
And every day of every one of those years meant ten dollars for Stella, at least
another ten for food and medicine and miscellaneous expenses.

And Rolfe was supposed to stand for this without a murmur of protest; he
was—yes, Mr. Webb was making it quite clear—he was supposed to stand for it
gladly, just because Mother had gone out of her way to keep the trust fund intact,
until now.   As if that were Rolfe's fault!   He hadn't asked her to pay for his education, the summers in France, all the rest of it, out of her own earnings.   It
was her business, how she chose to spend her salary.   And yet, now that there
was no more salary, he was to be penalized, his very life was to go down
the drain!

Well, he *wouldn't* stand for it.   They were dealing with a man, not a mouse.
And no ordinary man, either; he would show them, once and for all, the caliber
of Rolfe J.   The dream, the vision of himself as a man among men, touched with
genius, ruthlessly molding his own destiny, had never been more vivid.   He
would—

"As I say," Mr. Webb was concluding, as he shuffled his papers back into their
folder, "I'm glad you're taking a sensible attitude about this.   Even if you weren't,
it wouldn't make any difference.   There's not a thing you can do about it."

That was what Mr. Webb thought.   Rolfe knew better.   It had hit him in the
second before Mr. Webb stopped speaking: the flash of crystal understanding, and
the resolution.

Nothing he could do about it?   Ah, but there was, there was.   Something so
obvious, so necessary and right (or why should Mother, simply by living, cheat
him of what was rightfully his?) that even a fool like Mr. Webb ought to see it.
He didn't though.   There was a gleam of satisfaction in his granite eyes as he said
good-night.   He thought he had scored, in this little talk of theirs.   He thought
he had taken Rolfe down a notch or two.

Out in the hall, Rolfe paused a moment, waiting for his heart to stop pounding.
Then he let himself into Mother's apartment and called cheerily, "Anybody home?
How about a glass of sherry?"

Mother was in bed—Stella always got her settled for the night before she left—
but bright-eyed, obviously brimming over with news.   She was a fat little woman,
with a halo of white curly hair.   "You'll never guess what happened to me today,"
she began, while Rolfe poured the sherry.   "I was approached by an ex-narcotics
addict!"

"What?   Now really, Mother—"

"Really.   Oh, a strictly business approach.   He wants me to help him write a
book.   'I Was a Narcotics Addict'—that sort of thing.   I must say, he doesn't
look like a man with a lurid past.   Quite presentable.   I don't know why I—
Maybe it was his missionary zeal that put me off.   This project seems to be kind
of a crusade with him."

"That's normal, isn't it?"   said Rolfe.   "Look at the reformed drunks that go
around spreading the good word.   I suppose it works the same with dope addicts."

"I suppose.   Or maybe it was his name.   It's Borden, and all I could think of was that little verse about Lizzie Borden taking an axe . . . It's awful to have a free-wheeling mind like mine.''

They both laughed. Rolfe became aware of a prickle at the back of his neck, a tremor of obscure excitement. But he kept his voice casual.

"You turned him down, then?''

"No, I told him I'd think it over and let him know tomorrow. It *would* be fun, you know." Just the thought made her look, for a moment, quite like her old busy, enthusiastic self. "And then supposing it turned out to be a best seller and we all got rich.''

"I wasn't thinking of the money," said Rolfe truthfully. "Nice as it would be. I was just thinking how much you'd enjoy having something to do again.''

"You think I'm being silly?" she asked wistfully. "You think I ought to do it?" She waited or his answer, and at once the illusion of vigor vanished. For in the old days she would not have needed Rolfe's advice, she would have known her own mind. Now uncertainty clouded her eyes. Her whole face sagged into lines of doubt, almost of fear. But it was the delicacy of her temple that fascinated Rolfe. Above her plump cheek it was slightly sunken and threaded with blue. It looked fragile as an egg shell.

"Good Lord, Mother, I've never seen the man, so how can I tell! And I've been wondering, how'd he happen to get in touch with you?''

"Well, he works in a bindery, a book bindery. Someone there suggested an editor, who in turn suggested me. So he looked me up in the phone book—''

"If you want me to look him over when he turns up again tomorrow," said Rolfe, "I'll be glad to . . .''

The deal was clinched next day, on the spot. Mother, now that Rolfe had disposed of her original vague doubts, was frankly delighted at the prospect. So was Borden.

Only Stella held out. She cornered Rolfe as he left; she had been lurking in the kitchen, waiting to speak her piece. Which she did, in an ominous whisper. "I don't like it, Mr. Jackson. I just think you and your mother are taking an awful chance, letting that dope fiend in here three evenings a week. Oh, I know. He claims he's cured. I've heard that one before. They're none of them ever cured. Not for sure. I don't like it. Not one little bit.''

Good old Stella. Under her white nylon uniform she wore what appeared to be a suit of armor; it jutted out in ridges across her meaty shoulders and back. Lumpy wriggles of varicose veins showed through her white stockings. And she dyed her hair shoe-polish black. As ugly as ever, and yet Rolfe regarded her with something very like affection. Good old doubting Stella.

"*Sh,*" he whispered back. "The only reason I'm going along with it is that she needs something to keep her occupied. It's brightened her up already. Don't worry, I'll make sure she's never left alone with him. That's why I insisted on meeting the fellow, to make sure he seemed all right.''

"All right!" Stella snorted. "With those gooseberry eyes of his, and those long twitchy hands? Gives me the shivers just to think of him.''

But even Stella seemed to forget her doubts as two weeks, three weeks, went by, with no danger signals from Borden. Rolfe found it necessary to remind her now and then, in an unobtrusive way.

He himself was busy exploring. He had been quick to sense Borden's potentialities. But they would remain only potentialities until he had found the way to use them. To use them he must know his man, through and through.

He found the whole project almost alarmingly easy. No one could have been more cooperative than Borden, either in striking up a friendship or in promoting the exploration of his own character. The circumstances were favorable too. In his capacity as watchdog, Rolfe was always present on Borden evenings, for Stella—having first given Mother her early dinner and settled her in bed—left at seven thirty. Rolfe did not intrude on the book sessions, which were held in the bedroom; he lounged in the living room, pretending to read, waiting for Borden to emerge, ready with his suggestion—so natural—that they drop into the bar and grill next door for a sociable drink. Borden snapped at the invitation like a hungry dog at a bone. The drink or two often stretched out to dinner and beyond: a whole solid evening of analyzing Borden.

It was a subject that fascinated them both. Borden's experiences as a psychiatric patient had left him with an insatiable interest in his own mental processes. Sometimes he would work himself up into a transport of confession, like a religious convert glorying in the spectacle of his remembered sins. His prominent green eyes dilated even more than usual, and he would sway on his bar stool, making jerky gestures or running his hand through his lank blond hair.

At other times he was coldly objective. "It's a classic type," he would say. "The rejected child." And he would tick off the "classic" elements—the family-deserting father, the indifferent mother, the succession of even more indifferent substitute parents. The few friends he had managed to make always ended by sloughing him off—frightened away, probably, by the violence of his attachment to them. For he was violent. He was so famished for affection that he could not help it.

"You'll never know what it's meant to me, meeting you and your mother. You've always had friends, so you can't possibly understand—" He broke off with an embarrassed laugh, and went on more calmly. "You see, it's not just a question of getting cured of the dope habit. You've got to get cured of whatever it was that made you turn into a dope addict in the first place. That's where you can't ever be sure. I'm 'cured' now, and I can stay 'cured' as long as I've got my job at the bindery, and the book to work on, and most of all you and your mother. But let something go wrong, maybe the least little thing—"

It was the truth. When Rolfe tested it out a few nights later by breaking a dinner date they had made, Borden's face turned quite white and into his eyes flashed a look of desperate presentiment: here it was again, the pattern as before. Rolfe and his mother, like all the others, were going to cast him off. He wrote Rolfe a cringing, overwrought letter: What had he done to offend Rolfe? How could he make amends? It took Rolfe several days to quiet the fears he had set off with his trivial slight.

He was excited, even a little bit scared, at how easy it was going to be.

The crucial slight, he decided, must come from Mother, because the full force of Borden's devotion was focused on her rather than on Rolfe.   It would have to be faked.   Though Borden sometimes made Mother nervous ("He's so intense, poor fellow!") still she sympathized with him; she would stick with him as long as he behaved himself.   Of course if she thought for one minute that he had gone back to drugs . . .

A little manipulation by Rolfe, and that was exactly what she thought.   She couldn't understand it when Borden failed to turn up for three sessions in a row. (The doctor, Rolfe had explained to him, felt that Mother might be overdoing; she was showing signs of strain.)   Why didn't Borden call?   Why didn't he explain? ("Whatever you do, please don't call her," Rolfe had cautioned.   "It would only upset her, and we're trying to keep her as quiet as possible.")   She fretted.   She hoped against hope—until Rolfe, commissioned to investigate, brought back a report that confirmed her worst fears.

Of course there was nothing to do but call the whole project off.   They couldn't risk letting Borden come back now, under any circumstance.   But Mother didn't know when she had been so disappointed in anyone.   And just when she had thought he was doing so well!   She had a good cry over it.   Then—with Rolfe's help—she wrote the letter that had to be written to Borden.

It was all that was needed to push Borden over the edge.   A prey, as always, to his own insecurity, he had been suspicious from the first.   "You're not telling me the truth," he had raged to Rolfe.   "It isn't doctor's orders.   She hasn't been overdoing.   I've offended her somehow, the way I always do, with everybody I've ever cared about.   She wants to get rid of me.   Doesn't she?   Doesn't she?   Why won't you admit it?"   And Rolfe had been just kind enough, just evasive enough, to keep him simmering.

He had expected an immediate explosion after the letter.   But it was several days before he heard from Borden.   No letter this time.   None of the frantic telephone calls he had grown used to.   His doorbell rang very late one night, and there was Borden—an ominously different, glassy-eyed Borden who at first seemed to have nothing to say and then suddenly burst into a flood of abject pleading.   He couldn't stand it, that was all.   They had to give him another chance.   It was true that he had lost his job and hocked most of his clothes (he was not even wearing a jacket, though the night was raw and windy) but only because he couldn't stand it, they couldn't do this to him, another chance and he would be all right again.

"But that's why I've been trying to get hold of you!"   Rolfe broke in—all sincerity, the distressed friend eager to help.   "I've told Mother all along she was being unfair.   Only I didn't know where to find you, and here she is, all but convinced that she ought to give you another chance—"

"Let me see her!   Now!   Right away!"   Trembling with excitement, Borden jerked himself out of his chair.   "I'll do anything, anything.   Let me see her. You come with me, Rolfe, she'll listen to you—"

"Are you crazy?" said Rolfe coldly.   "At this hour of the night?   And you in the shape you're in? We wouldn't have a prayer. I'll tell you right now, I'm not doing one thing for you unless you pull yourself together. Is that understood? You've got until tomorrow night. Let's say tomorrow night at nine thirty. We can meet next door at the bar, and if you're okay I'll take you to see Mother and I'll do all I can for you. But remember, it's up to you.''

"Anything, I told you I'll do anything—'' Borden drew a long, shaky breath. "Can't we make it earlier?'' he whispered. "It's so long to wait. Nine thirty. I don't know if I can wait.''

"You'd damn well better,'' Rolfe told him. "I can't make it till then.''

He thought he never was going to get rid of the fellow. Borden promised, over and over again. Agonized hope flared in his eyes; he knew that if he could just see Mother, speak to her for only a minute, he could convince her. He apologized, he explained, he all but licked Rolfe's hand in a transport of gratitude.

When he was leaving, as an afterthought, Rolfe lent him his own sports jacket. It seemed like the least he could do.

He may have slept some, during what was left of the night, but very little. Mostly, he paced the floor and planned. And as the hours of the next day slid by into afternoon, into evening, a mystical calm spread through him. Here was what he had waited for all his life—the moment (and of his own choosing, brought about by his own contrivance) that would change Rolfe J. in one incandescent flash from vision to reality. Soon, very soon. A bare half hour from now. He had only to slip down the fire escape and into Mother's bedroom through the window he had surreptitiously unlatched when he said goodnight to her, and then—and then—

It would take a very few minutes. He knew so well the exact location of the paperweight, on the desk beside her bed. He knew so well the way she would be lying, with the blanket pulled up to her chin and above it that egg-shell temple exposed, waiting for the blow. Asleep. She would be fast asleep. She would never know what hit her. Or who. Or why.

Back up the fire escape, because he could not afford the risk of being seen in the elevator. A few minutes later he would emerge from his own apartment quite openly, take the elevator to the street floor, and go into the bar next door. Most likely Borden would already be there, wild with anticipation. "Come on,'' Rolfe would say, "Mother's expecting us.'' And into the apartment house they would go, up in the elevator to Mother's door, where Rolfe would suddenly pause in the act of turnig his key in the lock. "Oh, damn!'' (slapping his pockets) "I forgot my pipe. I'll just run up to my place and get it. Go on in, I'll be right back.'' Opening the door, he would call in to Mother the business about the pipe, just as though she could hear. Up to his own place again. Five, ten minutes.

When he came back, Borden would have discovered what had happened in the bedroom. He might be standing there, stunned; he might—even better—have fled in panic. Rolfe's story to the police would fit, in any case. "I never trusted the guy,'' he would say. "Stella can tell you. I made a point of always being here, when he came for his sessions with Mother. But it never occurred to me— It couldn't have been ten minutes. Just while I went upstairs for my pipe. I shouldn't have left him there. God, if only I hadn't!'' As for what Borden would try to tell the police— Well, who was going to take the word of a hophead? He didn't have a prayer. Like as not, before it was all over, Borden, along with everybody else, would become convinced of his guilt.

It had been snowing lightly, Rolfe found when he stepped noiselessly through his window. The fire escape steps looked ghostly under the thin white coat. The windows of the two floors between him and Mother's apartment were dark. So was the church next door. No one to see or hear him. Everything was just as he had planned: the swift, silent descent, Mother's window opening smoothly under his hands, his leg thrusting inside, feeling for the floor, avoiding the little chintz chair . . .

He was inside. And suddenly nothing was as he had planned: the paperweight was not there on the desk. He stumbled into the medicine table, setting off a nervous clash of silver against glass, and still there was no stir or sound from the hump in the bed. His own rapid breathing unnerved him; he could not make it slow down. He became aware of a smell in the room, and that too was wrong because it was unfamiliar—pervasive, yet not like Mother's medicine; sweetish, yet not like her dusting powder. The smell of fear? Might Mother, having heard the intruder, be lying there frozen with terror? It could not be that Rolfe himself was afraid.

It was just that he could not see to find the paperweight. But to turn on the lamp would be to meet Mother's eyes . . . Again he groped over the desk; for a moment he thought he had it, his fingers closed convulsively, and at once a snatch of wistful music tinkled out. Horrified, he clapped the lid back on the damned-fool contraption: one of those musical cigarette boxes. Mother loved such trinkets. He braced himself for what must surely come now—some movement, some sound from the bed. It did not come. He held his own breath, listening for hers. It was not there.

He turned on the lamp.

The shock came not so much from what had been done to Mother—after all, he himself had planned it—as from the fact that it had been done without his realizing it. For his first nightmarish conviction was that his memory had betrayed him, tricked him by blanking out. How could I have done it, he thought, and I have absolutely no recollection of it? Why, there I was, fumbling around for the paperweight, when all the time I had already . . .

The paperweight was on the bed, where it had been dropped once it had served its purpose. Mother's smashed-in head lay sideways on the pillow. She had put up quite a struggle for her poor life; one fat dimpled hand reached vainly toward the telephone, and her eyes, glazed and terrible with knowledge, stared up at him. She had known who hit her, and why.

It could not have been Rolfe. At last his mind grasped the truth. Memory was not playing tricks on him. Someone else had beaten him to it, had carried out his plan for him. A glance around the room, and he had the answer. The someone else was Borden. There across the chintz chair was Rolfe's jacket, the one Borden had borrowed last night. Maybe he had left it here on impulse— simply shucking off anything connected with Rolfe or his mother—or maybe on purpose in the hope (the dirty little rat) of implicating Rolfe. Well, Rolfe wasn't having any of that. He had come down in his shirt sleeves. With a feeling of triumph he slipped into the jacket. The comfortable set of it on his shoulders seemed to steady him.

Not that he was really shaken, of course. Not Rolfe J. Naturally it was a jolt, to find that Borden had come barging in ahead of time. But only a minor jolt, only momentary.

How had the fellow gotten in? The open fire-escape window? No, Rolfe remembered. There had been a key to Mother's apartment, an extra one, in his jacket pocket. Finding it must have been the spark that set Borden off. There right in his hands was the means of cutting short the agony of waiting; he could not resist using it. And Mother—taken by surprise, unaware that she was supposed to be on the verge of giving Borden another chance—would not have minced words. A flat, harsh turndown. What followed was inevitable.

Yes, there was the key on the desk, where Borden must have tossed it when he came in. Rolfe reached for it. And hesitated.

Supposing the police didn't believe him? He had never doubted that he could convince them of a lie. But now, in a chilling flash, he saw the situation as it would look, for example, to someone walking in on him at that moment. Standing there with the weapon in his hand (hastily, he slipped it into his pocket), the open fire-escape window behind him . . .

But of course nothing like that was going to happen. It wouldn't take them long to catch up with Borden, and he would crack. He had none of Rolfe's stamina, he was sure to crack. Guilty as he was, he might already be turning himself in. He would spill everything—the jacket borrowed from Rolfe, the extra key accidentally left in the pocket.

So it was a mistake to wear the jacket away. He must leave everything just as it was. And it would be a mistake to call the police quite yet. Because the other key to Mother's apartment was upstairs, on his chest of drawers; and it would be hard to explain why, with it lying there, Rolfe had chosen to come down the fire escape. Thank God he had thought of it in time! He drew a breath of relief at the simplicity of what he had to do—another trip up the fire escape for his key, down again in the elevator, back here to the bedroom (he must remember to lock the fire-escape window) and then the distraught call to the police. He had it made.

All the same, he had one leg through the window when he realized he was still wearing the jacket. The near-blunder shook him; it gave him a grim glimpse of how treacherous his mind could be. But must not be. Would not be.

The trouble was that everything happened at once: he discovered in his hurry to shed the jacket why Borden had left it behind. There was blood on the sleeve; it was already beginning to stiffen. And he heard the voice and the footsteps. His whole body locked in a paralysis of listening. Someone was in the apartment. Someone who was moving through the living room, on toward the bedroom. That fool Borden must have left the door ajar, simply walked out and . . .

Move. Get out of here. But get out of the jacket too, the damning jacket, because the footsteps were appallingly close now! At the last moment his arms and legs unlocked, but only to a flurry of witless jerks that neither got him through the window nor out of the jacket. And it was all too late. He was lost. Ignominiously straddling the window sill, with one arm still trying to fumble its way out of the jacket, he looked into the granite eyes of Mr. Webb and knew that disaster was upon him.

Complete disaster. He felt Rolfe J.—the masterful man of destiny—disintegrate, once and or all, into the reality of what Mr. Webb saw—a pudgy, guilty wretch, caught red-handed and babbling (somehow that was the worst of all, that he could not stop babbling) an incoherent story that no one was going to believe.

"Tell it to the police," said Mr. Webb, and reached for the telephone.

So Rolfe went on babbling to the police that they must find Borden, all they had to do was find Borden. He babbled on and on.

They found Borden. What was left of him. He had either fallen or jumped from the window of his room to the alley below. Nobody knew exactly when. Or why. As the police said, who knew what made hopheads do any of the screwball things they did?

Luck had been with Borden—until he went out the window, of course. Nobody had seen him entering or leaving Mother's apartment. Nobody had seen him wearing Rolfe's jacket; there was only Rolfe's word that he had ever borrowed it. Only Rolfe's word, which nobody believed.

Yet there was nothing else for Rolfe to do but to go on hopelessly telling the truth. At the very end, while he was waiting in the death cell, he said, "I am guilty. I did not do it, but I am guilty."

A garbled sort of confession? Or just some more crazy babbling? No one recognized it for what it was. The deepest truth of all.

JACK RITCHIE

The Third Call

At 1:20 in the afternoon I phoned Stevenson High School and got through to Principal Morrison.

I spoke through the handkerchief over the mouthpiece. "This is no joke. A bomb is going to explode in your school in fifteen minutes."

There were a few seconds of silence on the other end of the line and then Morrison's angry voice demanded, "Who is this?"

"Never mind that. I'm not fooling this time. A bomb is going off in fifteen minutes."

And then I hung up.

I left the gas station, crossed the street, and returned to the main police station. I took the elevator to the third floor.

My partner, Pete Torgeson, was on the phone when I entered the squad room.

He looked up. "Stevenson High School just got another one of those calls, Jim. Morrison is having the school evacuated again."

"Did you get the bomb squad?"

"I'm doing that right now." He dialed and completed the call to Room 121, giving them details.

The enrollment at Stevenson was 1800 and all the students were out of the building by the time we arrived. Their teachers, following the instructions we had given them the last two times the school had received phone calls, were keeping them at least two hundred feet away from the building.

Principal Morrison was a large graying man wearing rimless glasses. He left the group of teachers at the curb and came forward. "The call came at exactly 1:20," he said.

The bomb unit truck and two squad cars pulled up behind our car.

My son Dave lounged against the wire fence with a half a dozen of his buddies. He waved. "What is it, Dad? Another bomb scare?"

I nodded. "And let's hope it's nothing more than a scare this time too."

Dave grinned. "I don't mind a bit. We were just going to have a history exam."

Morrison shook his head. "I'm afraid that most of the students regard this as nothing more than a welcome break in the routine."

Several more details of men arrived from headquarters and we began searching the building. We finished the job at 2:30 and I went back to Morrison. "It was another hoax. We didn't find a thing."

Morrison ordered the students back to their classes and then took Torgeson and me to his office.

"Did you recognize the voice?" Torgeson asked.

Morrison sat down at his desk. "No. It was muffled and indistinct, just as before. But it was a male voice. That much I'm certain about." He sighed. "I'm having the attendance records checked right away. Are you sure it's one of the students?"

"In cases like this, it usually is," Pete said. "A boy decides he hates one of the teachers or the whole school because he's getting bad marks. So he uses this way to get what he thinks is revenge. Or maybe he just thinks the whole thing is a roaring joke."

The attendance records were brought to Morrison. He glanced at them and then passed them over to us. "Ninety-one absences. About average."

Pete and I went over the names of the absent students. I knew that Bob Fletcher would be there, but that didn't matter. I hoped that Lester Baines had come back to school in the afternoon.

"Fletcher's here," Pete said. "But he's out, of course." His eyes went back to the list. "And Lester Baines was absent." He ran down the rest of the names and then looked up and smiled. "Just Lester Baines. He's our boy."

Morrison had Lester's records brought in. He shook his head as he read. "He's seventeen. No disciplinary problem at all, but he's absent a lot. His grades are pretty bad. He failed in two subjects last semester."

Pete was looking over Morrison's shoulder. "Do you know him?"

Morrison smiled wanly. "No. A principal knows fewer of the students than any teacher."

Torgeson lit a cigar. "This looks like the end of this one, Jim. You should look more cheerful."

I got to my feet. "I just don't like to see any boy get into trouble."

We drove to the Baines home. It was a medium-sized two-story house much like any of the others in the block.

Mr. Baines was tall and blue-eyed. The smile left his face when he opened the door. "You here again?"

"We'd like to talk to your son," Pete said. "Lester wasn't at school today. Is he sick?"

Baines' eyes flickered and then he said, "Why?"

Pete smiled faintly. "The same thing we were here for before."

Baines let us in reluctantly. "Lester's at the drug store. He'll be back in a few minutes."

Torgeson sat down on the davenport. "He isn't sick?"

Baines watched us narrowly. "He had a cold. I thought that it was best to keep him home today. But it wasn't so bad that he couldn't go down to the drug store for a coke."

Pete's face was bland.   "Where was your boy at ten-thirty this morning?"

"He was right here," Baines snapped.   "And he didn't make any phone calls."

"How do you know that?"

"This is my day off.   I was with Lester all day."

"Where is your wife?"

"She's out shopping now.   But she was here at ten-thirty.   Lester didn't make any phone calls."

Pete smiled.   "I hope so.   And where was Lester at 1:20?"

"Right here," Baines said again.   "My wife and I will swear to it."   He frowned.   "Were there two calls today?"

Pete nodded.

We sat in the living room waiting.   Baines fidgeted nervously in his chair and then got up.   "I'll be right back.   I've got to check some of the upstairs screens."

Pete watched him leave the room and then turned to me.   "You're letting me do all the talking, Jim."

"It doesn't take two for something like this, Pete."

He lit a cigar.   "Well, everything turned out all right.   We won't have to lose sleep on this one."   He picked up the phone on a table at his elbow and listened. After a while he put his hand over the mouthpiece.   "Baines is on the upstairs extension.   He's calling around.   He doesn't know where his son is."

Pete kept listening and after a while he smiled.   "Now he's talking to his wife. She's at the supermarket.   He's telling her about us.   She's supposed to say that Lester was at home all day and made no phone calls."

I was looking out of the picture window, when a blond teenage boy turned up the walk and came toward the house.

Torgeson saw him too and put down the phone.   "There's Lester now.   We'll try to have a few fast words with him before his father comes down."

Lester Baines had a new sunburn and he carried a rolled-up towel under his arm. His normally cheerful face sobered when he stepped into the house and saw us.

"Where were you today, Lester?"   Pete asked.   "We know you weren't at school."

Lester swallowed.   "I felt pretty rotten this morning and so I stayed home.

Pete indicated the towel under his arm.   "Is there a wet pair of swimming trunks in there?"

Color came to Lester's face.   "Well—around nine this morning everything seemed okay again.   Maybe I didn't have a cold.   I mean, maybe it was just an allergy or something and it cleared up."   He took a deep breath.   "So I decided to go swimming, get some sun."

"All day?   Didn't you get hungry?"

"I took along a few sandwiches."

"Who did you go with?"

"Nobody.   Just me."   He shifted uneasily.   "Was there another one of those phone calls?"

Pete smiled.   "If you were feeling so fit, why didn't you go to school in the afternoon?"

Lester's hands worked on the towel. "I was going to. But the next thing I knew it was after one o'clock and I couldn't have got back in time anyway." He went on lamely, "So I just decided to swim some more."

"If you were just going to be away for the morning, why did you take the sandwiches along?"

Lester's color deepened and he finally decided to tell the whole truth. "I didn't have a cold today. I just stayed away from school. Mom and Dad don't know that. There was going to be a civics test this morning and a history test in the afternoon, and I knew I'd flunk them both. I figured that if I studied tonight I'd be able to pass make-up tests tomorrow."

We heard the footsteps coming down the stairs and waited.

Baines stopped when he saw us with his son. "Don't tell them anything, Lester. Let me do the talking."

"I'm afraid it's too late or that now," Pete said. "Your boy admitted that he wasn't in this house today."

Lester's voice showed panic. "I didn't make any of those calls. Honest, I didn't!"

Baines moved beside his son. "Why keep picking on Lester?"

"We're not picking on Lester," Pete said. "But we're reasonably certain that one of the students did the phoning. However, all of the calls came during times when classes were in session. And that means that only a student who was absent could have made them."

Baines wasn't impressed. "I'm sure that Lester wasn't the only student absent today."

Pete conceded that but went on. "The first of the three phone calls came eighteen days ago. We checked the attendance records at Stevenson at that time and found that ninety-six students had been absent at the time it was made. Sixty-two of those were boys and we talked to all of them—including your son. Your boy was home at that time with a cold . . . and alone. You were at work and your wife was attending the birthday party of a friend. However, your son denied making the call and we had to accept his word for that."

Lester appealed to his father. "I *didn't* make that bomb call, Dad. I wouldn't do such a thing."

Baines met his eyes or a moment and then turned back to us, his face expressionless.

Pete continued. "The second phone call came this morning at ten-thirty. We went over the attendance records again and discovered that only three boys had been absent on both this morning and on the day of the first phone call."

Baines' face showed a faint hope. "Are you checking the other two boys?"

"We were about to do that, but then another bomb scare call was made this afternoon and we were saved the trouble. We went back to the attendance records. One of our three suspects had returned for the afternoon session and therefore could not have phoned."

"What about the other boy?" Baines demanded.

"He's in a hospital."

Baines grasped at that. "Hospitals have phones."

Torgeson smiled faintly. "The boy caught scarlet fever while he was out of the state with his parents last weekend. He's in a hospital five hundred miles away from here—and the phone calls were all local."

Baines turned to his son.

Lester paled. "You know I never lie to you, Dad."

"Of course you don't, son." But there was doubt on Baines' face.

The front door opened and an auburn-haired woman stepped inside. Her face was pale, but determined, and it took her a moment to get her breath.

"I just stepped out for a moment to go shopping. Otherwise I was here all day. I'm sure I can account for every moment of Lester's time."

"Mom," Lester said miserably. "It's no use. I played hookey all day today and they know it."

Pete reached for his hat. "I'd like both of you to talk to your son tonight. I'm sure you can do that much better than we can." He put one of our cards on the table. "We'd like to see all three of you tomorrow morning at ten."

Outside, when he pulled our car away from the curb, Pete said, "We might find ourselves in for a hard time, if they decide to keep lying for their son."

"Suppose it wasn't somebody from the school?"

"I hope it wasn't. But you and I know that the chances are ninety-nine out of a hundred that it was." Pete sighed. "I don't like to see things like this. The bomb scare is bad enough, but what's happening to that family now is a lot worse."

I checked out of the station at five and got home a little after five-thirty.

My wife, Nora, was in the kitchen. "I read in the paper that there was another bomb scare at Stevenson this morning."

I kissed her. "And one this afternoon. That one happened too late to get into the paper."

She lifted the cover off the pot roast. "Did you find out who made the calls?"

I hesitated a moment. "Yes. I think we have."

"Who was it?"

"One of the students. A Lester Baines."

Her face showed pity. "What would make him do something like that?"

"I don't know. He hasn't admitted making the calls yet."

She studied me. "You look tired, Jim. Is something like this a little worse than usual?"

"Yes. A lot worse."

Her eyes showed worry, but she smiled. "Supper's just about ready. Why don't you call Dave? He's out in the garage trying to get that car of his to run."

Dave had the carburetor on the work bench. He looked up. "Hi, Dad. You look beat with the heat."

"It was a hard day."

"Find the fiend?"

"I hope so."

Dave had the gray eyes of his mother. He frowned. "Who was it?"

"A boy named Lester Baines. Do you know him?"

Dave peered down at the parts before him. "Sure."

"What kind of a boy is he?"

Dave shrugged. "I just know him to talk to. Seems like he's all right." He still frowned. "Did he admit making the calls?"

"No."

Dave picked up a screwdriver. "How did you narrow it down to him?"

I told him the method we had used.

Dave seemed to have trouble with an adjustment. "Is he in a lot of trouble?"

"It might turn out that way."

"What do you think will happen to him?"

"I don't know. He's never been in trouble before. He might get probation."

Dave thought about that. "Maybe he did it as a joke. I mean nobody got hurt. All he did was stop school for a while."

"A lot of people could have gotten hurt," I said. "It wouldn't have been a joke if there had been a panic."

Dave's face seemed slightly stubborn. "We have fire drills all the time. Everything goes off okay."

Yes, and that was what I had counted on when I called. I didn't want anyone to get hurt.

Dave put down his screwdriver. "Do *you* think Lester did it?"

"He could have."

Yes, Lester Baines could have made those first two phone calls. And I had made the third.

Dave was silent for a while. "Dad, when the school got the first phone call, did you talk to all the boys who were absent?"

"Not myself. But the department got around to seeing all of them."

Dave had a faint wry smile. "I was absent that day, Dad. Nobody talked to me."

"I didn't think it was necessary, son."

And I hadn't. Other men's boys might have done such a thing, but not my boy. But now I waited.

Dave spoke reluctantly. "I was absent this morning too."

"Yes," I said.

He met my eyes. "And that narrowed it down to how many boys?"

"Three," I said. "But we discovered that one of them couldn't possibly have made the call. He was in a hospital out of the state." I watched Dave. "And that left us with just two suspects. Lester Baines—and you."

Dave had trouble manufacturing a grin. "Some luck, huh? I was at school this afternoon when the third phone call came and so that left just poor Lester."

"That's right. Poor Lester."

Dave licked his lips. "Is Lester's dad standing by him?"

"Of course. That's the way dads are supposed to be."

Dave seemed to be perspiring slightly. He worked silently at the carburetor for a minute or two. Then he sighed and met my eyes. "Dad, I think you'd better

take me down to headquarters.   Lester didn't make those bomb calls.   I did.''
He took a deep breath.   "I did it as a joke.   I just wanted to pep things up.   I
didn't mean anything wrong.''

I hadn't wanted to hear those words, and yet now I felt a pride that I had a son
who wouldn't let someone else suffer for his own mistakes.

"But, Dad, I just made the first two calls.   Not the one this afternoon.''

"I know.   I made that particular call myself.''

His eyes widened.   And then he understood.   "You tried to cover up for me?''

I smiled tiredly.   "It was something I shouldn't have done, but a father doesn't
always think too clearly when it involves his son.   And I was hoping that it might
turn out to be Lester after all.''

Dave wiped his hands on a rag and there were a few moments of silence.

"I guess I ought to tell them I made all of the calls, Dad,'' Dave said.   "There's
no sense in all of us getting into trouble.''

I shook my head.   "Thanks, son.   I'll tell them what I did.''

And now when Dave looked at me, I had the feeling that somehow he was proud
of me too.

"We'll have supper first,'' I said.   "And then we'll phone Lester's father.   A
half an hour won't make much difference.''

Dave smiled wryly.   "It will to Lester and his dad.''

I made the phone call as soon as we got back to the house.

RUFUS KING

Damon and Pythias and Delilah Brown

Within this subtropical dreamland of alcoholic divorcees, in this bar-studded playground of the suspicious rich, in this Florida of sunshine, palm trees, nag and dogtracks, bars, jai alai, bolita, bookies, bars, surf-swept beaches, a moon, and bars, lived a young married lady with the first name of Delilah, her surname being Brown.

It happened that Delilah Brown was one of those special young women who crop up every now and again like Cleopatra or Circe or Pompadour or Gypsy Rose Lee, and who drive otherwise sensible men straight out of their wits.

In a case like hers mere looks do not matter, although Delilah had plenty, such as titian hair, deep-sea eyes, good bones and good bumps to go with them. It is the inner woman that counts, that certain ferrous quality, always in a state of magnetic flux, that can draw a man with even the trace of a nail in his head right into a condition of animal, mineral, and vegetable collapse.

The hunting ground through which Delilah scalped when off duty from her job as hostess in Grandmother Katy's Kitchen was the seaboard town of Halcyon, a homelike little community somewhat to the north of Miami. Apart from its seasonal glut of shrimp pink tourists, the place is inhabited largely by retired yankees, disillusioned motel owners, heat-baked construction workers, somewhat larcenous bar operators and an assortment of deep down Southern crackers.

(Word lore note: the term cracker in its Southern sense has nothing to do with a barrel or Nabisco. It derives from the early Florida settlers' prima donna habit of cracking their whips over the flanks of their oxen, mules, or horseflesh—and sharp-eared little Susie, as a consequence, saying to her pea-shelling mother, "Hark, Ma, here comes a cracker," and Mother understanding her perfectly.)

Well, Delilah was a cracker and her husband Pythias Brown was a cracker and Pythias' construction-boss-and-best-friend Damon Lang was one too.

Although the boys' friendship was on a common plateau of unshatterable fondness, the economic stature of Pythias and Damon were far apart. The Langs had prospered abundantly through several generations of turpentine stands, citrus groves, and eventually valuable real estate, leaving the resultant boodle in Damon Lang's husky, well-molded hands—a provocative situation which more than frequently caused Delilah Brown to think, think turgidly.

If (she would turgidly think) I were married to Damon instead of to Pythias, I would have that kidney-bean-shaped swimming pool, that Jaguar and that 65-foot dream yacht, and I would have unlimited charge accounts at Burdines and at Jordan Marsh, instead of an installment rating at Sears Roebuck and a credit card with Texaco.

Damon, per se, never clearly entered the picture because men to Delilah were simply men—handy rungs on a ladder to an ultimate Monaco or an Aga Khan.

Now Delilah was not the type of girl who sits idly by and lets her dreams remain dreams.   When she positively decided she wanted something she would put her well adjusted thinking cap on her titian hairdo and sort out all practical approaches to her goal.   The basic solution to her immediate dream-compulsion was, naturally, for Pythias to be evaporated into outer space and for her ensuing state of pathetic widowhood to be rectified posthaste by a marriage with good, dependable, protective, and filthy rich Damon Lang.

What had sparked this lethal thought process into activity was the irritating announcement by Damon of his engagement to a svelte snowbird, a Miss Ethel Chalice, whose Westchester family wintered in Fort Lauderdale.   Miss Chalice was generally considered by Delilah's coterie to fall loosely within the category of a female meat-head, due to her absurd interest in puppet shows, ceramics, ballet, Aldous Huxley, and kindred paranoiac subjects.

Delilah was not alarmed, she was simply spurred from a contemplative jog trot into a gallop.   She was personally satisfied that the Chalice nuisance was little more than a resigned move on Damon's part of accepting second-best.   He was definitely the marrying male, and as pal Pythias had removed his one true passion (herself) from the market, a sensible ceremony with the Westchester drip was his best out.   The wedding was scheduled for December, leaving Delilah a comfortable margin of three months for arranging her husband's encore act to the Sputniks.

How?

Suffocation?   Blunt force?   Gunshot?   Ice pick?   Rat poison?   Delilah considered them all, judicially chasing their drawbacks about in her clever young head while she seated and soothed and politely kidded the stuffed customers in Grandmother Katy's Kitchen, or as she glowed magnetically while downing several cool ones at a neighborhood tavern, or especially while she and Pythias were involved in the (to her) shopworn gestures of love after the two-o'clock curfew had eased them away from the taps.

It took about three weeks of speculative prospecting before she hit pay dirt, in what satisfied Delilah as a recipe for the perfect crime.   Reasonably simple, enchantingly original—this it was—and leaving her grief-shocked self trimphantly in the clear.

All she needed was a goat.

Delilah pin-pointed this goat in the bulging, perspiration-moistened person of a Dr. Hillegas Dow.   Dr. Dow was also a cracker—in fact, everyone concerned in this simple pastiche on homicide was a cracker except for the sheriff's deputy and the B.C.I. man who were shortly to be slapped with the case in the middle of a sopping wet and windy night.   And, of course, the peripheral Ethel Chalice.

Delilah knew Dr. Hillegas Dow both inside and out, being on liquid terms of gossiping intimacy with a Mabel Oestringer who held down the job of nurse-receptionist at Dr. Dow's small clinic. Delilah knew him to be licensed in chiropody and as a naturopath, facts that apparently barred him from practicing in any of the hospitals, and that he had had to establish his private clinic in order to cash in. She was further happy in the conjecture that his professional ethics were as flaccid as a dying girdle and that his one-and-only god was the fast buck.

Definitely, Dr. Dow appeared not to be what even his kindest colleague would call a dedicated man. He was reputed to be far more interested in the pattings and pinchings of the comely than in therapeutically patting the ill. He was undoubtedly one of the exceptions to the rule that can be found in any line of professional work.

During a pre-dawn hour of the Wednesday-Thursday night of October 16th, while Pythias breathed deeply in guileless sleep, Delilah explored the pockets of his slacks and then arranged the first ingredient of her recipe for wishing him a bon voyage. Needless to say, it was not three cups of sifted flour.

The weather forecast for Halcyon and vicinity (said the 6 o'clock A.M. newscaster) *calls for fair skies and mild temperatures today and Friday . . .*

"Nuts," said Delilah, snapping off the radio set and getting back into bed.

"What did you say, sugar?" Pythias asked drowsily.

"I said nuts."

"Why?"

"Because the man said clear weather."

"Good. Damon and I have that job to inspect over on Bricknel."

"You got about one hour more sleep coming. Turn over and take it."

Friday:

The weather forecast for Halcyon and vicinity calls for party cloudy skies today with occasional showers late tonight and Saturday . . .

"And just why only occasional?" Delilah said irritably, snapping off the set and getting back into bed.

Saturday:

The weather forecast for Halcyon and vicinity calls for partly cloudy skies and increasing showers over the weekend . . .

"That's better," said Delilah.

Sunday.

. . . A low-pressure area in the Caribbean will cause an increase in the rainfall both today and Monday. Motorists are advised to exercise special caution while . . .

"Now that's my boy," said Delilah, getting back into bed and landing a solid punch on the back of Pythias' solid neck to wake him up.

"How—when—what's the idea, sugar?"

"Do you know what day it is tomorrow?"

"Yes."

"Well, what?"

"Monday. Look, Del, this is the one morning in the week when I can sleep—"

"What else day is it besides Monday?"

"Damon and I got that Harrison job to look over."

"And is that all that Monday October the twenty-first means to you?"

"Isn't it enough?"

"Wake up and listen to me, you bleak catfish.   Monday is my birthday."

"Why?"

"*Why?*"

"Sure, why.   Last year it was in November.   Come to think of it, the year before last it was June."

"So this year it's tomorrow."

"Del, honey, if it's that leopard-spotted velvet stole you're thinking about at Japeson's—"

"I am thinking about no leopard-spotted velvet stole at Japeson's or at any other cut-rate trap.   I am thinking that tomorrow is my day off from Grandmother Katy's kind home for old mice, and that I want you and Damon to give me my yearly birthday party irregardless of the date."

"Okay, sugar.   How about knocking it off now so I can get some sleep?"

"I want both you and Damon to take me for a charcoal broil at Tropical Joe's. Damon is marrying that pixy potroast-special in six or seven weeks, and this may be our last good party like old times.   Just the three of us all alone together.   Just Damon, just you, and just me."

"Look, babe, don't. choke it to death.   I said yes.   I'll give him a buzz, if I can for one more time get back to sleep again."

And so with the few medical facts Delilah had gleaned from Mabel Oestringer, along with the rather less than flattering portraiture of Dr. Hillegas Dow, and with one pertinent bit of information she had casually lifted from Damon, and with the time now set for the launching, the deadly casserole was ready for the oven.   Hot. 375 degrees.

"Wella, wella, well," said Tropical Joe with his celebrated originality as he watched Damon and Pythias and Delilah steer a homing-pigeon course from the wet doorway to the wet bar, "if it isn't the Three Muscatels."

Delilah smiled magnetically back at Joe's greeting and automatically counted the house: ten parboiled tourists, three deadpan crackers with their lady friends, and one stupefied ex-jockey with an Amazon lush.   Not at all bad for a storm-flooded Monday night.

She herded her mutually devoted escorts through some sets of martinis (Pythias), manhattans (Damon), old-fashioneds (herself) and then over to a table for charcoal-broiled steaks and beer.

The long established pattern of their threesome get-togethers held, with Pythias and Damon absorbed in construction business chitchat, and Delilah occupied in stoking away the groceries and in exchanging the eye with any mobile individual in pants.

Several hours and a good many squat ones later, Delilah rang the departure bell. The pattern continued to hold.   As usual, she drove.   As usual, Pythias lapsed into a state of negligible consciousness on the seat between herself and the painlessly un-consolidated Damon.

Windshield wipers battled against a tropical downpour that blurred road visibility through a sheeting of water, and Delilah held the speed down to twenty-five while glissading over slick blacktop until, vague in the distance, a chaste neon sign announced the clinic of Dr. Hillegas Dow.

It was a lonesome span of road, made melancholy on one side by scrub palmettos and on the other by a hyacinth-choked canal.   She had scouted the route several times before tonight, and knew exactly the location of a tall Gru-gru palm tree with its thorn-spiked trunk and large top of feather leaves that stood close by the entrance drive of the clinic.

Perfectly cool in her head, despite a warm lower down flush from the evening's liquid potpourri, Delilah swept a mental eye across this moment in which the show was to start.   Her devoted consorts were both ripe for a good night's sleep with their eyelids already comfortably composed, a single-edged safety razor blade was ready in her bag, and the rain-lashed highway fore and aft was empty of traffic.

She took a skipper's look at the looming Gru-gru palm tree, depressed the accelerator, swung the wheel, braced herself, and muttered, "Gold Coast, here I come!"

The effects were reasonably spectacular.   Pythias and Damon lunged in unison against the windshield, to their somewhat detriment, splintering it.

Delilah, having prepared herself against impact, suffered little beyond a momentary loss of breath.   Swiftly, she took the single-edged razor blade from her bag.   Swiftly, she used it.   Then she jumped out onto the clinic driveway and started a crescendo of screams.

They were agreeably effective.   Dr. Hillegas Dow emerged from the clinic and ran towards the screamer.   He was followed by his nurse-receptionist, Miss Mabel Oestringer.   By the time they reached the wrecked car, Damon had sufficiently recovered from shock to struggle out and take some befuddled steps over to Delilah, who adjusted herself about him warmly.

Delilah went into her act.   It was important that she establish her concern for Pythias, and even though her gears remained enmeshed with Damon, she cried desperately to Dr. Dow, "Help Pythias! He's still in the car! He may be bleeding to death!"

It is interesting to note that Damon promptly dropped Delilah like a hot potato, even while her physical contact was shooting through him with bolts of fire.   He lunged for the car.   And even though both young men were of equal tonnage and size, Damon managed under the press of anxiety to extricate Pythias and to carry him on a trot towards the clinic, crying "Snap into it, Doc! He's bleeding like a stuck pig."

Dr. Dow snapped.   What had initially struck him as being nothing more than an interesting motor accident was now translated into a source of cash, in what had been an otherwise cashless evening.   First aid, he decided, then at least a week of expensive recuperation in the clinic.

"Shall I phone for an ambulance?" Mabel Oestringer suggested as she trotted beside him.

"Certainly not!" And Dr. Dow added, as a conscience-quieting clincher, "The man would be dead before an ambulance could possibly get here."

This made little sense to Mabel, but then little ever did beyond the delicious properties of vodka and her weekly take home pay of $42.60.

Throughout this group-trot along the driveway, Delilah did not lose her impressario touch. She aligned herself beside Damon and established her loyalty as a wife by hysterically saying into Damon's closer ear, "If Pythias dies I'll kill myself. It was all because I didn't control the skid. And I'd rather end it all than go on living with the horrible thought."

It worked to an extent, for Damon called time out from his deep anxiety over Pythias, fleetingly, to admire Delilah's noble self-recrimination and noble anguish.

"Forget it, Del," he snapped soothingly, while hustling on with his bleeding-to-death burden. "That road was pure vaseline. Even a bulldozer could skid on a night like this."

Within the clinic's antiseptic walls, the command post fell to Dr. Dow, and in all truth the doctor was neither a complete dud nor a quack.

He directed Damon to place Pythias on a surgical table, and was disturbingly aware that the situation was critical. Obviously, Pythias had lost and was losing a dangerous amount of blood from a wrist slash that had severed an artery. Odd, Dr. Dow thought abstractedly as he went about compressing the flow.

Odd, in the sense of the wound's location. The minor head and face lacerations were understandable, but unless Pythias had struck out in some witless moment of thrashing, and a shard of windshield glass had sliced the artery . . .

"He must have an immediate transfusion—and I mean immediate."

"I'll give it," Damon said, adding with earnest selflessness, "He can have my last drop."

"Have you ever donated, Mr. Lang? Do you know your type?"

"Yes. Type A."

"You absolutely sure?"

Damon took out his wallet and leafed through its plastic compartments.

"Here, Doc. Take a look."

"Oh, stop quibbling and give it to him!" Delilah cried. "His poor, dear skin looks like a slice of boiled liver." Her agitated voice rose higher still. "Give him blood!"

"Miss Oestringer—"

"Yes, Doctor?"

"Please take Mrs. Brown into the waiting room and keep her there. Perhaps one of the yellow capsules."

"Yes, Doctor."

The clinic's waiting room was principally a matter of chairs, ash-tray stands, and Mabel Oestringer's desk. Mabel shook out a barbiturate.

"Want this, hon, or a slug?"

"Both," Delilah said.

Mabel produced vodka.

"Join you," she said, doing so, and then dialing the telephone.

"Who are you calling?"

"Sheriff's office."

"Why?" Delilah's voice held an edge.

"Well, somebody has got to, hon," Mabel said reasonably. "Anytime now, a patrol car will maybe spot the mix-up heap and will then ask why it was not reported and we'll be in a snit—oh, hello? Sheriff's office? Chuck? Well listen, honey boy, this is Mabel and . . ."

Some twenty minutes later honey boy blew in, with his big fullback body creating the effect of a minor atmospheric disturbance in the quiet room.

"Chuck, I want you should meet Mrs. Delilah Brown," Mabel said.

Chuck did so and suffered the usual male reaction upon first facing Delilah, of having been blasted by a pleasing booby trap. This over, he said to Mabel, "Bill is down investigating the wreck. What gives in here?"

"Bill?" Mabel looked puzzled. "Isn't Bill B.C.I.?"

"He is. Happens Bill was in the office and losing his shirt at stud. He just came along for the ride. And now, ma'am, Mrs. Brown? Could I have just what happened?"

But Dr. Dow appeared and broke in upon Delilah's Sarah Bernhart interpretation of the dramatic night. Dr. Dow was both a bewildered and a badly shaken man.

He said, "He's dead."

It is fantastic how swiftly during a moment of absorbing triumph, disaster can strike and the tired old cliché about the cup that slips on its journey to the lip can get in its deadly licks.

Never had Delilah so richly enjoyed the sweet and pitless fruits of success. Beneath her Academy performance of just-widowed grief, she was one utterly satisfied and contented cat. She had even managed to radiate through her quiet sobbing a few hot shafts at Bill, the Bureau of Criminal Identification man, who had finished with his examination of the wreck and for the past twenty minutes had been closeted with Chuck and Dr. Dow in the room where Pythias was lying in the long sleep.

Twenty minutes?

Remotely, the length of time—for what after all should have been a simple look-see—was beginning to overlap Delilah's mood of total security. The thought seeped through her complacency: there is danger in that man. Something he knows. But how could he? And what? She worked on the problem, while Damon's worthy right arm encircled and comforted her port side and Mabel bolstered up the starboard.

"I feel so lost—so alone," she sobbed.

"You've got me, Del," Damon said. "You've always got me."

"And me," Mabel said.

"Thank you, both of you," Delilah sobbed simply, while in her coldly calculating thoughts the questions continued: What does that man know? From the wreck? From what is taking place in that room in there right now?

The razor blade?

Scarcely.   She had tossed it into the shrubbery, and on a storm-lashed night such as this . . .

"Pythias was my very best friend," Damon was saying in a voice charged with restrained emotion.   "And you were everything to him, Del.   It is my aim and my duty to shelter you as Pythias would shelter you, if—if he were still—"

Damon's honest baritone voice broke, and Delilah was engaged in the twin thoughts of how perfectly Damon was reacting according to plan and how silly were her unreasonable doubts when that B.C.I. man came back into the room with a purposeful stride.

Bill carried his six foot two inches of whipcord intelligence and superlative B.C.I. training over to the trio.

"With your permission, Mrs. Brown?" he said.

Without waiting for the permission but just taking it for granted, Bill lifted Delilah's bag from her lap and dumped out its contents onto the receptionist desk. His manner was so quietly assured, so officially confident of being within his legal rights (which he wasn't, and knew it) that the trio of competent young adults watching him were momentarily changed into hypnotically transfixed children.

He was about to pick up the wallet from among the trivia in Delilah's bag when his attention was caught by a small cardboard guard.   He held it up carefully by its edges.

"You find these shields on new single-edged safety razor blades," he said.

Bill set it to one side back on the desk.

"The blade itself will be looked for," he said, "in the shrubbery near the wreck, after sunup."

"Damon, sugar," Delilah sobbed (she was still at it), snuggling closer with Damon's arm, "what is the man talking about?   Make him stop."

"Something in the nature of a razor blade was used to cut an artery in your husband's left wrist, Mrs. Brown," Bill said.   "The location and nature of the wound rules out the probability of its coming from windshield glass."

Delilah froze into a cold, clear-thinking cube of ice.

"It *was* the windshield glass that made my dear, dead husband bleed.   And what is more," she added, to restore the situation clinchingly back where it belonged, "I screamed my head off getting him help so that Dr. Dow could see to it that he got an immediate transfusion and his life be saved.   Why should I move both heaven and earth to save him if I had been so foolishly cruel-hearted as to want him to bleed to death?"

"It was the transfusion that killed him," Bill said.   "It was the transfusion that was *meant* to kill him, Mrs. Brown."

"Don't say that!" Damon cried in horror, releasing Delilah for the second time that evening like a hot potato.   "My blood—no, not *the blood I gave*—"

"Yes, Mr. Lang.   It was your blood that killed him.   Wrong type.   Mr. Brown died from cardiac and cerebral embolism due to your blood corpuscles collecting into clumps.   Dr. Dow recognized the symptoms during the transfusion, when he had got over his shock and thought back about it—skin turning blue—rapid pulse—

labored breathing—death—happens most likely when the donor's blood is type AB and the recipient's type is O.   Cases on record about it."

"But Pythias's blood was type AB too.   Same as mine," Damon said, drifting deeper into the horror of it all.

"No, his blood group was type O.   Dr. Dow has just finished testing it."

"Dr. Dow don't know his blood-testing, or any other kind of testing, from horse feathers," Delilah insisted inelegantly.   "My husband's type was AB.   It's marked right on his driver's license."

Bill selected Delilah's license from its cellophane folder in her wallet.

He studied with satisfaction the small box in its lower right-hand corner labeled BLOOD TYPE.   A space provided on licenses by the State of Florida, for the operator to print in his own blood group, for swift use in case of an automobile accident when an instant transfusion would be required.

"I see that your type is B, Mrs. Brown.   Did you print it in yourself?"

"I did and what of it?"

"Just that our handwriting expert will testify it matches the B you added on your husband's license—after you had changed the original O into an A by drawing a line down on either side of it and straightening its curved bottom into a crossbar. Like they change the cattle brands out west.   Showed up plain under Dr. Dow's microscope, Mrs. Brown."

Bill added—as Damon groaned in tortured horror, and as Mabel plunged for the vodka, and as Delilah changed into a shrieking female—"Weirdest murder weapon I ever came across in my life."

RICHARD M. ELLIS

Glory Hunter

When the buzzer buzzed at the front entrance, Homer Doyle set down his mug of lukewarm tea—he never drank coffee after midnight—and rose from his chair behind the desk. He crossed the lobby to the heavy glass door and clucked disapprovingly at the young man smiling in at him. He released the latch and pushed the door open a few inches.

"I thought my sister might have turned up," the young man said eagerly. "I know it's late, but—"

"Almost three o'clock in the morning," Homer Doyle said with some asperity. "Your sister isn't here. Perhaps she went to some other hotel."

The young man's sandy brows puckered in a frown. "No. She was definitely supposed to come straight here from the airport. I don't understand it."

"She might have met someone on the plane—"

"Oh, no. Betty isn't that kind of girl," the young man said, looking a bit shocked.

Doyle grunted dubiously. He had been night-clerking at the Cragmore, a small hotel for women, more than long enough to decide that almost any girl was that kind of girl. He said, "Well, I'm sorry, she just hasn't shown up. No one has checked in since you were here earlier."

He started to pull the door shut.

"Could I come in long enough to use the phone?" the young man asked. He gestured to the dark, deserted street stretching into the hot summer night on either side of the Cragmore's lighted entrance. "There doesn't seem to be another place open along here. I want to call the—the police. I really am worried about Betty."

Homer Doyle hesitated.

The Cragmore was run very much like the nearby YWCA; no male visitors were allowed inside the building after midnight, when the front door was locked. "Propriety" and "Cragmore" were synonymous.

Doyle nodded. After all, the boy was obviously only concerned with locating his sister, and there was a phone booth just inside the lobby.

Inside, the young man waited while Doyle shut and locked the door. The rather large lobby was in shadow; the only lights on were Doyle's reading lamp behind the registration desk, and the tiny yellow bulb above the elevator.

"Certainly different from when I was here before," the young man said. "The place was swarming with girls then."

Doyle nodded vaguely. The boy had come in around ten or ten-thirty last night, inquiring for his sister who had supposedly arrived in the city earlier in the evening.

Perhaps she had, but she hadn't checked in at the Cragmore. The young man, who had given his name as Bob Ed Lambeth, had hung around for several minutes with a sort of polite but dogged persistence until Doyle had gone through the registration cards twice with the same result. Finally, after a long look around the then busy lobby, the young man had left.

Now Doyle said, "The phone's over there. I suppose you've checked to make sure your sister's plane arrived on schedule last night?"

"What? Oh, yes." Lambeth fumbled in a pocket of his sports jacket. "I think I'll need change."

Doyle sighed and turned toward the desk. He took two steps, and then his head suddenly exploded in a great burst of white light followed by a shower of sparks that died into nothingness.

He woke to find himself in his familiar chair behind the registration desk, but with a most unfamiliar pain throbbing in his head. He groaned and tried to lift his hands. He couldn't move. He blinked dazedly up into the concerned face of the young man who had wanted to use the phone.

"Thank goodness," Lambeth said. "I was afraid I'd hit you too hard, Mr. Doyle."

"What—"

"Would you like a drink of water?"

Doyle shook his head, winced, and again tried to lift his hands. Then he saw that his arms were bound securely to the arms of the chair, with some kind of heavy cord that also encircled his chest, holding him firmly against the back of the chair.

Lambeth was saying, "I'm sorry I had to slug you but I couldn't be sure you weren't carrying a gun or something. I had to play it safe."

"Gun?" Doyle said dazedly.

"After all, you are down here on the ground floor alone, and there's no house detective or anyone like that in the hotel; just you and the manager, Mrs. McVey, and of course she's fast asleep in her room up on the top floor."

Along with the throbbing in his head Doyle began to feel anger, most of it directed at himself. This kid with his guileless air and fresh-scrubbed face had taken Doyle in completely.

Doyle swore under his breath. Then he glanced toward the small safe set into the wall behind the desk. The safe had been closed, but not locked; now its door was ajar.

Doyle snapped, "I see you've cleaned out the cash box. I hope the fifty bucks you found in there is enough, because that's all there is."

Lambeth didn't appear convinced. "I don't—"

"Of course, I might have all of five dollars in my wallet," Doyle added bitterly.

"Six, as a matter of fact," said Lambeth, with a deprecating smile. "I searched you while you were unconscious. I also found a gun in this little drawer under the counter here. I'll just take that along . . . But I'm really not interested in money, or guns. This is what I was looking for." From the desk he picked up four sheets of stiff paper, floor plans of the hotel, one for each of the four upper floors. Small removable tags indicated which rooms were occupied and which were not.

Doyle stared.

Lambeth said lightly, "No, I'm not still trying to find my sister. Actually, I imagine Betty's sound asleep at this hour, in her own bed at home. Way out in Seattle, Washington. She really did stay here once, though, when she came east on a visit. She told me all about this place. Thought it was very nice. Very quiet and respectable."

Doyle frowned uncertainly at the young man. He noticed that in spite of Lambeth's casual chatter and outwardly calm manner, there was a sheen of perspiration on his face, and his hands were trembling.

"You've got all the cash in the place," Doyle said. "Why are you hanging around?"

"It's not quite three-thirty yet," said Lambeth, nodding toward the wall clock. "There's nothing to do but wait."

"Wait for what?"

Lambeth made an abrupt gesture. "Do you like this job?"

"Now, listen—"

"It sounds like it would be—interesting. Night clerk in a hotel for women, one man alone with all these girls. I'll bet you could write a best-selling book about your experiences, huh? Even at your age, it must be interesting."

"Are you kidding?"

Lambeth shrugged, his pale gaze again flicking to the clock. He took off his jacket and folded it neatly over a corner of the desk.

He said, absently, "I suppose if you were the lecherous type, you wouldn't have this job in the first place. Not in a respectable place like this is supposed to be . . . Well, it's almost time. I'll just—"

"Time for what?" Doyle cried. "What the hell is all this?"

As he spoke, Doyle struggled against the cord that bound him to the chair and discovered that there was a certain amount of give in the loops encircling his left arm and the arm of the chair on that side. He immediately stopped his efforts; Lambeth didn't seem to notice.

Lambeth was busy. He had taken off his shirt, and Doyle saw that the young man's naked, hairless chest was covered with curious designs done in greasepaint; jagged streaks of red and green radiating from a bright yellow spiral.

Now Lambeth took a tiny mirror and a stick of yellow greasepaint from his trousers pockets and carefully drew crude stars on his clean-shaven cheeks and a sunburst on his forehead.

Doyle watched, his eyes bulging.

"Just an added touch," Lambeth said, with an embarrassed grimace. "It's the kind of thing that goes over big in the newspapers."

"Sure. Uh-huh," said Doyle soothingly. Until now he had been more annoyed at his own gullibility than afraid of Lambeth. The kid was hardly the type to inspire terror, but if he was a psycho, that was something else again.

Lambeth eyed the clock. "Three-thirty. Good. That's the time my father died, some years ago. Three-thirty on a hot summer morning . . . He died of acute alcoholism, Mr. Doyle. Driven to it by my mother. How does that grab you?"

Doyle tried to moisten his dry lips with a tongue that felt like parched leather. "I—I'm sorry—"

Lambeth burst out laughing. "Don't be. Just between us, my old man died of a coronary, but the other way sounds much more interesting."

"Sure."

"Well, to work," Lambeth said briskly. "I've looked at these floor plans. I believe the top floor is best. I see there are seventeen guests on that floor, most of them in single rooms. That'll make it easier, you know."

"What are you—"

"See, I can go quietly from room to room, using this master key I found in the safe. With just one girl to deal with in each room—except in a couple of cases where there are two—there won't be any unnecessary uproar or bother."

Doyle shook his aching head. He wondered if he might be having some kind of weird hallucination; but the pain was real enough, and so was the needle-pointed ice pick that Lambeth had taken from a sheath attached to his belt.

Doyle sat there, frozen, while the young man tucked the chart of the top floor under one bare arm and with a casual nod walked around the end of the desk and started across the lobby. He was humming softly.

"Wait," Doyle croaked. "Listen, you can't mean—"

"Sure I do," Lambeth said, his face shining with sweat and greasepaint. "What the heck, I'll soon be twenty-four, and who's ever heard of Robert Edward Lambeth? Nobody. But in a few hours, Mr. Doyle—in a few hours I'll be the most famous man in the country—in the world."

"But—"

"I'll be down as soon as possible. Then I'll untie you, and we can call the television stations and the newspapers—and the cops, I suppose." Lambeth grimaced. "Don't worry about a thing, Mr. Doyle. After all, you'll be the man who took my surrender. Wish me luck."

Lambeth reached the elevator and slid open the door. He stepped inside and, with a last cheerful nod, punched the button and the door slid shut.

Whimpering, Doyle strained and tugged at the cord; almost at once his left arm was free.

"My God," he panted. "Seventeen—he'll kill . . ."

Now his right arm was free, and only the cumbersome loops of cord around his chest held him in the chair. If he could free himself before the elevator reached the top floor, there was an emergency switch that would override the controls inside the elevator itself, stopping it between floors.   If Doyle could just reach that switch in time . . .

He glared across the dim lobby at the indicator above the elevator door.   The hand of the indicator was moving slowly past 2 and on toward 3.

Doyle tried to stand up but he was still entangled in the stiff new cord.   He groaned.

That psycho would kill those women, one by one, entering their rooms and stabbing them with that ice pick before they knew what was happening, and Doyle had no doubts remaining that Lambeth meant to do just that.   Seventeen . . .

It would be the most horrible crime . . .

Lambeth would be famous, all right.   Oh, yes!

At last Doyle was able to stand up partially, his eyes glued to the elevator indicator; it had reached 3, and there was only 4—and then 5, the top floor.

There was still time, though.   The switch was on a panel in an alcove behind the desk, only a few steps from where Doyle was struggling to push the last loop of the cord down past his hips so that he could step out of it.

Famous?   Lambeth would be more than famous.   There would be hours of television about him, miles of newsprint devoted to him, magazine articles, books— if Homer Doyle didn't stop him in the next few seconds.

And what about the man who caught Lambeth? Right now it would mean nothing. But afterwards, after seventeen murders . . .   That man would be almost as famous as Lambeth!

Doyle stood there in a sudden blinding agony of indecision.

Then, slowly, he sank back into the chair.   He stared in fascination at the elevator indicator.   Then he slowly pulled the last loop of the cord back up around his waist.

After all, not only the young have dreams of glory.

PAULINE C. SMITH

Linda Is Gone

The young woman remembered a small town and long-ago winter snow, or did she? She remembered it now but would not tomorrow. She remembered a family and a young man in a house on a tree-lined street; a yesterday memory almost gone today. She remembered a summer picnic—noise, games, laughter, and cars on the highway in the distance . . .

"What's your name, chick?" asked the guy in the shiny new 1963 convertible.

"Linnette," she had said, knowing it was not exactly that, but liking the sound of it on her tongue, so that she repeated the name, "Linnette," with its soft roll and decisively final click.

"Linnette. Yes, it fits you," he had said, and she felt the name wrap around her narrow shoulders and hold her small waist with comfort. She looked at the sound of it with big blue eyes and smiled at the sight of it with too-thin lips painted to provocative inducement.

She caught the name and held its reality within the unreality of that which surrounded her.

At one time or another on that day in the park almost everyone claimed to have seen Linda, but no one could remember at which time or other she had been seen. Who counts hours of a summer day at an all-out picnic?

The rolling, heavily wooded park was throughly searched and the hobo jungle at its very edge, down by the muddy river, "was gone over with a fine-tooth comb," the police chief said. "We can't find hide or hair of her," and admitted he didn't know what to do next.

Who gets lost in a town like this with nothing but prairies and farmland on each side? Who? *Only Linda, wouldn't you know, who thinks she's so much, acting like she's better than anybody else. Newly married, too . . .*

How about her husband? Maybe he killed her and buried the body.

Kenneth? Kenneth Borchard? That'd be like killing the goose that laid the golden eggs. Anyway, he was crazy about her. Where would he bury the body?

Oh, there's a million places for a kid like that with a car.

Perhaps there were, especially a kid who'd come from trash. After all, his father had killed his mother in a drunken rage and turned the shotgun on himself. You can't get around that kind of blood.

Kenneth seems a nice sort of kid.

Sure he is, as long as things go along all right. Maybe things didn't go along all right and he did to his wife what his old man did to his mother.

Oh! Maybe so . . .

They grilled Kenneth; but first they talked to Linda's father, Leland Krebs, city councilman and owner of the feed store.

Up to that point, the father's secret thought had been that Linda had gotten peeved or hurt about something and hightailed it to the highway to hitch a ride to nowhere, and he was scared. His daughter, such a pretty, shy, sensitive and usually tractable little doll had hightailed it off twice before—not that anyone else knew about those times, of course. The first was when she was twelve and got a shameful D on her report card, and again when she was sixteen and wasn't invited to a party of her peers. He had found her, the first time, down the railroad yards waiting for a freight; and the second, on a country road hoping for a hitch. Both times she had returned home peaceably as soon as her father assured her that he would force the teacher to raise her grade and would throw a party for her equal to two of the one to which she had not been invited.

When the police chief sounded out Leland Krebs he did so carefully, with one eye on Krebs' civic importance and the other on his own career. "You know we've done all we can, Mr. Krebs," he said, spreading his hands helplessly. "We've combed the county and alerted the agencies. We've been thinking . . ." using the editorial "we" in order to spread the blame around, "we've been thinking, how about your son-in-law, Kenneth Borchard?"

"How about him?" Krebs answered thoughtfully, and wondered, indeed, how about Kenneth Borchard?

It was right after Linda had graduated from high school that she had proclaimed, "Now I want only to marry Kenneth Borchard."

"What?" Krebs exploded.

Linda's mother, Minnie Krebs, quivering protoplasm of inadequacy, folded her hands over her breasts and breathed fast.

"Kenneth Borchard?" boomed Linda's father. "He's just a kid, and scum to boot. You're too young to get married anyway."

Leland Krebs was wrong on two counts and right on one. Kenneth was a kid chronologically only, having lived twice as long as his years in order to establish a reputation out of nothing, making him probably less scum and more of a man than most of the so-called men in town. That Linda was too young to be married was the truth. Linda was too young for almost anything.

She withdrew. The moment her father dared to bring forth argument, her lips closed tight so that only the lipstick peaks were left, her eyes went blank and her face took on a hightail-escape look.

"Well, let's talk it over," suggested her father, and her mother let her hands drop from her breasts.

Kenneth was, really and truly, very crazy about Linda. She was what he aspired to, having the diffidence, modesty, lovely purity and aloof dignity he worshiped, yet felt he could never attain.   He almost fell out of his 1950 heap the night she primly proposed.   "We'll be married," she announced as if she were planning an afternoon tea.   "Right away."

"How can we, for Pete's sake?   I haven't even got a job except for that piddlin' boxboy job down at the market.   I was thinking of using that scholarship I got and going to State—"

"You won't have to," Linda said, offering him a substitute for education. "Daddy'll give you a job in the feed store.   A *good* job.   And we can live with my folks until you work yourself up.   Daddy said so."

Kenneth was overwhelmed, first by the fact that his life was being arranged, then by the one who was doing the arranging.   "Linda," he choked, and kissed her somewhat less chastely than he had ever before kissed her.

They had been married a little less than two months that August 17th, 1963, the Saturday Linda disappeared from the park picnic.

"I never saw her again after I left the house that morning to go to my job at the feed store," Kenneth explained, remembering the morning following the night before that had tied him up in knots.   What did Linda think other married people did in bed—sang hymnal duets?   Played word games?   Held hands?   It was another of those times that she called him a beast and coldly withdrew herself to the far side of the bed as if he were scum, and yes, she had told him he was that, too.

"I left at eight," related Kenneth, remembering the cold, white face on the pillow, eyes closed against him, folded hands holding the sheet tightly shut like a veil of purity.   "She went to the park with her folks—early.   I didn't get away to go until five."

"After you got there," the chief of police asked, "didn't you see her?"

"No," Kenneth said.   Nor had he looked, but he wouldn't tell that part.   It was his sin of omission that he hadn't looked for her.   He hadn't wanted to.   He still felt the words "beast" and "scum" like insulting handprints on his sensitive face, loving her, loving her on his knees, loving her abjectly and loving her with a tentative passion.   It was the last that made of him a scummy beast and sent him, in the park, to the beer keg, not to search out his wife.

"Didn't you look?" asked the police chief, making the question an accusation.

"Well . . ."   and Kenneth said sure he looked, too loudly, as if he were lying. "But I didn't see her.   And, gosh, she could have been anywhere.   You know how it was.   There were all those games and people milling around . . ."

So then the police chief questioned the picnickers as to whether or not they had seen Linda's husband.   Most people had, or thought they had, at one time or another, late that day; but no one could remember at which time or other, between five and eight o'clock when it began to get dark, that they had seen him, if at all.

"It was eight o'clock when I began looking," Kenneth said.   "Everybody began to look then."

Between five and eight, the chief of police reasoned cannily, during that time the people didn't know when or even whether or not they had seen Kenneth, he could have taken his wife from one of the wooded areas off in his car and killed and buried her.   Or he could have found her alone, killed her on the spot, dragged her away and buried her.

What else?   She couldn't be found, so she must be dead and covered up.

Kenneth was formally charged and took up residence in one of the four cells in the jailhouse.

The young woman was accustomed to the slipping away of things, ideas and memories, to leave her on ankles of air, so now that winter was here with no change in the climate, she was not really surprised.   She remembered only now and then a small town with winter snow, but was that memory from out of her past or something she might have read?

There was a new man here in the house where she was living.   At least she thought he was new, and remembered another house, a family, another man, and wept for she knew not what.

"The trouble with you, Linese, is you're always crying," she heard from some-where, with the name her only reality, or almost reality, and not the speaker.

Was it her name or was it *nearly* her name?   Her hands reached up to catch and hold the name tight.   She *must* hold something tight, but she wanted not to be held herself.

She remembered, in subliminal flash, a picnic and noise and games, and im-mediately lost the memory, to weep again.

The snow was thick in drifts around the courthouse during Kenneth Borchard's trial, where the town judged him guilty and innocent, whichever way the wind blew, looking upon him with delighted excitement or the publicity he had produced, and with suspicious reserve just in case he actually was a killer.

The chief of police took a neutral no-comment stand, causing everybody to know that he thought Kenneth Borchard guilty as hell because, after all, a live girl had not been found, had she, even though he, in his wisdom, had led the search?   So, there must be a dead girl somewhere and Kenneth Borchard killed her.

Leland Krebs' mind was fixed from the very first instant the idea had been placed there.   *I should have watched her more closely.   She had the closed-in, ready-to-hightail-it look that morning.*   "Sure he did it," he told sympathetic listeners. "I take him into my home, give him a job, let him marry Linda and he kills her."

Minnie Krebs said nothing.   Minnie Krebs never said anything about anything.

The trial was a farce, but played seriously and with solemnity, since it offered the defense attorney an opportunity to practice criminal law and allowed the pros-ecution to prosecute more than vandalism and theft.   By their combined inept efforts, Kenneth was convicted of murder two and sentenced to twenty years.

The man in the room with the palm fronds at the window asked the young woman where she had been that day.

"What day?" she countered quickly.

"Yesterday.   Dammit, Linese," he cried in frustration, "Wednesday, August

17th. The year is 1966, in case you've forgotten, and you probably have. So, where were you? I come home from work and you're off someplace. Where in hell were you?''

Blankly, she gazed at and through him. ''I was looking,'' she said, ''for a park filled with trees, and a picnic.''

''Oh, man,'' he moaned, ''it's always that. You're forever looking for something. Some damn park . . . some damn street . . . snow in winter . . . and in California. You get these streaks and you're off in limbo. I've had it. You understand? Another time . . . just one more time you're not here when you're supposed to be . . .''

''Where is here?'' she asked.

On August 17th, 1966, there in the state penitentiary, Kenneth Borchard had completed the work necessary for his B.A. degree and looked forward to earning his master's. He rarely thought of Linda—after all, they had been married less than two months three years ago, hardly long enough to remember and too long ago to conjecture upon.

Leland Krebs erected a granite memorial to his daughter in the park while he privately wondered where she really was.

Minnie Krebs never did see the memorial, for she rarely left the house. ''In deep mourning,'' her husband described her seclusion, but the general opinion was that she was locked up in the house because she was just plain crazy . . . ''Always was a little nutty, you know.''

The young woman felt as if the carpet of grass beneath her feet bent and swayed more than usual, much more than usual. She staggered over sliding carpet, arms outstretched for balance, feet running for safety, and reached the bench to throw herself down upon it and laugh with triumph at outwitting this slippery world.

She smiled and nodded the hours away, catching at thoughts that flickered in her mind, catching and losing them, chuckling at their passing, amused by the kaleidoscope of color and butterfly-wing movement of these scampering pictures in her brain.

People strolling by noticed and remarked upon her.

''Maybe she's high on something.''

''A drunk, more than likely.''

''Hey, what's with her?''

''She's a kook. This park collects 'em.''

Only two old gentlemen, chess opponents, saw her from the beginning and observed her through the hours. ''Look at that woman, drunk as a coot,'' one said to the other as her steps stuttered toward the bench. ''Don't like to see women drink.''

''This is 1968. Women drink all the time,'' declared the other, moving his knight three squares forward and two squares sideways while his friend's eyes were off the board.

They watched her between moves and commented on her condition, and after several hours of inattentive chess, came to the conclusion that the woman on the bench was not drunk at all, but had some wires crossed.

"So what do we do?" one asked the other.

"Call someone, I suppose."

"Call who?"

"The police, maybe."

They folded their board and boxed the chessmen and walked across the palm-tree-lined park to stand on the curbing and await a prowl car that regularly patrolled this downtown street. While they waited, they discussed the significance of their discovery, building stories, each topping the other, that caused their old eyes to gleam with inventive delight.

"Maybe she murdered someone and went off her rocker," came the final pinnacle of suggestion, and they stood there in double horror, sure that one should have stayed to see that the killer remained where she was while the other went for help.

Neither had offered to return and stand watch by the time the patrol car came slowly down the street. Both leaped to attention, arms upraised, voices squeaking with age and self-importance.

The two officers walked across the park with the two old men who were frantic now with fear that the woman might be gone and they would be tagged as a couple of imaginative old idiots. But no, she was still there, still smiling and nodding, still talking to her thoughts with little trills of sound.

One officer stood, the other knelt on a knee before her, getting no answer to his questions until he asked her name. She looked back at him. She caught a thought. Her lips thinned to a fine line of contemplation. "Linn . . ." Dissatisfied, she shook her head. "Linn," and shrugged, accepting this new narrow view of a horizon which had done nothing but fluctuate for as long as she could remember, though she could not remember long nor accurately.

"Where do you live?" she was asked, replying that she did not live at all, and spoke of a park, peering through the frame of the kneeling officer's bent arm.

He rose up from his knee and looked at his partner who offered a slight nod. He leaned down and gently touched the woman's shoulder. "Come with me. Would you come with me, please?" he asked.

Linn nodded. She stood and staggered, clutching at the officer's arm, glad of the support. "Oh, yes," she said, "it is very slippery in the world in which I live."

When, in 1968, Kenneth Borchard was turned down for parole, he plunged back into his education. After his master's, he started studying law, never thinking of Linda now that he had become maturely introspective enough to realize he had lost nothing, through her, but his freedom.

That year, Leland Krebs retired from active participation in the feed store and gave some thought to hiring a private detective to investigate the disappearance of his daughter. Then, on second thought, he decided to let the situation lie quietly for fear she might be found, and Kenneth freed.

It had been so long since anyone had seen Minnie Krebs, they had all forgotten her existence.

The day-room attendant stood at the window watching two male patients in their daily attempt to carry a trash barrel from a spot by the fence to a pick-up junction fifty yards away. Each being obsessively right-handed, one grabbed a side handle with his right hand and walked forward, following the other in a continuous frustrated circle.

The attendant turned her back on the window, knowing the argumentative fury that would ensue, also knowing it would not be resolved, and stepped to her desk that was placed so as to offer a wide-swept observation point to include all the patients in the day room, the four at a card table playing a spirited no-rule game, the catatonic in steady gaze of the ceiling, the furious knitter making knots of her work, and the young woman who wrote the letter.

She was always writing a letter which, when finished, she folded, placed in an envelope, licked closed and addressed to nobody.

The day-room attendant was emotionally interested in these letters, probably because she would like to write letters too, and also had no one to whom she could write. "You're new here," a nurse told her. "Everyone new gets interested in her. Each new doctor pores over the letters. He compiles them, compares them, trying to figure out whether hers is a process schizophrenia or a reactive schizophrenia, and tries to talk to her and gets nothing back and the letters pile up, all of them pretty much the same, about a picnic in the park and snow in the winter; and finally he throws them all away. Then another doctor comes along and the same things happen. Sure, it's interesting at first, but then . . ." and the nurse shrugged. She had watched the woman for three years, ever since her admission to this California State Mental Hospital in 1968. She had seen the gradual slide from tractable noncommunication, with only occasional flashes of useless memory, to moody isolation filled with letter-writing—the letters all signed with the name "Linn" finally shortened to "Lin."

"Who is she, really?" the attendant asked.

"Who knows?" the nurse said. "Even she doesn't know who she is."

By 1971, Kenneth Borchard knew enough law so that he was in great demand by his fellow inmates for the drafting and submission of writs of habeas corpus and certiorari. He considered his eight years in prison as well-spent and never once thought about whose absence it was that had put him there and whose continued absence kept him there.

Leland Krebs had, long since, eased his slightly shifting conscience with the excuse that since Kenneth Borchard must have put the withdrawn, ready-to-hightail-it look on his daughter's face that August morning of 1963, he could rot in prison for all of him.

Minnie Krebs sat vacant-eyed and non-moving in her room.

On that summer day of 1971, no one member of the mental hospital staff could be absolutely sure what it was that had brought Linda out of her darkness and into identity.   The doctors gave credit to psychotherapy; technicians to shock treatment; the nurses thought, of course, their chemotherapy had turned the trick; but the day-room attendant knew it had been the letters—the letters that had retained her interest, if not that of the nurses or doctors—those blank envelopes handed her each day, which she discussed in monologue, asking the questions, "Who is it you write to?" and "Where do you write each day?"—-always unanswered until today, August 17, 1971, when "Lin" handed her the envelope addressed to Kenneth Borchard in a small Midwestern town, with the name, Linda Borchard, written in the upper left-hand corner.

The chief of police answered the station-house phone and was startled into frozen silence at what he thought he heard.   Finally, unlocking his tongue from the roof of his mouth, he stammered in repetition that, yes, a Kenneth Borchard did live in town, or used to, and yes, he was married to a girl by the name of Linda, who . . . *The hell you say* . . . and the police chief fished for a handkerchief to wipe away the sweat that poured down his brow from the significance of the words he was hearing.

Five minutes later, he was explaining to Linda's father why he didn't think it was his daughter whom they said was in that asylum way out there in California—how could it be, with the Borchard kid in prison for killing her, and her buried somewhere nobody'd found yet?

Leland Krebs *knew* it was Linda, his joy at the miracle of having her restored to him so pure that he forgot Kenneth Borchard, her husband, in prison for her murder.   He flew off to California to claim his child, with the firm resolution that he would anticipate her future moods and wishes and always endow her with, and surround her with everything her heart desired so that never again would she get the hightail look on her lovely face and leave him bereft.

Minnie Krebs, unroused by news of her daughter, continued to survey the wall of her bedroom that she had so catatonically surveyed for almost eight years, and the chief of police said it certainly went to prove he sure couldn't find a dead body when there wasn't any dead body to find, so nobody could blame him, could they? He was just glad Mr. Krebs had his daughter back . . . oh-damn-now-the-state-authorities-would-have-to-be-notified-and-they'd-find-out-it-had-been-his-recom-mendation-to-keep-that-kid-locked-up-and-throw-away-the-key-because-he-was-a-killer-like-his-father-before-him . . .

Kenneth, notified that he was no murderer after all, immediately submitted his own writ of certiorari as well as habeas corpus, along with a judgment against the state for wrongful detention and cruel and inhuman treatment.   He became so involved with the legal processes of gaining his freedom, establishing his full civil rights and acquiring a profitable return on his time of incarceration, he forgot to think of Linda until, once the legal red tape of the Midwestern penitentiary was untangled and the institutional bureaucracy of the California State Mental Hospital bogged down to exhausted simplicity, he saw her again and knew damned well that she hadn't been worth a minute of those eight years in prison.

"This is Kenneth, my dear," Leland Krebs said to his daughter, clicking the consonants and rounding the vowels to form a clear and understanding statement. "Kenneth Borchard, my dear, your husband," the last said with a flicker of remorse.

Linda knew who Kenneth was, she knew with immediate and total recall that completely eradicated the past eight years from her life. It was summer, there had been a picnic in the park . . . "Such a nice picnic," she said, her voice a childish treble, and Kenneth, remembering his eight-year-long picnic, hated her.

Minnie Krebs stared at the wall of her room without knowing of her daughter's absence or return, and the town was shot through with guilt, each individual townsperson feeling his own particular pang of conscience, wanting to make it up to Kenneth, so that when he set up his law practice they flocked to his office with their real and imagined troubles—and he took care of them and prospered.

With the money he received from his suit against the state (the largest sum ever paid for wrongful detention), he built a house above the wooded park, a showplace, an estate.

The townspeople pointed it out to each other, pridefully and with comments.

He deserves it. If anybody deserves success, it's him.

Who would have thought, ten years ago . . .

Even two years! With him still in prison then and her out there in California. How he could have been so forgiving, I'll never know—not letting us dump the chief off the police force or Krebs off the council, and taking back that wife who caused it all and treating her like a queen . . .

Yeah. Beats me. But then, you don't find many like Mr. Borchard.

That you don't. He's a prince.

Kenneth Borchard walked through the park every day, his law office being at one side of it and his home on the other. Sometimes he walked across the close-cropped lawns and cement walkways to approach his house from the front. Other times, he went around and through the woods and climbed the hill, entering his house through the rear. He learned much about the park and its growing things and felt the firmness of the ground under his feet after a dry spell, its sponginess after rain. He learned how much rain could cause it to muddy and cling soggily to a stick thrust into it and how a lesser rain made it so friable that the stick entered easily and the soil broke away cleanly. The soil was just right after this September rain in 1973. The time was right too, after two years of freedom, success and public respect. At five-thirty in the evening, the woods were deeply shadowed; by six, the hill would be in dusk; and by six-thirty, it should be quite dark.

He entered the lighted kitchen, whistling. Linda turned from the stove and lifted her cheek, withdrawing it the moment he had brushed it with his lips. She spoke of the chops she was frying to inedibility, blaming the butcher. She spoke of her daddy, who had visited her that day as he did each day, but she did not speak of her mother whom she had forgotten, as had everyone else in town. She spoke of the gardener who had been rude, and the house being too much to care for . . .

Her world, now so small and solid, with snow in the winter and a park to be seen from her windows, that she must pick at it for its small solidity, its park and its snow in season, with her solidly small mind that had dwelt upon parks and snow for eight lost years.

Kenneth promised to speak to the butcher and gardener. He fervently promised to install a housekeeper, this last a promise he planned to keep for himself.

He looked at his watch—almost six—and glanced through the kitchen windows, now nearly dark beyond the light. With abortive gestures of assistance, he attempted to hurry Linda's dinner preparations and, typically obstinate, she put barriers in the way.

First, she asked him to mix martinis; she who rarely drank. "You don't have to get to that chamber of commerce meeting until eight," she pointed out in childish treble, which was true.

Then she decided to serve the dinner in the dining room instead of conveniently in the kitchen.

She set the dining table, drank her martini, and burned the chops until 6:30. He could have killed her then, and felt his fists tighten. He should have been in the act of doing so, according to his timing.

Perversely, while he was consulting his watch and refiguring his time, Linda decided on another martini before sitting down to the table. Fifteen minutes for the drink, a half hour for dinner, fifteen minutes to clear the table and get the dishes done—that meant it would be 7:30 before he could kill her, and he sure as hell couldn't kill her, drag her down to the woods, bury her, get back to the house, call Krebs and leave for the chamber meeting by a quarter of eight . . .

So he reached across the martini pitcher, folded his hands around her long slim neck and pressed tight.

Kenneth Borchard was sure that she was definitely dead by 6:37, and dropped her body to the kitchen floor. He stood still for one moment of recapitulation, mentally adding the tasks that she should have done to those he had so meticulously planned for himself, changed the order of his schedule and raced upstairs to her closet, where he lifted out the new fall coat. He carefully closed the door and walked slowly down the stairs, catching his breath.

In the kitchen, he knelt to thrust Linda's limp arms into the coat sleeves. He memorized her clothing, brown slacks, tan sweater. It was 6:50 and he began to smell the chops that had burned dry. He jumped up, turned off the flame, stuffed the chops down the garbage disposal and filled the pan with water to soak. While the disposal was running, he dumped the limp salad and looked around wildly for any more food that should have been eaten during an ordinarily composed dinner, scraped a pan of green beans and turned back to Linda.

In death, her eyes were wide and blue, with no less expression than they had held in life, her thin lips drawn back and parted. Kenneth was devoutly glad that she was dead at last.

It was seven o'clock and this part of the operation was but a mechanical replay of plans long in the making—the gardener's boots and gloves, the wheelbarrow and shovel from the tool shed out back—hoisting the body from the kitchen floor to the wheelbarrow to trundle it through the dark, and down the grassy hillside to the edge of the woods that fringed the park.   A softly cool wind blew through the trees and clouds collided in the sky, denoting another rain, which was good, provided it did not start for a couple of hours.

The soil was exactly as he knew it would be, easy to slice through, just compact enough so that he could lift out shovelfuls of sod and lay them aside, friable so that he could work quickly.   He began to sweat in the cool breeze and pulled off his suit coat, laying it across the body, and worried—-would he have enough time to change his shirt—what time was it now?   He couldn't make out the digits or the hands of his watch in the dark of the trees and the overcast of the sky.

He worked quickly, digging the grave narrow but deep, regularly measuring its depth by the handle of the shovel, the sod on one side, soil on the other, until he was satisfied.

He laid down the shovel carefully and fanned his arms to dry his shirt of per-spiration.   He picked up his suit coat from the body, put it on, shrugged it in place, then tipped the wheelbarrow so that the body fell into the trench he had dug. He bent, careful not to kneel in the soft earth, and straightened her out, then he shoveled in the soil, tramping it with the gardener's boots.   When the grave was filled within three inches, he fit the clods of sod over it, tramping these down, and using the shovel, scattered the soil that had been displaced by her body, so that it fell in small secret heaps under the trees and in the turf.

He placed the shovel in the wheelbarrow and pulled it after him up the hill.   The kitchen windows provided a path of light to the tool shed.   He looked at his watch: 7:30.   He'd done a beautiful job!   He upended the wheelbarrow, hung up the shovel, placed the gloves on the workbench, toed off the boots and placed them exactly as he had found them.   He shook his trouser legs into their impeccable crease, closed the door of the shed and walked to the kitchen.

There were the dirty pans!   At 7:32!

He walked to the hall, lifted the phone and dialed the Krebs' number.   He put a hearty note into his voice.   "What say I pick you up a little before eight and we go on together to the C. of C. meeting?   No point in using two cars."   He hung up and raced to the kitchen and groaned.   He took off his coat again and tossed it to a chair, then he unbuttoned and rolled up his shirt sleeves and tackled the pans.

He finally found a box labeled "scouring pads" and was finished by 7:45—all the pans put away, the kitchen in order.   He stacked the dishes in the dining room, tossed the silverware into a drawer, whisked off the tablecloth, folded and put it away, remembering to put the centerpiece back on the table.   It was 7:48.   He looked at his hands, rolled down his shirt sleeves.   He wouldn't have time to change.

He hurried to the living room, turned on the TV set, piled the pillows at the end of the divan, and punched them as if a head had rested there.   He left only one lamp burning.

He turned off the lights in the dining room, grabbed his suit coat from the kitchen chair and put it on, buttoning one button, and took a quick look around the tidy kitchen, glancing at his watch: 7:52.   He turned off the kitchen lights, slammed the door, made sure it was locked and ran for the garage.

He picked up Krebs at 7:59 and arrived at the meeting by 8:10 where he maintained an attentive attitude without hearing a word of the business, so intent was he upon listening for hopeful rain against the windows.   With rain, even a gentle rain, the trampled grass of the grave would spring up again and the scattered soil would sink into the ground . . .

Had the meeting been a long one, Kenneth would have suggested to Krebs, with a light and teasingly conspiring chuckle, that he come home with him to explain the lateness of the hour; but since the meeting was over at nine o'clock, he opened the car door for his father-in-law and offered his alternate suggestion.   "Sir," he said, "it's still early.   I'll drive you up to the house first, we'll have a nightcap and then Linda and I'll both take you home.   She can use the fresh air after an evening in front of the TV set—at least, that's where she was when I left and I'll bet she's still there . . ."

The rain began just as he unlocked the back door and opened it to the sound of a familiar commercial tune.   He laughed with relief and called, "Hi, honey," telling Krebs to go on in while he mixed the drinks.

He waited then, in an ecstasy of frozen excitement.   Through the patter of quickening raindrops against the windowpanes, it came at last, the "Linda" cry, a confusion of sound within the sound of the commercial, and Kenneth loosened his muscles, eager for activity, and loped to the living room to stand and stare at the dented pillows, then at the television set that rolled its picture.

"Linda," he bawled up the stairs, and took them, two at a time.   He made a purposeful clatter, charging from room to room, turning on lights and slamming doors.   He raced down the stairs, snapped off the television set and brushed Krebs aside as he searched the downstairs rooms, closets, cupboards, even the furnace room beneath the house.

He ran from the kitchen, slammed the door of the tool shed, turned on the garage lights and came back in, soaked.   He walked to the hallway, shoulders slumped, dialed a number and ordered the police in a voice carefully broken.   "The chief of police," he added with a sob.

Then he turned toward his father-in-law and said, "She's gone.   It is happening again, just as it happened before," watching him, watching the dawning realization on Leland Krebs' round father-face as the sudden knowledge assailed him that Linda was gone and it was indeed happening again, but not as it had before.   This time, he could not accuse Kenneth Borchard of the crime that he had committed, having once accused him of the uncommitted crime.

The police chief, there in minutes, eager to rectify rash conceptions and past misjudgment, solemnly listed the clothing worn by the missing woman: brown slacks, tan sweater, new brown fall coat, no handbag, therefore no identification. The chief shook his head.   "Well, about all we can do is put out an APB on her," he said, as Kenneth Borchard was sure he would, "and concentrate on the asylums between here and California," with an apologetic and somewhat resentful glance toward Leland Krebs, to whom he didn't owe one damn thing.

The townspeople now had not only a hero and a prince, but a romantic martyr. Minnie Krebs continued to stare at the wall of her room unaware that her daughter had gone and returned, only to go again. Leland Krebs sat with her much of the time.

Kenneth Borchard knew at last that Linda had been worth every minute of his eight years in prison, now that he had paid her back for them . . .

C. B. GILFORD

Frightened Lady

Noel Tasker learned about the murder when he arrived home from the office. That was about five-forty-five on Tuesday. He drove through the entrance of Camelot Court and took the left drive. The right drive was his own, but he often took the left in order to pass by Gaby's apartment. Not that he would ever dare to stop in during daylight hours, but perhaps only to see if her car were there, or maybe, as had happened once, to see a man escorting her out the door. Despite the fact that he didn't own Gaby—and she had reminded him of that often—the experience had caused him a pang of jealousy. Masochistically, he continued to check on her now and then.

The sight which greeted him on this Tuesday, however, was not of Gaby's being escorted to a shiny new foreign sports car. There were four vehicles parked before her door today, three police cruisers and a white ambulance; and there was a crowd on the green lawn.

Noel Tasker braked to a quick stop, not wisely perhaps, but instinctively. That was Gaby's door standing wide open, with a policeman just outside it to fend off the crowd. He leaped from the car, then realized it was not his place to show such concern, and sauntered over to join the crowd.

"What's going on?" he asked the nearest man.

"There's been a murder."

Noel began to shake. He hoped the fact wasn't noticeable to his neighbor. The next question was infinitely more difficult. "Who was it?"

"A woman. I think her name was Marchant."

Gabrielle Marchant! His Gaby!

He was sick. He wanted to run, to find a private corner somewhere where he could let go, but also he wanted to stay there. He wanted to find out . . . the answers to a million questions. What had happened? Who had done it? A crazy thought ran through his head, of going up to the policeman at the door and saying, "Let me in, Officer. I was the dead woman's lover; one of her lovers, I mean."

Now his thoughts went pell-mell. *One* of her lovers! That guy he had seen picking up Gaby, taking her out in his fancy, expensive, foreign car. He ought to tell the police about that guy. He was probably the one who killed her! Describe the guy, describe the car . . .

"I hear she was good-looking." The man beside him was continuing the conversation.

"Yes . . ." Noel answered absently.

"You knew her?"

"Well, I . . ."

He stopped. Another thought was seeping into his reeling brain. If Gabrielle Marchant was suddenly murdered, *all* her lovers would be suspect, wouldn't they? Not that Noel Tasker was in any way implicated in her death; but now that she was dead, he didn't want to be implicated in her *life*.

"You knew her?"

"Well, I—I knew who she was."

"You've seen her?"

"Well, yes."

"Good-looking?"

"Well, depends. Depends on what you like. I guess she was, sort of."

He walked away from the man, who could have been a plainclothes detective, or a busybody sort who might report to the cops that he was talking to someone who acted very upset and nervous. So Noel returned to his car and drove away because now he was no longer mourning for the loss of Gaby, or shocked at her death. He was frightened.

He wheeled around the police cars and the ambulance, trying to go slowly, trying not to attract attention. He drove all the way to the far end, then back again on his own street, and parked in his own carport. The adjacent spot was empty. Leona hadn't arrived yet. He was thankful for that.

Once inside his own apartment, he felt a little better, but he was still shaking. He fixed himself a drink, heavy on the bourbon, easy on the soda. His hands trembled through the operation. He took a long swallow, then carried the rest of it into the bedroom. There he yanked off his jacket and tie. Afterward, though he didn't want to, he walked to the window.

There was only one thing out there on the rear lawn to suggest that there might be something wrong in Gabrielle's apartment—a cop; a uniformed cop standing at the rear door—just standing there. Maybe he was guarding the door, but there was no crowd in the rear; all the activity was out front.

Noel sipped at his drink, hoping to quiet the trembling in his hands. The view out this window was too painfully familiar, but he stayed there nevertheless, staring.

It had been while standing at this window that he'd first seen Gaby. She had moved in last spring, and on the first sunshiny day she had appeared. What was the distance between the two buildings, between the window where he stood now, and Gaby's back door? Two hundred feet? Maybe a little more, but the view had been good.

Gaby had come out that day to begin her summer tan, wearing one of the tiniest bikinis Noel Tasker had ever seen. Gaby had the figure for it: legs long, graceful, so aware of their own perfection that they seemed to be posing; a slim waistline that emphasized the curves above and below; a bust that bulged out of the little bra. She arranged herself on a chaise longue, and Noel Tasker stared.

Through the months of May and June, he continued to stare, whenever Gaby was out there on the lawn and Leona was absent from the apartment.   He even bought binoculars to achieve a more intimate view, and hid the instrument in his briefcase, a place where Leona never peeked.   During May and June, the sunbather's skin changed from creamy ivory to creamy golden.

In July, Noel became Gaby's lover.

It hadn't been easy to manage—nor difficult.   He had observed her living habits, clocked her movements, and so was driving by one morning when she'd had car trouble and was able to give her a lift downtown.   Afterward there'd been a "chance" meeting at the office where she worked, followed by cocktails the same afternoon; then two dinner dates, and finally, by appropriate degrees and the passage of time, home to bed.

All very discreet.   His job had always demanded his being away a few evenings, calling on clients, attending a meeting now and then.   The evenings out had become merely a bit more frequent.   Leona had something of an after-dark life of her own. She was a secretary, and a very good one, with an income that topped Noel's whenever his sales slipped, as they often did.   So she had nightwork occasionally, and the businesswomen's club she belonged to, and her duplicate bridge.   Thus it hadn't been too hard for Noel to see Gaby a couple of evenings a week.

Poor Gaby, so beautiful and yet so undemanding; though a divorcée, she hadn't been looking for a husband, or even strings.   Because she was beautiful, she had plenty of men.   All Gaby had ever seemed to want was a good time.   Who could have wanted to kill her?

Noel finished his drink and fixed himself another.   It was six-fifteen now and Leona wasn't home yet.   Was she supposed to be on time tonight or was she staying downtown?   His mind was blank.

Miserable, he drank and waited.   He couldn't quite believe or accept the new fact yet.   Gaby was dead.   Her beautiful body had been . . . what?   Shot? Strangled?   Knifed?   Did it really matter?   The beautiful body was dead, destroyed.   There would be no more of those stolen hours together, no more excitement, no more ecstasy.   It wasn't fair! He'd had such a good thing going, and someone . . . someone . . .

The sound of a key in the door lock spun him around.   He mustn't be caught staring out this window!   Force of habit, as if poor Gaby were out there sunning. He ran from the window and was back in the living room when Leona walked in.

He guessed instantly that she already knew about the excitement in the neighborhood.   She was pale, flustered, which was unusual for her.   She stared at him. She was even trembling.   That was fortunate in a way.   Perhaps she wouldn't notice his symptoms.

"A woman was murdered on the other street," she announced.

Not seeming to care whether or not he already knew, she passed him and marched into the bedroom.   He watched her go.   She always marched.   She'd grown stout and matronly, and the martial stride seemed to fit her.   He followed her after a moment.   There she was, at *his* window, the window through which he had watched Gaby.

"A woman named Gabrielle something . . ."

He said nothing. He wasn't going to be so foolish as to furnish the last name.

"It must have been pretty terrible. They say it was a maniac. She was all cut up."

He bit hard into his lower lip, and steadied himself against the doorjamb. The images pounding into his brain were red and horrible, but somehow he had already guessed. Gaby was no ordinary woman. She would have been murdered in no ordinary way. Cut up! He who had known her body so intimately could visualize the grimmest interpretation of those words.

"It must have been a sex maniac," Leona said. Suddenly she turned from the window and confronted him. "She used to sunbathe out there. Did you ever see her?"

He sensed the danger and reacted. Gaby was dead. He had to protect himself. Every man who had a window overlooking that lawn must have seen her. Not to have noticed her would be suspicious in itself. "I remember a sexy gal, if it was the same one. A brunette?"

Leona nodded. "I think she was a brunette."

He swallowed hard. He could scarcely change the subject and ask what was for dinner. "Cut up, you say? You mean . . . ?"

"Sliced. With something real sharp. Maybe a razor." She staggered suddenly to the bed and sat. "A sex maniac, Noel," she whispered. "There's a sex maniac loose in this neighborhood."

That night was a strange one. The August dusk was redolent with the scents of chrysanthemums and of terror, full of the sounds of cicadas and soft human conversation. The inhabitants of Camelot Court gathered outside in groups, which seemed safer than being alone inside, and rumors were rife.

The corpse had been taken away, thoroughly sheeted, of course, but covered, as everyone knew, with ghastly wounds. The crime had been discovered by a woman named Maxine Borley, who lived across the hall and who'd been, apparently, Gabrielle's only female friend. Maxine had heard the TV playing inside the Marchant apartment, had knocked, received no reply, had opened the unlocked door and walked in. Whether or not Maxine was supposed to give out details, she had: blood all over the place, the body nude, lying in the doorway between the bedroom and the living room; so many cuts that she couldn't count, and so much blood that it was hard to see where the cuts were. One detail was certain, however. There'd been a man's old-fashioned straight razor beside the body.

The news was passed in hushed tones up and down both streets of Camelot Court. Men shivered, women visibly trembled, and they all said what Leona had said.

"There's a sex maniac loose around here."

Leona didn't want to go back into the apartment, not yet at least. The streets and walks of Camelot were well-lighted, and for the moment there seemed to be safety in numbers outside. She hung tightly onto Noel's arm as they walked about. Women generally stayed close to their husbands. Mostly there were couples living in Camelot. If there were other single women like Gabrielle Marchant, they weren't in evidence on this night.

Whenever neighbors met, they always talked about the same things. Gabrielle

Marchant had had boyfriends, lovers.   A disappointed lover could have killed her. *Could* have.   But why, then, the butchery?   If he'd had to use a razor, one slice across the throat would have been sufficient—unless he were insane.   Had Gabrielle Marchant been beautiful enough to drive one of her lovers insane?   Possibly. She'd been sexy, all right, and she'd displayed herself pretty freely out on the lawn and by the pool.   So the murder could also have been committed by a stranger. Why necessarily a stranger?   Why not some frustrated guy who lived in Camelot? A maniac *inside* Camelot?   That, of course, was the most frightening possibility of all, because, as every woman seemed aware, a maniac might kill again.

Eventually the impromptu group discussions had to break up, people had to get their sleep.   The maniac wouldn't strike again tonight.   The place was crawling with cops.   The Marchant apartment was sealed off, guarded by the police.   Police cruisers came and went frequently.   Somebody said plainclothesmen were roaming. Certain of Gabrielle's immediate neighbors had already been questioned.   There were reporters around, too, who also asked questions.   Too many alert people were around tonight; not a good night for a murderer to prowl.

Noel and Leona went home together.   Noel had a drink while Leona locked windows, closed venetian blinds, tucked draperies around their edges, wedged chairs under doorknobs front and back.   In their bedroom finally, they performed the rituals of retiring.

Noel glanced covertly at his wife during the process.   She was realistic enough at least not to affect slinky, transparent nightgowns.   Her lavender pajamas ballooned over her heavy breasts, thick waist and generous haunches.   He discovered that he couldn't even remember what she'd looked like when they were married thirteen years ago.

Could a woman like Leona really be in danger from the same "sex maniac" who had murdered Gaby?   It seemed impossible.   Sex maniacs would have certain standards.   They obviously enjoyed murdering women, but judging from the choice of Gaby, such maniacs must prefer murdering beautiful women.

When Noel and Leona climbed into bed, with Noel suddenly wondering why after all these years they still slept together in a double bed, Leona snuggled up close.   "Noel," she whispered, "I'm scared," and she proved it by trembling violently.   "You will protect me, won't you, Noel?"

"Yes," he promised, though he didn't mean it even then.   "I'll protect you."

The next morning Lieutenant Kabrick of Homicide arrived.   He was a squat, square man, powerful-looking as a bear.   He didn't smile, merely nodded and showed his identification.   "You must be Mr. Tasker."

"Yes."

"May I come in?"

Noel stepped aside.

"Mrs. Tasker at home?"

"She just left for work."

"Maybe I can catch her later.   While I'm here, I'd like to ask you a few questions."

"Questions?"   Despite gritted teeth and clenched fists, Noel's trembling started again.

"About the murder of Gabrielle Marchant." The lieutenant seemed not to notice the trembling. "Did you know Miss Marchant?"

The question Noel had realized would come eventually, the question he dreaded; he had thought of a dozen answers, none of which he liked particularly, but he had to say something. "Not exactly know . . ."

"What does that mean, Mr. Tasker?"

"Well, I can't say that I knew her. But I . . . Well, I guess like everybody else, I—I knew who she was."

"How was that?"

"Well, I—I saw her . . . from a distance . . . outdoors . . . several times, I guess."

The lieutenant stared enigmatically, then nodded.

"Can I look around?"

"You mean . . . search?"

The stare continued, unblinking. "I just wanted to see what view of the Marchant apartment you have from here."

"Oh." Noel didn't know whether to feel relieved or not. He led the way into the bedroom, pulled up the blind.

The lieutenant stood at the window for a long time. "Good view you had here," he said.

"Yes, my wife and I appreciate the open space."

"They tell me Miss Marchant was a sunbather."

Noel made no comment.

"Those several times you said you saw her, Mr. Tasker, must have been when she was sunbathing."

"Yes, I guess so."

"You don't remember that well? They tell me she was rather spectacular."

"Well, it's some distance . . ."

"A couple hundred feet, I'd say." The lieutenant turned away from the window. "I suppose you read about the case in the paper this morning."

"Yes."

"Well, like it said, although the body wasn't discovered until Tuesday afternoon, we're certain that the crime was committed on Monday evening. Between nine and eleven P.M. is what the doc says. There was no forcible entry. The murderer just rang the doorbell; probably the front door, but maybe it was the back door. That's why I'm here, Mr. Tasker. I wanted to find out whether you or your wife saw anything strange in the vicinity of the Marchant apartment on Monday night."

"I wasn't here!" Noel was bursting to reveal his alibi. Even if they connected him with Gaby otherwise, they couldn't pin the murder on him. "I didn't come home at all. Monday. I mean, I didn't come home until real late. It was a lot later than eleven. Maybe one or one-thirty. We had a dinner and a sales meeting, and afterward I had some drinks with a couple of guys."

Lieutenant Kabrick nodded slowly. "Okay, Mr. Tasker, so you didn't see anything. How about your wife?"

"I don't know."

"Was she home?"

"She didn't say.   Sometimes when I'm not going to be here for dinner, she eats out, too.   I think maybe that's what she did.   But I don't know what time she got home."

"If she had noticed anything peculiar, she'd probably have mentioned it to you, I guess.   Everybody around here has been very cooperative.   They want to find the killer."

Noel tried to stay calm.   It wasn't easy.   "I don't know what we could have seen if we'd been home," he said.   "It's pretty far away, and it was dark."

The lieutenant nodded.   "But you never can tell," he said.   "That's why we're asking everybody here in the complex.   And of course, maybe we ought to be interested in other times besides Monday night.   The fact there was no forcible entry into the apartment doesn't prove anything, but it's possible that the murder was committed by someone known to Miss Marchant.   This will come out in the papers maybe later today, Mr. Tasker, but the medical examination didn't indicate rape."

Noel started.   "Then it wasn't a sex murder?"

"I didn't say that.   There are all different kinds of sex murders.   But it doesn't seem to have been a rape-murder.   I've got a little theory on it myself.   Maybe it was a revenge murder."

"Revenge?"   Noel stuffed his hands into his pockets to hide their trembling.

"Like, maybe, a jealous lover.   Or a rejected lover.   Miss Marchant was attractive.   We don't know how many men there were in her life.   So that's why I'm asking you about other times besides Monday evening.   Did you ever notice what people came and went over across the way?   We're trying to find out what men hung around Miss Marchant."

The guy in the expensive foreign car!   Would it be smart to mention that incident? To admit that he had deliberately driven down the other street and noticed the guy? Stay out of it, Noel told himself.   Stay far out.

"Can you give us any information along that line, Mr. Tasker?"

"No, I'm afraid I can't."

The lieutenant shrugged.   "Well, thanks, Mr. Tasker," he said on his way out. "Tell your wife I may stop by.   And also tell her not to worry.   We'll catch the guy.   We've gone over the place for prints, and we've lifted quite a few.   Some of them may have been left by the murderer."

When the lieutenant had gone, Noel sank onto the sofa.   Fingerprints! He hadn't thought about fingerprints.   His own would be all over Gaby's apartment . . .

He spent the day worrying about fingerprinting, and then that evening his worries were suddenly over.   The story appeared in the newspaper, either deliberately leaked by the police for purposes of their own, or uncovered by an enterprising reporter.   A most important fingerprint had been found in the Marchant apartment. Since the print did not belong to the deceased, it had to belong to the murderer. Who else but the murderer, since it was imprinted on the murder weapon, and in blood?

So whatever other strange prints they found around the apartment, they wouldn't even bother to check them, would they?   Everybody's apartment must be full of fingerprints. People come and go. Even in and out of bedrooms? Of course, innocently. But it didn't matter. The police had a print of Gaby's murderer now, and that would be the only one they'd check out thoroughly, through the F.B.I. files in Washington, or however they did it.

Noel felt so relieved that he wanted to talk about the case now, and the only person he had to talk to was Leona. He showed her the newspaper the moment she arrived home.

"They'll catch that maniac now," he announced. "The police found a bloody fingerprint on the razor."

Leona grabbed the paper and read it without bothering to sit down. Was she actually frightened by all this murder business? Or was she pretending? Do unattractive women like to pretend they're desirable, even to a homicidal maniac?

"Well," she said finally, "they'll catch him now. They've got a fingerprint of him. Then we can all relax." She went to the kitchen, transferred TV dinners from the freezer to the oven, and afterward retired to the bedroom. He didn't follow her there. After Gaby, the sight of Leona's changing clothes had become rather an obscene spectacle.

Then, just before the TV dinners were ready, Lieutenant Kabrick arrived, and it was a different Noel Tasker who received him this time. Gaby was gone, the moments of ecstasy would be no more; but Noel Tasker was alive and safe, and now he was confident.

"Lieutenant," he fairly bubbled, "you came to see my wife, didn't you? Honey, the detective's here! Sit down, Lieutenant. Read all about it in the paper—the bloody fingerprint on the razor. Have you located the matching print in your files yet?"

Kabrick sat down, tentatively, on the edge of a chair. "No, I'm afraid not," he said.

Leona came in, wearing Bermuda shorts. She didn't look good in them. Kabrick rose politely, anyway, and introduced himself.

"Mrs. Tasker, were you at home Monday night? We're canvassing to see if any of the neighbors noticed anything or anybody around the Marchant apartment that night."

"I wasn't home," Leona answered quickly, and by remaining standing made the lieutenant stand too.

"When did you get home, Mrs. Tasker?"

"It must have been midnight." She trembled. "And to think I drove in here, and parked my car, and walked to my door . . . and there was a maniac hanging around . . ."

"We think he was gone by then, Mrs. Tasker."

"Lieutenant," Noel interrupted, "sit down. Care for a drink? Cup of coffee?"

Kabrick refused both, but he did sit down. Leona sat on the sofa.

"I guess if you're still asking questions," she ventured softly, "that means you haven't caught the man yet."

"Not yet."

"Then no woman is safe."

The lieutenant shrugged. "We go on the assumption," he said, "that no woman is ever safe. The world is full of nuts. But that doesn't mean that this murderer will strike again. He may have been a friend of Miss Marchant, you see, and may have killed for revenge or jealousy."

Again Noel was tempted to mention the guy with the foreign car, but he resisted. He was out of it now, and he wanted to stay out.

"There was no rape involved," Kabrick pointed out, "and probably not even attempted rape. You see, we're convinced that Miss Marchant was attacked from behind."

"Behind?" Noel echoed, really curious. "With a razor?"

"Very simple," Kabrick explained. "Miss Marchant was a small woman, short, about five-one. That made this method of attack easy. The murderer was right-handed, we believe. Standing behind Miss Marchant, he reached over her left shoulder, cupped her chin in the palm of his left hand, forced her chin upward, bringing her head back, and tightened her neck. Then with his right hand he reached across her right shoulder and simply drew the razor across her throat. Somehow that M.O. suggests deliberation to me. I don't go with the maniac theory. So the other women around here may be safer than you think, Mrs. Tasker."

Leona didn't give up. She wanted to feel that she was in danger, Noel felt certain, because she wanted to feel desirable. "He cut her all up, though," she argued. "Only a maniac would do that."

"The body was mutilated after she was dead," Kabrick said. He sat back farther in his chair and surveyed both his listeners. "I could be wrong, of course," he went on. "I'm always theorizing, but in Homicide you have to. There's this matter of the blood. You know what M.O. means, Mr. Tasker?"

"*Modus operandi,*" Noel answered confidently.

"That's right. The criminal's method of operation. The way he commits the crime. Now, what are the advantages of attacking the victim from behind in a razor murder?"

Noel thought. "Surprise?"

"Maybe. And the victim has less chance to protect herself with her arms. You can get right to the vital spot. But there's another advantage. The murderer doesn't get too much blood on himself."

"Really?" Noel asked in admiration.

"That's a very important advantage. It minimizes the problem of disposal of bloody garments. Which can be quite a problem. Plenty of murders have been solved by the discovery of bloody clothes."

"But Miss Marchant was cut up," Noel objected. "The woman who discovered the body said there was blood all over the place."

Lieutenant Kabrick slouched in the depths of the chair and smiled. "There was and there wasn't," he said. "Now, let's say Miss Marchant is dead from a cut throat. She's lying more or less face up on the floor. Only one cut so far. There's a lot of blood, mostly on the front of the corpse. And on the razor and the murderer's hands, of course. But now the victim is dead, quiet, easy to cut on. From here on, the murderer can proceed very carefully, avoid getting blood on himself. You see, there was one very peculiar fact. Although there's blood on the carpet in nearly every direction, there are no footprints in the blood. Wouldn't you say the murderer was being very, very careful?''

"Seems so," Noel admitted.

"Now tell me," Kabrick pursued, "what kind of maniac do we have, then? One seized with blood lust, who wants to cut and cut, who wants to mutilate, to butcher? Yes, all that. In a sense, every murderer is a maniac. But this is one who has other things on his mind, too. Like the problems of disposal of bloody clothes and bloody shoes.''

Noel was calm now, completely absorbed. "What about the bloody fingerprint on the razor?'' he demanded.

"Two explanations. Remember, no killer is completely sane. Explanation one, then: he deliberately wanted to leave a clue to his identity for the thrill of the risk involved. Explanation two: he saw something, heard something, got scared, and ran, before he was quite finished. Although there were plenty of slashes, incidentally, the job did look a little unfinished. Maybe that sounds strange, but I've seen quite a few of these cases—'' Kabrick broke off suddenly, glanced at his watch, and stood up. "Maybe I got too graphic," he said to Leona. "What I really wanted to do was to make you feel a little better, a little safer maybe. Because I think that killer was interested in only one woman.''

He walked to the door. "If at any time either of you does remember any little item about Miss Marchant, whether it seems important to you or not, I hope you'll let us know.''

The detective was gone, but Leona continued to sit there, pale, shivering, staring at nothing.

"What's the matter?'' Noel asked. Perhaps he was beginning to enjoy her fear, now that his own was past.

"I'm afraid," she said.

He smiled indulgently. What reason did she have to be afraid? Who would want to murder her? Only himself, her husband, and even he didn't have any special reason to do it at the moment.

Life, however, has a way of changing. The best-laid plans and all that. For Noel Tasker, who didn't have any plans, best-laid or otherwise, things could still go awry.

Lieutenant Kabrick and his cohorts did not bring the murderer of Gabrielle Marchant to justice. The police, it was said, did a thorough job on the Marchant apartment, ripping, so the rumor went, the paper from the walls and the carpeting from the floors, to no avail. They gave up finally, and disappeared from the scene. The management of Camelot Court didn't try to rent the redecorated apartment apparently. They were too busy trying to fill their other vacancies. Nervous renters drifted away when leases expired. Other nervous renters stayed, among them Leona Tasker, seeming to enjoy the little tremors of apprehension which went up and down their spines whenever they had to walk through the dusk and night of advancing autumn. The tremors all the more enjoyable being experienced in safety. The killer did not strike again.

Noel Tasker, who possessed enough masculine animal vitality to have interested the likes of Gabrielle Marchant, somehow lacked the moxie to achieve very much in the world of commerce. His business career went from bad to worse. His customers fell to the blandishments of competitors. His boss kept him on, but cut his drawing account and issued vague threats. Noel considered trying to find another mistress to fill the emptiness in his life, but discovered with dismay he couldn't afford the luxury. He remembered Gaby, who had never demanded much, and he brooded.

To Leona, however, although she might continue to cringe in mock terror at the thought of the lurking maniac, life down at the office was kinder. She received a promotion, a minor executive title, rather unusual for a female.

"Do you get a company car?" Noel sniped at her when she told him the news. His own company car, he knew, might be taken away from him any day.

"No," she admitted, "but my other fringe benefits have been increased. I've got fifty thousand dollars' worth of company-paid life insurance now."

It became only a matter of time, therefore, before Noel Tasker steeled himself to the obvious decision. Time, meanwhile, was running out.

He didn't know how long he could hang onto his own job. An unemployed man with a wife insured to the tune of fifty thousand bucks might look just a little too suspicious. Then also, his job, with all the night work it entailed, was his only source of alibis.

The "maniac" had not been as obliging as he might have been. When he failed to commit further crimes, Lieutenant Kabrick's theories of revenge and jealousy gained strength. Even worse, the women of Camelot Court were ceasing to be terrified, Leona included.

Oh, they played the little game as long as they could, especially when a bunch of them were together; half a dozen thirtyish and fortyish females, some past their prime, some never having had any, all cackling about how the killer could be hiding in any shadow, ogling their charms, and lusting to slice those charms like so much baloney. Baloney indeed!

So it would be a favor to those old hags to give a new little boost to their adrenalin production. Actually, the hags were rather important to Noel's plan. They would be sure to testify, when the time came, that Leona Tasker had been for months deathly afraid of the fate which eventually befell her.

M.O. Noel had it memorized. Lieutenant Kabrick had been most obliging; the newspapers too. Everybody knew the M.O., and they'd recognize it when they saw it again. Too bad about the lieutenant's theories. He'd have to change his mind.

The straight razor was easy to obtain. Noel picked one up on an out-of-town trip. There'd have to be one difference about the razor, though. There'd be no bloody fingerprint on it this time. But then the M.O. is not always precisely the same, is it? A criminal, even a maniac, learns as he goes along.

The worst risk involved the alibi. What it amounted to was simple: he had to be in two places at the same time. Not easy, perhaps, if one is supposed to be at dinner with a single customer and at home with one's wife simultaneously. But what about a larger social occasion, where one might slip away for a few minutes without the absence being noted, and yet where a dozen half-inebriated witnesses might swear that, "Sure, old Noel was here with us all evening"?

Life cooperated with Noel Tasker on this one score. A business convention was coming to town.

"Are you going to be home on Thursday night?" he asked Leona.

"Why shouldn't I be?" she asked him. Her persistent terror had reduced her out-alone-after-dark activities. "I suppose you'll be at your old convention party. Well, I'll be here watching TV."

Thursday night it would be, then.

Qualms? Still? Right down to the wire? Oh, yes, indeed, but the choice was inevitable—and bitter.

On the one hand, he could continue as he was. Losing his present selling job, he might of course get another; such as selling encyclopedias from door to door, for instance. Leona could support him—and become more and more possessive of him, more and more demanding. Ever since the Marchant murder, under the pretense of being afraid, she had required more affection, snuggling a bit closer every night in bed, and on Saturday and Sunday mornings lingering there for a bit of dalliance. After Gaby, he could endure Leona even less.

But with fifty thousand, plus their joint savings account, he could go somewhere else, start over. Maybe fifty thousand wouldn't last forever, maybe he'd eventually be back in the same bind he was in now; but fifty thousand would buy a lot of time, and somewhere along the route he might pick up another Gaby. Hell, he didn't have to plan all the way to his old age. More important was to enjoy the little bit of youth he had left.

Was there really any choice? Thursday night it had to be.

At the convention-opening banquet on Thursday evening, Noel Tasker tried to impress his presence upon as many conventioneers as he possibly could. He slapped backs, pumped hands, told jokes. Also he pretended to drink—but only pretended. He stayed cold-sober.

The dinner dragged on, his nerves frayed, but nobody noticed such details. He hung on grimly. Afterward there were cigars, and much milling about. Then, finally, the time he was waiting for: the chairs and seating arrangements all got a bit confused because the lights went out, a special forty-five-minute film on new developments in the industry. He had forty-five minutes, therefore, of invisibility.

Only a waiter or two could have observed his exit. He didn't use an elevator. He had parked in the street, so no parking attendant was involved. He drove home in twelve minutes. No one, he was fairly certain, observed his arrival in Camelot Court. Now that it was autumn, people stayed indoors, never noticed the comings and goings of their neighbors.

Only Leona welcomed him, rather amazed. She was attired in nightie and robe, with her dyed black hair in curlers—but she smiled at him.

"What are you doing home so early?" she asked.

"It was boring," he said.

She didn't question that.

He went into the bedroom and disrobed.   When he emerged again, stark naked, with one hand, the right hand, the razor hand, behind his back, she did have a question.

"Noel, what on earth?"

He smiled.   He shrugged.   "I told you it was boring at the dinner.   I thought there might be something more interesting here."   He had to get her off that sofa, to maneuver her into the required position.

"Noel!   You've had too much to drink!"

He shook his head.

"A girl must have jumped out of the cake—"

"And gave me ideas?   Maybe that was it."   The seconds and minutes were ticking away, and she was playing coy, taking her time.   "How about it, Leona?"

"I just put my hair up . . ."

"Take it down."

She slowly placed the bookmark in her book, laid the thing carefully aside—and smiled.   "Noel," she said.   "You're positively wicked tonight."

"Yes, I am," he admitted.   "I'm waiting."

She rose slowly, ever so slowly.   Then she paused, in the very middle of the room, and slowly . . . slowly undid the belt of her robe.

"Take it off," he invited.   "The draperies are closed."   They were.   He had made sure of that.

She shrugged out of the robe and stood there, just in the nightie.   "Shall I take this off too?" she asked, simpering.

"Why not?"

She started—and he started to slip around behind her.   *How glad I am,* he thought, *that Gaby wasn't raped that night.   That would have been a most difficult M.O. to stick to.*

She was halfway out of the nightie—a good situation, he decided impatiently— when he stepped to a position directly behind her, grabbed her hair, curlers and all, pulled upward and backward, and gritting his teeth in a supreme effort of will, pulled the razor across her throat.

Oh, the blood!   He hadn't dreamed how far it could spurt, and he hadn't dreamed, either, how powerful a woman Leona was, or how powerful any woman, in the very process of bleeding to death, could be.   She lunged sideways, trying to escape. He hung onto her hair.   She fell toward the sofa, and he hung on.   She grabbed for the coffee table, and he hung on.   She reached for a heavy ashtray there, her hands and arms all covered with blood now.   She reached for the tray . . . for a weapon?   He hung on.   He weighted her body down with his own.   He couldn't allow her to turn on him, couldn't let her swing on him with that tray.   He couldn't afford a lump on his head.

Then, when he was afraid she would never, ever succumb, she suddenly sagged. They stayed together for a moment, her head and arms on the table, he riding on her back, her life's blood pouring out, reddening the table, the ashtray, and the floor beneath.   Finally—he knew it somehow—she was dead.

He wasted a precious minute, perhaps two, before he could bring himself to the next, and the most difficult, phase of the project.   He'd had no appetite at the banquet, had eaten as little as possible, but now he felt ready to vomit.   A horrible thought bounded around in his brain; could his vomit be analyzed and compared with the menu served at the banquet?

He rallied.   The M.O.   Follow it or fail.   Impersonate the maniac, or let it look like a rational crime, a husband murdering his wife for a rational motive, fifty thousand dollars.

So he dragged the now inert body away from the table, laid it face up on the floor.   Blood still gurgled from the throat wound.   The razor was bloody, his own hand was bloody—but he hadn't stepped in the stuff.

He went to work with his eyes closed, then realized he might cut himself, which would never do.   Follow the M.O.   He'd heard the story about precisely what had happened to Gaby.   Maxine Borley, who had discovered Gaby's body, had authored the story, so it had been an eyewitness account.   Now, he hoped that Maxine had gotten it straight.

Finally he was finished—except for that one item, the one slight difference in this second crime.   The murderer must not leave his fingerprint on the razor.   Noel could have worn gloves, of course, but then he would have had to dispose of bloody gloves.   No, his way was simpler.   Using a corner of Leona's nightie, he rubbed blood off the razor, dropped the weapon into a red pool, then soaked the nightie in the same pool.   No crime lab could ever lift a print now off that mess.

Finally, there was himself.   Lieutenant Kabrick had been so right.   This particular M.O. didn't splash much blood on the murderer.   His clothes were in the bedroom, of course.   There were no bloody footprints; just hands and arms.

To make totally certain, he took a shower; not a leisurely shower, but thorough, including his hair.   The night air would dry it.   Afterward, he climbed back into his clothes.   When he walked from the bedroom back through the living room, he didn't glance at the body on the floor.

He locked the door as he went out.   Nobody saw him return to his car, get in, and drive off.   In twelve minutes he reached the hotel.   He was even able to park in the same spot he had vacated earlier.

The movie was just ending when he rejoined the conventioneers.   Now he drank for real, slapped more backs, pumped more hands, told more jokes than he had before, but he was thinking all the time.   He solicited comments about the film, and his obliging companions told him everything about the film he needed to know.   Kabrick wasn't going to trick him that way.

It was late when he left the hotel.   He didn't really want to leave.   He would have preferred to stay there with some of the out-of-town guys, sleep on the floor or something, but he chose to go home, like a faithful, loving husband should.

He drove more slowly this time, taking about twenty minutes.   He parked, walked up the path, opened the door with his key.   He had left the light on, so he didn't need to flip the switch.   There was Leona, lying just where he had left her.   Good, faithful, dependable Leona.

He dialed the number of the police, and in a broken voice reported the crime.

*   *   *

Noel Tasker did spend the rest of that night in a hotel, after all, at Lieutenant Kabrick's suggestion, so the police investigation team could have the apartment.

Noel slept fitfully.   His emotional condition was no act for the police.   He really was in a state almost of shock.   Committing the murder had been no easy thing.

The lieutenant found him at the hotel at eleven on Friday morning.   He hadn't stirred.   The lieutenant knocked, and Noel opened the door willingly.

"Leona had a right to be terrified, didn't she?" he began.   "It was that same maniac, wasn't it?"

The lieutenant shrugged and sidled to a chair.   "Same?" he echoed after he had sat.

Noel stared.   "Wasn't it?   I saw the razor."

"No prints on the razor this time," Kabrick informed him.

Deep inside, invisibly, Noel smiled.   *One thing done right*.

"There were bloody prints on the coffee table and on an ashtray though."

"The killer's?"

"No, your wife's."   The lieutenant glanced up.   His eyes were hard, implacable.   "Funny thing.   We caught it right away.   A print of your wife's, on the table and on the tray, matched the print on the razor in the Marchant apartment."

Noel sat on the edge of the bed, slowly, carefully.   Things were beginning to spin.

"Let's talk, Mr. Tasker," the lieutenant said.   "We've got a lot of things to talk about.   Like maybe how your wife was the one who killed Marchant.   And why she killed her.   And then, finally, if your wife killed Marchant, who killed your wife?   Now, Mr. Tasker, I've got a theory . . ."

Noel stopped listening.   Why, why should Leona have cut Gaby's throat?   He couldn't think of a reason—but perhaps it would occur to him later.

DONALD E. WESTLAKE

Come Back, Come Back . . .

Detective Abraham Levine of Brooklyn's Forty-Third Precinct was a worried
and a frightened man.   He sat moodily at his desk in the small office he shared
with his partner Jack Crawley, and pensively drew lopsided circles on the back of
a blank accident report form.   In the approximate center of each circle he placed
a dot, drew two lines out from the dot to make a clock-face, reading three o'clock.
An eight and a half by eleven sheet of white paper, covered with clock-faces, all
reading three o'clock.

"That the time you see the doctor?"

Levine looked up, startled, called back from years away.   Crawley was standing
beside the desk, looking down at him, and Levine blinked, not having heard the
question.

Crawley reached down and tapped the paper with a horny fingernail.   "Three
o'clock," he explained.   "That the time you see the doctor?"

"Oh," said Levine.   "Yes.   Three o'clock."

Crawley said, "Take it easy, Abe."

"Sure," said Levine.   He managed a weak smile.   "No sense worrying beforehand, huh?"

"My brother," said Crawley, "he had one of those cardiograph things just a
couple months ago.   He's just around your age, and man, he was worried.   And
the doctor tells him, 'You'll live to be a hundred.' "

"And then you'll die," said Levine.

"What the hell, Abe, we all got to go *sometime.*"

"Sure."

Abraham Levine was fifty-three years alive, twenty-four years a cop.   A short
and chunky man, he wore plain brown suits and dark solid-color ties, brown or
black plain shoes.   His hair was pepper-and-salt grey, trimmed all around in a stiff
pseudo-military crewcut.   The crewcut didn't go with the face, roundish, soft-
eyed, sensitive-lipped, lined with fifty-three years' accumulation of small worries.

"Listen, Abe, you want to go on home?   It's a dull day, nothing doing, I
can—"

"Don't say that," Levine warned him.   "The phone will ring."   The phone
rang as he was talking and he grinned, shrugging with palms up.   "See?"

"Let me see what it is," said Crawley, reaching for the phone.   "Probably nothing important. You can go on home and take it easy till three o'clock. It's only ten now and—Hello?'' The last word spoken into the phone mouthpiece. "Yeah, this is Crawley."

Levine watched Crawley's face, trying to read in it the nature of the call. Crawley had been his partner for seven years, since old Jake Moshby had retired, and in that time they had become good friends, as close as two such different men could get to one another.

Crawley was a big man, somewhat overweight, somewhere in his middle forties. His clothes hung awkwardly on him, not as though they were too large or too small but as though they had been planned for a man of completely different proportions. His face was rugged, squarish, heavy-jowled. He looked like a tough cop, and he played the role very well.

Crawley had once described the quality of their partnership with reasonable accuracy. "With your brains and my beauty, Abe, we've got it made.''

Now, Levine watched Crawley's face as the big man listened impassively to the phone, finally nodding and saying, "Okay, I'll go right on up there. Yeah, I know, that's what I figure, too." And he hung up.

"What is it, Jack?" Levine asked, getting up from the desk.

"A phony," said Crawley. "I can handle it, Abe. You go on home."

"I'd rather have some work to do. What is it?"

Crawley was striding for the door, Levine after him. "Man on a ledge," he said. "A phony. They're all phonies. The ones that really mean to jump do it right away, get it over with. Guys like this one, all they want is a little attention, somebody to tell them it's all okay, come on back in, everything's forgiven.''

The two of them walked down the long green hall toward the front of the precinct. *Man on a ledge,* Levine thought. *Don't jump. Don't die. For God's sake, don't die.*

The address was an office building on Flatbush Avenue, a few blocks down from the bridge, near A&S and the major Brooklyn movie houses. A small crowd had gathered on the sidewalk across the street, looking up, but most of the pedestrians stopped only for a second or two, only long enough to see what the small crowd was gaping at, and then hurried on wherever they were going. They were still involved in life, they had things to do, they didn't have time to watch a man die.

Traffic on this side was being rerouted away from this block of Flatbush, around via Fulton or Willoughby or DeKalb. It was a little after ten o'clock on a sunny day in late June, warm without the humidity that would hit the city a week or two farther into the summer, but the uniformed cop who waved at them to make the turn was sweating, his blue shirt stained a darker blue, his forehead creased with strain above the sunglasses.

Crawley was driving their car, an unmarked black '56 Chevvy, no siren, and he braked to a stop in front of the patrolman. He stuck his head and arm out the window, dangling his wallet open so the badge showed. "Precinct," he called.

"Oh," said the cop. He stepped aside to let them pass. "You didn't have any siren or light or anything," he explained.

"We don't want to make our friend nervous," Crawley told him.

The cop glanced up, then looked back at Crawley. "He's making *me* nervous," he said.

Crawley laughed. "A phony," he told the cop. "Wait and see."

On his side of the car, Levine had leaned his head out the window, was looking up, studying the man on the ledge.

It was an office building, eight stories high. Not a very tall building, particularly for New York, but plenty tall enough for the purposes of the man standing on the ledge that girdled the building at the sixth floor level. The first floor of the building was mainly a bank and partially a luncheonette. The second floor, according to the lettering strung along the front windows, was entirely given over to a loan company, and Levine could understand the advantage of the location. A man had his loan request turned down by the bank, all he had to do was go up one flight of stairs—or one flight in the elevator, more likely—and there was the loan company.

And if the loan company failed him too, there was a nice ledge on the sixth floor.

Levine wondered if this particular case had anything to do with money. Almost everything had something to do with money. Things that he became aware of because he was a cop, almost all of them had something to do with money. The psychoanalysts are wrong, he thought. It isn't sex that's at the center of all the pain in the world, it's money. Even when a cop answers a call from neighbors complaining about a couple screaming and fighting and throwing things at one another, nine times out of ten it's the same old thing they're arguing about. Money.

Levine's eyes traveled up the facade of the building, beyond the loan company's windows. None of the windows higher up bore the lettering of firm names. On the sixth floor, most of the windows were open, heads were sticking out into the air. And in the middle of it all, just out of reach of the windows on either side of him, was the man on the ledge.

Levine squinted, trying to see the man better against the brightness of the day. He wore a suit—it looked grey, but might be black—and white shirt and a dark tie, and the open suit coat and the tie were both whipping in the breeze up there. The man was standing as though crucified, back flat against the wall of the building, legs spread maybe two feet apart, arms out straight to either side of him, hands pressed palm-in against the stone surface of the wall.

The man was terrified. Levine was much too far away to see his face or read the expression there, but he didn't need any more than the posture of the body on the ledge. Taut, pasted to the wall, widespread. The man was terrified.

Crawley was right, of course. Ninety-nine times out of a hundred, the man on the ledge *is* a phony. He doesn't really expect to have to kill himself, though he will do it if pressed too hard. But he's out there on the ledge for one purpose and one purpose only: to be seen. He wants to be seen, he wants to be noticed. Whatever his unfulfilled demands on life, whatever his frustrations or problems, he wants other people to be forced to be aware of them, and to agree to help him overcome them.

If he gets satisfaction, he will allow himself, after a decent interval, to be brought back in. If he gets the raise, or the girl, or forgiveness from the boss for his embezzling, or forgiveness from his wife for his philandering, or whatever his one urgent demand is, once the demand is met, he will come in from the ledge.

But there is one danger he doesn't stop to think about, not until it's too late and he's already out there on the ledge, and the drama has already begun. The police know of this danger, and they know it is by far the greatest danger of the man on the ledge, much greater than any danger of deliberate self-destruction.

He can fall.

This one had learned that danger by now, as every inch of his straining taut body testified. He had learned it, and he was frightened out of his wits.

Levine grimaced. The man on the ledge didn't know—or if he knew, the knowledge was useless to him—that a terrified man can have an accident much more readily and much more quickly than a calm man. And so the man on the ledge always compounded his danger.

Crawley braked the Chevvy to a stop at the curb, two doors beyond the address. The rest of the curb space was already used by official vehicles. An ambulance, white and gleaming. A smallish fire engine, red and full-packed with hose and ladders. A prowl car, most likely the one on this beat. The Crash & Rescue truck, dark blue, a first-aid station on wheels.

As he was getting out of the car, Levine noticed the firemen, standing around, leaning against the plate glass windows of the bank, an eight foot net lying closed on the sidewalk near them. Levine took the scene in, and knew what had happened. The firemen had started to open the net. The man on the ledge had threatened to jump at once if they didn't take the net away. He could always jump to one side, miss the net. A net was no good unless the person to be caught *wanted* to be caught. So the firemen had closed up their net again, and now they were waiting, leaning against the bank windows, far enough away to the right.

Other men stood here and there on the sidewalk, some uniformed and some in plainclothes, most of them looking up at the man on the ledge. None of them stood inside a large white circle drawn in chalk on the pavement. It was a wide sidewalk here, in front of the bank, and the circle was almost the full width of it.

No one stood inside that circle because it marked the probable area where the man would land, if and when he fell or jumped from the ledge. And no one wanted to be underneath.

Crawley came around the Chevvy, patting the fenders with a large calloused hand. He stopped next to Levine and looked up. "The phony," he growled, and Levine heard outrage in the tone. Crawley was an honest man, in simple terms of black and white. He hated dishonesty, in all its forms, from grand larceny to raucous television commercials. And a faked suicide attempt was dishonesty.

The two of them walked toward the building entrance. Crawley walked disdainfully through the precise center of the large chalked circle, not even bothering to look up. Levine walked around the outer edge.

Then the two of them went inside and took the elevator to the sixth floor.

The letters on the frosted-glass door read: "Anderson & Cartwright, Industrial Research Associates, Inc."

Crawley tapped on the glass. "Which one do you bet?" he asked. "Anderson or Cartwright?"

"It might be an employee."

Crawley shook his head. "Odds are against it. I take Anderson."

"Go in," said Levine gently. "Go on in."

Crawley pushed the door open and strode in, Levine behind him. It was the receptionist's office, cream-green walls and carpet, modernistic metal desk, modernistic metal and leather sofa and armchairs, modernistic saucer-shaped light fixtures hanging from bronzed chains attached to the ceiling.

Three women sat nervously, wide-eyed, off to the right, on the metal and leather armchairs. Above their heads were framed photographs of factory buildings, most of them in color, a few in black and white.

A unifomed patrolman was leaning against the receptionist's desk, arms folded across his chest, a relaxed expression on his face. He straightened up immediately when he saw Crawley and Levine. Levine recognized him as McCann, a patrolman working out of the same precinct.

"Am I glad to see you guys," said McCann. "Gundy's in talking to the guy now."

"Which one is it," Crawley asked, "Anderson or Cartwright?"

"Cartwright. Jason Cartwright. He's one of the bosses here."

Crawley turned a sour grin on Levine. "You win," he said, and led the way across the receptionist's office to the door marked: "Jason Cartwright PRIVATE."

There were two men in the room. One was sitting on the window ledge, looking out and to his left, talking in a soft voice. The other, standing a pace or two away from the window, was the patrolman, Gundy. He and McCann would be the two from the prowl car, the first ones on the scene.

At their entrance, Gundy looked around and then came over to talk with them. He and McCann were cut from the same mold. Both young, tall, slender, thincheeked, ready to grin at a second's notice. The older a man gets, Levine thought, the longer it takes him to get a grin organized.

Gundy wasn't grinning now. He looked very solemn, and a little scared. Levine realized with shock that this might be Gundy's first brush with death. He didn't look as though he could have been out of the Academy very long.

I have news for you, Gundy, he thought. *You don't get used to it.*

Crawley said, "What's the story?"

"I'm not sure," said Gundy. "He went out there about twenty minutes ago. That's his son talking to him. Son's a lawyer, got an office right in this building."

"What's the guy out there want?"

Gundy shook his head. "He won't say. He just stands out there. He won't say a word, except to shout that he's going to jump whenever anybody tries to get too close to him."

"A coy one," said Crawley, disgusted.

The phone shrilled, and Gundy stepped quickly over to the desk, picking up the receiver before the second ring. He spoke softly into the instrument, then looked over at the man by the window. "Your mother again," he said.

The man at the window spoke a few more words to the man on the ledge, then came over and took the phone from Gundy. Gundy immediately took his place at the window, and Levine could hear his first words plainly. "Just take it easy, now. Relax. But maybe you shouldn't close your eyes."

Levine looked at the son, now talking on the phone. A young man, not more than twenty-five or six. Blond crewcut, hornrim glasses, good mouth, strong jawline. Dressed in Madison Avenue conservative. Just barely out of law school, from the look of him.

Levine studied the office. It was a large room, eighteen to twenty feet square, as traditional as the outer office was contemporary. The desk was a massive piece of furniture, a dark warm wood, the legs and drawer faces carefully and intricately carved. Glass-faced bookshelves lined one complete wall. The carpet was a neutral grey, wall-to-wall. There were two sofas, brown leather, long and deep and comfortable-looking. Bronze ashtray stands. More framed photographs of plant buildings.

The son was saying, "Yes, Mother. I've been talking to him, Mother. I don't know, Mother."

Levine walked over, said to the son, "May I speak to her for a minute, please?"

"Of course. Mother, there's a policeman here who wants to talk to you."

Levine accepted the phone, said, "Mrs. Cartwright?"

The voice that answered was high-pitched, and Levine could readily imagine it becoming shrill. The voice said, "Why is he out there? Why is he doing that?"

"We don't know yet," Levine told her. "We were hoping you might be able to—"

"Me?" The voice was suddenly a bit closer to being shrill. "I still can't really believe this. I don't know why he'd—I have no idea. What does he say?"

"He hasn't told us why yet," said Levine. "Where are you now, Mrs. Cartwright?"

"At home, of course."

"That's where?"

"New Brunswick."

"Do you have a car there? Could you drive here now?"

"There? To New York?"

"It might help, Mrs. Cartwright, if he could see you, if you could talk to him."

"But—it would take *hours* to get there! Surely, it would be—that is, before I got there, you'd have him safe already, wouldn't you?"

She hopes he jumps, thought Levine, with sudden certainty. *By God, she hopes he jumps!*

"Well, wouldn't you?

"Yes," he said wearily. "I suppose you're right. Here's your son again."

He extended the receiver to the son, who took it, cupped the mouthpiece with one hand, said worriedly, "Don't misunderstand her. Please, she isn't as cold as she might sound. She loves my father, she really does."

"All right," said Levine. He turned away from the pleading in the son's eyes, said to Crawley, "Let's talk with him a bit."

"Right," said Crawley.

There were two windows in the office, about ten feet apart, and Jason Cartwright was standing directly between them on the ledge. Crawley went to the left-hand window and Levine to the right-hand window, where the patrolman Gundy was still trying to chat with the man on the ledge, trying to keep him distracted from the height and his desire to jump. "We'll take over," Levine said softly, and Gundy nodded gratefully and backed away from the window.

Levine twisted around, sat on the windowsill, hooked one arm under the open window, leaned out slightly so that the breeze touched his face. He looked down.

Six stories. God, who would have thought six stories was so high from the ground? This is the height when you really get the feeling of height. On top of the Empire State building, or flying in a plane, it's just too damn high, it isn't real anymore. But six stories—that's a fine height to be at, to really understand the terror of falling.

Place ten Levines, one standing on another's shoulders, forming a human tower or a totem pole, and the Levine in the window wouldn't be able to reach the cropped grey hair on the head of the top Levine in the totem pole.

Down there, he could make out faces, distinguish eyes and open mouths, see the blue jeans and high boots and black slickers of the firemen, the red domes atop the police cars. Across the street, he could see the red of a girl's sweater.

He looked down at the street, sixty-six feet below him. It was a funny thing about heights, a strange and funny and terrifying thing. Stand by the rail of a bridge, looking down at the water. Stand by a window on the sixth floor, looking down at the street. And from miles down inside the brain, a filthy little voice snickers and leers and croons, "Jump. Go on and jump. Wouldn't you like to know how it would feel, to fall free through space? Go on, go on, jump."

From his left, Crawley's voice suddenly boomed out. "Aren't you a little old, Cartwright, for this kind of nonsense?"

The reassuring well-known reality of Crawley's voice tore Levine away from the snickering little voice. He suddenly realized he'd been leaning too far out from the window, and pulled himself hastily back.

And he felt his heart pounding within his chest. Three o'clock, he had to go see that doctor. He had to be calm; his heart had to be calm for the doctor's inspection.

At night—He didn't get enough sleep at night anymore, that was part of the problem. But it was impossible to sleep and listen to one's heart at the same time, and of the two it was more important to listen to the heart. Listen to it plodding along, laboring, like an old man climbing a hill with a heavy pack. And then, all at once, the silence. The skipped beat. And the sluggish heart gathering its forces, building its strength, plodding on again. It had never yet skipped two beats in a row.

It could only do that once.

"What is it you want, Cartwright?" called Crawley's voice.

Levine, for the first time, looked to the left and saw Jason Cartwright.

A big man, probably an athlete in his younger days, still muscular but now padded with the flesh of years. Black hair with a natural wave in it, now mussed by the breeze. A heavy face, the chin sagging a bit but the jawline still strong, the nose large and straight, the forehead wide, the brows outthrust, the eyes deep and now wide and wild. A good-looking man, probably in his late forties.

Levine knew a lot about him already. From the look of the son in there, this man had married young, probably while still in his teens. From the sound of the wife, the marriage had soured. From the look of the office and the apparent education of the son, his career had blossomed where his marriage hadn't. So this time, one of the exceptions, the trouble wouldn't be money. This time, it was connected most likely with his marriage.

Another woman?

It wouldn't be a good idea to ask him. Sooner or later, he would state his terms, he would tell them what had driven him out here. Force the issue, and he might jump. A man on a ledge goes out there not wanting to jump, but accepting the fact that he may have to.

Cartwright had been looking at Crawley, and now he turned his head, stared at Levine. "Oh, no you don't!" he cried. His voice would normally be baritone, probably a pleasant speaking voice, but emotion had driven it up the scale, making it raucous, tinged with hysteria. "One distracts me while the other sneaks up on me, is that it?" the man cried. "You won't get away with it. Come near me and I'll jump, I swear I'll jump!"

"I'll stay right here," Levine promised. Leaning far out, he would be almost able to reach Cartwright's outstretched hand. But if he were to touch it, Cartwright would surely jump. And if he were to grip it, Cartwright would most likely drag him along too, all the way down to the sidewalk sixty-six feet below.

"What is it, Cartwright?" demanded Crawley again. "What do you want?"

Way back at the beginning of their partnership, Levine and Crawley had discovered the arrangement that worked best for them. Crawley asked the questions, and Levine listened to the answers. While a man paid attention to Crawley, erected his facade between himself and Crawley, Levine, silent and unnoticed, could come in on the flank, peek behind the facade and see the man who was really there.

"I want you to leave me alone!" cried Cartwright. "Everybody, everybody! Just leave me alone!"

"Look up at the sky, Mister Cartwright," said Levine softly, just loud enough for the man on the ledge to hear him. "Look how blue it is. Look down across the street. Do you see the red of that girl's sweater? Breathe in, Mister Cartwright. Do you smell the city? Hark! Listen! Did you hear that car horn? That was over on Fulton Street, wasn't it?"

"Shut up!" screamed Cartwright, turning swiftly, precariously, to glare again at Levine. "Shut up, shut up, shut up! Leave me alone!"

Levine knew all he needed. "Do you want to talk to your son?" he asked.

"Allan?" The man's face softened all at once. "Allan?"

"He's right here," said Levine. He came back in from the window, signalled to the son, who was no longer talking on the phone. "He wants to talk to you."

The son rushed to the window. "Dad?"

Crawley came over, glowering. "Well?" he said.

Levine shook his head. "He doesn't want to die."

"I know that. What now?"

"I think it's the wife." Levine motioned to Gundy, who came over, and he said. "Is the partner here? Anderson?"

"Sure," said Gundy. "He's in his office. He tried to talk to Cartwright once, but Cartwright got too excited. We thought it would be a good idea if Anderson kept out of sight."

"Who thought? Anderson?"

"Well, yes. All of us. Anderson and McCann and me."

"Okay," said Levine. "You and the boy—what's his name, Allan?—stay here. Let me know what's happening, if anything at all does happen. We'll go talk with Mister Anderson now."

Anderson was short, slender, very brisk, very bald. His wire-framed spectacles reflected light, and his round little face was troubled. "No warning at all," he said. "Not a word. All of a sudden, Joan—she's our receptionist—got a call from someone across the street, saying there was a man on the ledge. And it was Jason. Just like that! No warning at all."

"The sign on your door," said Crawley, "says Industrial Research. What's that, efficiency expert stuff?"

Anderson smiled, a quick nervous flutter. "Not exactly," he said. He was devoting all his attention to Crawley, who was standing directly in front of him and who was asking the questions. Levine stood to one side, watching the movements of Anderson's lips and eyes and hands as he spoke.

"We are efficiency experts, in a way," Anderson was saying, "but not in the usual sense of the term. We don't work with time-charts, or how many people should work in the steno pool, things like that. Our major concern is the physical plant itself, the stucture and design of the plant buildings and work areas."

Crawley nodded. "Architects," he said.

Anderson's brief smile fluttered on his face again, and he shook his head. "No, we work in conjunction with the architect, if it's a new building. But most of our work is concerned with the modernization of old facilities. In a way, we're a central clearing agency for new ideas in industrial plant procedures." It was, thought Levine, an explanation Anderson was used to making, so used to making that it sounded almost like a memorized patter.

"You and Cartwright equal partners?" asked Crawley. It was clear he hadn't understood a word of Anderson's explanation and was impatient to move on to other things.

Anderson nodded. "Yes, we are. We've been partners for twenty-one years."

"You know him well, then."

"I should think so, yes."

"Then maybe you know why he suddenly decided to go crawl out on the ledge."

Eyes widening, Anderson shook his head again. "Not a thing," he said. "I had no idea, nothing, I—There just wasn't any warning at all."

Levine stood off to one side, watching, his lips pursed in concentration. Was Anderson telling the truth? It seemed likely; it *felt* likely. The marriage again. It kept going back to the marriage.

"Has he acted at all funny lately?" Crawley was still pursuing the same thought, that there had to be some previous build-up, and that the build-up would show. "Has he been moody, anything like that?"

"Jason—" Anderson stopped, shook his head briefly, started again. "Jason is a quiet man, by nature. He—he rarely says much, rarely uh, *forces* his personality, if you know what I mean. If he's been thinking about this, whatever it is, it—it wouldn't show. I don't *think* it would show."

"Would he have any business worries at all?" Crawley undoubtedly realized by now this was a blind alley, but he would go through the normal questions anyway. You never could tell.

Anderson, as was to be expected, said, "No, none. We've—well, we've been doing very well. The last five years, we've been expanding steadily, we've even added to our staff, just six months ago."

Levine now spoke for the first time. "What about Mrs. Cartwright?" he asked.

Anderson looked blank, as he turned to face Levine. "Mrs. Cartwright? I— I don't understand what you mean."

Crawley immediately picked up the new ball, took over the questioning again. "Do you know her well, Mister Anderson? What kind of woman would you say she was?"

Anderson turned back to Crawley, once again opening his flank to Levine. "She's, well, actually I haven't seen very much of her the last few years. Jason moved out of Manhattan five or six years ago, over to Jersey, and I live out on the Island, so we don't, uh, we don't *socialize* very much, as much as we used to. As you get older—" he turned to face Levine, as though instinctively understanding that Levine would more readily know what he meant "—you don't go out so much anymore, in the evening. You don't, uh, keep up friendships as much as you used to."

"You must know *something* about Mrs. Cartwright," said Crawley.

Anderson gave his attention to Crawley again. "She's, well, I suppose the best way to describe her is *determined*. I know for a fact she was the one who talked Jason into coming into partnership with me, twenty-one years ago. A forceful woman. Not a nag, mind you, I don't mean that at all. A very pleasant woman, really. A good hostess. A good mother, from the look of Allan. But forceful."

The wife, thought Levine. *She's the root of it. She knows, too, what drove him out there.*

And she wants him to jump.

Back in Cartwright's office, the son Allan was once again at the phone. The patrolman Gundy was at the left-hand window, and a new man, in clerical garb, at the right-hand window.

Gundy noticed Levine and Crawley come in, and immediately left the window. "A priest," he said softly. "Anderson said he was Catholic, so we got in touch with St. Mark's, over on Willoughby."

Levine nodded. He was listening to the son. "I don't know, Mother. Of course, Mother, we're doing everything we can. No, Mother, no reporters up here, maybe it won't have to be in the papers at all."

Levine went over to the window Gundy had vacated, took up a position where he could see Cartwright, carefully refrained from looking down at the ground. The priest was saying, "God has his time for you, Mister Cartwright. This is God's prerogative, to choose the time and the means of your death."

Cartwright shook his head, not looking at the priest, glaring instead directly across Flatbush Avenue at the building across the way. "There is no God," he said.

"I don't believe you mean that, Mister Cartwright," said the priest. "I believe you've lost faith in yourself, but I don't believe you've lost faith in God."

"Take that away!" screamed Cartwright all at once. "Take that away, or I jump right now!"

He was staring down toward the street, and Levine followed the direction of his gaze. Poles had been extended from windows on the floor below, and a safety net, similar to that used by circus performers, was being unrolled along them.

"Take that away!" screamed Cartwright again. He was leaning precariously forward, his face mottled red with fury and terror.

"Roll that back in!" shouted Levine. "Get it out of there, he can jump over it! Roll it back in!"

A face jutted out of one of the fifth-floor windows, turning inquiringly upward, saying, "Who are you?"

"Levine. Precinct. Get that thing away from there."

"Right you are," said the face, making it clear he accepted no responsibility either way. And the net and poles were withdrawn.

The priest, on the other side, was saying, "It's all right. Relax, Mr. Cartwright; it's all right. These people only want to help you; it's all right." The priest's voice was shaky. Like Gundy, he was a rookie at this. He'd never been asked to talk in a suicide before.

Levine twisted around, looking up. Two stories up, and the roof. More men were up there, with another safety net. If this were the top floor, they would probably take a chance with that net, try flipping it over him and pasting him like a butterfly to the wall. But not here, three stories down.

Cartwright had turned his face away from the still-talking priest, was studying Levine intently. Levine returned his gaze, and Cartwright said, "Where's Laura? She should be here by now, shouldn't she? Where is she?"

"Laura? You mean your wife?"

"Of course," he said. He stared at Levine, trying to read something in Levine's face. "Where is she?"

Tell him the truth? No. Tell him his wife wasn't coming, and he would jump right away. "She's on the way," he said. "She should be here pretty soon."

Cartwright turned his face forward again, stared off across the street.   The priest was still talking, softly, insistently.

Levine came back into the office.   To Crawley, he said, "It's the wife.   He's waiting for her."

"They've always got a wife," said Crawley sourly.   "And there's always just the one person they'll tell it to.   Well, how long before she gets here?"

"She isn't coming."

"What?"

"She's at home, over in Jersey.   She said she wouldn't come."   Levine shrugged and added, "I'll try her again."

The son was still on the phone, but he handed it over as soon as Levine spoke to him.   Levine said, "This is Detective Levine again, Mrs. Cartwright.   We'd like you to come down here after all, please.   Your husband asked to talk to you."

There was hesitation from the woman for a few seconds, and then she burst out, "Why can't you bring him in?   Can't you even *stop* him?"

"He's out of reach, Mrs. Cartwright.   If we tried to get him, I'm afraid he'd jump."

"This is ridiculous!   No, no, definitely not, I'm not going to be a party to it. I'm not going to talk to him until he comes in from there.   You tell him that."

"Mrs. Cartwright—"

"I'm not going to have any more to do with it!"

The click was loud in Levine's ear as she slammed the receiver onto the hook. Crawley was looking at him, and now said, "Well?"

"She hung up."

"She isn't coming?"   It was plain that Crawley was having trouble believing it.

Levine glanced at the son, who could hear every word he was saying, and then shrugged.   "She wants him to jump," he said.

The son's reaction was much smaller than Levine had expected.   He simply shook his head definitely and said, "No."

Levine waited, looking at him.

The son shook his head again.   "That isn't true," he said.   "She just doesn't understand—she doesn't really think he means it."

"All right," said Levine.   He turned away from the son, trying to think.   The wife, the marriage—A man in his late forties, married young, son grown and set up in his own vocation.   A quiet man, who doesn't force his personality on others, and a forceful wife.   A practical wife, who pushed him into a successful business.

Levine made his decision.   He nodded, and went back through the receptionist's office, where the other patrolman, McCann, was chatting with the three women employees.   Levine went into Anderson's office, said, "Excuse me.   Could I have the use of your office for a little while?"

"Certainly."   Anderson got up from his desk, came around, saying, "Anything at all, anything at all."

"Thank you."

Levine followed Anderson back to the receptionist's office, looked over the three women sitting against the left hand wall. Two were fortyish, plumpish, wearing wedding bands. The third looked to be in her early thirties, was tall and slender, good-looking in a solid level-eyed way, not glamorous. She wore no rings at all.

Levine went over to the third woman, said, "Could I speak to you for a minute, please?"

She looked up, startled, a bit frightened. "What? Oh. Oh, yes, of course."

She followed him back into Anderson's office. He motioned her to the chair facing Anderson's desk, himself sat behind the desk. "My name is Levine," he said. "Detective Abraham Levine. And you are—?"

"Janice Shapleigh," she said. Her voice was low, pleasantly melodious. She was wearing normal office clothing, a grey plain skirt and white plain blouse.

"You've worked here how long?"

"Three years." She was answering readily enough, with no hesitations, but deep in her eyes he could see she was frightened, and wary.

"Mister Cartwright won't tell us why he wants to kill himself," he began. "He's asked to speak to his wife, but she refuses to leave home—" He detected a tightening of her lips when he said that. Disapproval of Mrs. Cartwright? He went on. "—which we haven't told him yet. He doesn't really want to jump, Miss Shapleigh. He's a frustrated, thwarted man. There's something he wants or needs that he can't get, and he's chosen this way to try to force the issue." He paused, studying her face, said, "Would that something be you?"

Color started in her cheeks, and she opened her mouth for what he knew would be an immediate denial. But the denial didn't come. Instead, Janice Shapleigh sagged in the chair, defeated and miserable, not meeting Levine's eyes. In a small voice, barely audible, she said, "I didn't think he'd do anything like this. I never thought he'd do anything like this."

"He wants to marry you, is that it? And he can't get a divorce."

The girl nodded, and all at once she began to cry. She wept with one closed hand pressed to her mouth, muffling the sound, her head bowed as though she were ashamed of this weakness, ashamed to be seen crying.

Levine waited, watching her with the dulled helplessness of a man whose job by its very nature kept him exposed to the misery and frustrations of others. He would always want to help, and he would always be unable to help, to really help.

Janice Shapleigh controlled herself, slowly and painfully. When she looked up again, Levine knew she was finished weeping, no matter what happened. "What do you want me to do?" she said.

"Talk to him. His wife won't come—she knows what he wants to say to her, I suppose—so you're the only one."

"What can I say to him?"

Levine felt weary, heavy. Breathing, working the heart, pushing the sluggish blood through veins and arteries, was wearing, hopeless, exhausting labor. "I don't know," he said. "He wants to die because of you. Tell him why he should live."

Levine stood by the right-hand window, just out of sight of the man on the ledge. The son and the priest and Crawley and Gundy were all across the room, watching and waiting, the son looking bewildered, the priest relieved, Crawley sour, Gundy excited.

Janice Shapleigh was at the left-hand window, tense and frightened. She leaned out, looking down, and Levine saw her body go rigid, saw her hands tighten on the window-frame. She closed her eyes, swaying, inhaling, and Levine stood ready to move. If she were to faint from that position, she could fall out the window.

But she didn't faint. She raised her head and opened her eyes, and carefully avoided looking down at the street again. She looked, instead, to her right, toward the man on the ledge. "Jay," she said. "Jay, please."

"Jan!" Cartwright sounded surprised. "What are you doing? Jan, go back in there, stay away from this. Go back in there."

Levine stood by the window, listening. What would she say to him? What *could* she say to him?

"Jay," she said slowly, hesitantly, "Jay, please. It isn't worth it. Nothing is worth—dying for."

"Where's Laura?"

Levine waited, unbreathing, and at last the girl spoke the lie he had placed in her mouth. "She's on the way. She'll be here soon. But what does it matter, Jay? She still won't agree, you know that. She won't believe you."

"I'll wait for Laura," he said.

The son was suddenly striding across the room, shouting, "What is this? What's going on here?"

Levine spun around, motioning angrily for the boy to be quiet.

"Who is that woman?" demanded the son. "What's she doing here?"

Levine intercepted him before he could get to Janice Shapleigh, pressed both palms flat against the boy's shirt-front. "Get back over there," he whispered fiercely. "Get back over there."

"Get away from me! Who is she? What's going on here?"

"Allan?" It was Cartwright's voice, shouting the question. "Allan?"

Crawley now had the boy's arms from behind, and he and Levine propelled him toward the door. "Let me *go!*" cried the boy. "I've got a right to—"

Crawley's large hand clamped across his mouth, and the three of them barreled through to the receptionist's office. As the door closed behind them, Levine heard Janice Shapleigh repeating, "Jay? Listen to me, Jay, please. Please, Jay."

The door safely shut behind them, the two detectives let the boy go. He turned immediately, trying to push past them and get back inside, crying, "You can't do this! Let me go! What do you think you are? Who is that woman?"

"Shut up," said Levine. He spoke softly, but the boy quieted at once. In his voice had been all his own miseries, all his own frustrations, and his utter weariness with the misery and frustration of others.

"I'll tell you who that woman is," Levine said. "She's the woman your father wants to marry. He wants to divorce your mother and marry her."

"No," said the boy, as sure and positive as he had been earlier in denying that his mother would want to see his father dead.

"Don't say no," said Levine coldly. "I'm telling you facts. That's what sent him out there on that ledge. Your mother won't agree to the divorce."

"My mother—"

"Your mother," Levine pushed coldly on, "planned your father's life. Now, all at once, he's reached the age where he should have accomplished whatever he set out to do. His son is grown, he's making good money, now's the time for him to look around and say, 'This is the world I made for myself, and it's a good one.' But he can't. Because he doesn't like his life, it isn't *his* life, it's the life your mother planned for him."

"You're wrong," said the boy. "You're wrong."

"So he went looking," said Levine, ignoring the boy's interruptions, "and he found Janice Shapleigh. She wouldn't push him, she wouldn't plan for him, she'd let *him* be the strong one."

The boy just stood there, shaking his head, repeating over and over, "You're wrong. You're wrong."

Levine grimaced, in irritation and defeat. *You never break through,* he thought. *You never break through.* Aloud he said, "In twenty years you'll believe me." He looked over at the patrolman, McCann. "Keep this young man out here with you," he said.

"Right," said McCann.

"Why?" cried the son. "He's my father! Why can't I go in there?"

"Shame," Levine told him. "If he saw his son and this woman at the same time, he'd jump."

The boy's eyes widened. He started to shake his head, then just stood there, staring.

Levine and Crawley went back into the other room.

Janice Shapleigh was coming away from the window, her face ashen. "Somebody down on the sidewalk started taking pictures," she said. "Jay shouted at them to stop. He told me to get in out of sight, or he'd jump right now."

"Respectability," said Levine, as though the word were obscene. "We're all fools."

Crawley said, "Think we ought to send someone for the wife?"

"No. She'd only make it worse. She'd say no, and he'd go over.

"Oh God!" Janice Shapleigh swayed suddenly and Crawley grabbed her arm, led her across to one of the leather sofas.

Levine went back to the right-hand window. He looked out. A block away, on the other side of the street, there was a large clock in front of a bank building. It was almost eleven-thirty. They'd been here almost an hour and a half.

Three o'clock, he thought suddenly. This thing had to be over before three o'clock, that was the time of his appointment with the doctor.

He looked out at Cartwright.   The man was getting tired.   His face was drawn with strain and emotion, and his fingertips were clutching tight to the rough face of the wall.   Levine said, "Cartwright."

The man turned his head, slowly, afraid now of rapid movement.   He looked at Levine without speaking.

"Cartwright," said Levine.   "Have you thought about it now?   Have you thought about death?"

"I want to talk to my wife."

"You could fall before she got here," Levine told him.   "She has a long way to drive, and you're getting tired.   Come in, come in here.   You can talk to her in here when she arrives.   You've proved your point, man, you can come in.   Do you want to get too tired, do you want to lose your balance, lose your footing, slip and fall?"

"I want to talk to my wife," he said, doggedly.

"Cartwright, you're *alive*."   Levine stared helplessly at the man, searching for the way to tell him how precious that was, the fact of being alive.   "You're breathing," he said.   "You can see and hear and smell and taste and touch.   You can laugh at jokes, you can love a woman— For God's sake, man, you're *alive!*"

Cartwright's eyes didn't waver; his expression didn't change.   "I want to talk to my wife," he repeated.

"Listen," said Levine.   "You've been out here two hours now.   You've had time to think about death, about non-being.   Cartwright, listen.   Look at me, Cartwright, I'm going to the doctor at three o'clock this afternoon.   He's going to tell me about my heart, Cartwright.   He's going to tell me if my heart is getting too tired.   He's going to tell me if I'm going to stop being alive."

Levine strained with the need to tell this fool what he was throwing away, and knew it was hopeless.

The priest was back, all at once, at the other window.   "Can we help you?" he asked.   "Is there anything any of us can do to help you?"

Cartwright's head swiveled slowly.   He studied the priest.   "I want to talk to my wife," he said.

Levine gripped the windowsill.   There had to be a way to bring him in, there had to be a way to trick him or force him or convince him to come in.   He had to be brought in, he couldn't throw his life away, that's the only thing a man really has.

Levine wished desperately that *he* had the choice.

He leaned out again suddenly, glaring at the back of Cartwright's head.   "Jump!" he shouted.

Cartwright's head swiveled around, the face open, the eyes shocked, staring at Levine in disbelief.

"Jump!" roared Levine.   "Jump, you damn fool, end it, stop being alive, *die! Jump!* Throw yourself away, you imbecile, JUMP!"

Wide-eyed, Cartwright stared at Levine's flushed face, looked out and down at the crowd, the fire truck, the ambulance, the uniformed men, the chalked circle on the pavement.

And all at once he began to cry. His hands came up to his face, he swayed, and the crowd down below sighed, like a breeze rustling. "God help me!" Cartwright screamed.

Crawley came swarming out the other window, his legs held by Gundy. He grabbed for Cartwright's arm, growling, "All right, now, take it easy. Take it easy. This way, this way, just slide your feet along, don't try to bring the other foot around, just slide over, easy, easy—"

And the man came stumbling in from the ledge.

"You took a chance," said Crawley. "You took one hell of a chance." It was two-thirty, and Crawley was driving him to the doctor's office.

"I know," said Levine. His hands were still shaking; he could still feel the ragged pounding of his heart within his chest.

"But you called his bluff," said Crawley. "That kind, it's just a bluff. They don't really want to dive, they're bluffing."

"I know," said Levine.

"But you still took a hell of a chance."

"It—" Levine swallowed. It felt as though there were something hard caught in his throat. "It was the only way to get him in," he said. "The wife wasn't coming, and nothing else would bring him in. When the girlfriend failed—"

"It took guts, Abe. For a second there, I almost thought he was going to take you up on it."

"So did I."

Crawley pulled in at the curb in front of the doctor's office. "I'll pick you up around quarter to four," he said.

"I can take a cab," said Levine.

"Why? Why, for the love of Mike? The city's paying for the gas."

Levine smiled at his partner. "All right," he said. He got out of the car, went up the walk, up the stoop, onto the front porch. He looked back, watched the Chevvy turn the corner. He whispered, "I *wanted* him to jump." And he thought, "It's crazy. How would that have kept my number from being up?"

Then he went in to find out if he was going to stay alive.

JAMES HOLDING

Once Upon a Bank Floor

I usually buy a mystery story magazine to kill the tedium of a plane ride, but this time I didn't need it. The man who had the window seat beside me was better than any magazine.

He was middle aged and dressed conservatively but rather carelessly. He had a double chin and bushy brows over gentle brown eyes. When I sat down in the aisle seat beside him before take-off, he glanced casually at me. I wanted to start a conversation but just couldn't do it. And he didn't say anything until we were airborne and had unsnapped our seat belts.

His opening remark was purely tentative, a friendly overture. He said, "I see you're a mystery story fan," his eyes going to the magazine in my hand.

"Not really a fan," I said, "but I find them a pleasant way to pass the time on a plane ride."

"I'm not really a fan, either," he said. "I read mystery stories as much to keep up-to-date on the new criminal techniques as anything else."

"That could mislead a lot of people," I said, making a pleasantry of it, "into thinking you were a crook reading your trade journals."

He grinned disarmingly. "It's not as bad as that," he said. "I work for a bank. Banks deal in money, and money draws criminals. I want to be ready for trouble if they try anything on the bank where I work, that's all." He added companionably, "My name's Colbaugh."

"Mine's Dickson," I said. "Glad to know you." He said, "I was mixed up in a bank robbery once myself, at the Merchants National Bank in . . ." He named a small California town. "So I know how unexpectedly such things can happen."

"It sounds exciting," I remarked idly.

He shrugged. "You could call it exciting, all right." He leaned back in his seat and closed his eyes, evidently considering the amenities preserved.

But I wanted to get the story out of him, hear him tell it. "Tell me about it," I said.

"You'll be bored," he protested, opening his eyes again. "But all right. It's not a very long story. And it happened twenty years ago. I was a kind of assistant-assistant cashier at the bank—a clerk, really. We had a night depository

314

at the bank where the town's merchants could deposit their cash for safekeeping after their stores closed up for the night.   And as all the stores stayed open until nine o'clock on Thursday evenings in those days, there was always a good bit of cash to be found in our night depository on Friday mornings.''

"I know how that goes," I said.   "I own a sporting goods store in Fresno."

"Oh, really?   That's a nice part of the country.   Well, one of my jobs was to get down to the bank early in the mornings and clean out the deposits in the night depository so I could have them all tallied and on the assistant cashier's desk when he arrived for work at opening time.   So I was always the first one there; other employees would begin to drift in about fifteen minutes before opening time, but I had the bank to myself for a good half hour each morning.   And I kind of liked it, you know?   It made me feel responsible to have the run of the place before anybody else got there.''

I nodded comprehendingly.

"Well, one morning I left my house about eight o'clock as usual, and I was standing on my regular corner waiting for the bus that I rode to work, when a gray Ford sedan came along and stopped beside the bus stand and the driver leaned over and asked me if I wanted a lift downtown.   I said sure and got in beside him when he pushed the car door open for me.''

"In a mystery story," I said wisely, "you'd have been suspicious of the guy for offering you something for nothing.   You'd have said no thanks and waited for your bus.''

"Very probably.   But it never entered my mind there was any hanky-panky afoot that morning.   I got into the Ford and only then realized that there were two other men sitting in the back seat behind the driver and me.   The thing that struck me most forcibly about them, was that the one on the right held a long-barreled revolver of some sort in his hand, and it was pointed right at me.   The gun didn't have any sights on the front.   I remember noticing that in my shock and surprise.''

"Sounds like a Woodsman with the sights filed off," I said.   "Kind of a target pistol.   I sell them in my store.   That joker must have been a crack shot to work with a sporting gun like that.''

"As far as I was concerned, he certainly was!   I didn't say or do a single thing to attract attention to my plight, I can assure you, because the man with the gun told me not to.   And that was a plenty good enough reason for me.''

"We drove to the bank in dead silence, but at a very sedate speed.   The driver stopped the Ford at the rear of the bank where I always went in, just as though he knew all about my daily routine.   The bank backed on a narrow lane, or alley, and the rear door was used only by employees.   At that early hour, the lane was deserted.

"The man with the gun said to me, 'Here we are, Buster.   Out.'   He motioned for me to get out of the car.   He and the other man in the back seat got out, too.   The gun-bearer was tall and blond and skinny, painfully thin.   The other fellow was chunky and had fuzzy black hair growing down the back of his neck all the way to his collar, I remember that.   The tall one said to the driver, 'Stay with the crate,' and then to me, 'Now, let's open up and go inside, if you don't mind.' His voice was cool and polite and unhurried, as though he did this sort of thing every day. Maybe he did.

"I couldn't see much point in arguing when that long gun barrel was poking into my back, so I got out my keys and opened the door. As I put the key in the lock, my sleeve pulled back, and I saw by my wrist watch it was only 8:15—still quite a while before I could expect the bank guard or any of our other employees to show up. But I knew the time lock on the vault was set for just a few minutes before the bank opened, and I was pretty sure they couldn't do anything about *that*, unless they waited for opening time.

"We went inside. The tall man shattered any frail hopes I'd entertained with four words. He said to me, 'The night depository, Junior,' and I realized then that they *did* know what my routine was. They must have watched me for a few mornings to see what I did. I believe that's what they call 'casing the joint,' isn't it, Mr. Dickson?''

Colbaugh looked at me expectantly, as though wanting me to compliment him on his command of thieves' argot, derived, no doubt, from his reading of mystery stories. I said, "Yeah." It *was* strange to hear the expression come from the lips of this dignified middle-aged bank clerk.

"They forced me," he continued, "toward the night depository receptacle in the wall of the bank inside the front door. In those days, they didn't have solid ranks of all-glass, electric-eye doors for bank entrances the way we do now. Our bank just had a regular steel-frame front door with glass in it down to knee-height like any store door. And, there was a venetian blind on the inside of this door to keep the afternoon sun out of the eyes of Mr. Johnson, one of our vice presidents, whose desk was just to the right of the entrance. This blind was lowered after the sun moved around into Mr. Johnson's eyes every afternoon. And, it was left like that—lowered—until I came to work the next day, when I raised it as my first official act each morning on my way to clean out the night depository." Mr. Colbaugh turned his serene eyes on me and said deprecatingly, "You can see I had a lot of odd chores to do around the bank, Mr. Dickson. I was almost the janitor, really." He laughed before he went on.

"Even with the gun in my back, habit was strong in me that morning; I reached out automatically to raise Mr. Johnson's venetian blind on the front door as we went by. But the man behind me with the gun said, 'What do you think you're doing? Freeze!' I froze. I said, 'I raise this blind every morning. I was just going to draw it up . . .' 'Today,' he said, 'we won't raise it, Junior. If you don't mind. You think we want every jerk on the sidewalk to see what's going on in here?'

"I thought I ought to make some token effort, at least, to resist the robbers, so as we approached the night depository, I said, in what I fear was not a very convincing voice, 'I can't open this thing. It takes a special key. The assistant cashier carries the only key, and he won't be here till the bank opens.'

"The short man didn't say anything, merely pulled a gun out of his pocket and went to stand beside the front door, looking out into the street through the slats of the lowered blind but hidden from the eyes of anybody outside. But the tall thin man jabbed his gun barrel harder than ever into my spine. 'Don't give me that, Buster,' he said. "I know who opens this thing every morning. *You.* So fly with it. And don't make me wait. My nerves are getting pretty jumpy.' He didn't sound a bit nervous to me."

"But *you* must have been," I put in.

Mr. Colbaugh nodded vigorously. "I was terrified. Almost stiff with fright. I got out my key to the depository box and opened it up as meek as Moses. What else could I do?"

"I would have done the same," I consoled him.

"This was Friday morning, and there was quite a large amount of cash and a lot of checks in the depository from the merchants' Thursday night receipts. The tall man grunted with satisfaction when he saw how much was there. 'Clean it out,' he ordered me, 'and put it in this.' He held out a black briefcase to me.

"I did as he said, but I moved as slowly as possible without it seeming too obvious. Maybe I could delay them a little, I thought. But, when the money and the checks were all in the briefcase, it was still only eight-thirty.

"I was beginning to wonder what they intended to do with me when they left. I didn't feel sanguine about that at all. I'd seen their faces. I could describe them to the police. I could identify them. And, I'd ridden in their Ford and could identify it, too, for I'd memorized the license number when I got out of the car at the rear of the bank.

"The tall man said, 'Lay down on the floor, buddy . . . on your back.' I did so. Right in the middle of the marble lobby. I felt very foolish, I can tell you. And very exposed, too. For the short man at the front door could keep me covered with his gun and watch out the door, too.

"The tall man took a look at his wrist watch. And just then the telephone rang. It was the telephone on Mr. Johnson's desk by the front door. It sounded like a fire alarm in that empty bank. I was so startled, I jumped, if you can really jump when you're lying flat on your back on the floor. The tall man stooped over me and prodded me in the stomach with his gun.

" 'Get that, you!' he barked at me. All his polite coolness was gone now. 'Answer that phone! And make it sound natural, Buster, or you'll never live to take another phone call! Move!'

"The phone was ringing for the third time. 'Hold the receiver away from your ear,' he warned me, 'so I can hear it, too.'

"I got up from the floor and went over and picked up the telephone, with the tall man right beside me. The short one hadn't said anything, but his gun was trained on me, now. I cleared my throat and said, 'Hello?' into the receiver, loud and clear. 'Is this the Farmers National?' came the tinny inquiry, as I held the receiver so the tall man could hear it.

"His gun was boring into my back. 'Yes, sir,' I said into the phone.

" 'How late do you stay open this afternoon?' the voice asked. I looked at the bandit beside me and raised my eyebrows.

" 'Tell him!' he whispered.

"I said into the phone, 'We close at three-thirty, sir.'

" 'Thanks,' came the answer, and we could both hear the sharp click that sounded as the caller hung up.

"I put down the phone.   There was sweat on my forehead and I felt sick.   I looked at the short man's gun that was aimed at my mid-section from five feet away, and my knees shook.   The tall man let out his breath in a 'whoosh' of relief.

" 'Okay, Shiner,' he said to his pal, 'back to the door.'   And to me, 'And you get back where you were, Buster.'   He waved his gun at me.   I lay down on the floor again.

" 'Plenty of time, Shiner,' he called to his partner, then.   'Watch the kid, here. I'm going to take a look in the tellers' cages.'

"He went out of my sight, then, and I could hear him jerking open the cash drawers and swearing when he found them empty.

"I could see the minute hand on our big wall clock above the New Accounts desk moving with tiny jerks; one jerk for eve.y thousand years, it seemed to me. It made four of these jerks by the time the tall man was satisfied that he wasn't overlooking anything in the tellers' cages.   I could have told him we always locked up the cash in the vault.

"He came out into the lobby again where Shiner and I were, the briefcase in his left hand, his gun in his right.   He motioned Shiner toward the rear door of the bank, the way we'd come in.   So they weren't going to wait for the time lock on the vault.   They were leaving.   I could hear my heart thudding against the marble floor, as though the floor were a sounding board.

"Shiner left his post by the front door.   'What about him?' he asked the tall one, pointing his gun at me.

" 'Put him out,' the other one said matter-of-factly, 'the way I told you.' "

Mr. Colbaugh turned and looked at me with a smile softening his mouth and crinkling up his eyes.   "I can tell you, Mr. Dickson, I was awfully scared at that point.   I didn't know whether they meant to kill me or just knock me out, or what. 'Put him out' could have meant anything.   Then I saw Shiner reversing his gun in his hand and leaning over me and swinging the butt at my head, and that's all I saw for a while."

I said, "The banking business has more hazards than I'd realized."

"It has indeed," he said.   "I found out later that the bandits had another car waiting for them half a mile away, and that the Ford had been stolen.   They were from out of state, it developed, and unknown in our town.   So they didn't think it necessary to kill me.   They just put me out of business while they made their getaway."

"So what happened?" I asked, the way a good listener should.

"The police took them easily as they emerged from the rear door of the bank," Colbaugh said.   "The driver of the Ford was already in custody.   The police had the bank surrounded."

We could hear the motors change pitch as our plane started to let down for a landing.

"The police!" I said, astounded.   "Where'd *they* come from?"

"Johnny Sampson sent them."

I looked at him blankly. "Who was Johnny Sampson?"

"We went to high school together," Colbaugh said. "He was my best friend in the bank, a teller."

"What made him send for the police?"

"When he telephoned the bank and asked the closing time, I told him 3:30. But he knew it closed at 3:00. So that was his signal. To call the police."

I reached up for my hat and coat as I saw the airport runways coming up to meet us.

"You mean that telephone call was rigged?" I asked. "You had it all arranged with Sampson beforehand?"

"Sure." He smiled, pleased at my surprise. "That's what I meant when I said I liked to be ready for trouble at the bank. Johnny and I had it all worked out."

"Wait a minute," I protested. "Even so, how did Sampson know he should call you that particular morning? Did he do it every day?"

"Oh, no. Johnny was a bachelor," Colbaugh said, as though that explained everything. "He always ate his breakfast around the corner at Mother Hague's Coffee Shop before coming to work at the bank. He passed the bank entrance to get to the coffee shop at the same time every morning—8:20. And if he ever saw that the venetian blind on the bank's front door was still lowered when he went to breakfast, he was supposed to telephone the bank and ask what time it closed. If I answered and gave him the wrong closing time, call the police. If anybody but me answered, call the police. If nobody answered, call the police. You see how simple it was?"

"Very simple," I said, "if anything as complicated as that can be simple. What if you were sick and didn't come to work some morning and, therefore, failed to raise the venetian blind?"

"If I was sick, my wife phoned Sampson at his home before he went to breakfast and told him the venetian blind would be down when he passed it."

"How about Sampson, though? Suppose *he'd* been sick on the day of the hold-up?"

"An unlikely coincidence," Colbaugh said. "I guess that would have been just too bad for me and the night deposits."

I unfastened my seat belt as I felt the wheels touch down. "I'd say it was too bad for you anyway, wasn't it? You were the 'inside' man of your live burglar alarm system. You took the chances. You got knocked silly by the hold-up men, while your friend Sampson ate bacon and eggs in Mother Hague's Coffee Shop."

We stood up.

"Yes, that's true, I suppose," Colbaugh conceded. "But we were young. And, as you suggested earlier, it *was* exciting. You have no idea, Mr. Dickson, how exciting it is to see a gun butt being swung at your head and then not be sure until two hours later when you regain consciousness, that you haven't been murdered!"

I said, "Are you still with Merchants National?"

"Yes, still at the same old stand. So's Johnny Sampson. He's the president of the bank now."

"Good for him. Virtue's reward. And what's your job these days, Mr. Colbaugh?"

"I'm chairman of the board," he said, smiling. "Still taking the chances, you see."

"Now, I've got the whole story," I said ambiguously. "Right down to the present."

We walked down the ramp into the airport terminal together. I was slightly behind him. My topcoat was over my right arm. On impulse, when we got inside the terminal lobby, I pushed my forefinger into his back, under cover of my topcoat, and said, "Turn left, Mr. Colbaugh, and go into the men's room, will you?"

He reacted quite calmly. His eyes widened a little as they swiveled toward me. He stiffened slightly, and I could feel his back muscles come up under my finger for a second. Then he said, "The washroom? Why?" But he kept on walking.

"Now don't tell me that your assistant cashier has the only key to *this*," I said. "Here we are. Go on in."

We went in. It was a slack time; the washroom was empty, as I'd hoped.

When the door swished shut behind us, I took my forefinger out of Colbaugh's back and he turned toward me. He really looked at me this time, tilting his head back to gaze up into my face. And he got it right away.

He said, "You've taken on a good bit of weight since then, Dickson. And changed your name. Do you really own a sporting goods store in Fresno?"

"I was anticipating there a little," I said, smiling at him. "I *clerk* in a sporting goods store, and I have a wonderful opportunity to buy into it if I can raise two thousand dollars by the end of this week."

"Oh," Colbaugh said. "You're going straight, then?"

"I'm trying to, since I got out." I held up my finger. "I don't file the sights off my guns anymore, you see?"

He said, "Why don't you swing a loan?"

"Did you ever know anybody who would lend money to an ex-con? I've tried."

"You didn't try our bank."

"I was going to. At least I went to your bank this morning to make an appeal to you personally, if you still worked there."

"Why didn't you?"

"I lost my nerve when I saw your line-up of loan officers and vice presidents. I knew they'd nix me for sure. It had to be you or nobody."

"So you followed me onto the plane, is that it?"

"Yes. I happened to see you walk through the bank with your hat and coat and overnight bag and get into the airport taxi. I recognized you right away. So, I followed you to the airport and bought a seat on the same flight."

He nodded, his face expressionless. "Two thousand dollars?"

"That's all. And I have no collateral, Mr. Colbaugh."

He allowed himself a tight smile. "You told Shiner to put me out that day, Dickson. He clubbed me with a gun. And remember I was just a kid."

"I know it. And I'm not proud of it. But think of it this way, Mr. Colbaugh. Wasn't your successful prevention of that bank robbery the first thing that made your bank management really *notice* you and Sampson? Isn't that what triggered the whole series of promotions that led you both to the top jobs you have today?"

I watched him narrowly, temporarily forgetting to breathe. For this was the only weapon I could use in my second hold-up of Colbaugh.

He didn't say anything for a minute, thinking it over. Then, his lips curled up a trifle, and I began to breathe again.

"You know," he said, "I think you're right, Dickson. It *was* through you that I first drew favorable notice at the bank. I never thought of it like that before, but in a sort of cock-eyed way, I suppose I owe you something for it. And so does Sampson."

"How about a thousand dollars apiece? You could call it a personal loan, Mr. Colbaugh. And I'll pay it back."

He made up his mind quickly. "I believe you will, at that," he said. He got out his checkbook and wrote out a check to cash for two thousand dollars. As he handed it to me, and we shook hands, he said curiously, "Why'd you bring me in here? Why not brace me in the plane or out in the lobby?"

I looked around at the bare white-tiled walls of the washroom and grinned at him. "No venetian blinds in here," I said.

EDWARD D. HOCH

Warrior's Farewell

Some early morning fishermen had found the body, washed up on the sandy beach like a great dead whale cast aside by nature, and it was only a few hours until the authorities identified the man as Sam Zodiak, an unmarried used car dealer and petty gambler.

I read the item in the afternoon editions of the paper with great interest because at one time Sam Zodiak had probably been my best friend. He was a large man in every way, and when I first knew him he was an army sergeant, looking very much the part. That was something like fifteen years ago, in a place called Korea that most of the kids today don't even remember.

I was young and sort of frightened in those days—frightened of a place I didn't know and people I didn't understand. Prowling the streets of Seoul at night, lonely and far from home, I was thankful for the company of a man like Sergeant Zodiak. Unlike the others, he wasn't particularly interested in picking up any of the girls who cluttered the bars of the city, and he managed to stay reasonably sober during the hours we'd spend together.

"You know, Corporal," he'd say over a beer at a crowded back table in one of those smoky places, "I just look forward to doing my job every day. Sometimes I think the two most important words in the language are *war* and *justice*. And they're not a great deal different from each other, if you're fighting a just war like this one. They're invaders, and they got to be killed. It's as simple as that."

"You talk like a career soldier, Sarge." I liked to kid him about it.

"I'll stay in as long as they need me, that's for sure." He took the cigar out of his mouth. "Justice! That's what we got to deliver."

"What about when you get home?" I sipped my beer. "A lot of the fellows talk about going back to school."

"Hell, I'm too old for that. I'm over thirty already. No, I'm going to get me a little lot and sell used cars. That's where the money is. Then maybe I'll take off an afternoon a week and go out to the racetrack or something. I like to see them ponies run."

"They say it might be a long war here, Sarge."

He puffed on the cigar for a minute. "Well, then I'll stay a long time. First things first. We got to end this thing."

Two weeks later we went into battle together, one of the last big engagements before the truce was signed, and I saw for myself exactly what he meant. It was a bloody scrap, not far from the 38th Parallel, in an area of hilly farmland that had changed hands at least twice before. The planes had softened up the area, leaving only the old stone farmhouse standing roofless in the sun. We came over the hill with our rifles ready, backed up by a BAR and mortar team, and immediately exchanged fire with a retreating enemy squad. It was the better part of an hour before we'd taken the farmhouse and decided we could hold it till morning.

After an hour or so of scouting the area, we flushed out a Korean farmer who'd been hiding in a ditch. He didn't look quite right, but then none of them ever did to our eyes. He seemed friendly enough at first, and pretty soon the PFC who was guarding him put down his carbine to light a cigarette. It was his first and last mistake. The farmer made a dive for the rifle and got off two quick shots before I ran up and clubbed him to the ground with my own weapon. The PFC was dead.

"He's a North Korean officer," I said, ripping away the farm clothes to reveal the last vestiges of a uniform beneath. "I guess we came on too fast for him to get away."

"Damn spy!" Sergeant Zodiak muttered. He was the ranking noncom, and he had to decide what to do with the man. "Too bad you didn't kill him." The man was bleeding from the temple but otherwise seemed to be suffering no ill effects from my blows.

"It was faster to slug him, Sarge. I didn't want him spraying bullets around the place. Shall we send somebody back with him?"

"With the kid dead, we can't spare a man."

"We leave him tied up in the farmhouse, then. They'll find him tomorrow."

Sergeant Zodiak shook his head. "And let him kill somebody else, maybe? No, there's only one way to handle his kind." He reached out and took the carbine from me.

"He's a prisoner of war, Sarge!"

"Like hell he is! He's out of uniform. He's nothing but a spy and a murderer, and as such he can be executed."

"Without a trial?"

But Sergeant Zodiak half turned toward the prisoner and fired a quick burst from the carbine, ending the discussion. The man's head jerked back in the shock of death and he went down hard in the tall grass of the field.

We left him there with the other bodies, and nobody ever mentioned it again.

Sergeant Zodiak surprised me and everyone else when he didn't re-enlist for another tour of duty. He returned to the States with me, and we were discharged together in San Francisco. I moved east after that, spending a couple of years finishing my education at a little college in Ohio, but all the time I kept in touch with Zodiak, and an odd sort of friendship seemed to grow between us.

I saw him once after college on a trip out west, and we went on a two-day drunk that was unlike any of our subdued army outings. Sam had his used car lot and was making a pretty good living at it. Drinking together on that visit, I think we both realized for the first time the bond of friendship that existed between us. Six months later, when I married a girl I'd met in college, Sam Zodiak came east to be my best man.

After that, I didn't hear from him for something like a year, until he phoned me one evening and told me he was getting married. "That's great news, Sam," I told him, meaning it. "I was beginning to think you'd never do it."

"I want you out here for it," he said. "Best man, the whole deal."

"Just let me know the date and I'll be there."

Sam had left San Francisco and was living in a smaller ocean community in a neighboring state. I flew out there on my vacation, although the wedding was still a month away. I was anxious to meet the girl Sam Zodiak had finally chosen.

I never did meet Ann. On the very night I was flying out, an exmental patient who lived in the next block from her went wild and shot his wife. Then he went out on his front porch with the gun, saw Ann running across the street toward the house, and shot her dead. He wounded two others before the police managed to subdue him, and I arrived at the airport to find that tragedy had struck Sam Zodiak.

"I don't know what to do," he told me the next day. "I'm just lost and going around in circles. Ann was a nurse, always wanting to help people. We were just getting out of the car when she heard the shots and went running. Crazy! I should have grabbed her. I should have held her back. I should have done a hundred things."

"It wasn't your fault."

"The hell of it is, this fellow Gondon will get off free. There's not even a death penalty in this state any more."

"They'll put him away for a long time."

"A few years in a mental hospital and he'll be walking the streets a free man. I know."

I stayed for the week, trying to calm him, and I thought I'd succeeded pretty well. His prediction proved to be correct, though, and George Gondon was never brought to trial for killing Ann. The others recovered from their wounds, including his wife, and Gondon was sent to the state hospital for treatment.

I went back east to my own wife and, though the correspondence with Sam Zodiak continued, we saw no more of each other for three years. Then one day I received a brief letter from him, enclosing a newspaper clipping. It told how a man named George Gondon, recently released from a mental hospital, had been shot and killed during an apparent robbery. Sam's only comment on the clipping was a single sentence in his letter: *This is what I call justice, not revenge.*

Shortly after that, I changed jobs and became a purchasing expediter for a large chemical firm. One of my duties was a monthly trip to a supplier in Sam's city. Suddenly we were seeing each other again, on a regular basis.

One night, over beers, I asked him how he was doing.

"Darned good. The used car business is a little off, but I'm making it up at the track. Even own part interest in a racehorse now."

"That's great, Sam." I found myself trying to read the backward lettering on the neon sign in the bar's front window. "There's something I've been wanting to ask you," I said finally.

"Fire away, boy!"

"That clipping you sent me a few months back, about that fellow who killed Ann."

"Yeah?" I could read nothing into his expression.

"Well, Sam . . . How should I say it?"

"I'll say it for you," he told me quietly. "It's no mystery, really. The thing's in the Bible. An eye for an eye, and all that stuff. There's not even a death penalty in this state anymore."

"I know." Suddenly my blood had turned cold.

"I know what you're thinking. You're remembering that time in Korea."

"No."

"I was right then, and I'm right now. He killed Ann, and nobody punished him for it. What was I supposed to do?"

I couldn't answer that. I didn't want to answer it. I just wanted to get away from there as quickly as I could.

After that, I started cutting down on my visits with Sam Zodiak. Sometimes I'd sneak into town for a day and not even tell him about it. I saw the signs for his used car place around town, and I knew he must be doing pretty well, but I didn't want to see him anymore.

About a year after George Gondon's death, the city where Sam lived was the scene of a particularly brutal sex murder involving a fourteen-year-old girl. She'd been found in the trunk of an abandoned car, and it took the police only an hour to trace the ownership of the vehicle and send out a ten-state alarm. The suspect was arrested in San Francisco a few days later and brought back to Sam's city under close police guard. The newspapers reported that the man had confessed to the killing.

There were maybe a hundred people outside police headquarters when the suspect, a young man named Asker, arrived. As he was led into the building between two detectives, a single shot from somewhere across the street hit him in the back of the head, killing him instantly. In the near panic that followed, the killer made a clean getaway.

I read the newspaper accounts of the killing with a gnawing sense of urgency. It couldn't be Sam Zodiak again, it just couldn't be, yet I had to know, to be certain. I arranged to fly out there the following weekend.

I wired Sam that I was coming, and he met me at the airport, smiling and friendly as ever, despite the fact that I'd seen little of him during the past year. "How you been, boy? How's the wife? Any kids yet?" He was the same old Sam, and I instantly regretted the suspicions which had been breeding in my mind; regretted them until I remembered Gondon and the Korean thing.

Later, over dinner, I ventured into the object of my trip. "I read about the killing of that fellow, Asker, at police headquarters. Awful thing."

"Awful? Asker's crime was awful, his killing wasn't."

"He hadn't even stood trial yet."

Sam Zodiak waved his hand. "What good would a trial have been? There's no death penalty in this state anymore."

"No." I lit a cigarette and tried to keep my hand from shaking. "Then you think his killing was justified?"

"Of course."

"Just like George Gondon's."

"Just like it. The people of this state never had a chance to vote on capital punishment. The legislature and the governor just got together and abolished it. You think that's right?"

"For some people it's hard to tell the difference between right and wrong. You killed Asker, didn't you?"

He eyed me slyly across the table. "Justice was done."

"Sam, Sam! What's happening to you?"

"It's not me—it's the modern morality—or lack of it." He focused on me with wide, intent eyes. "People look at me and what do they see? A used car dealer, a petty gambler. I suppose I'm the sort of guy who's supposed to have no morals at all. And yet, look at the rest of them! Condoning every sort of violence, every excess. The murderer today is to be pitied—because of his tragic childhood, or low IQ, or mental illness, or economic blight. They don't execute murderers anymore, they send them to the hospital, or to prison for a few years. And then they turn them free to kill again."

I had to get out of there, into the fresh air where maybe it wouldn't seem so much of a bad dream. Sam paid the check and left with me, strolling at my side with one arm around my shoulders like the old army buddy he was. "I'm a warrior in the battle for justice," he said. "A warrior."

"I think you're mad," I told him. "How long are you going to keep this up?"

The sly look was back on his face, not entirely hidden by the night. "You're a buddy, so I'll tell you something. You'd never prove it to the police anyway, so I'm safe in telling you. There've been five of them now, five of them since last year. The others were downstate, and didn't make such splashy headlines."

"*Five!*"

"All criminals, all *murderers* who'd escaped the death penalty because of our laws."

We were strolling across the bay bridge, with the lights of the harbor obscured by the nightly mists. I turned to him, for a moment speechless from the horror of what he was telling me. Then I said, "You really think you have the right?"

Sam Zodiak stared straight ahead at the deserted bridge. "I have three others on my list already."

It was then that I pushed him with all my strength, saw him grasping frantically at the railing before he toppled over, with the beginnings of a scream cut short as he hit the murky waters below.

They found his body the following morning, while I was still in town, and though I read the account in the afternoon paper with a growing sense of relief, there was one thing that nagged at my mind—one tiny, troublesome thing.

When he'd realized what I was doing, in that last second before his face vanished from sight, Sam Zodiak hadn't looked really angry. Instead, there'd been a sort of challenge in his expression.

As if he were saying to me, *See what I mean!*

WENZELL BROWN

Death by Misadventure

There warn't no two ways about it. Red Emma was the fattest woman in the whole o' Pisquaticook County. That was until Bessie Bellinger come round. Then I reckon you'd have to flip a coin to decide which one was fatter than the other.

Who could have guessed there'd be so much fussin' and feudin' over a matter of avoirdupois? But then there wouldn't never have been no real trouble, at least not the killin' kind, if it hadn't been for Joe Dongan and the yen he had for buxom females.

Looks like I'm gettin' ahead of my story. Mebbe I better start the cart rollin' by tellin' about the Ringside Diner. Bein' as how I'm County Sheriff I don't get much call to go over to Bancroft, which is the biggest town hereabouts, but when I do, I always make it a point to drop into the Ringside and put on the feedbag. There ain't no fancy trimmin's about their fare, just plain Maine food, the kind that sticks to your ribs, and plenty of it, but I reckon that's good enough for any man.

Nigh on to twenty years ago, Joe Dongan bought up the diner with money he'd saved up in the prize ring. He'd been a heavyweight boxer in his day and had a cauliflower ear and a flattened-out nose to prove it. Me, I ain't never studied up on the fight game, but people 'round tell as how Joe was goin' great guns, and might have been the champ if he had got the breaks. I ain't disputin' their claims but I reckon you got to take 'em with a pinch of salt, considerin' local pride and all.

One thing's for sure, Joe ain't no chucklehead. In no time at all he's got a flourishin' business, and 'taint long afore he's expandin', buildin' hisself a bowlin' alley and sports arena. Joe rates as a solid citizen too, awardin' high school athletic trophies and settin' up a scholarship at the state university. But a lot of folks in Bancroft got it figured that Emma Foley's the real brains behind Joe Dongan.

Nobody rightly remembers when Red Emma first drifted into town or where she come from. But one day there she is a-settin' on a high stool in back of the cashier's counter at the Ringside Diner, greetin' everybody as comes in with a big warm smile and that boomin' voice of hers.

Emma ain't no beauty. She's got carroty hair, a slew of freckles, broad, flat cheekbones, and the build of a lumberjack. Just the same she's all woman. When she smiles her face lights up deep inside, so a man feels sort of happy just lookin' at her.

Plenty of people put a heap o' store by Red Emma. Ain't never no reason for an honest man to go hungry in Bancroft, and nobody knows when Emma puts a meal on the cuff. But she don't stand for no hanky-panky. Let a feller start cussin' or cuttin' up mean in the Ringside and she lays it on the line. It's either shut up or get out, and Emma don't take no back talk. She's got enough beef, and Joe's taught her enough judo tricks, so she don't have no trouble at all frog-marchin' a drunken truck driver right out onto the street.

Same with the high school kids. The diner's a hangout for the teenagers, 'specially after the late movies. Emma likes to see 'em have a good time but there's a limit to what she'll take. None of 'em dare sass her back. At least not more'n once. I reckon it's partly because of her Bancroft ain't got much of this here juvenile delinquency you read so much about in the papers.

Big as she is, there's more'n one man's gone sweet on Emma. But she ain't never had eyes for no one save'n Joe Dongan. Trouble is Joe's got a wife, though you might say in name only. Poor Lulie Dongan was always a puny little thing and not very bright. Joe married her afore he turned twenty. Warn't more'n a year afterward when they had to put her away in a sanitarium up 'Gusty way. Joe takes care of all the bills and visits her when he can but, accordin' to what I hear, Lulie don't even recognize him. She just sits starin' into space when he comes.

Most ways Maine folk tend to be sort o' narrer-minded but I never do hear much criticism of Joe and Emma, not even when she rents a cottage on the Shore Road north of Cripple's Bend and Joe's car is parked up there most nights and weekends. Course Joe could have shucked Lulie and tied up with Emma. But that ain't the way they call the play, and folks think the better of 'em for it. Everyone takes it for granted they'll get spliced if they ever have a chance.

That's the way things is standin' when Bessie Bellinger enters the scene. She's Ralph Napier's mother-in-law. Now the Napiers have been livin' in Bancroft since it was founded. They owned the paper mill and practically run the town at one time. But that ain't sayin' that Ralph was popular. He was a snooty kid with a hankerin' for licker, fast cars and faster women. I had him in once for speedin' and he paid his fine like he was doin' me a favor.

An Ivy League college don't improve Ralph none, nor a couple of years in New York. When his daddy died, Ralph come back and settled down in the old Napier house on Cedar Street, bringin' his bride with him. Even if I don't cotton to Ralph, I got to admit he knows how to pick a wife. Doris Napier is pretty as a pitcher and right pleasant too. And that bein' the case, there ain't no need for Ralph to play the field no more.

Everything's hunky-dory until Doris' widdered mother came to live with 'em. Now Bessie would attract a heap of attention in a town a lot bigger'n Bancroft. She's built along the lines of an outsized kewpie doll, all pink and white and dimpled. She has a pile of auburn hair, touched with gray, sparklin' brown eyes and a complexion like a fresh peach. When she joggles down the main street the youngsters giggle and pass mockin' remarks, but more'n one old buck stops to ogle her.

Now I know a fat woman ain't stylish, but I reckon there's a lot of men gets tired of the scrawny females he meets up with nowadays. And there ain't no denyin' there's plenty of attractive curves to Bessie. It ain't only that, she's what you might call the quintessence of femininity. She dresses to the nines with broadbrimmed hats, high-heeled shoes, and plenty of ribbons and fancy gewgaws. Her plump little hands are soft and warm and covered with diamond rings, and she always smells of expensive perfume.

More'n once I find an excuse to pass the time o' day with her. She's got a croonin' sort of voice and a laugh like dried leaves a-rustlin' in the wind. Even if I do feel sheepish admittin' it, she puffs a man up and makes him feel like he can really roar.

'Taint no time at all afore the town's a-buzzin' with speculation as to whether Bessie or Red Emma is the fattest. I reckon you toss 'em on the scales and Emma'd win by a few pounds. But Miss Daisy Lunt, the librarian, pretty well sums up the situation when she points out that ain't a fair comparison. Emma's carryin' a load of bone and muscle, while Bessie's all soft and rollin'.

In a town the size of Bancroft, gossip makes the rounds fast. Neither Bessie nor Emma is takin' kindly to the jokes linkin' them together. Everyone's a-wonderin' what'll happen when they meet face to face.

The Ringside Diner is smack in the middle of Bancroft's main street, and most any day Red Emma's a-settin' in the winder for anyone to see. A couple of times Bessie stops in front of the diner, her lips pursin' in and out while she's pretendin' to read the menu in the winder, but really sizin' up Emma. Seems like she don't care for what she sees, because each time she gives a sort of sniff and goes on her way. As for Emma, she sits stony-faced like she don't know that Bessie's a-peerin' in at her.

Then one day Bessie flounces into the Ringside and settles herself down at one of Minnie Martin's tables. She orders clam chowder and preens a bit while she's waitin'.

Pretty soon Minnie slides a big frothy bowl in front of her, filled with clams, 'taters, onions, celery and such, with a great gob of rich yeller butter swimmin' around on top. Bessie crumbles a few crackers in the bowl and stirs 'em up, sort of holdin' herself away from it, like she's scared one of them clams is going to jump up and bite her.

After a while she raises a spoonful to her mouth and takes a weeny bit of a sip. She puckers up her lips, sighs and lays the spoon down. She nibbles at a dill pickle, makes a little move and sets that down too.

Red Emma's takin' it all in from behind the cashier's counter. Ain't nobody ever turned up their nose at her clam chowder afore. Matter of fact, tourists from all over the country go clean out of their way for a shore dinner at the Ringside Diner. She's smilin' but anyone who knows her can recognize the danger signs. Her eyes are bright and shiny, and her lips are pressed back hard against her teeth in a forced smile.

Bessie calls for her check and Minnie, the waitress, comes over, all flustered, and hands it to her. By this time everybody in the diner is watchin'

"I hope there's nothin' wrong," Minnie quavers.

"Oh no, I'm not very hungry," Bessie says, sweet as you please. "You might not guess it to look at me, but I eat like a bird."

Minnie says, "Isn't there anything else I can get you?"

Bessie shakes her head, still smilin'. "I don't think so, dear. I have a very delicate appetite and well—" She looks down at the heavy, chipped, crockery bowl and the tin spoon.

Minnie flushes and starts apologizin' but Bessie cuts her off. "It's not your fault, darling."

She digs around in her oversized handbag, hauls out a fifty cent piece and tucks it under the napkin for a tip. Then she sails over to the cashier's counter with the check and a dollar bill in her hand.

Emma's all a-bristle now. She's still got her fixed smile on but it's wearin' mighty thin.

She says, "There won't be any charge, Mrs. Bellinger."

"But I insist."

"We don't want dissatisfied customers."

"Land's sake! Did I make any complaint? I didn't say a thing!"

Emma's gettin' rattled and her words snip off real sharp.

"We don't want your money or your patronage. Do you understand?"

Bessie's got more experience at this kind of game. She coos, "Really, you can't force food down people's throats. Do you make everyone who comes in here eat what's put in front of them? Why, mercy sakes, you'd think I was a naughty child."

Things is just gettin' set to be right interestin' when who walks into the diner but Joe Dongan. Emma sees him and slices off whatever retort she's about to make.

Joe comes up behind Bessie and puts a hand on her arm. She bridles a bit, and Joe says, "I'm sorry, Mrs. Bellinger. Is something wrong?"

Bessie gives her chuckling laugh. "Not a thing except, well, I'm feeling a trifle peckish. I ordered some clam chowder and your—er—cashier seems to think I'm obliged to eat it. Otherwise, I'm banned from the Ringside Diner."

Joe scowls at Emma. She gives him a baffled look and turns away. Joe's voice grows firmer. "Ridiculous, Mrs. Bellinger. You're always welcome here."

"Well, I'm glad to hear that," says Bessie. "I must say you've been very kind and considerate."

While he's been talkin', she's been sidlin' toward the door, leavin' the dollar bill on the glass counter. Joe's movin' right along with her.

Out on the street they stop and chat for a while. Nobody inside can hear what they're sayin', but Bessie's smilin' and gesticulatin', while Joe has a silly grin on his ugly pan. 'Taint long afore Joe leads her over to his shiny black car that's parked at the curb. He helps her into the front seat, gallant as all get-out, and then runs around the car to jump in beside her.

Red Emma's watchin' like a cat. She's so mad she's all a-tremble, and her fingers is clampin' the dollar bill so hard she rips it to shreds.

Pretty soon the word is spread all over town that Joe Dongan is squirin' Bessie

Bellinger around, takin' her for drives in his car, escortin' her to the Beacon Theatre on Sat'dy nights, and even tryin' to teach her to bowl.

Nobody has to be a mind-reader to know that Red Emma is burned up. She takes to moonin' around the cashier's desk, and a-starin' out the winder like she ain't seein' a thing. What's more, she's right snappish with the customers, and that ain't like Emma at all.

Then comes a crisis. Lulie Dongan up and dies, and Joe is free to marry, at last. But it looks like mebbe Emma's been a-waitin' all these years just to get cut out by Bessie Bellinger.

Seems like most everybody in Pisquaticook County is pitchin' for Emma, claimin' as how Joe Dongan's givin' her the dirty end o' the stick. Feelin' runs high against Bessie Bellinger too, 'specially as the widder's supposed to be loaded, while Emma ain't got a red cent save'n what Joe's a-payin' her.

There's plenty of snickerin' goin' on behind Joe Dongan's back, but nary a soul has got the guts to say nothin' to his face. That is, nobody 'cept Ralph Napier. Now it's general knowledge that Ralph ain't doin' so well in a business way, and he's been bankin' on comin' into a packet when his mother-in-law dies. Mebbe that's just gossip, but sure as shootin' Ralph views Joe's courtship o' Bessie with a jaundiced eye.

Ralph ain't makin' no secret of how he feels about Joe. Course he ain't puttin' it on a money basis. Accordin' to him the Napiers has always been gentlefolk, while Joe Dongan's a roughneck and not far from a gangster. The idea of Joe linkin' himself up to the Napiers, Ralph says, is enough to make him sick to his stomach.

The showdown comes late one night when Joe's bringin' Bessie home from a picnic on the beach. Ralph's waitin' up for them and he lights into Joe, orderin' him out of the house. Ain't much Joe can do but leave. Later on that night the neighbors say there's big goin's-on at the Napier place, with Ralph and Bessie a-hollerin' and givin' each other what-for, while Doris is tryin' to cool 'em both down and not succeedin' too well.

Bessie and Joe keep right on seein' each other, but Joe don't go 'round to the Napier place no more. Instead, they meet at the Ringside Diner, right under the nose of Red Emma. And that spells more trouble, seein' as how Joe and Emma ain't hardly on speakin' terms these days.

Things is bad enough but Ralph Napier makes 'em worse. One night he comes chargin' into the diner with whiskey on his breath and fire in his eye. He tries orderin' Bessie home, and when she says as how she won't go, he grabs for her wrists and starts tryin' to yank her to her feet.

That's too much for Joe Dongan. He bellers for Ralph to let her loose. Now Ralph ain't much for size but he's a fightin' cock of a man, 'specially when he has a few drinks under his belt. He faces Joe in a boxer's stance with both fists raised. Joe just wades in, takin' two or three hard punches without even gruntin'. Then he's got Ralph by the scruff o' the neck and the seat o' the pants. He lifts him right off the floor, carries him to the door and tosses him out on the sidewalk.

Ralph jumps up and rushes Joe but he's way out of his class. Joe plants a big palm in Ralph's face and gives a heave that sends Ralph head over heels into the gutter.

By this time quite a crowd is gathered 'round. Ralph gets up and shakes himself and starts toward the door again but some of the men hold him back. Ralph's face is all aflame and he's fit to be tied, but I reckon even he knows he's a fool to mix it up with Joe Dongan.

After that things just ride along for a while. Joe don't give up seein' Bessie but he seems to have patched things up with Red Emma. He's dividin' his time equal between the two women. The town bookie's takin' bets on which one of 'em will hook Joe. The odds is still heavy on Bessie, but Emma's creepin' up all the time.

Meanwhile Ralph Napier's doin' a lot of plain and fancy drinkin' and, as soon as he's had over three drinks, all he can talk about is how he's going to get even with Joe Dongan.

"I'll kill the bum," he boasts. "Some day I'll murder him."

Up in Icy's Grill it gets to be a standard joke.

"How you going to do it?" the boys ask. "You going to tackle him again with your fists?"

Ralph just wags his head and looks wise. "I'll fix him, all right. Needn't any of you fellows worry about that."

The way I look at it the whole town's sort of to blame for the tragedy that follows. Here's Ralph Napier spittin' murder and, instead of takin' him serious, everyone's laughin' at him and eggin' him on.

As County Sheriff I ain't got no authority in Bancroft and it ain't rightly my affair. All the same, I drop by the office of Steve Roper, Bancroft's Chief of Police, and chew things over.

Steve ain't worried. He says, "I've known Ralph Napier since he was knee-high to a grasshopper. I ain't sayin' Ralph ain't given to violence when he's had a few drinks. But he wouldn't pull a kill in cold blood. He's too almighty fond of his own skin. Anyway, I reckon Joe Dongan is capable of takin' care of himself."

I don't like it, but I've spoke my piece and there ain't nothin' more to do but keep my big mouth shut.

Like I said, Emma's got a cottage on a wild stretch of the Shore Road. She ain't usin' it much of late, doin' most of her sleepin' in her room above the diner. But I reckon the next time I get a chance I'll have a word with her. After all, the cottage is in my territory.

I drop around there on a Sat'dy afternoon, not expectin' no trouble. First thing I see is Emma's car parked on the circular drive of her house. Alongside of it is another car, and I don't have to look twice to recognize Ralph Napier's white sports car. I sit in the county car for a while, mullin' things over and not likin' what I'm thinkin'.

Finally I lumber out o' the car and mosey up to the house. Red Emma's a-settin' on the porch with a cocktail glass beside her. In a rattan chair opposite her is Ralph Napier, lookin' like a cat with a bowl of cream.

Ralph rolls his eyes up at me with that insolent way he's got. He says, "Surprise, Sheriff! What brings you to Emma's hidey-hole?"

I'm plum out o' words. Ain't nothin' wrong with Emma and Ralph havin' a drink together but, sure as sin, that ain't the way Joe Dongan'll look at it. I got a shrewd suspicion Ralph's stirrin' up trouble, and Emma's playin' along in the hope of makin' Joe jealous and winnin' him back. It's a plan that can backfire. I don't like it one little bit.

Emma gives me her warm breezy smile.

"Have a cocktail, Sheriff. Please do. It's quite a drive out here."

I don't go in for these here fancy drinks. When I drink at all, I like my licker straight. But I'm in need of some time, so I gives her a nod.

She's still busy with the cocktail shaker when I hear the roar of an engine in the drive. Don't seem like more'n two shakes of a lamb's tail afore Joe Dongan's slammin' the screen door back on its hinges.

He strides across the porch toward Ralph. Now I can move right fast when I have to, even if I am a bit long in the tooth. I shoves in between them and it's lucky I do. Joe understands I ain't the sort o' man to be pushed around and he stops dead in his tracks, glarin' at me. Then I see him look past me and his eyes pop out and his mouth goes slack with disbelief.

I swing around to Ralph Napier. He's sittin' cool as a cucumber, one leg danglin' over the rattan arm of the chair. He's got a black automatic in his hand, the snout pointin' square at Joe's heart.

He lowers the gun when he sees me lookin' at him and grins. He says, "Maybe you don't believe it, Sheriff, but you just saved Joe's life. If he'd laid a finger on me, I would have plugged him. I'd have been within my rights too. Self defense, and you'd have been a witness to prove it. After all, a prize-fighter's fists are lethal weapons."

"Mebbe so. Mebbe not. You'd still be in a peck o' trouble," I warn him. "Have you got a license for that gun?"

"You know I have, Sheriff." He's right about that. He belongs to a pistol club and he's a crack shot.

Joe hollers, "You leave Emma alone or I'll ram your teeth down your throat."

Ralph turns to me. "You heard him threaten me, Sheriff."

I says, "Shut up. Both of you. You, Ralph, get a-movin'. You ain't got no rightful business here."

Ralph's eyes grow round and innocent and his voice as smooth as cold cream. "Now listen, Sheriff. I've got a right to call on Emma if I feel like it. She's free, white and twenty-one. Dongan hasn't got any strings attached to her. Not legal ones anyway. Of course, if Emma asks me to leave, that's different. It's her house. But it seems to me like Dongan is trying to cut his cake two ways."

We all look at Emma. She says real soft, "I wish you'd go, Ralph. You too, Sheriff. I want to talk to Joe."

I follow Ralph out to his car. He shows his teeth in a nasty little grin afore he tucks himself behind the wheel. I wait until he's disappeared afore I head out.

A look back shows me Joe and Emma on the porch, both of 'em standin' stiff and awkward.

When I get home I talk things over with Maw. There's a storm brewin', there's no doubt o' that. Ralph Napier's as smart as he is mean, and he's needlin' Joe Dongan into an attack where there'll be a killin'.

Maw heaves a sigh. She heaps all the blame on Bessie Bellinger. She says, "There ain't nothin' that woman reminds me of so much as an overdressed marsh-meller. Now if we could only feed her some reducin' tablets, mebbe Joe would come to his senses and fergit about her."

I says, sort o' ruminatin' about, "It ain't going to be so easy as all that. Mebbe I could have another talk with Steve Roper and persuade him to pick up Ralph's gun license."

"It won't help none," Maw vows. "Ralph can always lay his hands on another gun. 'Taint no problem around here. Seems to me like the key is Red Emma. She's got plenty o' hoss sense. If we put our heads together we might work somethin' out."

I don't know what Maw had in mind, and I never do get to find out because tragedy hits even sooner'n I expect. Funny thing too. I seen it happen and there warn't a tootlin' thing I could do to stop it.

The very next night I get a call from up Granger way. A chicken farmer, name o' Hixon, has got himself a bellyful of corn licker from a still and is beatin' up on his wife. I knew this feller, Hixon. Mild as a field mouse when he's sober, and mean as tarnation when he's lickered up. Ain't nothin' for me to do but head up to Granger and take him over to the police barracks until he cools off.

It ain't no night for drivin'. Rain's been fallin' most of the day and it's snapped off real cool, freezin' the puddles along the edge of the road and makin' the asphalt slippery as the underside of an eel.

I take it slow and easy, crawlin' along the Shore Road, where the banks drop down to jagged rocks with the surf poundin' over 'em and throwin' spray thirty feet high. I'd just hit the curve where the road makes a big half circle around Benson's Bay when I see the headlights flashin' toward me. Even from where I am, I can tell they're going too fast. I suck in my breath and pull the car into a cuttin', so as to be out of the way.

When I look again there's not one pair o' headlights but two, racin' lickety-split along the twistin' road. With the bright moonlight and the way the road angles, I can make out Joe Dongan's big sedan in the lead, with Ralph Napier's white car doggin' his tail.

There's a blast of a horn and the sports car draws up beside the sedan. They're bowlin' along a narrer road with scarce room enough for two cars to pass. They ain't more'n inches apart. It's like the crazy drag races some of the teenagers pull from time to time, but a lot more deadly. A stand o' pine trees is on one side o' the road and, on the other, nothin' but a white guardrail to break the fall off the cliff-side into the ocean.

The lights jounce and bounce around and seem to blend together. I reckon Ralph is tryin' to force Dongan off the road, but Joe ain't havin' none of it. He's edgin' over to Ralph's car.   And then what I been a-fearin' all along happens. The slap of metal as the two cars hit is like a peal o' thunder.   For seconds they cling together, then they're spinnin' hard toward the guardrail.   They crash through, both of 'em plungin' onto the rocks below.   There's another crash and a rumblin' when they hit.   Then the echoes die away and there ain't no sound but the pounding of the surf.

I'm shakin' all over.   I get the car into gear but there ain't no sense hurryin'. It ain't possible for a man to survive a crash like that.   There ain't a thing can be done for either Ralph or Joe 'til the tow cars can come with their grapples, and that won't be 'til mornin'.

I reckon, if you want to be technical about it, you could call it double murder or mebbe double suicide.   Or mebbe you could attach the blame to Ralph Napier or Joe Dongan.   But all you'd be accomplishin' by that is airin' a lot o' dirty linen in public.   The coroner's verdict called it "death by misadventure" and when you come to think on it that ain't such a bad name for what happened.

Afore the inquest I have a long chat with Red Emma.   Seems like Ralph Napier's been givin' her a hard time.   He's been a-moonin' around after her, claimin' that's the way to make Joe jealous and bring him back to his senses.   Emma don't want no truck with such tricks.   She says she'll win Joe fair and square or not at all.

But Ralph won't stay away.   He's sittin' in her front room on Sunday night when Joe comes bustin' in.   Joe stands in the doorway, lookin' 'em both over.

He says, "Well, Ralph, I'm glad you're here.   I got news for you and Emma, and this way I can get it all off my chest at once.   Me and Bessie's took out a marriage license and we're plannin' to get hitched in Portland next week.   What's more, there ain't nobody stoppin' us so there ain't no use tryin'."

Ralph jumps up, his face all livid.   He yells, "You'll never marry Bessie except over my dead body."

Joe says, "I'm marryin' her."

Ralph goes for his gun the same as he done when I was there.   He's got it lined up on Joe's chest and his knuckles is white on the trigger.   Mebbe he would've shot Joe and mebbe he wouldn't.   He's so excited he fergits all about Emma.   She comes up in back of him and slaps down hard on his wrist.   The gun explodes, the bullet splinterin' into the floor.

Joe moves fast then.   He loops a heavy right to Ralph's jaw that lifts him plum off his feet and slams him into the sofa.   Then Joe wheels and strides away.

Ralph ain't hurt bad.   Emma helps him to his feet.   He stands there groggy, shakin' his head and feelin' his jaw.   Then he rushes out to his car.   Emma follows him as far as the yard.   The tail lights of Joe's car are already winkin' a long way down the road.   But Ralph takes off after him like a cat with salt on his tail.

That's the last that Emma hears about either of 'em until I bring her news of the wreck.   She has to admit that Ralph was out for blood that night.   On the other hand it was Joe's car that rammed Ralph's and drove it through the guardrail. Mebbe both of 'em had killin' on their minds, or mebbe neither one.   No one can tell for sure, savin' they're both dead.

Well, everybody's mighty curious as to what'll happen next between Red Emma and Bessie Bellinger.   Already they'd been feudin' and fightin' and ready to cut each other's throats.   Emma's lost her man to Bessie, only for Bessie to lose him for good, and her son-in-law to boot.   So it seems like the feud is slated to go on forever.   But that ain't the way it works out.

Instead o' that, they get real chummy.   Even though Joe was plannin' to get spliced to Bessie, he hadn't got around to changin' his will.   Red Emma inherits his estate, includin' the Ringside Diner.

She runs it just the way she did when Joe was alive, settin' up in front, with a big smile for everybody as comes in.

As for Bessie, if she's a-grievin' over Joe she don't show it no more'n Emma does.   Her doctor's gone and put her on a diet, and she's shed a lot o' weight. That means she and Emma ain't rivals no longer.   Things have come around full circle, just like they was afore Bessie Bellinger showed up in town.   There ain't no two ways about it.   Red Emma's the fattest female in the whole o' Pisquaticook County.

LAWRENCE BLOCK

With a Smile for the Ending

I had one degree from Trinity, and one was enough, and I'd had enough of
Dublin, too.   It is a fine city, a perfect city, but there are only certain persons that
can live there.   An artist will love the town, a priest will bless it, and a clerk will
live in it as well as elsewhere.   But I had too little of faith and of talent and too
much of a hunger for the world to be priest or artist or pen warden.   I might have
become a drunkard, for Dublin's a right city for a drinking man, but I've no more
talent for drinking than for deception—yet another lesson I learned at Trinity, and
equally a bargain.   (Tell your story, Joseph Cameron Bane would say.   Clear
your throat and get on with it.)

I had family in Boston.   They welcomed me cautiously and pointed me toward
New York.   A small but pretentious publishing house hired me; they leaned toward
foreign editors and needed someone to balance off their flock of Englishmen.   Four
months was enough, of the job and of the city.   A good place for a young man
on the way up, but no town at all for a pilgrim.

He advertised for a companion.   I answered his ad and half a dozen others, and
when he replied I saw his name and took the job at once.   I had lived with his
books for years: *The Wind At Morning, Cabot's House, Ruthpen Hallburton, Lips
That Could Kiss,* others, others.   I had loved his words when I was a boy in Ennis,
knowing no more than to read what reached me, and I loved them still at Trinity
where one was supposed to care only for more fashionable authors.   He had written
a great many books over a great many years, all of them set in the same small
American town.   Ten years ago he'd stopped writing and never said why.   When
I read his name at the bottom of the letter I realized, though it had never occurred
to me before, that I had somehow assumed him dead for some years.

We traded letters.   I went to his home for an interview, rode the train there and
watched the scenery change until I was in the country he had written about.   I
walked from the railway station carrying both suitcases, having gambled he'd want
me to stay.   His housekeeper met me at the door.   I stepped inside, feeling as
though I'd dreamed the room, the house.   The woman took me to him, and I saw
that he was older than I'd supposed him, and next saw that he was not.   He
appeared older because he was dying.   "You're Riordan," he said.   "How'd you
come up?   Train?"

"Yes, sir."

"Pete run you up?" I looked blank, I'm sure. He said that Pete was the town's cab driver, and I explained that I'd walked.

"Oh? Could have taken a taxi."

"I like to walk."

"Mmmmm," he said. He offered me a drink. I refused, but he had one. "Why do you want to waste time watching a man die?" he demanded. "Not morbid curiosity, I'm sure. Want me to teach you how to be a writer?"

"No, sir."

"Want to do my biography? I'm dull and out of fashion, but some fool might want to read about me."

"No, I'm not a writer."

"Then why are you here, boy?"

He asked this reasonably, and I thought about the question before I answered it. "I like your books," I said finally.

"You think they're good? Worthwhile? Literature?"

"I just like them."

"What's your favorite?"

"I've never kept score," I answered.

He laughed, happy with the answer, and I was hired.

There was very little to do that could be called work. Now and then there would be a task too heavy for Mrs. Dettweiler, and I'd do that for her. There were occasional errands to run, letters to answer. When the weather turned colder he'd have me make up the fire for him in the living room. When he had a place to go, I'd drive him; this happened less often as time passed, as the disease grew in him.

And so, in terms of the time allotted to various tasks, my job was much as its title implied. I was his companion. I listened when he spoke, talked when he wanted conversation, and was silent when silence was indicated. There would be a time, his doctor told me, when I would have more to do, unless Mr. Bane would permit a nurse. I knew he would not, any more than he'd allow himself to die anywhere but in his home. There would be morphine shots for me to give him, because sooner or later the oral drug would become ineffective. In time he would be confined, first to his home and then to his room and at last to his bed, all a gradual preparation for the ultimate confinement.

"And maybe you ought to watch his drinking," the doctor told me. "He's been hitting it pretty heavy."

This last I tried once and no more. I said something foolish, that he'd had enough, that he ought to take it with a little water; I don't remember the words, only the stupidity of them, viewed in retrospect.

"I did not hire a damned warden," he said. "You wouldn't have thought of this yourself, Tim. Was this Harold Keeton's idea?"

"Well, yes."

"Harold Keeton is an excellent doctor," he said. "But only a doctor, and not a minister. He knows that doctors are supposed to tell their patients to cut down on smoking and drinking, and he plays his part. There is no reason for me to limit my drinking, Tim.   There is nothing wrong with my liver or with my kidneys. The only thing wrong with me, Tim, is that I have cancer.

"I have cancer, and I'm dying of it.   I intend to die as well as I possibly can. I intend to think and feel and act as I please, and go out with a smile for the ending. I intend, among other things, to drink what I want when I want it.   I do not intend to get drunk, nor do I intend to be entirely sober if I can avoid it.   Do you understand?''

"Yes, Mr. Bane.''

"Good.   Get the chessboard.''

For a change, I won a game.

The morning after Rachel Avery was found dead in her bathtub I came downstairs to find him at the breakfast table.   He had not slept well, and this showed in his eyes and at the corners of his mouth.

"We'll go into town today," he said.

"It snowed during the night, and you're tired.   If you catch cold, and you probably will, you'll be stuck in bed for weeks."   This sort of argument he would accept.   "Why do you want to go to town, sir?''

"To hear what people say.''

"Oh?   What do you mean?''

"Because Rachel's husband killed her, Tim.   Rachel should never have married Dean Avery.   He's a man with the soul of an adding machine, but Rachel was poetry and music.   He put her in his house and wanted to own her, but it was never in her to be true, to him or to another.   She flew freely and sang magnificently, and he killed her.

"I want to learn just how he did it, and decide what to do about it.   Perhaps you'll go to town without me.   You notice things well enough.   You sense more than I'd guessed you might, as though you know the people.''

"You wrote them well.''

This amused him.   "Never mind," he said.   "Make a nuisance of yourself if you have to, but see what you can learn.   I have to find out how to manage all of this properly.   I know a great deal, but not quite enough.''

Before I left I asked him how he could be so sure.   He said, "I know the town and the people.   I knew Rachel Avery and Dean Avery.   I knew her mother very well, and I knew his parents.   I knew they should not have married, and that things would go wrong for them, and I am entirely certain that she was killed and that he killed her.   Can you understand that?''

"I don't think so," I replied.   But I took the car into town, bought a few paperbound books at the drugstore, had an unnecessary haircut at the barber's, went from here to there and back again, and then drove home to tell him what I had learned.

"There was a coroner's inquest this morning," I said.   "Death by drowning induced as a result of electrical shock, accidental in origin.   The funeral is to-morrow.''

"Go on, Tim.''

"Dean Avery was in Harmony Falls yesterday when they finally reached him and told him what had happened. He was completely torn up, they said. He drove to Harmony Falls the day before yesterday and stayed overnight."

"And he was with people all the while?"

"No one said."

"They wouldn't have checked," he said. "No need, not when it's so obviously an accident. You'll go to the funeral tomorrow."

"Why?"

"Because I can't go myself."

"And I'm to study him and study everyone else? Should I take notes?"

He laughed, then chopped off the laughter sharply. "I don't think you'll have to. I didn't mean that you would go in my place solely to observe, Tim, though that's part of it. But I would want to be there because I feel I ought to be there, so you'll be my deputy."

I had no answer to this. He asked me to build up the fire, and I did. I heard the newspaper boy and went for the paper. The town having no newspaper of its own, the paper he took was from the nearest city, and of course there was nothing in it on Rachel Avery. Usually he read it carefully. Now he skimmed it as if hunting something, then set it aside.

"I didn't think you knew her that well," I said.

"I did and I didn't. There are things I do not understand, Tim; people to whom I've barely spoken, yet whom I seem to know intimately. Knowledge has so many levels."

"You never really stopped writing about Beveridge." This was his fictional name for the town. "You just stopped putting it on paper."

He looked up, surprised, considering the thought with his head cocked like a wren's. "That's far more true than you could possibly know," he said.

He ate a good dinner and seemed to enjoy it. Over coffee I started aimless conversations but he let them die out. Then I said, "Mr. Bane, why can't it be an accident? The radio fell into the tub and shocked her, and she drowned."

I thought at first he hadn't heard, or was pretending as much; this last is a special privilege of the old and the ill. Then he said, "Of course, you have to have facts. What should my intuition mean to you? And it would mean less, I suppose, if I assured you that Rachel Avery could not possibly be the type to play the radio while bathing?"

My face must have showed how much I thought of that. "Very well," he said. "We shall have facts. The water in the tub was running when the body was found. It was running, then, both before and after the radio fell into the tub, which means that Rachel Avery had the radio turned on while the tub was running, which is plainly senseless. She wouldn't be able to hear it well, would she? Also, she was adjusting the dial and knocked it into the tub with her.

"She would not have played the radio at all during her bath—this I simply *know*. She would not have attempted to turn on the radio until her bath was drawn, because no one would. And she would not have tried tuning the set while the water was running because that is sheerly pointless.   Now doesn't that begin to make a slight bit of sense to you, Tim?''

They put her into the ground on a cold gray afternoon.   I was part of a large crowd at the funeral parlor and a smaller one at the cemetery.   There was a minister instead of a priest, and the service was not the one with which I was familiar, yet after a moment all of it ceased to be foreign to me.   And then I knew.   It was Emily Talstead's funeral from *Cabot's House,* except that Emily's death had justice to it, and even a measure of mercy, and this gray afternoon held neither.

In that funeral parlor I was the deputy of Joseph Cameron Bane.   I viewed Rachel's small body and thought that all caskets should be closed, no matter how precise the mortician's art.   We should not force ourselves to look upon our dead. I gave small words of comfort to Dean Avery and avoided his eyes while I did so. I sat in a wooden chair while the minister spoke of horrible tragedy and the un-knowable wisdom of the Lord, and I was filled with a sense of loss that was complete in itself.

I shared someone's car to the cemetery.   At graveside, with a wind blowing that chilled the edge of thought, I let the gloom slip free as a body into an envelope of earth, and I did what I'd come to do; I looked into the face of Dean Avery.

He was a tall man, thick in the shoulders, broad in the forehead, his hair swept straight back without a part, forming upon his head like a crown.   I watched his eyes when he did not know that anyone watched him, and I watched the curl of his lip and the way he placed his feet and what he did with his hands.   Before long I knew he mourned her not at all, and soon after that I knew the old man was right.   He had killed her as sure as the wind blew.

They would have given me a ride back to his house, but I slipped away when the service ended, and spent time walking around, back and forth.   By the time I was back at her grave, it had already been filled in.   I wondered at the men who do such work, if they feel a thing at all.   I turned from her grave and walked back through the town to Bane's house.

I found him in the kitchen with coffee and toast.   I sat with him and told him about it, quickly, and he made me go back over all of it in detail so that he could feel he had been there himself.   We sat in silence awhile, and then went to the living room.   I built up the fire and we sat before it.

"You know now," he said.   I nodded, for I did; I'd seen for myself and knew it and felt it.   "Knowing is most of it," he said.   "Computers can never replace us, you know.   They need facts, information.   What's the term?   Data.   They need data.   But sometimes men can make connections across gaps, without data. You see?''

"Yes.''

"So we know."   He drank, put down his glass.   "But now we have to have our data.   First the conclusion, and then backward to the proof.''

My eyes asked the question.

"Because it all must round itself out," he said, answering the question without my giving voice to it. "This man killed and seems to have gotten away with it. This cannot be."

"Should we call the police?"

"Of course not. There's nothing to say to them, and no reason they should listen." He closed his eyes briefly, opened them. "We know what he did. We ought to know how, and why. Tell me the men at the funeral, Tim, as many as you remember."

"I don't remember much before the cemetery. I paid them little attention."

"At the cemetery, then. That's the important question, anyway."

I pictured it again in my mind and named the ones I knew. He listened very carefully. "Now there are others who might have been there," he said, "some of whom you may not know, and some you may not remember. Think, now, and tell me if any of these were there."

He named names, five of them, and it was my turn to listen. Two were strangers to me and I could not say if I'd seen them. One I remembered had been there, two others had not.

"Get a pencil and paper," he told me. "Write these names down: Robert Hardesty, Hal Kasper, Roy Teale, Thurman Goodin. Those will do for now."

The first two had been at the funeral, and at the cemetery. The other two had not.

"I don't understand," I said.

"She had a lover, of course. That was why he killed her. Robert Hardesty and Hal Kasper should not have been at that funeral, or at least not at the cemetery. I don't believe they're close to her family or his. Thurman Goodin and Roy Teale should have been at the funeral, at the least, and probably should have been at the cemetery. Now a dead woman's secret love may do what you would not expect him to do. He may stay away from a funeral he would otherwise be expected to attend, for fear of giving himself away, or he might attend a funeral where his presence would not otherwise be required, out of love or respect or no more than morbid yearning. We have four men, two who should have been present and were not, and two who should not have been present but were. No certainty, and nothing you might call data, but I've a feeling one of those four was Rachel Avery's lover."

"And?"

"Find out which one," he said.

"Why would we want to know that?"

"One must know a great many unimportant things in order to know those few things which are important." He poured himself more bourbon and drank some of it off. "Do you read detective stories? They always work with bits and pieces, like a jigsaw puzzle, find out trivia until it all fits together."

"And what might this fit into?"

"A shape. How, why, when."

I wanted to ask more, but he said he was tired and wanted to lie down. He must have been exhausted. He had me help him upstairs, change clothes, and into bed.

I knew Hal Kasper enough to speak to, so it was his shop I started in that night. He had a cigar store near the railroad terminal and sold magazines, paperbound books, candies and stationery.   You could place a bet on a horse there, I'd heard. He was thin, with prominent features—large hollow eyes, a long, slim nose, a large mouth with big gray-white teeth in it.   Thirty-five or forty, with a childless wife whom I'd never met, I thought him an odd choice for a lover, but I knew enough to realize that women did not follow logic's rules when they committed adultery.

He had been at the funeral.   Joseph Cameron Bane had found this a little remarkable.   He had no family ties on either side with Rachel or Dean Avery. He was below them socially, and not connected through his business.   Nor was he an automatic funeral-goer.   There were such in the town, I'd been told, as there are in every town; they go to funerals as they turn on a television set or eavesdrop on a conversation, for entertainment and for lack of better to do.   But he was not that sort.

"Hi, Irish," he said.   "How's the old man?"

I thumbed a magazine.   "Asleep," I said.

"Hitting the sauce pretty good lately?"

"I wouldn't say so, no."

"Well, he's got a right."   He came out from behind the counter, walked over to me.   "Saw you this afternoon.   I didn't know you knew her.   Or just getting material for that book of yours?"

Everyone assumed I was going to write a novel set in the town, and that this was what had led me to live with Mr. Bane.   This would have made as much sense as visiting Denmark in order to rewrite *Hamlet*.   I'd stopped denying it.   It seemed useless.

"You knew her?" I asked.

"Oh, sure.   You know me, Irish.   I know everybody.   King Farouk, Princess Grace—" He laughed shortly.   "Sure, I knew her, a lot better than you'd guess."

I thought I'd learn something, but as I watched his face I saw his large mouth quiver with the beginnings of a leer, and then watched the light die in his eyes and the smile fade from his lips as he remembered that she was dead, cold and in the ground, and not fit to leer over or lust after.   He looked ever so slightly ashamed of himself.

"A long time ago," he said, his voice pitched lower now.   "Oh, a couple of years.   Before she got married, well, she was a pretty wild kid in those days. Not wild like you might think; I mean, she was free, you understand?"   He groped with his hands, long-fingered, lean.   "She did what she wanted to do.   I happened to be there.   I was a guy she wanted to be with.   Not for too long, but it was honey-sweet while it lasted.   This is one fine way to be talking, isn't it?   They say she went quick, though; didn't feel anything, but what a stupid way, what a crazy stupid way."

So it was not Hal Kasper who had loved her; not recently, at least.   When I told all this to Joseph Cameron Bane he nodded several times and thought for some moments before he spoke.

"Ever widening circles, Tim," he said.   "Throw a stone into a still pool and watch the circles spread. Now don't you see her more clearly? You wouldn't call Kasper a sentimental man, or a particularly sensitive man. He's neither of those things. Yet he felt that sense of loss, and that need to pay his last respects. There's purpose in funerals, you know, purpose and value. I used to think they were barbaric. I know better now. He had to talk about her, and had also to be embarrassed by what he'd said. Interesting.''

"Why do we have to know all this?''

"Beginning to bother you, Tim?''

"Some.''

"Because I am involved with mankind," he quoted. "You'll learn more tomorrow, I think. Get the chessboard.''

I did learn more the next day. I learned first to forget about Roy Teale. I had not recognized his name, but when I found him I saw that he was a man who had been at the funeral, as he might have been expected to be. I also learned, in the barber shop, that he was carrying on a truly passionate love affair, but with his own wife. He sat in a chair and grinned while two of the men ragged him about it.

I left, knowing what I had come to learn; if I'd stayed much longer I'd have had to get another haircut, and I scarcely needed one. I'd taken the car into town that day. It was colder than usual, and the snow was deep. I got into the car and drove to Thurman Goodin's service station. Mr. Bane usually had me fill the car at the station a few blocks to the north, but I did want to see Goodin. He and Robert Hardesty were the only names left on our list. If neither had been the woman's lover, then we were back where we'd started.

A high school boy worked afternoons and evenings for Goodin, but the boy had not come yet, and Thurman Goodin came out to the pump himself. While the tank filled he came over to the side of the car and rested against the door. His face needed shaving. He leaned his long hard body against the car door and said it had been a long time since he'd put any gas into the car.

"Mr. Bane doesn't get out much any more," I said, "and I mostly walk except when the weather's bad.''

"Then I'm glad for the bad weather." He lit a cigarette and inhaled deeply. "Anyway, this buggy usually tanks up over to Kelsey's place. You had better than half a tankful; you could have made it over there without running dry, you know.''

I gave him a blank look, then turned it around by saying, "I'm sorry, I didn't hear you. I was thinking about that woman who was killed.''

I almost jumped at the sight of his face. A nerve twitched involuntarily, a thing he could not have controlled, but he might have covered up the other telltale signs. His eyes gave him away, and his hands, and the movements of his mouth.

"You mean Mrs. Avery," he said.

His wife was her cousin, Mr. Bane had told me. So he should have been at her funeral, and now should have been calling her Rachel or Rachel Avery. I wanted to get away from him!

"I was at the funeral," I said.

"Funerals," he said. "I got a business to run. Listen, I'll tell you something. Everybody dies. Fast or slow, old or young, it don't make a bit of difference. That's two twenty-seven for the gas."

He took three dollars and went into the station. He came back with the change and I took it from him. My hand shook slightly. I dropped a dime.

"Everybody gets it sooner or later," he said. "Why knock yourself out about it?"

When I told all this to Joseph Cameron Bane he leaned back in his chair with sparkle in his eyes and the ghost of a smile on his pale lips. "So it's Thurman Goodin," he said. "I knew his father rather well. But I knew everybody's father, Tim, so that's not too important, is it? Tell me what you know."

"Sir?"

"Project, extend, extrapolate. What do you know about Goodin? What did he tell you? Put more pieces into the puzzle, Tim."

I said, "Well, he was her lover, of course. Not for very long, but for some space of time. It was nothing of long standing, and yet some of the glow had worn off."

"Go on, Tim."

"I'd say he made overtures for form's sake and was surprised when she responded. He was excited at the beginning, and then he began to be frightened of it all. Oh, this is silly, I'm making it all up—"

"You're doing fine, boy."

"He seemed glad she was dead. No, I'm putting it badly. He seemed relieved, and guilty about feeling relieved. Now he's safe. She died accidentally, and no one will ever find him out, and he can savor his memories without shivering in the night."

"Yes." He poured bourbon into his glass, emptying the bottle. Soon he would ask me to bring him another. "I agree," he said, and sipped at his whiskey almost daintily.

"Now what do we do?"

"What do you think we do, Tim?"

I thought about this. I said we might check with persons in Harmony Falls and trace Dean Avery's movements there. Or, knowing her lover's name, knowing so much that no one else knew, we might go to the police. We had no evidence, but the police could turn up evidence better than we, and do more with it once they had it.

He looked into the fire. When he did speak, I thought at first that he was talking entirely to himself and not to me at all. "And splash her name all over the earth," he said, "and raise up obscene court trials and filth in the newspapers, and pit lawyers against one another, and either hang him or jail him or free him. Ruin Thurman Goodin's marriage, and ruin Rachel Avery's memory."

"I don't think I understand."

He spun quickly around. His eyes glittered. "Don't you? Tim, Timothy, don't you truthfully understand?'' He hesitated, groped for a phrase, then stopped and looked pointedly at his empty glass. I found a fresh bottle in the cupboard, opened it, handed it to him. He poured a drink but did not drink it.

He said, ''My books always sold well, you know. But I had a bad press. The small town papers were always kind, but the real critics . . . I was always being charged with sentimentality. They used words like *cloying* and *sugary* and *unrealistic.''* I started to say something but he silenced me with an upraised palm. ''Please, don't leap to my defense. I'm making a point now, not lamenting a misspent literary youth. Do you know why I stopped writing? I don't think I've ever told anyone. There's never been a reason to tell. I stopped, oh, not because critics were unkind, not because sales were disappointing. I stopped because I discovered that the critics, bless them, were quite right.''

''That's not true!''

''But it is, Tim. I never wrote what you could honestly call sentimental slop, but everything always came out right, every book always had a happy ending. I simply *wanted* it to happen that way, I wanted things to work out as they *ought* to work out. Do you see? Oh, I let my people stay in character, that was easy enough. I was a good plot man and could bring that off well enough, weaving intricate webs that led inexorably to the silver lining in every last one of the blacker clouds. The people stayed true but the books became untrue, do you see? Always the happy ending, always the death of truth.''

''In *Cabot's House* you had an unhappy ending.''

''Not so. In *Cabot's House* I had death for an ending, but a death is not always an occasion for sorrow. Perhaps you're too young to know that, or to feel it within. You'll learn it soon enough. But to return to the point, I saw that my books were false. Good pictures of this town, of some people who lived either in it or in my mind or in both, but false portraits of life. I wrote a book, then, or tried to; an honest one, with loose threads at the end and—what was that precious line of Salinger's? Yes. With a touch of squalor, with love and squalor. I couldn't finish it, I hated it.''

He picked up the glass, set it down again, the whiskey untouched. ''Do you see? I'm an old man and a fool. I like things to come out right, neat and clean and sugary, wrapped with a bow and a smile for the ending. No police, no trials, no public washing of soiled underwear. I think we are close enough now. I think we have enough of it.'' He picked up his glass once more and this time drained it. ''Get the chessboard.''

I got the board. We played, and he won, and my mind spent more of its time with other pawns than the ones we played with now. The image grew on me. I saw them all, Rachel Avery, Dean Avery, Thurman Goodin, carved of wood and all of a shade, either black or white; weighted with lead, and bottomed with a circlet of felt, green felt, and moved around by our hands upon a mirthless board.

''You're afraid of this,'' he said once. ''Why?''

''Meddling, perhaps. Playing the divinity. I don't know, Mr. Bane. Something that feels wrong, that's all.''

''Paddy from the peat bog, you've not lost your sense of the miraculous, have you?   Wee folk, and gold at the rainbow's end, and things that go bang in the night, and man a stranger and afraid in someone else's world.   Don't move there, Tim, your queen's *en prise*, you'll lose her.''

We played three games.   Then he straightened up abruptly and said, ''I don't have the voice to mimic, I've barely any voice at all, and your brogue's too thick for it.   Go up to the third floor, would you, and in the room all the way back, there's a closet with an infernal machine on its shelf—a tape recorder.   I bought it with the idea that it might make writing simpler.   Didn't work at all; I had to see the words in front of me to make them real.   I couldn't sit like a fool talking at a machine.   But I had fun with the thing.   Get it for me, Tim, please.''

It was where he'd said, in a box carpeted with dust.   I brought it to him, and we went into the kitchen.   There was a telephone there.   First he tested the recorder, explaining that the tape was old and might not work properly.   He turned it on and said, ''Now is the time for all good men to come to the aid of the party.   The quick brown fox jumped over the lazy dog.''   Then he winked at me and said, ''Just like a typewriter; it's easiest to resort to formula when you want to say something meaningless, Tim.   Most people have trouble talking when they have nothing to say.   Though it rarely stops them, does it?   Let's see how this sounds.''

He played it back and asked me if the voice sounded like his own.   I assured him it did.   ''No one ever hears his own voice when he speaks,'' he said.   ''I didn't realize I sounded that old.   Odd.''

He sent me for bourbon.   He drank a bit, then had me get him the phone book.   He looked up a number, read it to himself a time or two, then turned his attention again to the recorder.

''We ought to plug it into the telephone,'' he said.

''What for, sir?''

''You'll see.   If you connect them lawfully, they beep every fifteen seconds, so that the other party knows what you're about, which hardly seems sensible.   Know anything about these gadgets?''

''Nothing,'' I replied.

He finished the glass of whiskey.   ''Now what if I just hold the little microphone to the phone like this?   Between my ear and the phone, hmm?   Some distortion?   Oh, won't matter, won't matter at all.''

He dialed a number.   The conversation, as much as I heard of it, went something like this:

''Hello, Mr. Taylor?   No, wait a moment, let me see.   Is this 4215?   Oh, good.   The Avery residence?   Is Mrs. Avery in?   I don't . . . Who'm I talking with, please? . . . Good.   When do you expect your wife, Mr. Avery? . . . Oh, my! . . . Yes, I see, I see.   Why, I'm terribly sorry to hear that, surely . . . Tragic.   Well, I hate to bother you with this, Mr. Avery.   Really, it's nothing . . . Well, I'm Paul Wellings of Wellings and Doyle Travel Agency . . . Yes, that's right, but I wish . . . Certainly.   Your wife wanted us to book a trip to Puerto Rico for the two of you and . . . Oh?   A surprise, probably . . . Yes, of course, I'll cancel everything.   This is frightful.   Yes, and I'm sorry for disturbing you at this—''

There was a little more, but not very much.   He rang off, a bitter smile on his pale face, his eyes quite a bit brighter now than usual. "A touch of macabre poetry," he said. "Let him think she was planning to run off with Goodin. He's a cold one, though. So calm, and making me go on and on, however awkward it all was. And now it's all ready on the tape. But how can I manage this way?"

He picked up a phone and called another number. "Jay? This is Cam. Say, I know it's late, but is your tape recorder handy? Well, I'd wanted to do some dictation and mine's burned out a connection or something. Oh, just some work I'm doing. No, I haven't mentioned it, I know. It's something different. If anything ever comes of it, then I'll have something to tell you. But is it all right if I send Tim around for your infernal machine? Good, and you're a prince, Jay."

So he sent me to pick up a second recorder from Jason Falk. When I brought it to him, he positioned the two machines side by side on the table and nodded. "I hate deception," he said, "yet it seems to have its place in the scheme of things. I'll need half an hour or so alone, Tim. I hate to chase you away, but I have to play with these toys of mine."

I didn't mind. I was glad to be away from him for a few moments, for he was upsetting me more than I wanted to admit. There was something bad in the air that night, and more than my Irish soul was telling me so. Joseph Cameron Bane was playing God. He was manipulating people, toying with them. *Writing* them, and with no books to put them in.

It was too cold for walking. I got into the car and drove around the streets of the town, then out of the town and off on a winding road that went up into the hills beyond the town's edge. The snow was deep but no fresh snow was falling, and the moon was close to full and the sky cluttered with stars. I stopped the car and got out of it and took a long look back at the town below, his town. I thought it would be good right now to be a drinking man and warm myself from a bottle and walk in the night and pause now and then to gaze at the town below.

"You were gone long," he said.

"I got lost. It took time to find my way back."

"Tim, this still bothers you, doesn't it? Of course it does. Listen to me. I am going to put some people into motion, that is all. I am going to let some men talk to one another, and I am going to write their lines for them. Do you understand? Their opening lines. They wouldn't do it themselves. They wouldn't start it. I'll start it, and then they'll help it play itself out."

He was right, of course. Avery could not be allowed to get away with murder, nor should the dead woman's sins be placed on public display for all to stare at. "Now listen to this," he said, bright-eyed again. "I'm proud of myself, frankly."

He dialed a number, then poised his index finger above one of the buttons on the recorder. He was huddled over the table so that the telephone mouthpiece was just a few inches from the recorder's speaker. The phone was answered, and he pressed a button and I heard Dean Avery's voice. "Goodin?"

A pause. Then, "This is Dean Avery. I know all about it, Goodin. You and my wife. You and Rachel. I know all about it. And now she's dead. An accident. Think about it, Goodin. You'll have to think about it."

He replaced the receiver.

"How did you . . ."

He looked at my gaping mouth and laughed aloud at me. "Just careful editing," he said. "Playing from one machine to the next, back and forth, a word here, a phrase there, all interwoven and put together. Even the inflection can be changed by raising or lowering the volume as you bounce from one machine to the other. Isn't it startling? I told you I have fun with this machine. I never got anything written on it, but I had a good time fooling around with it."

"All those phrases—you even had his name."

"It was *good* of you to call. And the tail syllable of some other word, *happen*, I think. The two cropped out and spliced together and tossed back and forth until they fit well enough. I was busy while you were gone, Tim. It wasn't simple to get it all right."

"Now what happens?"

"Goodin calls Avery."

"How do you know?"

"Oh, Tim! I'll call Goodin and tell him how my car's broken down, or that he's won a football pool, or something inane, and do the same thing with his voice. And call Avery for him, and accuse him of the murder. That's all. They'll take it from there. I expect Avery will crack. If I get enough words to play with, I can have Goodin outline the whole murder, how it happened, everything."

His fingers drummed the table top. "Avery might kill himself," he said. "The killers always do in that woman's stories about the little Belgian detective. They excuse themselves and blow their brains out in a gentlemanly manner. There might be a confrontation between the two. I'm not sure."

"Will it wait until morning?"

"I thought I'd call Goodin now."

He was plainly exhausted. It was too late for him to be awake, but the excitement kept him from feeling the fatigue. I hated playing nursemaid. I let him drink too much every day, let him die as he wished, but it was not good for him to wear himself out this way.

"Goodin will be shaken by the call," I told him. "You'll probably have trouble getting him to talk. He may have closed the station for the night."

"I'll call and find out," he said.

He called, the recorder at the ready, and the phone rang and went unanswered. He wanted to wait up and try again, but I made him give it up and wait until the next day. I put him to bed and went downstairs and straightened up the kitchen. There was a half inch of whiskey in a bottle, and I poured it into a glass and drank it, a thing I rarely do. It warmed me and I'd needed warming. I went upstairs and to bed, and still had trouble sleeping.

There were dreams, and bad ones, dreams that woke me and sat me upright with a shapeless wisp of horror falling off like smoke. I slept badly and woke early. I was downstairs while he slept. While I ate toast and drank tea, Mrs. Dettweiler worried aloud about him. "You've got him all worked up," she said. "He shouldn't get like that. A sick man like him, he should rest, he should be calm."

"He wants the excitement.   And it's not my doing."

"As sick as he is . . ."

"He's dying, and has a right to do it his own way."

"Some way to talk!"

"It's his way."

"There's a difference."

The radio was playing, tuned to a station in Harmony Falls.   Our town had one FM station but the radio did not get FM.   Mrs. Dettweiler always played a radio unless Mr. Bane was in the room, in which case he generally told her to turn it off.   When she was upstairs in her own room, the television was always on, unless she was praying or sleeping.   I listened to it now and thought that he might have used it for his taping and editing and splicing.   If you wished to disguise your voice, you might do it that way.   If Dean Avery had never heard Thurman Goodin's voice, or not well enough to recognize it, you could work it well enough that way. With all those words and phrases at your disposal. . . .

Halfway through the newscast they read an item from our town, read just a brief news story, and I spilled my tea all over the kitchen table.   The cup fell to the floor and broke in half.

"Why, for goodness . . ."

I turned off the radio, thought better and reached to pull its plug.   He never turned it on, hated it, but it might occur to him to tape from it, and I didn't want that.   Not yet.

"Keep that thing off," I said.   "Don't let him hear it, and don't tell him anything.   If he tries to play the radio, say it's not working."

"I don't . . ."

"Just do as you're told!" I said.   She went white and nodded mutely, and I hurried out of the house and drove into town.   On the way I noticed that I held the steering wheel so tightly my fingers had gone numb.   I couldn't help it.   I'd have taken a drink then if there'd been one about.   I'd have drunk kerosene, or perfume—anything at all.

I went to the drugstore and to the barbershop, and heard the same story in both places, and walked around a bit to relax, the last with little success.   I left the car where I'd parked it and walked back to his house and breathed cold air and gritted my teeth against more than the cold.   I did not even realize until much later that it was fairly stupid to leave the car.   It seemed quite natural at the time.

He was up by the time I reached the house, wearing robe and slippers, seated at the table with telephone and tape recorder.   "Where'd you go?" he wanted to know.   "I can't reach Thurman Goodin.   Nobody answers his phone."

"Nobody will."

"I've half a mind to try him at home."

"Don't bother."

"No?   Why not?"   And then, for the first time, he saw my face.   His own paled.   "Heavens, Tim, what's the matter?"

All the way back, through snow and cold air, I'd looked for a way to tell him— a proper way.   There was none.   Halfway home I'd thought that perhaps Providence might let him die before I had to tell him, but that could only have happened in one of his novels, not in this world.

So I said, "Dean Avery's dead. It happened last night; he's dead."

"Great God in Heaven!" His face was white, his eyes horribly wide. "How? Suicide?"

"No."

"How?" he asked insistently.

"It was meant to look like suicide. Thurman Goodin killed him. Broke into his house in the middle of the night. He was going to knock him out and poke his head in the oven and put the gas on. He knocked him cold all right, but Avery came to on the way to the oven. There was a row, and Thurman Goodin beat him over the head with some tool he'd brought along. I believe it was a tire iron. Beat his brains in, but all the noise woke a few of the neighbors and they grabbed Goodin on his way out the door. Two of them caught him and managed to hold him until the police came, and of course he told them everything."

I expected Bane to interrupt, but he waited without a word. I said, "Rachel Avery wanted him to run away with her. She couldn't stand staying with her husband, she wanted to go to some big city, try the sweet life. He told the police he tried to stop seeing her. She threatened him, that she would tell her husband, that she would tell his wife. So he went to her one afternoon and knocked her unconscious, took off her clothes and put her in the bathtub. She was still alive then. He dropped the radio into the tub to give her a shock, then unplugged it and checked to see if she were dead. She wasn't, so he held her head under water until she drowned, and then he plugged the radio into the socket again and left.

"And last night he found out that Avery knew about it, about the murder and the affair and all. So of course he had to kill Avery. He thought he might get away with it if he made it look like suicide, that Avery was depressed over his wife's death and went on to take his own life. I don't think it would have washed. I don't know much about it, but aren't the police more apt to examine a suicide rather carefully? They might see the marks on the head. Perhaps not. I don't really know. They've put Goodin in jail in Harmony Falls, and with two bloody murders like that, he's sure to hang." And then, because I felt even worse about it all than I'd known, "So it all comes out even, after all, the way you wanted it, the loose ends tied up in a bow."

"Good heavens!"

"I'm sorry." And I was, as soon as I'd said the words.

I don't think he heard me. "I am a bad writer and a bad man," he said, and not to me at all, and perhaps not even to himself but to whatever he talked to when the need came. "I thought I created them, I thought I knew them, I thought they all belonged to me."

So I went upstairs and packed my bags and walked all the way to the station. It was a bad time to leave him and a heartless way to do it, but staying would have been worse, even impossible. He was dying, and I couldn't have changed that, nor made the going much easier for him. I walked to the station and took the first train out and ended up here in Los Angeles, working for another foolish little man who likes to hire foreigners, doing the same sort of nothing I'd done in New York, but doing it at least in a warmer climate.

Last month I read he'd died. I thought I might cry but didn't. A week ago I re-read one of his books, *Lips That Could Kiss*. I discovered that I did not like it at all, and then I did cry. For Rachel Avery, for Joseph Cameron Bane. For me.

CHARLOTTE EDWARDS

Television Country

I'm not asking you to believe it, you understand. In a way, I don't even want you to. You have no idea how lucky you are if you can't believe it.

Harry and I have to believe it. We have to live with it. We try to. Only Harry flies now, traveling the great wide swing of his territory, especially the round trip to Phoenix and Tucson. It gets him home sooner. Besides which, really you know, it's safer.

And anyhow, I'm not much good with Harry away any more. I haven't been for quite a while. I get nervous and have strange dreams.

Ever since the trip home from Tucson.

We left about two, after Harry had seen his last dealer. We were both pretty quiet, packing things in the company station wagon. We stood for a moment at the door of the cool impersonal room, which we had personalized, and Harry's arm was tight around my waist.

That moment stands very clear and sharp all by itself in my mind. It was the last of something, of completely peaceful sleep perhaps, or of asking questions which always had logical answers, or of trusting the perimeter of the human mind.

As we drove away from the sprawling place, I could hear splashing in the pool. It seemed strange that it would all go on after we were back home.

The car's broad nose turned toward the north and west. Harry's arm lay across the back of the seat and his fingers touched my shoulder lightly.

"We're going back another way," he said. "They say a new piece of freeway has been opened. Used to be rough and very lonely, but I took it because it's a little shorter."

The road laid itself out long and slender, slightly bumpy from heavy truck travel, and we were on our way back to California.

If you have ever stretched out a map of the United States, you know how it is. The Eastern half is pale green and yellow, blackened with the printing of hundreds of town and city names. About the beginning of Texas in the south and the Dakotas in the north, the color changes, ripens to orange streaked widely with the purple of mountains, and there aren't enough towns to dim the bright shades. Somehow it gives you the feeling of the hot dry country itself.

We weren't ten miles out of Tucson before I felt the map come alive under us, before us, on either side of us. Empty and wide-flung, the desert spread lavishly to rocky hills that weren't quite mountains, that had jagged scalloped tops, that looked two miles away and turned out to be twenty, or forty.   The clear pure air distilled the sky with its tatters of silken clouds.

The miles moved sleekly under Harry's good tires.   The air conditioning hummed around us.   The windows, shut tight, made a compartment as remote from the land as any in a train.   Yet, somehow, I was part of it.

Harry didn't talk much, nor did I.   It had been a good and perfect thing, this trip together, from the beginning.   You see, he travels most of the time.   We're not together much, not nearly so much as we would like to be.

Harry and I have a good thing going for us, and have had from the start.   We like each other.   Every moment shared is precious.   But with three teen-aged girls, and his being away so much, those moments squeeze pretty thin sometimes.

So Harry said to me, "Myra, come on, go with me this time.   The girls can take care of themselves."   He came over and kissed me on the forehead.

You'd think a woman would get used to a little thing like that and not find herself alerted along the nape of her neck, and mush on the edges of her heart.

I looked into his eyes, and they were pleading.   He wanted a few days, alone, quiet, with me there to talk it all over with, a swim together, a long slow drink before dinner, dressing up a little and eating at nice places.

Talk about divided loyalties.   A woman is like an apple pie.   Without supervised cutting, only crumbs are left for the last in the kitchen.   Personally, I hide pies and cut Harry's wedge first and biggest.   In everything else, though, he seems to get the snips and bits.

When I began to shake my head, he removed his hand and went back to his chair.   I didn't like the way his shoulders looked.   Not a bit.

Which is how I happened to go with Harry.   It took some doing, and Mrs. Mackintosh down the street to supervise, but off we went, me with a white dacron waltz-length gown and matching peignoir the girls gave me for Mother's Day.   It's a ridiculously young outfit, but I knew someday I'd feel ruffly enough to wear it. And I did, in Phoenix and Tucson.

I couldn't remember our first honeymoon, by the time the second one was over. But Harry's hand on my arm from time to time made speech unnecessary.

We stopped in a little town called Casa Grande, where Harry always visited a faded cafe for coconut cream pie.   Such a pie I shall never taste again, unless we walk into the same restaurant in the same town.

But nothing could force me to do that, of course.   Nothing, or nobody or ever.

It was so hot that we were both dappled with moisture when we got back to the car.

"This is the long haul to Yuma," Harry said.   The pie and coffee seemed to have restored him.   "There's only the next town of Gila Bend, and then it's all empty desert."

I looked around.   It was beginning to be just that.   "How could they bear it? How did they ever get across down here?"

"That's a good question," Harry agreed.

My gaze went back, hypnotized, to the window. It looked familiar, in patches.
Then I realized why.

"This is television country," I cried.

"Indian country," Harry corrected. "Arizona still has more Indians than all
the other states together."

He swung his arm toward the bushes that studded the sand. "Mesquite."

"My goodness," I reacted. It was the last phrase I spoke for a long time.

This thing began to happen to me. I began to get the feeling of history underneath
me. I felt history and loneliness, panic and terror, courage and grief, spreading
out from either side of me. I looked up at the sun, which defied the spattered
clouds. I thought of how quickly my arms and legs had turned red, then brown,
in five short days. I thought of five days on the desert instead of our ten air-
conditioned hours. I watched the forests of tall cactus, weirdly shaped, like one
long pointing finger surrounded by a clenched fist. I watched the strange hard
mountains in the distance, and counted up their infinite layers of rock and shale as
the road wound through the nearer hills. I shivered and was suddenly giddy.

"I can turn this down if it's too cold." Harry reached toward the air button.

I shook my head. Quite suddenly the narrow road divided, grew broad, and
became a freeway. The car purred with pleasure and Harry said, "Ah, that's
better."

We went through the little town of Gila Bend on a breath. The houses, stores,
all except the gas stations, were dun and washed out, dried like bones.

Then we were alone again, Harry and Myra, alone as we hadn't been even in
the motel. Alone in a sort of backward immortality, as if we were once again in
the age of our ancestors, who came this way and made a place for us in California.
I wished that I had asked my grandmother more questions about her parents. Or
that somebody had written it all down in the family Bible.

"The thing you have to be careful of," Harry volunteered cheerfully after a long
silence, "is that they mean what they say on those 'Soft Shoulders, Sand' signs.
You see, if you get off the rim of the road, two things can happen. Either the
sand catches your wheels and you roll over and over in the mesquite—"

"Harry, really," I protested.

"Well," he argued defensively, "it's so. Or else it throws you out of control
and you go skidding across the freeway and smack into a car coming the other
way."

There weren't, I realized, many cars coming the other way. Harry was right.
This was a very lonely way home. "I'm not going to get a night's sleep when
you're gone from now on," I said lightly.

As they say in old-fashioned books, little did I know.

He laughed. "Forewarned is forearmed, honey," he comforted. "See, I stay
in the fast lane. Only one kind of soft shoulders I'm not afraid of." He patted
them.

"It would be awful just to get stuck," I volunteered moodily.

We had stayed at the motel until the last minute of the sign-out time. Now it was beginning to get dusky around us. Not a fast dusk, laying itself smooth in purple, just a haze, like fog, beginning at the very top of the farthest hills and letting itself down carefully, an inch at a time, toward the earth.

My eyes were on the sky one moment, then on the road the next.

"Harry," I screamed, "look out!"

Harry's arm was off the back of the seat, his two hands were struggling with the wheel, his leg was a slamming force against his ankle and foot on the brake. The screech seemed to fill the world. The woven rubber feeling of the car was fluid and sickening.

We careened from the fast lane into a semi-circle, careened back from the center, wheels grinding on the right side in the sand of the soft shoulder of the road.

I waited in utter calmness for us to roll over and over into the mesquite. But we didn't. Harry had managed to stop the car.

His anger was louder than the air conditioner. "What the hell," he yelled, "did you scream like that for?"

"You almost hit him," I cried. "The old man in the middle of the road. You were headed right for him."

"What old man? I didn't see any old man." Harry opened the door on his side and stepped out. He peered back down the road. "I don't see any old man," he insisted.

He stomped around the car. The right rear wheel was deep in the sand. I knew it before he called the knowledge to me, unbalanced as we were.

I jumped out, glanced quickly both ways, and ran back down the empty road to the old man. He stood there, not two feet from where I had first seen him. He looked dazed and worried, as well he might after such a close call.

"Thank God we missed you," I threw at him, running, getting to him, trying to see if he was hurt in any way.

He swung around to stare toward me. I stopped short, aware of the late afternoon heat which somehow seemed to have gotten into my heart and had set it steaming and bubbling like a kettle.

It was television country, all right, I thought distractedly, and this old boy was right out of the small screen in the living room. A thick patina of sandy dust lay all over him. Under it I made out an old flat hat, rags of brown clothes, a bag on his shoulder on which was hitched a heavy pick and shovel. I peered closer, ignoring my heart, ready to yell for Harry, and looked at his face.

Did I say the houses of Gila Bend were dun and dried bones? I knew nothing. This old face was dun and dried bones, with a skimpy white beard too tired to fly in any wind. Buried somewhere under the shadow of the hat brim, under the dirt and sharp eyebrows, were old eyes I could only sense, and weariness which came out from them in waves.

"You must be almost in shock," I found myself saying. "Come along with me. The car is cool. And we have some ginger ale. Sit awhile, until my husband digs us out, and then we can take you where you're going."

"You headed for Mexico?" His voice was faint in the stillness, far away, as weary as his eyes.

"No," I said. I remembered that Harry had told me that to our left, the south, it wasn't far to the border, and that up ahead there was a turn, beyond Yuma, at Calexico, where you could almost step across the line.

Harry called, his voice sharp in all the sudden silence, loud in contrast to the old man's. "Hey, Myra, give me a hand! Myra!"

He was bent over the back fender, pushing against the heavy resisting sand. I knew, somehow, that he hadn't seen me leave the car, that he thought I was still in there, air-conditioned and waiting.

I reached one hand toward the old man. "Come on," I coaxed softly, the way I used to handle the middle girl, the shy one. "Come on and get cool, and have something to drink."

He moved with a dry shuffle, as if all the juice were out of his joints, and very very slowly. I matched my steps to his, a little ahead of him, my eyes on the road to see that tragedy didn't come roaring at us, as it so nearly had.

We were beside the car when Harry looked up. "Isn't it enough," he said fiercely, "that you go suddenly berserk and get us into this fix without—" He looked beyond me. His mouth and cheeks and eyebrows went lax all in one movement. "For the love of God," he whispered.

"He was there, you see, Harry," I said with pure reason. "You must have been blinded by the sun, or looking off at an angle—because there he was, Harry, right in the middle of the freeway—" It hit me, the enormity of it. I shivered a little.

"You can use my shovel," the dry old voice walked its great distance, "if'n you want. But not my pick. I gotta use my pick when I find my water hole." He reached creakily back to his pack. He put two thin-veined hands around the handle. The skin of his wrists was etched deep on the bones, burned red as blood. He pulled the shovel free, and heaved it, missing Harry by inches.

"Hey!" Harry cried. Some of the color came back into his face.

The old man wasn't looking at Harry. He stared at the car. He shook his head and closed his eyes and opened them again. "Still there," he muttered.

I opened the back door. "Get in," I offered. "Rest a little."

He backed away from me. He shook his head fiercely. "Not me. If'n you'll just finish with my shovel. I got to find my water hole. I been lookin' and lookin'. It's gotta be here. It should be here. I can't rest easy till I find my water hole."

Harry said sharply, "Myra, get in the car."

I stared at him.

"Do as I tell you," he commanded. Any authority he'd shown was minor compared to his total maleness. "Shut the door and lock it. Lock all of them."

I went close to him. "He's just a tired old man, Harry," I whispered "He must have walked miles. We haven't passed a town in hours. He's a—a prospector or something—" It sounded as if I were begging.

Harry said, "Get—in—the—car!"

He began to dig rapidly. I minded him. Like one of the girls, having to take an order without explanation, I obeyed my husband. But once inside, I reached for a bottle of ginger ale and the opener, then I ran down the window and held the foaming stuff toward the old man.

"Myra," Harry called warningly. His shovel moved with deep precision, loud and scratching, fast, straining, racing to the finish.

The old man hesitated, then he moved in that strange bony way toward me. I held the bottle out as far as I could, so that he wouldn't have to touch me.

He took it. He put it to his cracked lips. His Adam's apple raised and dropped twice. Then he spat the fizzy stuff, away from me, toward the highway, lifted the bottle high and threw it with a crash to the nice new freeway pavement.

"Gahh," he choked.

I pulled myself back into the car.

"I gotta find my water hole," he muttered, making a sing-song affair of it now. I can't rest easy till I find my water hole. All them years, baking, baking, stone ovens, baking, no water like my water hole, can't rest easy."

Harry came around the side of the car. He was soaked and patched with sweat, and the shovel swung heavy in his hand.

"Here we are, Old Timer," he cried. It sounded like TV again. But there was something false and too hearty in Harry's voice, something strange and young and frightened. "Thanks. Those pebbles ought to do it." He paused. "No water holes around here," he added.

The old man took his time about reaching for the shovel and fastening it back in place. "Lot you'd know," he breathed thinly.

Harry pulled a handkerchief, very white in the slow-pushed dusk, from his back pocket and worked it over his soiled and perspiring face. "Where you from?" he asked the old man.

We both saw it, I know we did. The shadowed eyes pinched and turned sly. "Ain't from Yuma," the voice was defiant. "Ain't never been to Yuma. Never. Whole life."

"We're going that way," Harry said. I knew it was against his will and better judgment. I knew it was his good heart, and his feeling of guilt for not seeing the old man in the first place. "Thanks for your shovel, we're ready to head on. Want a lift?"

It happened then. The old man stood a foot taller, his eyes went wild with fear and rage. His thin hands knotted into fists, and the burned wrists were livid. His mouth turned to a grey vacancy.

"No, you don't," he shrilled, high, like an animal. "You don't get me back there again. Not you nor no man's army. Yuma." The word came out like spit in the air. "I gotta find my water hole. My own good pure water from my own water hole. Nobody's goin' to shut me up in that filth again. Them caves. Bake ovens. I dreamed my water hole. I can't rest easy until—you don't get me back there. Not ever."

He reached upward, strong and strangely young. The pick was in his hand with the suddenness of a quick drawn gun. "Now git," he shouted. "Git, both of you, whoever you are and wherever you're from. Leave me be to find my water hole or I'll rip you into long strips of meat."

Harry was in the car before I could open my mouth to scream. The motor turned at once, praise new cars. The rear wheel slashed a few empty rounds, then took hold. We skidded out onto the pavement.

Not so fast, though, that we couldn't hear the harsh clank of the pick against the left back fender, and the harsh uplifted shriek of the old man.

"I can't rest easy," he ranted. "I can't rest easy."

I heard him twice, somewhere in the midst of my shuddering, before the sound of the motor and the blessed hum of the air conditioner drowned him from my ears.

Harry's hands on the wheel were shaking. "Crazy old coot," he muttered. "Nutty old fool. Walking the freeways looking for water."

I started to cry. I cried for quite a while and Harry didn't say a word to stop me. If he'd been a woman I'm sure he would have done the same thing, instead of just drawing long breaths on his cigarette and swearing under them.

When we neared Yuma, Harry spoke for the first time. "There's a sign on the edge of town I've noticed before." He sounded calm and himself again. "It points the way to the Territorial Prison. I think we'd just better stop off there and tell the authorities about that guy."

"You think he was an escaped prisoner?" I asked. Crazy, yes. Driven mad from the sun, I'd thought. But a prisoner?

Harry nodded. "Add it up."

We rode in silence, following the green sign. We went through streets which were just turning on lights in the brown twilight. We swung to a dead end, and crossed a series of railroad tracks. We lifted up a sharp hill and around a curve.

Yuma Territorial Prison was spread out before us at the top of the hill.

It was our fault, of course, for not knowing more about Arizona history. California, sure. But not Arizona.

Yuma Territorial Prison—and Museum! 1825.

Adobe, old rocks, broken-down walls. Sun-burned brick. Crumbling. Hanging on. It was every television Western, every sheriff who fought to get the prisoner to the Territorial Prison before a gang could lynch him.

Tragic. Horrible. Man's inhumanity to man. The tiny dug-out cells, chipped from the heavy rock hill. Great rusted crossed bars before them. Great rusted rings to manacle men, set in the center of them.

"Caves," the old man had cried. "Filth. Ovens," he had shrilled with those blood-red wrists raised high.

I was ill. I was very ill.

Suddenly and completely all history was in me. The place where I stood, the old yard, dirt packed to stone by other feet, the yard where a hundred years ago men took their pathetic limited exercise and yearned out over the green country. Because it was green, even in the twilight, the land below was rich and green, watered by the silver thread of the Colorado River. History climbed up into my legs and feebled them, and went on into my stomach and nauseated it, and caught my heart and squeezed it dry.

It was the same with Harry. We stood there, the two of us, Myra and Harry on a second honeymoon, and for a long time we were too weak to walk back to the car. We were too gone in the past to think of the old man.

It was only when we were once again down the hill, moving very slowly because the steering wheel looked big and dangerous in Harry's trembling hands, once more across the railroad tracks, that we thought of him and looked at each other.

You have to be married quite awhile to share a strong thought, a question, an answer, and agree without words, the way we did. Harry picked up speed, swung the car out of Yuma, and began to retrace the distance back to the spot where the old man had been so shockingly and suddenly in the middle of the freeway.

It turned dark all at once, as if somebody had snapped a switch off in a bright room. I suppose there were stars, but we didn't see them. Perhaps there was a moon, but it gave us no light. All we saw, the two of us, straining our eyes, was the road, black and wide, in the modern beam of our headlights, unreeling like film, roll after roll of it, black, shiny, full of miles.

"We have to find out," Harry said, some time, any time, a long time. "We have to try to find him."

"Yes," I breathed. "Yes."

I don't remember how long it was. Years of night and road and the motor all seemed to push against dead air. We slowed at last, caught by the familiar shape of a hill, the one beside which the car had skidded and lashed into the sand.

We slowed for another reason too.

On the opposite side of the freeway red and white blinker lights flashed in crazy syncopation. As we drew closer, going very gently now, we saw yellow barricades, thrown up rapidly, haphazard. A spotlighted sign read SLOW—DETOUR.

Harry parked at the side of the road, careful to stay off the sand, yet give maximum passing space. He kept the lights on. He opened the door and signaled me out. He took my hand. We ran across the road, across the narrow center divider and to the detour sign, the busy reflectors flashing their warning.

There was a police car at the far side. The officer called, "What do you want?"

I could almost hear Harry swallow. "The old man," he cried thickly. "Was he hit? What happened here?"

The officer came into the aura of the reflectors, his face mottled a flashing red and white. "Don't know anything about any old man. Damnedest thing, though. Look at it and see for yourselves."

The barricades were a neat fence, framing a large chipped hole in the freeway. The hole wasn't neat, though. It was ragged, as though it had been worked at in frenzied haste. It gaped in the nice new pavement like a great tear in the seat of a new pair of pants.

And filling it, brimming it, cupping it, shimmering in the red and white lights, was a clear shining pool of water!

We turned, not caring what the officer thought. We ran, still hand in hand, two utterly terrified children in a night too big and dark for us, a land too spread and wild. We ran toward the security of our modern, sensible, air-conditioned, motorized world.

Just before we reached the car, Harry stumbled, fell to one knee, caught himself, and came up with something in his hand.

It was a pick, ancient and rusty and very efficient.   It was damp on the edges from water finally discovered.

After how many years?   Oh heaven, after how long a time?

"I can't rest until I find my water hole."

Harry's arm stretched high and frantic.   He threw the pick with all of his strength toward the unseen mesquite bushes.

"I can't rest until I find my water hole."

All right, as I said before, you don't have to believe it.   You're lucky if you can't.

Maybe Harry and I would be lucky too, in time.   They say all experiences dim, and a sensible explanation can be made for almost anything.

But we have to live with it.

You see, the best mechanics in town, or in the city, cannot seem to straighten out the sharp narrow gouge in the center of the left rear fender of Harry's company station wagon.

DAN J. MARLOWE

Art for Money's Sake

My name is Carl Widner. I have none of the characteristics people usually associate with men of daring. I'm balding, pink-cheeked, far too short, and on the wrong side of sixty. On the other hand, I'm a chain-smoker who is loaded with nervous energy, I drive a bright red sportscar, I'm a *young* sixty-four, and I know I'm considered something of an eccentric by my associates at the museum.

I have a background in daring too. All my life I've been reading mystery stories and planning perfect crimes. What began as an intellectual exercise prepared me for reality. Spurred to action by circumstances, I had just such a plan in operation.

It was really very shortsighted of the museum trustees. After a hundred years of laissez-faire operation in regard to employees' retirement ages, they suddenly decided to invoke a mandatory retirement-at-sixty-five clause. The word reached me eventually in the restoring and retouching section which I had headed for fifteen years. At the moment my total worldly assets approximated $900 plus my car. Since my combined museum pension and social security would barely keep me in the quantities of unfiltered cigarettes to which I was accustomed, the precipitous action of the museum board left me no alternative but to feather my nest against my fast approaching involuntary retirement.

I borrowed $2,000 that afternoon and wrote an airmail letter that night. I enclosed the $2,000 in the form of a bank draft. Three weeks later I received a notice from the air express office at the local airport that they were holding a package for me.

I drove to the airport, weaving in and out of traffic. Upon the occasion of one of his infrequent rides with me, my young assistant, Henry Sansom, remarked in an awed tone: "Mr. Widner, you really *use* a car!"

I skidded to a stop in the NO PARKING zone at the airport terminal building. There were several signs with arrows pointing toward the location of airport facilities. I climbed from the car and followed the set of arrows marked AIR EXPRESS.

Five minutes later I returned to the car carrying a large, flat crate. The policeman must have arrived a couple of minutes sooner. He gave me an impersonal glance as I placed the crate on the passenger's-side bucket seat and then got into the car. He continued to write in his summons book as he stood with one foot on my rear bumper. It irked me that this crass arbiter of automotive injustice seemed determined to ignore me personally.

When he bent to get the license number, I gunned the car forward. The bumper was yanked from under his foot as I pulled into the moving traffic stream. The discomfited minion of the law was still rolling on his back in the dust when the airport disappeared from my rear-view mirror.

Twenty minutes later I parked outside my studio apartment. I'm fond of the place. It has one large room with a skylight, and the walls of the room are covered with my paintings. I'd prefer to have the walls bare and the paintings sold, but I've become reconciled to the fact that we live in an imperfect world.

The apartment also has a small bedroom, a bath, and a kitchenette. A cleaning woman takes care of those three rooms for me, but I don't permit her to touch anything in the studio. The floor is littered with cigarette butts and the twisted remains of paint tubes. There is no order in the haphazard placement of cabinets, easels, drawing tables, and paint boxes. The entire atmosphere, in fact, is perfect for the creation of rare and original works of art.

The critics are all agreed, unfortunately, that I have never created anything that was rare, original, or a work of art. Their attitude and their aspersions are all the more dastardly when it's considered that never once have I asked for their opinions. Almost as much as the museum board, the critics were responsible for forcing me into my chosen course of action.

Have you ever heard of Hans van Meegeren? Quite simply, he was a genius, the world's greatest art forger. He created Verméers so perfect that even Jan Vermeer would have thought they were his own. And van Meegeren's deceptions might never have been detected at all if he hadn't confessed due to a bizarre combination of circumstances.

At the end of World War II, van Meegeren was put on trial by the Dutch for selling national art treasures to the Nazis. The only way he could hope to avoid a prison sentence was to admit that he'd painted the "masterpieces" himself. He wasn't believed, of course. The critics and experts had all certified his paintings as genuine Vermeers. To prove his point, he created another Vermeer in his jail cell, and the experts all had to admit that they'd been wrong.

Van Meegeren's story always appealed to me because he showed up the critics from whom he'd suffered just as I had. His first forgery was begun for no other reason than to fool them. A profit motive was soon involved, however. In all, van Meegeren created six false Vermeers which he sold for a total of $3,200,000. One might be able to find fault with his ethics but never with his arithmetic.

If you're not an artist yourself, you can't possibly imagine the knowledge, skill, and patience the man needed to bring off his coup. Each new painting had to be the equal of a genuine Vermeer. It had to be consistent with the master's known works. It had to be a subject which Vermeer himself might have selected. The color, the perspective, and the style of execution all had to be as technically perfect as a genuine Vermeer.

But that's not the half of it. In addition to making Vermeer the subject of years of intensive study, van Meegeren had other difficulties to overcome. A painting is made up of four layers: the support, usually canvas or wood; the painting ground, the prepared surface upon which the picture is painted; the paint itself, made from particles of colored pigment suspended in a medium such as linseed oil; and finally a film of varnish to give brilliance to the colors and to act as a protective covering.

A forger not only must be a fine artist, he must choose his materials with care. A modern canvas would never pass for a canvas 200 years old.   The modern weave is too uniform, obviously the product of a superior technology.   A forger must also know what pigments were used by the artist he's imitating, because many of the pigments in use today are comparatively recent discoveries.

A forger must know, for instance, that Renaissance painters used ultramarine for the blue in their canvases; the Prussian blue wasn't discovered until 1704; that cobalt blue first appeared in 1802; and that synthetic ultramarine, first used in 1824, is distinguishable from the natural product because it lacks impurities and its particles are all the same size.

A forger must have similar knowledge of all other color pigments.   He must be careful to use nothing that will date his work earlier than he intends.   A simple error like using a modern brush made from hog bristles instead of a period-piece brush made from badger hair can destroy the illusion of authenticity.   If brush bristles are discovered in a painting, they had better be the right kind.

Although I didn't plan to forge a Vermeer, I did plan to employ many of van Meegeren's tested techniques.   Before I was finished, I expected to have enough money to end my days on the French Riviera, surrounded by beautiful, bikini-clad mermaids.   When I dream, you understand, I really dream.

In the studio I found a claw hammer and pulled the nails from one end of the crate I'd brought from the airport.   Out came the most expensive piece of trash I'd ever owned.   It was a painting by Albretti, a Renaissance artist so minor that few people have ever heard of him.   I'd gone $2,000 in debt to purchase the painting from a private collection.

What I planned to do was produce a Delgardi, and my newly acquired canvas had been painted in Delgardi's own studio.   Albretti had been one of Delgardi's least accomplished students, but the materials he used were identical with those employed by the master.   As soon as I made up my mind to paint a Delgardi, I knew this was the type of support I had to have.

Van Meegeren again had pointed the way for me.   Knowing that old wood or canvas can't be faked successfully, he bought old paintings of minor artists of the proper time period, removed their work, and substituted his own.   He once paid $400 for a painting just for its support and later sold the "Vermeer" he created upon it for $700,000.

I began the tedious task of carefully removing the varnish and the paint of Albretti's work.   The next day I stayed in the museum until long after closing. When I was sure I was alone, I took several color photos of the museum's most recent acquisition, a Delgardi madonna that had been in the private collection of a Spanish family for centuries.   The museum had acquired it at auction in Sotheby's London showroom.   I examined the painting in detail, and was delighted to find that the support for the Delgardi was in every way identical to the support I was salvaging from the Albretti.   So far, so good.

I'm not stupid.   I knew I couldn't hope to create a painting that would be accepted as a long-lost Delgardi. I didn't know enough about the master's style and technique to create something totally new as van Meegeren had done with his Vermeers. The years I'd spent restoring and retouching old masters, however, more than qualified me to copy any existing Delgardi.

By the time the photo lab delivered my color enlargements of the Delgardi madonna, I had removed all traces of the Albretti from my support and had collected pigments and brushes of the proper period. I got right to work then duplicating the Delgardi masterpiece.

My plan was simplicity itself. First I would duplicate the museum's painting, then I would remove the original from the museum and leave the copy in its place. Next I would announce that while trying to restore my Albretti I had discovered another painting underneath, identical to the one on display in the museum. After that it would be up to the experts to decide which was the genuine Delgardi and which was the work of a copyist.

Just to make sure there could be no mistake, I used a little cobalt blue on a couple of spots to give my copied Delgardi a date too late for the original. This would show the experts beyond a shadow of a doubt that the copy hanging in the museum was indeed a copy.

I couldn't afford to be in a hurry. I allowed the painting to age for a few months, then brushed on a coat of special varnish. The next-to-final step was to place the canvas in an oven and bake it delicately until a network of fine cracks spread over its entire surface. I sprayed it then with a thin coating of ancient grime I'd scraped from my original Albretti.

I had a key to the museum because I often worked weekends. That same night I let myself into the museum and turned off the alarms guarding the collections of old masters. I substituted my copy for the original Delgardi and made my departure after the closest inspection showing the paintings to be presumably identical. Back in my apartment I gloated for most of the balance of the night over my "copy."

In the morning I called on the curator and told him about my fantastic discovery. He telephoned the chairman of the museum board, and the excitement began. No one doubted for an instant that the Delgardi madonna in the museum display case was the same one that had always been there. The only question to be resolved was which painting was authentic. I was glad I'd had the foresight to put the two spots of cobalt blue on the forgery, because I didn't have much faith that the experts would come up with the right answer unless there was an obvious flaw.

They used X rays, alcohol tests, spectroscopic analyses, and a few tests unknown to me. It took several weeks, but no one hurries where a half-million-dollar painting is concerned. Then one Saturday afternoon, as I was lounging in the apartment, reading a travel brochure about the Riviera, I received a phone call from the curator. It was the unanimous opinion of the experts that the painting on display in the museum was the genuine one.

I was staggered. "Are you sure?" I asked.

"We're certain. There's no doubt at all. We even found traces of cobalt blue on the museum's Delgardi."

"But doesn't that *prove* it's a copy?" I argued. "Cobalt blue wasn't discovered until the early 1800's." It annoyed me that I had to do their thinking for them too.

"On the contrary. It proves the painting's age. You understand that if a copy was made from your painting, it would have had to be done hundreds of years ago, before Albretti covered it. Besides, anyone able to duplicate a Delgardi would know enough to use the proper pigments. Everyone knows how recent cobalt blue is. The cobalt blue that was used undoubtedly occurred when the painting required retouching, perhaps 150 years ago. An artist doing retouching, as you very well know, Carl, is concerned with color and effect, not in using pigments identical to those of the original painter."

I stared at the far wall. "Then what about *my* painting?" I asked finally.

"A copy. It wasn't uncommon for students to duplicate the works of their teacher, including the signature. Yours is most likely the work of Albretti. It's an uncommonly fine job, everyone agrees, but then, you see, he painted over it. We can't imagine any artist covering such fine work unless he knew it was a copy and placed more value upon the original work he planned to put over it."

The infuriating part of it was that their logic made a certain weird sense. Or could it be that I was the victim of the experts' commercialism rather than their stupidity? After all, the museum had half a million tied up in the painting on their wall.

I paced the room while I tried to think. I now owned a "copy" of a Delgardi by Albretti instead of a mediocre Albretti original. The "copy" was worth more than the original, but hardly enough to pay my debts and transport me to a lifetime of ease on the French Riviera.

The irony of it struck me afresh. That was *my* work hanging in the museum. I had fooled all the experts, or so they were prepared to swear. Hundreds of people would stop in front of the Delgardi in the museum every day and admire the skill of the artist, who was me. Art magazines would publish articles praising the painting. And it would all be for my work. It was exactly what I'd always dreamed of during those scarifying moments while reading the critics' cutting reviews of my work.

Wasn't that better than going to the Riviera?

Of course it was.

I might not be able to retire to a life of leisure, but after all, when a man passes sixty, bikini-clad mermaids present a problem not even van Meegeren could solve.

HILLARY WAUGH

Nothing but Human Nature

Captain of Detectives Mike Galton, or "the old man" as he was known to his underlings, looked down at the woman's body. It was dressed in a nightgown and a blue flannel robe and lay on the kitchen floor in a crumpled heap. The woman was a brunette, thirty-three years old, and perhaps twenty pounds overweight. Whether she was pretty or not was hard to tell from the way her head was smashed. The instrument that did the damage, a length of lead pipe, lay beside her. There was a bag of groceries on the kitchen table, and the back door was open.

"Photo been called?" the old man asked William Dennis, the young detective beside him.

"Yes, sir, and the M.E."

The old man turned and went back to the little front parlor where Joseph Eldridge, the dead woman's husband, sat twisting his hands between his knees. A policeman stood nearby, trying to look invisible.

"That piece of pipe," the old man said to the husband. "Did that come from somewhere in the house?"

Joseph Eldridge focused on the detective's face. He was a lean, handsome man in his mid-thirties though now he looked harrowed and white. "No," he said, shaking his head. "I never saw it before."

"You want to tell it again—exactly what happened this A.M.?"

"I went to do the marketing, same as every Saturday morning—"

"You do the marketing?"

"My wife teaches school all week. I want—wanted her to relax on weekends."

"You work, Mr. Eldridge?"

"Me?" He looked startled. "Yeah. I sell insurance." Then he said, "I didn't touch her money, if that's what you mean. We lived on what I make."

"But she taught?"

Joseph Eldridge nodded. "She taught because she loved teaching. She didn't want to give it up when we married, and I didn't make her." He sighed deeply.

Mike Galton nodded. "And you do the marketing Saturday mornings. Tell me about this morning."

Eldridge shrugged and looked down at the floor. He spoke in a choked voice.

"There's nothing to tell, really. I went to the supermarket, I bought the week's groceries, I drove home, came in the back door and—and found her."

"Any idea who did it?"

He shook his head slowly. "I can't imagine."

Detective Dennis said, "Did you go into the bedroom?"

Eldridge nodded. "When I called you. The phone's in there."

"You touch anything?"

"No."

Dennis said to the old man, "The bedroom's been ransacked, Captain. The bureau drawers, the closets."

Galton said, "You have valuables in the house, Mr. Eldridge?"

"Not anything much. A few dollars maybe, and May had a couple of rings that might have been worth a little—a hundred bucks or so."

The photographer arrived and Galton and Dennis took him out to the kitchen. Then the medical examiner came and was also shown the scene.

Galton returned to the husband. "What time did you go to the store, Mr. Eldridge, and what time did you get back?"

"I left the house around nine o'clock, give or take ten minutes. I wasn't noticing the time."

"Somewhere between eight-fifty and nine-ten, then?"

"That sounds about right."

"And you got home?"

"I didn't notice. I came in. I saw her. I guess after that I just stopped thinking."

"Can you give me a rough idea what the time was?"

Eldridge tried to think. "About half an hour ago, I suppose. I phoned the police, and then—" He looked up. "Wait, I do remember. The clock in the store said twenty of eleven when I was checking out. Five minutes to load the car and five minutes to get home here— Call it about ten minutes of eleven when I found her."

"How long have you been married, Mr. Eldridge?"

"Ten years in June."

"No children?"

"No."

"Did she have any enemies that you know of?"

"She couldn't have. Everybody loved her."

"Any relatives?"

"Her mother, two brothers and a sister. But they live on the west coast."

The old man went back to the kitchen. The medical examiner told him the woman had been beaten to death with the pipe. The photographer said he'd got his pictures and did the captain want him to dust for fingerprints?

"See if you can get anything off the pipe," the old man said. "And the drawers in the bedroom. I understand the bureaus have been ransacked."

Dennis said, "Do you believe the burglar theory?"

The old man shrugged. "It's possible there was a burglar. It's possible Eldridge killed her and faked the burglary. It's possible someone else killed her and faked the burglary." He said to the doctor, "Do you think she was beaten unnecessarily—by someone who hated her rather than someone who wanted to rob her?"

The doctor said he couldn't venture an opinion. He sat down at the kitchen table to fill out his papers.

The body was lying face up now, and Captain Galton said to Dennis, "See if you can find a sheet or something and cover her."

Policewoman Jenny Galton came through from the living room. She was a young and pretty redhead, but poised and experienced despite her youth, for she was Mike Galton's daughter.

"Hi, Pops," she said. "I hear I'm to search a body." Then she saw the dead woman and she sobered. "That's not very pretty," she said. "It's a homicide, then?"

Galton said, "It's a homicide, pet, and a nasty one."

While Jenny searched the apparel on the body, Galton went outside for a look around. The house was a tiny brick bungalow in an area of tiny brick bungalows, packed together on midget lots with one-car garages in back and just room for a driveway between. Joseph Eldridge's station wagon was standing in front of the garage and two steps from the stoop. In the back were two more bags of groceries like the one on the kitchen table.

Detective Dennis came out to join him. "No fingerprints on the pipe," he said, "and it doesn't look like there's going to be anything on the bureau knobs either." He smiled wryly. "We aren't left with much."

"We never are when there are no witnesses." Galton sighed and turned to the porch steps. "Well, I guess the next step is to canvass the neighborhood, see if there've been any strangers around—salesmen, vagrants, and the like—and see if anybody can tell us anything about the Eldridges. I'd like to know whether his grief is as real as it looks."

A sheet was over the body when they came back in, and Jenny told them the woman was missing her wedding and engagement rings. Otherwise there was nothing to report.

"You get any ideas when you examined the body, kitten? Any female intuition?"

She said, "If you mean do I think Mr. Eldridge is telling the truth, I don't know. Nothing I found is inconsistent with his story. It could have happened like that."

The captain went on into the little bedroom. The police photographer was putting away his fingerprint equipment and shaking his head. "Just smudges," he said. "One partial on the bureau top but it looks like the woman's."

The old man and Dennis brought Mr. Eldridge into the bedroom then to make a search. He looked through the drawers and his wife's purse. He found there was no money in the purse and her jewelry box was missing from the drawers.

"You got any insurance on the jewelry?" Dennis asked him.

Eldridge shook his head. "It wasn't worth that much."

The old man showed him a note on the telephone pad. It said: "Membership comm. Tues. at 4:00."

"May wrote that," Eldridge told him. "They usually meet at the church on Mondays. I guess it got changed."

"Do you know when she received the call?"

"I don't have any idea. It wasn't when I was around."

"Do you know who would have made the call?"

Eldridge said it was probably the committee chairman. Her name was Mrs. Bertha Crump, and the old man found her number in the address book on the phone table.

Dennis took Eldridge back to the living room while Galton got the woman on the line. Yes, she told him, she was the one who called May Eldridge about the change. She'd called her just that morning, in fact.

"Do you know what time this morning, Mrs. Crump?"

"About quarter past nine. Why, is something the matter?"

"Yes, something is the matter. But can you say for sure that you made the call at quarter past nine?"

"Well," Mrs. Crump said hesitantly, "I wouldn't want to swear to it. But I do know that I don't make phone calls before nine o'clock, and Mrs. Eldridge was the fourth person I talked to about the change. It couldn't have been before quarter past nine. Of that I'm sure."

"It was Mrs. Eldridge who answered the phone?" Galton said.

"Yes."

"How long did the two of you talk?"

"Oh, perhaps two minutes. Usually I'd talk longer, but I had five others to call so I didn't want to dally."

"Did she mention her husband at all?"

Mrs. Crump said no, and asked again what the trouble was.

Galton told her, helped her over her shock, and questioned her some more, but the answers didn't change.

When he hung up, Galton went back to Eldridge and had him tell the story over again two more times. It came out the same way, but with two additions. He knew nothing of Mrs. Crump's phone call, for he had already left. He knew of nobody who could support his alibi.

The hearse pulled into the drive and two morgue attendants came through the back door with a stretcher. Galton watched them lift the body onto it with practiced precision and take it out. He sent the patrolman back to his beat and, with Detective Dennis, started a canvass of the neighborhood to see what they could learn.

The brick bungalow abutting the Eldridges' driveway was their first stop and the door was answered by a trim young bottled blonde in shorts and halter. Galton showed his badge, apologized for the intrusion, and explained about the death next door.

"Yeah," the woman said. "I saw the hearse. You say she was killed, huh? Gee, that's terrible."

"Did you know them well, Mrs.—ah—"

"Jenks. Mimi Jenks. No, I didn't know them except to say hello to."

"What about Mr. Jenks?"

The woman laughed. "Mr. Jenks sends me an alimony check once a month. That's all I know about him or care."

Galton said, "Oh." Then he said, "Can you tell me anything about this morning? Did you see anybody or hear anything next door?"

Mrs. Jenks frowned in thought. Then she said, "I heard their car go out at nine o'clock. I can't think of anything else."

"Did you say nine o'clock?"

She shrugged. "Well, it might not have been exactly nine o'clock. It might have been two or three minutes after."

"How do you remember the time so well?"

She laughed. "That's easy. I got up at nine. I looked at the clock. And I had just got out of bed when I heard their car start up."

"And you saw or heard nothing else?"

"Nothing else. Until the hearse."

"You didn't hear his car return?"

She shook her head. "I only heard it go out because the bedroom's on that side of the house and the window was open."

"I see." Galton pursed his lips. "One more question. You know anything about what kind of a marriage they had? Did they get along or fight, or what?"

Mrs. Jenks said she didn't have any idea. All she knew was she never heard them fight. She never heard anything from them at all.

"I see. Now, one last thing. It's very important. Are you absolutely sure it was nine o'clock when he drove away?"

"Absolutely, because I looked at the clock when I got up and then I did my exercises by the window for fifteen minutes and I remember the car wasn't there. Why is that so important?"

"Because it supports his own story that that's when he went shopping."

"I see. I'm his alibi, in other words?"

"Yes, you could call it that."

"I'm glad I can help."

"So are we. You'll be asked to testify, of course."

She smiled. "Any time."

Galton and Dennis tried the family on the other side of the Eldridges' but they could not help at all, nor could anyone else in the neighborhood. No one had noticed suspicious strangers around. No one had seen Eldridge go to the supermarket.

The old man and his youthful companion returned to police headquarters at half past twelve. The chief was there and so was Jenny.

"We're up a tree," Dennis told the chief. "Absolutely no clues." He went on to explain the problem. Mr. Eldridge left the house between nine and nine-five. Mrs. Eldridge received a phone call from Mrs. Crump between nine-fifteen and nine-twenty, between nine-twenty, when she hung up, and ten-fifty, when Mr. Eldridge returned, someone came in the back door, beat Mrs. Eldridge to death with a pipe, ransacked the bureaus in the bedroom, and made off with a box of inexpensive jewelry and the few dollars in Mrs. Eldridge's purse.

The chief said, "Is that how you see it?" to the old man, but Galton's attention was on his daughter.

"You're a right pretty girl, kitten," he said.   "Now that I notice, I'm struck by that fact."

She laughed and told him he was dotty.

"No, I'm not dotty, I'm serious.   What are your measurements, thirty-eight, twenty-three, thirty-six?"

"That's reasonably close.   Why?"

"Because when you go home for lunch, you're going to change into your prettiest dress.   Then we're going to see what kind of an actress you are."

Jenny, the chief, and William Dennis all were curious, but the old man merely said very mysteriously, "Wait and see."

At half past two that afternoon, the old man rang Mrs. Jenks' doorbell again. He smiled and said he was sorry to trouble her but could she come down to headquarters so they could take her statement?   She said she'd be glad to oblige and got her coat.

On the way he told her how much he appreciated her cooperation and she said she was only doing her duty.   As an innocent man's only alibi, she had to testify.

"Yes," the old man said, "except, you will be pleased to learn, the burden is no longer solely on your own shoulders.   We've found someone else to verify his alibi."

"Oh?" she said, and turned to look at him.   "Who?"

"A young woman he knows.   She's come forward to testify that she saw him enter the supermarket at ten minutes past nine."

Mrs. Jenks said, "Oh," again, in a strange voice.

The chief and William Dennis were in the squad room when the old man brought Mrs. Jenks in.   He introduced her and told her that they'd take her statement in just a few minutes, and if she'd wait in the other room . . . He took her to the door and there was Jenny, sitting on the couch in her prettiest dress, her hair just so, looking as luscious as chocolate cake.   "This is Miss Murphy, Mrs. Jenks," the old man said.   "She's the one I was telling you about, the one who saw Mr. Eldridge in the supermarket.   Isn't that right, Miss Murphy?"

Mrs. Jenks stopped dead in the doorway but "Miss Murphy" didn't seem to notice.   "That's right," she said brightly.   "Joe came in at exactly ten minutes past nine.   I know because I was looking at my watch."

Captain Galton smiled with approval, but Mrs. Jenks didn't smile at all.   "She's a liar," she said.

Miss Murphy put her nose in the air.   "I ought to know when Joe came in," she said.   "I'm the one who was looking at my watch."

"She's a liar," Mrs. Jenks repeated in a louder voice.   "Because Joe Eldridge didn't leave his house until half past nine."

"Half past nine?" the captain said.

"Half past nine," she told him.   "Because that's how long it took that two-timing cheat to bash in his wife's head.   And he didn't go to the store for five more minutes after that because he got blood on his shirt and had to change it.   I know, because the bloody one is in the bottom of my laundry bag, wrapped around her jewelry box."

Captain Galton said, "Is that right?" but Mrs. Jenks wasn't paying any attention to him.

She was pointing at "Miss Murphy" and saying, "So if you think you're going to run off with him to the Virgin Islands while I'm left holding the bag, forget it. He's going to jail.   And I'm going to put him there."

She told it all to the detectives and a tape recorder, how Eldridge promised her marriage and a life of Caribbean luxury in return for a murder alibi.   Then they got the district attorney in and she went over it again.   After that, they sent two policemen out with a warrant for Mr. Eldridge's arrest.

In the squad room, Detective William Dennis and the chief of police looked at Captain Galton and shook their heads.   "Absolutely amazing," they said.

"It's nothing but human nature," the old man replied.   "I figured the moment she thought a younger and prettier girl was also lying to save Eldridge's neck, she'd blow his alibi to kingdom come."

Dennis said, "That, I understand.   But how did you know she and Eldridge were a twosome to begin with?   That's what amazes me.   What tipped you off?"

The old man said, "Human nature again, Bill.   Put a sexy young grass widow next door to a handsome free-lance insurance agent whose wife is away at work all day and you can expect there's going to be a situation.   And when the wife has ten years' worth of teaching salary lying around unspent, you know the answer to that situation isn't going to be divorce, it's going to be murder.

"We had the murder, so one look at the woman next door was all I needed to know the whole story.   It wasn't the piece of pipe or the missing jewelry or the stories they told that gave it away.   It was her shorts, her halter, and her bleached hair."

C. B. GILFORD

Murder, 1990

The case of Paul 2473 really began when he discovered the old book. He recognized it instantly for what it was, because he had once been through the Micro-filing Section where they were recording some old-fashioned but worthy volumes on genetics before destroying them. But the sight of this book, obviously an uninspected relic of the dim past, provoked a simultaneous curiosity and dread in him.

He'd been marching with the Thursday Exercise Platoon over a country back road, and now they were enjoying their ten-minute rest period, lying by the roadside among the grass-strewn brick ruins of some ancient building. Paul was bored— Thursdays always bored him intensely—and both his mind and eye were casting about for something of interest to focus upon.

Which was why his gaze had roamed over the crumbling, disintegrating wall beside him. He saw the aperture almost immediately. At this particular spot, the bricks seemed to have fallen down against a still standing portion of the wall so as to make a small igloo or cave. A tiny, cozy, rain-proof den, he thought, for some small wild thing. A few of the little beasts always seemed to survive the best efforts of the decontamination squads which constantly scoured vacant areas.

Paul turned over and lay on his stomach so that he could peer into the dark hole, and saw the book. He knew instantly, of course, what the proper procedure was. He should take the thing, not open it, but hand it over instead to the Platoon Leader. He'd been taught that all such objects pertaining to the former civilization could be either valuable or dangerous. He had no more right to destroy the book than he had to look at it.

Half-intending deceit but not fully decided, he checked first to see if he was being observed. The Leader was nowhere in sight. The members of the Platoon were all prone, none of them close to Paul, and none of them paying the least attention to him. Tentatively, still not committed to disobedience, Paul reached into the hole, grasped the book and drew it out.

It was small, light, and seemed ready to fall apart at his touch. Trembling, but overwhelmed by curiosity, he lifted the cover and glanced at the fly leaf. *The Logic of Murder*, he read.

For a moment, he experienced a dismal disappointment. The word "logic" had some meaning for him, though vague.   The last word, "murder," was completely and totally mysterious.   The book was useless if he knew absolutely nothing of its subject matter.   But as he pondered it, he was not so sure.   The book might teach him what "murder" was.   And "murder" might be something vastly entertaining.

"Everybody up!"   The Platoon Leader's shrill bark of command came from far away through the trees.

In the instant before the somnolent members of the Platoon could rouse themselves and stir from the matted grass, Paul 2473 came to a momentous decision.   He thrust the little book inside his shirt.   Then he got up, stretched, and walked back to the road where the files were forming.

In his cubicle, Paul 2473 re-invented the ancient stratagem of schoolboys.   Every evening during the few minutes he had to himself, he held the little book behind the afternoon edition of *The News of Progress,* and thus, while seeming to be immersed in the sort of reading that was his duty, he was actually engaged in a forbidden pastime.   He practiced this little deception in case the wall television screen chose at any time to look in on him.

As he read, though more and more conscious of the dangers involved, he grew more and more fascinated by what he found in the little book.   Gradually, by piecing together scattered references, he began to arrive at some conclusions.

Murder, he discovered with something of a shock, was the taking of a human life.   It was a completely new and hitherto undreamed-of idea to him.   He knew that life did not go on forever.   He knew that elderly people sometimes got sick, were carted off to some medical building or physiology laboratory or clinic, and then were never seen again.   Death, he also knew, was usually painless—unless there was a specific, scientific reason for the authorities to decree it should not be—and so he had neither considered death much nor feared it.

But murder had apparently been a phenomenon of the previous civilization in which the authorities not only did not arrange human death, but were actually opposed to individuals who took such matters into their own hands.   Yet the practice, though accompanied by danger, seemed to have been amazingly popular.   Paul 2473 shuddered at the barbarism of it, but could not stop reading.

But as he came to understand the title of the book, he discovered that although murder was hideous, it had been in its own past environment rather understandable.   In a society where people had chosen their own mates at random, murders had been committed out of sexual jealousy or revenge.   In a society where the authorities had not provided sustenance for the population, murders had been committed to acquire wealth.

As he read on, Paul was treated to the full panorama of homicidal motivations, both sane and insane.   There was a chapter on methods of murder.   There were sections on the detection, apprehension, and punishment of murderers.

But the conclusions of the book were the most amazing part.   "Murder," it was stated emphatically, "is a much more widespread crime than statistics indicate.   Many murders are committed without premeditation, in the heat of emotion.   Those who commit such murders are quite often brought to justice.   Much more successful at evasion, however, are the murderers who plan their crimes beforehand.   The bulging files of unsolved murders are predominantly of this variety.   In the battle of wits between murderer and policeman, the former has all the advantage.   Although the findings of various statistical studies have varied somewhat, they all point inescapably in one direction.   Most murders go unsolved.   Most murderers live out their natural lives in peace and safety and the enjoyment of the fruits of their efforts.''

Paul 2473 was thoughtful for a long time after he finished the book.   He recognized the peril of his own position more than ever.   The new civilization simply could not afford to let this book be disseminated, to allow humanity to realize how recently it had emerged from primitive savagery.   He himself had therefore broken an important rule in reading the book, and he saw now why it was an important rule.   If he were found out, he would surely be reprimanded, demoted, perhaps even publicly disgraced.

But he did not destroy the book.   Instead he hid it inside his mattress.   The notion of murder, like some inventor's dream, intrigued him, and he devoted all his spare time to thinking of it.

He even considered mentioning it to Carol 7427.   He saw Carol 7427 almost every evening at Recreation, and on many occasions had gone into the Caressing Booths with her, more often than with any other girl.   He had taken Compatibility Tests with Carol 7427, and was hoping for a Three-Year Assignment with her, a Five-Year if he could get it.

That first evening after he had finished the book, he came very close to confiding in her.   She came into the Recreation Center still in her work slacks, but they fitted her so neatly and snugly that he did not mind.   He gazed at her close-cropped blonde hair, at her bright blue eyes and clear skin, and he thought about the Mating Assignment.   It would be very nice to share a double cubicle with someone, to have someone to talk to, really talk to, someone to whisper to, out of reach of the microphones, someone with whom to discuss strange and fascinating and bizarre ideas, such as murder and what civilization must have been like when individuals dared to murder one another.

He maneuvered her over into a corner, away from the Group Conversation on Radiation Agriculture.   "Would you like to know a real secret, Carol?" he asked her.

Her long lashes blinked at him, and her color heightened prettily.   "A secret, Paul?" she breathed.   "What kind of a secret?"

"I've broken a rule."

"Really!"

"A serious rule."

"Really!"   She was enthralled.

"And I've discovered something that's terribly interesting."

"Tell me!"   She leaned closer to him.   She had taken a perfume tablet, and her exhalations enchanted him.

"If I told you, you'd either have to report me, or you'd be in the same dangerous position I'm in."

"I'd never report you, Paul."

"But I wouldn't want to get you into trouble."

She looked disappointed and began to pout.   But her reaction pleased him. They shared the same spirit of adventure and curiosity.   He wouldn't tell her now. But when the Mating Assignments came out—next week for sure—when they shared a cubicle, then he would give her the book to read, and they could discuss the wonders of homicide for hours and hours.

That was the day that Paul 2473 definitely decided he was compatible with Carol 7427.   And surely the Tests, scientific as they were, would bear him out.

But the Tests didn't.   He saw the results on a Thursday, as he came back from Exercise.   The enormous poster almost covered the bulletin board, and it read, "Five-Year Mating Assignments for Members of Complex 55."   Confidently he raced down the list.   But it was with horror that he made two discoveries.   Carol 7427 was paired with Richard 3833, and he had drawn Laura 6356.

Laura 6356 for five years!   A simpering, dumpy little thing with mouse-colored hair.   Was she the sort with whom they thought he was compatible?   And Richard 3833, who was to have exclusive possession of Carol for five years, was a beast, a swaggering, arrogant beast.

Paul contemplated his future with indignation.   He was now in the age group to which the Caressing Booths were no longer allowed.   The authorities had found that at this age a worker would be more productive if he had a settled and well-defined social pattern.   Therefore, the Mating Assignment meant that he would be tied exclusively to Laura 6356, while Carol would be just as exclusively the companion of Richard 3833.

He and Carol would scarcely see each other!   There would be no cozy cubicle for them.   No stealthy little discussions after hours about his wonderful book.

The book!!!

It was by no devious, hesitant line of reasoning that Paul 2473 came to a conclusion about committing murder.   It posed itself instantly as the solution to his problem.   His mind traveled briskly through the check list—motives, methods, risks.

Certainly the motive was there.   He was to be mated with an incompatible person, while his compatible person was to be mated with someone else.   As he referred to his handbook for possible variations to remedy this situation, he perceived that a purely emotional murderer might choose to eliminate Carol to prevent Richard's getting her.   But that line of action would not obtain Carol for himself, and it would leave him with Laura.

A double murder was necessary then.   Richard and Laura.   A bit more complicated in the execution, but the only procedure that would guarantee satisfaction.

The details of the method he left for later.   But he did choose a weapon.   Or rather, necessity chose it for him.   He had no gun, nor means of obtaining one. He had no knowledge of poisons, nor access to any.   Richard 3833 was bigger and stronger than he, and Laura 6356 was hardly a frail creature, so strangulation and all such feats of overpowering violence were impossible to him.   But he could get a knife, and he could sharpen it adequately.   And he knew enough physiology to know how a knife should be used against the human body.

Finally, he tried to calculate the risks.   Would they catch him?   And if they did, what would they do to him?

It was then that something really amazing occurred to him.   As far as he knew, there was no crime called murder in the statutes.   If there were, he surely would have been aware of it.   They were lectured often enough on things they should do and things they shouldn't do.   At the head of the list, of course, was treason to the state.   This included such things as sabotage, insurrection, and subversive activities of all sorts.   Below treason on the list were the crimes of sloth, failure to fulfill work quotas, failure to attend meetings, failure to maintain mental and physical health.

And that was it.   Murder wasn't listed, nor any of the other crimes often connected with murder—no fraud, none of the old attempts to gain material wealth by violence.   Paul realized that he lived in an ideal civilization, where there was an absolute minimum of motivation for crime.   Except the one that he had found— when some official made an obvious error in grading the Compatibility Tests.

Now the amazing thing then was simply this.   Without the crime of murder even mentioned in the law books, the state simply possessed no apparatus for dealing with murder.   There was no organization, no experienced detectives, no laboratory scientists trained in sifting clues, none of the things or people that the book had said existed in the old civilization.   With just a little reasonable caution and planning then, the murderer of this new, enlightened age could take the au-thorities completely by surprise, catch them utterly unprepared.   And he could commit his crime in absolute safety!

This realization set Paul's heart to beating fast, and set his mind to scheming. The Mating Assignments would go into effect just as soon as the plan for the shifting of cubicle occupancy could be drawn up.   This would, he knew, take a week. As it turned out, he had plenty of time.   He was ready to begin operations in two days.

His job gave him an initial advantage.   As an air filtration maintenance engineer, he was free to rove throughout the entire area of Complex 55.   No one would question his presence in one place or his absence from another.   All he needed was a work schedule that would take him on a route in the vicinity of first one of his victims and then the other.

Thursday came, and he had to waste a whole afternoon trudging about with the Exercise Platoon.   On Friday, however, luck turned in his favor.   As he glanced at the sheet which listed the air filtration trouble spots he was to visit that morning, he knew the time had come.

He carried his sharp steel blade tucked into his belt under his shirt.   In his soft-soled, non-conductive shoes he padded noiselessly along the antiseptic corridors. His work schedule was tight, but the route was perfect.   He could spare a minute here and there.

He arrived first in the vicinity of Richard 3833.   The latter worked in Virus Chemistry, had his own private corner where he could work more efficiently out of sound and view of his fellows.   Paul found him there, absorbed in peering through a microscope.   "Richard," Paul greeted him softly, "congratulations on your Mating Assignment.   Carol's a fine girl."

There was always a chance, of course—perhaps one in fifty, or a hundred—that a microphone would be eavesdropping or a television screen peeking in on them. But Richard—and Laura too, for that matter—had never caused any trouble.   So they would not be under special surveillance.   And very seldom did the guards monitor anyone during working hours.   The small risk had to be taken.   He would conduct his business as quickly as possible though.

"Thanks," Richard said.   But his mind wasn't on Carol.   "Say, while you're here, take a look at this little beast on this slide."   He climbed off his stool and offered his place to Paul.

Paul took an obliging look, and managed surreptitiously to turn a couple of adjustment knobs while he was doing it.   "I can't see a thing," he said.

Richard patiently went back to re-adjusting the knobs.   His broad back was turned to Paul, all of his attention concentrated on the microscope.

Paul slipped the knife from under his shirt, chose the exact point to aim at, and struck hard.

Richard's reaction was a startled grunt.   His hands clutched at the counter top. Before he sagged, Paul withdrew the blade, then stood and watched as his victim slumped into an inert heap on the floor.   Then very carefully he wiped the bloody knife on Richard's shirt, and left the laboratory immediately afterward.   No one saw him go.

Within four minutes from the time he stabbed Richard 3833, Paul arrived at the Mathematical Calculation Section where Laura 6356 tended one of the huge machines.   As in the case of Richard, Laura worked practically alone, out of contact with the other girls who did similar work on similar machines.   Her only companion was the monster itself, an enormous panel of switches, buttons, dials, and blinking lights of all colors.

Laura saw her visitor out of the corner of her eye, but her fingers continued to type out information for the machine.   She was a very conscientious worker.

"Hello there, Paul," she said with a little giggle.   She had scarcely noticed him before the Mating Assignments came out, but since that time she had grown very feminine.   "Don't tell me our cubicle's ready to move into!"

Did she imagine that he would make a special trip to bring her news like that? He maneuvered to a position behind her and groped under his shirt for the knife.

Possibly she imagined he was going to caress her, despite the fact that such things were strictly forbidden during working hours.   Her chubby shoulders trembled expectantly, awaiting his touch.   He plunged the knife in quickly.

She did not sag to the floor as Richard had done, but instead fell forward over her keyboard.   The machine continued to hum, its lights continued to flash, as Laura's dead weight pressed down upon the keys.

The machine will be giving some inaccurate answers, Paul thought with grim amusement as he withdrew the knife and wiped it on the sleeve of Laura's blouse.

But then as he went away and back to his own work, another, pleasanter thought occupied his mind.   Carol 7427 and Paul 2473 now had no mates.   Surely it would be logical—and the easiest thing to do in view of the compatibility scores— for the Committee to assign these two orphans to the same cubicle.   For five years, subject to renewal, of course.

He had not known what to expect.   He could not predict how the rulers of Complex 55 would react.   The book was an inadequate guide in this respect, since it dealt with the phenomenon of murder in the old civilization.

Murder always had the power to excite interest, the book said.   Especially if the victim was well known, if the method of murder was particularly gruesome, or if there was some sensational, scandalous element involved.   The newspapers featured detailed description of the crime, then followed along as it unraveled, and finally—if the murderer was caught—reported on the trial.   The whole thing could drag on for weeks, months, even years.

But in Complex 55, *The News of Progress* was circulated that afternoon without containing any mention of an unusual happening.   At Recreation that evening, nothing seemed amiss, except that Richard 3833 and Laura 6356 were missing.

Paul saw Carol there, and realized he had not spoken to her since the Mating Assignments were published.   He managed to detach her from her companions, and carefully asked her:

"Where's Richard?"

She shrugged.

"I don't know.   I haven't seen him."

He was overjoyed at her attitude.   Richard was missing and she didn't seem in the least concerned, as if she had never read the Mating Assignments.   Probably she didn't care for him at all.   When this was all straightened out, she'd be quite willing to accept a new arrangement without mourning for Richard.

He stayed with her most of the evening, in a happy, languorous state.   He was even beginning to believe that the authorities, confronted with a new problem outside the realm of their rules and experience, might even decide to hush the matter up, pretend it never happened, in the hope that the rank and file, if kept ignorant of the idea of murder, would never think of indulging in it.

By the time he retired that night, Paul had convinced himself of the soundness of this theory.

Reveille on Saturday morning shattered his illusions.   In fact, he wasn't even certain it was reveille because the high-pitched buzzer seemed to sound louder and more insistent.   And also at an earlier hour.   It was still dark outside his single window.

He climbed into his clothes quickly and joined the others out in the corridor. They were all as startled as he was, very meek, slightly uneasy.

"Forward . . . march!"

They tramped in long files to the end of the corridor, plunged down the iron stairs on the double, emerged into the courtyard where light awaited him.   All the floodlights on the roofs and the high walls had suddenly been turned on.   In their harsh glare platoons and companies formed quickly and stood at stiff attention. There was no talking in the ranks, no complaining at being routed out at this early hour. An atmosphere of fear and foreboding settled over the whole place.

Paul felt it. Even if he had known of no reason to be afraid, the others' fear would have communicated itself to him. Nothing quite like this had ever happened before. Surely nothing pleasant was in store.

What were they going to do? There would be an announcement probably, stating that two people had been killed. And what then? Would they ask the guilty party to identify himself? Or ask if anyone could volunteer any information?

Then quite strangely, he felt calm. If they had brought everybody out here, that meant they didn't know who was responsible, didn't it? That was encouraging. Of course it appeared now that there would be an investigation of some sort. Questions asked. Whereabouts checked. He would have to be careful. But the main thing to remember was that the authorities did not yet know who the murderer was. And if he could keep his wits about him, they need never know.

But there was no announcement from the loudspeakers. The long ranks of silent men were left to contemplate the unknown, to nurse their fears. Perhaps the authorities had planned it this way, to let those fears wreak their psychological mischief for a little while before the questions began.

Half an hour went by, and still the dawn did not appear. Yet no one broke ranks. No one coughed or shuffled his feet. The only sound was the moan of the night wind over the high walls.

What bothered Paul the most was the floodlights. They seemed to be shining directly into his eyes. He could blink against the glare, but he discovered that if he tried to close his eyes for a few seconds, his body had a tendency to sway. He didn't dare call attention to himself by falling down or even by swaying too much. So he tried to endure the glare, tried to think of the pleasant things that would happen when this ordeal was over.

And it had to be over sometime. The whole machinery of Complex 55 with its hundred thousand members could not be halted and disrupted indefinitely because two of those members had been murdered. People were taken off to die every day, and their places were filled with recruits from the Youth Farms. There would be some excitement and tension for a while, but sooner or later things would have to return to normal.

Normal . . . a mating cubicle with Carol . . . somebody to talk to . . . talk to privately . . . an end to the deadly aloneness . . . even with the microphones and the television screens, he knew that mated couples could manage a certain degree of privacy.

"Company Number One! Right face! Forward march!"

A sound of trampling feet, and a hundred men left the courtyard.

By listening to the shouted commands that followed, Paul could estimate where they had gone. To the Recreation Hall adjoining the Dormitory. Whatever was happening to them, whatever processing they were going through, was being done in the Rec. That didn't sound too ominous. If they had marched out the gate, he might have felt more uneasy.

A few more minutes passed. Possibly a quarter of an hour. The lights were becoming unbearable, and there was still no sign of dawn. But Paul was in the second company. Perhaps he could manage. But there were pains shooting up and down his legs. A slight dizziness attacked him momentarily. The floodlights danced before him. He closed his eyes tightly, but they could not be shut out. The dance became weird.

"Company Number Two!"

He marched, fawningly grateful for the exquisite feeling of being able to move again. Yes, they were going to the Rec. Two guards held the doors ajar, and the entire company tramped into the big place.

More lights, but no longer painful. A buzz of human voices pitched low. The company was taken to the far end, then formed in a single file. They were held at attention no longer, but still the men could not relax. Their fears had been worked on too long. They were silent, refusing to speculate among themselves.

Finally, the single file became a queue, and began moving through the small door. Paul was perhaps the twentieth man in line. It seemed to him that the men ahead of him moved through the door at a rate of one every thirty seconds or so. He awaited his turn, still calm, confident that the huge scale of this maneuver indicated desperation and helplessness on the part of the authorities.

Then he saw around the shoulders of the man ahead of him, saw through the door into the room beyond. There was no one and nothing there, but a nurse with a tableful of hypodermic needles beside her.

He could have either laughed or cried with relief. They were only giving shots. Oh, of course, it perhaps meant a plague scare. Or a test of some new serum. Or even a possibility of bacteriological warfare—and they were being given a precautionary antidote. It had nothing at all to do with his two insignificant little murders.

When his turn came for the needle, he endured the small sting with supercilious disdain. After the long ordeal in the courtyard and his occasional uneasy imaginings, this was a small enough price for reassurance.

Yet the effect of the shot was rather strange. There was scarcely any pain in his arm, but there was an odd lightness in his head. Surely, he thought, he wasn't going to faint in this moment of triumph.

But then he lost all awareness of himself as self. He did as a guard told him. He walked into the next room. There a man in a white coat and a very penetrating stare confronted him.

"Did you stab two people to death yesterday?" the man asked.

Somehow there didn't seem to be any choice, but to answer with the truth. Perhaps it had been the shot.

"Yes," he said.

There was a big trial. He was dazed throughout most of it. But it wasn't for his benefit anyway. It was rather for the edification of all the members of Complex 55.

Then afterward they put him in a glass cage at one end of the courtyard. He was strapped there in an upright position.   More than a hundred wires were inserted into various portions of his body, and ran down through the floor and thence out into a control box where there was a button for each wire.   His torturers were the members of Complex 55 themselves, who were expected to display their devotion to civilization by pausing in front of the cage whenever they had a moment and pushing a few of the buttons.   The result was exquisite pain, which made him scream and writhe inside his bonds, but which was never fatal.

Once a day, of course, the loudspeaker reminded him and all the others why he was there.   "Paul 2473," it would intone, "in wantonly and wilfully destroying two pieces of valuable state property, Richard 3833 and Laura 6356, committed sabotage, and is a traitor to the state."

But his miscalculations had not ended there.   One of the most frequent visitors to the cage, and one of the most enthusiastic buttonpushers, was Carol 7427.

PAUL W. FAIRMAN

Panther, Panther in the Night

Inf this final account—the end of the Cozenka story—satisfies you, you're an exceptional person. It didn't come anywhere near satisfying me. But then, I'm a pretty ordinary person. I like things neatly tied up and rounded off at the corners.

And I don't like murder.

Or at least I keep telling myself that I don't. But the fact remains—I'm a writer. I make my dubious living reporting on extraordinary people and places and things. So perhaps I was subconsciously conditioned to stand back and let it all happen.

I hope not, but I can't be sure.

I was even witness to the tragedy in a professional capacity. I'd interviewed Cozenka in New York on her arrival from Africa and had been invited to drop out to "their little hideaway," as she termed it, to look over the animals she'd brought back.

She and Peter Wyndham.

And I certainly had no reason to suspect that I was being invited for any other reason.

I was getting the story for a top magazine and had a liberal expense account, so the trip into the Southwest, halfway across the country, was no problem—merely a pleasant excursion on someone else's money.

Thus, a week later, I was picked up at a lonely whistle stop and driven twenty miles to Ken Bender's place by a chauffeur in a custom-built station wagon, a pith helmet, and what appeared to be the hiking uniform of an African scoutmaster.

Of course, Cozenka is no stranger to you, her picture having appeared in every important magazine and newspaper in the nation, the sultry Eurasian beauty's romance with Ken Bender holding the national spotlight strictly upon its own merits.

A glamour natural; the merging of oriental loveliness with Texas oil millions; east is east and west is west and the twain met head on to make a fool out of Kipling.

There was plenty of post-marriage ammunition too. Cozenka's love of Africa, the safari, and all the noble beasties of jungle and veldt. Ken Bender's apparent acceptance of handsome Peter Wyndham as Cozenka's guide and companion both here and abroad. The money he poured out like water at her slightest whim, turning a portion of his endless lands into an African replica as a sanctuary for the animals she brought back and couldn't bear to part with.

A colorful background with ever-potent possibilities news-wise.

So the three of them were in the papers as often as Khrushchev and that was the situation when the knobby-kneed chauffeur dropped me off in front of Bender's twenty-room lodge.

Bender himself was waiting for me and there was nothing stiff about our meeting because I'd interviewed him several times before and we'd gotten on well together.

A big, shapeless man without veneer or polish; no touch of the sophistication one would expect in the man Cozenka chose as a husband.

He seized my bag and crushed my hand and bellowed, "Marty, you old wrangler! Great to see you. Zenka's down at the sheds with Pete. A sick monkey or something. How about a brandy? And by the way, you've never seen this place before. How do you like it? Great place, isn't it?"

That was Ken Bender; a man who seemed always to be tumbling eagerly forward through life; a study in clumsiness, physical and otherwise. But honest, open, and as friendly as a stray pup.

"Nice of you to let me come," I said. "I'm finishing up a piece on Cozenka's latest trip and I'm out here to check on the deer and the antelope, African style."

"Great," he boomed. "Stay a month. Stay a year. But now, how about that brandy?"

So we had a couple of Texas-sized snifters and then—because it never occurred to Bender that anyone ever got tired—we headed for the sheds.

The trip was a five-minute drive into the heart of the Dark Continent—a million-dollar never-never land carefully recreated out there in the middle of nowhere.

And there were animals to go with it. I saw a pair of sullen water buffalo, a giraffe nibbling its mate's ear way up there in the stratosphere, a rhino in its own private puddle, and a zebra that looked completely bored with the whole impossible business.

Cozenka and Wyndham were not in the monkey house, but in a shed further on where we found them standing very close together in front of a cage that housed a gorgeous black leopard.

Very close indeed, I thought. But Bender took no notice at all and I couldn't help wondering about his blindness. I couldn't help thinking also what the scandal sheets would do with an eyewitness account of this situation.

Not that I'd ever had any dealings with such outfits. I merely wondered about the true relationship between Bender and the woman he'd married.

Nor did Cozenka react from guilt. As we approached, she dazzled us with her famous smile and flowed into Bender's arms and when he kissed her I envied him.

There was something about Cozenka that conjured up visions in a man's mind—in my mind at any rate; thoughts of Javanese dancing girls, ancient temples, orange-robed Buddhist monks, and fragrant tropical nights. Arrestingly attractive, she still symbolized beauty rather than radiated it; a beauty so fragile I was loath to reach for it even with my mind for fear it would shatter like a Ming vase.

Moreover, Cozenka needed no atmospheric background. She could produce this illusion in riding britches, a cocktail gown, or—so I suspected—even an old flour sack.

She turned from Bender's kiss to give me her hand and say, "How wonderful of you to find us way out here, Marty darling. You must stay a long, long time. You know Peter of course."

I knew him mainly as Cozenka's eternal shadow. He was a striking brute of a man who'd proved it wasn't necessary to look like Gregory Peck in order to fill the white hunter role to perfection. He was blond and made the most of it; a shock of carelessly perfect sunbleached hair conspired with bushy, overhanging eyebrows to give him just the correct touch of masculine ruggedness. Yet he would have been at home in a dinner jacket at the Savoy.

He took a bulldog pipe from his mouth just long enough to say, "Payne, old fellow—delighted to see you looking so fit," and put it back again.

I replied in kind and we turned our attention back to Cozenka. She was gripping Bender's arm and staring into the leopard's cage as though hypnotized. "Darling," she said, "if I'd lived in pagan times I'm sure I would have worshipped the cat god. Just look at him crouching there in all his savage black symmetry! What murderous thoughts he must be thinking. How he must hate us!"

Bender smiled, more at Cozenka than at the cat, and said, "I sure wouldn't want to meet him on a dark night with a gun in my—"

"Watch it, Payne! Stand away! Have a care, man!"

The warning came from Wyndham—rapped out sharply—and I jumped as though bee-stung.

"Sorry," he went on. "Didn't mean to frighten you, but those cats are the soul of treachery—that one in particular. A little closer and you could have lost an arm. You certainly could have."

"Sorry," I mumbled, still shaken.

"Not the right kind of cage for his breed. He should really be paneled off with steel netting."

I viewed the beast with new respect. It lay facing us, satiny black except for the white star on the sleek head that rested gracefully between its barbed front paws, looking more classically beautiful than dangerous.

But I saw that Wyndham could well have been right. The animal's eyes, though motionless, were pools of living green flame and I was able to read into them all the hatred and treachery of which Cozenka and Wyndham had spoken.

Cozenka broke the silence with a laugh.

"Come, darlings," she said, "Marty will give us a bad press—bringing him here to be scared to death by our lovely Demon. We must try now to be good hosts and perhaps he will forgive us."

"Right you are," Bender said heartily.

"Quite," Wyndham intoned and put a match to his pipe.

And good hosts they were, with a dinner few cosmopolitan restaurants could have hoped to match; with coffee and brandy on the screened patio later, where Bender—boring and voluble—told of his pre-millionaire struggles; where Wyndham's manner implied he was graciously contributing his presence; and Cozenka, without effort, overshadowed everyone and everything with her electric aura.

It was either a trio that represented rarely achieved compatibility, or a lot of color and personality wasted on the desert air—I couldn't tell which.

But late the following afternoon, a new insight into the picture was furnished by Bender himself.   He and I had ridden out together, Bender acting as guide so that I might get some idea of how much land he owned.

We each had a canteen strapped to our saddles and gradually it dawned on me that Bender's had been filled with brandy, most of it having gone into the big man by the time we started.

I realized this when he began swaying in his saddle and we were drawn down to a walk.   Then he stopped his horse and got off and sat down on a rock and said, "They're going to kill me, Marty old pal.   They're going to kill me as sure as—"

He stopped and rubbed a big hand over his face as I got off my own horse and sat down on the rock beside him.

"I think maybe you've had a little too much sun and brandy," I said.

"Sure, I'm drunk—as drunk as I ever get—but I always keep my head."   He shook it groggily as though to prove it hadn't gone anywhere, and said, "Were you ever in love, Marty?"

"A couple of times.   But I was always too busy to follow it up."

"There's love," he said, "and then again—there's love."

"I don't quite follow you."

"The kind that's a good thing and the kind that's dope, a drug—all the drugs on earth rolled into one.   And when this second kind hits you, you're done, man—finished—all washed up but good."

It was beginning to be a little embarrassing, but I could hardly ride away and leave him there; at least, that was the excuse I gave myself for sitting tight with both ears wide open.   "You were pretty lucky in that particular department," I said.

"You're crazier than a spooked herd."   And there seemed to be more weariness in his voice than drunkenness.   "I got cursed the day I set eyes on her and I've been cursed ever since."

I measured my next question carefully.   On one side, I put the wisdom of minding my own business; on the other, the fact that he'd opened the subject, not I, and I asked, "Is it Wyndham?"

He thought that over, giving the impression of a bewildered man trying to penetrate the logic behind a swarm of flies.   "No.   He's incidental.   It's me—the way I feel about her—because if I didn't feel the way I do, I'd throw him right out and kick him clear back to Africa."

"Exactly how *do* you feel about her?"

"Like I said—she's dope to me.   I want her so bad it makes me sick—so bad I ain't been the same man since I met her.   She's so damned important to me that I'm afraid to open my mouth about Wyndham or that idiotic zoo or traipsing off to Africa or anything else.   Scared for fear she'll walk out on me.   The way it is now I'm willing to settle for whatever little bit of affection she'll give me."

"I'd say that's a pretty dangerous attitude. Aren't you afraid it's just the kind of thing that might kill her love for you altogether? I don't think a woman like Cozenka could care a great deal for a spineless man."

He looked at me in disgust, for being so stupid. "Her love for me? Why, you fool—there isn't any. There never was. She told me that when I chased her all over the world, begging her to marry me. But I was willing to settle for any scraps she was willing to kick my way, so long as she'd give me a chance to make a fool of myself on a permanent basis."

"I don't think that's the situation at all. I think that somehow you've completely lost your perspective. What actual proof do you have that she doesn't love you?"

"Are you blind? Look at me. I know what I am. A big loudmouthed slob— not her kind at all. The only excuse for me being in the same county with her is that I've made a lot of money and Cozenka needs money like she needs God's breath."

I raised a hand in protest. "Now wait a minute—"

But he rushed on. "I know how she looks to you, Marty. The way she looks to all the men she isn't married to—a woman of beauty and warmth—but that's only on the outside. Actually, she takes everything she can get and gives nothing in return."

"Then why don't you face up to what you've got to do. Get her out of your system. Divorce her. Pay her off. You can afford to make it worth her while."

"Sure I can—financially, but that's not how it is. In plain words, I can't. If I sent her away, I'd be on her heels begging her to come back before she'd gone no more than a mile."

So this was the reason for his blindness where Wyndham was concerned. Not blindness at all, but a fear of accusing Cozenka of anything lest she walk out on him.

I could partially understand his position, having been around Cozenka's beauty enough to realize it would be dangerous to fall in love with her. I said, "Look here, Bender. You've got to take hold of yourself. Because one thing is certain, the answer doesn't lie in the direction you're going. In fact, I think you're distorting the whole situation."

He was a man who needed reassurance and he snatched pathetically at what I was offering.

"Do you really think so?"

"It's obvious. Give things a little more time. Then, if you can't see that you're wrong, go away alone somewhere and think it all out. You'll land on your feet, believe me."

"That's a good idea."

"And forget this nonsense about your life being in danger. You're way off base with that kind of thinking."

He jerked suddenly to his feet and said, "Sure—sure. Sorry, Marty—putting my problems on you this way."

I wanted to make him understand that I thought none the less of him for it; that I saw the outburst for what it was, not the maudlin whining of a weak man, but rather, the blowing of a strong man's safety valve. "You needed to get it off your chest," I said.

"We can forget it then?"

"Of course."

He scowled. "Look—if you've got any idea of putting this little talk into the piece you're writing about my wife—"

"Now you know I wouldn't do that."

Again he was abjectly sorry. "Sure you wouldn't. Forget I said that too."

He grinned now. "I really do things up right, don't I? When I sound off, I pick a writer out here for a story—"

"You did nothing of the kind. You picked a friend."

"Thanks, Marty. And now we'd better get back to the lodge. You'll be plenty saddle sore tomorrow, I bet."

We headed back and I was glad he'd blown off. I was sure it had done him some good, especially getting that murder fantasy out of his system.

But it wasn't fantasy at all.

They killed him that night.

They killed him right under my nose.

The evening began pleasantly enough. We had as fine a dinner as the night before and another session on the patio with Bender having sprung back to his old self. The waw he felt about Cozenka was quite obvious.

Cozenka fairly outdid herself as the gracious hostess and showed Bender such marked affection that I felt he had to be wrong in his doubts of her love.

"Darling, shall I change? Shall I look beautiful for you and our guest in an exquisitely beautiful evening gown?"

"You look just fine in that riding outfit, honey, and I know Marty feels the same way about it."

That sort of thing, with Wyndham sitting back—as he had the night before—and generously lending his presence and its continental glamour.

It was Bender who suggested the movie, an hour-long affair that we watched in his den; the color-film record of Cozenka's last trip; a dazzling parade of lions, tigers, zebras, monkeys, and ton after ton of elephant with Cozenka and Wyndham always showing off to good pictorial advantage.

Cozenka tiptoed out before the film ended. The three of us watched it to the finish, then went back to the patio to wait for her.

I visualized her returning in some ravishing Parisian creation and looked forward to it with anticipation. But I was disappointed. When she came back, a little while later, she was still wearing the riding habit.

Then, some ten minutes later, the curtain came up on the heart of the drama.

It was raised by a running man, a man in coveralls, who rushed into the patio breathing heavily, his voice reflecting unrehearsed fear.

"The leopard, Mrs. Bender! The black cat! It got loose! It ain't in its cage!"

Cozenka stiffened and Wyndham sprang to his feet.

She asked, "You mean he's out and running around in the shed?"

"He's running around loose on the grounds—anywhere. I came by on my midnight check and—"

"You went into the shed and baited him!" Cozenka shrilled, and it was the first time I had ever heard her speak in other than throaty, liquid tones. "You disobeyed orders, you stupid, senseless clod!"

"I didn't—"

"You angered him."

"No. No. Why should I?"

"Because you are a fool! You know Mr. Wyndham and I are the only ones who tend him. All others are ordered away. He was quiet as a lamb when we left him at five o'clock."

The man wouldn't be cornered into any damaging admissions. He shook his head stubbornly. "I just did like I always do—opened the shed door and flashed my light—no more. And the first thing I saw was the cage door open. I stayed just long enough to make sure he wasn't anywhere in the shed. Then I ran up here to tell you."

Wyndham's eyes met Cozenka's. "The cat could have broken out," Wyndham said.

"Not unless he was annoyed. This fool—"

"I'm not so sure. We debated putting a heavier lock on the cage—don't you recall? And the upper windows were open. Fifteen feet would have been no problem to Demon."

"This oaf is to blame," Cozenka insisted.

Wyndham turned to the man. "Go around to the kitchen and wait there until you're sent for. We don't want anyone roaming the grounds until something's done."

The man left, obviously hurt by Cozenka's ill-treatment, and Wyndham tried to smooth her down.

"It doesn't really make any difference who's to blame," he said. "We both know what has to be done now. We'd better get at it."

He didn't have to draw her a picture, for her anger flared even higher.

"No! I refuse. I will not see him destroyed—shot down like a common alley cat. He is the royalty of his kind. It would be a sacrilege."

Wyndham's face was grim. "I agree. It's a bloody shame. But better the cat than—"

"Not so fast," Bender cut in. He'd remained silent, leaving decisions to the experts, but as Cozenka's shoulders drooped he put his arms around her and scowled at Wyndham. "Zenka loves that cat. We aren't going to just walk out and kill it simply because you think that—"

"But Peter is right, my love. Demon is a killer. It is his nature to kill. We must think of the helpless human life at stake. We have no other choice."

Wyndham knocked the ashes from his pipe. "You people stay as you are. I'll go out and get a wind on him. It shouldn't take very long to do that."

But Cozenka objected. "Alone? You would leave me here to wait and suffer? Peter, sometimes you have no regard for how—"

"But this is a man's job."

"When have I not done as well as a man? I am as capable as you."

Wyndham shrugged, appealing silently to Bender as the latter said, "You and I will handle it, Pete. Zenka stays here with Marty."

Cozenka brightened as she kissed Bender. "No, you and I, my love. We two—together. We will find our beautiful Demon. Our bullets alone will destroy him."

She appeared to be throwing this as a challenge at Wyndham. The Englishman shrugged again. "Very well. Let's get about it. No telling what deviltry that killer is up to. I'll swing to the west of the sheds. You two take the eastern side. We should turn him up in fairly short order."

So they trekked off into the night with lights and rifles. I stayed behind, happy to agree that my experience with an air gun at the age of ten hardly qualified me for a job Wyndham wouldn't even allow the animal handler to attempt.

I saw them off, three flashlights bobbing in the gloom, and then sat back to wait.

But no finishing shots broke the heavy silence and it grew lonely there on the patio. I waited awhile longer and then got up and went back into the den where we'd left the brandy.

It was more comfortable there—and safer, with four stout walls around me instead of the patio screening. Much safer, until I raised my eyes and looked straight into those of the black leopard.

It had come in the window; the soft thud of its four paws on the thick carpeting and there it was, death in a satiny black skin.

I dropped my brandy and my first thought—when my brain functioned again— was why had the beast sought me out? There must have been others far more conveniently located.

Then a lot of thoughts skittered through my head: disgust with myself for not having had the sense to close the window; resentment at my hosts for not realizing I wouldn't have the sense and had to be reminded; anger at the leopard for looking so incredibly evil as it squatted there obviously understanding my predicament and enjoying it.

There was no chance to reach the door even if I'd had the strength to get up out of my chair. There was nothing in my favor except a faint hope—something I'd heard somewhere—that certain animals ignore you if you remain motionless.

I remained motionless, but the cat did not ignore me. It came up on its four sturdy legs and stretched fore and aft as it contemplated the coming slaughter. It opened its maw and showed me its fine white teeth.

It moved toward me, slowly, gracefully.

Then, as its whiskers practically brushed my paralyzed knees, a suspicion was born in my mind. It was soon quite clear to me that the ape-jawed expression was only a grin, that the menacing rumble in its throat was not a snarl, but a purr.

And immediately the cat verified my dawning doubt as to its ferocity by rolling over on its back to make kittenish passes at me with open paws.

The animal was as tame as a house cat. Lonely out there in the dark, it had seen my open window and come in search of company. It quite obviously wished misfortune to no one.

Reaction drained me of what little strength I had left, and I was on the verge of a nervous giggle as I extended a timid hand of friendship and actually patted the beast's head.

But we were given little time to cement relations because a few moments later a shot sounded somewhere out on the grounds—a sharp report that brought the cat to its feet, and sent it back to the window where it crouched, a black bundle of uneasiness.

Then scream upon scream from the same direction as the gunfire sent the leopard back out the window into the protecting night.

I left also, through the patio, guided by the continuing screams, until I saw a light to the east of the sheds. I ran hard and came finally upon Cozenka crouching over the still body of Ken Bender. They were both within range of a flashlight that lay on the ground nearby, its beam marking the bloody wound in Bender's chest.

It took no medical experience—only common sense—to know that Bender was dead.

Cozenka had stopped screaming. Her face was empty, her eyes stared and she swayed rhythmically back and forth.

"I killed my love. Oh! Oh, God forgive me, I killed him."

I knelt down. "How did it happen?"

She stared at me as though not comprehending. I shook her, rather roughly, by the shoulder. "How did it happen?"

"We were hunting separately. I was not using my light—watching for the glow of Demon's eyes. My darling must have veered over—gotten in front of me. But Demon was here. I swear it—I swear it. I saw the green of his eyes. I was sure he charged me as I fired. But of course it was—"

A pounding of feet cut off her flow of words and Wyndham arrived. He took in the scene like a white hunter should—no panic, no shock. "What's happened here?"

"Cozenka shot Ken. She thought he was Demon. She thought he had green eyes."

If Wyndham found my tone sarcastic, he gave no sign as he turned away to sweep his light in a circle. "The cat isn't here now," he said. "Go to the sheds. Bring a blanket to cover the body and someone to stay with it. Leave him one of the guns. Then you take Cozenka back to the lodge. I've got to keep going until I find that bloody cat."

"It shouldn't be too difficult," I retorted. "Just sit by an open—" But he'd trotted off into the night and I went about obeying orders.

Ten minutes later, leaving a stunned guard with the body, I led the now-silent Cozenka back to the lodge. As we entered the patio, we heard the bark of Wyndham's gun from beyond the lodge. A few minutes later, he returned to find us waiting for him in the den.

He knocked off a stout shot of brandy before saying, "What a mess! What a bloody mess!"

Both Cozenka and I asked the obvious question silently, with our eyes, and Wyndham nodded. "I found him in that brush patch, out away from the house—on the den side. I got in a good, clean shot. He's dead."

Cozenka had recovered somewhat, to just the extent that would be expected after what she'd been through. I paid her unspoken tribute as an actress when she said, "My love is dead. My beautiful, beautiful love."

"Are you referring to your husband, or the cat?" They both looked at me sharply. I wondered suddenly about my own chances of surviving the night, and pondered the wisdom of keeping silent.

But my sense of outrage was too great. "I should have paid more attention to what Ken told me this afternoon," I said.

Wyndham waited.

Cozenka asked, "What did my darling tell you?"

"Your darling said you two were planning to kill him. I think he was indirectly asking me for help, but I was too thick to understand. And by the way, I don't like to seem pickishly technical, but shouldn't someone call the police?"

"I took care of that on the way in," Wyndham said. "The County Sheriff. He comes from Kenton—a small village. A half hour's drive."

"You were speaking of Ken," Cozenka said. "But you're lying, of course. What sort of nonsense are you—"

"I took it for that, but I was wrong. I thought he was a little drunk and emotionally upset. But he obviously knew more than I let him tell me."

At this point, Wyndham won my respect as a cool operator if not as a human being. He sat back, masking the concern he must have felt, listening, saying nothing.

Excitement intensified Cozenka's foreign way of speaking. "Marty, darling— has this terrible tragedy shocked away your reason? What madness in heaven's name is this—what delirium?"

"Stop it. Your whole murder plot went down the drain. The cat that Wyndham was so desperate to shoot just now paid me a visit earlier—just before you shot Ken Bender down in the coldest kind of blood. The cat was lonely. It wanted to be petted and played with. It was as tame as a kitten."

"What utter insanity. If Demon was here, you're fortunate to be alive!"

"Perhaps I am. But I was never in any danger from the cat. The soul of treachery Wyndham spoke of out in the shed lies elsewhere—the cat never possessed it."

Wyndham was still content to let me do the talking, and Cozenka had assumed the role of a cruelly persecuted innocent. "But why, Marty? Why? What motive could I have had? Why would I kill the man who gave me everything?"

"He did give you everything. But all his love and money couldn't change the fact that he was a crashing bore—a big, clumsy, childlike man with only one qualification for your exquisite attentions. He was rich as Croesus. He, in short, had plenty of dough—you know, money. So you were quite willing to take everything he had except the one thing he wanted you most to accept. Himself."

"Marty—please—"

"So you figured out a foolproof way to kill him and have it called an accident. So foolproof it almost worked."

Wyndham had exhibited only one sign of uneasiness. He'd let his pipe go cold.

He took it out of his mouth, now, and said, "Do you plan to tell all this to the sheriff, old man?"

"I do.   That is, unless you feel you can explain away two corpses as easily as one.   There's a rifle standing two feet from your hand."

Wyndham smiled a thin smile.

"Good heavens, no.   In fact with things as they are now, it will be deuced difficult to explain away one."

Cozenka had no doubt been frightened, but she drew courage from Wyndham's refusal to panic.   "Marty, you're being very, very foolish."

"That's right, old fellow," Wyndham added.   "I don't think you'll get very far with the constable—not with that silly yarn."

"I see no reason why he shouldn't be interested."

"Oh, no doubt he will be, but the cat's dead.   And the law likes witnesses to such startling bits of revelation."

He was right, of course.

I began to realize how right, when I talked to the sheriff.   He was a small man with a hat and boots that appeared too large for him.   He came to the lodge in an officially marked station wagon, and the first thing he did after looking at the body was to go to the phone and call the coroner.

He talked to Cozenka privately, then to Wyndham.   I had no opportunity to learn what they'd said, although I was inclined to think they would both stick to their original story.

He questioned me last, in the den, alone also, and I told him the whole miserable story, beginning with Bender's fears and ending with my accusations before he'd arrived.

He listened politely, putting in a question here and there.   Then, when I'd finished, he said, "Those are pretty grave charges, Mr. Payne."

"I'm aware of that."

"And are you aware that you have nothing with which to support any of it?"

"There's my word as a reasonably honest citizen."

He'd spent a great deal of time outdoors and there were skeins of tiny wrinkles at the corners of his clear blue eyes.   These made him appear to be looking into a high wind as he studied me and said, "A newspaperman too."

"I beg your pardon?"

"I said you are a newspaperman."

Not quite that, but I saw no point in explaining the difference.   "What's that got to do with it?" I asked.

"Nothing, maybe.   But you *are* out here looking for a story.   These poor people haven't been left alone ten minutes since they got married.   Writers and newshawks snooping around—snooping in their business—practically peeking in their bedroom windows."

I could have explained also that the publicity they gave her was very important to Cozenka, but the sheriff was too close to antagonism as things now stood.   "I don't see what that's got to do with the case.   I really don't."

"Well, you might find it real easy to exaggerate—make yourself a sensational story. The leopard, for instance. Are you sure it was tame? Are you dead certain you know the difference between a purr and a snarl?"

"If it wasn't tame, why didn't it attack me?"

"Conceding it was there in the first place, I can't say. Maybe it was blinded by the light and didn't see you. Or maybe it was more interested in hiding than in killing someone at that particular time."

"All right. Suppose we concede that it was vicious and I was just lucky. That still puts the cat in the den with me when Cozenka claims she saw it out by the sheds."

The sheriff shook his head. "She didn't tell me that. She said she *thought* she saw it. She's making no claim that it was actually there."

I began to heat up under the collar. "Sheriff, tell me. Are you on their side?"

"I'm not on anybody's side. I'm interested only in the facts. But you don't have to worry about that. You'll get a chance to tell your story at the inquest tomorrow—that is, if you still think it's a good idea."

"Why shouldn't I tell the truth?"

"You should, by all means. But in matters of this kind, the truth has to be supported by a little tangible evidence and I don't think you've got much."

"It seems to be my word against theirs."

"And I'd give a little thought to the libel laws, Mr. Payne. You can be certain Mrs. Bender's legal battery will know all about them. They might take a dim view of unsupported accusations. You could get into serious trouble."

"I'll think it over."

"In the meantime, it's Mrs. Bender's wish this tragedy doesn't leak out—at least until after the inquest tomorrow."

"And you're cooperating with her?"

"Why not? She has a right to privacy. So don't try to use a telephone tonight. If a mob of reporters flood down on us, I'll know who to blame."

I was angry with him even while knowing I had no right to be. Actually, I'd given him nothing to sink his teeth into. The "word of a decent citizen" bit wouldn't hold water in court. I'd suspected that even before talking to the sheriff. But to let those two icy-veined killers get away with it—

I boiled over that for awhile and then remembered what he'd said about the inquest.

Put up or shut up.

He was right. If I went ahead with my accusations, I could get myself into a serious jam.

I retired to my room before the coroner arrived and no one bothered me any more that night. Only my conscience, as I pondered the advisability of keeping my mouth shut.

Ken Bender, a fine man who hadn't deserved it, had been murdered by two calculating killers. I knew it. Yet there was absolutely nothing I could do.

Nothing except pace the floor all night thinking about the old chestnut—*there is no perfect plan for murder*. The killer always makes a small mistake—one that gets him convicted and hung.

But where was the mistake here?   This one was so good, they could get away with it even when luck turned against them.   Certainly it was only their bad luck that had sent that black cat into the den.

And yet their plan hadn't been seriously damaged.

I knew now the reason for Wyndham's almost casual attitude when I'd accused them.   A much faster thinker than I was, he knew instantly that things would work out as they'd planned.

Of course, he hadn't threatened my life.   There was no need for him to.

And I realized that the perfect murder was not only a possibility, but a fact. The fallacy in the old saying was that the perfect ones were never uncovered.

Fuming and fretting, I finally got to sleep—so late I didn't wake up until ten the next morning.   I showered and shaved and went downstairs to find the sheriff alone in the dining room with a cup of coffee and a notebook.

He was neither friendly nor hostile as he looked up.   Simply impersonal.

"Good morning, Mr. Payne.   Sleep well?"

"Not very, but that's beside the point.   Do you still think the death of Ken Bender was nothing more than an accident?"

"Nothing's happened to change my mind."

"By the way, I didn't get your name last night.   You do have a name, don't you?"

"Henderson—Milt Henderson."

His answer was annoyingly mild, and I was fully aware that I was deliberately trying to irritate him—using him as a target for my own frustrations.

And the keen-eyed little lawman sensed the same thing because he said, "I don't want you to misunderstand what I said last night, Mr. Payne."

"Misunderstand?   Why should you care one way or the other?"

"For two reasons.   I do my job and I don't want anyone to think otherwise."

"And the other?"

"This case is going to cause a national stir when it breaks.   As a reporter on the scene, your copy will be in demand and you could easily make me the goat. You could make it look like I covered up for Mrs. Bender—that her money and position made me tip my hat and say yes, ma'am, and no, ma'am.   Do you see?"

"And that isn't true?"

He scowled for the first time since I'd known him.   "You're damned right it isn't.   Mrs. Bender and Wyndham get no more from me than any other resident of my county.   You know yourself you've got nothing that will stand up.   So go find something that will hold up in court, Mr. Payne.   You do that and I'll back you to the limit.   But don't expect me to accuse people of murder when it isn't proved."

He was right, of course, and maybe what he said was just what I needed.   At any rate, it started me thinking along positive lines instead of sitting around feeling sorry for myself because nobody would believe me.

Not that it reaped any immediate harvest.   With Sheriff Henderson's parting instructions to be on hand for the inquest that had been scheduled for two o'clock, I wandered out toward the sheds trying to figure out a way to back my story with some proof the law would recognize as such.

There had to be a hole in their scheme somewhere.

I think now my anger was centered mainly around having been played for a fool. Cozenka's invitation, putting me on the scene at the time of the murder, had not been coincidental.   I'd been carefully chosen as an amiable, not-too-bright slob who would automatically back up their play and give it the prestige of a witness whose copy appeared nationally in top magazines.   An accessory, in essence, to bolster the vicious plot with blindly sympathetic testimony after the fact.

This made me mad.   Together with the sheriff's prodding, it forced my mind to labor mightily and bring forth a hunch, one that sent me rushing back to the lodge and up to Cozenka's room.

She answered my knock, incredibly beautiful in a black lace gown.   She'd done something to her eyes to make them appear red from weeping, and the sight of her—even with what I knew—was a strain on my determination.   Could this sorrowing creature be anything but a grieving wife?   I had to bring in a quick image of her as she must have looked with her rifle aimed at Bender's chest.

"You have come to apologize, Marty dear?   Then I will accept your sorrow. I will forgive you.   Do come in."

I went in and found Wyndham sitting on the edge of the window seat with a scotch in his hand.   The streaming sun turned his blond thatch into a halo.   He looked like a good friend for one to have in time of grief.

He said, "Hello, Payne," and then knocked off the rest of his drink.

With what I had in mind, I didn't want their antagonism.   All I wanted was a little time alone in Cozenka's room.   Not that I was sure I would find what I hoped to, but it was the logical place to look and the sooner the better.

So I smiled engagingly at Wyndham and patted Cozenka's hand.   "I guess I was a little cruel last night, but Ken was my friend.   Perhaps we can—"

Wyndham, pipe in hand, suddenly turned grimly serious, the first hint of hostility that he'd shown.   "I'm afraid it isn't quite as simple as that, Payne."

"I don't understand."

"Good lord, man!   You aren't so stupid as to believe you can throw vicious charges all around the place and walk off scot-free, are you?"

"But we were all upset last night.   I—"

"You called us murderers to our face.   You also gave the same ridiculous story to the sheriff.   That means it will get around.   Your ugly accusations are no doubt on every tongue in the place right this minute.   Do you think we can just stand by under such circumstances?"

"What do you plan to do?"

"Drag you into court.   Sue you to the limit.   Any other course would indicate fear of your charges on our part.   Therefore, in countering, we must strike deep, so the magazine you're representing must also be named as a defendant."

Wyndham took a baleful puff on his bulldog.

"I wouldn't be surprised if when we get through with you, you'll not only be a pauper, but you'll be blackballed in every editorial office in the country."

Obviously, Wyndham had considered all aspects and decided they had nothing to fear from me.   That made his sudden turn to the offensive entirely logical.   An attack of the sort he'd outlined would block me off permanently from gaining any official sympathy.   I would become a persecutor of upstanding manhood and the defamer of a woman crushed by tragedy.

I wondered who the executive of this team was—Wyndham or Cozenka?   The turnabout could have been advocated by either of them.   I turned to Cozenka.

"Do you really think I deserve this?"

She chose to pout.   "But, Marty darling, you said cruel things to Pete and me. We have our good names to think of.   And the world must know how deeply I loved the man I married."

"I think I know.   And there's something else.   I think you loved Demon.   I think you truly grieved for the animal when he had to be sacrificed."

"I did love him because I love beauty.   And Ken loved him too.   I loved Demon, yet I did not flinch from turning my rifle on him to save human life."

"And the fact that you hit Ken only added to your grief."

"Marty—you are so cruelly sarcastic."

She was right.   I was doing a bum job of placating them and I knew I had to get out of the room or there would be fists flying.   "I'm sorry it sounds that way."

"You are cruel—cruel—"

Then my clumsy approach worked inadvertently in my favor and Cozenka flared into sudden resentment.   "We were waiting here for a visit from Mr. Henderson. He has been so kind—so thoughtful.   But we will not wait.   We will go to him. I cannot stand your presence a moment longer."

"She's telling you to get out, Payne.   That should be clear, even to you."

I got out, hoping Cozenka meant what she said about going to the sheriff.   I was in trouble—with only the slimmest chance of clearing myself, and very little time left for even that.

I went back to my own room at the end of the hall where I could watch Cozenka's door through the keyhole.   And a few moments later, she and Wyndham emerged and went downstairs.

The moment they vanished, I was out of my own room.   And before they reached the bottom of the stairs, I was snooping through Cozenka's personal belongings like any other common sneak thief.   I didn't enjoy it.

It was a big room and there was a lot to go through and I spent the most uncomfortable fifteen minutes of my life.   I heard them back at the door every time I opened a fresh closet, but I kept right on, reconciled to being caught in the midst of things if it should happen that way.

They didn't return and I found what I was looking for—or hoped I had.   There was no way of really telling.   I didn't have enough time, because my discovery, like the hunch it had sprung from, came too late to give an opportunity for complete investigation. I could only sneak out of the bedroom and trot downstairs with my find in my pocket—before they came hunting for me—to attend the inquest.

I only had time enough to say a small prayer and hope I had what I needed to trip up Cozenka, Wyndham and Company.

There were six men on the coroner's jury—all recruited on the premises from among the help—the coroner himself being a Doctor Wendell whom—I later learned—hadn't even told his wife what had happened there at the Bender lodge.

Such was the prestige and power of Bender's millions. The same millions, I thought nervously, that might soon be turned like cannon in my direction.

Doctor Wendell was a man in his sixties, quietly efficient, with something of a judicial bearing. He was admirably suited to the job of presiding. He'd obviously been briefed by the sheriff as to my contribution to the general confusion, because he regarded me with marked interest as I entered and took my seat.

But there was no over-leaping of routine procedure. He questioned Cozenka first, and she did very well, so well that every man in the room wanted to come forward and comfort her personally. Not that they were callous and unmindful of Bender's tragic taking off, but he was dead and absent and Cozenka was very much alive and present.

And she was Cozenka.

Wyndham came next and he also handled himself beautifully. They both stuck to the story as it was originally laid out in their plan. Cozenka tearfully admitted her carelessness in acting hastily—admitted it most convincingly—and they lied with sincerity about the exceptional viciousness of the cat, giving justification to Cozenka's nervousness and fatal mistake.

In short, they stuck to their story right down the line.

Then the slightest of chinks appeared in their armor, the first one since Cozenka's shot had rung out the night before. This when Wyndham leaned casually forward and placed his lips close to my ear.

He said, "A deal, old man. You can only hurt yourself with that fool yarn about a tame cat, so let's call it a stalemate. Forget the nonsense and I'll forget what I said upstairs. No point in our flailing each other."

"You're scared," I whispered.

"Not scared. Just sensible. And you should follow suit, because you know damned well that if you open your mouth I'll crucify you."

With that cheerful reminder, I was called to the stand.

Doctor Wendell, possibly from a keen sense of the dramatic, worked backwards in his questioning. He started with my hearing the shot and the screams and running out to investigate. I verified everything Wyndham and Cozenka and the watchman had told him of the actual tragedy, a girl—recruited from the late Mr. Bender's small office force—taking down every word meticulously. Then Doctor Wendell jumped clear over to the arrival of the sheriff and the removal of the body.

After that, he fired a question that was the business, the showdown. "I understand that shortly after Mr. and Mrs. Bender and Mr. Wyndham left the lodge to hunt down the leopard, you had an extraordinary experience.   I'd like to hear about it.''

This was my last chance to back down.

And I won't deny that I was frightened for my career and future as I agreed with Doctor Wendell that it had been most extraordinary and gave it out, for the record, exactly as it had happened.

There was a time of silence after I'd finished, probably longer to me than anyone else.   I used the time to steal glances at Cozenka and Wyndham.   Cozenka was crying softly into her handkerchief, crying in a way that made the coroner's jury hate me and my story—I was sure of that.

Wyndham took it with perfect aplomb, tamping tobacco into his pipe as though he had been indirectly accused of nothing more than swatting a troublesome fly.

Finally Doctor Wendell spoke.   ''Mr. Payne, do you have any proof whatever, other than your unsupported word, that the incident in the den, the coming and going of the leopard, actually occurred?''

''I hope so, but at the moment I can't be sure.''

''That's a pretty ambiguous statement.''

''I realize that, but it's all I can tell you at the moment.''

''When do you expect to be able to tell us more?''

''When we run this off and see what's on it,'' I said, and took from my pocket the reel of sixteen-millimeter film I'd found on a shelf in one of Cozenka's closets.

''You don't know what's on it?''

''No.   I haven't had time to check.''

''How did you happen to come into possession of this film?''

''As a result of what I hope will turn out to be logical thinking on my part. From observation, I believed that Mrs. Bender entertained a definite affection for the black leopard named Demon, that she was sincerely sad when the cat had to be sacrificed as a part of her plan.

''So it seemed strange to me that the leopard did not appear anywhere in the hour-long film covering her last trip to Africa.   I viewed the film last night, and saw enough to convince me that Mrs. Bender considered motion pictures of her activities over there and the animals she captured as being very important.

''So why no pictures of the animal she obviously regarded more highly than any of the others?

''From that point I proceeded on the belief that such films or stills actually existed and went about hunting for them.   This is what I found and only viewing them will prove me right or wrong.''

But I knew I was right.   Cozenka went pale as death and while Wyndham didn't jump up and break any windows, he tightened up in a manner that was almost the equivalent for a man of his self-control.

Cozenka did spring to her feet.

''No!   No!   He is wrong.   He is deliberately torturing me.   That film is most personal.   I beg you not to run it off.   You have no right to shame me!''

She was making a desperate all-out effort and Doctor Wendell was most polite in his ruling.   ''I'm very sorry, Mrs. Bender, but this is an investigation into a man's death and as such takes precedence over any personal feelings. Grave charges have been raised. Is there a film projector available?''

It was all there: highlights in the taming of a black leopard named Demon; shots mainly of Wyndham and the cat that could probably have been used in a course of instruction on how to take the viciousness out of jungle cats; a record from the time Wyndham first entered Demon's cage, somewhere in Africa, to the high point where Cozenka frolicked with the happy and gentle beast on the sylvan meadow.

There was a sound track, too, and during the final sequence I couldn't resist turning to Sheriff Henderson to say, "I think you will agree, Sheriff, that the cat is purring, not snarling.''

I was instantly regretful. After all, Henderson hadn't been against me. He'd only been doing a difficult job as well as he could.

The verdict said nothing about accidental death. It merely stated that Kenneth Bender had died of a gunshot wound under circumstances that warranted further investigation, and it enjoined Sheriff Henderson to continue with that investigation.

I wish I could report that the film did the trick—confounded two vicious murderers and that full payment was demanded.

But I can't. That wasn't how it finally worked out.

I left the lodge, of course, but I stayed on a few days in the sheriff's town. Some disturbing rumors made me seek him out.

He was busy in his office and so I got right to the point. "What's this I hear about charges being dropped against Mrs. Bender and Wyndham?"

"Nothing was dropped. Charges were never made. The grand jury, upon advice of the County Attorney, refused to indict.''

"And how did that gross miscarriage of justice come about?"

"Through orderly, logical thinking.''

I was thoroughly disgusted.

"Then we'd better have more disorderly and illogical thinking. It's an outrage.''

"I can understand your point of view,'' Henderson said, "but let's look at facts as they really are.''

"I've looked at them.''

"But you haven't seen them as they are. What was there, really, that would have a chance of getting a guilty verdict from twelve jurors?"

"Proof that their vicious cat was as tame as a kitten.''

"Sure, but that isn't proof. It's merely a point for argument in court. Bender and Wyndham would have had a battery of the country's finest defense attorneys, but even a mediocre one would have thrown doubt upon whether a black leopard, regardless of the evidence, is ever really tame.

"And their reason for hiding the fact could have been any of several that would have nothing to do with murder. Mrs. Bender could admit not being the hunter she claimed to be; that she wanted the prestige of owning a vicious cat without the danger.''

He stopped to light a cigarette and then added, "Do you see my logic?"

"I'm beginning to.''

"And your story about Bender's fear of death probably wouldn't even be admitted as evidence."

"I see."

"And one last point. Would you care to go before a jury made up principally of men and try to get Cozenka Bender convicted on the evidence we have?"

I thought it over for a moment. "No, but just the same they're both guilty."

"I think you're right," he agreed. "And now, how about a drink? I'll buy."

Perhaps there is some consolation in the fact that Cozenka and Wyndham gained nothing but tragedy from the tragedy they instigated. So it seemed.

They were both dead within six months after Cozenka fired her fatal bullet.

Wyndham, in Africa where he was pounded into the mud by a water buffalo after he missed a hundred-foot shot and had no time for a second.

He went back there, alone, two months after Bender's death. And three months later, Cozenka was killed when her sports car rocketed off the road one dark night.

It would be nice to think that she did away with herself because she couldn't face the guilt of her crime. But if her death was other than an accident, it was probably because Wyndham refused to step into Bender's shoes, and she realized that his clinging to her had been for the money she no doubt settled on him, not for love of her.

I think she truly loved Wyndham; ironically, in the same hopeless way Bender had loved her. And perhaps realization that Wyndham was the one man in this world that she couldn't have was sufficient grounds for suicide.

Then too, there's another possibility. Could I have been wrong from the beginning?

As Sheriff Henderson said, my conversation with Bender probably wouldn't have been allowed in court, and there were many reasons why Cozenka could have covered the true situation relative to Demon.

One thing is certain. Even though I was sure of their guilt, I wouldn't have wanted to pull the switch personally on either of them. Not on the evidence that I actually had.

So, in the final summing up, I was sure of only one thing.

The cat was tame.

E. X. FERRARS

Perfectly Timed Plot

Rina Evitt's eyes were stretched wide with fear. Staring across the room at her husband, they were not quite focused.

"It'll never work," she said shrilly. "Never."

"It'll have to." Harry Evitt's voice was as empty of feeling as hers was charged with it. His nervousness was in his feet. With one heel, he was trying to kick a hole in the costly gray rug before the fire. "Yes, it'll have to," he said without excitement, without doubt, without eagerness.

Rina dropped her head into her hands. Her hair tumbled over them as her fingers clawed her bursting temples. She had thick, bleached hair, with a sheen that was bright but lifeless. Her face was long, with slackly handsome features and big, wide-spaced eyes.

"I'll make a mess of it—there isn't time—there's too much to remember."

Knowing what she could do when she tried, her husband was not much troubled.

"You'll remember, all right," he said. "It's just the timing that matters. The rest's easy. But make sure you get the timing right."

He shifted his weight from one foot to the other, dug the back of one heel into a new patch of the rug and gave a fierce twist to his foot.

"You've got to be sure the others leave on time," he said. "And you've got to be sure you get Minnie out into the drive with them, to see them off, so that you can come back in here and change the clock and make that telephone call without her knowing. And you've got to time that exactly. But the rest of it's easy."

Rina jerked her head up, staring at him again.

He was a man of middle height, softly covered in flesh, dressed in a dark gray suit, a white shirt, a dark blue tie, all good, all inconspicuous. He had a round, white face, moulded into insignificant features, and had thinning dark hair brushed back from a low curved forehead.

With her eyes on that calm, dull face, Rina said, "You haven't just thought of all this, Harry—not just today. You've had it ready for a long time, in case George ever found out about the money. You have, haven't you?"

"All right, I've had it ready," Evitt said. "And a good thing I did, I'd say."

"You've had it all ready, yet you never told me . . ."

"You know that's what I'm like," he said.   "You ought to be used to it by now."

She swayed her head from side to side, not quite shaking it, not quite nodding. Crouched in her chair, shrunk into herself, she looked small, helpless and harmless. In fact, she was a tall woman, thin, but big-boned and strong.   But her apprehension had dwarfed her.

"I'm not used to it," she said, "I never shall be."

Evitt's pale pink lips twitched at the corners in a faint expression of satisfaction. But life never remained long in his face.

"Remember—get them all out into the drive," he said, coaching her again with patience, with understanding, but with relentlessness.   "Then run in and change the clock and make the telephone call.   Make sure Minnie stays outside long enough for you to do that.   Get her worrying about the roses.   Or fertilizers. Anything.   You can handle her."

"But the other part of it," Rina said, "suppose *that* doesn't work. Suppose—"

"It will."

"No, it's too difficult.   It's too complicated.   There are too many things to go wrong."   Her voice had leapt again into shrillness.

After a short silence, Evitt answered evenly.   "All right then, what do we do instead?"

When she did not answer, he said, "Go and get changed now, Rina.   Put on your green dress.   Get the room ready.   There isn't much time to spare."

She looked round dazedly.   "The room's all right, isn't it?   Just as usual."

"The room's fine."   His pride in the room escaped into his voice for a moment.

It was a room of which they were both proud.   The floor was of mahogany woodblocks.   The picture window showed them a sweep of lawn, some early daffodils blooming in rough grass under bare trees, distant roofs and still more distant hills, the tranquil English countryside.   The antique furniture had been bought after careful study of the best magazines.   There was central heating.

"The tea's all ready," Rina added.   "I've just got to get out the bridgetable and the cards."

"Get them out then," Evitt said.   "Keep busy.   Don't sit and think.   It won't help you."

"And you . . . ?"

He walked over to her.   He put his hands under her elbows and with slow deliberation hauled her up out of her chair.

"Don't think about me either, my dear."

She was slightly the taller of them, even without her high heels.   Face to face with him now, she could look over his head to the window, to the cluster of leafless trees and the gray-green line of the low hills beyond them.

"You can do it, Rina," he said, his hands tight on her arms.   "I am certain of it."

"I suppose I can do it," she said.   "But I don't like it."

"Do you think I like it?"

He did not like it. He was terrified of what he had to do and of what might result from it for himself and for Rina. He was a calculating rather than a violent man. But calculations can go very easily wrong, and then what is there left but violence?

Rina's bridge-party broke up at six o'clock. It always did. Two of the four women who met every Wednesday to play had to catch a bus home from the end of the road at ten minutes past six. So when the hands of the grandfather clock in the corner pointed to ten minutes to six, the losers groped in their handbags, paid out shillings and pence to the winners, re-hashed the blunders and disasters of the last rubber and made peace with each other. It was a scene which repeated itself week after week.

"Not my lucky afternoon," Minnie Hobday said in a tone of unusual heaviness. She smoothed back one of her straying locks of gray hair, but left several others, disturbed by the high wind of play, to droop around her square, mild face and support its gentle, sheepdog quality. "I'm getting too old for this game."

Rina, sitting on her left, scribbling on a scoring-pad before her, tapped Minnie on the wrist with her pencil, a gesture that Rina seemed to be fond of. The pencil was of emerald green, tipped with gilt, and matched the emerald green woolen dress and the heavy gold bracelet of intricate design that she was wearing.

"It isn't age that's the trouble," she said, smiling. "You've got something on your mind, Minnie. Isn't that so?"

"No, it's age," Minnie Hobday said insistently. "I never had much of a memory for cards, and soon I suppose, in just a few years, I shan't have any at all."

The truth was, however, that she had a great deal on her mind, that she was very worried, because for the last three days her husband George had barely spoken to her, and today he had gone to London without telling her the reason, all of which was decidedly quite unlike him.

But even if Minnie had reached the stage of wanting to confide in someone the terrible suspicion that had been torturing her all day, the suspicion that George was not well, that he had symptoms so fearful that he had not been able to bring himself to tell her about them, but had gone off alone to London to consult a specialist, it would never have occurred to her to confide in Rina Evitt. Though the two women had never had a quarrel, and during the five years since Rina's marriage to George's partner in the firm of Hobday and Hobday, auctioneers and estate agents, had made a habit of these weekly bridge afternoons, and of performing all sorts of small neighborly acts for one another, Minnie had never even begun to grow intimate with the younger woman.

She was sorry for this. It would have been far better for all of them if she and Rina had been able to become as friendly as George was with Harry. But Rina, so Minnie, blaming herself, explained it, was young, was smart, had travelled, and apparently, in other places, had known really interesting people. So she could hardly be expected, could she, to be anything but bored by Minnie Hobday?

Minnie had always been aware of the boredom in Rina, of the emptiness, of the need for something more than she had. And it was Minnie's belief that it would always be for more and more.   Whatever Rina had would never be enough.   Still, it had been clever of Rina to realize that she had something on her mind.   Ordinarily, she seemed so wrapped up in herself, so like a child in a daydream, that you would no more expect her to notice a shade of worry on an elderly face than, come to think of it, you would expect her, all of a sudden, to be interested in the names of two undistinguished shrubs, growing near the gate, and which had been growing there for years.

So perhaps something was happening in Rina, some change, some development. That would be nice, Minnie thought, walking out to the gate with the other two women, and identifying the shrubs as a laurustinus and a hypericum uralum.   But turning to Rina to tell her this, Minnie found that she had just turned back into the house, and this surprised her somewhat.

Minnie did not leave then, for George had said that he would call for her on his way home from the station, and Rina was expecting her to wait for him.   Returning to the house, Minnie found Rina setting a tray with a decanter and four glasses on it on the low, tile-topped coffee-table.

"I didn't see why we should wait for the men," Rina said.   "A drink is what you need to cheer you up a bit.   I suppose it's Michael you're worrying about, but you shouldn't, you know.   He's all right, that boy.   I'm fond of him."

Michael was the Hobdays' son, and because of a certain carelessness that he had sometimes shown in the handling of a fast car, he had more than once given his parents cause to worry about him.   But recently he had been almost sensible.

"No, I'm not worried about Michael," Minnie said.   "Really, I'm not worried about anything."   She took the glass that Rina held out to her and glanced at the clock.   George should be here at any moment, she thought; the suspense of the long day, thank heavens, would soon be over.

However, it was not as late as she had thought that it must be, or so she believed until, a minute or two later, she happened to glance at her watch.

In surprise, she exclaimed, "That clock's wrong, Rina!"

"Not *that* clock," Rina said emphatically.

"It is, it's ten minutes slow," Minnie said.   "George ought to be here."

Rina shook her head.   There was a smile in her wide-spaced candid eyes.   "It's the most reliable thing on earth, Minnie, and so it should be, considering what care Harry takes of it—and what he paid for it."

"But this watch of mine is quite reliable too.   I've had it for twenty-two years, and I never had to adjust it more than about two minutes in a month."   Because of her worry, Minnie sounded querulous.   "It's a very good watch.   And the thing is, it always has been."

Rina turned to the fire.   She stirred the smoldering logs with the toe of her shoe. Her pale hair, swinging forward, hid her face and its tense expression.

"Perhaps it needs cleaning," she said.

"I had it cleaned two months ago.   No, I'm sure it's the clock that's wrong. George ought to be here . . ."   The sound of strain in her voice checked Minnie.

"All right," Rina said equably.   "I'll tell Harry.   But talking of Michael, he's a crazy thing, but really so nice.   Everyone thinks so.   And even if he and George do cross one another, at times, you shouldn't make up your mind it's all Michael's fault."

Frowning vaguely, Minnie wondered why Rina kept dragging Michael in.   "I don't know what you mean about him and George crossing one another," she said. "They're ever such good friends nowadays.   Of course, Michael went through a difficult time.   All boys do."   She stopped, because she thought that she had heard footsteps outside on the gravel.

Rina had heard them too.   "There's Harry," she said.

"Or George."   Relying on her watch rather than on the Evitts' clock, Minnie believed that her husband's train must have reached the station about ten minutes ago, and she knew that by the short cut across the fields, he needed only five minutes to reach the Evitts' house.

"Yes—or George," Rina said, and with long strides went quickly out of the room.

Nervous and impatient, thinking of the dire news that George might be bringing her, Minnie made one of her random selections of an untidy lock of hair and smoothed it back from her forehead.   At the same time she did her best to arrange a placid smile on her face.   But it was Harry Evitt, not George, who received the smile.

"Ah, Minnie!" he said with pleasure.

"Good evening, Harry," she said.   "You haven't seen George, I suppose?   He was going to call in for me."

Evitt looked at the clock.

"Wasn't he coming on the six-twenty?   That's only just due now."

"But that clock's slow," Minnie said.   "It's half past six."

"*That* clock isn't slow," Evitt said, almost as Rina had said before him.

In a shriller voice, as if it mattered which was wrong, the Evitts' clock or her watch, Minnie said, "Well, by my watch it's half past six already.   George ought to be here.   He said he was going to come straight here and not go to the office."

The Evitts exchanged puzzled glances.

"Well, let's check it on the telephone," Harry Evitt said.   "You may be quite right, Minnie.   If you are, I expect it's just that the train's late, but if you like, I'll walk to the station and just make sure . . . make sure . . ."   He stopped, as if he were uncertain of precisely what, in the circumstances, he ought to make sure.

Rina had already gone to the telephone.   She picked it up, spoke into it and put it down again.

"The operator says it's six-twenty-one by the clock in the exchange," she said, and picking up the glass of sherry that she had left behind when she had gone out to meet her husband, she drank it down and began to choke.

Evitt hit her between the shoulders.   The sound his hand made, striking her, was surprisingly loud and hollow-sounding.

Wiping moisture from her eyes, Rina said hoarsely, "It's really Michael Minnie's worried about.   That row they had."

"That was nothing," Evitt said.   "Nothing at all.   Have some more sherry, Minnie.   George'll soon be here."

But even an hour later, George had not as yet arrived at the Evitts' house.

The Evitts said that he must be coming on a later train.   Minnie agreed with them, and decided not to wait for him any longer.   Evitt saw her down the short lane to her home.   He went with her as far as her gate, then walked off into the darkness, while Minnie walked up the path to the door, a door set in a jutting Victorian porch, that opened into a roomy but drably papered hall, across which an electric clock faced her, noisily whirring.   Comparing her watch with the clock, she saw that her watch was fast, but only by three minutes.

That was at seven-forty.

At seven-fifty-five the police arrived.   George had not come home by a later train.   He had returned from London, as he had said that he would, on the six-twenty, the ticket-collector quite clearly remembering his handing in his ticket. Then George had started to walk across the fields, directly to the Evitts' house.

At the time when his body was discovered, under a hedge and with his head battered in, he had been dead for at least an hour.

Detective Inspector Ronald Tewson was very interested in Minnie's watch.   Had she or had she not re-set it at the Evitts' when she found that it and their clock did not agree?   But Minnie by then was not in a state to give him an answer on which he could place much reliance.

In grief, at first, she had maintained a dreadful, vacant composure.   She had told the police all that she could, but had grown quietly more dazed and incoherent, till her son Michael, a tall boy of nineteen, who had been summoned home from a cinema, had led her upstairs to her room and the doctor had given her an injection that made it possible for her to rest.

As he watched her go, not losing her gentle restraint, but only her mind, Tewson, who could almost deceive himself that he could take murder in his stride, felt something in himself that he dreaded, the sense of pressure, caused, as he knew, by extreme anger.   For this, he was certain already, was a cold-blooded crime, and of all kinds of crime, that was the kind that made his own blood hottest.   But with that anger in him, he always wore himself out, suffered more than was useful to anyone, and jumped to unwarranted conclusions.   The unwarranted conclusion to which he jumped before that night's work was over was that George Hobday had been murdered by his partner, Harry Evitt.   All that funny business about the clock and the telephone call to the exchange . . .   It was too convenient.   But Tewson was not going to have anyone else saying anything of that sort yet.

"We haven't a thing against Evitt at the moment," he said dourly to Sergeant James Geary, at one o'clock in the morning, as the two men gulped tea in Tewson's office.   "That's the fact.   Not a solid thing except that Mrs. Hobday doesn't think she reset her watch before she got home.   Doesn't *think* so!"   He shook his head despairingly.   "A solid fact, d'you call that?"

Geary was a younger, heartier man than Tewson.

"Look," he said, "it's the telephone call that's the only trouble, isn't it?   The fact that they've confirmed it at the exchange that Mrs. Evitt did ring up and ask the time at six-twenty-one—which made the Evitts' clock right and Mrs. Hobday's watch wrong, and put Evitt right here in the room with Mrs. Hobday when Hobday's train got in, and for an hour afterwards.   That's all that worrying you, isn't it?''

Tewson nodded his head, in furious parody of a definite nod of agreement.

''Of course a little thing like motive doesn't worry me,'' he said, his lips drawn back in a tight, ugly smile.

''You'll find that in the books of the company, I shouldn't wonder,'' Geary said. ''There's been talk around for some time, about where Evitt was getting his money from.   When you've talked to that accountant Hobday went to see in London . . .''

''Go on and teach me my job,'' Tewson said.   ''It's that telephone call you're going to put me right on, isn't it?''

''There were two telephone calls,'' Geary said.

''That's right,'' Tewson said, ''there probably were.   One to the exchange and one to nowhere, and the one Mrs. Hobday heard was the one to nowhere.   It could have been like that.   Only if it was, I don't like it.''

Geary was disappointed that his thinking had already been done for him.

''Why not?'' he asked.   ''It's nice and simple.''

''Simple!'' Tewson said, as if the mere sound of the word made him ill.

''Look,'' Geary said, ''they arrive for the bridge-party—Mrs. Hobday and the two other women—and they play for a couple of hours.   All three have got watches, but not one of them says anything then about the clock being slow.   And the party breaks up at the usual time, because two of them have to catch a bus.   And they all go out in the garden together to see the two ladies off, and Mrs. Hobday also goes to look at some shrubs, because Mrs. Evitt suddenly got interested in knowing what they are.   But for some reason, instead of going with Mrs. Hobday to look at the shrubs, Mrs. Evitt doubles back into the house, and when Mrs. Hobday follows her, she's setting out drinks in the living room.   But by then Mrs. Evitt had three or four minutes to herself, and that would be plenty to ring up the exchange, get told that the time was six-twenty-one, then put the hands of the clock back to six-ten.   Well then, presently Evitt comes in.   It's really six-thirty, and he's met Hobday at the station, started across the fields with him, done him in and gone on home.   But the clock says it's only six-twenty, and when Mrs. Hobday says the clock's wrong, they make a fake call to the exchange which convinces the old lady for the time being that her watch is wrong.   Now tell me what's the matter with that?''

''Only that her watch wasn't wrong when she got home,'' Tewson said, ''or only three minutes wrong, which doesn't signify.   Or—'' he rubbed the side of his jaw thoughtfully ''—or I should say doesn't seem to.''

''But it's her watch not being wrong that proves all this,'' Geary said.

Tewson gave a weary shake of his head.   ''Evitt—a man like Evitt—he'd have thought of that, Jim.   But when we saw him, he wasn't scared.   Things had worked out just as he meant them to.   So he's got something else up his sleeve, and that means there's something else coming, something for us to trip over and send us flat on our faces.   Yes . . .''   Tewson stopped as the telephone rang at his elbow, then, as he reached for it, repeated somberly, ''Yes, something else is coming.''

His conversation on the telephone lasted for some minutes.   When it was over, he looked expressionlessly at Geary, then leaned back in his chair, stared up at the dingy ceiling and muttered, "Didn't I say something else was coming?"

"What was it?" Geary asked.

"That was young Hobday," Tewson said.   "His mother's watch is now thirty-five minutes fast.   In about six hours, it's gained nearly half an hour.   What do you make of that, Jim?"

In disgust, Geary exclaimed, "That means her watch *was* wrong at the Evitts'. She must have re-set it there and forgotten doing it.   And it had already gained another three minutes by the time she got home.   It's hopelessly out of order.   Or did anyone get a chance to tamper with the watch?"

"The boy says not.   He says she talked to him quite sensibly for a little while when he got her alone before the injection hit her, and she was quite sure no one had had a chance to tamper with it."

"Then you aren't going to be able to swash Evitt's alibi so easily, are you?"

"Because of the sheer coincidence that her watch, her good watch, that she's had for twenty-two years, went wrong the same evening as her husband was mur-dered?"   Still staring at the ceiling, onto which, at one time or another, he had projected most of his problems, Tewson shook his head.   "No," he said definitely.

"Then someone did tamper with it—stands to reason someone did," Geary said.

"Yes."

"The boy?"

"Why?"

"Working with Evitt, perhaps.   There's this story that he was on bad terms with his father."

"The Evitts' story.   No one else supports it."

"But then . . ."   Geary found himself staring at the ceiling.   But he was unable to draw from it the inspiration that Tewson seemed to find there.   Once more he fixed his eyes on Tewson's face, which at that moment was almost as gray, as lined and as blank as the ceiling which he was able to put to such good use.

"But then no one but Mrs. Hobday could have tampered with the watch," Geary said.   "Mrs. Hobday herself.   Only why should she do it?   She seemed fond of her old man.   So why should she do that to protect Evitt?"

"Just let me think, Jim," Tewson answered.   "Just let me think."

In the morning, Harry Evitt did not go to the office.   He knew that this was a mistake, but he was afraid to leave Rina by herself.   The day before she had done her part well.   Both in the handling of Minnie Hobday and of the police, she had shown the nerve and resourcefulness which he had known would be roused in her by excitement and the presence of an audience.   But in the morning, after a night quite without sleep, alone in the house, she was not to be trusted.

He knew that she ought to go round to the Hobdays' house to inquire after Minnie, but he doubted if he could make her go.   She clung to him, needing to be continually reassured that all had gone as he had planned.   So when, in the middle of the morning, the police reappeared, Evitt felt from the start at a disadvantage.   He felt that he must explain his own presence at home, when surely, of all times, he was needed at the office, and that he must apologize for Rina's failure to be the kind, concerned friend of the bereaved woman that would have seemed only natural under the circumstances.

"My wife's so upset, Inspector . . .   A bad night . . .   Perhaps a prowler around somewhere . . .   Afraid . . .   You understand . . ."

The words limped out uncertainly.   They weren't the right words, Evitt knew, even as he produced them.   A murderer should never explain or apologize.

What made it worse was that, for all the notice that Tewson seemed to take, Evitt might not have spoken at all.   Tewson had followed him into the living room, had nodded briefly to Rina, who had risen from her chair by the fireplace, then she had stood glancing around the room with the air of looking for something. The fact that he had the air of knowing just what he was looking for made Evitt's plump hands turn to ice.

He crossed to Rina's side.   Standing on the gray hearth-rug with his shoulder touching hers, he reached automatically for the warmth of the fire.   But yesterday's wood fire, for decorative purposes only in the well-heated room, was a heap of ashes.

"I came to tell you," Tewson said, "that Mrs. Hobday has withdrawn the statement she made to us yesterday evening that your clock was wrong.   She believes now it was her watch that was wrong.   Since it was practically speaking right when she reached home, she suspected you at first of having altered your clock and lied to her about your call to the exchange, in order to create a false alibi for yourself.   But she now believes she must have unthinkingly re-set her watch while she was here."

Tewson had been looking at the grandfather clock while he was speaking, but now his eyes rested on Evitt's face.

Evitt gave a grave nod, almost a bow.   He was striving to assume a solemnity of sorrow for his dead friend and partner.   It made a certain slowness of utterance, while he chose his words, seem understandable.   But it was difficult to keep his feet still.

"I see," he said.   "May I ask what made her change her opinion?"

"Her watch went on gaining after she got home," Tewson said.

"Ah, I see.   Just an unfortunate coincidence, then."

"Was it?"   Tewson gave a tightlipped, ferocious smile.   Then he moved away. He crossed to the telephone and stood looking down at it.   "That's what she herself believes it was.   An unfortunate coincidence.   But I'm not sure . . ."   He had picked up a little writing-pad from beside the telephone, the kind of pad intended for the jotting down of messages.   From across the room its cover had looked as if it were of tooled leather, of emerald green and gold.   But in fact it was of painted metal, cold to the touch of his fingers.   "I'm not sure that I agree with her.   Mrs. Evitt, what did you do with the pencil that belongs to this pad?"

Rina started.   Evitt could feel the trembling begin in the arm that was pressed against his. But her voice was only a very little higher than usual. No one who did not know her well would have noticed it. With an audience to play to, he thought, you could always rely on her.

"The pencil?" she said. "Why, I—I don't know. Isn't it there?"

"I mean the pencil," Tewson said, "a green and gold pencil, with which, as Mrs. Hobday told me this morning, you kept tapping her wrist yesterday afternoon, her left wrist, all the time you were playing bridge—tapping her watch too pretty often, of course."

"Did I do that?" Rina asked. "I don't remember. Oh, but you don't mean that *that* could have upset her watch?"

Evitt took it up quickly. "No, Inspector, surely you aren't suggesting that you can deliberately make a watch go wrong—because I take it that that's what this might imply—by giving it gentle little taps with an ordinary pencil?"

"Not with an ordinary pencil, no," Tewson said. "That isn't what I'm suggesting. But I know these pads. The pencils that go with them have magnets in them. That's to make them hold onto the metal covers of the pads, the idea being that you won't mislay them. Neat, if you can be bothered with that sort of thing. And if you keep on tapping a watch with a quite powerful magnet, you can make it go very wrong indeed. You can't tell *how* wrong, of course. You can't tell if it'll go fast or slow or stop altogether. All you can be pretty sure of is that with that magnet drawing at the works, they're going to be badly enough upset to make the watch useless as evidence against a fine old clock like that and a faked call to a telephone exchange. Now where *is* that pencil, Mrs. Evitt?"

There was silence in the room. For a moment the Evitts stood close to one another, both tense, wary and wooden-faced. Then Rina drew away from her husband, clawed suddenly at his round, empty face with her nails and started to scream at him.

JACK RITCHIE

#8

I was doing about eighty, but the long flat road made it feel only that fast.

The red-headed kid's eyes were bright and a little wild as he listened to the car radio. When the news bulletin was over, he turned down the volume.

He wiped the side of his mouth with his hand. "So far they found seven of his victims."

I nodded. "I was listening." I took one hand off the wheel and rubbed the back of my neck, trying to work out some of the tightness.

He watched me and his grin was half-sly. "You nervous about something?"

My eyes flicked in his direction. "No. Why should I be?"

The kid kept smiling. "The police got all the roads blocked for fifty miles around Edmonton."

"I heard that too."

The kid almost giggled. "He's too smart for them."

I glanced at the zipper bag he held on his lap. "Going far?"

He shrugged. "I don't know."

The kid was a little shorter than average and he had a slight build. He looked about seventeen, but he was the baby-face type and could have been five years older.

He rubbed his palms on his slacks. "Did you ever wonder what made him do it?"

I kept my eyes on the road. "No."

He licked his lips. "Maybe he got pushed too far. All his life somebody always pushed him. Somebody was always there to tell him what to do and what not to do. He got pushed once too often."

The kid stared ahead. "He exploded. A guy can take just so much. Then something's got to give."

I eased my foot on the accelerator.

He looked at me. "What are you slowing down for?"

"Low on gas," I said. "The station ahead is the first I've seen in the last forty miles. It might be another forty before I see another."

I turned off the road and pulled to a stop next to the three pumps. An elderly man came around to the driver's side of the car.

"Fill the tank," I said. "And check the oil."

The kid studied the gas station.   It was a small building, the only structure in the ocean of wheat fields.   The windows were grimy with dust.

I could just make out a wall phone inside.

The kid jiggled one foot.   "That old man takes a long time.   I don't like waiting."   He watched him lift the hood to check the oil.   "Why does anybody that old want to live?   He'd be better off dead."

I lit a cigarette.   "He wouldn't agree with you."

The kid's eyes went back to the filling station.   He grinned.   "There's a phone in there.   You want to call anybody?"

I exhaled a puff of cigarette smoke.   "No."

When the old man came back with my change, the kid leaned toward the window. "You got a radio, mister?"

The old man shook his head.   "No.   I like things quiet."

The kid grinned.   "You got the right idea, mister.   When things are quiet you live longer."

Out on the road, I brought the speed back up to eighty.

The kid was quiet for a while, and then he said, "It took guts to kill seven people.   Did you ever hold a gun in your hand?"

"I guess almost everybody has."

His teeth showed through twitching lips.   "Did you ever point it at anybody?"

I glanced at him.

His eyes were bright.   "It's good to have people afraid of you," he said. "You're not short anymore when you got a gun."

"No," I said.   "You're not a runt anymore."

He flushed slightly.

"You're the tallest man in the world," I said.   "As long as nobody else has a gun too."

"It takes a lot of guts to kill," the kid said again.   "Most people don't know that."

"One of those killed was a boy of five," I said.   "You got anything to say about that?"

He licked his lips.

"It could have been an accident."

I shook my head.   "Nobody's going to think that."

His eyes seemed uncertain for a moment.   "Why do you think he'd kill a kid?"

I shrugged.   "That would be hard to say.   He killed one person and then another and then another.   Maybe after a while it didn't make any difference to him what they were.   Men, women, or children.   They were all the same."

The kid nodded.   "You can develop a taste for killing.   It's not too hard.   After the first few, it doesn't matter.   You get to like it."

He was silent for another five minutes.   "They'll never get him.   He's too smart for that."

I took my eyes off the road for a few moments.   "How do you figure that? The whole country's looking for him.   Everybody knows what he looks like."

The kid lifted both his thin shoulders. "Maybe he doesn't care. He did what he had to do. People will know he's a big man now."

We covered a mile without a word and then he shifted in his seat. "You heard his description over the radio?"

"Sure," I said. "For the last week."

He looked at me curiously. "And you weren't afraid to pick me up?"

"No."

His smile was still sly. "You got nerves of steel?"

I shook my head. "No. I can be scared when I have to, all right."

He kept his eyes on me. "I fit the description perfectly."

"That's right."

The road stretched ahead of us and on both sides there was nothing but the flat plain. Not a house. Not a tree.

The kid giggled. "I look just like the killer. Everybody's scared of me. I like that."

"I hope you had fun," I said.

"I been picked up by the cops three times on this road in the last two days. I get as much publicity as the killer."

"I know," I said. "And I think you'll get more. I thought I'd find you somewhere on this highway."

I slowed down the car. "How about me? Don't I fit the description too?"

The kid almost sneered. "No. You got brown hair. His is red. Like mine."

I smiled. "But I could have dyed it."

The kid's eyes got wide when he knew what was going to happen.

He was going to be number eight.

BRYCE WALTON

All the Needless Killing

He sat eating his regular morning orange and watching the narrow road below through spots of hemlock and pine. Gray and brown stone jutted out in split sections around him, and rose into a jumble of glacial rock blotched with red lichen.

He seemed to doze, but he was alert, listening, hearing everything—particularly the multiple teeming and droning of insect hordes in damp rock and leafy mould, and the flitting of gentle birds in the leaves. There were almost no visitors to this sequestered section at the north end of the lake anymore. He would have heard unwanted intruders, but there were none. He heard her station wagon drive in, though, a little after ten, the regular time.

It turned in through the second-growth timber, headed toward the denser wooded area. He stood up, wiped his prim mouth with a clean blue bandanna, brushed dust from his corduroy trousers. Then, holding the handkerchief by opposite corners, he twirled it until it formed a taut effective tool for causing death by strangulation.

There was about him the manner of a mild man. The expression on his thin pale face was bland and his movements usually restrained and paced. But now as he started down through the rocks, he moved with a peculiar surefootedness, in quick, explosive and eager little leaps, suggesting those of a mountain goat.

She got out of the station wagon and stretched, a not unattractive woman whose slight chubbiness made her seem younger than she was, and helped to smooth out what would otherwise have been a few hard lines around her eyes and mouth. She wore slacks, not too tight, hiking boots, a loose khaki blouse with rolled-up sleeves. She had her peroxided hair tied in a pony tail with a red ribbon.

Sunlight through the leaves speckled her with shade. She took a deep breath. It had rained during the night. This morning was cooler than the others had been. Quaint animal life chattered and ran about. Snowdrops were open and forsythia broke in sprays of yellow. All ecstatic stuff for outdoor types, no doubt. But she did not consider herself an outdoor-type girl. Still it was a pleasant moment. And because it was pleasant, it reminded her of the city. She hoped soon to go back to Manhattan. One way or another.

She got the leather bag from the front seat, slid the strap over her shoulder. She opened the back of the station wagon, took out a cigar box lined with cotton, the killing-bottle, and two sandwiches and a thermos of martinis, put them into the bag.   Then she got the butterfly net out and swished it delicately in the air.

This might, or might not, be another long unrewarding day.   But it would alleviate the nauseating monotony of being the wife of a farmer.   Especially a New England farmer, who happened to be wealthy.   New England farmers were stereotypes of something; she wasn't quite sure what, except that it was tight-lipped, rigid, narrow and terribly grim.   Anything, in a word, but pagan.   Still, there were times when a girl, who had not always been blessed with security and leisure, should not complain.

She studied the ripe buzzing air and camp shadows with predatory eyes.   A bright yellow butterfly flitted past on a vagrant breath of breeze and she skipped after it, swinging her butterfly net about in what appeared to be that specialized joy reserved only for hunters stalking prey.

At one P.M., she lay down by an aged elm, ate sandwiches, sipped a martini, then stretched out pleasantly tired, and with her forearm over her face, she closed her eyes.

It was the killing-bottle . . .

He watched her through a curtain of briar.   His slightly enlarged eyes studied her through thick lenses like those of a microscope.   After having watched her loathsome antics for three days, he knew that she possessed exceptional strength and agility for a woman.   Overpowering her was out of the question, for he was a rather frail man and detested the physical.   If she frightened easily, she would hardly keep coming daily into these so-called ghoul-haunted woods (the local natives were extremely superstitious) to hunt alone, therefore the paralyzed fear reaction could not be depended upon.   The surprise attack seemed the only suitable approach.

He watched her until he felt sure she was sleeping soundly.   He padded noiselessly in a circle, crept up behind the elm and peered around and down at the reclining figure.

He ran the slightly oily and damp rope of bandanna through his pink hands.   He studied the movement, the sound of her breathing.   She would hardly be awake before he slipped the handkerchief under her head and brought the ends together and twisted gently.   Not too much pressure, of course, slow gentle application reducing consciousness, but not obliterating it.   She would lie breathing as though asleep.

He looked at the killing-bottle beside her.   It was about the size of an ordinary fruit-jar, perhaps bigger.   There was the horrible column of cotton wool coiling up to the glass stopper.   There it was, her lethal chamber, her big-game hunting apparatus.

A slight smile, not so bland upon closer examination, appeared on his lips.   There was a hint of cruelty in it.   If it was cruelty, it was no ordinary kind, but the reserved, implacable judging and sentencing of a breaker of sacred laws by a creature of righteous wrath.

He slipped on a pair of tight brown suede gloves. She would lie there afterward, still breathing. He would release the stopper and the huntress would snuff up the almond-scented fumes. She wouldn't wake up, wouldn't mind at all because it was a safe and pleasant smell. It was always so difficult to understand why cyanide of potassium should be lethal. But it always was. And one long whiff of it would be all that was required.

He slipped around the tree, over protruding roots. He crouched. The handkerchief stretched taut between his hands. Slip it quickly beneath her head, twist, hold—

The bandanna ducked, slid—scooped empty air!

He fell to his knees off balance, and felt an amazingly light touch along his right arm, a digging under his shoulder. Then the world gyrated. It was a blur. It smeared in a senseless pinwheeling rush of mingled leaves, sky and whirling rocks.

He hit on his upper back with an unpleasant jarring thud. She was leaning against the tree watching him as he sat up and blinked. He felt his neck. He rolled his head around a few times carefully, experimentally. His look, when he saw her, showed fear, but more outraged dignity mixed with sadness. He tensed as though to run away as he stood up.

"I'm sorry," she said, smiling in a warm but guarded manner. "But you scared me. I hope you're not hurt."

"I'm not sure," he mumbled and spat a fragment of leaf from his lip. He twisted, trying to determine if he was hurt. "I don't believe so."

They stared at one another for a while.

"Sure you're not hurt?" she asked.

He managed a nervous smile and began brushing leaves from shirt and trousers. "I suppose not."

Her smile broadened. It was the friendly expression of a thoroughly confident person. "First time I ever had to really use the old judo. You'd be surprised how many girls are taking it up these days."

"Yes, it was a surprise."

"Well, I'm glad there was no harm done."

His watery distorted eyes blinked at her, then around at brush, trees, and rocks, back to her. He reached down, picked up his hornrimmed glasses, and put them on. "Of course I should apologize and I do," he said, more at ease now. "Your actions were perfectly understandable. I should explain mine. You see, I was supposed to meet an—ah—friend here. Hardly anyone ever comes in here, so naturally I thought you were she."

She proffered a pack of cigarettes. He gracefully declined; he didn't use them.

She lit one for herself, and continued to study him with a friendly curiosity. Smoke formed two horns rising from her nostrils.

"Well," he finally said. "Again, I'm sorry. But I'd better move along. I don't want to miss my friend."

"Wait," she said. "Would you like a martini?" She lifted the thermos.

He moistened his lips. He shifted uneasily. "I really shouldn't."

"Please do; you could use it right now." She watched his face as she added, "You see, I know who you intended to meet here. *Me*."

He tensed again. His eyes widened, bulged slightly. "What?"

"I wish you wouldn't be afraid," she said.

"Why—why should I be?"

"That's right, you shouldn't." She poured a martini into the thermos top and handed it to him.

He took it in a dazed, reflexive gesture and gulped it hastily. His high pale forehead was damp.

"More?"

"I—"

She poured the topful of martini. He sat down heavily on a rock and gripped the drink between both hands.

"I haven't lived in Sawmill County long," she said in a casual, conversational manner. "I'm Barbara. What's your name?"

"Jim," he said in an almost inaudible voice.

"Well, Jim, I came out here to live with my husband right after we were married a few months ago. That's the custom, you know." She smiled. He flashed a quick dutiful smile in return. Obviously, smiling was hardly one of his regular habits. "I was curious. I've always been curious. I learned a lot in a short time. One of the first things I heard about was Loon Woods. About how several people died around here during the past two summers."

Jim sipped his martini and sat rigidly on the edge of the rock.

"Four people. Two last summer, two the summer before. Three women, one man. I love mysteries and I found out more."

She lit a cigarette.

"Yes," he said faintly. "What did you find out?"

"They were of different ages, from various parts of the county. One, a woman, was from another state. The four who died weren't related. They didn't have a thing in common, Jim, but what they happened to be doing when they died. They were catching butterflies—with one exception, which isn't really an exception the way I see it. One of them, the man, was catching beetles."

"If you were that curious, you must have found out more."

"Oh, yes. But I guessed at things too. The two ladies who died summer before last were found poisoned, poisoned by the fumes from their killing-bottles. The man catching beetles last summer was poisoned by the bite of a water moccasin. The woman that summer was also poisoned by fumes from her killing-bottle. She fell, the bottle broke a few inches from her face; she inhaled the fumes."

"Something of a coincidence," Jim said.

"It certainly was, wasn't it? The three women all dying in the same way. Our local Sheriff Reed thought it was simply a coincidence. But then he seems to be a very stupid and complaisant fellow. Not much imagination. The two women summer before last—it was easy to see them as accidents. The two last summer raised doubts in some people's minds, but not Sheriff Reed's."

"And what about you?" Jim asked.   He had finished his second martini.   His face was slightly flushed.   He started to protest, but mildly, as she poured him a third.   "Thank you, thank you very much," he said.   "I seem to need these."

She was watching a number of gaudy butterflies fluttering about in the dappled shade.   Her face softened.   "Dear, beautiful, harmless things," she whispered.   "There's so many of them around here now.   People have been scared off from coming in here much, haven't they?   Now it's as if those dear gentle things know where they're safe and protected from capture and cruel execution."

He started.   He leaned toward her.   His face softened, and his watery eyes seemed brimming with ineffable sadness.   "Yes, they realize they have a refuge here.   Many birds do too.   This has become a kind of sanctuary."

She nodded and for a while they shared an unspoken affinity, with the heat of the day flickering visibly upward from the loam and leaves.

"So," she said finally.   "What about me, you ask?   I'll tell you.   I kept thinking about what those people had in common—their murdering of God's innocent.   And because I felt so strongly their evil—I got a hunch, Jim.   I got a hunch about how and why they had really died."

Jim sipped his martini and his face was wistful and at the same time tense with interest.   "Yes, I understand, you know.   I, too, see those people as murderers."

"Of course.   A few people realize the sacredness of life, of all life, from the smallest nit to the glorious elephant.   Isn't that what you mean?"

His mouth dropped open.   He nodded as though partially stunned.   "Oh, yes, yes," he sighed.

"And I thought about it and there was my hunch.   There were facts too, Jim.   The poetic justice of their deaths.   I knew it wasn't a coincidence.   And then I found out that someone had seen a stranger near here twice just after those deaths.   A stranger.   A stranger because everyone around here knows everyone else.   And this stranger couldn't be described exactly.   Could have been a number of people.   But it wasn't anyone from around here.   I decided that those four people had been killed, Jim."

He couldn't quite pull his fixed gaze from her face.   There seemed to be a kind of rapture in her expression as if her own words had placed her under an euphoric spell.

"You see," she said, with a look of rapture, "it was more than just a hunch.   I understood the need to do what someone had done to those people.   I began to feel closer to the—I'd rather not say killer, but executioner.   I understood why he did it, the need for justice."

"You did?" Jim whispered.

"Oh, yes.   Before I left the city I belonged to many societies and organizations.   We did our best to stop the senseless slaughter of life—especially all the small gentle things that have never harmed anything or anybody.   We can do so little, but the few of us who care should do what we can, shouldn't we?"

"Yes."

"Not just words.   Words are no good, are they?"

"No."

"Blood calls for blood." She clenched her fists. "Oh, I hate cruelty more than anything in the world!"

He leaned forward. His eyes were brighter as the cloudiness left them. "So do I." Then he shrank back and he kept staring at the killing-bottle and the butterfly net. "But you've been capturing them too. They suffer so horribly there, shut up in the bottle. I've seen them, how they flutter and beat and break themselves against the glass walls. I've seen them clinging to that ghastly cotton wool. How they strain and gasp for a last breath of living air."

A look of horror, only hinted at before, now lay full and undisguised upon Jim's face. He slid away from her across the rock, still clutching the top of the thermos.

She shook her head slowly. Her smile was sad and compassionate. "You don't understand, Jim. I wanted to meet someone else who felt as I did. I wanted to meet you. That's why I've come out here almost every day for the last month. I guessed that you might come here once in a while to guard your sanctuary. Now I've found you, and you've found me."

"You lie," he said softly. "You're lying. This is some kind of a trap, isn't it?"

"Please!" She seemed almost on the verge of crying. "You must believe the truth, Jim. I've often felt like doing what was done to those vile, vicious people. But I never had the courage. Someone did, somewhere, I knew. I wanted to know that person."

"No, no!" He sat rigidly balanced on the edge of the rock. He started to sip more of the martini, but stopped—as though it had suddenly became distasteful. "You're like the others. You didn't mind murdering those lovely things, just to find me, and trap me."

"There's no one else around. No one has ever followed me, Jim, you know that."

He didn't answer.

"And even if I was an expert at judo, would I come out here alone to trap someone most people would regard as a vicious murderer?"

"Vicious—that isn't true. They died painlessly. That's more than can be said for the countless helpless creatures they tortured and killed!"

"I know that, Jim. Believe me. I know you could never be cruel. I know that you're dedicated to fighting cruelty, and avenging the gentle small things of this world. I am too, Jim. Believe me, I am too. Please believe me. Look."

She opened the cigar box. She walked toward him slowly, and he sat trembling with some odd hypersensitivity. He glanced reluctantly into the box.

"I've only caught a few, Jim. And they're all cabbage butterflies, don't you see?"

He nodded slowly.

"There are some kinds of butterflies that are dangerous pests, Jim. You must admit it. Just as there are locusts that destroy. There are mosquitoes and other kinds of pests. Only man kills for pleasure, but there are harmful kinds among all species. Isn't that true?"

He hesitated, then gave a quick nod of assent. But he wouldn't look at the box anymore. "Undeniably, you're right," he said. "Yes, you're right about the cabbage butterfly. And there are other noxious insects that should be destroyed, just as is the case with men."

"But there are not many insects that deserve such a fate, Jim. And you can see that I've caught only the harmful ones."

"Yes. The list of destructive lepidoptera is relatively insignificant." He seemed to relax a little. She refreshed his martini, and he began to sip again.

His face was soon flushed, and his breathing fast. She put her hand over his hand, and they sat there together side by side on the rock holding hands for some time, communing in an inner quiet that seemed flawless and unbreakable.

Then they finished the batch of martinis and talked in excited discovery of one another. He talked about the brief but glorious life of the butterflies and other insects, how they lived their own brilliant but strange cycle in only a few hours sometimes, to finally be killed by nature's way, by the frost. Everything had been planned to balance out, and man was destroying the balance, destroying the world itself.

She asked him again to trust her. She would be back again tomorrow, she said. He could meet her there in the same place. He could watch, be certain she was not followed, finally be convinced that she was not part of any sort of trap.

They met there the next day. She waited over an hour under the elm until suddenly he appeared, moving out of the leaves silently. She had two thermos bottles of martinis this time, and they enjoyed themselves with a steady lessening of strain and suspicion.

He talked about when summer would be over; the blossoms would come to seed and the fledglings to flight. The knowing squirrel was already hoarding its winter harvest. Soon feathered migrants would be heading south and the cricket would seek a sheltered place. The sun would cross the celestial equator, he said, and summer would be officially dismissed. But the squirrels, chipmunks and woodchucks and robins knew nothing of these precise hours or minutes. They did well enough, he said, without clocks or calendars. He felt it in his blood too, he said, just as they did. And just as she did, she was quick to point out. No need to check anything by manmade instruments of measurement to know. Indeed not, she said. They didn't have to look at the sun's shadow. How unimportant precise moments were, he said, except in man's statistics.

Cause and effect, nature's cosmic balance. Man was destroying it all.

"God, Jim," she said with an almost savage intensity, "if we could only do more to save millions of little lives."

They met the next day, the day after, and then almost every day. Soon he was waiting for her. It was a lonely world for their kind, they agreed. They sat until the sun went down and the cicada droning of the hot afternoon began to fade and the insect chorus began.

She pointed out a dead robin, then another.

"You know what killed them?" she said. "What is killing birds by the thousands every day, Jim?"

He caressed the small inert puff of feathers, then turned away.

"Man is killing them, Jim.   The farmers around here are killing everything with their pumps of poison sprays.   You know that, don't you?"

"Oh, yes, I know that!"

"Every day, Jim, with their pumps and vile hoses smearing poison over the land. Millions—billions even—are being killed now.   It poisons the larvae and pupae and they never are allowed to live.   And that kills the birds too, because they eat the insects and the larvae.   That's what kills these robins, you know."

"I know."   He sank down to his knees and remained there for some time, his head bowed.

She whispered with a harshly accusing tone.   "We're quibblers and piddlers, Jim.   We are, you know.   You made your gesture, didn't you, but how insignificant it was compared with what they do every day.   They slaughter millions every day.   And you've struck back, yes, but what have you and I accomplished? Four people!   They didn't use sprays.   They killed a few, but how does that compare with the billions that are being slaughtered here day in and day out?"

"I know, I know," he moaned softly.   He raised small clenched fists.   "What can I do?   I used to try to convince others.   I published pamphlets.   I made speeches at the university, but they laughed at me finally.   People think I'm abnormal in some way, a kind of—well—a crackpot.   That's what they say about our kind.   I can only do a little.   Sometimes it seems to be driving me crazy because I'm alone and helpless and frustrated and no one cares!"

"Now you listen," she said and turned him around and they looked steadily into each other's face.   "You can do a great deal more.   With one act you can save millions and millions of sacred little lives."

As she continued talking and he listened, his eyes grew abnormally bright behind his thick-lensed glasses.   He bent slightly forward and his breath came faster.   He kept nodding in agreement, his head moving in quick jerking little motions like a bird's.

"I know their habits," she said.   "I can help.   I know when they work and where to find them.   I'll tell you when and where to strike!"

"Not a few," he whispered.   "But millions and billions saved.   The birds saved!"

"Yes, yes!"

He began to sway in a subtle rhythm to the intensity of his feelings as she gave him vital information.   The insect chorus rose around him.   It was only a whispering of the wind and the rustling of leaves at first.   Then it swelled from the throats of the most abundant life on earth, the pygmy hordes celebrating their season in the sun, the late afternoon of their life.

The insect chorus rose in his ears like thunder, the humming, scratching, singing drone swelled and seemed to explode in his head . . .

He was there in the storage shed, under the damp corrugated tin roof, early.   He was there alert and ready before five A.M. Above him on a rack of two-by-four planks were the barrels of deadly parathion used to spray crops, used to heartlessly slaughter millions of sacred living things. A few pests must be killed, therefore go on and kill everything, kill all the beautiful gentle things, kill the butterflies and velvet-winged moths, kill the beautiful Swallowtail and the Macaons and Purple Emperors and lovely iridescent peacock-winged Pavitos, kill the Holly Blues, and the Tornoasoladas and magnificent golden-wing Tortoise-shells. And finally there would be nothing, nothing but silence where the robins had once come back in the spring.

He stood in the shadows waiting, with the spray tank beside him and the nozzle ready in his hand. A tinge of dawn filtered through the cracks in the shed and he heard the plaintive screech of a barn owl and then the back screen door of the farmhouse snapped shut.

He waited and listened to the clopping of heavy shoes approaching the door of the shed.

It did not matter who it was, of course. He was one of the killers and soon he would die so that millions might live. Blood calls for blood. The workings of justice are indeed secret and incalculable. This one now, and the others later, one by one. He remembered what she had told him and she was so right about it, about so many things. There was enough poison in one small killing-bottle to kill the inhabitants of an entire town. But how to administer it? How much more logical it was to select those who were directly responsible for the indiscriminate murder of millions, eliminate them on the spot. Painlessly of course, or comparatively painlessly, and with poetic justice, as she had pointed out, with their own vile, suffocating, poisonous spray!

He peered through a crack between the warped boards. He saw a shadowy figure only a few yards from the shed now, a tall man in a straw hat with a ragged brim, a pair of levis, a faded blue denim jacket.

Jim inhaled deeply and raised the handle of the spray pump. That man was not at all a hated object. He could be regarded objectively, without malice, merely as a thing to be eliminated for purposes that no sane man should reasonably question.

The man stepped through the doorway. He stopped, startled, uncertain. Jim pushed down the pump handle and a pale stream caught the man flush and hissing in the face. The man screamed and clawed at his eyes. He ran blindly into the side of the shed and fell as Jim coolly continued to pump while aiming the nozzle with unerring accuracy and singleness of purpose.

Barbara sat pale and tearless at the kitchen table, as if too shocked, too stunned, to cry. Sheriff Reed watched her with awkward sympathy, his small black eyes in a porcine face avoiding her direct gaze. He finished the coffee in one sucking gulp and stood up.

"Better get that fella into the town jail," he said. "Guess I better."

"More coffee?" she asked listlessly.

"No, thank you, Ma'am. I got here quick as I could when you telephoned. But I guess I couldn't have helped much nohow."

"No one could have done anything," she said. "A few drops of parathion on the skin can kill a person in minutes if they don't get treatment. My—my husband was just drowned in it by that—that awful person!"

"Well, we got him, Ma'am, thanks to you. Pretty good shootin', only it's kind of a good thing you didn't hit him in a vital spot. That would have been too easy on him."

"Darrell thought it was a robber and went out to see," she said. "That was all—"

"I reckon he was at least a thief. He don't look like no thief though. Identification says he's a college professor from over in Lakeville."

"He—he must have been crazy or something," she said thinly.

"Can't ever tell about people."

"I don't care. I've lost my Darrell!" She turned away and bit her lip.

"Fine man," Sheriff Reed said. "Hard worker and steady as a rock. Never harmed nobody. Well—" he hesitated. "—he was a good provider and I reckon he left you comfortable set up—I mean moneywise?"

She nodded. The farm plus fifty thousand in insurance was indeed comforting. She would sell the farm, rent a penthouse on Park Avenue. No more scrounging for television roles or being a stand-in for much less talented actresses than herself. If she still felt so inclined, she would buy a lead in a Broadway show, and—

She put her head down on her folded arms and began to cry.

Sheriff Reed patted her shoulder. "You just let it all out now, Ma'am, that's what you need. I'll take that fellow on in. Why, the poor guy's liable to bleed plumb to death. And you're right, I think he's buggy. He won't say anything. Every time you pick him up he falls down on his hands and knees again."

She seemed too broken up to answer. He backed quietly out the kitchen door.

There was some claim to his being insane.

But he was articulate and disclaimed any inability to distinguish right from wrong.

He knew very well right from wrong and passionately explained how right he had been in killing people . . .

They strapped down his wrists to the arms of the chair. His ankles were clamped. Steel doors slammed. He stared at the glass enclosure of the chamber. Faces studied him curiously through the glass, and the faces began to blur as if the glass were steaming over.

He hadn't realized for some time what was really happening to him. It was as though he had been sleep-walking and had suddenly awakened.

And now he knew.

He knew when the cyanide pellets dropped into a bucket of acid under his chair and the fumes drifted up into a mist before his face.

He smelled the fumes and he saw the faces pressing against the glass and watching him through the glass and he knew well enough.

It was the killing-bottle.

EDWARD D. HOCH

A Melee of Diamonds

The man with the silver-headed cane turned into Union Street just after nine o'clock, walking briskly through the scattering of evening shoppers and salesclerks hurrying home after a long day. It was a clear April evening, cool enough for the topcoat the man wore, but still a relief at the end of a long winter. He glanced into occasional shop windows as he walked, but did not pause until he'd reached the corner of Union and Madison. There, he seemed to hesitate for a moment at the windows of the Midtown Diamond Exchange. He glanced quickly to each side, as if making certain there was no one near, and then smashed the nearest window with his silver-headed cane.

The high-pitched ringing of the alarm mingled with the sound of breaking glass, as the man reached quickly into the window. A few pedestrians froze in their places, but as the man turned to make his escape a uniformed policeman suddenly appeared around the corner. "Hold it right there!" he barked, reaching for his holstered revolver.

The man turned, startled at the voice so close, and swung his cane at the officer. Then, as the policeman moved in, he swung again, catching the side of the head just beneath the cap. The officer staggered and went down, and the man with the cane rounded the corner running.

"Stop him!" a shirt-sleeved man shouted from the doorway of the Diamond Exchange. "We've been robbed!"

The police officer, dazed and bleeding, tried to get to his knees and then fell back to the sidewalk, but a young man in paint-stained slacks and a zippered jacket detached himself from the frozen onlookers and started after the fleeing robber. He was a fast runner, and he overtook the man with the cane halfway down the block. They tumbled together into a pile of discarded boxes, rolling on the pavement, as the man tried to bring his cane up for another blow.

He shook free somehow, losing the cane but regaining his feet, and headed for an alleyway. A police car, attracted by the alarm, screeched to a halt in the street, and two officers jumped out with drawn guns. "Stop or we'll shoot!" the nearest officer commanded, and fired his pistol into the air in warning.

The sound of the shot echoed along the street, and the running man skidded to a halt at the entrance to the alleyway. He turned and raised his hands above his head. "All right," he said. "I'm not armed. Don't shoot."

The officer kept his pistol out until the second cop had snapped on the handcuffs.

"Damn it!" Captain Leopold exploded, staring at the paper cup full of light brown coffee that Lieutenant Fletcher had just set before him. "Is that the best you can get out of the machine?"

"Something's wrong with it, Captain. We've sent for a serviceman."

Leopold grumbled and tried to drink the stuff. One swallow was all he could stomach. The men in the department had given him a coffee percolator of his very own when he'd assumed command of the combined Homicide and Violent Crimes squad, but on this particular morning, with his coffee can empty, he'd been forced to return to the temperamental vending machine in the hall.

"Get me a cola instead, will you, Fletcher?" he said at last, pouring the coffee down the sink in one corner of his office. When the lieutenant came back, he asked, "Phil Begler's in the hospital?"

Fletcher nodded in confirmation. "There's a report on your desk. Phil came upon a guy stealing a handful of diamonds from the window of the Midtown Diamond Exchange. The guy whacked him on the head with a cane and started running. They caught him, but Phil's in the hospital with a concussion."

"I should go see him," Leopold decided. "Phil's a good guy."

"They identified the fellow that stole the diamonds and hit him as Rudy Hoffman, from New York. He's got a long record of smash-and-grab jobs."

Leopold nodded. "Maybe Phil Begler's concussion will be enough to put him away for good."

Fletcher nodded. "Hope so, Captain, but there is one little problem with the case."

"What's that?" Leopold asked.

"Well, they caught Hoffman only a half-block from the scene, after a young fellow chased and tackled him, and fought with him till a patrol car arrived. Hoffman got $58,000 worth of diamonds out of that window, and he was in sight of at least one person every instant until they arrested him."

"So?"

"The diamonds weren't on him, Captain. No trace of them."

"He dropped them in the street."

"They searched. They searched the street, they searched him, they even searched the patrol car he was in after his arrest. No diamonds."

Leopold was vaguely irritated that such a simple matter should disrupt the morning's routine. "Haven't they questioned him about it?"

"He's not talking, Captain."

"All right," he said with a sigh. "Bring him down. I'll have to show you guys how it's done."

Rudy Hoffman was a gray-haired man in his early forties. The years in prison, Leopold noted, had left him with a pale complexion and shifty, uncertain eyes. He licked his lips often as he spoke, nervously glancing from Leopold to Fletcher and then back again.

"I don't know anything," he said. "I'm not talking without a lawyer. You can't even question me without a lawyer. I know my rights!"

Leopold sat down opposite him. "It's not just a little smash-and-grab this time, Rudy. That cop you hit might die. You could go up for the rest of your life."

"He's just got a concussion. I heard the guards talkin'."

"Still, we've got you on assault with a deadly weapon. With your record, that's enough. We don't even need the felony charge. So you see, you're not really protecting yourself by clamming up about the diamonds. Even if we don't find them, we've still got you nailed."

Rudy Hoffman merely smiled and looked sleepy. "Those diamonds are where you'll never find them, cop. That much I promise you."

Leopold glared at him for a moment, thinking of Phil Begler in a hospital bed. "We'll see about that," he said, and stood up. "Come on, Fletcher, we're keeping him from his beauty sleep."

Back in Leopold's office, Fletcher said, "See what I mean, Captain? He's a hard one."

Leopold was grim. "I'll find those damned diamonds and stuff them down his throat. Tell me everything that happened from the instant he broke the window."

"I can do better than that, Captain. The kid who chased him is outside now, waiting to make a statement. Want to see him now?"

Neil Quart was not exactly a kid, though he was still on the light side of twenty-five. Leopold had seen the type many times before, on the streets usually, with shaggy hair and dirty clothes, taunting the rest of the world.

"You're quite a hero," Leopold told him. "Suppose you tell us how it happened."

Quart rubbed at his nose, trying to look cool. "I work over at Bambaum's nights, in the shipping department. I'd just finished there at nine o'clock and was heading home. Down by the Diamond Exchange I saw this guy with the cane smash a window. I wasn't close enough to grab him, but as he started to run away this cop rounds the corner. The guy hit him with the cane, hard, and knocked him down. Now, I don't have any love for cops, but I decided to take out after this guy. I ran him down halfway up the block, and we tussled a little. He tried to conk me with the cane too, but I got it away from him. Then he was up and running, but the other cops got there. One cop fired a shot in the air and it was all over."

Leopold nodded. "How long was the robber—Rudy Hoffman—out of your sight?"

"He wasn't out of my sight. Not for a second! I went right after him when he knocked the cop down. Hell, I thought he might have killed him."

"You didn't see him throw anything away, into the street?"

"Not a thing."

"Could he have thrown anything away as he raised his hands?"

"I don't think so."

Fletcher interrupted at this point. "They caught him at the entrance to an alleyway, Captain. Every inch of it was searched."

Leopold turned back to Neil Quart. "As you've probably guessed, we're looking for the diamonds he stole. Any idea what he might have done with them?"

The young man shrugged. "Not a glimmer. Unless . . . We were wrestling around some boxes."

"They were all checked," Fletcher said. "Everything was checked. The police were there all night, looking."

"You still did a good job," Leopold told the young man. "You weren't afraid to get involved, and that's what counts."

"Thanks. I just didn't like to see him hit that cop."

Outside, Fletcher asked, "Satisfied, Captain?"

"Not by a long shot. What about Hoffman's clothes?"

"We went over every stitch, including his topcoat. Nothing there."

"All right," Leopold decided, grim-faced. "Let's go see where it happened."

The Midtown Diamond Exchange still showed the scars of the previous night's robbery, with a boarded-up window and a little pile of broken glass.

The assistant manager, who'd been on duty the previous evening, was a sandy-haired man named Peter Arnold who looked pained by the whole affair.

"Just tell us how it was," Leopold told him. "Everything you can remember."

"It was just closing time, a few minutes after nine. The other clerk had gone home, and I'd locked the front door. That was when I heard the window smash and saw him scooping up the diamonds."

"Let's go back a bit, Mr. Arnold. How many diamonds were in the window?"

"Dozens! We had a few large rings mounted on cards giving the prices, and then we had perhaps twenty-five or thirty smaller stones, unmounted. A melee of diamonds, to use the trade term—although that usually refers to stones of less than a quarter carat. Most of these were larger."

"They were valued at $58,000?"

Peter Arnold nodded sadly. "I've already heard from our New York office about it."

"Do you always leave that many diamonds in your store window?"

"Not at all. They're in the window only while the store is open. My first duty after locking the door would have been to remove them from that and the other display windows and lock them in the vault for the night. I had just locked the door and was starting for the window on the other side when I heard the smashing of glass. I looked over and saw this man scooping the diamonds out of their trays. The window alarm was ringing, of course, and as he started away Officer Begler appeared around the corner."

"You know Phil Begler?"

The jeweler nodded. "He's been on this beat maybe four or five years. Usually he's, right around this corner, but at nine he goes up to direct traffic out of the parking ramp in the next block. It was only a fluke he happened to get back just when that man broke the window."

"Any idea what he did with the diamonds during his escape?"

"I'm baffled. If he'd dropped them, I should think at least a few would have been found."

Leopold walked to the boarded-up window, and pulled aside the black velvet drape so he could peer into it. The diamond trays were still there, speckled with broken glass, but there were no gems. "He got everything?"

"No, there were four rings on cards and six unmounted stones that he missed, but he made a good haul. We estimate $58,000, or even a bit more."

Leopold let the drape drop back into place. He took out a picture of Rudy Hoffman. "Ever see him in the store before the robbery, casing the place?"

"I don't remember him, but of course someone else may have been on duty."

"I'll leave this picture with you. Show it to your manager and the clerks. See if anyone remembers him."

"You think it was well-planned?"

"He got rid of the diamonds somewhere, and that took planning."

On the way out, Leopold paused at the little pile of broken glass and bent to examine it.

"Find something, Captain?" Fletcher asked.

"Ever think about how much broken glass and diamonds look alike, Fletcher?"

"Are there any diamonds in that pile?"

"No, just broken glass."

On the way back downtown, Fletcher said, "They did an X ray on Hoffman too, in case you're thinking he might have swallowed them."

"Never considered it for a moment." He stared through the car's dirty windshield at the passing scene. Police headquarters was separated from the main Union Street shopping area by some ten blocks of abandoned, run-down buildings— many of them doomed by a much-postponed urban renewal project. Those that still had tenants housed record shops and adult bookstores on their lower levels, renting the rooms above to bearded young people and transient types. It was a shabby section of the inner city, but the crime rate was not as high as might be expected.

"They should tear it all down," Fletcher commented.

"I suppose they will, one of these days." Leopold had another thought. "What about the men who searched the street? Could one of them have pocketed the diamonds?"

Fletcher thought about it. "We've got some bad eggs in the department, Captain—like any other city—but I'd trust any of the men who were out there last night. I know them all, from Begler on down. They're honest cops."

Leopold said no more until they reached his office. Then he asked Fletcher to bring him Rudy Hoffman's clothing. They went over each piece together, though the clothes had been searched earlier, and they found nothing.

Leopold frowned and went to stare out the window at the crowded parking lot that was his only view. "How about a wig, false teeth, something like that?"

Fletcher shook his head. "Nothing, Captain."

Leopold turned suddenly. "Damn it, Fletcher, why didn't I think of it before? There's one thing we've completely overlooked, one thing that's missing from Hoffman's possessions!"

Fletcher looked blank. "What's that, Captain?"

"The cane, of course! The silver-headed cane he used to break the window and crack Phil Begler's skull! Where is it?"

"I suppose they've got it tagged as the weapon.   It would be in the evidence drawer, or else already at the D.A.'s office, for presentation before the grand jury."

"Find it, Fletcher, and let's take a look at it."

Lieutenant Fletcher was back in five minutes, carrying a long black walking stick with a silver head in the shape of a ball held by a bird's claw.   Leopold snorted and turned it over in his hands.

"Doesn't really go with Hoffman somehow," Fletcher commented.   "Not his style."

"No."   Leopold turned it over in his hands, and tried to twist off the top.   It seemed solid, as was the shaft of the cane.   "He probably stole it from somewhere. There's certainly nothing hidden in it."

"Let's think about it," Fletcher suggested.   "Maybe something will come to us by morning."

Leopold glanced at his watch and nodded.   It was after three, and he wanted to stop by the hospital and see Officer Begler on his way home.   "Good idea," he agreed.   "See you in the morning."

"Say, how about coming over for dinner tonight, Captain?   Carol was saying the other day that she hasn't seen you since the Christmas party."

"Thanks, Fletcher.   I could use some of your wife's cooking, but let's make it another time.   Give her my best, though."

He drove over to Memorial Hospital and spent a half hour with Begler, who grinned from beneath his bandages and seemed in good enough spirits.   Leopold paused in the lobby to chat with a couple of nurses, and then headed home to his apartment, encountering the rush-hour traffic he usually tried to avoid.   Driving along Union Street, he remembered the empty coffee can in his office and pulled over at a neighborhood grocery.

The place was cluttered and crowded.   He picked up a can of coffee and found a clerk to take his money.   "Anything else, sir?"

Leopold shook his head.   "That's it."   Then he noticed the dark-haired girl who'd entered behind him.   She pretended to be choosing a loaf of bread, but she was really watching him.   No one takes that long to choose bread, he knew, and when she finally moved up to the clerk with her selection her eyes were still on Leopold.

The clerk slipped the coffee can into a paper bag, and Leopold left the store. Before he could cross the sidewalk to his car he heard the girl's voice behind him. "You're a detective, aren't you?"

He turned to her with a smile he hoped was friendly.   She was a good-looking girl, in her early twenties, but her face seemed drawn and tired at the moment. "You might say that."

"Do you want the loot from the Midtown Diamond robbery?"

In all his years of police work, nothing like it had ever happened to him before. He'd spent a full day trying to locate the diamonds that had disappeared by some sort of magic, and now this girl walked up to him outside a grocery store and offered them, just like that.

"Do you know where it is?"

She nodded.   "I can take you there, if you'll promise not to arrest me or my boyfriend."

"Who is your boyfriend?"

"Names aren't important.   He didn't have anything to do with the robbery. Have I your promise?"

"Then how'd he get the diamonds?"

"He's supposed to take them to New York and sell them—you know, like a fence.   I don't want any part of it.   I want you to take them."

"How'd you know I was a detective?"

"I followed you from the hospital.   You were visiting that policeman who was injured.   I went there to find out how he was, and a nurse pointed you out as a detective."

"You're concerned about Officer Begler?"

"Certainly.   I never knew it would be anything like this when Freddy agreed to handle the stuff.   I want out of it, before we all end up behind bars."

"Can you take me to the diamonds?"

She glanced quickly down the street and nodded.   "Leave your car here.   We'll go in mine."

He followed her to the corner and slid into the front seat of a little foreign sedan, still clutching his pound of coffee.   She drove like a demon, weaving in and out of the rush-hour lines of traffic.   In five minutes they'd reached the run-down section of Union, where the buildings waited for demolition, and he knew this was her destination.   She parked the car and led him up a narrow flight of dimly lit stairs to an apartment above a vacant barber shop.   In view of the long-haired residents, Leopold could easily understand why it had been forced to close.

"Is Freddy here?" he asked the girl, shifting the coffee to his left hand so his right would be near his gun.

"Who told you his name?" she asked, startled.

"You did."

"All right.   No, he's not here.   If he knew what I was doing, he'd probably kill me!" she prophesied.

She unlocked the door and led Leopold into a drab, dim living room.   A large white cat came running to meet her, and she knelt to stroke its fur.   "Where are the diamonds?" he asked her.

"This way.   In the kitchen."

He followed her out, expecting a trap, expecting a seduction, expecting almost anything but the little leather pouch she took from the breadbox and opened before his eyes.   She poured them out on the counter—big diamonds, little diamonds, some in rings but most unset.   Leopold simply stared, almost at a loss for words. "There are all of them?" he asked finally.

"Yes."

"How did Hoffman get them to you?   He's in jail."

"He has an accomplice who brought them to Freddy.   Now take them and go, before he comes back!"

But as Leopold's hand closed over the little pouch of diamonds, they heard a sound at the apartment door.   It was a key in a lock, and a moment later they heard the door open.

"Is that him?" Leopold whispered.

"Yes, yes!   He'll kill us both!"

"Go out and try to stall him."

She hurried through the swinging kitchen door, her face white, and Leopold looked around for a way out.   There was only a door to a dead-end pantry, and a window that looked out onto a back alley.   He tried the window and found it painted shut, unbudging.   He turned back toward the door to the living room, listening to the muffled voices on the other side, and slipped the revolver from his holster.   He stared down at the jewels for a moment and an idea came to him.

Two minutes later, he stepped through the swinging door with his gun drawn. "Hold it right there, Freddy."

There was a gasp from the girl and Freddy turned, startled at the voice, but it took him only an instant to realize what was happening.   "You damned little double-crossing tramp!" he shouted at the girl.   "Glenda, I'll kill you for this!" He started for her, but Leopold waved him back with the gun.

"You'll kill no one.   I'm Captain Leopold of Violent Crimes, and if anything happens to her I'll have you behind bars."

"What did she tell you?"

"She brought me here to give me the diamonds, to try and save your skin, but somebody beat us to them.   They're gone."

Freddy was on his feet.   He was a little man with mouselike features, and he moved now like a rodent who discovered the trap does not even contain a piece of cheese.   "What do you mean, they're gone?   They can't be gone!"

Glenda's eyes had widened in wonder, as she tried to decide what Leopold was up to.   "Look for yourself," he told Freddy, and lowered his gun.

The little man lost no time in getting to the kitchen.   He tore through the breadbox, the wastebasket, the cupboards, while Leopold stood in the doorway. Finally, after ten minutes of searching, he asked, "Where are they, Glenda?   Get them now!"

"It's like he said, Freddy!   Honest!"

"You hid them somewhere," he accused.

"No!   Honest!"

"Would she have brought me here if she'd hidden the diamonds somewhere else?"   Leopold argued.

Freddy eyed him with open distrust.   "How do I know they're not in your pocket?"

Leopold put away his gun and raised his arms.   "You can search me if you want."   Now that he'd seen Freddy in action, he knew he didn't need the gun to take him, if it came to that.

The little man stepped close, eyeing Leopold, and ran his hands carefully over his body, checking his topcoat and pants cuffs and sleeves.   It was a good search, but he found nothing.   Leopold removed his gun to show the inside of the holster, then opened the revolver itself to show that the chambers held nothing but bullets.

"What's in the bag?" Freddy asked.

Leopold smiled. "A pound of coffee. I was on my way home when Glenda contacted me."

Freddy took out the coffee can and looked into the bag. Then he replaced it in disgust. "All right, I believe you—but if the diamonds aren't here, where are they?"

"I'm as anxious to get them as you are," Leopold assured him. "It seems to me there's only one other person who could have them."

"Who's that?"

"The guy who brought them to you in the first place—Rudy Hoffman's accomplice."

Freddy thought about that. "Why would he take them?"

Leopold shrugged. "With Hoffman in jail, maybe he figured he could keep the loot for himself. By delivering the diamonds to you, and then stealing them back, he'd be in the clear."

"Yeah," Freddy said, beginning to go along with it. "That damned double-crosser would pull something like this!"

"Want to tell me who he is?"

Freddy's eyes narrowed in distrust. "I'll handle it, cop."

"Look, you're on very thin ice. If I catch you with those diamonds, I could arrest you for receiving stolen property."

Freddy thought about it. "No," he decided, "I'm not telling you. Maybe the guy didn't take them."

Leopold sighed and turned to the girl. "Glenda, who is Hoffman's accomplice?"

"I don't know. I didn't see him."

"She's telling the truth, cop. I'm the only one who knows, besides Hoffman—and he's not about to talk. Even if he gets sent up, it wouldn't be for too long, and when he gets out he can still work his sweet little scheme in other cities."

"Are you part of his scheme?"

"I was going to fence the gems, that's all. Don't bother taking notes, though, because I'll deny everything."

"If you won't tell me who the accomplice is, call him up. Tell him you know he took the stuff and get him over here."

That idea seemed to appeal to the little man. "Yeah," he said slowly. "Maybe I could do that."

"If I get the diamonds and the accomplice, Freddy, you're off the hook."

"All right, I'll call him."

He walked to the phone and Leopold shot Glenda a look that told her to play along with him. Given a bit of luck, he'd have the accomplice and get her off the hook with Freddy.

"Hello? This is Freddy Doyle. Yeah, yeah . . . Well, something's gone wrong. The diamonds are missing . . . You heard me, missing! . . . Well, you damned well better get over here to the apartment . . .   Yeah, right now! And if you've got those stones, you better have 'em with you!''

He hung up and Leopold said, ''That was good.   Did he admit taking them?''

''Hell, no!   He thinks I'm pulling a double cross, or that's what he said anyway. He'll be here.''

They sat down to wait, and Leopold watched the darkness settle over the city. He felt good, knowing the next hour's work would probably wrap up the case. ''Get me a drink,'' Freddy ordered the girl at one point, and she hurried out to the kitchen.

It was just after seven o'clock when the buzzer sounded and they heard someone starting up the stairs.   ''Expecting anyone else?''   Leopold asked.

''No, that'll be him.   Better be careful—he might have a gun.''

''Let him in.   I'll be right behind you at the door.''

While Glenda stood terrified in the kitchen doorway, Freddy Doyle opened the apartment door.   He peered into the now-darkened hall and asked, ''Is that you . . . ?''

Leopold cursed silently.   He tried to step back quickly and pull Freddy with him, but it was too late.   Three quick shots came with deafening suddenness from the darkness, and Freddy toppled backward into his arms.

''Stop!'' Leopold shouted.   ''Police!''

He heard the running footsteps on the stairway, and allowed Freddy's limp body to sag to the floor.   Behind him, Glenda was screaming.   Leopold made it to the banister and fired a shot down the stairway, but he had no target.   The street door was yanked open, and Freddy's assailant was gone.   By the time Leopold reached the street there was no sign of him.

He climbed the stairs and went back into the apartment.   Glenda was on the floor, kneeling in a widening pool of blood.   *''He's dead!''* she shouted, close to hysterics.

''I know,'' Leopold said, feeling suddenly old.   He walked to the telephone and dialed headquarters.

Fletcher found him in his office, staring glumly at the wall.   ''I came as soon as I could, Captain.   What happened?''

''I bungled, that's what happened, Fletcher.   I was trying to pull off a neat trick, and I got a guy killed.''

Fletcher sat down in his usual chair, opposite the desk.   ''Tell me about it.''

Leopold ran quickly over the events of the evening, from his visit to the hospital, through the shooting of Freddy Doyle.   ''I didn't think our man was desperate enough to commit murder,'' he admitted.

''Why would he kill Doyle?''

''Because he saw it was a trap.   Maybe the bullets were aimed at me, too, but Doyle was in the way.   I suppose he suspected something when Freddy called to say the diamonds were missing, because he knew he hadn't taken them.''

''But where were they?'' Fletcher asked.   ''You said you saw them.''

Leopold nodded. "They're right here—my one accomplishment for the night."
He took the can of coffee from its paper bag. "I had only a couple of minutes
alone in that kitchen, but I got the idea that Freddy could lead me to Hoffman's
accomplice if he thought the accomplice had returned and stolen the diamonds back
again. So I used a can opener to open the bottom of this coffee can part way.
I emptied just enough coffee into the sink so there'd be room in the can for this
pouch of diamonds. Then I bent the bottom shut the best I could, and capped it
with this plastic lid they give you, just so no coffee would run out. When Freddy
was searching for the diamonds, he actually lifted the can out of its bag, but the
top was still sealed and he never thought to examine the bottom."

Fletcher opened the pouch and spilled a few of the gems onto the desk top. "A
clever trick, Captain."

"Clever—except that now Freddy is dead and we've got a murder on our hands.
Our man isn't one to stand still for games."

The lieutenant was frowning down at the gems. "If Hoffman used an accomplice, it had to be somebody who came in contact with him during those few
minutes after the robbery. He couldn't have hidden the diamonds anywhere,
because the street was searched, and there's only one person he had physical contact
with—only one person he could have slipped the jewels to."

Leopold nodded. "I've been thinking the same thing, Fletcher. Put out a
pickup order on Neil Quart."

The young man sat uncomfortably in the interrogation room chair, looking from
one to the other of them. "What is this, anyway? You drag me down here at
midnight like a common criminal? Just this morning I was a hero!"

"That was this morning," Fletcher said.

Leopold sat on the edge of the desk, close to the man in the chair.
"Look, Neil, I think it's time you told us the whole story. It's not just robbery
now—it's murder."

"Murder! I don't . . ." He started to rise and Fletcher pushed him back in
the chair.

"Hoffman passed those diamonds to someone, who delivered them to a fence
and later killed the fence. You're the only one who had physical contact with
Hoffman after the robbery."

"But I ran after him! I wrestled with him! I held him till the police got there!
You know I did!"

"And while you were conveniently holding him, he slipped you the diamonds."

"No! You're crazy! I didn't . . ."

Leopold began pacing the room. "There's no other way it could have been.
You have to be the accomplice, Quart."

"Look, it doesn't make sense! He was getting away! Why should there be
this elaborate scheme to pass me the diamonds when he was getting away with
them? If I hadn't grabbed him, he'd have made good his escape."

Leopold thought about that, trying to sort out the facts in his mind. What Neil

Quart said made sense, too much sense. "Where were you tonight around seven o'clock?"

"Working in Bambaum's shipping department, like every night. You can ask them."

"All right," Leopold said with a sigh. "Get out of here. Go on home. We'll check it in the morning."

Fletcher looked surprised. "But Captain . . ."

"It's all right, Fletcher. I was wrong—again. This is my night for being wrong."

Fletcher followed him back into his office. "Let me fix you some coffee, Captain."

Leopold handed over the can. "I've lost it, Fletcher. I can't even think straight anymore. I jump on some poor kid and try to make a murderer out of him. I get some guy killed for nothing."

"You recovered the diamonds, Captain."

"Yeah."

Fletcher was filling the coffee pot. "Well, Hoffman sure did something with those diamonds. He had them when he hit Officer Begler, and he didn't have them when they grabbed him a few minutes later."

Leopold sat up straight. "How do we know that, Fletcher?"

"What? Well, hell, he sure didn't crack Begler's skull because he *wasn't* carrying the diamonds."

"Fletcher," Leopold said very slowly, "I think that's exactly what he did."

They were waiting for Peter Arnold in the morning, when he unlocked the door of the Midtown Diamond Exchange. He glanced up, surprised, and said, "Captain Leopold! You look as if you've been up all night."

"I have," Leopold said, following him inside the store. Fletcher came too, but stayed by the door. "I've been getting people out of bed, checking on your finances, Arnold. I didn't want to make another mistake."

"What?"

"It was a damned clever plan, I have to say that. I suppose Rudy Hoffman thought it up, and then got friendly with some jewelers around town till he found one who needed the money."

"I don't know what you're talking about."

"I think you do, Arnold. You closed the shop at nine o'clock the other night, and quickly removed the diamonds from that window. Rudy Hoffman came by as scheduled, broke the window and ran. You pocketed the diamonds and called the police. Then you took the diamonds to Freddy Doyle, who was supposed to sell them. The plan had a great advantage—Hoffman didn't have to spend precious seconds scooping up the loot in the window, and if he were arrested a block or two away, he'd be clean. No diamonds, no evidence. He probably planned to dump the cane and topcoat and keep on going. Only Officer Begler wasn't where he was supposed to be, directing traffic. Hoffman knew it was too soon to be arrested—right by the window. He didn't have the diamonds and the whole plot would be obvious, so he hit Begler with the cane and ran. That's when he had more bad luck—a young fellow named Neil Quart chased after him. You had the diamonds all the time, but unfortunately Hoffman didn't even have a chance to pretend he'd dumped them. We had an impossible crime on our hands, even though you didn't plan it that way."

Peter Arnold continued staring at them. He ran a damp tongue over his lips and said, "I assume you have some proof for all this?"

"Plenty of proof. You're in bad financial trouble, and aiding in the theft of your company's diamonds was an easy way out for you. We've got the gems back, and with you in jail I'm sure Hoffman can be persuaded to tell it like it was."

"There were witnesses who saw Hoffman at the window, though."

"Yes, but they only saw him reach inside. He would hardly have had time to scoop up all those loose diamonds, and only you, Arnold, actually said you saw him do that. You said you saw it while you were locking the door, even though there's a velvet drape at the rear of the window that keeps you from seeing anything from inside the store. You didn't see him take the diamonds because he never took them. They were already in your pocket when he broke the window and started running."

"I don't—"

"You panicked when Freddy called you, and especially when you saw me in the doorway with him. You recognized me, of course, and started shooting. That alone told me the killer was someone I'd questioned in connection with the case."

Peter Arnold moved then, as Leopold knew he would. It was only a matter of guessing whether the murder gun was in his coat pocket or behind the counter. His hand went for his pocket, and Fletcher shot him from the doorway. It was a neat shot in the shoulder—the sort Fletcher was good at.

Arnold toppled against a showcase, crying and clutching his shoulder, as Leopold slipped the gun from his pocket. "You should have dumped this in the river," he said. "We could never have made the murder charge stick without it."

Fletcher locked the front door and called for an ambulance. They had to get Arnold patched up, and booked for murder and robbery, and then they could both go home to bed.

MARY BARRETT

One for the Crow

Ed chose the fast route, the new highway which was engineered to bypass Ozark and go directly into the hills. Had he taken the old road south from Springfield, he probably would have lived a longer and a happier life. He certainly would have enjoyed a more pleasant trip along a more scenic route than the one he elected.

About twenty miles out of town, on the old road, he would have come upon a scene with the misty charm of a French impressionist painting: from the hilltop, grapevines march down the slope in orderly rows; in the valley below, as if protected by the hills from change and blight, lies the clean, sleepy town of Ozark, Missouri.

From his vantage point on top of the hill, Ed would have seen the water tower rising white against the green hills beyond, and the iron-gray smokestack of the cheese factory. Had he then continued downhill, he soon would have come to an official sign: *Ozark, Pop. 800* and, on a nearby tree, a less formal but more enthusiastic announcement: *Welcome to Ozark, a good live town.*

Clattering across the Finley River bridge and passing an abandoned mill with its rusty wheel forever still, he would have arrived at the Ozark square where the red brick courthouse stands in the center.

There are always a few men sitting on shaded benches in front of the courthouse, chewing tobacco and occasionally exchanging a few words about the weather, the crops, chicken feed, pesticides. Any of these local experts could have warned Ed about the risks he was taking, but he might not have listened anyway, or heard what was said to him. He was that kind of guy. Besides, a warning of sudden death in such a setting would be difficult for anyone to believe, for the scene is deceiving. All appears to be peace and rural contentment; but primitive passions and strong hatreds are bred in the hills, and old ideas and old grudges die hard. Just five minutes' conversation with one of the fellows in front of the courthouse would have given him a warning, but to gain a little time, he missed his chance.

The powerful engine of his big rented car purred quietly under the hood as Ed looked out the window with distaste at the scrubby oaks and hickory trees struggling for life in the thin topsoil. He felt a city man's scorn for wasted space and a successful man's scorn for what he saw as failure.

"In this Godforsaken place," he said to himself, "the hillbillies will be glad for the chance at a little cash."

Ed had a reputation in Hollywood for always being on top of any job, and he was certainly going to be on top of this one with no trouble; *no trouble at all,* he thought.

He wheeled the car off the highway onto a likely-looking farm-to-market road. It was pitted from the winter freeze, and Ed was forced to slow down. A thin film of dust blanketed the weeds and wild strawberries growing on each side of the narrow road, but no matter. The air-conditioned car was sealed against intrusion by the environment.

Ahead appeared the first sign of habitation—a dilapidated farmhouse with a much-patched roof. One window was covered with cardboard, like a patch over a missing eye. A thin streak of smoke drifted from the chimney. A white hen clucked dispiritedly in the front yard.

Ed turned the car off the road onto dry grass, stopped and stepped out, slamming the car door. He looked around speculatively.

It was a clear, cloudless spring day, and after the steady hum of the car, the silence was startling. Far away, a meadowlark sang its pure notes.

Ed walked toward the house. "Hello," he called. "Anyone here? Anyone home?" There was no answer.

He rounded the corner of the house. There, bent low over the red earth, was a tall, bony man in faded blue overalls. His skin, tanned to leather, was bare to the sun over the bib of the overalls.

"What's the matter with you?" Ed demanded. "Didn't you hear me?"

The man didn't look up. He said shortly, but with no animus, "I heard you. Long ways off."

Ed came closer. "What are you planting there?"

The man at last stood up. He looked Ed in the eye and said, "Corn," the monosyllable discouraging conversation.

Ed tried to remember what he knew about corn. It was very little. He had seen some pictures, though, and they didn't look like this.

"I thought you planted corn in furrows," he said.

"Some do. Where there's not much rain. Plenty of rain here. Plant corn in hills. Four seeds to a hill."

"Why four?"

The man explained, matter-of-factly, "One for the cutworm, one for the crow, one for the dry rot, and one to grow."

"Oh," Ed said, unenlightened. "When will it come up?"

"Tassels out about July," the man answered. Then, clearly dubious, he asked, "You thinking to grow corn hereabouts?"

"Oh, no," Ed said hastily. "I'm just looking for local color."

The man looked around at the familiar greens and browns of his landscape, and then inquisitively back at Ed.

"The way people talk," Ed explained, "their customs, their folkways. Those things."

The farmer frowned; whether disapproving or puzzled, it was impossible to tell.

"Reckon you better come inside, then, and talk to Ma. She knows all about folks' ways." Moving to the back door, he added, "I'm Luke Anderson. This is our place, Ma's and mine, since we lost our son."

Ed followed him through a squeaking screen door into the kitchen. It was cool and dark after the bright sun outside.

A woman with gray hair stood at a stained sink, shelling beans.

Luke said, without preamble, "This fellow wants to know about our ways."

The woman turned to them, her face expressionless. She wiped her hands on her cotton apron, slowly and deliberately. She inspected the visitor as she might have scrutinized a mule offered for sale. Like her husband, the woman was browned by the sun; and like him, she was economically lean, without an ounce of unnecessary flesh.

She pulled a straight wooden chair up to the kitchen table and put her hands on the oilcloth, palms down, as if preparing for a seance. Luke and Ed sat down too.

"Why do you want to know our ways?" she asked with guarded curiosity.

"We want to make a movie here in the hills," Ed said. "The setting has to look authentic. Real, you know." He was uncertain how much these ignorant people could understand. "We want to cast local people, in minor roles, of course. And we'll pay."

The woman was clearly not impressed. She looked at him sharply from star-tlingly-light blue eyes. "They done made a movie once, nearby."

"I know," Ed said. It had been a disaster. Every possible thing had gone wrong—the entire cast sick, equipment breaking down and even disappearing, and the director actually dropping out of sight, never to be seen again. That had caused quite a stir in the press. It was, in fact, the only thing which saved the movie from being a box-office disaster. No one particularly mourned the loss of the director. He hadn't turned out any good work in years.

The woman said, "Those other movie folk built cabins and pretend barns from stuff they brought with them. Those things are still there. Maybe you could use them for your movie and not mess up a new part of the hills?"

Ed smiled indulgently. *These people are so naive.* "I'm afraid that won't do. That old set is much too artificial. We need virgin territory. Of course, we'll improve on it some. But the old site is ruined for our purposes."

The woman spoke quietly, "That's how it seems to us, too—spoilt. Spoilt for living. Spoilt for farming. Spoilt for looking at. You think to do that here, on the side of the hill? Spoil it?"

"Not at all," Ed said impatiently. *Don't these hicks understand anything?* "We'll bring new life to this place. Lots of tourists will come just to watch us shooting. There'll be new business, new money pouring in, lots of action."

A glance passed between husband and wife which Ed could not interpret. The woman put both hands on the table and pushed herself to her feet. "Since you're here, you best stay on for dinner," she said.

The meal was quickly served. She put the plates on the oilcloth. Ed looked dubiously at the food.   There were ham hocks, beans, and hot corn bread, with fresh warm milk.   Ed managed to choke down enough not to offend.   He thought wistfully of a cold martini and rare roast beef.

"I'll red up the dishes," the woman said.   "You men go along to the front porch.   We can set in the shade and talk awhile."

Ed followed Luke through the living room.   The shades were down, and the room had the dimly lit appearance of being underwater.   The faded carpet was worn through to the floor in places.   A sofa, tilting on three legs, was covered with an afghan.   Ed thought with satisfaction, *We can use this.   It certainly looks authentic.*

They stepped out onto the porch.   The floorboards were warped, and for a moment the wavy effect made Ed dizzy.   They sat down in straight wooden chairs, identical to those in the kitchen.   The woman soon joined them.

They looked through the haze of the warm afternoon across the yard to a hill beyond.   A wasp buzzed busily at his nest in a corner under the roof.

"That hill over there," Ed said.   "We could use that in several scenes.   It looks easy to climb."

The woman glanced at him.   Her voice was soft but clear.

"Some say that hill should be let be.   Most folks won't go there for any reason."

"Oh?" Ed asked, intrigued.

"It's the Bald Knob," Luke said, as if that explained everything.

"Bald Knob?" Ed asked.

The woman explained, "A bald knob is nothing but a hill with no trees growing on top.   This one's different, though."

"It's where the Bald Knobbers met," Luke said.

The woman leaned her head against the back of her chair and gazed off into the distance.   "Was a time," she said, "when roads were bad and town too far away.   We hadn't no pertection of the law.   No one to see that cows wasn't stolen nor strangers didn't come, causing trouble."   She paused and looked at Ed.   If he found any significance for himself in the statement, however, he gave no indication.

She went on: "Some of the men hereabouts got together to make themselves the law officers.   They had their meetings atop that bald knob there.   Sometimes at night a person could see their bonfire.   It was a good sight.   Made a body feel safe, to know someone was there, caring.

"Then real trouble set in.   Some outsider come and set to build himself a fancy house on Bald Knob.   He liked the view, he said.   We never had much truck with outsiders.   They never seem to catch our ways of thinking.   This man was extra bad, building there on Bald Knob where our men had their meetings, and not understanding why that was wrong.   He brought a curse to the hills and to all the folks hereabouts.   We knowed 'twas him all right.   No one else was new in these parts.

"There wasn't no rain for months on end.   The cows went dry.   The hens stopped laying.   Folks was hungry, and we couldn't see no way out of our trouble.   It was the outsider and the strangeness he brought to the hills.   The hills don't tolerate no alien ways. Something had to change. So the Bald Knobbers came in the dark one night and killed him where he lay."

She paused to let the point strike home.

"Then the real lawmen came from Ozark. They heard of what was done, and they said our men had to be punished. The Bald Knobbers came to trial, and the jury said they had to be hanged. One of those was our son."

The tone of her voice hadn't altered in any degree with that statement, and Ed could almost imagine that he hadn't heard it correctly.

"The real lawmen had trouble, though, when it came to carrying out what they wanted to do. No one hereabouts would do the hanging. Those men were our own, and nobody would have it on his soul to kill their own folks. So the law sent off to Kansas City for a real hanging man."

Luke prompted, "Brought his own ropes."

"Yes. And built the gallows, one for each man, twelve in a row right there on the courthouse square. People come from miles around to watch.

"On the hanging morning, they brought the Bald Knobbers from the jailhouse— some men, and some just boys not yet to razor growed. Our son was one not yet a man."

The woman was silent for a moment, in tribute to the blindness of justice. "But then a strangeness come. Seemed like that hanging man just couldn't get his job done. There was something didn't want our folks to hang. Some say the rope he brought from Kansas City was green, and stretched. That's as may be. Maybe it was something else. Anyways, the trap would spring and a man would drop through, stretching that rope with his weight, and dangle there with his feet bouncing on the ground. You can't break no man's neck that way.

"When it was all over, they couldn't hang but two. At last, they just give up and let the others go. No one had the heart for any more. The Bald Knobbers were let go free and told to go away, somewheres else. They never been seen since."

She gazed at the top of the hill. "And yet, there's some folks say their spirits never left. Some say that at least one Bald Knobber never went away at all. Sometimes you can see a bonfire on Bald Knob at night. Some say the Bald Knobbers do pertect us yet. From strangers and the like."

Only the wasp, buzzing, made a sound in the still air.

Ed said, "That's quite a story. I'm going to climb that hill and see how things look on top."

Luke said quietly, "I wouldn't, if I was you."

The woman said, "Go, if you want." There was warning in her tone—and promise.

Across the still afternoon a mournful, cooing sound came from far away.

"Rain crow," Luke announced. "Means rain soon, for sure."

Ed looked up, unbelieving, at the clear sky, and smiled complacently. "Well, I'd better go take a look at Bald Knob now, before the deluge."

He set out across the dry, brittle grass. In a few minutes Luke and the woman saw him start up the hill. Then he passed from sight among the oak trees.

The two stood up.   "It'll be all right, Luke," the woman reassured, putting her hand on his arm.   "He's there.   I know he is.   He'll take care of everything. Just like he done before, with that other movie man."

They went indoors.

Night came.   Ed didn't return.   A watchful person might have thought that he saw a fire burning on top of Bald Knob as darkness set in.

Then the storm struck.   Lightning flickered on the horizon.   The first huge, spattering drops of rain fell, bringing the odor of moisture on dry land.   A howling wind bent the trees.   Then torrents of water poured from the sky.   Lightning bolts flashed and thunder bounced from hill to hill.

Luke and the woman looked at one another wordlessly, and went to bed.

The morning sun shone on a world washed clean and shining.   Luke and the woman set out up the hill.   Ed's footprints were washed away.   There was no sign that anyone had been there before them.

Luke found him just below the tree line.   Above where Ed lay, the hilltop was bare.   The big oak tree which lay on top of him had been split by a lightning bolt. Under it, Ed was crushed like a bug under a man's heel.

The woman spoke softly: "Get him out from there, Luke.   We'll plant him in the hill, where we planted the other man."

Luke bent to the job.

"It was our son again," the woman said with pride.   "He lured that man under the oak tree.   Any hill man knows better than to go under a tree in a thunderstorm."

Luke intoned, "One for the cutworm, one for the crow . . ."

HENRY SLESAR

Happiness before Death

T he psychiatrist's voice, in some ventriloquial effect, seemed to be emanating from his framed diploma over his head. The engraved scrawl lent majesty to his otherwise mundane name: Harold Miller. Studying the splendid loops and swirls, Werther Oaks wondered if Dr. Miller had supplied his own signature to be grandly redesigned by the fine Italian hand—or was it Viennese? He squinted and made out the place of matriculation: New Jersey. Where have all the Viennese psychiatrists gone? Dr. Miller seemed to realize he wasn't listening. Throat-clearing followed.

"I'm sorry," Werther said. "I'm having trouble concentrating. What you're saying is—well, I can't really believe what you're saying."

"I know," Dr. Miller said, the voice now emanating gravely from its natural source. "It's not an easy thing to hear about one's own wife. But I honestly believe it's so, Mr. Oaks. That overdose was no accident. As Freud once said, there *are* no accidents."

"It's just hard to comprehend. I mean, about Sylvia. With all she has." A wry addition: "I don't mean to include myself, of course. I haven't been a bad sort of husband, but I don't ask you to accept that."

"And I didn't ask you here to point an accusing finger either."

Werther looked at Miller's fingers. They were short and stubby. Werther's hands were exquisite. He had been a hand model when he met Sylvia at the Grosse Pointe Country Club. When she learned of his odd profession, she had smiled insultingly. Later, on the terrace, she had wondered aloud what it would be like to be touched by a pair of famous hands.

"Dr. Miller," Werther said, "my wife swore to me that she took those extra pills purely by mistake. Are you telling me that it was deliberate?"

"I'd say it was the expression of an unconscious wish. Because, you see, the fact that your wife has 'everything' doesn't mean that she has—*everything*. Do you see what I mean?"

Werther considered slapping Sylvia that night, with one of his famous hands. Instead, he framed her face between his palms and planted a gentle kiss on her lips. The slap would have surprised her less.

Two months later, despite the anguish of her friends, who bluntly called Werther a fortune hunter and worse, they were married. On their honeymoon, she had seized him by the wrists and exulted, "Now they're mine!"   He made a joke about giving his hands in marriage, and Sylvia had laughed.   It was the last time he'd heard her laugh.

"Well, she's not exactly a cheerful woman," Werther told the psychiatrist.   "I knew that from the moment I met her.   She has fits of depression, but I never thought of them as being terribly serious."

"She tells me that she would lock herself in her room for three and four days at a time."

"Well, yes, she does that now and then.   It's her way of getting away from all the pressures."

"What pressures?"

"Having money doesn't take away obligations," Werther said, actually parroting Sylvia's financial manager, Vossberg.

"Ah," Miller said, looking almost Viennese now.   "But having money doesn't always guarantee emotional health."

"Won't buy happiness?"

"To a psychiatrist," Miller said in deep tones, "that cliché is fraught with meaning.   And there, I think, is the key to your wife's problem.   The silver spoon she was born with is still in her mouth, and now it's choking her.   Perhaps to death."

Werther's eyes blinked several times.

"Money has made her miserable," Dr. Miller continued.   "Money has made her lead a life devoid of personal satisfaction.   She is unable to enjoy simple pleasures, and therefore she experiences *no* pleasure at all."

"Found *that* out," Werther murmured.   "But do you really think she's unhappy enough to kill herself?"

"Unless something is done," Dr. Miller said, "there may well be another 'accident' like the one two nights ago.   And this next one may prove fatal."

When Dr. Miller walked him out of the office, Werther offered one of his famous hands, and it was trembling badly.   Miller suggested that he get some rest, too.

Werther left the medical building and was surprised to find that it was still daylight.   His XKL was at the curb, overparked by half an hour, but he still took the time to walk around the block and think about what he had just learned.

Sylvia might kill herself.

Sylvia was so miserable that she was going to die of her misery.

The full import filled him up like a wineglass, and the effect was like champagne. If nobody had been watching, he would have leaped in the air with joy.

Velvet knew something was different about him, but waited with catlike contentment to let Werther make his own explanation.   She curled up on the floor beside him as he sat rigidly on the sofa, smoking a small brown cigar and inhaling it like the cigarettes he had eschewed.   She tugged one sock down to his shoes and rubbed his ankle.

"Thursday night," Werther said slowly, "Sylvia swallowed four sleeping pills, maybe five.   Said she made a mistake.   Thought they were aspirin."

"Who takes five aspirin?" Velvet asked logically.

"Ah," Werther said, realizing that he now sounded like Dr. Miller.

"Wushy-mushy-tushy, will you please tell me what's the big deal?"

He winced at the name, but it was something worth living with.   Velvet was the highest-paid girl in the Tilford Model Agency.   She never earned less than a hundred dollars an hour, which made her personal income higher than Werther's own allowance (dispensed by Vossberg).   Under the circumstances, he considered himself lucky to be Velvet's special friend.   They had met in the agency several months before his Grosse Pointe encounter with Sylvia.   (He had gone to Detroit to perform in a commercial for one of the auto companies.   "Watch these hands on this wheel and learn what's really new in auto engineering!")   When he had married Sylvia, Velvet had screamed at him for almost a full hour, ending up with a case of laryngitis that kept her from performing in a Silk-Creme commercial the next day.   Every month after that, she sent him a bill for the residuals she wasn't receiving.   He had finally paid his debt with a diamond bracelet charged at Tiffany. To this day, Vossberg thought he had presented the gift to Sylvia.

"My wife is going to kill herself," Werther said.   "That's the big deal."

"Are you joking?   Are you saying that for a *joke?*"

"Vel," Werther said with pained lips, "do you think I'd joke about such a thing?   Do you realize what it *means?*   We don't have to go through with the car business, with the whole chancy *brake* business, with that whole sticky, rotten, scary *murder* business!"

"Oh, Wushy," Velvet wailed, covering her ears, "don't say that word here. How can you *say* that word in my house?   Who knows who could *hear* you?   You know we promised never to say 'mm-mm'."

"We've been talking about mm-mm for six months," Werther said.   "And now poor Sylvia may mm-mm herself."

"*Poor* Sylvia?"

"Yes," Werther said.   "She's worse off than I thought—all mixed up inside, hates her own money.   That's a laugh, isn't it?   Her hating the money I love so much."

"You got to be crazy to hate money," Velvet said.   "Maybe that's why she's going to that shrink, because she's crazy."

"She's unhappy," Werther said, sighing out a trail of smoke.   "She's always been unhappy.   Because the money never meant anything to her—like it does to me, for instance."

"And me," Velvet said.   "Look, Werther, look," jabbing an inch-long nail at the corner of her eyes.   "Look at the crow's-feet starting.   In another year, down come the rates."

"There's no telling when she'll do it," Werther said.   "No telling when she'll try again.   Maybe next week, maybe next year, maybe two years from now."

"Hey!"

"The psychiatrist couldn't predict, he just doesn't know.   It all depends."

"On how *unhappy* she is?   Then make her unhappy, Wushy!"

"Yeah, fine, great."   He frowned.   "And the money, the will, the inheritance?

I'm hanging by a thread right now, and don't think Vossberg isn't standing by with a big pair of scissors. No," he said sadly, "I don't *want* to make that poor woman unhappy. I like her, Velvet, I really feel sorry for that poor miserable person."

"That's what I love about you," Velvet sighed, a soft cheek against his ankle. "You're a person with heart."

"So what I have to do," Werther said, "is *give* her an overdose of sleeping pills. Dr. Miller will swear she was ready for it, and nobody's the wiser."

Sylvia's eyes were closed when he entered the bedroom. His heartbeat accelerated as he went up to the satin-sheeted oval bed and put his hand close to her mouth. Her breath fogged his polished fingernails.

"Sylvia?" he whispered.

"I'm not asleep," she said. Her eyes came open and looked at him directly; her pupils were like black wells filled with unshed tears. "I was waiting for you. I wanted to hear what Dr. Miller told you."

"Now who said I saw Dr. Miller?"

"The scratch-pad near the phone. You wrote down his address. Obviously he called you. What did he say about me?"

"About you, nothing." Werther smiled. "He just wanted to know what kind of rotten husband doesn't watch what his wife takes out of the medicine cabinet."

"How dare he call you a rotten husband?"

"But I am," he said cheerfully. "Look at the hours I keep. If I had gotten home before ten that night, this wouldn't have happened."

"I know you work hard," Sylvia said. Of course, she knew nothing of the kind; she merely assumed that all men worked hard. Her father had made seventy million dollars by never leaving his office except to get his teeth cleaned. Werther, who now worked for the company her father had founded (American Bit & Drill), was actually the most indolent executive imaginable, which suited everyone just fine. An ignorant executive owes his colleagues an avoidance of diligence.

"Tell me the truth," Sylvia said. "What did Dr. Miller say about me? Did he tell you all my little traumas?"

"No," Werther answered. "He just said that you were a very wonderful person who hasn't been given a real chance to be herself."

For a moment, the wells of her eyes almost brought in a gusher.

"There must be something wrong with me, Werther. Why can't I *feel* happy? I know I *should* be happy, but all I feel is this emptiness inside. Werther, tell me what to do!"

"Right now, darling," her husband said, "just close your eyes and try to sleep. Remember, Vossberg will be here in the morning. You'll need your strength to put up with him."

"You're my strength, Werther," she said, and clutched at his beautiful hands.

The gesture choked him up. When her eyes closed again, still tearless, he felt moisture under his own lids. "Poor Sylvia," he whispered.

The next day, he flung all six darts at the target in his office, and then picked up the phone with determination.

"Velvet," he said, "I've got to talk to you."

"I'm listening."

"Not on the phone.   Are you going to the shampoo job?"

"All through.   Now I've come home to wash my hair."

"I'll meet you there."

He forced her to sit on the couch while he paced the floor.

"I can't do it," he said.

"What?"

"Don't get excited."   She wasn't; just baffled.

"I don't mean I've changed my mind.   I mean I just can't do it *now,* right now. It wouldn't be right."

"What wouldn't be?   Mm-mm-ing her?"

"Yes.   Mm-mm-ing her.   Not now, Velvet, I just can't."

"But you said now would be the best time, Wushy, on account of her psychiatrist *knows* she's suicidal, and he'll blame it all on *her,* not on you."

"I know what I said."

"Then why wait?   I mean, if she's miserable now, that's the time when she'd *do* it."

"But that's also the reason I *can't* do it, Vel.   Because she's miserable.   Because that poor lady hasn't known a day of really being happy in her whole life.   Choking on that silver spoon."

"What spoon?"

"Never mind," Werther said.   "The point is, she's had nothing to be happy about.   Not even me."

"But she loves you."

"I'm her strength," Werther said, now sounding like Sylvia.   "That's all I am to her.   But I haven't made her happy, and that isn't right.   It isn't fair, Velvet, to take all her money without giving her *something* in return."

"Gee, you're a funny sort of person," Velvet said, not without admiration.

"So what I was thinking," Werther said, "was that I might try to make her happy—really happy—before she dies."

"Huh?"

"I don't know if I can succeed.   I don't know if this Dr. Miller really knows what he's talking about, whether his theory is right—that money's spoiled her so bad she can't enjoy the simple things."

"What simple things?"

"You know.   Like the things in nature.   The sky when the clouds are getting together to discuss the rain . . ."

"Oh, Werther, that's beautiful!"

He had read it on a calendar.   "The sky when it's really worth looking at, and the way the ocean rolls, and the way the grass feels when you lie down on it after walking a little too far . . ."

"Yes," Velvet nodded, "yes, I know what you mean, Wushy.   I enjoy those things, too, but it's even nicer if you have money."

"No," he said.   "It's doing these things *without* money, without *paying* for them, without buying a *ticket* to everything and feeling you've got to enjoy them just because there was a price tag attached . . .   Don't you see what I mean?''

"Wushy, will you please tell me what you're going to do?''

"I'm going to take Sylvia on a trip—a special trip—no first-class arrangements, no fancy hotels, nothing that money can buy.   I'm going to see if she can be happy the way poor people can be happy, not giving a damn about tomorrow, just happy to be alive, and with each other, man and woman, sky, ocean, grass.   I know it sounds crazy, maybe *she'll* think I'm crazy, but I'm going to suggest it.   She's got it coming to her, Vel.   A little happiness before the end.   You know?''

"Yes,'' Velvet said, looking at him in awe.   "And you know what else I know, Wushy?   You're going to make me a wonderful husband.''

Sylvia was incredulous at first.   "A trip without money?   What on earth do you mean?''

He laughed.   "I knew you'd have that reaction, darling.   But I mean every word of it.   Oh, not that we'd be completely flat broke.   We'd take maybe four, five hundred dollars with us.   But we won't go to any of *those* places, we won't stop at hotels, we won't hire cars or do anything else that a couple of crazy kids couldn't afford to do.''

"Werther, I can't believe you're serious.   We've always spent a fortune on our trips—''

"And how much fun did you ever have?   Face it, Sylvia, how much have you enjoyed them?''

"But where would we go?''

"Where do Gypsies go?   Anywhere, everywhere!   No destination.   Off on the open road.''

"In a wagon?''

"How about a bicycle?   How about our feet?   Or our thumbs, for that matter?''

"You mean hitchhike?''

"Why not?   You've got a very pretty thumb; did I ever tell you that?''

"Coming from you, Hands, that's a compliment.''

He laughed like a boy.   "We'll be hoboes, darling.   We'll be vagrants, tramps, wanderers, nomads!   If we're lucky, maybe we'll even get ourselves arrested—''

"No thank you!''

"We'll eat hamburgers in roadside stands and pick blueberries in the woods. We'll stay at the cheapest motels and sign the register Mr. and Mrs. Smith so that no one will suspect that we're legitimately married . . .''

She was actually smiling.

"Werther, I think you're just a little mad.''

"But I want us to be completely mad, Sylvia.   I want us both to know what it feels like to breathe unconditioned air, and swim in unchlorinated water, and drink cheap wine and eat Mrs. Nobody's food and maybe beat the check if we're running out of cash . . .''

"I really think you mean this.''

"I want us to leave tomorrow—tonight—this minute—and not tell anyone where we're going, not even Vossberg; just grab whatever cash that's lying around and take off for parts unknown.   No letter of credit, no word to the bank, no suitcases—''

Sylvia gasped.

"Well, all right, one small suitcase, *small,* just very necessary things."

"Werther, it's the silliest idea I ever heard in my whole life.   I don't think we'd last more than a week doing such a thing."

"If we feel like it, we could stow away on a ship going to Europe.   We could probably bum our way across the entire continent."

"I've never seen you like this, Werther!"

"And I've never seen you really enjoy life, Sylvia," he said taking her into his arms.   "And that's why I want you to say yes."

"And you're sure we shouldn't tell Vossberg?"

Werther beamed with a sense of victory.

"We'll send him a postcard," he said jubilantly.   "We'll send him a card from some tacky gift shop, and we'll write—'having a wonderful time!   Glad you're not here!' ''

For the second time since he knew her, Sylvia laughed.

Velvet received Werther's letter two months later.   She had almost abandoned hope of ever hearing from him again, and her subsequent depression had taken its toll.   Three more crows had marched across her face in the interim, and like an augury, the agency received (and accepted in her name) an assignment to pose in a beer ad for ninety dollars an hour—ten percent downgrade.

She tore open the letter with such excitement that she lost half a dozen words on the second page.

The remains of the letter read as follows:

> Darling Vel,
>
> Sorry I haven't written, but the circumstances made it impossible. Sylvia and I have just returned from Big Sur, where we were staying in a commune which was notable for the fact that it was impossible, literally impossible, to tell the boys from the girls, at least through visual acuity. This was because the male half of the commune (I'm assuming there was a male half) had all decided that beards were "out" this year, even though long hair was still "in." As for myself, however, you will be interested to know that I have a luxuriant brown beard which makes me look a bit like Walt Whitman, I think, only younger and handsomer, if you'll pardon my vanity. Sylvia herself looks entirely different from the woman who left with me on our wild adventure two months ago. She hasn't worn one iota of makeup since the first week (she took half a dozen cosmetics with her when we started out, but she soon threw them away). Just the same, she never looked better. Her skin is brown as a walnut but as unwrinkled as a peach. She's lost at least ten pounds which I thought would make her into a scarecrow, but somehow it suits her very well.

She's terribly pleased about her svelte new figure but oddly enough she doesn't think of it in terms of what clothes she'll drape it in.   She has simply stopped caring about Halston and Yves St. Laurent and Madame Gres and about ever going back to fashionable restaurants or appearing at fashionable parties.   In fact, most of the things that Sylvia thought were necessary to the so-called "good life" no longer hold the slightest interest for her.   But the important thing I wanted you to know is that Sylvia is *happy*. I mean she's *happy*, Vel, she's never been happier or more contented in her entire life.   From the day we left (with exactly four hundred and twelve dollars in our pockets, and the solemn resolution to make it last two months) she found a whole new personality hiding inside that body of hers, a prisoner who was dying to come out and see the world as it really was.   I can't possibly tell you what these two months have been like.   Can you imagine eating goat as a main course for dinner, or sleeping in a haystack for two nights in a row, or riding in a boxcar with three drunken tramps who played the harmonica all night long in terrible cacophony, or getting a job picking apples and eating so many of them that you never wanted to see an apple again, or making friends with a gang of rock-and-roll musicians who took us on their bus all the way to Charlotte, North Carolina, a distance of sixty miles?   Vel, I can't tell you everything, but then we've got lots of time for you to hear the whole story.   All you need know for now is that I did what I thought was right, that I did what I knew I had to do, and now it's all over and finished, and Sylvia and I are coming back home.   She's a changed person, Vel, and a much happier person, but I wanted you to know that I haven't changed, not about the things that are important to me.   I'm sure you know what I mean.   So don't expect me to be in touch with you for several days.   You'll know why in just a little while. Meanwhile, all my love, and don't forget to burn this letter.

Werther

P.S.   I told you to burn this letter.   What are you waiting for?

Velvet burned the letter.

It was a week to the day that she read the news about Sylvia Oaks' tragic death. Only one newspaper, the *News*, considered the story important enough to relate outside of its obituary columns, but in all the papers which reported it, she was described as an "heiress."   The *Times* ran her picture, one obviously taken before her days of nut-brown skin and no makeup.   Most of the obituary was devoted to her father, not her; it was a sad, gratuitous insult, Velvet thought.   The cause of her death was listed as an overdose of sleeping pills.   She was survived by her husband, Werther.   The article in the *News* said she had been "depressed."
When Werther didn't show up the next day, or the day after, Velvet started getting anxiety attacks.   She didn't want to phone him at home; there might still

be mourners around who would raise eyebrows. However, when she still hadn't heard from him by the end of the week, she decided to risk a call. A maid answered, said that he was in conference, and Velvet hung up, more anxious than ever.

That night, Werther called and explained.

The conference was with Vossberg, the man Werther was always mentioning with huge bitterness. He had something to do with money. There were questions about the estate, about probating of the will, questions that Werther couldn't get answered. He sounded troubled. Velvet understood, of course. People who committed mm-mm would have to be troubled.

Finally, Werther called and said he was coming over. He sounded funny.

"You sounded funny," Velvet told him.

She looked at him and added, "You *look* funny."

"It's the beard," Werther said. "I shaved it off. My skin under it was white. The rest of my face is tan. That's why I look funny." He sat heavily on the couch, staring straight ahead.

"Wushy, you didn't learn to take *drugs* or something in that commune, did you?"

"No," Werther said, shaking his head, without moving his eyes.

"Then what is it? Why do you look that way?"

"I made her happy," Werther said dreamily. "I did what I said I'd do, Vel. I made Sylvia happy before she died. Then I gave her those pills, and she went to sleep, and she was smiling. I swear she was smiling when they found her."

"Is that why you're like this?" Velvet asked.

"No," Werther said. He looked down at his exquisite hands. He noticed that there were wrinkles on the back, like the tracks of a bird. Then he looked at Velvet.

"I just came from the lawyer's office," he said. "I found out what Sylvia did when we came back from our trip. She changed her will, Velvet."

"She *what?*"

"She gave it all away. All her money. She gave it all to charity. She wanted to be poor, because that's what made her happy.

"Happy," Werther repeated, the word sounding like the beginning of a dirge.

I Don't Understand It

W ell, I'd been on the road for two days, riding on the produce trucks from El Centro to Bakersfield, when a refrigerator van picked me up and took me straight through to the Salinas Valley. They let me out right where I was headed, too, in front of this dirt road about three miles the other side of San Sinandro.

I stood there on the side of the road, hanging onto the tan duffel with my stuff in it, and it was plenty hot all right, just past noon, and the sun all yellow and hazed over. I looked at the big wood sign that was stuck up there, and it said: JENSEN PRODUCE—PICKERS WANTED, and had a black arrow pointing off down the dirt road. That was the name of the place, sure enough.

I started up the dirt road, and it was pretty dry and dusty. Off on both sides you could see the rows and rows of lettuce shining nice and green in the sun, and the pickers hunched over in there. Most of them looked like Mex's, but here and there was some college boys that are always around to pick in the spring and summer months.

Pretty soon I come over a rise and I could see a wide clearing. There was a big white house set back a ways, and down in front an area that was all paved off. On one side was a big corrugated-iron warehouse, the sun coming off the top of that iron roof near to blinding you, it was so bright. About six flatbeds, a couple of Jimmy pickups and a big white Lincoln was sitting beside the warehouse. All of them had JENSEN PRODUCE done up in these big gold and blue letters on the door.

I come down there onto the asphalt part. Just to my right was four long, flat buildings made of wood, but with corrugated roofs. I knew that was where the pickers put down.

I walked across to the big warehouse. Both of the doors in front was shut, but there was a smaller one to the left and it was standing wide open.

Just as I come up to that door, this woman come out, facing inside, and sure enough she banged right into me before I could get out of the way. I stumbled back and dropped the duffel.

She come around and looked at me. She said, "Oh, I'm sorry. I didn't see you there."

Well, she was about the most beautiful woman I ever saw in my whole life. She had this long dark hair and green eyes with little gold flecks in them, and she was all brown and tan and her skin shined in the sun like she had oil rubbed on it.

She had on a pair of white shorts and this white blouse with no sleeves. Her hands was in little fists on her hips, and she was smiling at me real nice and friendly. She said, "Well, I don't think I've seen you before."

I couldn't say nothing right then. I mean, I never been much good around the women anyway—I can't never think of nothing to talk to them about—and this one was so pretty she could've been in them Hollywood pictures.

My ears felt all funny and hot, with her looking right into my face like she was. But I couldn't just stand there, so I kind of coughed a little and bent down and picked up the duffel.

I said, "No, ma'am."

"I'm Mrs. Jensen. Is there something I can do for you?"

"Well, I heard you needed pickers."

"Yes, we do," she said. "The hot weather came on before we expected it. We have to harvest before the heat ruins the crop and we're awfully shorthanded."

I started to say something about being glad to help out, but just then this big good-looking fellow in a blue work shirt that had the sleeves rolled up and was unbuttoned down the front so you could see all the hair he had on his chest, he come out of the door. The woman turned and saw him and said, "Oh, this is Mr. Carbante. He's our foreman."

I said, "How are you, Mr. Carbante?"

"Okay," he said. "You looking for work?"

"Sure."

"Ever picked lettuce before?"

"No, sir. But I picked plenty of other things."

"Such as?"

"Well, citrus."

"Where?"

"Down in the Imperial Valley."

"What else?"

"Tomatoes. Grapes and apples and celery, too."

"All right," Mr. Carbante said. "You're on."

"I sure do thank you."

This Mrs. Jensen was still standing there with her hands on her hips. She looked at me. "I'm sorry again about that bump."

"Oh, it's nothing."

"Good luck."

"Thanks."

"I'll see you later, Gino," she said to Mr. Carbante.

"Okay, Mrs. Jensen."

When she was gone, around to the side, Mr. Carbante took me into the warehouse. They had a criss-cross of conveyer belts in there, and packing bins lining one wall, and there was a lot of Mex women that was sorting out the lettuce heads and putting the good ones off on one belt to where they were trimmed and graded and packed, and putting the ones that wasn't any good off on another belt.

We went into a little office they had there, and Mr. Carbante give me a little book to keep track of how many crates I was to pick, and told me what they paid for each crate. Then he said what bunkhouse I was to sleep in and the bunk number and what time they give you supper and what time you had to be up and ready for work in the morning.

He just finished telling me all that when this old bird come into the office. He had a nice head of white hair and pink cheeks, and he stopped where we was and give me a smile. He must've been close to seventy, sure enough, but his eyes was bright and he looked to get around pretty good.

Mr. Carbante said, "This is Mr. Jensen. He's the owner."

"How do you do, Mr. Jensen?"

"Glad to know you, son. You going to work for us?"

"Yes, sir."

"Well, that's fine."

"Yes, sir."

"Did you want to see me, Mr. Jensen?" Mr. Carbante asked.

"Have you seen Mrs. Jensen?"

"Not since breakfast."

"All right, Gino," Mr. Jensen said, and he went on out.

I said, "Mrs. Jensen was right here with you, Mr. Carbante."

"Never mind, boy."

"Yes, sir," I said. "Is that Mrs. Jensen's husband?"

Mr. Carbante's eyes got all narrow. "That's right. Why?"

"Well, nothing," I said, but I was wondering how come old Mr. Jensen had such a young wife. People sure do funny things sometimes, specially when they get old.

Mr. Carbante said, "You just mind your own business and pick your quota every day, and you'll get along fine here. You understand that, boy?"

"Sure, Mr. Carbante."

"Okay, then. You'll be down on the south side. There's a couple of Mex's out there who'll give you the hang of it."

Do you know how they pick lettuce?

The way you do it is, you have this long knife, real sharp, and you walk in along the rows, which are about two feet apart, and you clip off the heads in close to the ground and put them in these field crates you drag along with you. When you get a crate filled, you leave it in there between the rows and then a truck comes along and picks up the crates and takes them up to the warehouse.

Now, it don't sound like much, me telling it like that, but there's plenty of little tricks to it, all right.

These two men that Mr. Carbante had told me about give me some tips on how to tell which heads was to be cut, and how to tell which ones had been chewed up by the aphids, and which ones had got the mildew or been burnt by the sun. I took to watching this one big fellow, whose name was Haysoos. He was pretty near pure black from the sun, and had tiny little eyes and thick, bushy eyebrows. But he sure knew what he was doing in that lettuce, clipping away like nobody you ever saw.

After I watched him for a while, I got onto the knack of it and started right in myself. I had my shirt off out there, and it was plenty hot. I was burnt up pretty good from being down in the Imperial Valley, but down there you was working citrus and didn't have to pick right in under the sun like that.

Just as I got my first field crate filled up, who should come down the road but Mrs. Jensen and Mr. Carbante. They was just strolling along, side by side, her with this big floppy straw hat stuck up on her head. She was smiling, and every now and then she would wave to one of the pickers out in the lettuce. Every one of them was looking at her, sure enough.

She got up to where me and Haysoos was working and stopped and give me a nice smile. "Hello, there."

"Hello, Mrs. Jensen."

"How are you doing?"

"Just fine."

This Haysoos smiled at her with teeth that was all yellow and said something in Mex, but I guess she didn't hear him. She started off down the road again. Haysoos watched her. *"Muy bonita,* hey? Such a beautiful woman, a man's blood boils at the sight of such a beautiful woman."

"She sure is beautiful, all right," I said.

"She likes you, hey *amigo?"*

"She's real nice and friendly."

"Haysoos she does not like. Not big ugly Haysoos."

"Oh, sure she likes you, Haysoos."

"Carbante is who she likes, hey? Carbante and a thousand others."

He turned away and started in to pick again. I didn't know what he'd meant, but I didn't want to say nothing so I just turned away too and went to work in my own row.

The next day I was pretty sore from the stooping over, but I'd had a nice sleep the night before and it didn't bother me too much. I'd got the hang of picking the lettuce now, and I was clipping along at a nice pace.

One of the trucks come around with sandwiches and milk for us at noontime, and we sat there on the side of the road to eat. Well, while we was eating, here comes Mrs. Jensen down the road again.

She come right up there to where we was, smiling at everybody, and asked us if we all had enough to eat. Some of the college boys called out some things I didn't understand, and most everybody laughed, and Mrs. Jensen laughed right with them.

This Haysoos was sitting right near where I was. He kept watching Mrs. Jensen. "Everyone but Haysoos, hey?" he said.

"How was that?"

"A man's blood boils."

He sure said a lot of funny things, that Haysoos.

Saturday come around before you knew it and that was when we was to get paid. After supper we all went to the office in the big warehouse with the little books we had and old Mr. Jensen and Mr. Carbante totaled up the number of crates we had picked and give us our pay, all in cash money.

When we was all paid, old Mr. Jensen stood up and said that he was going off to Salinas for the next few days on business, and that Mr. Carbante was to be in charge and if we wanted anything we should see him.   After that he went out and got into his big Lincoln and drove off down the road.

I went back to the bunks then, but most of the other pickers, they was going off into San Sinandro to drink in the bars.   A couple of them asked me if I wanted to come along, but I said I wasn't much for the drinking.

I lay down on my bunk and started to read this movie magazine one of the college boys had.   I sure like to read them movie magazines, all about the Hollywood people and the houses they have and the fine clothes and everything.   Someday I'm going to have me all them things, too.

Well, I lay there and pretty soon it got dark outside.   But it was awful hot in there and I got up and went out to get some air.   It sure hadn't cooled down much.

I walked down by the other bunks and come around the south end of the second one, and I heard all this commotion inside.   There was a window right there and I stopped by that and looked inside to see what it was all about.

There was this bunch of pickers in there, about six of them, and they was all pretty well oiled up.   They had a couple of empty wine jugs lying around on the floor, and they was passing this other one around from one to another.

And who should be right there in the middle of all of them but Haysoos.   He was sitting on one of the bunks, his eyes all glassed over.   He got the jug and took a long one out of there, and it passed on to the next one.   He wasn't whooping it up or nothing, like the rest of them was, but just sitting there on that bunk, kind of staring at the floor.

Well, while I watched, the rest of them started out the door and one had the wine jug.   They called back to Haysoos, but he just sat there and didn't answer them at all.   Then Haysoos was alone, and I heard the rest of them going off down the road singing some kind of Mex song.

Old Haysoos found another jug somewhere and had one you would hardly believe from it.   He wiped off his mouth with the back of his hand and then stood up and wobbled around some.   I could see his lips moving like he was talking to himself, but I couldn't hear none of it.

I got tired of watching him and went back to my bunk and lay down again, and it wasn't so hot anymore.   Pretty soon I went to sleep.

I woke up right away when I heard the sirens.   They was really loud.

I jumped off my bunk and ran outside, and there was a lot of the other pickers there, too, just come back from San Sinandro.   They was all running up toward the big white house.

I commenced to running up there with them, and I thought how it must be that the big white house had caught fire somehow and what a terrible thing that would be.   But when I got up there, I saw that it wasn't fire engines that had made the sirens, but police cars.   There was three of them there, and a big ambulance, and they all had these red lights going round and round on their tops.   There was a couple of policemen, too, holding the pickers back and telling them not to come any closer.

I wedged in there, and the pickers that had been there for a while was talking pretty fast.

". . . right there in the bedroom."

"She had it coming."

"They both did."

"Yeah, but not *that* way."

"Who found them?"

"Somebody heard the screams."

"But they didn't get him?"

"Not yet."

"He must have gone through the fields."

"They've got the roads blocked."

"We'll get up a posse . . ."

I said to one of the college boys who had been talking, "What is it?   What happened?"

"You don't know?"

I said, "I was sleeping.   What is it?"

Just then the front door of the big white house opened and two fellows dressed in white and two policemen come out and they was carrying two stretchers.   They had to pass by where I was to get to the ambulance, and I looked at the two sheet-covered stretchers and what was on them.

I just couldn't believe it at first, but the college boys was talking again, telling about it, and I knew it had to be true.   I turned away, sick as anybody ever was.

The one college boy put his hand on my shoulder.   "Come on," he said, "we're going after him."

But I pulled away and run back to the bunks.   I had to get away from there. I couldn't stay there no more.

You know what that crazy Haysoos had done?

He'd killed Mrs. Jensen and Mr. Carbante, that's what.   He'd gone up to the big white house with that sharp, sharp lettuce knife of his and cut off both their heads.

I don't understand it, and I'm just so sick.   A fine lady like Mrs. Jensen and a nice man like Mr. Carbante.   Two of the swellest people you ever wanted to meet and know, and that crazy Haysoos had killed them both.

I just don't understand what could have made him do a terrible, terrible thing like that.

Do you?

RON GOULART

News From Nowhere

It was right there in the window, behind the dusty glass, next to scatters of tarnished metal jewelry, drooping peacock feathers, rusty faucets, collapsed hats and much-traveled suitcases: an enormous oil painting of Conway.

Conway, lean and smiling, wearing that broad-striped native poncho he'd always worn down there in Mexico, a small #1 brush cocked over his right ear and a wineskin clutched in his knobby right hand. Conway, smiling his gap-toothed smile, his big moustache bristling, and behind him the flat bright Mexican countryside; the view from the back room of the girl's house. Conway, a self-portrait he must have painted while they were down there all those months.

Right there in the front window of the News From Nowhere Junk Emporium, Conway smiled out on McAllister Street and all its run-down buildings and junk shops.

Andrew Paulin had forgotten to keep breathing. He coughed now and gasped in air through his open mouth. He was a tall blond man of thirty, about twenty pounds overweight and wearing a new gray suit. He'd been eating a chocolate almond bar and he threw it down toward the gutter. "Conway," he said aloud.

A heavy black woman in a green coat smiled at him as she passed.

Paulin licked his lips. He'd been in the News From Nowhere shop before. He liked to browse in the antique shops and junk stores that dotted San Francisco. Now that he only had to pretend to be working as a commercial artist he could take all the time he wanted to wander Union Street and Clement and McAllister. During the nine months he'd been back in San Francisco he'd been down here on McAllister as often as two or three times a week.

He went over to the door of the shop and grabbed the brass knob. The knob spun around and around in his hand and nothing happened. Paulin pressed his shoulder against the grimy door and shoved. "Don't tell me he's closed?"

There were a dozen signs pasted on the inside of the glass door. *Hi Class Junque. Choice Items Come From Everywhere To Nowhere. In case of emergency contact owner at Oakleaf Hotel, Eddy Street.*

After trying the door once more, Paulin shaded his eyes and tried to see inside the long, narrow junk shop. He couldn't tell if there were any more of Conway's paintings inside or not. He turned away.

He went back around the corner and climbed into his sports car. "I should have gone back to that studio of his and gathered up all his stuff,'' he said to himself. He left the curb and headed for Eddy Street. ''No, Conway had a couple of other places where he bummed studio space. There's really no way of telling where all he left his paintings. Now look, all that is back there is a picture of Conway in that fussy realistic style of his. New neorealism, didn't he call it? That's all it is. A self-portrait of Conway, so what. Nothing in it to link him with you. You might as well buy the thing and keep it out of sight, but you have to relax. Okay, it does show the girl's house, but nobody knows that besides you and Conway and the girl. And they're both dead.''

The hotel clerk at the Oakleaf had grown fat since he'd been tattooed, and the snakes and flowers on his chubby bare arms were dim and distorted. ''Who?'' he asked Paulin.

''The old guy who runs the News From Nowhere.''

''What's that?''

''A junk shop over on McAllister. You know the one.''

''Oh, you mean Mac.''

''Mac. Old guy who always wears a brown hat and rimless glasses.''

''He's eighty-two, can hardly see anymore,'' said the fat sixty-year-old clerk. ''Why you want him?''

''I want to buy something out of his shop.''

''What?''

''A painting.''

''Say, is this Tuesday?''

''Yes, it is.''

''Tuesday Mac closes up shop and goes over across the Bay to visit his in-laws.''

''You don't know where I might reach him?''

''Nope.''

''What time do you expect him back?''

''Not till after ten tonight.''

''Well, I'll call then.''

''Switchboard closes sharp at ten. You'll have to wait until tomorrow,'' said the tattooed clerk. ''That must be some terrific painting.''

Paulin backed off from the brown wood counter in the Oakleaf's small lobby. ''Nothing special, really.''

Driving home toward his Russian Hill apartment, Paulin said to himself, ''Don't go acting too anxious about the damn picture, now. I think you're right to want to buy it and get it out of the way. But don't make everybody wonder why. There's nothing to link you with Conway or the girl. Everyone—the papers, her family—accepted the crash. They believe she had an accident and was burned up in her car. Burned up along with the money she was carrying. You and Conway fixed that up. Just relax.''

At the signal at the bottom of his street he glanced over and saw a Chinese man in a station wagon watching him. He must have been talking out loud, moving his lips. He had that habit and he'd have to watch it, control it. He made himself grin over at the Chinese and shrug.   The light changed and he shot uphill toward home.

The shop door opened this time.   Paulin stepped inside the News From Nowhere junk store, squinting.   The long low room was dim, dusty.   He stepped over a fallen tuba with a feather boa in its bell.   "That's an interesting painting in the window," he said.

Behind a glass counter sat an old man in a brown coat-sweater.   He had a soft brown hat pulled down low on his bald head.   Sprawled on the streaked counter top were a dozen roller skates, a hacksaw, two cast-iron skillets, a Mason jar full of green marbles, three volumes of a 19th-century encyclopedia and two slices of whole wheat toast on a cracked china plate.   "Far as I can tell," replied old Mac. He touched his glasses, leaving dusty prints on the thick lenses.   "My sight is slowly diminishing."

"I think I might like to buy the painting.   How much?"

"Far as I can see, it's the work of an authentic artist."   Mac picked up the top slice of toast and broke it slowly in half.   "Twenty dollars."

Pretending not to be that interested, Paulin said, "That's a little steep."

"Fellow yesterday offered me fifty."

"Why didn't he take it, then?"

"He might come back today and do just that.   Twenty-five dollars.   You want it?"

"I thought you said twenty."

"The more we have to argue the higher the price climbs."

"Well, okay.   I'll buy it."

"No checks.   Twenty-five in cash."

Paulin got out his wallet.   "Have any more around by that particular artist?"

"Signed his name on it, didn't he?   I forget what he calls himself."

"I didn't really notice," said Paulin, drawing out two tens and a five.   "You wouldn't have anything else?"

The old man nodded.   "One more.   Out in back.   Cost you thirty-five dollars, that one will.   Want to take a look?   Go on through the little door over there, push it hard."

"Guess I might as well," said Paulin.   "He's an interesting artist, whoever he is."

"Likely he'll be famous someday and you'll make a fortune from your chicken-feed investment."

Paulin made his way around several small stuffed animals and to the door leading to the back room.   He pushed and the door swung lopsidedly open.

This room had a higher ceiling and was chill and damp.   Great dark bureaus and chairs hulked around the room, piles of ancient magazines, clouded mirrors, more jars of marbles.

Here was another painting by Conway.   Paulin inhaled, involuntarily bringing one hand up against his chest.   This one showed the girl.   "She was never very good-looking,'' Paulin said to himself.   ''The good-looking ones never seem to have money.   Ugh, that awful peasant blouse she always wore, showing off all her blotchy skin.''

He stepped closer to the big Conway painting, which was propped in a worn cane-bottom rocker.   ''When did he paint this thing?   Maybe before I met him down there.   He was trying to convince her she should be a patron of the arts even before I joined him.   I suppose you should feel sorry for her, wanting everyone around her doing beautiful things.''   Finally he grabbed up the unframed painting.   ''But I don't really feel anything.   I can live here in San Francisco for two or three years on that $50,000 we got out of her; longer if I take it easy.   That's all I feel about her.''

In the shop again, Paulin said, ''A nice bit of work.   I may as well take both of them.   Thirty-five did you say?''

Mac rubbed at his glasses and leaned toward the painting.   ''I forgot it was a picture of a pretty girl.   That should be worth fifty bucks at least.''

''She's not all that pretty.''

''Arguing merely ups the prices around here.''

''Okay, all right.   Here's the rest of the money.''

After he took the cash, Mac bent and reached under the counter.   A stuffed quail fell off a shelf and bounced on his stooped back.   ''Someplace I have some nice wrapping paper I can give you.''

''I imagine you get items in from all over.''

''From the four corners.''   Mac unfurled a spotted sheet of brown paper.   ''See if that'll fit around both of them while I dig you up a length of string.''

''For instance, I wonder where these two paintings came from.''   Paulin watched the old man shuffling off into a corner.

''Mexico.''   Mac knocked a model train off a sprung sofa and clutched up a ball of twine.

''Really.   Who brought them in?''

''Didn't get their names.''

''Two people?''

''Man and wife, as I remember, brought them in over the weekend,'' said Mac, cutting off a piece of twine.   ''At least I presume they were man and wife.   These days, and around Frisco, you never can tell.   Couple in their early forties, did some touristing down in Mexico.   Picked up these paintings, then decided they didn't want them after all.   No accounting for taste.   Here.''   He flung the string to Paulin.

Paulin had the two Conway paintings wrapped in the rough paper.   He took the twine and tied up the package.

''You do that pretty well.   Maybe you're an artist yourself.''

''Yes, I am,'' replied Paulin.   ''You wouldn't know the name of the couple, would you?   Where they might live?''

''This isn't a pawnshop,'' said Mac.   ''I have no need for biographical information.''

It was a calm spring day, and Paulin had walked all the way from his apartment. Leaving the News From Nowhere shop, he put the wrapped Conway paintings under one arm and began walking back toward Russian Hill.

"That was just like Conway," he said to himself as he walked the bright mid-morning streets. "Painting her exactly as she looked, not flattering her at all. He had great confidence in himself, no need for flattery. Charming, smiling. Well, it didn't do him much good. He's been dead at the bottom of that canyon for almost a year now. Apparently he hasn't been found yet. I didn't figure he would be. With the girl it was different. We wanted them to find her and believe the $50,000 was with her; $50,000 she told her parents she was going to use for good works among the Mexican poor; $50,000 Conway and I convinced her would finance the three of us in a wonderful remote art colony for long happy years. What an unattractive girl."

High above, gulls circled in the clear blue sky.

"Smiling Conway," Paulin said to himself. "I still don't like the way he treated her at the end, teasing her. Not just knocking her out quickly and dumping her in the car. No, he wanted her to know he was going to kill her, that he'd betrayed her. A fine sense of humor, Conway's. Well, in a way that made it easier to do it to him. Using a variation on the original plan and dumping him unconscious in that wreck of a car of his and sending him to the bottom of the canyon way out there in nowhere. Yes, and I got rid of him in time to save nearly all the $50,000 for myself."

He was breathing in a more relaxed way and he stopped at a hot dog stand on Van Ness and bought a chili burger. He ate it as he walked, smiling now to himself.

He saw the third painting eight days later. This was the worst of all. "It's me," Paulin said, stopping on the rainy street in front of the News From Nowhere Junk Emporium. In this Conway painting, Paulin was sitting out in the red-tile patio behind the girl's house down there in Mexico. The girl was there, too, standing in an archway behind Paulin. Conway must have done that one from memory, because Paulin never posed for it. Conway was good at that. He could look at you once and remember everything about you. Paulin had seen Conway do a painting of his parents years after they'd died, and it was perfect.

Mac was taking some sort of oily gears out of a cardboard box, wheezing as he did. "You're in luck." He wiped his hands on his brown pants and touched his hat. "I got another of those pictures in, by the artist you like so much."

Paulin waited for the old man to mention it was a portrait of him, but Mac's eyesight must have prevented him from realizing it. "Yes, I noticed as I was passing."

"Sixty bucks for this one. I figure this particular artist is so much in demand, at least by you, I may as well cash in on it."

Paulin looked from the stooped old man to the painting in the shop window. It made him very uneasy having the picture there, showing him with the girl like that. "I'll take it. Did you happen to buy this from the same couple?"

Mac fished a wrinkled slip of yellow paper out of the sweatband of his brown hat and then clamped the hat back on his bald head. ''Turns out these people got a dozen more by the same artist.''

''A dozen?''

''Don't know if they want to sell them,'' said the old man. ''See, when I showed interest they got the notion this particular artist was maybe hotter in the art world than they'd imagined. Many people suspect junk men are secret millionaires because of all the shrewd deals they pull. I'm going to have to go over there in my spare time and dicker. If it's worth it.''

''I could go,'' offered Paulin.

''You'd cheat me out of my markup that way.'' Mac unfolded the scrap of paper. ''Though maybe you could figure my commission in advance and then go and deal direct with these people.''

''How much would you want?''

''I'd settle for one hundred.''

Paulin sighed, got out his wallet. ''Okay, all right. Who are they?''

''Name is Henderson and they just moved into a new place out near Stinson Beach. You know where that is, over in Marin County.''

''Yes. Give me the address and phone number. I'll call them.''

''Haven't got a phone as yet,'' said Mac as he handed over the slip on which he'd written Henderson and the Marin beach address. ''Moving in, and you know how long it takes to get a phone installed. They tell me they're at home most every night.''

Paulin took the address, crumpling it in his fist.

The fog kept coming in. The Henderson house sat alone, ringed by pine trees, at the end of a short road that climbed up from the beach. The low shingle house was dark, and Paulin parked his sports car away from it, off the road under some oaks.

The mist rolled in across the ocean and came swirling up over the cliffside behind the house, spinning through the trees.

''Now, if they aren't home,'' said Paulin to himself, ''what difference does it make? If I can get the paintings without their seeing me, so much the better. It's likely all they have left will be here.'' He climbed quietly out of the car. ''They must have bought this stuff from someone who cleaned out Conway's studio. Or maybe somebody who stored some of his paintings for him. When Conway didn't come back for a while, whoever had the stuff got tired of holding it and unloaded. Anyway, I'll have to see what these Hendersons have got.''

The grass was high in the front lawn and, near a low rail fence, some sort of sign had fallen over. Paulin went directly to the front door and knocked. ''Just in case someone is at home.''

There was no response. After a moment Paulin slid a flashlight out of the pocket of his dark jacket and went quietly around the house. He found an unlocked window and raised it, then climbed in.

This was a bedroom. No paintings here.

He found them, seven pictures in all, lined up against one wall of the living room.

"Damn Conway," said Paulin. "I hadn't realized he'd documented our stay down there so well."

The three of them figured in most of the paintings: the girl, Conway and his smile, and Paulin. Even the girl's car, the one they'd put her in. There it was, sitting in the field near her house, with the three of them standing around, all looking happy. "Not expecting to die," he said.

Paulin checked out the other rooms in the Henderson house, but there were no more paintings.

He returned to the living room and studied the seven pictures again, swinging the beam of the flashlight from one to the other. "It's odd, in a way, so many of Conway's paintings should show up now," he said to himself. "You know, suppose this is some kind of setup? Oh, how could it be? Conway's dead, at the bottom of that canyon, far away in Mexico." Paulin went closer to the paintings. "You don't know for sure, do you? All you did was knock him out and put him in his car and roll it over. You don't actually know he's dead. Of course he's dead. How could he have gotten out of there?"

Paulin picked up the painting of the three of them standing by the girl's car. "Conway's car never caught fire, you know. You should have climbed down there and made absolutely sure he was dead. But he was dead. If he wasn't, where has he been all these months? Suppose he did get out alive somehow. He'd know I was coming back here to San Francisco. You know how patient he was with the girl and how he loved to toy with her. Suppose the paintings are new? Maybe he's been watching me for months, figuring out how I live, the pattern of it. He could have made fresh paintings and bribed that nearly blind old man to put them on display. Now he's got you over here and he's going to torture you, like he did the girl, and find out where you've got the rest of the cash hidden."

Paulin put the painting back against the wall. "Stop scaring yourself. Conway's dead and it's only a coincidence these old paintings have turned up now. Gather them up and get out of here."

Something made a faint noise elsewhere in the house.

Paulin looked down at his free hand, shining the flashlight on it. He rubbed his forefinger slowly over his thumb, feeling what was there. Then he said, "Oh, God."

It was wet paint.

KATE WILHELM

A Case of Desperation

Marge was hungry. She had used her lunch hour to pick up some plastic dolls for the PTA Fall Festival, knowing she would have time to eat between two and three-thirty, before the small branch bank reopened for the Friday evening rush. Now it appeared she was going to have to wait for Mrs. Ashton to come and collect the dolls.

Ralph, the other teller, grinned commiseratingly at her and left. The manager, Mr. Redmon, stood by the door, waiting for the minute hand to click into place, but before he could set the lock, two people arrived. Mrs. Ashton pushed her way into the bank. A tall slender man in a windbreaker followed her closely. Marge sighed her relief.

"Marge, my dear," Mrs. Ashton began at the door, and continued with no change in volume as she crossed the floor. "You don't know how I rushed to get here in time. Did you get them? I've lined up six mothers to make dresses. Did you ask Warren?"

Marge pointed to the carton near the door. "Fifty of them," she said, "forty-five cents each," and realized that she had done it again. Warren had been half asleep when she returned from the PTA board meeting last night, and she had been too tired to start the annual argument about the parents' show.

"Fifty?" Mrs. Ashton was saying. "At two dollars, that will bring a hundred dollars. That's fine. I'll just give you a check for these now. Right place for it, isn't it?" She laughed, and began scrawling out the check.

The man in the windbreaker was still standing at the wall desk, thumbing through a small notebook. Marge wished he'd make out his deposit slip, or whatever he had to do, and get in behind Mrs. Ashton. She really was hungry.

Without looking up, Mrs. Ashton asked, "Will Warren play for us?"

"I didn't get a chance to ask him yet," Marge said; at the quick look of reproach, she added, "I'm sure he will." He'd swear and have her on the defensive for a day or two, but in the end he would play.

"That's fine. I'll put him down," Mrs. Ashton beamed.

The stranger at the desk was just standing there, probably listening to every word. Marge wished Mrs. Ashton would give her the check and leave. She'd call home and tell Annie to let the children eat early. Then she would broil a

steak for Warren and herself later.   He liked to have time for a leisurely martini.
That would be the best way.

Mrs. Ashton waved the check back and forth, drying it.   "Will you be home
tomorrow?   I have some extra tulip bulbs . . ."

It was ten past two when she finally left, with the dolls.   Mr. Redmon locked
the door behind her, and glanced impatiently toward the last customer.

The man looked up, and for the first time Marge saw his face.   His features
were clear and strong, almost boyishly sensitive, but he was unsmiling.   He was
taller than Mr. Redmon, probably six feet plus an inch or even two, but that might
have been an illusion caused by his slenderness.   He wore a grey hat and slacks,
and a tan windbreaker over a white tieless shirt, and he carried a case that looked
more like a tool box than a briefcase.

He was coming toward her.   She started to smile, but didn't.   Mr. Redmon
looked frightened.   She noticed for the first time that the man was keeping his
right hand inside his jacket pocket.   Her eyes widened as his deep blue eyes held
hers.

"Don't get panicky, honey," he said softly, "but be careful, very, very careful."
He pushed the black bag across the counter top.

It was as if she had been emptied of all thought, and there was only a hollow
dread within her.   It was happening here at her bank!   Her fingers fumbled opening
the drawer and then were pushing money into the case.   Her eyes remained locked
with his.   It was forever—an instant—timeless, and he was reaching for it.

"That's fine, honey," he said.   "Now just as carefully walk around the end of
the counter and come out.   Bring your purse."

She shook her head and took a step backward, away from him.   For the first
time she saw the gun pointed at the very still figure of Mr. Redmon.   He nodded
at her to obey.   She walked around the counter and the three of them went back
to the small office.   The man taped Mr. Redmon's mouth and tied his hands and
feet, fastening him to his heavy mahogany desk.   He lifted the receiver from the
phone and set it on the desk.

"Listen, both of you," he said slowly.   "I've been thinking of this for a long
time, and I'm not going to be stopped.   You tell them I have her with me."   Mr.
Redmon's eyes pleaded and he shook his head violently.   The man ignored it.
"I don't want to hurt her, but it will be up to them.   And tell them," he said,
clipping the words, "the only way they'll get me is dead.   Just tell them I said
that."   He turned to Marge and motioned toward the door.

She didn't move, seemed unable to move.   He took her arm.   "Look at him,
honey.   He knows I mean every word I've said in here."

She looked from him to Mr. Redmon, and she found herself walking, the case
dangling from her hand where he placed it.   Using her keys, her car that was just
outside the bank, he drove several blocks to an above-the-street parking lot with
four decks.   The car wound around the ramp to the top, along the narrow passageway to the rear.

"Come on, honey.   We change here."   He made her slide under the wheel to
get out on his side.   He unlocked the door of a blue car and she crawled in without

being ordered.   He reached behind the front seat and pulled out an overnight bag, putting it on the seat at her side before he got in.   "You've been very sensible so far," he said, his eyes darting around at the other cars.   "Just a little more now and you can go.   Put this on."   He handed her a pink blouse and, when she didn't move, he edged the gun out of his pocket.   "Look, honey, you do exactly as I say or I'll knock you out and dress you myself."   The chill of his voice was more frightening than the gun.

She had trouble with her trembling hands as she unbuttoned her blouse, but finally handed it to him and put on the pink one.   It was a little loose, not noticeably. At his command, she handed him her earrings and stared at the blonde wig he took from the suitcase.   Impatiently he thrust it at her and she put it on.   Then he put her things and his windbreaker in the case, pulled on a coat that matched his slacks, and added a tie.   In all, it hadn't taken more than three or four minutes.   "What are you going to do with me?" she asked.

He began backing out.   "Just do exactly as I say and you'll have an adventure you can tell your grandchildren about."

"They'll catch you.   They always do."

"No!" he said intensely.   "For once I get to state the terms, and I'm not including being caught in them.   Either I make it with the money, or they kill me. But they won't catch me!"

Marge shuddered and moved closer to the door.

"There's a sweater and a purse on the back seat.   Get them."   She was straightening up again when he stopped and tossed a half dollar to a white-coated attendant.

When they drove away she was shaking visibly, the first reaction of shocked, frightened obedience crumbling.   Why hadn't she screamed in the lot?   She felt as though she were coming out from a deep dream, only now being consciously in control of her actions.   He couldn't act quickly enough to stop her if she could jump from the car at a stop sign or a red light.   They were out of the downtown area, and she looked out trying to remember the next red light.   About three blocks. If she could work the door handle . . . Cautiously she maneuvered one hand behind her back.   She couldn't halt her gasp of dismay when he turned into a side street, and then into an alley.   He stopped the car and pulled on the brake without turning off the ignition.   Hope flooded her.   Maybe he'd put her out there.

Casually he said, "I was in a prison camp in Korea and one of the guards taught me a kind of cute trick."   His hand reached out and took her wrist as he spoke, and his fingers moved up and down as though feeling for a certain spot.   Her eyes followed his fingers and then he was bringing her arm up behind her, her hand up to the shoulder blade, and higher.   Pain exploded in her shoulder and she screamed. He released her, and massaged her back as she wept.   "Every day he'd do that until I screamed.   Sometimes he'd throw my arm out of joint, sometimes not.   I never knew.   Got so I screamed before he touched me.   That seemed to please him."   Marge sobbed into her hands.   He waited until she stopped and then he said, "Sorry, honey.   I didn't want to hurt you, but you might as well understand that this isn't a game.   Your manager knew I meant it, and you might as well admit now that you do too. If I have to remind you again, you'll not use that arm for a long time. Keep off the door!'' He flicked on the radio and drove out of the alley toward the turnpike.

They were on the toll road before the announcer cut into the music. "We interrupt this program . . .'' He turned it louder and she listened to a recounting of the robbery, complete with their descriptions. Marge stared dully ahead. They were looking for her car, for a man in a windbreaker, and a woman with dark brown hair. She was a blonde beside a man in a conservative suit traveling in a car filled with vacation luggage.

The music resumed and she said, "You thought of everything, didn't you? But they'll find my car and get your fingerprints from it. They'll call in the F.B.I.''

He laughed. "They'll lift smudges from your car, just as they did in the bank. I was very careful.'' He glanced her way. "There will be road blocks and license checks; you remember to be just as careful, and there won't be any trouble.''

"Where are you going to take me?''

"You stay until I think I can make it alone.''

Her shoulder ached, and there was tightening in the back of her neck that she knew would bring on a violent headache within hours. The miles whizzed by at an alarming rate, and her expectations of an early pursuit faded as the monotony of the wind-filled ride wore her hopes to nothing. There had to be something he had overlooked. She leaned her head back against the seat and shut her eyes, trying to think.

At four-thirty he pulled off to the side of the road. "I have sandwiches,'' he said pleasantly, as if out for a Sunday picnic, "and a thermos of coffee. You did miss lunch, didn't you?'' His voice was low-pitched, naturally soft, the sort of voice that was never heard in a group larger than three.

The headache had arrived by then. She nodded briefly. While they ate, he studied a road map. "There's a toll gate ahead about four or five miles,'' he said. "They'll probably be looking over all cars. Now listen. We are Mr. and Mrs. Robert Thorne, from Gary, on our way to Raleigh, North Carolina, to visit your parents on our vacation. They might search the car, but I don't think they'll go through the luggage unless they get suspicious. So,'' he looked at her levelly over the paper cup of coffee, "if you want to get back to your husband and those two children again, don't make them suspicious.'' He watched as she sipped the steaming coffee. "What's wrong? You sick?''

"Headache,'' she answered.

He reached across her to the glove compartment and found a bottle of aspirins. It was half empty. He shook out two and handed them to her, watching until she swallowed them.

When she finished her coffee, he put the thermos on the seat between them. "Gives us a real homey touch, doesn't it?'' He worked the car back into the traffic, heavier and slower now. "They're stopped up there, all right,'' he said, grimly satisfied.

Marge felt herself tensing and she worked her hands together, feeling the palms moist and clammy.

"What's your husband do?" he asked and she started at the sound of his voice. "Ease up, honey," he murmured. "Tell me about your husband."

"He's a classified salesman for the telephone company."

"Away a lot?"

"He travels in the state."

"Make good money?"

"Yes," she said sharply. "Why?"

"Just wondered. Announcer said you were the mother of two kids. If he's such a hot-shot, why are you working?"

"That's none of your business!"

"Granted. Own your home?"

"Please," she cried. "Leave me alone! I can't talk!"

"Oh, yes, you can," he snapped. "I asked if you own your home. You talk if it chokes you."

They were driving at twenty miles an hour in spurts, and on both sides drivers were honking their horns and hanging out the windows trying to see what was happening ahead. Marge's rigidity had decreased at the persistent questioning, and she understood why he intended to keep it up.

"We have our own home," she said.

"Keep talking. Tell me all about it. When you got it, how much, what kind of furniture."

His hands gripping the wheel showed white at the knuckles, and a stab of fear went through her. What if he should panic? He might start shooting, or might try to break through the roadblock. She had seen it on television and in movies, and they always got killed. Almost hysterically she chattered about the house. It was four years old, split level with hemlocks and junipers. The lower level was the workroom where Warren once made some lawn furniture that they didn't use. Joanne had a birthday party on the terrace last week. She was ten; Larry was eight and played Little League ball, first base unless Hank showed up, and then he played in the field.

The car in front of them was moving again, and he jerked their car as he followed. Marge's voice faltered. What had she been saying? They stopped in sight of the toll gate and she thought, *Now!* The police would recognize her. She had to be ready.

"Split level!" he snorted in disgust.

"What's wrong with split level?" she said staring at the car ahead and willing it to move on. The line moved like a measuring worm gathering itself in, inching forward, and stretching out again. A uniformed officer approached the car in front of them and spoke with the driver. On the other side another trooper glanced in the rear.

"I didn't say anything's wrong with split levels, if they are on hillsides." The robber yelled, and the officer at the rear of the other car turned to look.

Marge stared at him terrified. She started to speak, but her tongue was frozen and nothing came out. He said, still in a loud, rough tone, "If you have to have a split level, dammit, have it! But don't expect me to like it!" The policeman was within a few feet of them and she knew he could hear every word.   "Now if you'll just shut up about split levels for the rest of this trip . . . Sorry, Officer."

"OK, Mac.   License, please."   He studied the license and compared the statistics with the man before he handed it back.   Briefly he glanced at Marge, and she trembled with anticipation.   He must see that something was wrong!   She felt tears forming in her eyes, and inside she was screaming, *I'm Marge Elliot!   Look at me!   See the wig!*   But he turned from them and flicked his eyes over the thermos and the luggage and fishing gear in the back, and waved them on.   *She would scream!   She'd make them notice!*   She felt his hand tighten on her wrist and she went limp.

They picked up speed almost immediately.   She felt weak from frustration. "You think you're so damned smart!   I hope they catch you and let me testify. I hope you rot in jail for the rest of your life.   You'll never get to spend a cent of the money."

"Wasn't planning to anyway," he said cheerfully and began to whistle.   "Oh, we ain't got a barrel of money . . ."

"You've had good luck, but it won't last," she continued, oblivious of the song, knowing only her rage at the stupidity of the troopers, at the clever way he manipulated her, making her play along with the grim farce, at her own cowardice.

"What's the name of your subdivision?"   He was ignoring her outburst as if she were a petulant child.

"Pleasant View," she snapped.

"Oh, no!   Pleasant View!"   He grinned broadly at the flush that raced across her face.

It was the first time he had smiled, and it made him look incredibly young and vulnerable.   Marge shivered at the thought.   Him vulnerable!   She thought of Warren, and irrationally she wondered if he would give Larry and Joanne their dinner on time.   They liked to eat at five.   What would he tell them?   Mother is going for a ride with a bank robber; eat your pork chop.   She shook off the thought.   They were with Annie.   He would be with the police somewhere, waiting to hear, smoking too much and swearing viciously, his face looking unshaved by now and dark with anger.   Had he sworn so when she met him?   She couldn't remember.   Probably not, or she would have been shocked by it.   *Yea, though I walk through the valley . . .*   She pushed that aside also.   That was her mother speaking through her mind, the conditioning of her childhood, behind her and meaningless now.   It shouldn't be; she was very active in church work.   She wished passionately she could return to the time when she knew someone would be there to take care of things when there was trouble.   For so long she had been self-sufficient, needing no one; where was that strength now when she did need it?

She was roused from her thoughts by the slowing of the car, and reluctantly she opened her eyes.   They were stopping at a filling station.   She kept her eyes turned away from him so he couldn't see the sudden hope that bloomed in them.

"Forget it!" he said in a whisper.   "You're not getting out, so relax."   He told the attendant to fill it, and they sat side by side as the gauge clicked and the bell rang, as the spray covered the windshield and was wiped off, and they were again on the highway.   The attendant had not looked at her once.

Marge felt that suddenly everything about her was too tight; her necklace was choking her and she pulled at it, finally taking it off and putting it on the seat between them.   Her fingers twisted her rings around and around, and she became aware of the moistness of her hands, and the heat of her girdle against her body. Her skirt was too tight, the band cutting into her waist, and her watch was uncomfortable on her wrist.   She knew her feet were swelling; she felt herself swelling all over.   The diamond on her finger caught the light and flashed as she turned it, and impatiently she pushed it around so only two narrow gold bands showed. There were red marks on the palms of her hands where she had gripped with her nails.   She looked at the watch and compared it to the car clock, not believing it was running at all.   It was Warren's Christmas gift from five years ago.   "Go buy yourself a watch.   Have it inscribed and everything.   Pick out a nice one." In spite, she had picked out an exceptionally nice one and now she stared at it dully, and ran her finger under the band, relieving the pressure of it on her skin.

"Are you all right?"   His voice startled her and she jerked reflexively.   "There's a rest park ahead," he said.   "We'll get out and walk up and down a few minutes. Don't faint on me now!"

Had she been near fainting?   She thought probably she had.   The tightness had gone into her chest, and breathing was a labored business.   The car stopped and they were walking briskly, his hand firm on her arm, his steps setting a fast pace. Another car pulled into the small park, and he was stopping her before a rustic brown outhouse.

"I'm going to stand right here," he said curtly.   "Don't get cute!"

There was nothing there.   Nothing.   Rough log walls, a smooth wooden seat with two covers, paper . . .   Tears filled her eyes as she looked about wildly, and she felt defeat once more.   She remembered her watch and yanked it off, leaving it on the seat.   The newcomers were exercising a small dog, the man whistling cheerfully, his wife throwing sticks for the dog to retrieve.   Marge walked back to the car, at his side, keeping her eyes on the ground.   His grip was painful on her arm; the two other people ignored them, and they were driving away again.

"What did you do?" he demanded after they were again on the road.   His fingers clamped on her wrist in a brutal grasp.

"Nothing."

"You're lying! I could see it on your face.   You were scared and pleased with yourself.   What did you do?"   He was holding his anger under tight control, but it showed in the way he gripped the steering wheel, in the working of his jaw muscles, in the steely fingers that paralyzed her arm.   He let go abruptly and flung it from him.   He said no more until the park was out of sight and the emergency lane was clear of cars on both sides of the road.   Then he pulled out of the driving lane and stopped the car.   "Tell me!"   His eyes burned into her, and she thought he was going to bring out the gun and shoot her.

"Nothing," she whispered.   "There wasn't anything in there.   I couldn't do anything!'' She felt her heart beating as though it were going to stop completely after a last wild adagio of its own. Without reason or forethought, she twisted in the seat and began to fumble with the door. She had to get out! He pulled her back and slapped her, snapping her head back. She fell halfway across the seat, with her face pressed down against the plastic of the covering. ''Please,'' she cried, ''let me go! Please let me out. Tie me up, or knock me out, or anything. I have to get out! I can't stand any more!'' She sobbed violently until there was nothing left in her. Wearily she pulled herself up and groped in the purse for a handkerchief.

''You've been saving that for a long time, haven't you?'' She raised her eyes at the quiet of his tone. He sat smoking calmly, not touching her or even looking at her. His anger was gone, leaving his thin face thoughtful and withdrawn, almost resigned looking. ''What's the matter, honey, can't a woman have a cry once in a while in a split level in Pleasant View?'' It was as if he weren't talking to her, or even thinking of her, but of something far away. The car came alive and rolled back onto the highway.

''Leave me alone. Just leave me alone.''

''Sure, honey. How old are you? Thirty-one, thirty-two? Doesn't matter. Your type I know,'' he said expressionlessly. ''Out of school, into the marriage parlor, a few trips to the maternity hospital and presto, all through being a woman. Soon as the kids are old enough to start school you go to work, and for the rest of your lives, you're as independent as hell. What makes you so damned afraid of being a woman?''

She was too tired to protest. It was pointless to argue with a man who had a gun in his pocket.

He told her to fix her makeup. She obeyed silently. Then he said, ''We're leaving the toll road at the next turnoff, and I want you to lie back with your eyes shut. You're a mess. I don't know how serious it was letting you out back there, and maybe I'll have to make you tell me about it. So be good to yourself and do it my way now.''

The phrase, '' . . . maybe I'll have to make you tell . . .'' droned through her mind. She wouldn't tell him about the watch. He couldn't make her tell. She moved her shoulder imperceptibly, and the instant stab of pain made a mockery of her resolution. She couldn't ever remember being hurt deliberately before. To be hurt and made to cry out and cower, just because he was big and had a gun . . . She hoped she'd see him chained and helpless. She would sit in the witness chair and tell them how he hit her, and she'd be the calm one, and he'd know he was going to prison because of her. She wouldn't tell him! Not even if he did hit her or twist her arm . . . She cringed at the remembered pain, and at the thought of breaking again under his will. She couldn't humble herself again to him. She couldn't.

She was too afraid to lie outright. He'd know. He might even kill her if she lied now. At first, she had been terrified and it had worn off, and then he had hurt her and frightened her again, not the same way. She had become afraid of the pain and the humiliation of being hurt, not of being killed. Now she thought she might not live to see Larry and Joanne again.   She felt her throat constrict, but she had no more tears, no more emotions to spend.   She lay with her eyes shut, trying to plan.

"Why did you do it?"   she asked after a long silence.   "You said you weren't planning on using the money."

"That's right.   But I needed it."

"Most people don't take up robbery.   Most people are willing to work for the money they need."

"Work!" he said contemptuously.   "You mean most people dream up ways to steal it without running the risk of arousing suspicions."

Marge swallowed her quick retort and said meekly, "I thought it might help if we talk.   I won't try anything, I promise."

"I bet."

"About the rest room . . ."

"Later," he snapped.   "There's the toll gate.   Be asleep!"

She tried to look dead.   The car stopped and change was jingled.   He asked about a good restaurant.   Inwardly, she could almost laugh.   His asking about a restaurant like any innocent tourist!   He was so clever, not overlooking a thing.   And she had outsmarted him.   When they caught him, she'd get the credit for keeping her head and giving them a lead.

He turned on the car lights and reduced speed as they approached the town.   "About the rest room?"

"I left my watch in it," she said defiantly.

"I see.   With your name on it, no doubt."

"My first name," she said.   What if the woman merely kept it?   Or if she handed it in and the police merely put it way down in a "lost and found" drawer?   Just Marge and Warren on it; who would comment on that, or connect it to the robbery?

Music blared from the radio and he turned it down.

"Well?" Marge said.   She looked away from the blazing eyes he turned on her.

"You want a medal?   I don't believe you!"

"What do I care about whether or not you believe me!   I've done nothing wrong!"   She took a deep breath and said more calmly, "I will cooperate with you.   Not because I want you to get away with it.   I just don't want to be hurt again, and I don't want anyone killed.   I hope they catch and execute you!"

"And you'd testify?"

"Gladly!"

He laughed, stopping it almost as quickly as it started.   "Okay, that's fair enough.   We know where we stand.   I'll try not to hurt you so you can return home and send your kids to school so they can grow up to become substantial citizens like their parents.   The boy can be like his father and the girl like you, making the same meaningless tracks on the same endless treadmill."

"That's insane!" Marge cried.   "You make it sound shameful to be normal."

She shook her head angrily.   He had no right.   He made her life sound hopeless and without purpose or meaning. Desperately she said, "You're sick. You said you were in a prison camp. They did something to you. They must have brainwashed you without you realizing it."

"Let's drop it," he cut in rudely. "The news is on."

They listened silently to a summation of the day's happenings, and a brief rehash of the robbery, with another description of both of them. Her car had been located and had given no clues that could be termed helpful.

They stopped at a drive-in and had hamburgers and coffee. Besides the coffee they drank, he had the thermos filled for later use. Then they were speeding down the highway again, as before the stop.

Away from the turnpike she became aware of the mountainous nature of the countryside, and wondered vaguely where they were. It didn't seem very important. They had been driving over eight hours and she was too tired to care. Before the silence became too heavy to interrupt she asked, "Are you married?"

"Isn't everyone?" he said cynically.

Marge followed it up quickly. "Do you love her? Is the money for her?"

"A kid gets taken out of college and told to kill or be killed," he said instead of answering directly. "Finally, he comes home and there's a girl he kissed in another lifetime smiling at him, holding a ring in her hand. Bang, he's married and has a family! No time to think or wonder what it's all about. I don't know. Maybe I did love her, maybe I still do. I don't know. It doesn't matter. I had to get out of it. She'll use the money until she finds a new guy to conjure it up and hand it over, in exchange for the privilege of being told what to do. It's not her fault," he added, sounding sad. "She does what she has to. I guess we all do."

"If you didn't like it, you could have changed it without this. Others do."

"Do they? Or do they just change partners and go on dancing to the same tired music?"

"That's going to sound pretty stupid when they put you in prison."

"I'm not going to jail. Remember, honey?"

She felt a chill at the sureness of his voice. "I suppose," she said quickly, "you'll issue bulletins from time to time telling the rest of us about the better life, now that you've found it."

"People could use them, don't you think?"

"The first step, of course, is to rob a bank. A man can't just run off. He has to provide for his family."

"Honey," he said mockingly, "don't you realize that's all most men are doing now? Providing. How long since you thought of your husband as a man and wanted him?" His laugh was harsh when she sucked in an indignant breath. "Bulletins!" he said. "That's an idea. First, I'd kick out all that extra junk— PTA meetings every week, Ladies' Auxiliaries, socials, and I don't give a damn if they are for the church, charity, or your old Aunt Suzy. A man gets tired of having his wife just coming in, or going out, or too busy on the telephone committee, or plain too tired. And every time a woman used sex as a club, she should become pregnant so she'd have nine months to meditate on its real meaning. There'd be damn few women able to hold jobs. Sex wasn't meant to be a club or a reward, and every time your men lose another round, you despise them a little bit more.''

"Stop it!" she cried. She bit back her denial. She wouldn't give him the satisfaction of arguing with him. Why was she even listening to it? What did he know about her and Warren? After fourteen years no woman got excited . . . She clenched her fists and drew up the image of Larry and Joanne, but her own plan to broil steaks and have martinis kept intruding. She knew what would have happened afterwards, and then she would have told him about playing the piano for school. And the robber had heard back in the bank. He knew.

"I'm through. It's no good anyway," he said tiredly, the mockery and bite gone. "We're all on the same merry-go-round and it's going too fast to see beyond the next horse, too fast to realize that the same paths that lead to it, can take us away. Once you're on and the music starts, you don't get off again."

She glanced at his brooding silhouette. *You did,* she thought. They drove and she became numb with fatigue. She put on the sweater and tried to arrange her legs so she could be more comfortable. She must have dozed, for suddenly he was awakening her. She was dizzy with the motion of the car.

"Want some?" he asked, offering her coffee. She shook her head and huddled against the seat. "It will warm you," he insisted.

It wasn't worth quarreling over, and she drank it even though it was sweetened and bitter. "We'll stop in about an hour," he said. "There's a city about forty miles ahead and we'll find a motel." She stiffened and drew herself up and he laughed bitterly. "Don't be a fool. After I get some rest, you're out of it."

"What do you mean?"

"Just that. There were sleeping pills in the coffee. They won't take full effect for an hour or so, and you'll sleep about eight hours. By then, I'll be gone." He sounded very tired. "When we get to the motel I'll help you in. Don't start yelling if you wake up and find me helping you. If we have to pull out because of anything you do, I'll kill you." His voice, desperate in his weariness, sounded of truth.

Sleeping pills, she thought. It would look perfect. A man and his wife not able to keep driving. He'd help her, and no one would notice anything. Occasionally she took sleeping pills and rolled about for hours before they had any effect on her. What if he overdosed her? If she could vomit . . .

"Relax, honey," he said, almost gently, and one of his hands covered hers in her lap. "Don't be scared now. You've been very brave, really. I couldn't tell from watching you a few times how you'd take it. I thought I might have to keep you out cold the whole trip, but you've been fine. You can be proud of yourself. Someday you'll look back on it and wonder if it really happened. You'll be a heroine on television, in the newspapers. Maybe a national magazine will buy your story. All the women in your subdivision will be jealous.''

He continued to talk quietly, keeping her attention for a long time before her mind began to wander away.

"No one should have to take pills to sleep," she murmured when his words ceased.

"I know." His fingers pressed her hand.

She was drifting along a wooded path feeling alive with excitement at what awaited her at the end . . . It was so nice not worrying or planning, knowing someone was taking care of things. Her hand touched his, the warmth of it spreading through her body. She sighed and relaxed.

She felt his hands on her, and she was walking, haltingly. "Does this look all right for tonight, honey?"

She made the effort to mumble, "Fine."

"OK, just put the bag down there," he said to someone else, and she drooped on his arm. She was unutterably weary and her time sense was gone. He put her down on the bed and pulled a cover over her.

"I'm sorry," she started thickly, and subsided when his hand removed the wig. He was stroking her hair, pressing her head back down.

"It's all right," he whispered. "Sleep."

The dream returned. They were very far up the path and the merry-go-round was nothing, a blur in the distance. He was close to her and the excitement was a glow that enveloped them both, and she slept deeply.

"Marge! Marge! Are you all right?" Someone was shaking her and shouting. She was too heavy and tired to pull away.

Another voice, "Take it easy, sir. The doctor's coming."

She climbed up through layers of mist that held her back, and rough hands hauled at her and cold wetness shocked her face. "Darling! Wake up! What did he do to you?" She moaned softly and worked at opening her eyes. "It's all right, Marge," Warren said. "They got your watch; the men remembered the car. They're chasing him right now. He won't get away." He was sitting on the side of the double bed pulling at her.

She stared at him and shook her head. "They won't catch him."

"Snap out of it, Marge! You're safe now. Listen!" There was a distant, lost sound of a siren somewhere in the grey dawn. As Warren shook her, Marge heard the rapid, faint reports of guns firing. They sounded once more. The siren's wail stopped abruptly and the morning became silent again.

She slipped from Warren's hands and lay back on the bed. She was fully clothed, and very, very cold.

"Where is that doctor?"

Outside someone was shouting, ". . . over the cliff . . ."

Marge squeezed her eyelids together but couldn't contain the tears behind them.

"Don't cry, Marge. Please," Warren said helplessly. "It's over now. You heard. He's dead. You'll forget when we get back home, back to normal. Please, don't. . . . Did he . . . harm you . . . ?"

She shook her head blindly, unable to speak. When he leaned down and touched her, she jerked away from him and buried her face in the pillow, where her abductor's head had rested.

PAUL TABORI

An Interlude for Murder

The loudspeaker cleared its throat and a genteel feminine voice said, "Leddies an' jentlemen, we rhegrhet to inforhm you that Flight One-Siss-Sevain to Montrheal will be delayed ninety minootes . . ."

Through the plate-glass windows of the upstairs lounge I stared at the tarmac. The lady was an optimist, I thought. I could see the mechanics swarming on the wings of the Super-Constellation. It looked as if we were stuck at Orly for the rest of the night. One engine was completely dismantled and they were just starting on the second. Unless they put in a relief plane . . .

I glanced at my watch. It was twenty minutes past five. Autumn dusk was beginning to sweep over the airfield. Half-a-dozen spotlights had been switched on around the stricken plane.

For a brief moment, I wondered whether I should take a taxi to Paris—no more than thirty minutes away. I might be lucky and find Martine at home. But then again, I might not. It was very bad manners to drop in unannounced on a girl friend you hadn't seen for six months. Besides, I'd been on the way since six o'clock in the morning and I was in no shape for a night of gladness. So I sighed and pushed temptation aside. If I was lucky, I'd be through with the job I was to do in Canada in less than a week—and Paris was a reasonably permanent fixture in the world even if Martine wasn't.

I turned towards the newsstand at the back of the lounge when the first champagne bottle popped off behind the screen. Some of my friends swear that I'm psychic about Moët-Chandon and Veuve Cliquot, not to mention Roederer or Sillery. They say that I can tell the vintage merely by ear. This, I must admit, is a slight exaggeration.

That first plop was followed by others. After the sixth, I stopped counting.

I sidled closer to the screen, casual-like. This sounded like a party. With time on my hands, the idea of crashing it was intriguing; so I ducked behind that screen.

My hunch had been right. There was a long heavily laden table in front of the windows with six waiters behind it. I'd landed at Orly or started from it forty or fifty times, so I knew that this room was normally part of the lounge, with armchairs and a TV set. Now it had been transformed into something different. It was L-shaped, with the short leg of the L ending in a staircase that led into the main lobby on the ground floor. At the back, someone had set up a tape recorder on a small table; there were also a couple of microphones and a good many portable spotlights about. All this spelled V.I.P. I wondered whether the current Premier—I had lost count of them, as usual—was flying somewhere. But there were no Sûreté men about—at least not any I could recognize, and I'd developed quite a knack for identifying officers of the law.

There were only three early arrivals in the room; and now one of them, a tall thin character in a loud suit, turned away from the table with a glass of champagne in his hand. His deep set eyes lit up and he addressed me in a mixed tone of surprise and well simulated pleasure:

"Why, if it isn't Adam Venture himself!"

"Hi, Burt," I said. Burt Bachelor was the Paris correspondent of the London *Globe*. "Going some place?"

"No. Just slumming." He drained his glass. "Where you been these last ten years?"

"Hasn't been ten years," I said, "only six months. I've been looking into oil."

He shuddered, not too delicately.

"You would," he said. "Found anything? Stole a few leases?"

I signalled to the nearest waiter and he handed me a glass. It was Veuve Cliquot—a good year, too. I drank and felt a whole lot better.

"Staying at the usual place?" Burt wanted to know.

"No—I'm just in transit. Off to Montreal as soon as they finish tinkering with our plane."

He stared at me, his eyes narrowed.

"I got it!" he hooted. "His Majesty's hired you as a bodyguard! How could ya, Adam? I know you'd stoop low—but *this* low . . ." I hadn't any idea what he was talking about and told him so. But when Burt, otherwise a most reasonable man, had a hunch, he stuck to it, however wrong. "Come on, Adam," he said. "Give."

I held out my glass to be refilled.

For a moment, I toyed with the idea of letting Burt hang himself with the rope of his own cleverness. I didn't know who His Majesty was, or why he should need a bodyguard. If I kept quiet, Burt would eventually provide this information. But it would take too long. So I said, "*You* tell *me*."

He looked around stealthily, but before he could speak, a whole crowd of people surged into the room. You know how it is with parties—one moment there are only a couple of people, the next it's jampacked. A woman with a hawk's nose and piercing eyes pounced on Burt, carried him off. I recognized her—Ginette Latour, who wrote a wicked and brilliant gossip column for the *Miroir*. This must be quite an important party for Ginette didn't turn up at anything but top-drawer occasions.

I nursed my drink, wedged between the table and one of the portable spotlights. I spotted André Daumon, the theatre critic, with his sharp little nose and flashing pince-nez. There was M. Grosbeck, the fat UNESCO department head; he stood next to one of the top models of Balmain, a tall, spectacular girl with an air of aristocratic disdain, entirely due to myopia; several ladies whose proud lineage gave them the right to be outrageously unfashionable; Granard, the young film director, trailing a Central European starlet whose picture appeared more often on magazine covers than it did on screens.   A large party, I thought, and a peculiar list of guests.   What was the director of the *Comédie* doing here, and the Under-Secretary of the Ministry of Fine Arts?   I didn't know either by sight, but Granard, standing close to me, was explaining who was who to his lady friend in a more than penetrating whisper.

I felt quite safe as a gate-crasher; there must be others.   There always were. Having reassured myself, I had my glass filled a fourth time.   Yes, it was a grand party, I decided; only the best champagne.

Someone poked me in the side.   A gangling youth in a pullover and blue jeans. He took up a position directly behind the spotlight.

A tall man in a dark suit was clearing a space opposite and setting up the microphone.   Still another was maneuvering a camera on wheels.   The curtain would go up any minute, I thought.   And I wondered who was topping the bill.

Then there was a sudden burst of applause, and the crowd parted.   A stocky old man wearing a Basque beret and a velvet jacket entered.   He was carrying a stick with a heavy, solid gold knob; clean-shaven, his thin lips barely parted in a cold smile, the broad black ribbon of his eyeglass giving him an oddly piratical look, he made a real entrance.   And now I understood what Burt had been talking about.   No one could mistake this square jaw, these beringed fingers, this royal presence.   A king who ruled far more than a country.   In Paris there was only one man nicknamed His Majesty.   *Sa Majesté*, as the French called him.   The fashion had started with the initials of his name—Serge Maillot.   S.M.   The initials appeared on the titles of every film he produced, directed, wrote and starred in, surmounted by a stylized crown; the same trademark was printed on the posters and the program of his own theatre that had stood for thirty years on the Boulevard Haussmann; there were few of his possessions that did not bear them.   Malicious rumor included his underpants among these.

But a moment after the royal entrance, I had stopped to think about monogrammed undergarments, His Majesty, or the occasion of the champagne party.   Escorted by two young men, a girl had followed Serge Maillot.   Her honey-colored hair held a glint of red; she was wearing a mink coat over a severely cut travelling suit. A gold charm bracelet was jingling on her left wrist.   I knew her a good deal better than Burt or M. Grosbeck or anybody else at the party.   Her name was Martine and, only seven months ago, I had wanted to marry her.

When I met Martine she was dancing at the Boul' Blanche.   Even among the nightclub's hand-picked beauties, Martine stood out.   In short, she was a peach, a lulu, a beaut.

I'm only thirty-five, but Martine—being a beaut, and all that—made me feel about twenty which is a good thing to happen to any man.   When I thought of her, I used the language of a sophomore.   She only drank champagne.   And at dawn, when the show ended, she went straight home to her small hotel in the Rue

Lhomond.   She liked men but, as she explained to me, she couldn't afford them—not until she had become the star of the Casino or the Tabarin.   For some reason, she didn't think much of the Folies Bergères.

And she, apparently, didn't think too much of me.   She allowed me to hold her hand.   Once, after I had offered to pay for her lessons in acrobatic dancing, she kissed me.   I wasn't permitted to kiss her back.   A month before I was called to the Middle East, I became so exasperated that I proposed to her.   She was very sweet about it, but said that she wasn't ready for marriage yet.   And, in any case, could I afford her?   I assured her that I could, and she then wanted to know for how long.   The most I could get out of her was a promise to "review the matter" when I got back from Bahrein.   She didn't even promise to write to me.

And now here she was, looking just as lovely as usual, standing near to His Majesty, Serge Maillot, the uncrowned king of French show business who was seventy if he was a day and who had been married four times, always to women a decade or two younger than himself.   I felt a tingling premonition.   I didn't have to wait long before the premonition turned into certainty.

Maillot stood, facing the crowd which had become an audience.   His strong face showed few lines of age.   Then the Under-Secretary stepped forward.   The tall man in the dark suit adjusted the microphone to the requisite height.   The lamps flared up.   The camera was trained on central figures.   Curtain up.

"Cher Maître," the Under-Secretary began, hooking his thumbs behind his lapels in the classic pose of modern orators, "and my dear Madame Maillot . . ."

He was looking at Martine and Martine smiled—faintly and modestly as befitted a young bride.   I wondered how long they had been married.   I couldn't remember what had been His Majesty's marital status when I left.   Had he been divorced or about to be?   But such things can be arranged easily and quickly if one is Serge Maillot.

". . . this is a great day for France," the Under-Secretary continued, well launched and good for at least fifteen minutes.   "A day of pride and of a little sadness. You are taking our immortal Molière to the New World.   Molière and his direct successor, his spiritual heir—namely, yourself . . ."

There was applause.   Maillot bent his head graciously.   Martine smiled.   The smile had become a trifle mechanical; in a minute or two, if she kept it up, it would turn into a grimace.

"We are proud that the Serge Maillot company is crossing the ocean to present the flower of the French theatre to our kinsmen in Canada.   Even the great United States, during this three-month tour, will have the opportunity of encountering the epitome of French culture . . ."

The Under-Secretary droned on.   I took the opportunity of edging closer to the front of the audience.   I'm a big man, but I can move softly.   Soon I was within a couple of yards of Serge Maillot and not very much farther from Martine.   Her smile had frozen and was going to crack any moment.   I hoped not before all the pictures had been taken.   This was the full works—newsreel, television, still photographers.   And from where I was standing, I could also see into the shorter leg of the L where two young men were tending a tape recorder.

At last the Under-Secretary finished; now it was the turn of the director of the *Comédie* who spoke briefly and quite well, assuring His Majesty that the good wishes of the entire French theatre accompanied him on his journey which was bound to be, like he was himself, fabulous.

"You have said once, my dear Serge," he wound up, "that all comedies had to end with marriage because that was the beginning of all tragedies.   I'm sure that you would revoke this *mot* of yours since your marriage to Madame Martine who is the brightest jewel in your distinguished company of artists."

There was applause again and Martine's smile was refreshed.   Maybe she blushed, too; I couldn't be certain what was makeup and what natural coloring.   In any case, Serge put a possessive arm around her shoulder and she tilted her head to give him a look of utter adoration.

And now it was the star's turn.   Maillot removed his arm from Martine's mink, shifted his cane to his left hand and grasped the microphone with his right.   The monocle glinted brightly in the spotlights.

"Your Excellencies," he said, and the famous voice, with its occasional and deliberate little squeaks, commanded instant silence, "my friends.   I . . ."

The face, the great face that had appeared in a hundred disguises yet always recognizable, on a thousand screens, twisted suddenly.   For a moment it was as if every muscle had become independent, as if every nerve was twitching to break loose.   And then Maillot fell forward with a resounding crash, dragging the microphone with him.   From where I stood, I could see the bare calf of his right leg because his trousers had slipped up with the fall.   The muscles at the back of his calf were twitching violently; then the leg straightened and was completely, horribly still.

It looked real ugly for a minute or two.   Women screamed; two of them fainted. Not Martine; she was standing, close to the wall, a yard or two from the crumpled, huddled figure, staring at it with eyes opened so wide that her face seemed nothing but eyes.   The camera went on grinding, the flashbulbs popped off.   Then there was a surge forward.   That was when I moved.   I knew if I didn't, we'd have a first-class panic on our hands. Crowds, whether of academicians or plumbers, react the same way to an accident or sudden death.   They want to see as much of it as they can, as close as they can.

I pushed and shoved and got through.   I raised my arms and roared out in my best French to keep calm, not to move.   That helped a little.   Then Inspector Jeannot, whom I knew, joined me and I felt relieved.   He was in charge of the airport police and he called for a doctor.

Soon an elderly man, with the red ribbon of the Legion in his buttonhole, struggled into the small empty space around the fallen microphone.   He knelt down, made his brief examination, and then looked up at Jeannot.

"He's dead," he said.

In the sudden and breathless silence that followed the confirmation of what was pretty obvious, a wild sound arose—laughter, loud and hysterical.   I swung around. It was Martine, her body pressed against the wall, gasping out the mad laughs as if they were cries of agony.   As I swiftly moved to her, she began to slide floorward.

I caught her halfway.   She did not seem to be surprised to see me.   She was still laughing as she struggled to say something.

"You know . . . you know what he said?"

"Martine!"

"The others . . ." she clung to me, her slim fingers digging into my arm, "the others . . . he told me . . . they were my wives.   B-but you . . . you will be my widow . . ."

Suddenly she went limp in my arms, and I was glad she'd finally fainted.

In the meantime, half-a-dozen of Jeannot's men had materialized.   They were herding the crowd out of the room; I heard the Inspector offering apologies and saying that it would be necessary to detain everybody for a little instant.   The policemen guided the notables and the hangers-on across the main lounge into the restaurant at the far end which, luckily, wasn't open for business yet.   I deposited Martine in a chair and scooped up a handful of ice from a bucket on the long table.   But as I was about to apply it to the back of her neck, Jeannot caught my hand.

"That can wait," he said.   "It is best if we dispose of M. Maillot's remains first."

Already the room was empty—except for two policemen, Jeannot, the doctor, the unconscious Martine and myself.   And of course the rigid, sprawled figure on the floor.   Someone had righted the microphone.   The spotlights still cast their glare upon the scene.   Outside—I just became conscious of it—a plane was taxiing to the take-off.

The two policemen lifted the body and carried it to the sofa near the head of the stairs.   As they deposited it with reverent care something fell soundlessly to the carpeted floor.   Jeannot and the doctor were near the window, talking softly; I bent down, as soon as the policemen had turned away, and picked up the object.   It was about five inches square, flat and shaped like a cigarette case.   But it wasn't a cigarette case.   For one thing, a thin silvery wire was attached to one end.   It was, I realized almost immediately, the battery of a hearing aid.

The fall had undoubtedly broken the wire.   I stepped up to the sofa.   At first glance I couldn't see the rest of the wire.   Then something glinted faintly.   Under the curious glance of the policemen, I lifted the broad black ribbon of the monocle.   The vanity of actors, I thought.   The wire of the hearing aid was fastened inside the ribbon; its final few inches were still entangled in Maillot's thick white hair and curled down to his ear.   He must have needed the thing very badly, to have worn it even in such a camouflaged form.   As I followed the trail of the wire with a hesitant finger, I stopped suddenly, having just touched Maillot's left ear.   I hesitated.   Though it was a ghoulish business, I had to make sure.   For a few moments, I rested my fingertips on the cheek of the dead man just under the cheekbone.   The flesh was cold and smooth to the touch.

"And what are *you* doing here, M. Venture?" Jeannot's voice said, so suddenly and so close behind that I almost jumped.

"Waiting for a plane," I said.   "I just drifted into the party—just happened to."

But you couldn't fool Jeannot.   We'd been on the same side in that business of the Boston heiress who'd disappeared from the George V without a trace; I was known to him as a reasonably upright citizen.   But that didn't give me any privileges.

"You know I didn't mean that," he said, gentle reproof in his soft voice.   "I mean—just now.   You aren't supposed to touch bodies, however famous."

I showed him the battery.   He took it into his blunt, nicotine-stained fingers. His glance followed the wire as mine had.

"*Tiens*, the doctor didn't tell me . . ."   He raised his voice.   "Dr. Varnel, if you please—"

The elderly, dignified doctor joined us.

"Was Serge Maillot deaf?" demanded the Inspector.

"No, of course not," the doctor said, a little testily.   "Hard of hearing, certainly, but only in the left ear.   I don't see what this . . ."

"You established the cause of death?" I interrupted, rudely, but I had to justify my presence.

"Yes.   It is beyond doubt heart failure.   After all, the *maître* was sixty-nine, and though he was remarkably fit . . ."

Jeannot interrupted this time.

"What's on your mind, M. Venture?" he demanded.

I hesitated.   What *was* on my mind?

"I've sent for the ambulance," the Inspector added, casually.   "The body is to be returned to the Hôtel Maillot."

"No autopsy?" I asked.

"Do you see any reason for it, M. Venture?"

I took a deep breath.   I was sticking my neck out, but after all that plane to Montreal hadn't been announced yet.   I might be around the whole night.

"Yes," I said.

Jeannot did a characteristic thing then.   He nodded to the two policemen who had listened to our conversation with puzzled interest.

"Take Madame Maillot to one of the V.I.P. waiting rooms," he said.   "Ask one of the stewardesses to look after her.   And keep your mouths shut."

For a moment, I had forgotten about Martine.   I glanced over to where she was. She had just opened her eyes and was looking around, dazed.   I resisted the urge to go to her.   To charge a woman with fickleness just after she had become a widow seemed in rather poor taste.

"Are you going to keep that crowd here?" I asked Jeannot.   There was a displeased murmur from the restaurant which very well might grow into something stronger emotionally.   Burt and a few other journalists had already made a couple of attempts to invade the L-shaped room, repulsed firmly but only temporarily by the policeman on guard near the screen.

"That depends," Jeannot said.

"Depends on what?"

"Whatever you are going to say, M. Venture.   And you'd better say it quickly. There are half a dozen people over there who could be very unpleasant if they were detained without good reason."

"There's no reason to keep them," I said. "Except for the technicians who handled the TV and radio equipment."

He gave me a long, level look. Then he walked away and I was left alone with the doctor and the mortal remains of His Majesty. I remembered Burt's remark about Serge Maillot and a bodyguard. Why would he need one? And why would Burt presume that I had been picked for the job? I wanted some answers to these questions.

The doctor cleared his throat.

"This is very unseemly," he said, shaking his head. "I have been Maillot's physician for thirty years. I can tell you . . ."

Before I could say something, Jeannot came back. His face was set; I recognized the symptoms. Someone had reprimanded him and he hadn't liked it.

"And now, if you please, M. Venture," he snapped. "What's on your mind?"

"Have you ever seen a man being electrocuted?" I asked.

His eyes narrowed. "No. Why?"

"I happened to be watching Maillot when he died . . ."

"This is absurd," the doctor said.

"Yes," I agreed. "Just as absurd as the fact that when I accidentally touched Serge Maillot's left ear it was hot."

Dr. Varnel stared at me; then he hurried to the still figure on the sofa. He straightened, looking puzzled.

"There is a slight difference in temperature," he announced. "But nothing remarkable. There is certainly no heat . . ."

"There wouldn't be," I pointed out. "More than ten minutes have passed since I touched him."

"So we have to take your word for all this?" Jeannot asked, a little maliciously.

"No. Not at all. An autopsy'd show the physiological changes both in the ear and the brain . . ."

"Would they, Dr. Varnel?" the Inspector asked.

The old doctor shrugged impatiently.

"Perhaps," he said. "But, of course, the effect of a strong electric shock is not dissimilar to that of a brain hemorrhage . . ."

"But you said it was heart failure," I reminded him.

"The symptoms were certainly consistent with cardiac paralysis," he said. "But one cannot be sure . . ."

" . . . without an autopsy," I finished his sentence.

Jeannot looked at me, then at the doctor. "If there is any reasonable doubt . . ." he said, then stopped abruptly, thoughtfully. "But how could such a shock occur? I was told the microphone and all the apparatus were tested."

"Yes," I said, a hunch I had suddenly becoming clear and loud. "But after all, Maillot brought along some apparatus himself—on his person."

Jeannot reached into his pocket and took out the battery of the hearing aid. He turned it over in his hand. He found the small hinge of the opening. While Dr. Varnel stepped back, disassociating himself from the proceedings, I bent over the small oblong box.

Inside, there was a delicate arrangement of wires and pencil-thin cylinders. They were all blackened, and the center was a mass of shapeless metal, melted and fused by what must have been tremendous heat.

Jeannot and I exchanged a glance; then we both moved to the sofa. The Inspector extracted the dead man's hearing aid. He then took a nail file from his pocket and pried it open. Inside there was a mass of charred carbon and shapeless metal. He said nothing, but placed the hearing aid, together with the battery, on the table next to the tape recorder. Then he turned to Dr. Varnel.

"I must ask for an autopsy," he said quietly. "Of course, it'll have to be performed at the police morgue. You're entitled to be present . . ."

The doctor was still nursing his hurt professional pride.

"But why?" he demanded. "What possible reason—"

"I'm afraid," Jeannot explained gently, "that there is a strong possibility of murder."

Dr. Varnel and the body had departed; Jeannot and I were alone. I wandered over to the long table and poured myself another glass of champagne. It was lukewarm and flat, just like my mood. It had started as a hunch, a flash of observation, followed by a brief elation over being right. But the elation had all gone. And I knew that I should've kept my nose out of the whole thing. And there was the charming widow. I didn't want to see her—not now. No doubt she had a perfectly good explanation why she hadn't waited for me. But I didn't want to hear it.

"Now, Venture," Jeannot said, "what do you know about all this?"

"Nothing—except what I told you. And I still don't see why you call it murder. It may have been an accident."

"A very strange accident. If all this installation was dangerous, why hadn't it caused trouble during the testing? Or during the Under-Secretary's speech?"

I shrugged. "I'm no electronics expert . . ."

"But, apparently, you can tell a man who's being electrocuted—when you see one." Jeannot's grin was friendly, but that didn't mean he was friendly. "All right—you tell me how and why."

This was grossly unfair and he knew it. "There's only one person who can answer you," I said hotly. "And that's the murderer."

He touched my shoulder briefly. "I apologize," he said.

"We know a little," I said, somewhat pacified. "The hearing aid and the battery—they've been subjected to an electric current of very high voltage. This must have been transmitted somehow by the microphone or its stand . . ."

"Let's have a look at the equipment."

We examined the microphone and drew a complete blank. There was nothing wrong with it—no trace of heat, no fused wires or melted metal parts. I traced its wire to the tape recorder. That, too, seemed perfectly okay. When I rewound the few dozen yards of tape on which the Under-Secretary's speech and the oration of the Comédie's director had been recorded, it worked perfectly.

"So it wasn't the microphone," Jeannot said, disappointedly.

"I don't know," I said.   "Perhaps we ought to ask the experts.   You've kept them, haven't you?"

"But they're the last people I want to ask."

"Why?"

"If you're right," he explained, "then I think they're all suspect."

"The more reason to question them."

"No."   He shook his head.   "I don't want to do that.   Not until I have a reasonable explanation of how Serge Maillot died.   Because if any of them knows, *he* is certainly not going to oblige with the information."

Jeannot thought for a moment, chewing his lower lip.   Then he stepped to the telephone which stood in the corner on a small white-painted stand.

"Is Camp there?" he asked.   "Inspector Jeannot wants him . . .   Yes, urgently."   He waited.   "Camp?   Could you come over to the upstairs departure lounge? . . .   No, at once . . .   We need your help badly . . .   Yes, of course, it's a police matter . . .   Thanks.   Thank you."

He put down the receiver and turned to me.   "That's André Camp, head of the radio-communications section of Orly.   He's a wizard, but he doesn't like to be disturbed."

"Nobody likes murder," I said, making conversation.   I added, for the same purpose, "I didn't know Serge Maillot had any enemies."

Jeannot threw up his hands at that.   "Any successful man, any celebrity has enemies," he said.   "You ought to know that.   And Maillot had a talent for making them.   Hundreds of actors whom he sacked, aspiring playwrights whose manuscripts he rejected, film technicians and stage hands to whom he was rude—and he could be very rude.   He had four wives and think of all the women he'd discarded and the husbands he'd enraged."

"It's a miracle," I said, "that he lived as long as he did."

"He thrived on his enemies," Jeannot said.   "And there was his war record . . .   You know, he kept his theatre open right through the Nazi occupation.   He made three films, too.   He said he did it to keep French culture alive.   Others had an uglier name for it.   Soon after the Liberation he was kidnapped one night by some young resistance fighters.   They took him to a cemetery where a hundred of their comrades were buried—all executed by the Germans.   He had to pay homage to them on his knees.   It shook him badly and for a year or two he retired.   Enemies!   I wouldn't know where to begin if I wanted to round them all up!"

There were quick, nervous steps on the stairs and a tall, thin man burst into the room.

"Now look here, Jeannot," he began, "I'm responsible for the safety of my airport!   You can't just drag me away . . ."

"If you could just tell us what you think of these . . ." Jeannot said, unruffled.   He held out the hearing aid and the battery.

Camp stared at them, his bony Adam's apple working.   "Any fool can tell you," he said.   "What kind of a game do you . . ."

Jeannot cut him short.   "Serge Maillot," he said, "died in this room less than an hour ago, we think it's murder.   This, by the way, is M. Venture, a friend of mine.   He has been . . . helpful.''

I didn't like the little pause before the last word, but Camp took no notice of it.

"Well, I'm not a policeman," he said impatiently.

"No, but you're a genius," Jeannot stated, quite matter-of-factly.   "So if you'd bend your great mind to our little problem . . .''

Camp snorted irritably.   "These things here," he poked at the pencil-shaped tiny objects in the battery, "are transistors.   And I haven't the faintest idea what they're doing in a hearing-aid battery . . .''

"What about this?" and Jeannot handed him the hearing aid itself.

Camp inspected it briefly.   He looked sour.   "Same thing," he said, "but they've been badly damaged.   A short circuit, maybe.''

"What would cause a short circuit in a hearing aid?" I asked.

He shrugged.   "Nothing, in theory.   The voltage is so low—it has to be, for safety—that a short is most unlikely.   Of course, I'm not an expert on these contraptions.   But somehow, quite obviously, both battery and earpiece have been subjected to very high voltage current.''

"We've thought of that," I said.   "But all the equipment's been tested—the microphone, the tape recorder, the spotlights—and it all appears to be in perfect working order.''

Camp scratched his head.   He looked a little less angry and a good deal more interested.   Then, without a word, he went to work.   He took the microphone to pieces, examined the cables of the portable spotlights, even peered into the camera itself.   His face became brighter and brighter.   Jeannot and I watched him, in respectful silence, until he came back to us.   His original impatience was gone.

"This is quite interesting," he said.   "You're right.   None of that equipment could've caused anybody's death.''   He beamed as if he were tremendously pleased by the totally negative result.

"That's delightful," Jeannot said.   "Maybe Maillot was killed by someone from Outer Space.   Or by a death ray.   Or—or he just died of indigestion.''

"Don't be frivolous, Jeannot," Camp said, pointing a long, bony forefinger at him.   "You should always be serious in the presence of intellect.   Maybe a great intellect.   Do you not agree, Jeannot?''

"You haven't looked at the tape recorder," I said.

Camp gave me a quick, searching look.   "No," he agreed.   "I haven't. Maybe I'm like a man who looks everywhere for an important key except in his watch pocket—because he's afraid to.   If the key isn't there, he's lost it, you see.'' He chuckled.   "But then again I may have other reasons.''

He continued to chuckle.   He was a changed man, because he was interested and stimulated.   He was a picture of a scientist in the presence of a riddle.

"Do you know anything about transistors, M. Venture?" he asked as he moved to the tape recorder and set it at replay.

"Not much," I said.

"They're devilishly clever things.   They can be used both for sending and receiving electrical impulses—sound waves, light waves, electrical waves. Their possibilities haven't been exhausted yet by any means. Just now they're using them, for instance, to record the incubation cycle of a king penguin's egg—to discover how humans can be adapted to intense cold. Then again, transistors are the most important part of space missiles and . . .''

"Really, Camp,'' Jeannot interrupted. "Serge Maillot was neither a penguin nor a spaceman. I fail to see . . .''

The fruity voice of the Under-Secretary came through the tape recorder's built-in loudspeaker. Camp turned it down until it became a faint mutter.

"You'll see, all in good time,'' he said, with dignity. "And of course, I might be quite wrong . . .'' he added, maddeningly.

We waited and watched.

We were sitting in a circle: the cameraman, his assistant, the four young electricians who had handled the spotlights, the tall fellow in the dark suit who turned out to be a TV director, the sound engineers in charge of the tape recorder, Martine and myself.

It was characteristic of Camp that as soon as he had proved his theory right, he had departed. He wasn't interested in the outcome, the practical application. He left the test to Jeannot and myself.

Martine was subdued, but she had gotten over her hysteria. She sat next to me, but hadn't spoken a word. I preferred it that way.

Jeannot stood in the middle of the circle, his hands in his pockets, and rocked on his heels.

"I am sorry to have kept you,'' he said. "But there are certain questions we have to clarify about M. Maillot's death.''

"What is there to clarify about a heart attack?'' the director, whose name was Riret, asked.

"It wasn't a heart attack,'' Jeannot said softly. "It was murder.''

Martine's eyes opened wide and I thought she would scream or faint again. But they must have pumped her full of sedatives; she just stiffened a little and leaned forward, her heart-shaped face white under the makeup. The others reacted with incredulity, startled interest, or low exclamations of surprise.

"But,'' the cameraman said, "we've a record of it on film. If you let us process it, and run it . . .''

"The film wouldn't show the murderer,'' the Inspector said. "Only the victim.''

One of the sound engineers giggled—sheer nerves. The other gave him a reproachful look.

"May we know how M. Maillot was killed?'' the director asked. "That is, if we are to accept this remote possibility.''

"I think we can show you,'' Jeannot said. He took the hearing aid and the battery from his pocket and held them dangling from his fingers.

That was my cue. I got up and moved to the tape recorder. I felt their eyes following me every step of the way. I looked at Jeannot. He nodded and I switched on the recorder.

". . . I'm sure that you would revoke this *mot* of yours since your marriage to Madame Martine," the director of the *Comédie* was saying, his disembodied voice with the over-precise diction sounding eerie in the silence, "who is the brightest jewel in your distinguished company of artists . . ."

Martine gave a slight, choking sound. The tape ran on. Applause. A hubbub of voices, dying down.

"Your Excellencies," Serge Maillot began, "my friends. I . . ."

And then—silence. Silence for several yards of tape, followed suddenly by a veritable cataract of sound—screams, shouts—ending with Dr. Varnel's barely audible announcement: "He's dead."

There was silence, too, as I switched off the recorder and went back to Jeannot's side.

"But what is this?" the cameraman asked. "You said you were going to show us how Serge Maillot was killed. All we heard was—"

"We can play it again," the Inspector said. "But perhaps you'll take my word for it. It's all there on that tape. The end of the Director General's speech, the applause, and then the few words Maillot spoke . . ."

"After that there was silence," the TV director said, his face puzzled.

"Yes," Jeannot nodded. "Silence. Yet the tape recorder was switched on. Why didn't we hear the thud of Maillot's body hitting the floor? Why the sudden gap?"

"Don't ask us," said one of the young technicians. "We wouldn't know."

"I'm not asking you. But we can try running the tape again. This time we'll demonstrate more fully."

He looked around as if seeking someone, making a choice. He stopped in front of one of the young sound engineers, a stocky, dark-haired fellow. The other was fair, with a nervous, sensitive face. "If you wouldn't mind," Jeannot said, and offered the battery and hearing-aid to the dark-haired young man. "Just slip it into your ear . . . That's right . . . It's quite safe, I assure you."

The young man hesitated, then obeyed. I was at the tape recorder again, waiting for Jeannot's signal. It was a long time coming. I glanced back. Martine was staring at the Inspector. The others looked as if they were waiting for some unusual parlor trick to be performed. I couldn't see the fair-haired young fellow because Jeannot's body blocked the view.

At last the Inspector nodded. Once again the fulsome sentences of the *Comédie's* director echoed. Once again there was applause, the hubbub, and then Maillot's speech. But this time he didn't get past the first three words. A chair went over with a crash. I jumped forward. The fair-haired young man had just torn the hearing aid from his colleague's ear. His other hand held a gun. His thin, sensitive face was twisted in a mad grimace—very much like the last expression of Serge Maillot before he had collapsed.

"So," he said, his voice a little hoarse, "so you've found out. Such clever people! I did it! The dog—he deserved to die a hundred times over. He kicked out my father from his company—and the Boche sent him to a camp—and there he died!"

"Put that gun down," Jeannot said calmly.

"She helped me!" the youngster cried, and the gun pointed now at Martine's breast. "It was she who changed the battery. I wanted to kill him, but she helped me. She wanted him dead, too!"

Martine's head was shaking in denial—her face pale, white.

Jeannot moved fast, very fast. But it wasn't fast enough. The gun exploded and then the young man turned tail—his footsteps clattering down the staircase. I was only a few yards behind him, but at the bottom I bumped into a fat woman who was just crossing from the perfume counter. I caught sight of the blond head; the young fellow was sprinting across the downstairs hall, past a group of passengers in one of the small departure bays. He tore open the glass door and went flying across the tarmac. By the time I was outside, a couple of policemen had joined me. I had a confused impression of a bus swinging out, people shouting and wheels screeching; somewhere in the distance, swallowing it all, the roar of engines being tuned up. As I dodged the bus, I could see the young engineer running across the tarmac. He had a good hundred yards' start. I put on a spurt, but I didn't gain much. Neither did the policemen. There were dazzling lights at the edge of the field where they were still working on the Super-Constellation. And then, as I got within fifty yards of him, I was dazed by the lights and had to slow down. As a consequence, I didn't see him rushing into that cluster of lights. I only heard the scream, high-pitched and long-drawn, as he ran into the flaying propellers. He must have been killed instantaneously, sucked into the whirling blades by the air-stream.

"Yes, we know all about him," Burt was saying as we sat—it seemed a year later, though it was only an hour or so—sipping champagne in the lounge. "His name was Demaine. It was quite true about his father, though Maillot couldn't have known what would happen to him when he dismissed him in 1942. Old Demaine was a drunkard. But of course the son would overlook that, so he could go on living with this obsession to get even . . ."

"Poor devil," I said. I felt empty and exhausted. I saw Martine's lovely face dissolving into fear and panic as she was taken away. Whether Demaine's accusation would prove true or not, it did not seem to matter. Most likely it was true. Finding out was Jeannot's job. I had the feeling that she'd married the old boy for his money and wanted him out of the way as soon as possible.

"But how did he do it?" Burt asked. "Jeannot wouldn't say. And if you could put it into plain language, for a poor dumb layman like myself . . ."

"I'm no expert," I said wearily. "It was Camp who figured it out. What Demaine did was simple enough. He replaced the battery with three transistors—or possibly, if Martine were mixed up in this thing, had her do it. The transistors acted as receiver. In the tape recorder, he had built another set—which was the sender. All he then had to do was to switch off the tape and switch on his sender. The transistors in the hearing-aid battery and the recorder were naturally tuned to each other . . ."

"For Pete's sake," Burt protested, "I said in simple language.   What I want to know is, what did he kill Maillot with?"

"Sound," I said.   "High-frequency sound.   You know that the human ear can only pick up certain frequencies.   You get below them and you hear nothing. You can go above them—with the mechanical gimmick Demaine fixed up—and if they're strong enough, they can kill.   That was why there was a dead spot on the tape.   The high-frequency sound had been transformed into heat when it passed through the hearing-aid battery.   It wasn't electricity but heat that melted part of the battery and the hearing aid itself.   And if I hadn't happened to touch Maillot's ear . . ."

Burt opened his mouth to ask, at a guess, another fifty questions.   But the loudspeaker above us cleared its throat and a male voice said, "Passengers for Montreal, Flight 167, are asked to proceed to the aircraft.   Passengers for Montreal, Flight 167—"

I picked up my overnight bag, walked downstairs, through the glass door, and into the darkness outside.

ELEANOR DALY BOYLAN

Death Overdue

"**A** library would make a good setting for a murder," said Allan Gifford pleasantly as Mrs. De Ware stamped his books and accepted a four-cent fine. "You know—corpse found in the D-to-F section, dead hand clutching page torn from book, librarian identifies murderer by tracing book with torn page—"

"I'm glad I'm to be the detective. For a minute I was afraid I was the murderer."

"You're lucky I didn't make you the victim."

Mrs. De Ware laughed, a surprisingly hearty laugh to emanate from a ninety-pound frame, thought Gifford with amusement and affection. She was sixty-five and pretty as a pansy, with snow white hair and lively brown eyes. Mrs. De Ware had been the librarian in the town of Stockton since her husband's death ten years before. "I intend to see that you get an anniversary dinner while I'm here this summer," Gifford had told her on his arrival several weeks before. A journalist and occasional writer of detective fiction, he'd taken a cottage in Stockton every July for the past seven years.

"Well, I'd say you have your summer's work cut out. What will you call it— *The Body in the Stacks?*" Mrs. De Ware began removing crayon marks from a copy of *The Wizard of Oz*.

"More likely *Gifford's Swan Song*. I'm through with the clue type."

He leaned against her counter, reluctant to go out into the heat again. He was the only person in the library and they were great friends. The good-natured little librarian had been endlessly obliging, reserving books for him, checking on facts, even sending the sixty miles south to Boston for references and information that her limited stock could not supply.

"Swan song? You're just feeling sorry for yourself. Typical writer's slump. Probably Martha's away."

"She is. Took the kids to visit her mother. No, if I write any more fiction it will be straight stuff. A pox on mysteries. Most sweltering work on earth."

Mrs. De Ware started to say something, then stopped and smiled at two girls who bounced into the library, brown and barelegged. They waved to her and headed for the magazine racks. She said, in a lowered voice:

"Speaking of mysteries, a rather interesting thing happened just before you came up this year. At least, I thought it was interesting and sort of detective story-ish. I was running our annual 'No Fine Week.' You know, you leave a basket out front

494

and put a notice in the paper inviting people to return books that are long overdue without having to pay any fine.   It's a way of corralling a lot of books that you'd probably never see again otherwise.   Well, one morning when I emptied the basket, there was a book dated October 18, 1944.   Sort of odd and creepy, don't you think?''

''Why creepy?''

She looked disappointed.   ''Oh, dear, I forgot you aren't a native.   The date wouldn't mean anything to you.   That was the day of the Paxton murder.   A girl by the name of Dorothy Paxton was—''

''Wait a minute—that name rings a bell . . .''   Gifford rearranged his long frame on the counter.   ''See if I remember: she was drowned—no, strangled—found by some lake or other, and there was a fellow she was going to marry.   I think they even brought him back from overseas for questioning.   But why do I remember her?   She was somebody in Stockton—somebody's daughter or sister or—''

''Daughter.   The mayor's.''

''Of course.   Mayor Paxton's daughter.   And he raised a hell of a rumpus but there was no conviction, as I recall, was there?''

Mrs. De Ware shook her head, beaming at him.   ''Now, that is rather interesting and dramatic, don't you think?   Especially since that 'some lake or other' where the body was found is Willow Pool just down the road from here.''

''Really?''   Gifford laughed.   ''Too bad the borrower didn't bring the book back on the day it was due instead of fifteen years later.   He might have seen the murderer!''

''But that's the delicious part: Miss Gill, the librarian then, used a different system of stamping.   She stamped the day that the book was taken *out*.   So the person could have seen the murderer after all.''

Mrs. De Ware winked at him triumphantly as her telephone rang; she answered, made a note, disappeared into the stacks and returned to say yes, *How to Raise African Violets* was in and she would reserve it.

Gifford looked into space and told himself not to be a fool.   This sort of luck didn't happen to him—or to anybody.   Million to one stuff.   Billion.

''What was the name of the book?   Can I see it?''

The librarian stooped and opened a bottom drawer.   She produced a discolored volume.   ''*Civil Defense: Its Importance in Your Community*.   Published in 1942.   Completely outdated, of course.   I didn't even bother to catalogue it again.''

''No record, I suppose, of who took it out.''

She shook her head.   ''Not that far back.''

Gifford took the book from her and opened the cover.   He stared at the faded red ink in which the date was stamped, thinking fondly what a lovely dust jacket it would make . . . a skeleton hand holding the date stamp, the red ink running down the page and turning into blood, the title on a library catalogue card, *Death Overdue*.   Then his journalist's mind jostled the fiction writer impatiently.   He said:

''Don't I remember a principal suspect, somebody they almost convicted?''

"Yes. A man named Ralph Addison. He died just last year."

"Has he any relatives? Anyone I can see?"

Mrs. De Ware looked alarmed, then severe. "Now, Mr. Gifford, I didn't tell you all this so you could go poking around town asking questions. You were in the dumps and I told you about the book to try and give you a lift. I'll be very cross if you embarrass me by—"

"May I just keep the book for a few days?"

"You may not." She plucked it from him and dropped it back into the drawer.

"Well, at least tell me some more about the Paxton murder."

"No, sir."

"You're a fine one. Get me all interested and curious and then clam up. I won't hurt your precious reputation. I won't even mention your name. Please let me take the book for—"

She shook her snowy head vigorously and turned to her card file. Gifford smiled and strolled to the door.

"If I find out anything interesting, I'll take you to dinner and tell *you* about it."

Mrs. De Ware did not deign a reply. She had walked over to where the girls were reading magazines and was chatting with them, her back to him.

The library, which occupied a low frame building together with the post office, was at the very end of a side street off Stockton's main thoroughfare. Beyond it were fields, a small pond called Willow Pool and the beginning of farmland.

Gifford stood on the library steps, deliciously envisioning someone else standing there fifteen years before, holding a book on civil defense and idly noticing a passerby, the color of a dress, the movement of a passing car. Was there a hazy or disregarded fragment of memory in the mind of someone in Stockton that could just mean . . .

"You're punchy from the heat," he chided himself. Well, this was his vacation, his family was away and if he wanted to squander a few days, it was cheaper anyway than golf.

From alternate baking sun to harboring shade, Gifford walked to the corner of Main Street and waved to Captain Nichols through the window of the barber shop. Stockton's elderly fire chief was just getting out of the chair and Gifford waited till he came out onto the street.

"Hello, Nick. Say, tell me something. I'm writing a story set around the time of World War II, and I want some information on how civil defense might have been run in a small town. Know anybody who could help me?"

The hale, leathery-faced fire chief grinned. "Bernie Waterfield would be your man. He was in charge of the whole thing for Stockton. Little Caesar, we used to call him."

"Took it pretty seriously?"

"Oh, Lordy. All over town with the helmet and the arm band and the rest of the gear. Lecturing people on how to detonate a bomb and all that. I remember back during the Paxton trial, Bernie was screaming that there shouldn't be so many 'important officials under one roof.' Drove you crazy. But I suppose somebody had to do what he did.''

Gifford seized his break. ''That Paxton trial must have been something.''

''Yeah, we were really on the map that year. Lot of the big names are gone now. Mayor Paxton's dead and Ralph Addison—''

''What sort of fellow was he?''

''Ralph? Not a bad guy, really. Kinda silly. Thirty-five and still a girl-crazy bachelor. He was chasing Dotty Paxton while her boy friend was in the service. Ralph was the last person seen with her the morning of the murder; they found her body late that afternoon. But then, a lot of fellows were after Dotty. She was the prettiest thing in town. I'm heading over to the diner. Come along?''

''Thanks, Nick, but I think I'll get right over and see Waterfield. Owns the drug store, doesn't he?''

Nichols nodded and Gifford strolled the half block to the pharmacy, debating his approach. He longed to ask Waterfield point blank if he had taken the book out of the library on that fateful day. But this would almost certainly mean a discussion of its delayed return which could embarrass Waterfield and involve Mrs. De Ware. No, he had promised her he would be circumspect.

Next best, then, was the ''I'm writing a story'' tactic he had used with Nichols. How those words covered a multitude of snoopings, grinned Gifford to himself as he turned into the welcome coolness of the drug store. He would edge as close to the subject as he could, and hope that Waterfield was a talker.

The soda fountain was crowded, but there was no one at the prescription counter. Gifford was greeted by Bernie Waterfield himself, a big, fleshy man in his sixties.

''My name's Allan Gifford. Could you fill out a prescription for a murder story?'' Then he laughed at the other's astonished face. Waterfield began to smile doubtfully.

He said: ''I hear *you're* the fellow who fills those out. Can't say I've read any of your stories. I'm not much on detective stuff.''

''Tell you my problem if you have a minute.'' Gifford rested his palms against the counter edge. ''I'm working on a fictional account of the Paxton murder. That is, I'm using the basic facts of the crime, but dressing it up with imaginary characters and events. One of my ideas is to make a principal witness out of the man who runs civil defense in the town, as I know you did. Now, on the day of the murder, this fellow goes to the post office to put up some air raid signs. I have him go to the post office because it's right down there by the library, you know, not far from Willow Pool where—''

The telephone in his work room rang and Waterfield, whose face had grown increasingly disapproving, excused himself. Minutes passed and he did not return. Then a boy appeared to say that Mr. Waterfield was very busy and could not talk to Mr. Gifford any more that day.

Disappointed, Gifford ordered a strawberry soda and pondered his change of luck. Had he been too flip? Small town citizens are inclined to be proud of their local color and the Paxton case had been big stuff and no joking matter. If

Waterfield were the humorless, officious character he'd been described as, Gifford could practically hear him telling the town that that "writer fellow" was going to rig up a story about the Paxton murder, adding a lot of trimmings and foolishness. Or perhaps Waterfield did not relish himself in the role of a chief witness, even in an imaginary capacity.   Or had Gifford appeared to make light of the glorious trappings of civil defense?

Gifford walked home, determined now to play it straight.   He needn't involve Mrs. De Ware; after all, the Paxton facts would be a matter of public record.   At his cottage, he made a list of acquaintances, tradespeople and officials of Stockton old enough to have reliable memories of the event.   Then he telephoned the drug store and Waterfield answered.

Gifford identified himself.   "I'm afraid I gave the wrong impression just now, Mr. Waterfield.   The fact is, I'm very seriously interested in the Paxton case and as far as I'm able, I intend to try and reopen it.   Some rather interesting new evidence has come to light (heaven forgive him, but he had to capture the interest of these people if he expected to get anything from them) and I have before me a list of persons that I intend to call and ask for interviews.   I wonder if you could give me twenty minutes tomorrow morning.   I promise it won't be any longer."

There was a pause, then Waterfield said heavily: "Any time tomorrow," and hung up.

Gifford made a half dozen more calls and lined up four appointments for the next day, appointments he was never to keep.

For the next morning's *Stockton Eagle* carried screaming headlines of the suicide of Bernard Waterfield.   He had shot himself, leaving a written confession to the murder of Dorothy Paxton.   As he read, stunned, Gifford's eye caught and fixed on one phrase in the account, and deep pity welled in him for little Mrs. De Ware.

That evening, still glowing from the praise of his editor, Gifford sat with Mrs. De Ware at a quiet table of the Lord Jeffrey Inn at Amherst.   Her eyes were red from weeping and Gifford occasionally patted her hand and told her to eat like a good girl.

"After all," he smiled, "this is a celebration for both of us.   But I do wish you'd told me Ralph Addison was your brother."

"Poor darling.   To have his name exonerated at last.   You don't know what it means."

"Admit that you deliberately baited me with that book, knowing I'd react like a bloodhound."

She nodded, giggled, and sipped her coffee.   Then her eyes grew sombre.   "For fifteen years I've felt sure that Ralph was innocent.   And he knew that I believed in him, but it didn't help very much.   Even though they couldn't convict him, the cloud never lifted.   You can imagine what it was like, right up to the day he died."

"I can.   It must've been tough.   Did you ever suspect Waterfield?"

"Yes.   From the beginning."

"Why?"

She fixed her eyes on her plate.   "Bernie courted me when we were both young. I knew the sort of man he was . . ."

After a moment, Gifford said: "Then, of course, the book coming back with that date on it must have cinched it for you. But why on earth wouldn't you let me *take* the book? You were driving me out to do your dirty work, why deprive me of an important piece of evidence?"

A waiter handed them dessert menus and withdrew. Mrs. De Ware studied hers intently. "Apple pie, fudge sundae, honeydew melon . . . Because there wasn't any evidence. There wasn't any book returned with the murder date on it . . ."

"But you told me—"

Mrs. De Ware smiled at Gifford's perplexity. "That book on civil defense was in a crate that we received from an estate last spring. When I saw the title, it reminded me of Bernie; he'd made such a nuisance of himself over the whole program. I began to think of how I might use it to expose him if he was guilty. I had the idea to rig the date. You should have seen me trying to make it look old and faded. The next step was to pick the right moment for putting you on the scent. Oh, good, here's my favorite: lemon meringue pie."

DONALD E. WESTLAKE

The Best-Friend Murder

Detective Abraham Levine of Brooklyn's Forty-Third Precinct chewed on his pencil and glowered at the report he'd just written. He didn't like it, he didn't like it at all. It just didn't feel right, and the more he thought about it the stronger the feeling became.

Levine was a short and stocky man, baggily dressed from plain pipe racks. His face was sensitive, topped by salt-and-pepper gray hair chopped short in a military crewcut. At fifty-three, he had twenty-four years of duty on the police force, and was halfway through the heart-attack age range, a fact that had been bothering him for some time now. Every time he was reminded of death, he thought worriedly about the aging heart pumping away inside his chest.

And in his job, the reminders of death came often. Natural death, accidental death, and violent death.

This one was a violent death, and to Levine it felt wrong somewhere. He and his partner, Jack Crawley, had taken the call just after lunch. It was from one of the patrolmen in Prospect Park, a patrolman named Tanner. A man giving his name as Larry Perkins had walked up to Tanner in the park and announced that he had just poisoned his best friend. Tanner went with him, found a dead body in the apartment Perkins had led him to, and called in. Levine and Crawley, having just walked into the station after lunch, were given the call. They turned around and walked back out again.

Crawley drove their car, an unmarked '56 Chevvy, while Levine sat beside him and worried about death. At least this would be one of the neat ones. No knives or bombs or broken beer bottles. Just poison, that was all. The victim would look as though he were sleeping, unless it had been one of those poisons causing muscle spasms before death. But it would still be neater than a knife or a bomb or a broken beer bottle, and the victim wouldn't look quite so completely dead.

Crawley drove leisurely, without the siren. He was a big man in his forties, somewhat overweight, square-faced and heavy-jowled, and he looked meaner than he actually was. The Chevvy tooled up Eighth Avenue, the late Spring sun shining on its hood. They were headed for an address on Garfield Place, the block between Eighth Avenue and Prospect Park West. They had to circle the block, because Garfield was a one-way street. That particular block on Garfield Place is a double row of chipped brownstones, the street running down between two rows of high stone stoops, the buildings cut and chopped inside into thousands of apartments, crannies and cubbyholes, niches and box-like caves, where the subway riders sleep at night.   The subway to Manhattan is six blocks away, up at Grand Army Plaza, across the way from the main library.

At one P.M. on this Wednesday in late May, the sidewalks were deserted, the buildings had the look of long abandoned dwellings.   Only the cars parked along the left side of the street indicated present occupancy.

The number they wanted was in the middle of the block, on the right-hand side. There was no parking allowed on that side, so there was room directly in front of the address for Crawley to stop the Chevvy.   He flipped the sun visor down, with the official business card showing through the windshield, and followed Levine across the sidewalk and down the two steps to the basement door, under the stoop. The door was propped open with a battered garbage can.   Levine and Crawley walked inside.   It was dim in there, after the bright sunlight, and it took Levine's eyes a few seconds to get used to the change.   Then he made out the figures of two men standing at the other end of the hallway, in front of a closed door.   One was the patrolman, Tanner, young, just over six foot, with a square and impersonal face.   The other was Larry Perkins.

Levine and Crawley moved down the hallway to the two men waiting for them. In the seven years they had been partners, they had established a division of labor that satisfied them both.   Crawley asked the questions, and Levine listened to the answers.   Now, Crawley introduced himself to Tanner, who said, "This is Larry Perkins of 294 Fourth Street."

"Body in there?" asked Crawley, pointing at the closed door.

"Yes, sir," said Tanner.

"Let's go inside," said Crawley.   "You keep an eye on the pigeon.   See he doesn't fly away."

"I've got some stuff to go to the library," said Perkins suddenly.   His voice was young and soft.

They stared at him.   Crawley said, "It'll keep."

Levine looked at Perkins, trying to get to know him.   It was a technique he used, most of it unconsciously.   First, he tried to fit Perkins into a type or category, some sort of general stereotype.   Then he would look for small and individual ways in which Perkins differed from the general type, and he would probably wind up with a surprisingly complete mental picture, which would also be surprisingly accurate.

The general stereotype was easy.   Perkins, in his black wool sweater and belt-in-the-back khakis and scuffed brown loafers without socks, was 'arty'.   What were they calling them this year?   They were 'hip' last year, but this year they were—'beat.'   That was it.   For a general stereotype.   Larry Perkins was a beatnik.   The individual differences would show up soon, in Perkins' talk and mannerisms and attitudes.

Crawley said again, "Let's go inside," and the four of them trooped into the room where the corpse lay.

The apartment was one large room, plus a closet-size kitchenette and an even smaller bathroom.   A Murphy bed stood open, covered with zebra-striped material. The rest of the furniture consisted of a battered dresser, a couple of armchairs and lamps, and a record player sitting on a table beside a huge stack of long-playing records.   Everything except the record player looked faded and worn and second-hand, including the thin maroon rug on the floor and the soiled flower-pattern wallpaper.   Two windows looked out on a narrow cement enclosure and the back of another brownstone.   It was a sunny day outside, but no sun managed to get down into this room.

In the middle of the room stood a card table, with a typewriter and two stacks of paper on it.   Before the card table was a folding chair, and in the chair sat the dead man.   He was slumped forward, his arms flung out and crumpling the stacks of paper, his head resting on the typewriter.   His face was turned toward the door, and his eyes were closed, his facial muscles relaxed.   It had been a peaceful death, at least, and Levine was grateful for that.

Crawley looked at the body, grunted, and turned to Perkins.   "Okay," he said. "Tell us about it."

"I put the poison in his beer," said Perkins simply.   He didn't talk like a beatnik at any rate.   "He asked me to open a can of beer for him.   When I poured it into a glass, I put the poison in, too.   When he was dead, I went and talked to the patrolman here."

"And that's all there was to it?"

"That's all."

Levine asked, "Why did you kill him?"

Perkins looked over at Levine.   "Because he was a pompous ass."

"Look at me," Crawley told him.

Perkins immediately looked away from Levine, but before he did so, Levine caught a flicker of emotion in the boy's eyes, what emotion he couldn't tell.   Levine glanced around the room, at the faded furniture and the card table and the body, and at young Perkins, dressed like a beatnik but talking like the politest of polite young men, outwardly calm but hiding some strong emotion deep inside his eyes. What was it Levine had seen there?   Terror?   Rage?   Or pleading?

"Tell us about this guy," said Crawley, motioning at the body.   "His name, where you knew him from, the whole thing."

"His name is Al Gruber.   He got out of the Army about eight months ago. He's living on his savings and the GI Bill.   I mean, he *was*."

"He was a college student?"

"More or less.   He was taking a few courses at Columbia, nights.   He wasn't a full-time student."

Crawley said, "What *was* he full-time?"

"Not much of anything.   A writer.   An undiscovered writer.   Like me."

Levine asked, "Did he make much money from his writing?"

"None," said Perkins.   This time he didn't turn to look at Levine, but kept watching Crawley while he answered.   "He got something accepted by one of the quarterlies once," he said, "but I don't think they ever published it.   And they don't pay anything anyway."

"So he was broke?" asked Crawley.

"Very broke. I know the feeling well."

"You in the same boat?"

"Same life story completely," said Perkins. He glanced at the body of Al Gruber and said, "Well, almost. I write, too. And I don't get any money for it. And I'm living on the GI Bill and savings and a few home-typing jobs, and going to Columbia nights."

People came into the room then, the medical examiner and the boys from the lab, and Levine and Crawley, bracketing Perkins between them, waited and watched for a while. When they could see that the M.E. had completed his first examination, they left Perkins in Tanner's charge and went over to talk to him.

Crawley, as usual, asked the questions. "Hi, Doc," he said. "What's it look like to you?"

"Pretty straightforward case," said the M.E. "On the surface, anyway. Our man here was poisoned, felt the effects coming on, went to the typewriter to tell us who'd done it to him, and died. A used glass and a small medicine bottle were on the dresser. We'll check them out, but they almost certainly did the job."

"Did he manage to do any typing before he died?" asked Crawley.

The M.E. shook his head. "Not a word. The paper was in the machine kind of crooked, as though he'd been in a hurry, but he just wasn't fast enough."

"He wasted his time," said Crawley. "The guy confessed right away."

"The one over there with the patrolman?"

"Uh huh."

"Seems odd, doesn't it?" said the M.E. "Take the trouble to poison someone, and then run out and confess to the first cop you see."

Crawley shrugged. "You can never figure," he said.

"I'll get the report to you soon's I can," said the M.E.

"Thanks, Doc. Come on, Abe, let's take our pigeon to his nest."

"Okay," said Levine, abstractedly. Already it felt wrong. It had been feeling wrong, vaguely, ever since he'd caught that glimpse of something in Perkins' eyes.

And the feeling of wrongness was getting stronger by the minute, without getting any clearer.

They walked back to Tanner and Perkins, and Crawley said, "Okay, Perkins, let's go for a ride."

"You're going to book me?" asked Perkins. He sounded oddly eager.

"Just come along," said Crawley. He didn't believe in answering extraneous questions.

"All right," said Perkins. He turned to Tanner. "Would you mind taking my books and records back to the library? They're due today. They're the ones on that chair. And there's a couple more over in the stack of Al's records."

"Sure," said Tanner. He was gazing at Perkins with a troubled look on his face, and Levine wondered if Tanner felt the same wrongness that was plaguing him.

"Let's go," said Crawley impatiently, and Perkins moved toward the door.

"I'll be right along," said Levine. As Crawley and Perkins left the apartment,

Levine glanced at the titles of the books and record albums Perkins had wanted returned to the library.   Two of the books were collections of Elizabethan plays, one was the New Arts Writing Annual, and the other two were books on criminology. The records were mainly folk songs, of the bloodier type.

Levine frowned and went over to Tanner.   He asked, "What were you and Perkins talking about before we got here?"

Tanner's face was still creased in a puzzled frown.   "The stupidity of the criminal mind," he said.   "There's something goofy here, Lieutenant."

"You may be right," Levine told him.   He walked on down the hall and joined the other two at the door.

All three got into the front seat of the Chevvy, Crawley driving again and Perkins sitting in the middle.   They rode in silence, Crawley busy driving, Perkins studying the complex array of the dashboard, with its extra knobs and switches and the mike hooked beneath the radio, and Levine tying to figure out what was wrong.

At the station, after booking, they brought him to a small office, one of the interrogation rooms.   There was a bare and battered desk, plus four chairs.   Crawley sat behind the desk.   Perkins sat across the desk and facing him, Levine took the chair in a corner behind and to the left of Perkins, and a male stenographer, notebook in hand, filled the fourth chair, behind Crawley.

Crawley's first questions covered the same ground already covered at Gruber's apartment, this time for the record.   "Okay," said Crawley, when he'd brought them up to date.   "You and Gruber were both doing the same kind of thing, living the same kind of life.   You were both unpublished writers, both taking night courses at Columbia, both living on very little money."

"That's right," said Perkins.

"How long you known each other?"

"About six months.   We met at Columbia, and we took the same subway home after class.   We got to talking, found out we were both dreaming the same kind of dream, and became friends.   You know.   Misery loves company."

"Take the same classes at Columbia?"

"Only one.   Creative Writing, from Professor Stonegell."

"Where'd you buy the poison?"

"I didn't.   Al did.   He bought it a while back and just kept it around.   He kept saying if he didn't make a good sale soon he'd kill himself.   But he didn't mean it.   It was just a kind of gag."

Crawley pulled at his right earlobe.   Levine knew, from his long experience with his partner, that that gesture meant that Crawley was confused.   "You went there today to kill him?"

"That's right."

Levine shook his head.   That wasn't right.   Softly, he said, "Why did you bring the library books along?"

"I was on my way up to the library," said Perkins, twisting around in his seat to look at Levine.

"Look this way," snapped Crawley.

Perkins looked around at Crawley again, but not before Levine had seen that same burning deep in Perkins' eyes. Stronger, this time, and more like pleading. Pleading? What was Perkins pleading for?

"I was on my way to the library," Perkins said again. "Al had a couple of records out on my card, so I went over to get them. On the way, I decided to kill him."

"Why?" asked Crawley.

"Because he was a pompous ass," said Perkins, the same answer he'd given before.

"Because he got a story accepted by one of the literary magazines and you didn't?" suggested Crawley.

"Maybe. Partly. His whole attitude. He was smug. He knew more than anybody else in the world."

"Why did you kill him today? Why not last week or next week?"

"I felt like it today."

"Why did you give yourself up?"

"You would have gotten me anyway."

Levine asked, "Did you know that before you killed him?"

"I don't know," said Perkins, without looking around at Levine. "I didn't think about it till afterward. Then I knew the police would get me anyway— they'd talk to Professor Stonegell and the other people who knew us both and I didn't want to have to wait it out. So I went and confessed."

"You told the patrolman," said Levine, "that you'd killed your best friend."

"That's right."

"Why did you use that phrase, best friend, if you hated him so much you wanted to kill him?"

"He was my best friend. At least, in New York. I didn't really know anyone else, except Professor Stonegell. Al was my best friend because he was just about my only friend."

"Are you sorry you killed him?" asked Levine

This time, Perkins twisted around in the chair again, ignoring Crawley. "No, sir," he said, and his eyes now were blank.

There was silence in the room, and Crawley and Levine looked at one another. Crawley questioned with his eyes, and Levine shrugged, shaking his head. Something was wrong, but he didn't know what. And Perkins was being so helpful that he wound up being no help at all.

Crawley turned to the stenographer. "Type it up formal," he said. "And have somebody come take the pigeon to his nest."

After the stenographer had left, Levine said, "Anything you want to say off the record, Perkins?"

Perkins grinned. His face was half-turned away from Crawley, and he was looking at the floor, as though he was amused by something he saw there. "Off the record?" he murmured. "As long as there are two of you in here, it's *on* the record."

"Do you want one of us to leave?"

Perkins looked up at Levine again, and stopped smiling. He seemed to think it over for a minute, and then he shook his head. "No," he said. "Thanks, anyway. But I don't think I have anything more to say. Not right now anyway."

Levine frowned and sat back in his chair, studying Perkins. The boy didn't ring true; he was constructed of too many contradictions. Levine reached out for a mental image of Perkins, but all he touched was air.

After Perkins was led out of the room by two uniformed cops, Crawley got to his feet, stretched, sighed, scratched, pulled his earlobe, and said, "What do you make of it, Abe?"

"I don't like it."

"I know that. I saw it in your face. But he confessed, so what else is there?"

"The phony confession is not exactly unheard of, you know."

"Not this time," said Crawley. "A guy confesses to a crime he didn't commit for one of two reasons. Either he's a crackpot who wants the publicity or to be punished or something like that, or he's protecting somebody else. Perkins doesn't read like a crackpot to me, and there's nobody else involved for him to be protecting."

"In a capital punishment state," suggested Levine, "a guy might confess to a murder he didn't commit so the state would do his suicide for him."

Crawley shook his head. "That still doesn't look like Perkins," he said.

"Nothing looks like Perkins. He's given us a blank wall to stare at. A couple of times it started to slip, and there was something else inside."

"Don't build a big thing, Abe. The kid confessed. He's the killer, let it go at that."

"The job's finished, I know that. But it still bothers me."

"Okay," said Crawley. He sat down behind the desk again and put his feet up on the scarred desk top. "Let's straighten it out. Where does it bother you?"

"All over. Number one, motivation. You don't kill a man for being a pompous ass. Not when you turn around a minute later and say he was your best friend."

"People do funny things when they're pushed far enough. Even to friends."

"Sure. Okay, number two. The murder method. It doesn't sound right. When a man kills impulsively, he grabs something and starts swinging. When he calms down, he goes and turns himself in. But when you *poison* somebody, you're using a pretty sneaky method. It doesn't make sense for you to run out and call a cop right after using poison. It isn't the same kind of mentality."

"He used the poison," said Crawley, "because it was handy. Gruber bought it, probably had it sitting on his dresser or something, and Perkins just picked it up on impulse and poured it into the beer."

"That's another thing," said Levine. "Do you drink much beer out of cans?"

Crawley grinned. "You know I do."

"I saw some empty beer cans sitting around the apartment, so that's where Gruber got his last beer from."

"Yeah. So what?"

"When you drink a can of beer, do you pour the beer out of the can into a glass, or do you just drink it straight from the can?"

"I drink it out of the can. But not everybody does."

"I know, I know. Okay, what about the library books? If you're going to go kill somebody, are you going to bring library books along?"

"It was an impulse killing. He didn't know he was going to do it until he got there."

Levine got to his feet. "That's the hell of it," he said. "You can explain away every single question in this business. But it's such a simple case. Why should there be so many questions that need explaining away?"

Crawley shrugged. "Beats me," he said. "All I know is, we've got a confession, and that's enough to satisfy me."

"Not me," said Levine. "I think I'll go poke around and see what happens. Want to come along?"

"Somebody's going to have to hand the pen to Perkins when he signs his confession," said Crawley.

"Mind if I take off for a while?"

"Go ahead. Have a big time," said Crawley, grinning at him. "Play detective."

Levine's first stop was back at Gruber's address. Gruber's apartment was empty now, having been sifted completely through normal routine procedure. Levine went down to the basement door under the stoop, but he didn't go back to Gruber's door. He stopped at the front apartment instead, where a ragged-edged strip of paper attached with peeling scotch tape to the door read, in awkward and childish lettering, SUPERINTENDENT. Levine rapped and waited. After a minute, the door opened a couple of inches, held by a chain. A round face peered out at him from a height of a little over five feet. The face said, "Who you looking for?"

"Police," Levine told him. He opened his wallet and held it up for the face to look at.

"Oh," said the face. "Sure thing." The door shut, and Levine waited while the chain was clinked free, and then the door opened wide.

The super was a short and round man, dressed in corduroy trousers and a grease-spotted undershirt. He wheezed, "Come in, come in," and stood back for Levine to come into his crowded and musty-smelling living room.

Levine said, "I want to talk to you about Al Gruber."

The super shut the door and waddled into the middle of the room, shaking his head. "Wasn't that a shame?" he asked. "Al was a nice boy. No money, but a nice boy. Sit down somewhere, anywhere."

Levine looked around. The room was full of low-slung, heavy, sagging, overstuffed furniture, armchairs and sofas. He picked the least battered armchair of the lot, and sat on the very edge. Although he was a short man, his knees seemed to be almost up to his chin, and be had the feeling that if he relaxed he'd fall over backwards.

The super trundled across the room and dropped into one of the other armchairs, sinking into it as though he never intended to get to his feet again in his life. "A real shame," he said again. "And to think I maybe could have stopped it."

"You could have stopped it?   How?"

"It was around noon," said the super.   "I was watching the TV over there, and I heard a voice from the back apartment shouting, 'Al!   Al!'   So I went out to the hall, but by the time I got there the shouting was all done.   So I didn't know what to do, I waited a minute, and then I came back in and watched the TV again. That was probably when it was happening."

"There wasn't any noise while you were in the hall?   Just the two shouts before you got out there?"

"That's all.   At first, I thought it was another one of them arguments, and I was gonna bawl out the two of them, but it stopped before I even got the door open."

"Arguments?"

"Mr. Gruber and Mr. Perkins.   They used to argue all the time, shout at each other, carry on like monkeys.   The other tenants was always complaining about it.   They'd do it late at night sometimes, two or three o'clock in the morning, and the tenants would all start phoning me to complain."

"What did they argue about?"

The super shrugged his massive shoulders.   "Who knows?   Names.   People. Writers.   They both think they're great writers or something."

"Did they ever get into a fist fight or anything like that?   Ever threaten to kill each other?"

"Naw, they'd just shout at each other and call each other stupid and ignorant and stuff like that.   They liked each other, really, I guess.   At least they always hung around together.   They just loved to argue, that's all.   You know how it is with college kids.   I've had college kids renting here before, and they're all like that.   They all love to argue.   Course, I never had nothing like this happen before."

"What kind of person was Gruber, exactly?"

The super mulled it over for a while.   "Kind of a quiet guy," he said at last. "Except when he was with Mr. Perkins, I mean.   Then he'd shout just as loud and often as anybody.   But most of the time he was quiet.   And good-mannered. A real surprise, after most of the kids around today.   He was always polite, and he'd lend a hand if you needed some help or something, like the time I was carrying a bed up to the third floor front.   Mr. Gruber come along and pitched right in with me.   He did more of the work than I did."

"And he was a writer, wasn't he?   At least, he was trying to be a writer."

"Oh, sure.   I'd hear that typewriter of his tappin' away in there at all hours. And he always carried a notebook around with him, writin' things down in it.   I asked him once what he wrote in there, and he said descriptions, of places like Prospect Park up at the corner, and of the people he knew.   He always said he wanted to be a writer like some guy named Wolfe, used to live in Brooklyn too."

"I see."   Levine struggled out of the armchair.   "Thanks for your time," he said.

"Not at all."   The super waddled after Levine to the door.   "Anything I can do," he said.   "Any time at all."

"Thanks again," said Levine.   He went outside and stood in the hallway, thinking things over, listening to the latch click in place behind him. Then he turned and walked down the hallway to Gruber's apartment, and knocked on the door.

As he'd expected, a uniformed cop had been left behind to keep an eye on the place for a while, and when he opened the door, Levine showed his identification and said, "I'm on the case. I'd like to take a look around."

The cop let him in, and Levine looked carefully through Gruber's personal property. He found the notebooks, finally, in the bottom drawer of the dresser. There were five of them, steno pad size looseleaf fillers. Four of them were filled with writing, in pen, in a slow and careful hand, and the fifth was still half blank.

Levine carried the notebooks over to the card table, pushed the typewriter out of the way, sat down and began to skim through the books.

He found what he was looking for in the middle of the third one he tried. A description of Larry Perkins, written by the man Perkins had killed. The description, or character study, which it more closely resembled, was four pages long, beginning with a physical description and moving into a discussion of Perkins' personality. Levine noticed particular sentences in this latter part: "Larry doesn't want to write, he wants to be a writer, and that isn't the same thing. He wants the glamour and the fame and the money, and he thinks he'll get it from being a writer. That's why he's dabbled in acting and painting and all the other so-called glamorous professions. Larry and I are both being thwarted by the same thing: neither of us has anything to say worth saying. The difference is, I'm trying to find something to say, and Larry wants to make it on glibness alone. One of these days, he's going to find out he won't get anywhere that way. That's going to be a terrible day for him."

Levine closed the book, then picked up the last one, the one that hadn't yet been filled, and leafed through that. One word kept showing up throughout the last notebook. "Nihilism." Gruber obviously hated the word, and he was also obviously afraid of it. "Nihilism is death," he wrote on one page. "It is the belief that there are no beliefs, that no effort is worthwhile. How could any writer believe such a thing? Writing is the most positive of acts. So how can it be used for negative purposes? The only expression of nihilism is death, not the written word. If I can say nothing hopeful, I shouldn't say anything at all."

Levine put the notebooks back in the dresser drawer finally, thanked the cop, and went out to the Chevvy. He'd hoped to be able to fill in the blank spaces in Perkins' character through Gruber's notebooks, but Gruber had apparently had just as much trouble defining Perkins as Levine was now having. Levine had learned a lot about the dead man, that he was sincere and intense and self-demanding as only the young can be, but Perkins was still little more than a smooth and blank wall. "Glibness," Gruber had called it. What was beneath the glibness? A murderer, by Perkins' own admission. But what else?

Levine crawled wearily into the Chevvy and headed for Manhattan.

Professor Harvey Stonegell was in class when Levine got to Columbia University, but the girl at the desk in the dean's outer office told him that Stonegell would be out of that class in just a few minutes, and would then be free for the rest of the afternoon.   She gave him directions to Stonegell's office, and Levine thanked her.

Stonegell's office door was locked, so Levine waited in the hall, watching the students hurrying by in both directions, and reading the notices of scholarships, grants and fellowships thumbtacked to the bulletin board near the office door.

The professor showed up about fifteen minutes later, with two students in tow. He was a tall and slender man, with a gaunt face and a full head of gray-white hair.   He could have been any age between fifty and seventy.   He wore a tweed suit jacket, leather patches at the elbows, and non-matching gray slacks.

Levine said, "Professor Stonegell?"

"Yes?"

Levine introduced himself and showed his identification.   "I'd like to talk to you for a minute or two."

"Of course.   I'll just be a minute."   Stonegell handed a book to one of the two students, telling him to read certain sections of it, and explained to the other student why he hadn't received a passing grade in his latest assignment.   When both of them were taken care of, Levine stepped into Stonegell's crowded and tiny office, and sat down in the chair beside the desk.

Stonegell said, "Is this about one of my students?"

"Two of them.   From your evening writing course.   Gruber and Perkins."

"Those two?   They aren't in trouble, are they?"

"I'm afraid so.   Perkins has confessed to murdering Gruber."

Stonegell's thin face paled.   "Gruber's dead?   Murdered?"

"By Perkins.   He turned himself in right after it happened.   But, to be honest with you, the whole thing bothers me.   It doesn't make sense.   You knew them both.   I thought you might be able to tell me something about them, so it *would* make sense."

Stonegell lit himself a cigarette, offered one to Levine, but Levine declined. He'd given up cigarettes shortly after he'd started worrying about his heart.

"This takes some getting used to," said Stonegell after a minute.   "Gruber and Perkins.   They were both good students in my class.   Gruber perhaps a bit better. And they were friends."

"I'd heard they were friends."

"There was a friendly rivalry between them," said Stonegell.   "Whenever one of them started a project, the other one started a similar project, intent on beating the first one at his own game.   Actually, that was more Perkins than Gruber.   And they always took opposite sides of every question, screamed at each other like sworn enemies.   But actually they were very close friends.   I can't understand either one of them murdering the other."

"Was Gruber similar to Perkins?"

"Did I give that impression?   No, they were definitely unalike.   The old business about opposites attracting.   Gruber was by far the more sensitive and sincere of the two.   I don't mean to imply that Perkins was insensitive or insincere at all. Perkins had his own sensitivity and his own sincerity, but they were almost exclusively directed within himself. He equated everthing with himself, his own feelings and his own ambitions. But Gruber had more of the—oh, I don't know—more of a *world-view*, to badly translate the German. His sensitivity was directed outward, toward the feelings of other people. It showed up in their writing. Gruber's forté was characterization, subtle interplay between personalities. Perkins was deft, almost glib, with movement and action and plot, but his characters lacked substance. He wasn't really interested in anyone but himself.''

"He doesn't sound like the kind of guy who'd confess to a murder right after he committed it.''

"I know what you mean. That isn't like him. I don't imagine Perkins would ever feel remorse or guilt. I should think he would be one of the people who believes the only crime is in being caught.''

"Yet we didn't catch him. He came to us.'' Levine studied the book titles on the shelf behind Stonegell. "What about their mental attitudes recently?'' he asked. "Generally speaking, I mean. Were they happy or unhappy, impatient or content or what?''

"I think they were both rather depressed, actually,'' said Stonegell. "Though for somewhat different reasons. They had both come out of the Army less than a year ago, and had come to New York to try to make their mark as writers. Gruber was having difficulty with subject matter. We talked about it a few times. He couldn't find anything he really wanted to write about, nothing he felt strongly enough to give him direction in his writing.''

"And Perkins?''

"He wasn't particularly worried about writing in that way. He was, as I say, deft and rather clever in his writing, but it was all too shallow. I think they might have been bad for one another, actually. Perkins could see that Gruber had the depth and sincerity that he lacked, and Gruber thought that Perkins was free from the soul-searching and self-doubt that was hampering him so much. In the last month or so, both of them have talked about dropping out of school, going back home and forgetting about the whole thing. But neither of them could have done that, at least not yet. Gruber couldn't have, because the desire to write was too strong in him. Perkins couldn't, because the desire to be a famous writer was too strong.''

"A year seems like a pretty short time to get all that depressed,'' said Levine.

Stonegell smiled. "When you're young,'' he said, "a year can be eternity. Patience is an attribute of the old.''

"I suppose you're right. What about girl friends, other people who knew them both?''

"Well, there was one girl whom both were dating rather steadily. The rivalry again. I don't think either of them was particularly serious about her, but both of them wanted to take her away from the other one.''

"Do you know this girl's name?''

"Yes, of course. She was in the same class with Perkins and Gruber. I think I might have her home address here.''

Stonegell opened a small file drawer atop his desk, and looked through it. "Yes, here it is," he said. "Her name is Anne Marie Stone, and she lives on Grove Street, down in the Village. Here you are."

Levine accepted the card from Stonegell, copied the name and address onto his pad, and gave the card back. He got to his feet. "Thank you for your trouble," he said.

"Not at all," said Stonegell, standing. He extended his hand, and Levine, shaking it, found it bony and almost parchment-thin, but surprisingly strong. "I don't know if I've been much help, though," he said.

"Neither do I, yet," said Levine. "I may be just wasting both our time. Perkins confessed, after all."

"Still—" said Stonegell.

Levine nodded. "I know. That's what's got me doing extra work."

"I'm still thinking of this thing as though—as though it were a story problem, if you know what I mean. It isn't real yet. Two young students, I've taken an interest in both of them, fifty years after the worms get me they'll still be around— and then you tell me one of them is already wormfood, and the other one is effectively just as dead. It isn't real to me yet. They won't be in class tomorrow night, but I still won't believe it."

"I know what you mean."

"Let me know if anything happens, will you?"

"Of course."

Anne Marie Stone lived in an apartment on the fifth floor of a walk-up on Grove Street in Greenwich Village, a block and a half from Sheridan Square. Levine found himself out of breath by the time he reached the third floor, and he stopped for a minute to get his wind back and to slow the pounding of his heart. There was no sound in the world quite as loud as the beating of his own heart these days, and when that beating grew too rapid or too irregular, Detective Levine felt a kind of panic that twenty-four years as a cop had never been able to produce.

He had to stop again at the fourth floor, and he remembered with envy what a Bostonian friend had told him about a city of Boston regulation that buildings used as residences had to have elevators if they were more than four stories high. Oh, to live in Boston. Or, even better, in Levittown, where there isn't a building higher than two stories anywhere.

He reached the fifth floor, finally, and knocked on the door of apartment 5B. Rustlings from within culminated in the peephole in the door being opened, and a blue eye peered suspiciously out at him. "Who is it?" asked a muffled voice.

"Police," said Levine. He dragged out his wallet, and held it high, so the eye in the peephole could read the identification.

"Second," said the muffled voice, and the peephole closed. A seemingly endless series of rattles and clicks indicated locks being released, and then the door opened, and a short, slender girl, dressed in pink toreador pants, gray bulky sweater and blonde pony tail, motioned to Levine to come in. "Have a seat," she said, closing the door after him.

"Thank you." Levine sat in a new-fangled basket chair, as uncomfortable as it looked, and the girl sat in another chair of the same type, facing him. But she managed to look comfortable in the thing.

"Is this something I did?" she asked him. "Jaywalking or something?"

Levine smiled. No matter how innocent, a citizen always presumes himself guilty when the police come calling. "No," he said. "It concerns two friends of yours, Al Gruber and Larry Perkins."

"Those two?" The girl seemed calm, though curious, but not at all worried or apprehensive. She was still thinking in terms of something no more serious than jaywalking or a neighbor calling the police to complain about loud noises. "What are they up to?"

"How close are you to them?"

The girl shrugged. "I've gone out with both of them, that's all. We all take courses at Columbia. They're both nice guys, but there's nothing serious, you know. Not with either of them."

"I don't know how to say this," said Levine, "except the blunt way. Early this afternoon, Perkins turned himself in and admitted he'd just killed Gruber."

The girl stared at him. Twice, she opened her mouth to speak, but both times she closed it again. The silence lengthened, and Levine wondered belatedly if the girl had been telling the truth, if perhaps there had been something serious in her relationship with one of the boys after all. Then she blinked and looked away from him, clearing her throat. She stared out the window for a second, then looked back and said, "He's pulling your leg."

Levine shook his head. "I'm afraid not."

"Larry's got a weird sense of humor sometimes," she said. "It's a sick joke, that's all. Al's still around. You haven't found the body, have you?"

"I'm afraid we have. He was poisoned, and Perkins admitted he was the one who gave him the poison."

"That little bottle Al had around the place? That was only a gag."

"Not anymore."

She thought about it a minute longer, then shrugged, as though giving up the struggle to either believe or disbelieve. "Why come to me?" she asked him.

"I'm not sure, to tell you the truth. Something smells wrong about the case, and I don't know what. There isn't any logic to it. I can't get through to Perkins, and it's too late to get through to Gruber. But I've got to get to know them both, if I'm going to understand what happened."

"And you want me to tell you about them."

"Yes."

"Where did you hear about me? From Larry?"

"No, he didn't mention you at all. The gentlemanly instinct, I suppose. I talked to your teacher, Professor Stonegell."

"I see." She got up suddenly, in a single rapid and graceless movement, as though she had to make some motion, no matter how meaningless. "Do you want some coffee?"

"Thank you, yes."

"Come on along. We can talk while I get it ready."

He followed her through the apartment. A hallway led from the long, narrow living room past bedroom and bathroom to a tiny kitchen. Levine sat down at the kitchen table, and Anne Marie Stone went through the motions of making coffee. As she worked, she talked.

"They're good friends," she said. "I mean, they *were* good friends. You know what I mean. Anyway, they're a lot different from each other. Oh, golly! I'm getting all loused up in tenses."

"Talk as though both were still alive," said Levine. "It should be easier that way."

"I don't really believe it anyway," she said. "Al—he's a lot quieter than Larry. Kind of intense, you know? He's got a kind of reversed Messiah complex. You know, he figures he's supposed to be something great, a great writer, but he's afraid he doesn't have the stuff for it. So he worries about himself, and keeps trying to analyze himself, and he hates everything he writes because he doesn't think it's good enough for what he's supposed to be doing. That bottle of poison, that was a gag, you know, just a gag, but it was the kind of joke that has some sort of truth behind it. With this thing driving him like this, I suppose even death begins to look like a good escape after a while."

She stopped her preparations with the coffee, and stood listening to what she had just said. "Now he did escape, didn't he? I wonder if he'd thank Larry for taking the decision out of his hands."

"Do you suppose he asked Larry to take the decision out of his hands?"

She shook her head. "No. In the first place, Al could never ask anyone else to help him fight the thing out in any way. I know, I tried to talk to him a couple of times, but he just couldn't listen. It wasn't that he didn't want to listen, he just couldn't. He had to figure it out for himself. And Larry isn't the helpful sort, so Larry would be the last person anybody would go to for help. Not that Larry's a bad guy, really. He's just awfully self-centered. They both are, but in different ways. Al's always worried about himself, but Larry's always proud of himself. You know. Larry would say, 'I'm for me first,' and Al would say, 'Am I worthy?' Something like that."

"Had the two of them had a quarrel or anything recently, anything that you know of that might have prompted Larry to murder?"

"Not that I know of. They've both been getting more and more depressed, but neither of them blamed the other. Al blamed himself for not getting anywhere, and Larry blamed the stupidity of the world. You know, Larry wanted the same thing Al did, but Larry didn't worry about whether he was worthy or capable or anything like that. He once told me he wanted to be a famous writer, and he'd be one if he had to rob banks and use the money to bribe every publisher and editor and critic in the business. That was a gag, too, like Al's bottle of poison, but I think that one had some truth behind it, too."

The coffee was ready, and she poured two cups, then sat down across from him. Levine added a bit of evaporated milk, but no sugar, and stirred the coffee distractedly. "I want to know why," he said. "Does that seem strange? Cops are supposed to want to know who, not why. I know who, but I want to know why."

"Larry's the only one who could tell you, and I don't think he will."

Levine drank some of his coffee, then got to his feet. "Mind if I use your phone?" he asked.

"Go right ahead. It's in the living room, next to the bookcase." Levine walked back into the living room and called the station. He asked for Crawley. When his partner came on the line, Levine said, "Has Perkins signed the confession yet?"

"He's on the way down now. It's just been typed up."

"Hold him there after he signs it, okay? I want to talk to him. I'm in Manhattan, starting back now."

"What have you got?"

'I'm not sure I have anything. I just want to talk to Perkins again, that's all."

"Why sweat it? We got the body; we got the confession; we got the killer in a cell. Why make work for yourself?"

"I don't know. Maybe I'm just bored."

"Okay, I'll hold him. Same room as before."

Levine went back to the kitchen. "Thank you for the coffee," he said. "If there's nothing else you can think of, I'll be leaving now."

"Nothing," she said. "Larry's the only one who can tell you why."

She walked him to the front door, and he thanked her again as he was leaving. The stairs were a lot easier going down.

When Levine got back to the station, he picked up another plainclothesman, a detective named Ricco, a tall, athletic man in his middle thirties who affected the Ivy League look. He resembled more closely someone from the District Attorney's office than a precinct cop. Levine gave him a part to play, and the two of them went down the hall to the room where Perkins was waiting with Crawley.

"Perkins," said Levine, the minute he walked in the room, before Crawley had a chance to give the game away by saying something to Ricco, "this is Dan Ricco, a reporter from the *Daily News*."

Perkins looked at Ricco with obvious interest, the first real display of interest and animation Levine had yet seen from him. "A reporter?"

"That's right," said Ricco. He looked at Levine. "What is this?" he asked. He was playing it straight and blank.

"College student," said Levine. "Name's Larry Perkins." He spelled the last name. "He poisoned a fellow student."

"Oh, yeah?" Ricco glanced at Perkins without much eagerness. "What for?" he asked, looking back at Levine. "Girl? Any sex in it?"

"Afraid not. It was some kind of intellectual motivation. They both wanted to be writers."

Ricco shrugged. "Two guys with the same job? What's so hot about that?"

"Well, the main thing," said Levine, "is that Perkins here wants to be famous. He tried to get famous by being a writer, but that wasn't working out. So he decided to be a famous murderer."

Ricco looked at Perkins. "Is that right?" he asked.

Perkins was glowering at them all, but especially at Levine. "What difference does it make?" he said.

"The kid's going to get the chair, of course," said Levine blandly. "We have his signed confession and everything. But I've kind of taken a liking to him. I'd hate to see him throw his life away without getting something for it. I thought maybe you could get him a nice headline on page two, something he could hang up on the wall of his cell."

Ricco chuckled and shook his head. "Not a chance of it," he said. "Even if I wrote the story big, the city desk would knock it down to nothing. This kind of story is a dime a dozen. People kill other people around New York twenty-four hours a day. Unless there's a good strong sex interest, or it's maybe one of those mass-killings things like the guy who put the bomb in the airplane, a murder in New York is filler stuff. And who needs filler stuff in the spring, when the ball teams are just getting started?"

"You've got influence on the paper, Dan," said Levine. "Couldn't you at least get him picked up by the wire services?"

"Not a chance in a million. What's he done that a few hundred other clucks in New York don't do every year? Sorry, Abe, I'd like to do you the favor, but it's no go."

Levine sighed. "Okay, Dan," he said. "If you say so."

"Sorry," said Ricco. He grinned at Perkins. "Sorry, kid," he said. "You should of knifed a chorus girl or something."

Ricco left and Levine glanced at Crawley, who was industriously yanking on his earlobe and looking bewildered. Levine sat down facing Perkins and said, "Well?"

"Let me alone a minute," snarled Perkins. "I'm trying to think."

"I was right, wasn't I?" asked Levine. "You wanted to go out in a blaze of glory."

"All right, all right. Al took his way, I took mine. What's the difference?"

"No difference," said Levine. He got wearily to his feet, and headed for the door. "I'll have you sent back to your cell now."

"Listen," said Perkins suddenly. "You know I didn't kill him, don't you? You know he committed suicide, don't you?"

Levine opened the door and motioned to the two uniformed cops waiting in the hall.

"Wait," said Perkins desperately.

"I know, I know," said Levine. "Gruber really killed himself, and I suppose you burned the note he left."

"You know damn well I did."

"That's too bad, boy."

Perkins didn't want to leave. Levine watched deadpan as the boy was led away, and then he allowed himself to relax, let the tension drain out of him. He sagged into a chair and studied the veins on the backs of his hands.

Crawley said, into the silence, "What was all that about, Abe?"

"Just what you heard."

"Gruber committed suicide?"

"They both did."

"Well—what are we going to do now?"

"Nothing. We investigated; we got a confession; we made an arrest. Now we're done."

"But—"

"But hell!" Levine glared at his partner. "That little fool is gonna go to trial, Jack, and he's gonna be convicted and go to the chair. He chose it himself. It was *his* choice. I'm not railroading him; he chose his own end. And he's going to get what he wanted."

"But listen, Abe—"

"I won't listen!"

"Let me—let me get a word in."

Levine was on his feet suddenly, and now it all came boiling out, the indignation and the rage and the frustration. "Damn it, you don't know yet! You've got another six, seven years yet. You don't know what it feels like to lie awake in bed at night and listen to your heart skip a beat every once in a while, and wonder when it's going to skip two beats in a row and you're dead. You don't know what it feels like to know your body's starting to die, it's starting to get old and die and it's all downhill from now on."

"What's that got to do with—"

"I'll tell you what! They had the *choice!* Both of them young, both of them with sound bodies and sound hearts and years ahead of them, decades ahead of them. And they chose to throw it away! They chose to throw away what I don't have anymore. Don't you think I wish *I* had that choice? All right! They chose to die, let 'em die!"

Levine was panting from exertion, leaning over the desk and shouting in Jack Crawley's face. And now, in the sudden silence while he wasn't speaking, he heard the ragged rustle of his breath, felt the tremblings of nerve and muscle throughout his body. He let himself carefully down into a chair and sat there, staring at the wall, trying to get his breath.

Jack Crawley was saying something, far away, but Levine couldn't hear him. He was listening to something else, the loudest sound in all the world. The fitful throbbing of his own heart.

HELEN NIELSEN

Pattern of Guilt

Keith Briscoe had never been a hating man. Disciplined temper, alert mind, hard work—these were the things that made for success as a police reporter, and in the fourteen years since he'd returned from overseas, too big for his old suits and his old job as copy boy, Keith Briscoe had become one of the best. Enthusiasm was a help—something close to passion at times, for that was the stuff brilliance was made of—but not hatred. Hatred was a cancer in the mind, a dimness in the eye. Hatred was an acid eating away the soul. Keith Briscoe was aware of all these things, but he was becoming aware of something else as well. No matter how hard he forced the thought to the back of his mind, he knew that he hated his wife. And the thought was sharp, clear.

It was Sergeant Gonzales' case—burglary and murder. Violet Hammerman, 38, lived alone in a single apartment on North Curson. She worked as a secretary in a small manufacturing plant from Monday through Friday, played bridge with friends on Saturday night, served on the Hostess Committee of her church Sunday morning and died in her bed Sunday night (Monday morning, to be exact, since it was after 2:00 A.M. when the crime occurred) the victim of one bullet through her heart fired at close range. Sergeant Gonzales was a thorough man, and by the time Keith Briscoe reached the scene, having responded with firehorse reflexes to the homicide code on his short-wave receiver, all of these matters, and certain others, were already established and Gonzales was waiting for the police photographer to complete his chores so the body could be removed to the morgue.

She wasn't a pretty woman. A corpse is seldom attractive.

"You can see for yourself," Gonzales said. "It's a simple story. No struggle, no attempted attack—the bedclothes aren't even disturbed. The neighbors heard her scream once and then the shot came immediately afterward. She should have stayed asleep."

She was asleep now. Nothing would ever rouse her again. Briscoe glanced at the bureau drawer that was still standing half-open. One nylon stocking dangled forlornly over the side. He fingered it absently and then, without touching the wood, stuffed it inside.

"Fingerprints?" he asked.

"No fingerprints," Gonzales said. "The killer must have worn gloves, but he left a pair of footprints outside the window."

There was only one window in the small bedroom. It was a first-floor apartment in one of the old residential houses that had been rezoned and remodeled into small units, but still had a shallow basement and a correspondingly high footing. Violet Hammerman must have felt secure to sleep with her one window open and the screen locked, but that had been a mistake. The screen had been neatly cut across the bottom and up as far as the center sash on both sides. It now hung like a stiffly starched curtain, that bent outward at the touch of Keith Briscoe's hand.

"Port of entry and exit."

"That's right," Gonzales said. "But the exit was fast. He must have made a running jump out of the window and landed on the cement drive. It was the entry that left the prints. Collins, shoot your flash under the window again."

Collins was the man in uniform who stood guarding the important discovery beneath the window. He responded to Gonzales' order by pointing a bright finger of light down on the narrow strip of earth that separated the house from the driveway. It was a plot barely eighteen inches wide, but somebody had worked it over for planting, and because of that a pair of footprints were distinctly visible on the soft earth.

"We're in luck," Gonzales explained. "The landlord worked that ground yesterday morning. Set out some petunia plants—ruffled petunias. Too bad. A couple of them will never bloom."

A couple of them were slightly demolished from trampling, but between the withered green the two indentations were embedded, like an anonymous signature. Briscoe shoved the screen forward and peered farther out of the window.

"It must be nearly six feet to the ground," he remarked.

"Sixty-eight inches," Gonzales said.

"The footprints don't seem very deep."

"They aren't—no heels. If you were down where Collins is, you'd see what I saw a few minutes before you walked in. Those prints are from rubber-soled shoes, 'sneakers' we used to call them when I was a kid. At closer view you can pick up the imprint of some of the tread, but not much. Those particular soles were pretty well worn. But you're thinking, Briscoe, as usual. That earth is soft. We'll have to measure the moisture content to get an idea of how much weight stood above those prints to make them the depth they are, but at first guess I'd say we're looking for a tall, slender lad."

"A juvenile?" Briscoe asked.

"Why not? Like I told my wife when she came home from her shopping trip last week, no wonder so many kids are going wrong. They come home from school and find their mothers dressed up in a sack with a belt at the bottom. That's enough to drive anyone out on the streets."

Keith Briscoe pulled his head in out of the window and ran a searching hand over the cut screen. It was a clean job. A sharp blade of a pocket knife could do the job. Gonzales could be right about the juvenile angle.

"You sound like a detective," he said.

"Gee, thanks," Gonzales grinned. "Maybe I'll grow up to be a hot reporter some day. Who can tell."

There was no sarcasm in the exchange.   Gonzales and Briscoe had been friends long enough to be able to insult one another with respect and affection.   Gonzales had a good mind and an eye for detail.   He also had imagination, which was to building a police case what mortar is to a bricklayer.

"We found a purse—black felt—on the driveway near the curb," he added. "People in the building identified it as belonging to the deceased.   There's no money in it except some small change in the coin purse, but there's this that we found on the top of the bureau—"

Gonzales had a slip of blue paper in his hand.   He handed it to Briscoe.   It was the deduction slip from a company paycheck.   After deductions, Violet Hammerman had received a check for $61.56.

"Payday was Friday," Gonzales continued.   "The landlord told me that.   He knows because he's had to wait for his rent a few times.   Violet Hammerman didn't have time to get to the bank Friday—she worked late—but she cashed her check at the Sav-Mor Market on Saturday."   Gonzales had another slip of paper in his hand now.   A long, narrow strip from a cash register.   "When she bought groceries to the sum of $14.82," he added.

There was such a thing as sounding too much like a detective.   Briscoe returned the blue slip with a dubious expression.   It was barely two-thirty.   Gonzales was a fast worker, but the markets didn't open until nine.   But Gonzales caught the expression before he could fit it with words.

"I'm guessing, of course," he said quickly, "but I'm guessing for a reason. $14.82 from $61.56 leaves $46.74.   Assuming she spent a few dollars elsewhere and dropped a bill in the collection plate, we see that Violet Hammerman's killer escaped with the grand sum of $40 or, at the most, $45."

"A cheap death," Briscoe said.

"A very cheap death, and a very cheap and amateurish killer."   Gonzales paused to glance at the slip of blue paper again, but it was no longer entirely blue.   A red smear had been added to the corner.   "What did you do, cut your hand on that screen?" he asked.

Briscoe didn't know what he was talking about, but he looked at his hand and it was bleeding.

"Better look in the bathroom for some mercurochrome," Gonzales said.   "You could get a nasty infection from a rusty screen."

"It's nothing," Briscoe said.   "I'll wash it off under the faucet when I get home."

"You'll wash it off under the faucet right now," Gonzales ordered.   "There's the bathroom on the other side of the bureau."

Gonzales could be as fussy as a spinster.   It was easier to humor him than to argue.   The photographer was finished with the corpse now, and Briscoe pulled the sheet up over her face as he walked past the bed.   A cheap death and a cheap way to wait for the ambulance.   Violet Hammerman had lived a humble and inconspicuous life, but she might rate a conspicuous obituary if he could keep Gonzales talking.   Of course, Violet Hammerman might not have approved of such an obituary, but she now belonged to the public.

"A cheap and amateurish killer," Briscoe said, with his hand under the faucet, "but he wore gloves, rubber-soled shoes, and carried a gun."

Leaning against the bathroom doorway, Gonzales rose to the bait.

"Which he fired too soon," he said. "That's my point, Briscoe. There's a pattern in every crime—something that gives us an edge on the criminal's weakness, and we know he has a weakness or he wouldn't be a criminal. It takes a mind, some kind of a mind, to plan a burglary; but it takes nerve to pull it off successfully. This killer is very short on nerve. One cry from the bed and he blazed away at close range. A professional wouldn't risk the gas chamber for a lousy forty bucks. Don't use that little red towel. Red dye's no good for an open cut."

Gonzales, with an eye for detail even when his mind was elsewhere. Briscoe put the guest towel back on the rack. A silly looking thing—red with a French poodle embroidered in black. It seemed out of place in Violet Hammerman's modest bathroom. It was more the sort of thing Elaine would buy. Elaine. He thought of her and slammed the faucet shut so hard the plumbing pipes shuddered.

"A killer short on nerve, but desperate enough to break into a house," Briscoe recapitulated, his mind busy forcing Elaine back where she belonged. "A forty-dollar murder." And then he had what he was groping for, and by that time he could face Gonzales without fear of anger showing in his face. "Sounds like a hophead," he suggested.

Gonzales nodded sadly. "That's what I've been thinking," he said. "That's what worries me. How much of a joyride can he buy for so little fare? I only hope Violet Hammerman isn't starting a trend."

Among his other characteristics, Sergeant Gonzales was a pessimist, and Keith Briscoe couldn't give him any cheer. He had troubles of his own.

Judge Kermit Lacy's court hadn't changed in four years. The flag stood in the same place; the woodwork still needed varnishing; the chairs were just as hard. If the windows had been washed, the evidence was no longer visible. Courtrooms could be exciting arenas where combating attorneys fought out issues of life and death, but there was nothing exciting about a courtroom where tired old loves went to die, or to be exhumed for delayed post-mortem.

The dead should stay dead. The thought tugged at Keith Briscoe's mind when he saw Faye sitting at her attorney's table. Faye had changed in four years. She looked younger, yet more mature, more poised. She wore a soft gray suit and a hat that was smart without being ridiculous. There had never been anything ridiculous about Faye—that was the only trouble with her; she always carried with her the faint aura of Old Boston. She looked up and saw him then. And when their eyes met, there was a kind of stop on time for just an instant, an almost imperceptible shadow crossed her eyes, and then she smiled. Keith walked to the table. He didn't quite know what to do. Was it customary to shake hands with an ex-wife—the sort of thing tennis players do after vaulting the net? He kept his hands at his side.

"You're looking good, Faye," he said. "Great, in fact."

Clumsy words, as if he were just learning the language.

"Thank you," Faye responded. "You look well too, Keith. You've lost weight."

Keith started to say "No more home cooking" and thought better of it. And he didn't look well. It wasn't just because he'd been up most of the night delving into the violent departure of one Violet Hammerman from this vale of fears; it was because he had that depth-fatigue look of a man who's gradually working up to an extended hangover.

"I keep busy," he said.

"And how is Elaine?"

That question had to come. Keith searched in vain for a twinge of emotion in Faye's voice. There was none. Elaine was a knife that had cut between them a long time ago, and old wounds heal.

"Elaine's fine," he said, and then he couldn't be evasive any longer. "Faye—" The bailiff had entered the courtroom. In a few moments the judge would walk in and there would be no more time to talk. "—I wish you'd reconsider this action. We have a good arrangement now. If you take the boys east, I'll never get to see them."

"But that's not true," Faye objected. "They can visit with you on vacations."

"Vacations! A few weeks out of a year—that's not like every weekend!"

"Every weekend, Keith?" Faye's voice was soft, but her eyes were steady. Faye's eyes were always steady. "You've had four years of weekends to visit the boys. How many times have you taken advantage of them?"

"Every weekend I possibly could! You know how my job is!"

Faye knew. The half-smile that came to her lips had a sadness in it. Now that he really looked at her, Keith could see the sadness. She was lonely. She must be lonely, bringing up two boys with nothing but an alimony check for companionship. Now she was bringing suit for permission to take the boys east— ostensibly to enroll them in prep school; but Keith Briscoe suddenly knew the real reason.

There were old friends back east to wipe out the memories—perhaps even an old flame.

Keith felt a quick jab of pain he didn't understand.

"I'm going to fight you, Faye," he said. "I'm sorry, but I'm going to fight you every inch of the way."

It was nearly eight o'clock that night before Keith got home to his apartment. Nobody came to greet him at the door except Gus, Elaine's dachshund. Gus growled at him, which was standard procedure, and made a couple of wild snaps at his ankles as he passed through the dark living room and made his way to the patch of brightness showing down the hall. At the doorway of Elaine's bedroom, he paused and listened to the music coming from the record player at her bedside. It was something Latin with a very low spinal beat. He listened to it until she came out of the bathroom wearing something French with an equally low spinal beat. Keith was no couturier, but he could see at a glance that Elaine's dress wasn't percale and hadn't been designed for a quiet evening at home. He could also see that it was expensive. He would know how expensive at the first of the month.

She looked up and saw him in the doorway.

"Oh," she said. "I didn't hear you come in."

Keith didn't answer immediately. He just stood there looking at her—all of her, outside and inside. The outside was still attractive. He could feel the tug of her body clear across the room.

"Do you ever?" he asked.

Elaine turned around and picked up an ear clip from her dressing table. She raised her arms to fasten it to her ear.

"Going out?" he asked again.

"It's Thelma's birthday," she said.

"I thought it was Thelma's birthday last week."

That made her turn around.

"All right," she said, "what's eating you? Have you been playing with martinis again?"

"I'm old enough," Keith said. He came across the room. She not only looked good, she smelled good. "I just thought you might want to stay home for one evening."

"Why? So I can sit in the dark alone and watch Wyatt Earp? This lousy apartment—"

"This lousy apartment," Keith interrupted, "costs me $175 every month. Considering certain other expenditures I have to meet, it's no wonder I devote a little extra time to doing what is known among the peasants as being gainfully employed. If I didn't, you couldn't look so provocative for Thelma's birthday."

Elaine picked up the other ear clip and fastened it in place. It was as though he hadn't spoken, hadn't reprimanded her. And then her face in the mirror took on a kind of animal cunning. She turned back toward him with knowing eyes.

"How did you make out in court?" she asked.

"We got a continuance," Keith said.

"A continuance? Why? So you can suffer a little longer?"

"I want my boys—"

"You want Faye! Why can't you be honest enough to admit it? You've always wanted Faye. You only married me because you couldn't have your cake and eat it too. That's your big weakness, Keith. You want to have your cake and eat it too!"

"I want a divorce," Keith said.

He hadn't meant to say it—not yet, not this way. But once it was said there was nothing to do but let the words stand there like a wall between them, or like a wall with a door in it that was opening. And then Elaine slammed the door.

"You," she said quietly, "can go to hell."

That was the night Keith Briscoe moved out of the apartment. He'd been spending most of his nights in a furnished room anyway, a room, a bath, a hot plate for the coffee and a desk for his typewriter. And a table for the shortwave radio alongside the bed. The typewriter had bothered Elaine at night, and that was when Keith did most of his work. He could pick up extra money turning police cases into fabrications for the mystery magazines. Extra money was important with two boys growing their way toward college.

But on the night he moved into the room to stay, Keith didn't work. He just sat and stared at the calendar on the desk and tried to get things straight in his mind. He had a one week's continuance. One week until he'd walk back into Judge Lacy's courtroom and see Faye sitting there calm and proud and lonely. Elaine was a stupid woman, but even the biggest fools made sense when the time was right. It was Faye that he wanted—Faye, the boys, everything that he'd thrown away. Elaine was a bad dream. Elaine was an emotional storm he'd been lost in, and now the storm was over and he was trying to find his way home through the debris. But a week wasn't very long. Perhaps his lawyer could find a loophole and get another stay. It was actually only six days until Monday . . .

On Sunday night, at a half hour past midnight, the shortwave radio rousted him out again.

Dorothy McGannon had a cheerful face even in death. She must have smiled a lot in life. Once her moment of terror was over, the muscles of her face had relaxed into their normal position, and she might have been sleeping through a happy dream if it hadn't been for the dark stain seeping through the blanket.

She was alone in the room, except for Sergeant Gonzales and company. She had lived alone, an unmarried woman in her late twenties. The apartment was small—living room, kitchen, and bedroom. It was on the second floor, rear, one of eight apartments in the unit. The service landing stopped about eighteen inches from the window where the screen was cut three ways and now poked awkwardly out into the night. It had taken agility to balance on the railing and slit that screen; it had taken even more to swing out onto the railing and escape after the fatal shot had been fired.

"Our boy's getting daring," Gonzales reflected. "Still nervous with the trigger, but daring."

"Do you think it's the same killer who got Violet Hammerman last week?" Keith asked.

Up until this point, nobody had mentioned Violet Hammerman. She was just last week's headline, forgotten by everyone but next of kin. But the cut screen and swift death were familiar. Gonzales, the pattern-maker, was already at work.

"That was a .45 slug ballistics got out of the Hammerman woman," he answered. "When we see what killed this one, I'll give you a definite answer. Unfortunately, there's no soft earth out on that porch landing—no footprints; but the method of entry is the same. That's a peculiar way to cut a screen, you know. It takes longer that way."

"But makes for a safer exit," Keith said.

"That's true—and this caller always leaves in a hurry." Gonzales turned back toward the bed, scowling. "I wonder if he kills them just for the fun of it," he mused. "Nobody heard a scream tonight. The shot, but no scream. Still, with five out of eight television sets still going, it's a wonder they heard anything."

"Did he get what he came for?" Keith asked.

Still scowling, Gonzales turned and looked at him. Then he nodded his head in a beckoning gesture. "Follow me," he said.

They crossed the small bedroom and went into the living room. They turned to the right and entered the kitchen alcove, which had one wall common to the bedroom and faced the living room door. The far wall of the kitchen was cupboard space, and one door stood open. On the sink top, laying on its side as if it had been opened hurriedly, was a sugar can which contained no sugar—or anything else.

"What does that look like?" Gonzales asked.

"It looks like Dorothy McGannon kept her money in a sugar can," Keith said.

"Exactly. She worked as a legal secretary. She was paid Friday and gave $10 to the manager of this place Friday night in payment for $10 she'd borrowed earlier in the week. He saw a roll of bills in her purse at the time—$50 or $60, he thinks. We found the purse in a bureau drawer in the bedroom—there was $5 and some change in it."

"The killer missed it."

"The killer didn't even look for it. That drawer stuck—it made enough noise to wake the dead—well, almost. It's obvious he didn't bother with the bureau, and that's interesting because it's what he did bother with last week. Instead, he came straight to the kitchen, opened the cupboard door, and now it's bare."

What Sergeant Gonzales was saying explained the frown that had grown on his forehead. It meant another piece of the pattern of guilt was being fitted to an unknown killer.

"He might have been a friend of the woman," Keith said, "someone who had been in the apartment and knew where she kept the money. A boy friend, possibly. She was single."

"So was the Hammerman woman," Gonzales reflected. "But no boy friend. We questioned the landlord about that, definitely no boy friend. But you're right—she was single. They were both single and both killed on Sunday night. It's beginning to add up, isn't it? Two murders, each victim a woman who lived alone, each one killed on a weekend after a Friday payday. Do you want to lay a small bet that's a .45 slug in the corpse?"

"No bet," Keith said. "What about groceries?"

"Groceries? What groceries?"

"McGannon's. Does she have any? Hammerman did, as I recall. Over $14.00 worth."

Gonzales looked interested. He glanced behind him at the living room door clearly visible from the kitchen.

"You're thinking again, Briscoe," he said. "A delivery boy—but, wait, Hammerman's groceries were paid for at the market. Still, it might have been a delivery boy. Tall, skinny. The lab says not over 150 pounds. It's worth looking into. I don't like the idea of a murder every weekend."

Dorothy McGannon did Keith a big favor getting herself killed when she did. It was a good enough story to keep him away from court until another continuance had been called, and that meant another week to try to reach Faye.   He caught her coming down the courthouse steps.   She was annoyed that he hadn't shown up—obviously, she thought it was deliberate, and Keith wasn't certain but what she was right.

"If we can go somewhere and have a drink, I'll explain," he suggested.

"I'm sorry, Keith.   I've wasted enough time as it is."

"But I couldn't help not showing.   I was on a big story—look."

He unfolded the late edition and handed it to her.   She hesitated.

"One drink to show there's no hard feelings," Keith said.

She consented, finally.   It wasn't a warm consent, but Keith took it as a major victory.   He drove her to a small bar near the news building where she used to meet him in the old days, when their marriage, and the world, was young.   Faye had always been a little on the sentimental side.   He led the way to their old booth at the back of the room and ordered a scotch on the rocks and a Pink Lady.   That was supposed to indicate that he hadn't forgotten.

"Make it a vodka martini," Faye said.

"You've changed drinks," Keith observed.

"I've changed a lot of things, Keith."

That was true.   Now that they were alone, he could see it.   This wasn't going to be easy.   Faye took a cigarette from her purse.   He fumbled in his pocket for a lighter, and then studied the situation in her eyes, lustrous over the flame.

"I've changed too," he told her.   "I'm working nights now, Faye.   Real industrious.   I've been doing a little writing on the side—may even get at that novel I used to talk about."

"That's good," Faye said.   "I'm glad to hear it."   And then she paused. "How does Elaine like it?"

Keith snapped the lighter shut and played it back and forth in his hands.

"Elaine and I aren't living together anymore," he said.   "I moved out last week."

He watched for a reaction, but Faye was good at concealing emotions.   She was like the proverbial iceberg—nine-tenths submerged.   If he'd realized that four years sooner, he wouldn't have been sitting there like a troubled schoolboy waiting for the report on a test paper.

"I'm sorry, Keith," she said.

"I'm not.   It's been coming for a long time.   It was a mistake from the beginning—the whole mess.   I don't know how I could have been so blind."

One drink together.   He didn't say much more; he didn't dare push her.   Faye was the kind who would walk away from him the minute he did.   But at least he had said the important things, and she could think about them for another week.

Not until he was back in that small furnished room did it occur to Keith that he was playing the fool.   He was trying to get Faye back when he didn't even know how to get rid of Elaine.   He sat down to work.   He pushed the problem back in his mind and concentrated on Sergeant Gonzales' problem.   The case was beginning to fascinate him.   What kind of a killer was it who would operate in this way? A half-crazy hophead, yes; but with enough animal cunning to make some kind of plan of operation. Now he understood what Gonzales meant by that pattern talk. If it were possible to think as the killer thought . . . Obviously, he'd been in Dorothy McGannon's apartment prior to the murder. Very few people kept household money in sugar cans anymore. Elaine kept money anywhere—scattered about the bedroom in half a dozen purses. The "cat-killer," as Keith had dubbed him in his latest story, would have a holiday if he slashed her window screen.

But how would he know? He thought of Elaine again—she wouldn't stay in the back of his mind. He thought of her alone in the apartment. What did she do all day? She never went to the market; she telephoned for groceries. But she didn't pay for them, except to give the delivery boy a tip. The bill, along with many, many others, came in at the first of the month. There were other deliveries; the cleaner, the liquor store . . . And what else? And then he remembered that in the early days of their marriage, before Elaine learned to go outside for her amusements, she'd been a pushover for all the gadgets peddled by the door-to-door trade. It was a thought, and an impelling one.

A gadget. It would have to be something easy to sell; getting the door slammed in his face wouldn't help the killer at all. He had to have a few minutes, at least, to size up the possibilities: learn if the woman lived alone, see where she went for the money when he made the sale. Perhaps he had a gimmick—the "I just need 100 more points" routine. There were other approaches, legitimate ones that could have been borrowed: items made by the blind, items made by the crippled or mentally retarded. Something a woman would buy whether she needed it or not.

The next day, Keith went to Gonzales with his idea. Together they paid another visit to the McGannon woman's apartment. They examined the drawers in that kitchen cupboard—all standard items from bottle opener to egg beater, but nothing that looked new. Gonzales moved to the broom closet.

"Sometimes peddlers handle cosmetic items," Keith reflected. "I'll have a look in the bathroom."

He went through the tiny bedroom and into an even tinier bath. There was no tub, just a stall shower and a pullman lavatory. He pulled open one of the lavatory drawers and then called to Gonzales. When Gonzales came into the room, Keith stood with a small guest towel in his hand. It was green this time, a sort of chartreuse green with a black French poodle embroidered at the bottom. "Familiar?" he asked.

And Gonzales remembered, because a red towel was bad for an open cut.

They made an inquiry at every apartment in the building where anyone was at home. Afterwards, they went to the apartment on Curson and interviewed all of the available tenants there. Out of it all, a picture emerged. In both cases, on the Saturday prior to the murder at least one tenant at each address remembered seeing a peddler with a basket on his arm entering the premises. One tenant at the Hammerman address, an elderly woman living with her retired husband, had actually stopped the peddler on the walk and conversed with him.

"He was selling little towels and things," she reported. "Real pretty and cheap, too. I bought two for a quarter apiece. Would have bought more, but a pension don't go far these days." But did she remember how the peddler looked? Indeed, she did.   A tall, gawky young man—hardly more than a boy.   "Not much of a salesman," she added.   "He didn't even seem to care about selling his things. I had to stop him or he would have gone right past my door."

He had gone right past all of the doors, apparently, except two—Violet Hammerman's and Dorothy McGannon's.   A check on the mailboxes at each unit indicated an explanation.   All of the other apartments in each building were occupied by two or more tenants.   The cat-killer concentrated on women living alone.

"That's great," Gonzales concluded.   "In this particular area we have the largest concentration of unmarried people of any section of the city.   Now all we have to do is locate every woman living alone and warn her not to buy a guest towel from a door-to-door peddler."

"Aren't peddlers licensed?" Keith said.

"Licensed peddlers are licensed," Gonzales said.   "But what's more important, merchandise of this sort is manufactured.   There's a code number on the tag inside. Keep your hat on this operation for a few days, Briscoe, and you may have an exclusive.   In the meantime, this whole area will be searched for a tall, thin peddler carrying a basket."

"Or not carrying a basket," Keith suggested.   "I don't think your man entered these buildings blind.   I think he had his victims selected days before the Saturday check-up.   I think he watched them, studied the location of the apartments— planned everything in advance.   He's probably out lining up next Sunday night's target right now.   He's making headlines, Gonzales.   Everybody has an ego."

Gonzales made no argument.

"You've really been doing some head work on this," he said.

"Yes," Keith answered, "I have."

There was more head work to do.

Keith went shopping.   He left Gonzales and found his way to one of the large department stores.   He located the linen department and wandered about the aisles avoiding salesladies until he found what he was looking for: guest towels in all the assorted colors, guest towels with jaunty French poodles embroidered at the bottom.

"Something for you, sir?"

A voice at his shoulder brought his mind back to the moment.

"No, no thanks," he said.   "I was just looking."

He walked away quickly.   He was doing too much head work; he needed some air.

That evening he went to see Elaine.   He still had his key and could let himself in.   Nobody met him at the door, not even Gus.

"He's at the vet's," Elaine explained.   He caught a cold.   They're keeping him under observation for a week."

She was in the bedroom doing her nails.   She sat on the bed, sprawled back against the pillows.   She barely looked at him when she spoke.

"I thought you weren't coming back," she said.

"I'm not," he told her.   "I only came tonight so we could talk things over."

"Talk?   What is there to talk about?"

"A divorce."

The hand operating the nail polish brush hesitated a moment.

"We did talk about that—last week," Elaine said.

He waited for several seconds and there was no sign of interest in his presence. He might have been a piece of furniture she was ready to give to the salvage truck. He walked past the bed and over to the window. Elaine's carpet was thick; he couldn't have heard his footsteps with a stethoscope. He went to the window and pulled aside the soft drapes. It was a casement window and both panels were cranked out to let in the night air. The apartment was on the second floor. Directly below, the moonlight washed over the flat roof of the long carport and caught on the smooth curve of the service ladder spilling over the side. The window itself was a scant five feet above the roof.

"You should keep this window locked," he said. "It's dangerous this way."

The change of subject brought her eyes up from her nails.

"What do you mean?"

"Haven't you been reading the papers?"

"Oh, that!"

"It's nothing to scoff at. Two women are very dead."

She stared at him then, because this wasn't just conversation and she was beginning to know it.

"Stop wishing so hard," she said. "You're almost drooling."

"Don't be stupid, Elaine."

"I'm not stupid—and I'm not going to let you scare me into letting you off the hook. What do you think I am, Keith? A substitute wife you can use for a while until you decide to go back to the home-fires and slippers routine? Well, I'm not! I told you before, you can't have your cake and eat it. You walked out on me— I didn't send you away. Just try to get a divorce on that and see what it costs you!"

It was two days later that Sergeant Gonzales called Keith to his office. There had been a new development in the case, one of those unexpected breaks that could mean everything or nothing depending on how it went. A call had come in from a resident of a court in West Hollywood. A woman had reported seeing a prowler outside her bedroom windows. Bedroom windows were a critical area with Gonzales by this time, and when it developed that the woman lived alone, worked five days a week and spent weekends at home, what might have been a routine complaint became important enough for a personal interview. True to his words, he was cutting Keith in on the story if there was one, and there was.

Nettie Swanson was a robust, middle-aged woman of definite opinions on acceptable and inacceptable human conduct.

"I don't like snoopers," she reported. "If anybody's curious about how I live, let him come to the door and ask. Snoopers I can't abide. That's why I called the police when I saw this fellow hanging around out back."

"Can you describe the man, Miss Swanson?" Gonzales asked.

"I sure can. He was tall—like a beanpole. Would have been taller if he hadn't slouched so much. Young, too. Not that I really saw his face, but I thought he must be young by the way he slouched. Can you give me any reason why young folks today walk around like they been hit in the stomach? And their faces! All calf-eyed like a bunch of strays trying to find their way back to the barn!''

"Miss Swanson," Gonzales cut in, "how are your nerves?"

Some people talked big and folded easily. Nettie Swanson was as collapsible as a cast-iron accordion. She listened to Sergeant Gonzales explain the situation and a fire began to kindle in her eyes. The prowler might come back, he told her. He might appear at her door sometime Saturday carrying a basket of items to sell. Would she allow a police officer to wait in her apartment and nab him?

"That's not necessary," she said. "I got a rifle back in my closet that I used to shoot rattlesnakes with when I was a girl in Oklahoma. I can handle that prowler."

"But he's not just a prowler," Gonzales protested. "If he's the man we think he is, he's already killed two women that we know of."

She took the information soberly. She wasn't blind, and she could read. And then her eyes brightened again as the truth sank home.

"The 'cat-killer'! Now, isn't that something! Well, in that case I guess I'd better leave things to you, Sergeant. But I've got my rifle if you need another gun."

Gonzales couldn't have found a more cooperative citizen.

Saturday. Keith sat with Gonzales in a small, unmarked sedan across the street from the apartment house where Nettie Swanson lived. It was an old two-story affair flanked on one side by a new multiple unit and on the other by a shaggy hedge that separated the edge of the lot from a narrow alleyway. The hedge was at least five feet high and only the mouth of the alleyway was visible from the sedan. But the entrance to the building was visible and had been visible for over an hour. Inside the building, one of Gonzales' men had been waiting since nine o'clock. It was nearly eleven.

Keith was perspiring. He opened the door next to him to let a little more air into the sedan. Gonzales watched him with curious eyes.

"You're even more nervous than I am," he remarked, "and I'm always an old woman about these things. You're working too hard on this, Briscoe."

"I always work hard," Keith said. "I like it that way."

"And nights too?"

"Nights too."

"That's bad business. We're not as young as we used to be. There comes a time when we have to taper off a little." Gonzales pushed his hat back on his head and stretched his legs out in front of him, giving the seat a tug backward. "At least that's what they tell me," he added, "but with five kids they don't tell me how. You've got kids, haven't you?"

Keith didn't answer. He looked for a cigarette in his pocket, but the package was empty. Down on the corner, just beyond the alleyway, he could see a drugstore. Drugstores carried cigarettes and no conversation about things he didn't care to discuss.

"I'm going for some smokes," he said.   "Tell our friend not to peddle his towels until I get back."

The drugstore was on the same side of the street as the apartment house they were watching.   Out of curiosity, he crossed over and walked past the front door. It was open to let in the air, but the hall was empty.   He walked past the alley and on to the drugstore.   He bought the cigarettes and walked back, still walking slowly because he was in no hurry to get back into that hot sedan.   Gonzales was right: he was nervous.   His hands trembled as he slit the tax stamp on the cigarette box.   At the mouth of the alley he paused to light a cigarette, and then promptly forgot about it and let it fall to the ground.

A few minutes earlier, the alley had been deserted.   Now a battered grey coupe was parked against the hedges about twenty feet back from the street.   He looked up.   The sidewalk in front of him was empty, but across the street Gonzales was climbing out of the sedan.   Gonzales walked hurriedly toward the front door of the building, a man with his mind on his business.   He didn't see Keith at all. The picture fell into place.   Keith went directly to the coupe.   It was an old Chevy, license number KUJ770.   He stepped around to the door and looked for the card holder on the steering post.   It had slipped out of focus, but the door was unlocked. When he opened the door, he saw something that had dropped to the floor of the car and was half hidden under the seat.   It was dirty from being kicked about, but it was blue and it had a black French poodle on it.   He dropped the towel to the floor and went to work on the card holder.   The registration tab slid into view: George Kawalik, 1376¼ N. 3rd Street.

Keith had the whole story in his hand.   Gonzales hadn't seen the coupe; he couldn't have seen it from the far side of the hedge.   He stepped back, intending to go after Gonzales, and it was then that he heard the shot.   He waited.   There may have been a shout from within the building.   He was never sure because what happened, when it did happen, happened very fast.   He had started around the edge of the hedge when suddenly the hedge burst open to erupt a head—blond, close-cropped, a face—wild, contorted with fear—and then a body, long but bent almost double as it stumbled and fell forward toward the coupe.   The door was wrenched open, and the face appeared above the steering wheel before Keith could orient himself for action.   He was already at the curb twenty feet away from the car.   He turned back just as the coupe leaped forward and was forced to scramble in fast retreat to avoid being run down.   The retreat came to a sudden stop as he collided with about a hundred and eighty pounds of mobile power which turned out to be Gonzales.

"Was that him in the coupe?   Did you see him?"

The coupe was a grey blur racing toward the corner.

"Did you see the car?   Did you get the number?"

Gonzales had a right to shout.   A killer had slipped through his fingers.   A two-time murderer was getting away.

"That fool woman and her rattlesnake gun!"

Keith recovered his breath.

"Did she fire the shot?" he asked.

"No—but she had the gun in her hand when she opened the door. Clancy, inside, didn't catch her in time. The peddler saw it and ran for the back door. It was Clancy who fired. Did you get the license number?"

Gonzales' face was a big, sweaty mask in front of Keith's eyes. A big, homely, sweating face. A cop, a friend, a man in trouble. And Keith had the whole story on a tiny slip of paper in his hand.

He didn't hesitate.

"No," he said. "I didn't get it. I didn't have time."

Who could tell when decisions were made? An opportunity came, an answer was given—but that wasn't the time. Time was a fabric; the instant called now was only a thread. But it was done. The moment Keith spoke, he knew that something his mind had been planning all this time was already done. The fabric was already woven. He had only to follow the threads.

There was a murderer named George Kawalik who killed by pattern. He found an apartment where a woman lived alone. He watched the apartment, located the bedroom window, waited until Saturday when it was most likely he would find her home and made his scouting expedition under the pretext of peddling pretty towels. Sunday night was pay-off night. He came, he stole, he killed.

There was another man named Keith Briscoe who had made a mistake. He didn't like to think about how or why he'd made it, but he had to think of a way out. He wasn't a young man anymore. A little grey had begun to appear at his temples, and he was beginning to feel his limitations. It didn't seem fair that he had to pay for the rest of his life for a flirtation that had gone too far. It seemed less fair that his sons had no father, and that Faye was becoming a lonely woman who took her drinks stronger and who was running away to find the love he wanted to give her.

After leaving Gonzales, Keith had time to think about all these things. He sat alone in the furnished room and laid them out logically, mathematically in his mind. He put it into a simple formula: Keith plus Faye equaled home and happiness; Keith minus Elaine equaled Faye. The second part was no certainty, but it was at least a gamble and Keith not minus Elaine was no chance at all.

He knew the odds against murder. George Kawalik would be caught. He was no longer a footprint on the earth or a faceless shadow tall enough to reach up and slit a window screen, lean and agile enough to hoist himself into a room. He now had a face as well as a body; he had a method of operation; more important, he had a car. Gonzales had seen the grey coupe fleetingly, but he'd seen it with eyes trained to absorb details. And Gonzales had an organization to work with. Even as he sat thinking about it, Keith knew what forces were being put into operation. The coupe would be found. It might take days or even weeks, but it would be found. In the meantime, George Kawalik would kill again. That was inevitable. The compulsion that drove him to the act, whether it was a mental quirk or an addict's desperate need for money, would drive him again.

And Sunday was the night for murder.

On Saturday evening, as soon as it was dark, Keith went on an expedition. The address in Kawalik's registration slip wasn't easy to find in the dark; it wouldn't have been easy by daylight. It was a run-down, cluttered neighborhood ripe for a mass invasion of house movers. Old frame residences with the backyards cluttered by as many haphazard units as the building code would permit. Far to the rear of the lot he found Kawalik's number. The unit was dark and the shades drawn. He wanted to try the door, but it was too risky. This was no time to activate Kawalik's nervous trigger finger. He walked quietly around to the rear of the unit. All of the shades were drawn, but one window was open. He stood close to it for a few moments, and it seemed he could hear someone breathing inside. He moved on. The back door had an old-fashioned lock that any skeleton key would open. He fingered the key ring in his pocket and then decided to wait. He left the unit and walked back to the garages, a barracks-like row of open front cubicles facing a narrow alley. The grey coupe was there.

Kawalik was holed in, the natural reaction to his narrow escape. That was good. Keith wasn't ready for him yet; he merely wanted to know where to find him at the proper time. He found his way back through the maze of units to the street, always with the uneasy knowledge that a crazed killer might be watching from behind those shaded windows. He'd almost reached the sidewalk when a voice out of the darkness brought him to a sudden halt.

"Looking for somebody, mister?"

A man's voice. Keith turned about slowly and then breathed easier. An old man stood in the lighted doorway of the front apartment. He had the suspicious eyes and possessive stance of a landlord protecting his property.

"I guess I had the wrong address," Keith said.

"What address you looking for?"

"A place to rent. A friend of mine told me he saw an empty unit here."

"Nothing to rent here," the old man answered.

"A unit with the shades rolled down," he said.

"That place is rented. The man who rents it works nights."

Keith went home then. The old man still looked suspicious; Keith was satisfied.

There was only one thing to do before returning to Kawalik. In the morning, Keith called Elaine. It was nearly noon, but she sounded sleepy. Elaine's nights were unusually long. He'd worked out his story carefully. He was working late that night, he told her, but he had to see her. It was important. How about midnight? Elaine protested. Thelma was giving a party.

"Not another birthday?" he challenged.

She still protested. What did he want that couldn't wait? Freedom, he told her.

"And you know what I told you," she said.

"That it would cost me. Well, I may have a way of raising the fare. You don't dislike cash, do you?"

She fell for it. She would be home by midnight.

He watched the apartment from the street. At midnight all of the lights were blazing. At one o'clock the front lights went out, and he moved around to the rear. At one-thirty, the bedroom light went out. Elaine thought he'd stood her up and had gone to bed. She couldn't have made a bigger mistake.

Twenty minutes later, Keith entered Kawalik's apartment by way of the back door. The place was dark. For a few seconds, he was afraid Kawalik had more nerve than he'd been given credit for and was out calling on some other victim chosen in advance, but the fear left him when he reached the bedroom. A faint glow of moonlight penetrated the window blind outlining a long body under the sheet on the bed. Keith had his own gun in his hand. He switched on the flashlight. It was Kawalik, but he didn't stir. Keith moved closer to the bed. Kawalik's eyes were closed and his breathing heavy. One arm was thrown outside the sheet. Keith's first hunch had been correct. The arm was tattooed with needle marks and the last jolt must have been a big one. Kawalik wouldn't awaken for hours.

It was a better break than he'd bargained for. He played the flash around the room, not wanting to risk the lights because of the eagle-eyed landlord up front. Item by item, he found what he needed: Kawalik's .45 in a bureau drawer, a pair of canvas shoes with smooth rubber soles in the closet, a pair of gloves, a basketful of colored guest towels. Keith thumbed through the basket until he found a pink one. Shocking pink. It seemed appropriate for Elaine.

In the bathroom, he located the pocket knife among other interesting items; a hypodermic needle, a spoon with a fire-blackened bowl, the remnants of an old shirt torn in strips. One of the strips was stained with blood. Kawalik must have gone deeper than he intended locating the vein. Another blood-spotted strip dangled over the edge of the lavatory. He started to play the light downward and then switched it off instead. He didn't breathe again until he was convinced it was a cat he'd heard outside the building. He left the place then, without a light, locking the back door behind him.

Half an hour later, Keith climbed through Elaine's bedroom window. He was breathless and scared. A dozen times he'd expected her to hear him sawing away at the screen and ruin everything; but the other tenants of their building had always been thoughtful about such things as late, late television movies at full volume, or all-night parties of vibrant vocal range. This night was no exception and so Elaine would be sleeping, as usual, with ear plugs and eye mask. He really didn't need Kawalik's rubber-soled shoes on the deep-piled rug, but he did need Kawalik's signature—the pink towel to deposit in the linen closet in the bathroom. In the dressing room he found two purses in plain sight. He took the money from them, jamming the smaller, an evening bag, in his pocket for subsequent deposit in the driveway below. That done, he went to the bed, leaned over Elaine and raised the eye mask. She awakened with a start, but she didn't scream. Elaine had nerve—nerve enough to stare at the shadowy figure standing over her bed until recognition came.

"Oh, it's you—"

And then she saw the gun in his hand. That was when Keith fired.

It was easy. Murder was easy. By the time he was safely in his car again, Keith was in the throes of an almost delirious elation. His nerves had been tauter than he knew; now they were unwinding with the power of a strong spring bursting its webbing. He knew how Kawalik felt when the shot in his bloodstream took effect: wild and free and about ten thousand feet up. Elaine was dead, and there wasn't a thing anyone could ever do to him. The noisy neighbors hadn't heard the shot, the evening bag had been dropped at the foot of the service ladder on the garage, the pink towel was in the linen closet, and ballistics would match the bullet in Elaine's body to the two other bullets they were holding from two other identical crimes. And the beauty of it all was that Kawalik, when they caught him, wouldn't be able to remember but what he really had killed her. There was nothing left to do but get the gun, gloves, shoes, and the money back into Kawalik's apartment. After that, he belonged to the inevitable.

The inevitable was Sergeant Gonzales. Keith didn't see the police car in front of Kawalik's place until it was too late to drive on. He had slowed down to park, and Gonzales recognized him.

"I see you got my message," Gonzales called.

Keith shut off the motor. He had no idea how Gonzales had located Kawalik so quickly, but he could play dumb. Dumb meant silence.

"I told them at headquarters to call you just as I was leaving. It seemed a shame for you to miss out on the finish."

"The cat-killer?" Keith asked, his mind racing.

"We got him. I tell you, Briscoe, I've had an angel on my shoulder on this case. Another lucky break. The landlord here got suspicious. Said a fellow had been prowling around the place last night and heard somebody again, tonight, so he called the police. The boys didn't find a prowler, but out in the garage they found something more interesting—"

Keith's mind raced ahead of Gonzales' words. He wasn't ten thousand feet up anymore, but he was still free. They'd have to look for the gun. He could help them do that; in the dark he could be a big help.

"—an old coupe," Gonzales added, "like the one they've been alerted for all day. They took a look. The front seat was full of blood."

In the dark he could help them find the gun and the gloves and the rubber-soled shoes—And then Keith's mind stopped racing and listened to Gonzales' words.

"Blood?" he echoed.

Blood, as on a strip of torn cloth in the bathroom. Blood, as what was soaking into Elaine's bedclothes and beginning to stain Keith's hands.

Gonzales nodded.

"I guess Clancy's a better shot than we knew. The cat killer won't climb tonight, Briscoe, or any other night. He's in there now so doped up he doesn't even know we've found him. It's a good way to kill the pain when somebody's blown a chunk out of your leg."

It wasn't really blood on Keith's hands; it was a gun. When he couldn't stand the weight of it any longer, he handed it to Gonzales. Gonzales would figure it out. A thread, a fabric, a pattern. Elaine had been right: he had a weakness, and a man with a weakness shouldn't play with guns.

DONALD HONIG

A Real, Live Murderer

I was waiting on the back porch, a trifle mistrustful of the dark. It was overly quiet and the trees seemed to be watching me dourly as if they knew I was going to do something I shouldn't. Even the wind had stopped. I could hear Pa snoring through the upstairs window in slow, breaking rhythms.

It felt as though I'd been standing there for hours, but it wasn't more than fifteen minutes. I'd gotten out of bed at ten of twelve and the midnight bells had come tolling over the meadows about five minutes after I'd come down. I was almost hoping that Pete wouldn't show up. But I knew he would. He was always out late at night anyway. He was the only one allowed out so late; or maybe he wasn't allowed; but either way, he was always around, looking for some mischief.

Pete had seen the murderer last night and had told me about it this afternoon while I was watering Pa's horse at the trough in front of the Dooley House. He'd promised to take me tonight, if I could get out. It had to be very late, he said, because we had to be sure the murderer didn't see us because he was going to be hanged shortly and everybody knows it's bad luck to be looked at by somebody who is going to be hanged. We couldn't go to look at him during the day because he'd be sure to see us. So we had to be sure he was asleep. I really wanted to see him too. I'd never seen a murderer before and I wasn't going to be done out of it now no matter what.

I heard him coming then. He was coming through the elms across the road. I could hear him in there. I went down the porch steps as light as I could and went across the back yard and climbed over the picket fence. I met him in the middle of the road. A full white moon had come over the trees and you could see almost like it was morning.

"I made it," I said.

"That's good," Pete said. He had his thumbs hooked inside his suspenders. He was wearing the Union Army forage cap that Clay Taylor had recently brought back from Virginia for him. Pete was the only one in Capstone who owned a hat like that and he wouldn't trade it for anything. He said it was as near as he could come to fighting Rebs; the War was in its second year then.

We went down to the crossroads and then along Grant Avenue's moonlit emptiness.

"You sure he won't see us?" I asked.

"Nothing to be worried about," Pete said. We walked between the ruts that the wagons made, on the shaggy grass that grew there.

"How many times have you seen him?"

"Twice," Pete said. "The last two nights."

"What does he look like?"

"You'll see. You'll see him good tonight. The moon is just right."

The jail stood off by itself, a long, low, oblong building. Down further were the Dooley House and Gibson's tavern and the stores, but they were quiet now, very quiet.

We lightfooted around behind the jail. High up in the long, whitewashed wall were the little cell-windows. Pete had moved the rain barrel under one of them and that was where the murderer was. Pete climbed up onto the barrel first and took hold of the bars and looked in, bending his face in close.

"Is he there?" I whispered, clasping my hands.

"Shhh," he said.

"Let me up," I said.

He moved aside on the barrel and I climbed on. I hooked my fingers into his belt and pulled myself up and took hold of the bars and held my breath and looked down into the cell.

He was lying on the cot, the murderer was, on his back, sleeping. The moon fell full and bright through the bars and showed him good. I recognized him now as a man I'd seen about town from time to time, Jimmy Grover. Mostly I'd seen him drunk. He was not a very large man but was sort of round. He had a short beard which lent a peculiar sadness to his reposing face. His hands were clasped over his chest and he looked just like any other man who is asleep.

"That's him," Pete whispered.

"He don't look so special," I said.

Then his eyes opened. They opened slow and mysterious and were looking right up at our faces in the bars. And he looked worse with his eyes open—he looked like he was dead. The way they had just opened like that, it was uncanny; they had opened and found us there, or more properly caught us, and were holding us, and there was nothing we could do about it. We couldn't move. We couldn't do anything but stare back, our fingers caught around the bars.

At first his eyes showed nothing, as if our faces peeping there were a continuation of his dream. Then they became startled and I could detect a tremor go through his body. But he didn't move yet. I think if he would have moved—if he would have so much as parted his hands—we would have gone over backwards off the barrel.

He spoke first.

"What do you want?" he said. He was a little afraid and perhaps a trifle indignant.

Neither of us spoke, could answer. He asked it again, his voice not so harsh this time.

"We don't want anything," Pete said.

"You must want something," the murderer said.

"Honest we don't," Pete said.

The murderer moved now, slowly, almost deliberately slowly so as not to alarm us. First his hands slid away and then he sat up on the cot, watching us.

"You've come to look at me, haven't you?" he said. "You must think I'm a strange specimen."

"Yes sir," Pete said, not precisely agreeing, but trying to be agreeable.

"If you've come to see a murderer, then you're wasting your time," the murderer said, sitting there in the moonlight and looking up at us as if *we* were the peculiar ones.

"You mean to say you're not a murderer?" I asked.

"I never killed anybody," he said.

"Then why are you here?" Pete asked.

"The jails are full of innocent men."

"But everybody says you're a murderer," Pete said stubbornly, as though trying to convince him.

Then he commenced to tell us his side of what had happened those few days ago when he'd got into his trouble.

"We'd been drinking some, Eddie Larsen and I," he said. "We'd got ourselves a jug from Gibson's and gone over towards the marsh in good spirits. On the way we passed the Misses Tabers and Doctor Howell, and Eddie, being in his state, sorta sassed them and I had to cuff him on the head to make him stop and he yelled at me for it and we went off arguing into the woods. That's what the Misses Tabers and the doctor told at the trial and they were right as far as they told; what was wrong was the conclusions that were made of it."

"You couldn't blame people for thinkin' it," Pete said.

"Maybe not. But it ain't right to hang a man for what people happen to conclude," Jimmy said hotly. Then he subsided a bit. "I'll tell you the rest, if you want to hear."

"We want to hear," I said.

"We finished the jug, Eddie and I, and he wanted some more. He said that there was probably some in Mattick's shed and that he'd go over there and steal a jug. I was in good spirits, but still in control of myself. No, I says, you can't go onto a man's property and steal from him, especially a man such as Mattick. But Eddie, he was of a mind and when he got like that there was no standing him off. The last I saw of him he was reeling down the road to Mattick's place. The next thing I know is two days later I'm arrested for the murder, for which they have not even found a corpse . . ."

"But lots of blood marks on the rocks near the road," Pete said.

"It's a far cry from real evidence," Jimmy said.

"They say you killed him and buried him somewheres," Pete said.

"Hang it, boy, I know what they say. And I say they're liars."

"They say you was awful drunk and did it without knowing and that now you don't remember," Pete said.

"That's what they say, and that ain't evidence," Jimmy said. He rose now and stood there in all dignity, the moon halfway up him, his legs standing in shadow. "You're looking at an innocent man, boys," he said.

"Then who is the murderer?" I asked.

"I don't know," he said.

"But you're stuck for it," Pete said.

"Unless a miracle happens," Jimmy said.

"Well you hang on," said Pete, "and maybe the miracle will come true."

We got down off the barrel then and went away. We walked up along the middle of the empty road.

"I don't know," Pete said, "but he looks innocent to me."

"Innocent or not, they're going to hang him sure. Pa said it yesterday."

"I don't like it," Pete said, starting to brood on it.

"A man can look innocent and not be."

"Or might well be too. I'll tell you, Gascius, once they hang a man it don't make no difference to him if they find later he was innocent after all. They can name a park or a horserace after him, but he's finished all the same, poor chap."

"But if he's innocent then where is Eddie Larsen? It's been more than a week now."

"Could be anywhere. Maybe waiting for them to hang old Jimmy and then come out of the woods and say wasn't it a fine joke he done. Some fellows has got humors like that."

"So what can we do?" I asked.

"We give it our every thought," Pete said as he hooked his thumbs into his suspenders.

Pete would think of something, I knew. The prospect was both intriguing and intimidating because often he let ingenuity outgallop prudence. His ideas often sounded as if they had been propounded in a nightmare and then been chased for two miles over stones and then fallen down a precipice into a rapids and gone over a waterfall and been thrown back onto dry land still on hind legs and still running.

I suppose I felt sort of sorry for old Jimmy. Justice in Capstone in the 1860's was brief and positive. Public opinion—which was the prejudices of the men who sat on Dooley's porch—generally decided if a man was guilty or not, and so the trial was generally a mere formality. If enough men said, "I reckon Jimmy Grover murdered Eddie Larsen," then that was the way it was to be no matter how hard Jimmy Grover's lawyer ranted.

So they had the gallows all fixed and waiting for Jimmy and it looked sure like he was going to dance on it.

The next day, just past noon, Pete popped up out of the bushes back of my yard, the Union Army cap askew on his head, his brown hair hanging out from under. That's all he did, never said a word, and then went back down into the bushes again. But that was enough. I went across the yard and into the bushes.

"Let's go," he said. I followed him across the road and into the elms where it was cool out of the sun. When he stopped I noticed he had in his hand three mighty peculiar things to be holding all at once: a hammer, a chisel, and a bugle.

"What's all that truck for?" I asked.

"We're going to spring old Jimmy," Pete said. I didn't bother to ask him how those things would fit in. The explanation wouldn't have made sense anyway, nor sounded feasible.   So I just followed along, as I had learned to do with him, waiting for some powerful revelation.

When we came into sight of the jail, Pete stopped and pulled me behind the livery stable.

"Now listen here," he said, handing me the bugle.   "I know you can play this. I want you to go in there and give the sheriff a serenade."

"Play him a serenade?" I asked.

"Sure.   Play him all those fancy tunes you regaled the town with at the last picnic.   Get in there and make lots of noise."

"Suppose he won't let me?"

"Tell him you've got to rehearse in a place that's got walls around, 'cause you got to play at the church dance on Saturday.   The sheriff is a simple-hearted fellow with compassion for his brother man.   He'll let you play for as long as he can stand it.   By that time I'll have broke the bars and hauled Jimmy out of there. Now get on."

I went around to the jail and stepped up onto the boardwalk.   The cider barrels under the shed, where the men usually sat, were empty; the men never liked to sit there when somebody was inside waiting to be hanged.   I opened the door and saw Sheriff Rice just coming out from the passageway where the cells were. "Hello, Gascius," he said.

"Can I practice my bugle here, Sheriff?" I asked.   "I'm up to play at the social on Saturday night and I need a place to practice.   They ran me out of my house."

"Why don't you go into the woods?"

"You can't judge it too good out of doors.   The sound waves go off and don't come back."

"Well," the sheriff said thoughtfully, a trifle dubious, "it probably constitutes undue cruelty, but we ain't got but one prisoner at the moment and he's getting a hempen collar soon anyway—so I guess it's all right."

So I stood straight up and took in a good breath and brought the bugle up to my puckered mouth and began blasting out some military calls my Uncle Herm had taught me.   It got too much for the sheriff to bear and he went out and sat down on a barrel while I filled the place with fine brassy noise.   And it was a good thing too that he went out, because each time I paused to pull in some fresh air I could hear Pete hammering and chipping in the back like a woodpecker with an iron nose. I must of stood there for a half hour, until my head cracked and I felt that my next deep breath would surely turn me inside out, and I had to stop.   I cocked my ear and couldn't hear Pete anymore and so I went outside.   Sheriff Rice was sitting clear across the street now, under a tree.

"You all finished, Gascius?" he called.

"Yes," I said.   "And I thank you kindly, Sheriff.   I sure thank you."

"That was mighty nice playing," he said, coming across the road.   He took a seat on the steps and I was glad for that.   I didn't want him going inside just yet.

Then I went down the road, putting my footprints in the dust as nonchalant as a prize heifer, and then cut back into the alley behind the livery stable and ran as quick as I could to the back of the jail.   There waiting for me was an unusual sight indeed. Pete had knocked the bars out all right, but he was having considerable trouble trying to get Jimmy to fit through the little window. He had him out to his waist and in fact you couldn't see any window at all and Jimmy looked as if he was bolted onto that wall without legs; his arms were going like they were demonstrating swimming. And Pete was jumping there, every so often grabbing an arm and giving it a tug but unable to do much good.

Then Pete saw me and whipped off his cap and whirled it round and round to put me into haste, and I came on the fly. He ran to meet me and grabbed me by the shoulders.

"We've got to get him through!" he said, all heated up.

I stuffed the bugle down into my pants and ran after him. We stopped under Jimmy and looked up at him and he looked back at us, hung up there like a fixture, bald head covered with sweat-beads, mouth open in the little beard but unable to speak anything (though that round wordless orifice spoke louder than any words), and his body jerking and quivering which led me to suspect that his legs were doing considerable thrashing behind him.

"Now take hold," Pete said to me, reaching up and taking an arm, "and take hold good. We're going to heave him out."

"Easy now, boys," Jimmy said.

"You leave out your breath and let it be that way," Pete told him.

Then we were pulling. At first it didn't seem as if he'd ever come out of there and then it seemed as if we were pulling him in two and I had a vision of the town hanging just his legs while the rest of him was being wheeled away by us, but then his eyes squeezed shut and his mouth too and his face grimaced and he was on the way. There was an awful scraping and scratching and ripping, but he was coming, inch by inch. The sides of the window gave off a little spurt of dust and then he popped right out, fast and unexpected—and Pete and I were both pulling suddenly a flying force and falling back and down as Jimmy fairly flew out of there and plummeted chest-down between us.

We lay there for a second, the three of us, tuckered out with exhaustion and surprise. But we'd done it. Jimmy groaned and tried to get up.

"What's the matter?" Pete asked as we got up and whipped the dust from us.

"It's my leg," Jimmy said. "I can't put weight on it."

He'd given it a good solid whack when he'd come down and now he couldn't walk. So Pete and I lifted him up erect and he put his arms around us and skipped along on one foot as we hurried him into the woods. We took him a little ways into a very secluded spot in the elm grove and sat him down in the bushes next to the brook.

"Here you are," Pete said. "At least you'll have some water if you want, till we can scare you up a horse."

"My leg feels like 'twas mule-kicked," Jimmy said, lying back, shutting his eyes. He looked a sight, what with the dust all over his vest and trousers and his trousers considerably ripped from his slide through the window.

"Anyway it's a far sight better than being hanged," Pete said, with that unimpeachable wisdom of his.

Jimmy opened his eyes and looked up at us, the sun and the leaves making speckles of shadow on his face, and his eyes filled with tears.

"I reckon I'm mighty obliged to you lads," he said.

"That's fine," Pete said. "Now you just lay quiet till we can rustle up some transportation for you. These bushes hide you pretty good, so you don't have to worry."

We left him there and hurried on back.

"Where do you reckon we can get a horse?" I asked Pete as we skipped through the woods.

"I don't know just yet," Pete said. "From a careless man probably. Let's just keep our eyes open."

When we got back, we found the place in a general furor. Men were running about and a group on horseback was gathering in front of the Dooley House. The dust was flying thick as smoke.

"See here," Pete asked a young lad in overalls, "what's going on?"

"Old Jimmy's got away," the lad said breathlessly.

We heard somebody shout out, "We should've hanged him when we had him."

I hadn't ever seen such activity in Capstone. It seemed that everybody was there, all the storekeepers in their aprons and the men from the tavern that never came out in daylight and all the farmers and their sons. Most everybody who had a horse was mounted and so there wasn't an idle horse about at all. The sheriff and his deputies went by us and the sheriff looked at me and I shuddered but he kept right on going toward a wagon full of men with rifles, never suspecting anything at all I guess, and jumped up into the wagon as fierce as a bear. Just then Eddie Larsen's father ran up onto Dooley's porch and shouted out:

"Listen here, you men!" And he held up two fingers and said, "Two hundred dollars reward to the man that brings him in, dead or alive!"

I looked at Pete and his face lighted up as if he'd received a benediction. His face was a map to his every thought and scheme.

"You can't do it, Pete," I said.

But he had his hand inside my arm and was steering me off into the alley. "I didn't say I would," he said. "But isn't that a pile of money? Think of the suit of clothes and the derby hat and the buckboard a fellow could buy with that. And it looks like they'll catch old Jimmy anyway since he don't have a horse and we can't get him one. It'd be a pity to have one of those far-spittin' farmers carry off that money, don't you think?"

"No, I don't think," I said. He was moving along real quick into the woods now and I had to skip over fallen trees to stay with him. "You can't do it," I said.

"You listen here," he said. "We don't know for sure if he's innocent or not anyway. *He* says he is, of course, but I don't suppose he'd have much trouble influencing himself of that. We're going against the whole town, ain't we? What's the chances of us being right and everybody else wrong? I ask you that."

"I'm against it," I said.

"Then the whole two hundred belongs to me."

"It's blood money."

"But he's most likely a murderer.   The more I think on it the more I feel convinced."

The idea was hot in his head and there was no stopping him.   I told him I'd have no part of it and so he went on ahead, slipping through to the elm grove as quiet as smoke.   I sat down on the trunk of a fallen tree and clasped my hands in my lap and tried not to believe anything that had ever happened.   A little bit of trumped-up disbelief can go a long way in mitigating a nervous conscience, or so I thought.

Then I heard Pete whistling through the woods and I jumped up and went hurrying, sure he'd changed his mind.   But he hadn't.   When I came to the brook he was standing there and Jimmy was stretched out as peaceful as last night.

"I tapped him with the chisel," Pete said.   "He never saw me either, so he can't tell."

"You might've killed him," I said.

"There's a difference in knocking a man out and killing him.   Now you give me a hand with him if you want to have a hundred dollars and be a hero too."

So we gathered him up by the wrists and the ankles and started toting him through the woods.

"I don't like a bit of it," I said.

"You ain't so pure yourself," he said.   "Standing there and playing that fool bugle makes you liable for jail yourself."

We carried him back to the yard behind the jail and laid him down.

"We'd best bring him around the front," Pete said.

"I'll tell you one thing," I said.   "They're going to hang him as soon as they let eyes on him.   It won't be so pretty either, if you've never seen a man hanged, and you're going to have to stand there and watch and know that you done it."

Well, that sobered him proper.   He looked down at Jimmy and began nodding his head like a man who sees he's been standing in syrup.

"I reckon they would too," he murmured.

"They're riding mean right now."

"Well, what are we going to do?"

"What we intended on doing in the first place—help him get away.   And the first thing is to get him away from here."

"I reckon you're right," he said, and that was more than a casual admission for Pete Mariah to make.   It was like a man crossing party lines.   "You're the first one ever to talk me out of something I'd fixed on," he said.

"And a good thing too," I said.

"Let me go around to the front and see what's going on."

While Pete did that, I dragged Jimmy into the edge of the woods and hid him in the brush.   He was sleeping real good.   Pete had given him quite a good tap it seemed.

A few minutes later Pete came hurrying back, shoving his cap around on his head.   He jumped into the bushes and crouched down.

"We've had some luck," he said.   "There's an empty wagon standing with a team right in front of Dooley's. Now here's what we do: I'll get up there and drive her off and swing her around behind the stable. You carry Jimmy over there and we'll load him on and take him down to Shantytown. They just love to hide fugitives there."

So, with some effort, I dragged Jimmy into the tall grass behind the stable and hid him there. I became a little uneasy thinking about the consequences I might have to face if I happened to be caught in it. That was one thing about Pete Mariah: he never concerned himself with the idea of consequences. You have to be born inordinately fearless to be like that. But if I could tell lies like Pete could then I reckon I'd be the same as him. He could turn mighty artful when the moment called for it.

So I hid there with Jimmy, without a lie or an explanation to my name, my head just like a pocket that's been picked clean. I put my ear on Jimmy's chest to test him out and he was still there, thank the Lord, with a rasp in him like dry straw.

Then Pete came swinging into the alley with the wagon, sitting up on the seat holding the reins. He swung the rig in behind the stable and jumped down.

"Come on, let's heist him in," he said.

"Won't it be risky," I said, "riding along with him in there like that?"

"It won't either," said Pete. "We've had some more luck."

The luck was in the shape of a long pinewood box that looked to me like a coffin. In fact I thought for sure it was a coffin until Pete, using the hammer and chisel which had sure become a couple of all-purpose instruments—pried it open and we saw that it didn't hold anything but some rocks. We threw the rocks away in the bushes and then picked up Jimmy and got him into the wagon bed and then into the box. He fit in pretty neat too. Then Pete made a couple of holes in the side for air; after that he put the lid back on.

"There," he said. "Now we can ride off and not worry about more'n we have to."

We got up on the seats and Pete lifted the reins and made the team turn around and go back down the alley. We came out onto Grant Avenue and rode past the Dooley House—and that was a long moment because we didn't know for sure where the owner of the wagon was—and down the grade. Once we cleared the crest of the grade, we put on a little speed and went rattling and bumping down the dirt road towards Shantytown where all the disreputables lived.

We'd gone a little ways when we heard ourselves being hailed from behind. Turning around we saw seven or eight men on horseback coming down on us.

"No sense trying to outrun them," Pete said. So he reined in and we sat there in uneasy quiet while the hoofbeats clattered louder and then we were surrounded by the men. Deputy Ned Casey was among them and I noticed Jack Mattick too and several other men I knew.

"This your rig?" Casey asked Mattick.

"That's it," Mattick said. "We left it in front of Dooley's while we went in for a sentimental drink. When we come out it was gone."

"We found it strayin' by itself," Pete said, just as nonchalant as a butterfly. "Just meanderin' along. Figured it belonged to somebody down near the creek."

"Well, it belongs to Mattick," Casey said. They all had a look at the box in the back and I figured this would be a fine time for Jimmy to wake up and start hollering. But he didn't. We jumped down and stood in the road. I looked at Pete, but he was offering nothing but profound innocence. He still had the hammer and chisel stuck in his belt, but nobody remarked on them.

Mattick dismounted and tied his horse behind the wagon and then climbed up into the seat and took the reins and shook them against the team.

"I reckon we'll be able to finish our business now," he said. He turned the wagon around then began moving slowly back up the grade, the men following. They were all very solemn and quiet.

We followed along after, watching the wagon bump along. "We'll have to tag along till they set that box down somewheres," said Pete.

"Suppose he wakes up in there?" I said.

"I hope he'll have sense enough to keep still. He'd better, at any rate. If he starts in a-rattlin' around in there then there's nothing anybody'll be able to do for him."

I was going to ask why Jack Mattick had bothered to seal up a box of rocks and what he might be intending to do with it, but I didn't get a chance because what we saw next happening took the breath right out of me. Mattick had drawn the wagon off of Grant and down towards the Baker Avenue Cemetery. Pete and I both had the same realization at the same minute, but we were too scared to speak it. We just watched.

Mattick got down and unhooked the tailboard and with some of the others was sliding the box off the wagon. Further up on a knoll inside the gate, among the headstones, we saw standing the preacher and some other people.

I wanted to yell out, but Pete he just grabbed my arm and said to me without taking his eyes away from the men carrying the box on up to the knoll, "You run off and steal the first shovel you see. Then get back here as fast as your legs know how. Do it all on the fly, otherwise we've seen the last of old Jimmy."

So while Pete sat down on the rocks behind the low iron fence, I dashed off for the first house in sight, away on the other side of the meadow. I whipped around into the yard and went into the shed there. I found a rake, hoe and shovel leaning against the wall and I took the shovel and went rushing away with it. A chap came down the back steps and said, "You there!" but he never had a chance; by the time he finished saying it, I wasn't there any longer. He chased me a little ways, but I knew I was carrying Jimmy Grover's life in my hand and there was nobody that could have flagged me down then.

When I got back to the cemetery, Pete was still sitting in the same place, cool as a winter's moon.

"They've planted him," he said, getting up, running his thumbs up and down inside his suspenders.

"What are we going to do?" I asked, lathered with sweat.

"The way I see it, we've got a little time."

"Poor Jimmy," I said.

"Never mind him," said Pete. "If we don't reach him in time you'll be the one to go through life with it on your conscience. So don't feel so sorry for him."

The preacher and the others watched as Mattick knocked in the headboard with a stone and then they came down from the knoll and through the gate.   They got on their horses and Mattick drove the wagon away with the preacher sitting next to him.   We waited a few minutes until they'd gone out of sight, then Pete jumped the fence and I went after him, shovel and all.

We spurted up to the knoll where the fresh earth had just been patted down. The headboard looked like the back of a chair and it had inked on it: DINK O'DAY DECEASED JUNE 8, 1862.   Dink O'Day was Mattick's handyman, a seedy nondescript who hung on around the farm and did some chores for his bed and board.

But we had no time to speculate.   Pete grabbed the shovel and started stabbing with it and the dirt began to fly.   The dirt hadn't been packed down too well and Pete was able to dig it out in big scoopfuls.   When his arms got tired, I took the shovel from him and then he took it back when I got tired, and then he was hip high and still going like convulsions when he struck wood.   We could hear Jimmy in there then, kicking and hollering, and the first thing Pete did was take the hammer and chisel and knock in an air hole on top where it might do some good.   Then he pried open the lid and Jimmy sprung up like there'd been a chain attached from the lid to his belt.   His hair, what little he had left of it, was fair stood on end and his eyes looked as if they'd never seen sky before.   He gulped twice before he could say a thing, his throat working and his shoulders heaving like he was trying to swallow an egg.

"Take it easy," Pete said.

"What happened?" Jimmy said.   "Where am I?"

"Somebody tucked you into a coffin and you near suffocated, if not for us," Pete said.

Jimmy jumped up then and looked around at the headstones and the carven angels and I guess it was a mighty discomforting feeling for him.   He started trembling as if his bones were coming loose and he took hold of Pete and said,

"G-get me out of here.   P-please get me out of here."

We did that, of course, but it wasn't easy either.   First we had to close up the coffin and fill in the grave again and make it look innocent.   Then we had to get Jimmy out of there via the back way.   Then Pete had the bright idea that with all the town looking for him, Jimmy wouldn't be very safe again in the woods (for didn't some mysterious stranger creep up behind him before and sock him on the head and, for some unknown reason, try to secretly bury him under another man's name?) and that the only safe place would be in my hayloft.

So we smuggled him up into there and put a horse blanket over him.   Then we went back to the Dooley House.   Most of the men were still out on the chase and Dooley in his white apron was sitting on the porch smoking a cheroot.

"They found him yet?" Pete asked as we came up there and leaned on the bannister.

"Nope," Dooley said, savoring his cheroot.

"Think they will?"

"He couldn't of got far."

"How'd he get out?"

"Sheriff says he must've been working on them bars for some time."

"Say," Pete said, rubbing his chin as if he had just thought of it, "I noticed they buried Dink O'Day today."

"Yep. He passed on a few days ago. Had a fit, Mattick said. They was in here taking a drink to his soul when the team strayed off, but they found it. Mattick said it was just like Dink to do that," Dooley said with a chuckle.

We strayed away then and Pete was in a cloud of thought; I could tell because he'd become so profoundly still. I gave him his head and didn't say anything. Sometimes, when he thought enough, it could come useful. We wandered along the road in that manner of quiet, him profound and me respectful. Every so often some men sped past on horseback pounding up the dust. The dust hung in the air, settling back like something very old. What with the men scouring the woods and back roads for Jimmy the town was most quiet, the sun hot and yellow on the houses. Just a few old men were sitting by watching things.

"First of all," Pete said, breaking his spell, "you've got to feel as I do, which means to have a low opinion of Jack Mattick."

"I've never thought much about him," I said.

"Well he's a nasty-tempered, foul-brained, whiskey-blooded son of a turtle. None of his friends are dainty I can tell you."

"Why do you suppose he was burying a box full of rocks?"

"We're going to inquire into that."

"How?"

"You meet me tonight at the crossroads and we'll see."

"Why tonight?"

"It's always better to do these things in the dark."

"What things?"

"Looking around."

"Say, you're not going to go fooling around up at Jack Mattick's, are you?" I asked.

"You just meet me, Gascius," he said. "Ten o'clock, at the crossroads."

I wasn't so cheered by the prospect, you can be sure. But I was being devoured by curiosity about what had happened to Eddie Larsen and why Jack Mattick should want to have buried an empty box. I think that next to the ague, curiosity is the most devilish affliction a body can be stung with; it's the most humanizing thing next to being born and can't be resisted so far as I know. So I spent the rest of the day in a state of collapsed resistance and later that night, after sneaking some food and water up to Jimmy in the loft, set off to meet Pete. He was there at the crossroads, as he said he'd be. The men were sitting on Dooley's porch under the bug-swarmed lamps, looking all tired and sour.

"Well," I said to Pete.

"They're in a state of mutters," he said, " 'cause they haven't found him yet. Eddie Larsen's father is still shouting two hundred dollars for Jimmy."

"I thought you'd got that off your mind."

"I have. But I can't very well get it out of my head, can I? Come on, let's go."

Mattick's place was off in the back near the marsh. It wasn't much of a place, sort of run down and not very good soil, and folks wondered how he made any living from it.   The truth was he was something of a dubious character who associated in Shantytown a lot and it was probably true that he made a lot of money that he shouldn't have.   Nobody in Shantytown ever worked, but they always had money, so you can figure it out.

We went off of the road and through the night-webbed trees, hearing the silly crickets peep-peeping all around us and they gave me the impression of black little lights not fit for human eyes to see.   We struck a path and followed it till it ran out, then pushed through the hawthorn that bunched around outside Mattick's.   There was a half moon just up and it gave us enough light to see where we were going.   We came out next to the house—it was little more than a cabin with a porch covered by a slanted roof.   There was a light going in one window, but otherwise the house was dark and no sound coming from it.

I was of a mind to tell Pete that this was futile and ill-advised and sure to touch off some bad luck, but it would have been like trying to explain to a dead dog. I followed him over towards the shed.   It stood a good ways from the house, past the well and some cords of wood.   Pete got the door opened and we went inside. There was a window and the moon gave a little light through it.   There wasn't very much to the shed.   It had an earthen floor and there was a shelf of ciderjugs, some full, some not, and an assortment of tools laying handy about and a harness and a barrel in one corner covered up by what looked like canvas.

"Doesn't appear to be much here," I said.

"Maybe not," Pete said, but not convinced, I could tell.   "Let's have a look into that barrel."   He went to it and pushed away the canvas.   The pale film of moonlight fell right onto the barrel and so we were able to have a good look.   And we looked and we saw and I wish I had never done it, because it was something I knew I'd never forget.   I was old enough to join the army for the last year of the War, going as bugler in a New York regiment, and I saw some service in Virginia and saw some dead men in a field once, but I never saw anything that looked like Dink O'Day looked that night in the barrel.

Dink was stuffed into that barrel real horrible—his feet were even up with his face as if they had been shoved in there after the rest of him, and his face was rolled over on one side.

"Pete," I said, all quavery and sick inside, "let's get out of here."

He saw the wisdom of that and we lit out of there.   Too scared to pass the house again (it looked the most ominous thing in the world now) we went the other way, went clear across the breadth of the farm, and took the long way around back to town.   We found the sheriff up on Dooley's porch with the men.   Pete hailed him down and we walked a little ways into the shadows.

"Sheriff, we've found something of interest," said Pete.   The sheriff looked at him kind of skeptical.

"Of powerful interest," I said, and he looked at me too.   He was a big man. He had on a slouch hat, the brim hung low over his face.

"Such as what?" he asked.

"A dead body," said Pete.

The sheriff never said another word, but he put his hands on both our backs and began pushing us along in the direction we'd come, doubtless taking for granted the body was that of Eddie Larsen, never even asking of us who, just pushing us on through that dark.

When we got up to the Mattick place he said, "Here?"

"In the shed," Pete said.

"In the shed?" the sheriff asked, incredulous.

"Yes sir," Pete said. "Tucked into the barrel there."

The sheriff headed for the shed. I liked the way he walked; he didn't care if he made noise or not. The one light was still on in the house, but Mattick didn't come out. The sheriff went into the shed and made for the barrel and had him a good look. Then he swore and said, "That ain't Eddie Larsen—that's Dink O'Day."

"He buried an empty box, Mattick did," I said.

That seemed to make the sheriff real sore and he headed right off for the house. While we were walking across the yard, Mattick opened the door and stood there in the lighted doorway. I guess that for a second he didn't know who it was because he said out, "Is that you, doctor?"

Then the sheriff, still walking, in powerful motion now, sure and steady and resolute, said, "What do you need a doctor for, Jack?" Then he was on the porch, in the light, facing Mattick, bigger than Mattick, and stronger, and with the badge, the authority; so when Mattick saw the shed door hanging open and he tried to break away he never had a chance, the sheriff moving—countermoving—with him and catching him by the arm and throwing him against the wall. Mattick gave the sheriff a fierce look like a caught animal.

"Dink died of a fit, eh?" the sheriff said. "Maybe from your fit, eh?" he said, taking Mattick by the shoulders and pulling him away from the wall and then throwing him back against it again.

"Lay off, Rice," Mattick muttered.

Then the sheriff collared him good and led him off while Pete and me followed behind and Pete said, "I've got it half figured in my mind."

But I couldn't figure it nohow and when it was all told then Pete confessed that it had been too complicated even for him to have totally figured.

What it was was this, as we heard Mattick tell it in the jail to the sheriff and all the others:

Mattick had caught Eddie Larsen in his shed trying to steal some cider and had lit out after him with a rifle. He shot him down and killed him. Then he'd sent Dink over to that doctor in Little Village, the other side of the marsh, and sold the doctor the body (the doctor was known to rob graves to get cadavers to do research on). Then Dink started getting frisky about it and tried to squeeze a little money out of Mattick and that had set off Mattick's fierce temper and he had choked Dink to death and then on the day of the funeral he decided he might as well sell Dink's remains to the doctor too, and so that was why he had planted the empty box. He'd been waiting for the doctor to come that night when we were there.

After it was all said and Mattick was locked up, the men took Pete and me over to the Dooley House for a sarsparilla drink.   It was then that Eddie Larsen's father (after vowing to skin that doctor) said, "It has just occurred to me, gentlemen, we all owe Jimmy Grover an apology."

"Wherever he is," somebody said.

"I know where he is," piped up Pete.

"Where?" old Larsen said.

"Well," said Pete, "I'll tell you, but it seems to me the last thing I heard you say regarding Jimmy Grover was that you was giving two hundred dollars for him."

When everybody finished laughing at the one we had on him, old Larsen said, "Well, boy, I had offered that money to see a man hanged.   It'll do my heart better to see him *not* hanged; so the money is still good."

Then the fastest thing anybody in Capstone ever did see was Pete and me rush out of there to fetch Jimmy from that loft and bring him back to respectable society.

Doctor Apollo

Dr. Kessler, a senior psychiatrist and head of the city's Mental Hygiene Clinic, read the morning paper and hurried to Central Homicide. Murder was his specialty. This could be a special kind of murder.

"The kid confessed," Lt. Reed said. "What else is there to know?"

"For you, nothing," Kessler said. "You have your murderer." His nose wrinkled. He disliked the crude odors of police stations. "How's he taking it?"

"Still happy. He didn't try to run or hide. Walked up to patrolman name of Casetta right after he did it, little after midnight, and held up his bloody little hand and the icepick. 'I'm Richard Gorman, sir,' he said. 'I just killed a man.' End of quote."

"He here now?"

"Nope, Juvenile Detention. We're finished with the punk."

"How did his mother take it?"

"How'd you expect she would?" Reed shook his head. "A real floozie. The kid caught her playing house with this guy Laramer. He doesn't want to see his Ma. He wouldn't talk with a public defender either."

Reed grinned. "Sorry, Doc, no previous record of juvenile delinquency, no anti-social tendencies. Normal, well-behaved kid who worked long hours after school in a factory just to help support his poor widowed mother and her assortment of suitors. His employer just can't get over what a nice gentle young man Gorman was. Neighbors think him the sweetest boy ever. You'll have it tough getting a loony diploma for Gorman."

"Just the same," Kessler said evenly, "he stabbed Laramer with an icepick. What was it—thirty-two times?"

"Give or take a few. But the D.A. is going to hang this one."

"You've done your job," Kessler said. His heavily-lensed glasses gave his angularly thin face a bird-like austerity. "Mine can only begin now, because I'm interested in *why* he did it."

"Look at his record! Crazy? Hell, Doc, he just lost his temper! Blew his cork. Can happen to anyone."

"Fortunately for you, Lieutenant, it doesn't always happen every time someone loses their temper."

"I can tell you why he did it. Very simple, Doc."

"Tell me in your simple, easy-to-understand language."

"He hated Laramer's guts. And with good reason. It doesn't make him crazy. Just a revenge killing. And he'll hang for it."

Walking past the park toward Juvenile Detention, Kessler watched a blurring stream of humanity swimming past like fish in a murky aquarium. Hate festered in all of them, but few of them committed murder. Such cases as Gorman's could help illuminate one of the darkest cellars of psychiatry: the psychology of action. Everyone hated, but few carried the emotion out of fantasy into reality and to its logical climax of murder. Why Gorman?

Also, Kessler was particularly interested in murder that resulted from family hatred. Hatred for the father by the son, for example, the classical Oedipus complex. Laramer had not been Gorman's real father, but he had certainly served as a substitute for his father.

On the surface, Gorman's case seemed amazingly similar to the classical patricide cases. Still, Kessler could not be certain until he had a talk with the boy, gave him a few psychological tests, interviewed some of his acquaintances, particularly his mother.

Possibly, for the good of science, Gorman deserved to be preserved from the hangman.

Gorman lay on his bunk in an isolated corner of the detention ward. Grey light through a barred window formed charcoal stripes across his face. A burly female matron resembling a pseudo-woman wrestler stood by the door. Kessler detested stupid miserly taxpayers who assured such attendants because of low pay.

He stood there, unobserved by Gorman, studying him with a deep clinical interest. A slim, rather handsome boy with short blond hair, straight even features. As he walked forward, Gorman sat up and smiled shyly. He was the kind of boy you like the moment you see him.

When Kessler introduced himself, said he was there to help Gorman, that he was no cop, no preacher, no lawyer, and that no one had sent him, Gorman merely smiled timidly and nodded.

It was difficult at first to win the confidence of criminals. But then, Gorman was not, technically, a criminal.

Kessler lit his pipe.

"I think I know how you feel now, Richard. A great relief. You feel free and good about everything now."

Gorman relaxed, appeared to be grateful for this unexpected and sympathetic understanding. A few selective questions elicited answers indicating that Gorman had lived a rather lonely life, misunderstood by everyone, and was, consequently, a stranger to himself.

Kessler explained that he was a doctor and that he only wanted to help Gorman understand something of what had happened. He wanted to be Gorman's friend. He was no judge; he did not blame Gorman for his deed because, though it was socially wrong, Kessler understood thoroughly that the deed had been completely logical to Gorman. "And now you feel good about it," Kessler said. "As if you had been sick at your stomach for a long time and finally managed to throw up."

"Yes," Gorman breathed. His eyes were brighter now. "Yes," he said again, eagerly, reaching out to Kessler like a lonely child who has finally found someone who will listen, who is interested, who won't laugh or ridicule, misunderstand or hit back with a club. "It's like that. Like a big weight was off me."

"I'll be back to see you as often as I can," Kessler said. "I hope you will talk freely, tell me everything you can about yourself, how you've lived, how you feel about things. About Laramer, your mother, your father."

"Why?"

"We want to know why you did it, Richard. For your sake and for the sake of society. You might say it's like looking for a kind of hidden cancer. If we find it, isolate it, we can cut it out."

"It won't bring Laramer back."

"But you're not dead, Richard. There's still a chance for you to return to society, live a normal healthy life. I'm sure you want to whether you can admit it to yourself now or not. But to do that, we must clear this thing up, Richard, understand it."

Gorman clenched his hands. "What's there to understand? I mean, I know why I did it. I hated his guts."

It was, Kessler thought, a most convenient term. One word. Hate. Launch wars with it. Blow up the world with it.

"Hate is common enough," Kessler said gently. "But why did you have to kill Laramer?"

"I hated him that much." Gorman put a cigarette between his lips. Kessler offered his lighter. "Thanks, sir," Gorman said and looked up at the barred prison window.

It was obvious that the boy was repressed, unaccustomed to talking. He began awkwardly, groping for words, but then the intensity of emotion seemed to assume command and he poured out his hostility and justifications, and was astonished by his own verbosity.

Everything had been good until his father was killed in an industrial accident five years ago. His father, he said, had been good to him, bought him things, boxed with him, taken him to the gym. His father and his mother quarreled a lot, but that was all right, because she was a nagger.

The small note recorder in Kessler's pocket faithfully preserved Gorman's testimony.

" . . . then when Dad died, she started having guys in all the time. I was like a stranger around there and she didn't care about me anymore except that I worked in the goddamned bakery and brought home my pay every week . . . and she didn't bother cooking for me anymore or helping me . . . but these guys, especially Laramer, she couldn't do enough for him . . . washing his underwear, cooking his meals . . . he didn't marry her, see, but he practically lived there, moved in, took over . . . and he was a lush, a drunken bum and he started beating hell out of me all the time, but she didn't care, didn't say anything . . . she just took my pay and bought things for Laramer, clothes and wine, cigarettes and beer . . . he started kicking me out of my own house and beating hell out of me . . . bigger than me and a tough kind of guy . . . and when he was there all night he wouldn't let me in the house, and I'd walk around, sleep in the park . . . and he hit her too . . . I'd come back in the morning and she'd have a black eye, two black eyes, but she'd be fixing him breakfast just the same, never fixing me any . . .''

"But you never told anyone about it, did you?'' Kessler said. "You could have told someone. That would have helped.''

"How? Who would have done anything? And anyway, I guess it was sort of an honor thing. Didn't want people to know what kind of woman she was. Like honor in the family . . .''

Highly moral cover-up for a deep unconscious conflict, Kessler thought. Love for the mother, hatred for the rival.

"' . . . and then I came in last night making plenty of noise so they'd know I was there . . . and they was in the bedroom and I heard them laughing at me . . . so I got the icepick and went in there . . . after that, like you say, I felt so good. I don't care what happens to me now. No matter what happens, it's better than what I had before. Who can live in that kind of setup? I had to do it. They can hang me or anything they want, I don't care. It was worth it.''

Gorman sat up suddenly and raised his fists toward the window. "I'm not sorry. He had it coming. I ought to have done it the first time I saw him! I ought to have killed him right then. I hated him, that's all. I hated his guts!''

A mask of interest covered Kessler's face as he sat and listened. But his thoughts were busy inside working out a neat clinical pattern. It certainly appeared to be another classical Oedipal complex situation, with interesting variations worthy of further study. There were the usual typical elements. The normal boy exploding into savage murder. His youthfulness. The murder occurring in his mother's bedroom. After the murder, no desire to avoid punishment. No guilt, no regret. The usual justification of family honor. It all added up. Kessler made his decision without bothering to interview Mrs. Gorman.

Richard Gorman certainly was worth saving from the hangman's noose.

Gorman was a fine specimen. For a moment Kessler saw him as a kind of golden-furred guinea pig, then guiltily dismissed the image as being too cruel. No, Gorman was a bit like cancerous tissue that should be isolated, preserved for study, in order to prevent the disease from spreading.

No, not quite that either. Gorman was like those canaries miners carry in cages to give warnings of the first approach of dangerous gases.

"That's all there is to it, sir. I hated his guts."
Weeks passed. It wasn't easy to get Gorman to think of himself in a less primitive manner, and in a more sophisticated and complicated way. It wasn't easy to get Gorman to delve deeper into the complex regions below the level of conscious awareness.

But Kessler managed it. Gorman's insights developed slowly bit by bit. Kessler talked to him, listened to him, gave him routine psychological tests.   The Rohrshach, word association, picture-frustration tests, an Intelligence test.   Gorman was illiterate, ignorant, but far from stupid.   Because of his being cut off from his true self, his school work had been a failure.   He had never read anything but a few comic books.

All of that changed slowly at first, then with astonishing rapidity.   Gorman became not only an omnivorous reader, but he proved to possess an amazing retentive memory.

He became fascinated with the literature recommended by Kessler, whom he began to regard as a kind of God.   And Kessler did not select Gorman's reading indiscriminately.   For he believed in giving a patient literature that seemed to have a special application to his problem.

Gorman's basic conflict situation derived from the Oedipus complex.   Kessler was certain of this, so he recommended *Hamlet*, and Sophocles, *King Oedipus*, *Oedipus at Colonus*, and the story of *Orestes*.   And he found it very interesting that Gorman identified himself with Hamlet, rather than with Oedipus, and seemed especially intrigued by the Closet Scene.

Gorman developed a sense of his own importance, worthiness, and responsibility for self.   Vital insights occurred with increasing rapidity.

"Sure," Gorman said.   "Plenty of guys' fathers die, and their mothers start making out with other guys, and plenty of guys hate their mothers' lovers.   But now I see how you can hate your mother's lover, even hate your own father because of their relationship with your mother."

But he had some difficulty understanding why Laramer was the same as his father, when Laramer was a drunken brutal bum, and his father had been a nice guy.

Kessler explained.   "Your father was dead, so you could idealize him.   He probably wasn't quite as perfect as you made him out to be.   You could switch all of your suppressed hostility toward your real father onto Laramer.   It was easier to hate Laramer openly, because he wasn't your real father, but at the same time had assumed your father's role.   Not only could you hate him openly, but you could let this desire to kill him build up in you.   And finally you could actually kill him, without guilt."

Gorman nodded.   His eyes were bright now with pride and awe of himself.   "Just like Hamlet," he said.   "Just like Hamlet in the book."

"That's right.   Just like Hamlet, Prince of Denmark."

Gorman stretched out on the bunk in the jail.   "It sure makes more sense to me now.   Here I thought I did it just because I hated his guts."

"Do you have some feeling now for why you did it, Richard?"

"Oh, sure.   Wasn't because I hated him.   Hate is only a symptom of a deeper conflict.   I hated him because he stood for my father.   And I always unconsciously hated my father, because I was always jealous of his position with mother.   So this hate built up inside me for years, but I kept it down and hidden and I didn't know it.   I couldn't do anything about it for a long time, not while Dad was alive, because I felt too guilty about wanting to murder my own father when all the time he seemed like such a nice guy. Then when Laramer came along, I could do it. It was sort of like Hamlet there too. And there was this phony family honor business. I understand all that now."

Kessler took off his glasses and wiped his eyes. "Yes," he whispered, barely able to control his own emotion. "The classical Oedipus complex. Just remember the dynamics of the complex. You acted from a primary repressed hostility against the father image as the envied rival for your mother's affection."

Kessler stopped himself. He had a tendency to slide off into a lot of technical jargon at times. He did not believe in that sort of thing, especially with illiterates. That stuff was for textbooks, stuffed shirts, intellectuals at cocktail parties, that stuff was canned language. Sometimes it was necessary for communication.

It was *very* necessary if you were to impress the Lunacy Commission.

Meanwhile, Gorman had, of course, been charged with murder, transferred from Juvenile Detention to jail, back to JD, back to jail, into homicide court.

Kessler prepared a voluminous brief that explained Gorman's deed in highly complex language and then he appeared before the Lunacy Commission.

Gorman had protested against the idea of being labeled crazy.

"But without a favorable recommendation to the court by the Lunacy Commission," Kessler explained, "they can hang you. You're charged with murder."

"But I wasn't crazy," Gorman said.

"Just the same I've got to convince the Lunacy Commission that when you killed Laramer you didn't know the difference between right and wrong." He tried to explain the technicalities of what constituted legal insanity.

"But we know I wasn't crazy," Gorman shouted, and almost broke into tears. "We've worked it all out. I was just the victim of a compulsion neurosis."

"I have to plead insanity to save your life, and that's what I'm going to do," Kessler insisted. "You're just beginning to awaken, just beginning to find out what life can mean. You've got to be saved."

So Kessler appeared to testify before the Lunacy Commission considering Gorman's case, and save him. After six hours of overwhelming clinical evidence, truly a virtuoso performance, he proved that Gorman was legally insane at the time of the murder, according to the definition of insanity the law provides. He proved the existence of irresistible impulse. He proved that Gorman suffered from an almost specific disorder in the discrimination between right and wrong, and that he had regarded as moral, and even heroic, a deed that was most abhorrent to the conscience of normal man.

The Commission accepted Kessler's opinion. Gorman was committed to a state asylum for the criminally insane.

Kessler deplored conditions in state asylums. Publicity to the contrary, he knew most of them for what they really were behind false fronts. Modernized bedlams, sadistic keepers, pitifully inadequate staff supervision.

He arranged for Gorman's subsequent transfer to a private sanitarium known as Green Valley Manor on which Kessler served as a part-time resident staff member and which he had helped found and develop.   Here conditions were ideal for the advanced treatment of those who could be saved.

Green Valley Manor resembled a lovely lakeside resort.   Parklike grounds contained numerous small cottages, each reserved for guests, some of whom were wealthy enough to pay fifteen hundred dollars a month, and a few others who paid what they could afford, which was sometimes nothing at all.   These special cases, such as Gorman's, were admitted on the recommendation of one of Green Valley Manor's clinical staff.

Fountains played in the shadows of Grecian columns, and Greek and Roman statues sometimes seemed to dance in the shaded glades.

On the day that Gorman was admitted to Green Valley Manor, Kessler personally showed him about the grounds.   They walked past the violent ward, and a building given over to shock therapy.   The building somewhat resembled an old world pavilion with fluted columns and a statue of Neptune replete with seaweeded triton. There was also a place called Seclusion Cottage, but Kessler assured Gorman that he would never become acquainted with it.

Kessler opened the door of Gorman's private cottage and they went in.   Gorman sat down and lit a cigarette and looked about him with shy gratitude, and seemed incapable of adequate comment.

"Well, Richard, this will be your home for some time.   I am sure you will find it much more comfortable and reasonable than conditions on the outside."

Gorman nodded.

"You can study and grow here with comparative freedom.   You may see me whenever you like.   You'll find understanding and sympathy here.   Few of those here are in any position to level the accusative finger.   Your new life begins here, Richard.   One day you'll go back out there, a healthy normal young man.   You'll marry, have kids."

"Thanks to you, sir."

Kessler smiled with slight embarrassment at the open worship in Gorman's voice and shining from his eyes.   Hastily, he said, "From now on you'll be more and more on your own.   You must start to become independent of me.   You must realize that no doctor is as important as you think.   I am not God—not even his cousin."

Gorman smiled timidly, but did not seem convinced.   This would be, it always was, the toughest part.   The breaking away from the analyst, finally launching oneself into the mainstream as a truly independent person.

The windows were open.   The scent of lilac and wisteria drifted on the warm spring air.   A hummingbird hung suspended in the window, framed like an iridescent and timeless picture.   Pleasant laughter drifted through the shading evening.

Kessler lit his pipe and secretly exalted in the remarkable progress of his patient.

He glanced up and Gorman was going over that special paper Kessler had prepared as a result of his interest in Gorman's case.   Parallel statements.   Excerpts from Hamlet that astonishingly resembled those made by Gorman who, at the time, had been almost an illiterate.

The original motivation for the paper had been Kessler's plan to write a book based on the Gorman case.   It seemed worthy of such treatment and, if handled properly, it might even become a bestseller.

> Gorman: I got so I couldn't sleep.   All night I had these dreams about being chased by Laramer, and it always ended up with my following him because he was scared of me.
> Hamlet: Sir, in my heart there was a kind of fighting that would not let me sleep.

> Gorman: I used to think I was crazy.   Every thought seemed to fit into that one thing—I got to kill Laramer.
> Hamlet: A document in madness: thoughts and remembrance fitted.

> Gorman: I don't want anything to do with women.   If I don't let them nab me, my mother will stop having men come around.
> Hamlet: Get thee to a nunnery!

> Gorman: My father came to me in a dream and said you're old enough to do something.   Don't let Laramer do these things to your mother.
> Hamlet: Let not the royal bed of Denmark be a couch for luxury and damned incest!

What an amazing transformation, Kessler mused.   Now Gorman comprehended emotionally and intellectually the basis of his compulsive murdering of Laramer. And now his attitude toward women would begin to change, just as Hamlet's had toward Ophelia.

Gorman understood so much, where before he had understood nothing, felt nothing but primitive hate.

Now that the old limbs had been cut from the tree, new, fresh, normal healthy limbs were free to grow.

Somewhere, someone was softly strumming a guitar.

Gorman looked up.   His face glowed.   "I figure that I, personally, am about at the grave-digging scene in Hamlet.   You know, where the Prince begins to see things right, and understands how he feels, really feels, about Ophelia?"

"Yes."   He even speaks so differently, Kessler thought.   Carefully, almost like an actor.

Gorman hesitated only a moment, then whispered, "I think—think I'd like to see my mother."

Kessler sat up rather stiffly.   "What?   Why?"

"I've been thinking about her so much lately.   I dream about her now.   I thought of her and it made me cry yesterday."   He went to the window and looked up at the evening sky.   " 'Thy sin destroyeth thee.' "

Kessler stared at him, puzzled.   And for some reason, a bit irritated.   Then he got a flash of insight into himself.   He had his own difficulties with women.   He had married once and was divorced, and now he was unmarried.   He had told himself that he remained single because he could not afford to devote necessary time to domesticity. Self-analytical work, however, seemed to reveal deeper motives, certain suggestions of hostility toward women. Now he recalled that one interview with Mrs. Gorman, and how vulgar and animal-like she had been—that is, as an impressive image. Not, of course, as a human being.

He managed quite successfully, he thought, in keeping his personal emotional problems out of his work. But for some reason now, he realized that he had been carefully keeping Mrs. Gorman out of this psychoanalytical process as much as possible.

And now, in retrospect, he recalled Mrs. Gorman's skirt, tight and revealing over wide hips, and the swell of large breasts, and the way her lips had curled as she invited him in. He had since felt only a sort of revulsion toward her because of her treatment of Richard, and her promiscuous, irresponsible nature.

"What was that, what did you say, Richard? Wasn't that part of a quotation from *Orestes?*"

Gorman half turned. "I think so. Anyway, I've been reading *Orestes* more and more, and thinking of my mother more. I'd like to see her. I feel different about her now. I feel like I could be—well—my real self with her now. But there's still this hostility toward girls. It isn't right. If I'm ever going to go back out there and live a normal healthy life, get married and have kids, I've got to like girls. That's an area that hasn't been dug into enough yet. It ought to be cleared up. Sir, I'd like to talk with my mother again."

"I—I think it can be arranged."

"Has she wanted to see me?"

Kessler shifted uneasily. "Why—why, yes."

"When can I see her?"

"When would you like to see her, Richard?"

"Soon as I can. It's like I'd never known I even had a mother. I know that unless I get straightened out with her, I'll never get well. I'll never like girls. She's the key. Like in the books."

Pleased, but still a bit upset by something, Kessler stood up.

"I'll see if I can have her out here tomorrow evening. Visiting hours are from five to seven. You can entertain her here in your private cottage."

"Thank you, sir. I think I can learn a lot of important stuff from her."

At five after seven the following evening, Kessler saw Gorman striding eagerly up the graveled walk toward the front porch of the administrative building where Kessler sat at a marble-topped table sipping brandy and smoking his pipe. Gorman waved, then hurried on and jumped up the steps three at a time. This evening the boy seemed positively radiant.

Gorman sat down opposite Kessler and stretched his legs and stared through the trees shading into evening and at the silent bats dipping and weaving against the sky.

"Well," Kessler finally said, "was it as enlightening as you hoped it would be?"

"Yes. I think this thing about girls will clear up fast now."

"You had a good visit?"

"I knew it would be. I left her there. I wish you'd see her again before—"

"Before what?"

"Before something happens to everything."

Kessler studied the boy, the flushed face, his high look of joy.

Gorman said, "I want to explain something first. We—we made some mistakes. Basically you were right. I mean the Oedipus complex. It was a family thing. But it wasn't all that—you see—"

Kessler was pleased, happy at this indication of the boy's self-sufficiency in working out his own problems. "Did you expect me to be omniscient? For me to know everything, that is?"

"I over-idealized you for a while, I think. But then I got to thinking of how we left mother out of the picture all along. I reread Orestes. And then I realized I didn't really have an Oedipus complex at all. It was an Orestes complex . . ."

Kessler frowned. "How do you figure that?"

"Aren't both those complexes sort of the same?"

"In a way. Both are varieties—"

"There's the overattachment to mother," Gorman said, watching the bats. "The hatred for women, the guilt—like with Hamlet—"

"Hamlet didn't kill his mother," Kessler said, irritated again.

"He would have though," Gorman said. "In the Closet Scene, remember? That's when he kills Polonius. He was ready for murder—the murder of his mother—or he couldn't have done what he did. He didn't know Polonius was there. But he hears him and he turns and stabs him, right through the curtain, right then and there, kills him. Polonius was a substitute for Hamlet's mother. Just as Laramer was a substitute . . ."

Kessler tried to interject something, he wasn't quite sure what.

Gorman turned, his eyes glowing. "So you see it adds up now. Overattachment to mother, then you have to kill her so you can be a man. So you can love another woman. It starts out attachment and ends up hate."

Gorman stood up and leaned toward Kessler, who felt an odd inability to move.

"When I was a kid, sex was taboo to me and my playmates. But it wasn't to her. She was no good. I dreamed I shot her with a rifle. I think of Orestes saying 'I kill thee not . . . thy sin destroyeth thee . . .' "

Kessler was running wildly down the curving gravel path, under blurring patches of shade and frozen green splotches of leaves. His breath came with difficulty, as if he were a fish out of water, as he ran down the steep path toward the private cottages by the little singing stream. His throat felt dry. There was some sort of terrible pressure in his chest as he ran, but he felt startlingly alive in some way, and his mind was frighteningly sharp.

Dimly behind him Gorman was running, following. His eager footsteps were unbelievably loud and cracklingly distinct on the gravel. And his voice called out over and over through the twilight like that of a plaintive child calling after an abandoning father.

Then Kessler was stumbling back out of the cottage and half-falling through the brush toward the rushing stream. He kept seeing Mrs. Gorman as something not human, lying there naked and lifeless on the bed. The limbs he saw as those of a partly broken statue found in an old ruin, and the threading lines of blood in her punctured face and from the knife wounds in her throat and breasts as cracks that appear in very ancient statues, perhaps of Athena, that indicate authenticity and that cannot really appear in imitations.

It's odd, he thought, but it's the first time I ever could look upon a dead woman.

And then Kessler knew. I hated her too, he thought. I always hated women.

He fell to his knees, half in the cooling water—in a shade so thick, it was the entire world of night after sundown.

Gorman knelt beside him, squeezing his shoulder and sobbing with ecstatic joy.

"I'm really well now, really purged. It wasn't complete, sir, before. I feel so much better now than before, like I got wings."

Kessler lifted cool water up and let it trickle on his face. He seemed to hear a strange chorus chanting through the shade. His eyes closed in a moment of intense reverie. Of all the myths, he had been least interested in that of Orestes. It was the one Greek tragedy he had neglected, and had never bothered even recalling until now.

In Mycenae, Greece, after the Trojan War, wasn't it? And Orestes, that young man of high birth and noble appearance, murdered his mother. He told the worthy citizens that he had done this thing because of his mother, because she had dishonored his family. She was guilty of adultery. He was tried in the city of Athens and was acquitted, and the Furies who pursued Orestes seeking vengeance for the murder were called off by Athena, the Goddess of Wisdom.

"It's all right now," Gorman was saying from somewhere a long way off. "It was just the wrong complex. We thought it was one, but it was the other. Now it's straightened out, though, isn't it? Isn't it, sir?"

Kessler dipped his hands in the cooling water and watched it curl back in a slow heavy fashion from his fingers like crystal syrup, and he remembered who it had been who told the young noble Orestes to kill his mother.

The chorus seemed to rise to a crescendo all around, drowned his thought as he whispered, "Look at me, Richard. Look at me—don't you know—my name is Apollo . . ."

HOLLY ROTH

The Pursuer

When the door of her apartment had clicked behind him, Talia got off the couch, went over to the door, and pushed up the button that engaged the double lock. Then she paused and waited for her knees to steady. When they were under control, she crossed the room and switched on a lamp. Then she went into the bedroom, turned on the overhead light, and turned off the recording machine. She walked to her bedside, forgot why she was there, and then remembered. She reached into the side compartment of the small desk that served as her bedside table and brought out the telephone. She dialed the operator, and when the voice said, "This is the operator. Can I help you?" she replied, "I want the police, please."

"What is your number, please?"

Talia held the receiver away and looked at it. Then she rehung it on its cradle.

She got the telephone book from beneath the desk and looked up the local precinct number and dialed it.

She started to speak almost before the man had finished his few words of precinct identification. "Now, listen to me," she said. "I understand that the first thing the police want is one's name and address. I'm not going to give you those, and I'm not going to stay on the phone long enough for you to trace the call. If you *can* trace dial calls." The afterthought seemed irrelevant, and for a minute her mind went blank.

"Look, lady." The voice at the other end was tired. "How about you tell me what you *are* going to tell me insteada what you're not?"

"No, I'm not going to tell this story to a dozen people a dozen times. I want someone important."

"All right! All right! But I can't give you to anyone else until I know who to give you to, can I? If I decide to plug you onto *anyone,* I gotta know which one, don't I? Different departments, different cops, different jobs. See?"

That made sense. She said, "I'm being blackmailed. That's why I don't want to tell it to everyone."

The voice turned faintly coaxing. "But how's anyone gonna come to see you if we haven't got your address?"

Talia was suddenly exhausted. She said, "I've always heard—read, understood—that the police were no help in matters of blackmail. That people either paid, or killed, or got killed. I—"

The policeman's voice turned serious. Until that moment he had been humoring her, but now something—her words? a truth?—had reached through to him. He said, "One minute, I'll connect you."

It was more than a minute. She wondered again about the tracing of calls and thought, I'll have to chance that.

The wire came alive. A new voice said, "Lieutenant Bonner speaking. What's this all about? Who's blackmailing who and why don't you behave and give us your name?"

A bully, Talia thought. Like Bart. A type she knew well. He would not be helpful. She brought her voice to a careful, unexcited monotone. If she could impress him with her steadiness, her sanity . . . "My name is Cory—"

"Well, Mrs. Cory—"

"Miss Cory. Please listen for a minute. I am being blackmailed. I was also—hit. And I was threatened with a knife. I want to tell someone about it. That's the law, isn't it?"

"Yeah, but—"

"And I don't want to tell a man at a desk, and then another man at another desk, and so on. So if you will just advise me—"

He roared. "*Wait* a minute! How can anyone—important or not—come to see you and talk to you if you won't give us your address? —What's your first name?"

"My phone is not listed. So what good would my first name do you?" But this was the police; unlisted phones wouldn't hinder them. She said, "I don't want anyone to come to see me." To come into her place, to clog her three quiet rooms, to add to the sacrilege that had already desecrated her living room . . . "I want to go there. But where do I go, whom do I ask for?"

He grunted. "All right, all right. You can come here. Write it down." He gave her the address. "If you come over right away you can ask for me. Lieutenant Bonner. *Are* you coming over now?"

"No." She couldn't. She wouldn't be able to make it.

"When, then?"

"In the morning?"

"In the morning ask for Lieutenant Corelli."

"How early?"

"He comes on at eight."

"Thank you."

"Wait! Look, lady—Miss Cory—if this stuff is on the level, how d'ya know you're going to be okay, safe, until tomorrow?"

"I'll be all right." She looked around the small room. "I'm safe here. Thank you." She hung up.

She said to the uniformed policeman behind the big desk on the platform high above her, "May I see Lieutenant Corelli, please?"

"What about?"

"I have an appointment."

He grunted, reached for an old-fashioned telephone with a standing mouthpiece and said, "Lieutenant Corelli." After a minute he said, "Lieutenant? A lady to see you. Miss—" He raised his eyebrows at Talia and then repeated after her, "Miss Cory . . . Yeah, Lieutenant." He hung up. "Upstairs." He nodded at the stairway just outside the door to the big room. "Second floor. End of the hall. Room two-ten."

She said, "Thank you," and went out to the stairs.

The door to Room 210 was open, and a heavy-set man in shirt sleeves sat facing her across an expanse of desk, his head bent over a mass of papers. Her first thought was that the desk was too big for the room; then she noticed the walls— they hadn't been painted, she thought, in at least ten years. She stood, waiting for a second, and then she knocked on the open door.

The man looked up.

There was an empty moment, after which he registered surprise as thoroughly as an actor who had been trained for a lifetime in the art. Then, in one hasty motion, he stood up. He said, "Miss Cory?" His voice, even in those two short words, struck her as beautiful. Every consonant got equal rights, and the tone came from deep within him. But deep wasn't far, she thought; he was only five eight or nine inches tall, a stocky man. He had a pleasant face, despite a network of wrinkles—premature wrinkles, she decided; he had reached no farther than early middle age.

"Yes. And you are Lieutenant Corelli?" He nodded. "Lieutenant Bonner told me—"

"Yes, I know. He left me a report. Come in, please. Sit down. And let me take your, ah, bag."

Reflexively, her grip tightened on the small but rather heavy box. "I'll put it right here beside the chair, thank you."

"Fine. Now will you start from the beginning? And may we have it taken down?" He added quickly, "If we decide we can help you I won't be permitted to do so until I have a statement. So it would save you from going through the explanation all over again."

. She nodded. "Certainly. I've come to make a statement. And my—stubbornness on the phone was just to avoid saying it all over and over again. I had no other reason."

His mouth turned upward in a slow smile. It grew very wide and she saw then where his wrinkles had come from. His entire face took part in the smile, and the exercise had told on it through the years. He said, "I shouldn't admit it, but I think you may have been smart. You sure would have told it a few times. If it's—important." He raised his voice and called, "Sergeant!" A man in uniform, its jacket unbuttoned, came through a door opposite her. Corelli said, "A statement to be taken, Sergeant." The man disappeared into the back room, reappeared with a shorthand book, and sat behind Talia, beside the open door. Not then or ever did she hear him speak.

Corelli said, "Start with your full name and address, Miss Cory."

She gave him that. He nodded. "And your age?"

"Almost twenty-eight."

"All right. Go on."

She went on: "Four months and three days ago, on January twenty-first, I came here from my home town, Lafayette, Iowa. It's a small town, sort of a suburb of Des Moines. Before I left—on December twenty-third—I shot and killed my brother, Bartholomew Cory."

The wrinkles in Corelli's face twitched. It was too mobile a face, she thought. It would distract her. She raised her eyes and fixed them on the wall above him and to his left. She would forever afterward remember the crumbling paint on the dirty green wall.

"Briefly—and there's no sense in being more than brief; if you want details you can wire Des Moines—Polk County—and they will send you records, I'm sure." On the periphery of her gaze, she saw the nod. "So, briefly, it was like this. My brother came home at three in the morning. Slightly after that, they decided. He had forgotten his keys so he climbed in through the dining-room window. He was drunk. They established that. It wouldn't matter, it wouldn't be—pertinent— except that it accounted for the odd noises he was making. Like a—an animal. Between the fact of the—the guttural noises, and the fact that he didn't sound like himself when he finally spoke, and the fact that after I warned what I thought was an intruder to stop or I'd shoot he still hurled himself through the window at me— well, I shot him. There was a—a hearing; the jury agreed it was an accident. That was—" She looked briefly back at the lieutenant and then refocused on the patch of wall. "That was that, I thought.

"But last night a man came, threatened me, hit—me, demanded money." She waited.

Corelli said gently, "Well, now you have to tell me about that, don't you?"

"No. The beginning only. He phoned me at my office, Krause & Kane, an advertising agency on Fifth Avenue. He said he knew all about me. He used my full name, Natalia Eileen Cory. He was—very threatening. He said he would come to my apartment at eight o'clock. So—"

"He asked for your address?"

She looked down at him. "No."

"But you told Lieutenant Bonner your phone is unlisted. Is that true?"

"Yes." She frowned.

"Well, we'll discuss it later. So he was going to come to your apartment at eight o'clock. And he did?"

"At five minutes past. —Do you have an electric outlet in here?"

"An elec—" He stared at her, but only for a second. Then he stood up so that he could peer over the desk. He looked down at the box and then up at Talia. He said softly, "Well, well," and a new set of muscles came into play on the expressive face.

"Sergeant," Corelli said, and composed himself for listening.

She hadn't played the recording back the night before. She hadn't been sure of how to do so and was afraid she might accidentally reverse and erase it; she had been too tired; and she had been, before her four hours' sleep, afraid to relive the experience.   Now she was relieved to find that the machine operated perfectly, and every sound came through with entire fidelity.   She made her mind as blank as possible and lapsed from rigidity just twice: when she first heard her own voice she felt and showed surprise, and when the cracking sounds came she winced with each blow.

By a quarter to eight she had been ready and waiting.   For the next ten minutes she sat, like a figure caught in a slip of the earth's rotation, motionless, weightless, thoughtless.   The couch faced the door, and her eyes, almost unblinking, were fixed upon that door.

The downstairs door buzzer didn't sound until five minutes after eight, and as she got up to push the release button she could not have said if the period since she had assumed her vigil had been a lifetime or a second.   But with the necessity of motion came thought and response.   She went into the bedroom and turned the switch on the recording machine, adjusted the box behind the door so that the rear crack of the partly open door was near it, and then went and stood at her front entrance.   When she heard steps in the outer hallway she opened the door without waiting for the knocker to be lifted.

The figure outside was shorter than she and very thin.   That was almost all she could see at first because the only light within her apartment came from two shaded lamps and, as a result, the stronger hall lights outlined him and made details difficult to discern.   But, even in that outline, there was something very odd . . .   And then she realized that she had interrupted his preparations; he had a handkerchief folded into a large triangle before his face, and his arms were raised as he tried to tie it behind his head.   The eyes above the handkerchief stared strainingly at her and she saw that he was shocked, probably because she had so nearly caught him undraped.   She had a moment's desire to laugh—this undernourished little man was not the figure of terror her frightened imagination had conjured.   And then she saw the eyes, and the menace, all the menace that had existed in her imagination—and more—was there.   The eyes had enormous pupils and a peculiar lack of focus, and when he spoke his reedy, high-tenor voice did nothing to lessen the threat.   He said, with a flat lack of intonation that sounded particularly odd in the high voice, "Close the door.   Just leave it a little open.   Right away!"

She obeyed, almost as a reflex action.

The voice came around the door: "Now turn off the lights in there."

She moved across the room and switched off her lamps.   The room was still surprisingly well lighted; on a spring evening, New York glows.

The door opened and quickly closed, and the latch clicked.

He said, "Sit down," and she sank onto the couch.

The small man moved with a sidling motion until he was in front of the wing chair that faced the couch; then he sat on its edge.   He did not remove his hat. (It looked too large for him, Talia thought, or was it because such juvenile types usually didn't wear hats?) The two screens—the hat's broad brim and the hand-kerchief—combined to make an amazingly effective shield.   She could see nothing but the narrow strip of face that contained the unnatural-looking eyes. His brows were in the shadow of the brim; his ears were hidden by the handkerchief; the hair at the sides of the head was identifiable as hair only because one knew it was there—but for all she could tell, it could have been purple. With only those straining, staring eyes as guide she couldn't begin to place the man. But perhaps she didn't know him.

He said, and there was venom in every high quavering note, "You're the kind that comes out on top. You always do. In every moment of your life. This time you kill a man, and what happens? You get away from everything and come out on top."

That was true enough, Talia thought numbly. Not that she had always come out on top, but that she had this one time.

He said, "So I'm going to even things a bit."

He seemed to be waiting. Talia said, "Yes?"

"I'm going to take some of your money."

"This is very foolish," Talia said evenly. "What you are discussing is called blackmail—"

The high voice reached higher, into a kind of piercing whisper: "Don't you call me foolish, and don't you dare patronize me! Understand?" There was hate in his voice and killing in his eyes, and she realized she was terribly afraid. It was a particularly dreadful fear to be made so frightened by so inconsequential a little man.

She kept her voice even and tried to keep any intonation, patronizing or otherwise, out of it: "What I'm trying to say is that I *don't* understand. To be blackmailed, a person has to have a secret worth paying to keep, and the money to pay with. I haven't either."

"That's part of your arrogance. You earn a hundred and fifteen dollars a week, don't you?"

She looked at him blankly. How did he know?

"Or didn't you ever bother to figure it out? Six thousand a year is a hundred and fifteen dollars a week. So you must take home just about ninety dollars a week."

He waited. She said, "Yes."

"Well, *I* don't. So we're going to share things a little more evenly. I want thirty dollars every week. That won't bring me up to ninety, but it'll put me ahead of you, and I want to be—I *belong* ahead of you."

"But *why* should I pay you? Even a nickel?"

He laughed. The sound was somewhere between a snicker and a neigh, and she had a momentary fear that she would be sick as she saw that his eyes, luminous and staring in the room's dim light, didn't change at all, didn't get even slightly narrower. "Would you like all those innocents in—the place you work—to know that you are a murderess? To know all about you?"

"No." She swallowed and went evenly on. "No. I wouldn't. But I wouldn't pay anyone anything to keep them from knowing. I might leave my job, and just get another one.   And if you told the people at the next job, then I'd get another, and so on forever.   If you earn less than I, I don't see how you could afford to keep following me around.   And I don't see what good it would do you.''

The man got off his chair and walked unsteadily toward her.   A minute later she realized she should have been afraid, but her immediate reaction was that he must have been even more frightened than she because his knees were shaking even more than hers.   But as he stood over her and she looked from his legs up to his eyes, she saw that it was not fear but rage that caused his trembling.   And then he slapped her.   He was wearing heavy brown-leather gloves.   Very unsuitable for the weather, Talia thought.   And felt the pain.   The heavy leather cracking across her face sounded like a shot in the quiet room.   A series of shots, she thought, as his hand fanned back and forth so that first the gloved palm hit her left cheek and then the back of the hand hit her right cheek, in a volley of slow, deliberate, stinging blows.   Talia sat as still as the rocking blows permitted, and stubbornly refused to let herself cry.   There was nothing so degrading as physical violence.   That was what had made Bart so dreadful.   But Bart had never hit *her*, Talia—he had never dared.   This little man, half Bart's size, dared, and he got away with it.   Because in his left hand, inches from her breast, he held a knife. The light gleamed off its long length in a single piercing ray, since its tiny width offered little surface for reflection; the knife had been honed until it was not much more than a stiletto.

Talia sat as still as possible.   She didn't want to die.   And the little man would kill her.   There was no doubt at all about that.

Then his hand stopped its deliberate fanning motion and he backed slowly away, back to the wing chair, and perched on its edge once more.   "Now," he said, and his voice sounded more relaxed.   "You see?   You mustn't be impertinent. Even if you are so bold that you don't care who knows you are a murderess, there are two other reasons to pay me.   One is that I'll kill you if you don't.''   He paused.   Then he said, "Do you understand?''

"Yes."   And she believed him.

"And the other is that I know something about that murder that no one else knows.   *You saw him—because the light was on.*   Didn't you?''

I'm not *sure* I saw him, Talia thought.   But the light *was* on.

"So I don't even have to warn you about staying away from the police.   You have a lot more to fear from them than I have.''   He stood up.   "I'll phone you. I'll tell you how to pay me the money.   Exactly thirty dollars every week.   In a post-office box, I think.   I won't see you for a while.''   He moved toward the door and put his hand on the knob.   Then he turned back and faced her.   "But later—after I've taught you your place—we're going to become very good friends. Intimate.''

The door closed behind him.   Gently.

When the recording had run its course, the sergeant had halted it, and she had refastened her eyes on the wall.

The lieutenant asked, "Those cracking sounds—is your face swollen, Miss Cory?''

"Yes."

"Um." Then the next words were snapped out. "Is that machine yours?" Her startled eyes came down to his. "No."

"Where'd you get it?"

"Borrowed it."

"Where?"

"From a neighbor."

"Name?"

"Richards. James Richards. He lives in the apartment directly below me. He also works for an ad agency, and he once told me that he sometimes taped TV and radio programs."

"He's a good friend? You told him why you wanted the machine?"

"No. He's only a—an elevator acquaintance." When she first moved in, Richards had tried to be somewhat more than that, but Talia—frozen into her solitude—had snubbed him. Last night he had been a little stiff at first, but was too nice to maintain the attitude. "I didn't tell him anything. I was going to say that I wanted it for the same reason he used it, but he asked no questions and so I didn't have to lie. He showed me how to work the machine, to run a tape, to erase. And that was all." Except that he had been very kind.

"Um. You behaved with—admirable—dispatch and forethought Miss Cory."

Was that sarcasm? She said, "I've read all the stories that everyone else has read about blackmail. This seemed the best way to handle it."

"Um." He sat back in his chair and then moved quickly forward again. She moved instinctively backward. *"Were* the lights on when you shot your brother?"

"Yes."

"And you didn't say so? To the police? To the court?"

"No one asked me."

"And you didn't volunteer the information."

It was a statement. She said nothing.

"Um. I gather that you were supposed to have shot at a prowler. *Did* you know who it was?"

No amount of rapid-fire questioning could draw a fast answer to that. She had spent hours thinking about it, and she thought again now. "No," she said at last. "Possibly—in that very last second—possibly I might have known. But it was too late then."

"Didn't you like your brother?"

Talia took a deep breath, and said, "That is beside the point, Lieutenant Corelli. Wire Lafayette if you're curious. The blackmail happened here; the—shooting— was in their—jurisdiction."

"Um." He smiled, but it was a pale, frosty imitation of its predecessors. He said, "Maybe it's foolish of me to tip you, but you seem competent enough to know where the cards lie. So . . . you tell me you were acquitted, Miss Cory. The law of the United States forbids double jeopardy. You cannot be tried twice for the same crime."

She looked at him levelly and then she too smiled. It was the first time she had smiled in that office, and a tiny reflection, a rather surprised reflection, shone back at her from the broad, dark face before her. She said, "Perhaps it's foolish of me to—to tip *you*, Lieutenant Corelli, but you look competent too. Certainly competent enough to find out the simple truth: I was *not* tried for my brother's death. Not even on a charge of manslaughter. There was merely an inquest. I could be put on trial at any time."

"I see." He stared at her with obvious curiosity. There was some other quality in his face, she thought—admiration? He said, "You realize, I imagine, that your statement here is not privileged. I am not a priest, or a lawyer, or a doctor."

"Yes, I know."

"Well, in view of that realization on your part, it was—courageous—of you to come here."

A compliment? Or a threat? She said nothing.

Corelli spoke briskly. "Now this"—he waved at the tape recorder—"this character. Description, please."

She shook her head. "Almost nothing." She explained about the hat and handkerchief. "He was short—"

"How short?"

"Perhaps five feet seven or eight."

Corelli smiled. "Everything is relative. To me that is 'average.' I am five feet eight."

"Oh. But you see, I—"

"You are taller. Yes."

"And also he seemed shorter because he was—diminutive. Thin. Slender. No shoulders to speak of."

"The voice seems very high. Is the recording sound accurate?"

"Yes."

"Um. Then could it have been a woman?"

"A woman?" It was a new thought and she gave it time. Then she shook her head. "I don't know. Perhaps. I don't think so."

"Color of eyes?"

"I don't know."

"But you saw them."

"Yes. But there were no lights on. I think they were colorless."

"Colorless usually means gray."

She shrugged helplessly.

"The same applies to the color of his hair?"

She nodded.

"But he seemed young?"

"Yes."

"His hands?"

"He wore gloves. Thick brown leather."

"You *could* see the color of those?"

She looked at him inquiringly, but the dark face was impassive. "Yes."

"Suit?"

"I don't know. I don't notice men's clothes. Men simply look well-dressed or badly dressed to me. Or gaudy or not gaudy. His suit was gray, I think. Shabby. Not well pressed." She wondered if he didn't believe in the man at all. Her description certainly wasn't very convincing. But there was that recording . . . She looked down at the box.

"I believe he exists, Miss Cory."

The mind-reading made her jump slightly.

"But it is possible," he went on, "that you could have something else—an ulterior motive—in mind. Let's suppose—just suppose—that you were to kill a short, thin man tomorrow. Or a woman. In your apartment."

It was too much to take in all at once, but she trod doggedly along his path of thought. And she got as far as an answer. "In view of my—my history, that wouldn't be very sensible of me, would it? Recording or no?"

He smiled slightly. "No, it wouldn't. But it was just one of several suppositions." He leaned forward. "Listen to me while I play it straight: If your story is the simple truth, there are several noticeable oddities." He put up a hand. "Don't interrupt. I didn't mean the oddities in *your* story; I said was playing it straight. I mean *general* oddities. Let's take the matter of identification: You can't identify this person; he just seems vaguely familiar. Right? But he knows"—he ticked the points off on his fingers—"your middle name, your address—although he would not have been able to find it in the telephone book—your salary. Taking just that much into account, it sounds as if he must work with you. Does that suggest anything to you? Incidents, peculiarities?"

The idea was merely shocking. She showed it. "I am new in my job, of course. I have made no friends in the office. Friends, yes, but not—" She stopped, looked a little helpless, and he nodded to show his understanding. "My position there is—remote. Removed." She struggled to explain. To him, and to herself. "No matter how calmly I seemed to take it, the—the business of my brother's death was—shocking to me. Like in major surgery, the whole body is jolted—well, my mind was jolted. And my habits. My—everything." She looked up at him, and he nodded again. "So my relationships at the office are not—not quite normal. I speak to and am friendly with my superior, Mr. Long, my office mate, Janet Furman, one of the telephone operators, the office boy, one man in the art department . . . a few others." She lifted a hand and let it fall. "And it's all impersonal." She made a discovery and voiced it: "Because *I* am impersonal."

"I understand. But it suggests little in connection with this blackmailer. We come to the second connection: He also sounds like someone you should be able to identify from the past. He discussed your past life. What you 'always' had done. Would you necessarily know everyone in Lafayette?"

She struggled with that. Then she asked, "Are you a New Yorker, Lieutenant?"

He raised his eyebrows. "Yes."

"Then you probably don't know about small towns, and they're hard to explain. It's like— You have high schools here in New York where they have as many as ten thousand students at a time, isn't that so?"

"I went to one."

"Well, then, after four years I imagine you know, in a way, those ten thousand people. Maybe you don't speak to them all, but years later if one becomes famous or if you find yourself with one of them at a party or on a—a committee or something, you'd both probably know you went to school together, isn't that right?"

He nodded appreciatively.

"Lafayette has about eight thousand inhabitants, and I know them all in that same way. There are people whom I do not know well enough to speak to on the streets of Lafayette, but if I passed one of them on Fifth Avenue we'd probably stop and speak. And we'd sound and feel and *be* really friendly."

"Now, that's very clear. So you rule Lafayette people neither in nor out of your speculations." He leaned across his desk. "At the end of our interview I'll take certain standard steps. For instance, I'll have a check made on possible known offenders. That will be a routine police step, and pretty damn foolish. This person is very vindictive about you, very personal. His approach and demands are those of an amateur. But still I'll make that gesture. In addition, I'll ask you to advise us of anything that occurs, any direct contact or anything merely unusual. Then, if and when the person actually approaches you again, I'll take decisive steps. If there should be an attack on you, or anything resembling it, we'll provide police protection. At the moment, there is not enough to warrant that.

"Now, these steps, until the man shows his hand more clearly, are largely defensive. But with the information I have I see no way to go out and *find* this man. Do you?"

She shook her head. He was obviously working up to something. She waited.

"But there *is* a possible way. He probably comes from, or has a connection with, Lafayette, Iowa. Enough to know details of your life. Enough to know that—the lights were on. If you will let me question you—?"

"You *have* been questioning me. I *have* let you."

"You forewarned me that the shooting that occurred in Iowa was not in my jurisdiction."

"Oh. About that. But that is irrelevant."

"I don't think so."

She felt helplessly caught. She could not live in a world in which the little man wandered freely—with a knife like a stiletto—looking for her. Neither could she relive that night before Christmas Eve, with its multiple horrors. But the lieutenant seemed to be saying, "Either you cooperate as I see fit, or I will make only routine gestures." In essence, he would do nothing unless he could put her through a hell. Why? she wondered, and couldn't imagine an answer. What mattered was that she was caught in a classic situation—between two impossibilities. This, a choice of impossibilities, was what drove people crazy. Well . . . the years of coping, existing, enduring that had stiffened her mind stood solidly behind her and gave her the solution, the simple solution: one of the impossibilities would have to be made possible. She asked, "Ask your questions." She wondered why he was looking at her like that. Had her stiffening of will been visible to the eye?

"Right. Who was in the house that night?"

"Everybody. That is, Mollie, Bart's wife; her mother; Junie, my little niece; and my father."

"But *you* dealt with what was supposed to be an intruder?"

"Why, yes." Her surprise showed. "I dealt with everything." She paused. "That sounds disgustingly martyred. It wasn't. It was sheer sense. My father is very, very old. Mrs. Bolling, Mollie's mother, was—is—an invalid. Junie is four years old." She spread her hands.

"And your sister-in-law? The mistress of the house?"

How wonderful it would have been, how simple, if Mollie had been the mistress of the house! "Mollie is timid, nervous. Frightened."

"All right. Now, what happened?"

Just like that. "Well, we heard the noise and—"

"Who's we? Everyone?"

"Oh, no. My father is deaf. Mrs. Bolling pays no attention to things." Except her own hypochondria. "Just Mollie and I."

"It woke you?"

In Lafayette, no one had asked that question directly. She said tonelessly, "I was up."

"Were you usually up at three in the morning?"

In Lafayette, they had accepted a whole set of contradictions without mentioning their existence, to say nothing of inquiring into them. She was fully dressed—so she was up; it was three in the morning, so her senses were blurred with sleep; it was three in the morning, so of course the lights were out. In Lafayette someone had said, "Night before Christmas Eve. Must have been wrapping packages, huh?" He didn't add, "In the dark?" Whichever of the sweet people it had been—and until that Christmas, Talia had not fully realized just how many sweet people there were in Lafayette—whoever it had been had spoken with a kind of tenderness and had not waited for an answer.

The words—the lie-by-implication—that it was the night before the holiday trembled on her lips, but she did not speak them. She said woodenly, "No."

"But you were up that night."

"Yes."

"Well, Miss Cory, why?"

There was a little pause and then he said, "My God, Miss Cory, don't tell me they never asked you that question!"

"No. They didn't."

He stared at her, his face unreadable. It was a homely face, but a very nice one. He was probably a very nice man. She hoped that he would not be the one who would make her life forever unlivable. Then he said something strange: "My God," he said, "they must love you very much in Lafayette."

Yes, she thought numbly, perhaps they had. She felt the tears coming and held them back as she had before—stubbornly. "I was up," she said coldly, "until about one-thirty or two because Mollie was up. Mollie was upset. Mollie was . . ."

How did one describe Mollie, who certainly wasn't crazy but whose fears and weaknesses and clingings sometimes pushed her to the border? How to describe Mollie, product of her mewling mother and vicious father, in a few well-chosen words? Talia found just one word: "Mollie was hysterical," she said frigidly.

"Why?"

"She got—gets—that way. That night she had decided that because Bart was out late he was drinking and that as a result he would—hit—her when he came home."

"And would he have?"

Talia looked back into the distance and discovered something. "Because she so clearly expected him to, he probably would have."

"I see. So you were up until one-thirty or two, you said, with your sister-in-law. And then?"

"Then," Talia said woodenly, "the phone began to ring."

"In *Lafayette?*"

Talia looked at him and then accepted the humor. It even helped. "You're quite right. People do not telephone at two in the morning in Lafayette. They're asleep. In most houses."

"But not in yours?"

"He called often."

"He did?" Corelli asked. And she again thought his voice beautiful.

"Yes."

"And who was this person who called in the night?"

"I don't know."

"What did he say?"

She no longer saw Corelli. She was back in the dark, echoing hallway, with its ceiling lost in the shadows two stories above her, with its ugly, time-blackened, cheap oak paneling; she was looking at the screeching black snake of a telephone, and listening to the whispering, insinuating voice. "I cannot tell you what he said. Unrepeatable things. Over and over. Almost every night. If I hung up, he called again, and I was afraid the ringing would wake everyone. When I left the receiver off the hook, Bart got furious. I was afraid if I did it often Bart would ask why, guess why."

"And why didn't you tell him? Tell the authorities?"

Her mind was still back in Lafayette, seeing the streets, the people on the streets, the library, the school she had gone to, the single traffic light on the corner of Oak and Third. "You don't understand small towns. My house, our household, was looked at queerly. For good reason, I suppose. We were not a—sensible group of people. And I didn't want this to be broadcast, so that people would think—"

"But these calls were *outside* you, outside your house."

"You certainly don't understand small towns," she said tonelessly. "They run on the principle that where there's smoke, there's fire. The voice talked constantly about 'my lover.' I never went out with anyone. When boys asked me, years ago, I said no. And they stopped asking. But he talked about 'my lover' and said—unrepeatable things. They would have tapped the phone. They would have heard what that voice said, and some of them would have repeated those—delicious bits of scandal, those—'' She came back out of Lafayette and said, ''That's why I was awake at three o'clock.''

''And your sister-in-law?''

''She had been asleep for a little while. But the noise, the noise of the—prowler—woke her. She called down over the banister.''

''And then went with you to investigate?''

''And then went to the third floor. After all, there was Junie. She had to protect Junie. She took Junie upstairs with her.''

''I see.'' She thought that perhaps he *did* see. He said, ''And you went into the dining room and shot the man. You thought it was the owner of the voice on the phone?''

''Yes. Exactly. That is . . .'' She stopped.

''At the very last minute you saw it was your brother.''

''Yes.'' He had a kind face, but it was also perceptive. Perhaps he was perceptive enough to understand . . . She sat very straight in her chair and looked directly at Corelli. ''I tortured myself for a while about that. But I won't permit myself to be weak and foolish and give in to imaginings like—like Mollie. Make my own purgatory. The voice had said he would come some night. And he—detailed—what he was going to do. So I was upset, very upset—and there is the whole answer. When I realized it was Bart, I was just about to fire the gun. If I had been normal, perhaps I could have stopped. I wasn't normal, I couldn't stop.'' She paused, and then, surprisingly, smiled faintly. ''While I'm getting it all out, there is this too. You were right in your assumption that I didn't like Bart. He was a mean man, a bully. And he was largely responsible for my being—caught. In that house. In Lafayette. Bart was—well, for instance, my father wanted desperately to go into a home, an old people's home, on the other side of Des Moines. A lovely place in lovely, green grounds. Papa is eighty-two, and he wanted the companionship of people his age, and the care that he needed but didn't want to burden me with. It was an intense desire, a daily prayer, and it was pathetic that he should be denied anything so logical. But Bart wouldn't let him go. Bart said Papa would be shaming him, but what was really in Bart's mind was the house. The house was Papa's, of course, and to get into the Templeton Home everyone has to sign over his property to the Home. It makes perfect sense—they take care of you until you die. Bart said Papa should give him the house and *then* apply to Templeton for entrance. Papa wouldn't do that; he wanted to pay his way.

''Multiply Bart's treatment of Papa by a hundred other such things and you know what Bart was like.''

''Um. Well, thank you, Miss Cory. This will all help—''

''I don't see how,'' Talia commented, out of honesty and a small bitterness at having been forced back to Lafayette.

''No?'' Corelli's wrinkles cooperated to form a vivid question mark. ''Well,

I'll explain, then. Almost every evil springs from a preceding evil. The smallest situations find their seeds in situations that preceded them. Life, all life, is a chain. Your sister-in-law, for instance, did not spring hysterically into being. So when you came here and admitted to the past event, I found it hard to ignore what I consider the plan of life. Out of a shooting like that, such things as your current experience grow. And, incidentally, the only way to break the chain is to—break it. Not try to bury a few links."

Suddenly, surprisingly, the wrinkled face reddened. "Quite a speech for a cop, I guess. But in a way it makes sense that a cop should feel like that, because every day we see those situations growing out of others. Sometimes we come in the middle. Other times we watch the first link forged."

It did make sense for a policeman to be aware of such a "plan of life," Talia thought. But she would have been willing to bet that he was unique in his ability to see and understand it.

The wrinkles had composed themselves to impassivity. "Besides," he said, and his voice was as brusque as he could make it, "in simple police terms, there is something particularly screwy about that recording. That voice on the phone in Lafayette—was it a very high voice, Miss Cory?"

"No." She stared rigidly at him. "It was no voice. He whispered."

"So?"

"It could be." She thought about it. "But this man, yesterday, he didn't say obscene things."

"No, because now he's gone into action."

Talia felt cold.

Corelli rose. "Thank you, Miss Cory. We'll be in touch with you."

Talia stood up very slowly. She reached for the box, but he said, "May we hold onto that?"

"But I have to return it."

"Oh. Well, tell you—leave it for the day and we'll rerecord it. You can pick it up this evening. That okay?"

She nodded.

"I probably won't be here. Just ask for it at the desk downstairs."

She nodded again.

"Thank you, Miss Cory. And—try not to worry."

She was dismissed. As she walked down the stairs, she thought, Not worry? It was only a little after ten o'clock when she rode up thirty-four stories and entered the glass box of an office that she shared with Janet Furman. She did not intend to explain her lateness, to compound small lies, but when she caught Janet looking at her swollen face she answered both unspoken questions with one explanation: "Went to the dentist this morning."

"Oh, you poor kid!" Janet's pleasant contralto was full of sympathy. "The dentist and bra copy, all in one day!"

Half an hour later, Talia struggled up out of lacy comments about the iron strength of sheer wisps of engineering steel and caught Janet's eye. The eye looked hastily away, but it had been filled with curiosity. It occurred to Talia then that one rarely came away from a dentist with *two* distended cheeks—and curiously reddened cheeks, at that.

She made no further explanations. Carl Neilson, who should have been in the art department, manufactured a reason to visit, and commented, "Gained weight, I see." Mr. Long did a doubletake. Even Billy, the office boy, on his interminable rounds of empty-the-outgoing-box and fill-the-incoming-box, looked sideways at her each time he entered their glass box.

She escaped at five minutes to five, to Janet's obvious astonishment; Talia was usually the last one out of the office. She went to the office-equipment store, gave the make and model number of Jim Richards' machine, and bought a fresh roll of tape. Then she stopped at the police station, where a different but no more cordial man sat behind the high desk and, after unnecessary and lengthy explanations on her part, searched for and relinquished the recorder. It had been leaning cozily against his foot.

Home in her apartment, she replaced the role of tape with the newly purchased one, closed and latched the machine, and carried it down a flight of stairs. But her knock on Jim Richards' door brought no response. She went down to the superintendent's apartment, explained that Mr. Richards would call for it, and left the recorder with him. She also got a scrap of paper from him and wrote a note to Richards, telling him where the recorder was and thanking him. She put the note in his mailbox and rode the squeaking elevator back to her apartment.

Then she made dinner, including soup. She drank the soup, scraped the lamb chop into the garbage, and went to bed. But, once there, she stared at the picture opposite her bed, saw the not intended patterns the city's glow brought to eerie life on the canvas, listened for the silent phone to ring, and slept finally at three in the morning. The experience of rigid wakefulness, the strained listening for a telephone's ring, and even the hour at which sleep became possible—none was new to her. But it had been a while since she had suffered it.

The next morning her swollen face had subsided and her cheeks were no longer red, but the result was as unfortunate as the abnormality had been. She looked worn, thin, and tired. She shrugged at the mirror; there was simply nothing to be done about it.

She existed through the day. If her drawn face, her increased remoteness, her total silence drew surprised glances, she was almost unaware of them.

In the late afternoon she was visited by an achingly familiar sensation. In Lafayette, in the early hours of the morning, Talia had increasingly often awakened to an oppressive sense of impending horror. She had inevitably come to associate the awakenings with the whispered phone conversations that almost invariably followed. She had been astonished and frightened by what clearly seemed to be telepathy—and also irritated, since she did not believe in telepathy. But some sort of telepathic phenomenon was certainly at work, whether she believed in the theory or not. There was one occasion when she lay in bed, stiff and tense, waiting, only to have the sensation suddenly depart. And then she knew he had changed his mind.

In the office that day, the feeling came upon her with a force greater than she had ever experienced. She looked up from her papers and through the glass partitions. There was nothing to see, just the usual people and their dimly repeated images, the usual desktops, with their usual clutter.

At five, Janet's swishing departure roused her and she went home. But the feeling of dreadful expectation traveled with her through the congested streets.

In her apartment building, the self-service elevator seemed to move very slowly. She finally reached her floor, opened the door, and then stood in rapidly diminishing light as the elevator door swung automatically to, depriving the black hall of the glow from its interior.

She stood still for no more than a second, and then her mind became acutely active and aware. It was almost as if the dullness she had experienced for two days had been a resting on the part of her mind, a saving-up of its energy in order that it might deal with the emergency she had known would come. And the last hour's fright had been the immediate warning. She took three long, entirely silent sidesteps away from the elevator, moving toward the far end of the hall away from her door. Then she stood still again, breathing in slow, shallow drafts, her mouth slightly open. No sound of her breaths came to her ears. And I am nearer my breathing than he is, she thought. The thought brought a touch of hysteria, and she coldly pushed it away. She might not know where he was, but neither did he know where she was. Not yet.

She devoted a second's thought to the possibility that she was imagining danger where none existed. But the hall lights could not have burned out, because there were three of them. The odds against three bulbs burning out at once were astronomical. Could there have been a short, a blown fuse, a power failure? . . . Her knowledge of electricity died there, and anyway, she realized, it was better to feel silly later than to walk into nameless horror just to prove her bravery to herself. It— And she heard the sound.

He was breathing. She thought with ridiculous pride, he's not as smart as I am. But why did she hear him now when she had not heard him during the preceding moment? Perhaps the elevator's noise—no, it was because *he was coming nearer*.

The hall was in the shape of a square. At her back was the elevator door; on her left was a blank wall—another building was built flush against it. The wall facing her opened to permit the stairwell and, to the far right, her own door. The fourth wall held the doors of the two other apartments. It was from the region of that fourth wall that the sound of breathing came.

But now, in the darkness, she could see—something. For a second she peered intently toward the right, and then, quickly, she dropped her eyelids until her eyes were almost entirely shuttered. What she had seen was a reflection of the little man's eyeballs. They had seemed luminous, she remembered. And he had kept them so wide, so unblinkingly, so trainingly wide.

She moved to her left and around the inverted corner with a big, silent, careful step, a thought-out, planned step. If this went on, they could go round and round forever.

Through her slitted lids she caught repeated glimpses of his shining eyes, increasingly clearer, increasingly nearer. She didn't understand how she could see them. To reflect light, there had to *be* light— And then she felt a terrible, convulsive pain in her chest. My heart leaped, she thought wonderingly. Because I know now that I can't even go round and round . . . She had realized that in a minute she would come to the end of the blank wall she was inching along, using her spread fingertips as a guide, and there, on her left, would be the stairwell, and a faint, almost imperceptible glow was rising from the floor below. It was not enough to light her hallway or to define her outline when she was flat against the wall as she now was, but there was light enough so that her figure would make a greater darkness as she passed it.

But when she made the right-angled turn, before she reached that area of faint light, she would come to the up stairs. They led to the roof, and no light came from that direction. So she would climb them.

Would he know and follow? Probably, she thought, very probably. But she had to try . . .

Jim Richards' voice, funneled up the stairwell, sounded puzzled and apprehensive. He said, "Miss Cory?" There was a moment of utter silence while the man beside her—so near now—stopped the rasp in his throat, apparently stopped breathing altogether. Then Richards said more urgently and more loudly, "Miss Cory!"

She had reached the stairs leading to the roof. She put her foot on the first step and heard the cracking sound as her heel jammed against the riser, and so she gave up silence entirely. She yelled, "Go back, Jim! Go back! He has a knife!" Then, on the second step, she fell.

She hit full on her chin, and in the moment that followed she was deafened by a roaring in her ears. Then she heard the steps, the pounding footsteps of what sounded like a dozen men. And a scuffling. She tried to push herself upward— to help Richards or to run?—and as she placed her hand flat on the stairs a shoe came crushingly down on her knuckles. And through the pain she knew the answer: she was getting up to help; to catch him; to end the nightmare forever. Her other hand went out with intuitive, lightning speed and grabbed the ankle that was flashing past her.

The man fell heavily, and she was aware almost at once of her mistake. The ankle was that of a big man, the weight that fell against her was that of a big man, and above her she could hear the receding footsteps; Richards would not be the first man; he would be the pursuer. And she knew that she had tripped the wrong man.

She twisted around on the step and sat up—it was surprisingly difficult to accomplish; she must have fallen harder than she had realized. She shook off the renewed roaring and blinked away a blackness within the blackness of the hall, and said in a voice that sounded distant but almost normal, "Mr. Richards, are you hurt? I'm sorry. Are you—" She stopped and looked down at her hand. Beside her hand. There was a glow, like the glow that the little man's big eyes had given off. But this was long and even more glittering. The faint light reflected off the long knife, and Talia gave up her fight, gave in to the inner blackness.

* * *

She was lying on her couch. Her head ached. She moved it gently to the left and discovered Jim Richards sitting in the wing chair. The knife was in his right hand and his left thumb was flicking the blade.

He looked up and said, "He left us a souvenir." He waved the knife, then put it on the end table beside him and came over to the couch's side. He asked gently, "Head hurt?"

Her voice sounded strained: "I'll be fine in a minute. I think I simply knocked the breath out of myself when I fell."

"You've only been—out—a few minutes. I didn't know what to do. I was considering cold towels, doctors, smelling salts . . . but who has smelling salts anymore?"

She smiled. It was an effort. "Not I," she said.

"I guessed that without looking. By the way, I did have to look in your pocketbook. For the keys."

"Of course."

He sat on the foot of the couch. "I heard the elevator—you know that squeaking noise it makes. Then I heard the gate up here, and then the door as it closed. All this was a sort of habitual notation; I had never realized that I hear it. But I do, and that is just the beginning of the pattern. There should be two more sounds—your door closing, and one step as your heel clicks across the floor there before you step onto the rug." He pointed at the door, and Talia saw how the familiar rug ended on the familiar parquet about two feet from the door.

"Because it was all subconscious, I wasted a minute or two before I thought it out, defined the lack. I got scared then. Immediately. Because of the recording."

Her lashes had been lying on her cheeks. They went swiftly upward.

"Recording?"

"When I picked up the machine last night, I checked it. Force of habit with mechanical gadgets. One roll was in backward. I fixed it, and then tested the machine. I heard your voice. Then I ran the tape. Forgive me—" He paused. "No, I'm glad I listened. It explains you." He smiled faintly. "Explanation was even good for my ego. I had been wondering if *anyone* could be as thoroughly repulsive as you seemed to find me."

"But I changed the tape," Talia said numbly.

"You must have changed the unused tape."

"Oh."

"What are you going to do with that—that record of viciousness?"

"I took it to the police. Yesterday morning. They made a copy."

"Good girl!" He looked astonished, but the astonishment faded slowly into something else. "Courageous," he said. "Wise."

"Courageous?" Corelli too had said she was courageous.

Color rose high on his cheekbones. He said, "Well . . ."

"You, too, interpreted the business about the 'lights being on'?"

"Too?"

"The policeman, a Lieutenant Corelli, understood it immediately. I explained to him. Shall I explain to you?"

"Not unless you wish to." He sounded stiff.

He was a good-looking man, which was probably why she had avoided him so diligently. He was also a nice man, and it was his effort not to pry that was making him sound stiff.

"I do wish to," Talia said. She pulled herself upward against the cushions, and then she told him the story. She found it easier to tell this second time, and she told it differently, not limiting herself to the barest facts, but permitting herself some interpretation and explanation. But no apologies; what had happened had happened.

When she had finished, Richards' first comment was a repetition of Corelli's but he said it with less surprise and more warmth. "You may not realize," he said, "how revealing their treatment of you is. They did everything they could, it seems, to make it easy for you. Such a reaction doesn't spring up, all uncultivated and untended. They must have been seeing your position, sympathizing with you, for many years."

Talia had not thought that through. Now she nodded.

"And after the inquest?" he asked.

"We—cleaned up. We were not only the loose ends of a tragedy; we were the dregs of Bart's rule. We had to be—tidied up. It was surprisingly simple—each of us simply followed our wishes. Papa went into Templeton and deeded them the house, of course. They'll sell it and realize enough to make Papa feel comfortable. Mollie and Junie went to Mollie's brother and sister-in-law. Bart left seven thousand dollars' insurance; I had insisted on insurance, but he had lied to me, after all. It was supposed to be fifteen thousand. Still, in Lafayette . . . Mollie's brother and his wife are sensible, unimaginative. He owns the department store, and Mollie can be useful. I think she'll be—she paused—"if not happy, at least content. The baby will be infinitely better off. Mollie's brother has no children, and Junie is very loveable.

"I came here. I had been a copywriter in Des Moines for the branch office of a Chicago firm. They offered me a transfer, but I wanted the break to be complete." She stared into the distance. "The only people who didn't come out well were Mrs. Bolling, Mollie's mother, and a sister of Mollie's. Mrs. Bolling went to stay with her. The sister lives in Flint, and among a whole series of terrible character traits, she's a hypochondriac. They are either going to have a commiserating good time, or, more likely, they're going to try desperately to outdo each other in rare and violent symptoms. I suppose I should feel sorry for them." Her faint smile said that she was trying and finding it difficult.

Richards asked, "And this—this 'little man,' you don't know, can't remember, who he is?"

She shook her head. "If you had asked me that question at noon today I'd have pointed out that I can't be sure there is anyone to know or remember. And I'd have said that no matter how likely it might seem there was no certainty that he did come from Lafayette. But this afternoon . . . It's hard to explain and it sounds ridiculous. Just that a feeling I used to have—a warning, almost—came back to me. That man's phone calls used to bring it on; today I was warned again. And although his voice is still not really familiar, something he said is the same. When he left here he explained he wouldn't see me soon and—and then he made some threats.''

"I remember.'' His pleasant mouth tightened.

"Well, the man who whispered used to do that. He'd talk and talk and then he'd say he wouldn't call again soon. But he'd call very soon. Today I began to know, without even realizing it, that it would be the same. That he'd come back right away.''

Richards got up, walked over toward the wing chair, and stood, with his back to her, looking down at the knife. He said, "Well, the police are the next step. If you'll tell me where the phone is—''

"Oh, no!''

He turned around, surprised. "But—''

"No,'' she said. "I'm too tired, first of all. I'd have to wait for them, and talk to them. And Corelli isn't there at night, so I'd have to go all over everything again. And they'd come here. They'd invade . . .'' She stopped.

There was a little silence and then Richards said, "It *is* a pleasant apartment, isn't it?'' The extent of his perception surprised her. "But you *must* tell them,'' he commented. "That knife has to be turned over to your lieutenant.''

"Yes. Of course. In the morning. I'll go over on the way to work.''

"Tell you what.'' Richards sounded brisk. "Suppose you let me do it. They'll probably want to talk to me anyway, since I tangled with the guy. I can't tell them a helpful thing—he got away like an eel—but they'll want a report. Then I'll meet you for lunch and tell you what they say. Okay?''

"It's an imposition—''

"As long as you don't object, it's not an imposition, but a settled fact. Fine. Now, about tonight. Do your feelings of—invasion—extend to me? If not, I think I'll camp on your couch.''

The feeling of invasion did *not* extend to him. She examined the realization with surprise. But it would be too much to accept. "I'll be all right,'' she said slowly. "There's really no need—''

"Same answer as before. As long as you don't object, it's not a matter of needs, but a settled fact.'' He smiled. "I'll be very comfortable. It's a surprisingly long couch for a lady's apartment. But then you're rather a long lady, aren't you?''

She slept well and immediately. When she awakened she found that she had overslept by fifteen minutes, and knew immediately that she was alone in the apartment.

The knife was gone from the end table and there was a note in its place. It started without salutation, and she wondered if he didn't know what to call her. "Miss Cory'' would have seemed foolish and "Natalia'' was rather overwhelming. He wrote:

"I am not at my best by the dawn's early light, and anyway I want to catch your cop before he goes out. I'll pick you up at noon at the cigarstand in the lobby of

your building. I *do* mean *noon*—not five seconds later—because I know a wonderful place to eat that has two flaws—five hundred other people know it, and it
has eight tables. I'll make a reservation, but they won't hold tables. Noon!

Jim

If you need me for any reason don't hesitate to call my office.''

She didn't need him, but when he called a little before eleven, she was pleased.
Richards said, ''Thought I'd better warn you that we're having company for
lunch. Your pal.''

''Lieutenant Corelli?''

''Yeah.''

She said, ''What are you so happy about? You sound different.''

''I am, as they say in books, jubilant. Look, Natalia . . .'' He paused.

''Talia.''

''Ah, that's a nice name—mighty nice. Well now, look: Lieutenant Corelli is
a happy man too. He's proud of himself for having done police work at a distance
of about a thousand miles. It looks as if you didn't do it, you see.''

Talia stared through the partitions. ''Didn't do it?'' she repeated.

Then her voice arose: *''Didn't shoot Bart?''*

A silence fell around her and she realized how loudly she had spoken. She
turned slightly in her chair and saw through a haze that Janet and Carl and Billy
were staring at her. So was Mr. Long, who was standing in the doorway.

There had been bedlam in the office, and the cessation of sound apparently
became noticeable to Richards too. ''What's going on there?'' he asked.

As she looked at the four, they quickly went back into motion. Mr. Long
continued out the door and the other three resumed their moving-day gestures,
which seemed to consist largely of loud conferences.

''Desks are being moved,'' Talia said into the phone. ''Please. What— Can
you explain what—''

''I shouldn't have shocked you like that, but I didn't want you to spend even
one more hour . . . Apparently they were so fond of you in Lafayette that their
only idea was to get the matter over with. So, after the, ah, autopsy, they looked
at the bullet and said, 'Ah, a bullet.' You said you had fired a gun, they found a
hunk of lead, and that was that. But when Corelli talked to them he suggested
they look around the woodwork, and they did, and what do you think they found?
A bullet, neatly embedded in the windowframe. A bullet from your brother's
service gun, the one you fired.''

''But why''—in the unreality of the moment her mind could grasp only the
simple, immediate facts. Take one thing at a time, she told herself, and started
with the first: ''Why would the lieutenant even think of such a thing?''

''Because the lights were on.''

''The lights were on?'' In her bewilderment her voice rose and she felt the
little stir behind her. I must keep my voice down, she thought dimly.

''My dear, there's nothing subtle about that. Corelli saw it immediately, I saw
it immediately, anyone would see it immediately. Only reason you didn't was
that you were so utterly convinced that you shot your brother. But—how did the

guy know about the lights *if he wasn't there*? You see? So they're going to—to find out about the angle of the bullet, and re-examine it to determine its make, things like that. No matter what, only one shot was fired from the gun you held and that was in the windowframe. See?''

No. Not quite. But enough to . . . "Oh, my," Talia said with insane inadequacy. "My," she said.

"You can say that again," Jim Richards said, still jubilant.

"Thank you." She was caught tightly in the grip of inadequacy. She tried again:

"*Thank* you."

Richards seemed to find it adequate. "We'll thank Corelli," he said. "You and I. At high noon."

Talia hung up slowly and then turned in her chair. Welling up in her was the desire to tell someone, anyone, to shout the news. She wouldn't, of course. But she substituted a smile for the unsaid words.

Janet looked at her over an armful of dusty folders. "Wow!" she said simply. "That must have been quite a conversation."

Carl Neilson said, "Sure sounded like it." He looked at Talia with longing admiration.

Janet said, "Billy, wait!" The office boy was tugging at a file cabinet. "You can't budge that alone! Anyway, the telephone thing on the side of the desk is on too short a wire. We can't move the desk any farther." She let out a small wail. "All I wanted was a little light and air, just a little light and air! The world is against me!" She dropped the folders on the floor beside her desk, which had been moved just far enough to partly block the door, and slumped into her chair, looking determinedly woebegone.

"Being in a—a fishbowl like this somehow makes it worse. I *ought* to have light and air."

Talia smiled at her. "Aren't fishbowls usually round?"

"We're the exotic kind of fish in the rectangular tanks."

"Are you sure you won't change desks with me?"

Janet shook her head with exaggerated despondency. "I'd love to, but my conscience simply won't let me."

Billy said, "The telephone man is in the building, Miss Furman. I saw him. Shall I get him and bring him up here?"

Neilson said, "Good idea. And then we can move the desk and file this afternoon."

"You could do it at noon," Janet said, with a bland face and a noticeable air of innocence.

Carl Neilson examined her suspiciously. "I'll bet you and Talia are going to lunch at noon."

Janet giggled.

"Oh, no, you don't," he added. "I am making like slave labor merely for the sly purpose of enjoying you girls' company. If you're not willing to give me at the very least advice and comfort you can requisition the stockroom for help—and wait a week or two—or three—or four."

"All right," Janet said meekly.   "Billy will bring the telephone man as soon as he can, and the two of you can come back after lunch."

"Sure."   Neilson smiled at Talia and went out, tailed by Billy.

Janet said, "Seems unfair of *me* to take advantage of his overpowering passion for *you* to get *my* desk moved.   But no one feels that way about me."

"Don't be silly," Talia said vaguely, and smiled brilliantly at Janet.   She would like to have sung, to have danced . . .   She turned back to her desk, and found that she was teeming with ideas.   She picked up a pencil.

Janet said, "It's five of twelve, Talia."   She was standing in the doorway.

Talia came abruptly out of her surprising absorption.   "Whoops!" she said.   "That gives me three seconds for lipstick."

Janet waved and left, and Talia grabbed her purse and started picking her way through the clutter toward the door.   As she moved around Janet's desk the office boy appeared in the doorway.   He said, "Miss Cory please, I couldn't find the telephone man."

"Well," Talia said, "that's all right, Bunny.   Janet will have to—"   She stopped.   She kept her eyes on the pile of file folders she had been about to step over, and after a controlled second she said, "I mean Billy, of course.   And about the telephone—"

"It doesn't matter.   That you finally recognized me.   After all, you've known me all your life so I knew you might see me someday."

Talia looked up.   A small boy—   No, a man.   He must be just about her age.   But how would anyone ever guess it?   She said, "Your glasses are different."

"You mean that horn-rims make such a difference?   You just never would have recognized me, huh?"

"You wore—silver rims."   And the pale eyes behind the thick glasses had always looked very small, looked very small now.   The glass she thought numbly, must be the reducing kind.   Like the wrong end of a telescope.

"I'm flattered."   The sarcasm had a cruel bitterness.

"And your hair, your hair was—"   How to describe Bunny Williams' hair?   It had been, not blond or fair, but colorless.   Colorless, and long but thin, lying limply on his head like bleached monkey fur.

"I dyed it.   I don't know why I bothered.   You wouldn't have seen me if I wore a placard.   If I'd called myself to your attention—if I'd slapped your face from side to side.   Hard."   He took a step forward and she saw his mouth.   She had never noticed his mouth before, but she had never really noticed him before at all, not as Bunny Williams nor as Billy, the office boy.   He had a tiny round mouth, like a rosebud.   "You never saw me at all, did you?   Not in the sixth grade, or the seventh, or the eighth.   Not at dances, not at graduation from high.   Not when I made a fool of myself by asking you on the picnic."

Had he done that?   She had no memory of it.   "I never went out with anyone—"

"A girl like you?   Don't try to give me that, I never knew who he was, your lover, but I knew I'd find him, and so I watched and waited, and then when I thought I had him—when I saw him crawling in that window, I was so *sure* I had him—and then it turned out to be that bully of a brother of yours. And the man I was waiting for got away. So I'll take you from *him*."

There must be something she could say. If she could divert him— "Then," she said, "you really shot Bart by mistake. They'll understand that it was a mistake."

"You never saw me. Never knew me. Not on the street. Not on the telephone. And when I came to your back door with groceries you said, 'Are you the new delivery boy?' and smiled. And you didn't know me at all. But you had known me all your life." The little rosebud kept opening and closing . . . She took a step backward.

He took a step forward. "Doesn't matter now, you snob. And it doesn't matter what you look like anymore. You're never going to snub people anymore. I've put it off too long; now I'm going to take care of you." He moved around Janet's desk, and Talia found herself beside her own desk, her back to the window. There were thirty-four stories of air behind her.

He said, "You have my best knife—"

She spoke quickly. "You can have it back. I'll bring it in tomorrow."

When the little rosebud smiled, it curled and opened a trifle. Talia felt her stomach turn in revulsion, and nausea rise. "No," he said. "You won't bring anything anywhere tomorrow. And anyway, I have another." And he had. He held his hand low in front of him, and there was the knife. She looked through the glass walls. Would no one see?

"It's lunch hour," Bunny Williams said. "All those high-paid snobs get out of here before twelve and they don't get back until after two. I go at exactly twelve-thirty and I get back at one-thirty, in time to punch the time clock. Did you know there is a time clock down in the stockroom?"

"No. I— You can't get away with this, Bunny. There are three girls out there. Behind you. Just look. And Mr. Long's door is open. He's still in there."

"I'm not turning my head. It's so unusual to have you look at me—straight at me—seeing me—that I'm going to enjoy it for a minute. Then . . ." He gave the knife a tiny wave, and the rosebud mouth curled at its edges.

"But why? Why?"

"Lots of reasons. I'll remove you from *him*. Was that him in the hallway last night? . . .

"I heard you talking on the phone before. 'Didn't shoot Bart?' you said. So I know that they finally decided to stop looking at you, smiling at you, touching, patting you—everyone could always look and smile and touch and pat. Except me. But you weren't around anymore so they looked at something else. The bullets, I suppose. So now I've got another reason: No one's going to do it for me, so I've *got* to do it. And anyway, I can't let you out of this office because now you know me. *How* do you know me? What finally made you see me? Tell me. Then when you're gone and there isn't anyone alive to prove to me all the time that I'm nothing, and I start to be something, then maybe I can play up whatever it was that made you know me. What made you know me?"

Talia stared at him.   He wasn't very near her yet.   If she ran . . .   But there was no quick way around that big desk.

"How?" he said insistently.

"How?   Oh, it was just—just the way you said, 'Miss-Cory-please.' In school you used to say, 'Miss-James-please' and 'Miss-Wetzel-please' . . ."

He took a step forward and she pressed her back against the windowsill.   For some reason, it had been wrong to tell him.   The thin little face before her, the small staring little eyes, the horrible, curled little mouth—all had twisted with a terrible hate.   "So you remember me because I was humble, is that it?   Maybe if I'd crawled on my belly up your back steps with your groceries *then* you'd have known me?"

She shook her head numbly and forced her eyes away from the contorted face.

And there, as her eyes stared over the hair that now looked exactly like monkey fur, was Richards.   And Corelli.   They were almost up to the doorway.   Corelli shook his head violently, and she looked quickly back at the face.

It was smiling.

"Don't bother," he said.   "I won't look around.   Why would they come? I'm just the little office boy, talking to the big lady.   And when I stick this knife in your throat no one's even going to notice.   Then I'll wipe it on your blouse and just walk quietly out of here.   Who'll think of me?   Who *ever* thinks of me? You see what you did when you made me so unimportant?   You took care of *yourself*."

He laughed, a little, high, throaty giggle.

"You see what—"   He stopped and his eyes shifted to her left.   Why? she wondered.   There was nothing beside her but thirty-four stories of air.   But . . . a window separated her and him from that air.   And then she knew what he was looking at.   The window was showing him a reflection—the whispery reflection of all the glass they were surrounded by; the reflection, however dim, of the two men behind him, who had reached the door . . .

He swung violently around to his right, and as his hand went out to help him keep his balance the knife in it whistled past her breast, an inch away.

There was a second of dead, motionless silence.   Two men were just inside the open door, standing side by side, facing the desk.   It was the same as it had been in her hall, Talia thought.   They were going to run around and around the desk like—like the Marx Brothers.   She felt hysteria rising . . .

Richards broke the stalemate.   He leaned down and put his hand flat on the desk and then, in a flashing motion, rose into the air.   The vault would bring him down within a few feet of Bunny.   But as he landed, Bunny moved.   He moved to his left.   But he *can't*, Talia thought in that interminable second.   The glass wall . . .

He rose in the air, only an instant after Jim had, and, like Jim, he went feet first.   Through the glass wall.   Jim stopped, looked at the jagged hole, and turned to Corelli.   But Corelli had gone out to the door of the next glass box.

Bunny hesitated briefly, and then he rose again, and again he went through the wall.   In the next box he didn't stop, didn't hesitate, didn't bother to see if Corelli was near. He just kept going, insanely, like an automaton on a pogo stick. Over the low wooden partitions, through the glass walls.

People came into view. Talia saw Mr. Long and the blank astonishment of his face, and then another of the shattering crashes exploded into the splintering echoes of its predecessor and she thought, But how many fish tanks are there? There can't be more!

She looked again and saw the vaulting figure; it was—all red. She looked away, and realized that something like silence had come. No one spoke, and then splinters of glass detached themselves and dropped away, making a diminishing little series of tinkling sounds, as if the wind had blown across a Christmas tree and the ornaments had moved gently together.

Into the new silence came voices. Movements. A girl emitted a long delayed scream. A babble arose and through it, quite near, she heard Corelli's voice. He said, "She all right? He didn't touch her?"

Richards said, "No, he didn't. She'll be all right."

And she knew she would be.

LAWRENCE PAGE

Final Arrangements

The idea had come to him suddenly, and he had been fascinated by it. At the time, it had been a ridiculous daydream—but the more he thought about it, the more sensible and imperative it became.

Early in the morning, he sat in the living room staring at the wall as was his custom. He would rise every day with the sun, make breakfast for Elsie and himself, and then sit lost in thought.

This practice of early morning meditation was a brief, daily escape from reality. For Elsie never came into the living room; she hadn't come in once in the last ten years of their married life.

She sat in a wheel chair in her bedroom. She sat silently, bitterly. Her silence was broken only when she was shrieking at him, complaining about this or that. When she wasn't upbraiding him, she habitually stared at him with contempt, reminding him that he was responsible for her condition.

For ten long years she had been impossible to live with, and so each morning Rutherford Parnell, to lessen the pain, slipped into his own peculiar euphoria.

"Rutherford!"

"Yes—yes—" Roughly her voice had jerked him back to the living room. "Yes, Elsie?"

"Well, come in here, *please!*" she shouted.

He arose with a vast weariness and walked into her room. It was dark (she never allowed him to raise the shades) and smelled faintly musty.

"This tea is weak!" she said, her voice a thin high-pitched squeal. "Weak, like you! Everything you try to do is weak, or cold or useless. But you don't have the decency to hire someone who can cook, do you?"

"Mrs. Casey will be over, as usual," Rutherford said, calmly. Mrs. Casey was the eighth in a line of women he had hired to be a companion for Elsie. "She can't be here to cook breakfast, you know."

"I know. And a sloppy breakfast *you* make. Leave me alone, now, Rutherford. Unless you'd like to take me for a drive!"

How many times in the past decade had he heard that statement: *Unless you'd like to take me for a drive.*

He closed the door and walked into the living room, stopping to look out the window. He saw Mrs. Casey coming up the front walk.

Mrs. Casey was a warm, kindly woman, and Rutherford enjoyed talking to her. The dead-weight of Elsie's personality had not thus far affected her manner.

He opened the front door. "Good morning, Mrs. Casey," he said.

She was thin and tall, with a smiling Irish face. But her Irish face wasn't smiling today. "Good morning, sir," she said. "I was wonderin' if I could talk to you, Mr. Parnell."

"Surely," Rutherford said, and felt ill at ease.

"Mr. Parnell," she said as she came into the house, "I'm afraid, sir, that I'll have to give notice. I've found a position that pays a good deal more money . . ."

"I understand, Mrs. Casey, I understand. You will be able to finish out the week, won't you?"

"Oh, surely, sir."

Rutherford would have liked to say, "It's really not more money that you want. You're leaving because you can't stand her. Isn't that the truth?" But he said nothing. Instead, he put on his hat and coat and walked out of the house.

It was a clear, sunny day. It was also the day Rutherford had picked to carry through the plan upon which he meditated morning after morning. He came to a halt at the bus stop on the corner and waited for Number 16, Downtown, as he had every weekday morning for ten years. He had sold the car, after the accident. But that hadn't removed the car or the accident from his thoughts. And Elsie never let him forget that he had been at the wheel that drizzling November night, and that it had been his error in judgment that had sentenced her to life in a wheel chair.

As he stepped into the bus, he nodded to the driver as he did every day; then he moved to the rear and took a seat by the window, as he did every day. But today, he left the bus three blocks before his regular stop.

A telephone booth stood nearby, just off the wide cement apron of a service station. He went into the booth and called his office.

"Mary?" he said. "Hello, Mary. This is Rutherford."

"Why, Rutherford—aren't you feeling well?"

"No, I'm not. That's why I called."

"You want me to tell Mr. Speaks you won't be in today? Oh, I do hope you feel better. It's not at all like you, being out for a day . . ."

The senior Krushman of Krushman and Sons, Funeral Home, adjusted the spectacles on the thin bridge of his nose. He cleared his throat, ever so gently; his smile, intended to express sympathy, suggested a slight nausea.

"May I be of help, sir?"

"I would be grateful," Rutherford said, very softly, very carefully, "if you handled all the details for me."

"Of course, of course," Krushman said. "I understand. I know this is a most trying time for you. May I please have the name of the departed one?"

"That won't be necessary," Rutherford said. "I've written the address on this slip of paper. And if you would come by this evening and—and—take the deceased."

Krushman cleared his throat, but not quite as gently this time. "It's a little irregular, I must say. And from whom, sir, will I get the necessary information?"

"When you arrive—you'll get it then. Eight o'clock tonight. Would that be all right?"

"Eight o'clock—yes, of course," Krushman said. "Now what type of funeral were you interested in?"

"The—the—"

"Departed one," Krushman put in helpfully.

"Yes," Rutherford said. "Yes, the departed one won't have many friends attending, I'm afraid."

Mrs. Casey expressed surprise that Rutherford had come home so early.

Rutherford smiled at her. "Take the rest of the day off, Mrs. Casey. I want you to get home early too. In fact," he produced a wallet, "I'll pay you off now *and* with a little bonus."

Mrs. Casey's Irish face was somber. "I hope I didn't offend you this morning, Mr. Parnell. You do know why I'm leaving, don't you? I told an untruth this morning, that I did. It's not—"

"I know why you're leaving. It's my wife you can't stand. And I certainly understand how you feel. Oh, I don't blame you one bit, Mrs. Casey, not one bit."

Mrs. Casey fidgeted in embarrassment.

"I hate her too. I wish she'd die, so I could be free. But she won't die. That would be a courtesy to me that's beyond her. If I could only walk away from her as easily as you can, Mrs. Casey."

Mrs. Casey, at this point, mumbled a quick goodbye, and her departure was clearly an escape.

"Rutherford! Rutherford, is that you?"

The voice from the bedroom was sharp, piercing, inescapable.

"Yes, dear," he said. "And I'm coming."

He took a moment to clench his fists, to steel himself, and then he strode into the bedroom. He went immediately to the windows, yanked up both shades. Sunlight filled the room.

"Rutherford!" she screamed. "Have you gone out of your mind!"

Rutherford took the poison he'd purchased at the drug store from his pocket, extended the package toward her. "I brought something for you," he said. "A little present. Something to help you escape your constant loneliness and bitterness."

"What are you saying? Pull those blinds down. You know I can't stand bright daylight at this hour, Rutherford! Has your incompetence gotten you fired now?"

"Angel," Rutherford said. "Did I ever tell you that you're beautiful? Because if I did, I was a liar and I want you to know about it!"

"You're insane!" she shrieked.

He moved out of the bedroom quickly and into the small kitchen, where he poured a large glass of milk. He was all too aware of her voice going on endlessly in the other room, and it spurred him on. He opened the package and, with a teaspoon, dropped two helpings of the rat poison into the milk.

Then, glass in hand, he strode back into her room.

"Don't try to make up to me—I hate milk and you know it!"

"But you drink it every night," he said. "And besides, I m not trying to make up to you. I haven't been able to make up to you in ten years!"

She burst into tears and put her head in her hands. The wheel chair creaked with her sudden movement. "You're horrible! Mother told me not to marry you! I should have listened to mother."

"Your mother never told you not to marry anybody. As soon as she saw a chance to get rid of you, she reeled me in like a prize catch. Even your father couldn't stand you!"

"Rutherford! You are horrible! Horrible!"

"Don't you want to hear the news, Elsie, about the present I bought you? Freedom. An escape for both of us. A chance to get away from each other!" He snickered. "After all, this present cost me over three thousand dollars!"

"Three thousand dollars! Where—where—"

"I cashed in my insurance, Elsie, dear. All the value of it. Three thousand, five hundred dollars and eighty-two cents. And I cancelled the term insurance. What about that!"

"Rutherford! You have gone out of your mind!"

"Just listen to me, will you? I've a proposition for you." He held the glass of milk steady, held it with both hands. "How would you like to go away to a rest home?"

"Don't be absurd," she said. "Is that your proposition?"

"That's what I thought you'd say."

He smiled—a gentle, sad smile—lifted the glass and drained it in one gulp. "You'll soon realize, Elsie dear, that things here weren't so rough for you . . ."

She didn't know what he meant—for a few minutes.

DAVID ELY

Countdown

The meteorologists had correctly forecast fine weather; everything seemed made to order that day. The offshore winds had swept away the clouds, the sky was a clear and trackless field of blue and the sun ranged well off toward the northern horizon, as if deliberately posted where it could not interfere with the great event taking shape on the earth below.

People had come by the thousands, in cars and buses and taxis, and the sandy waste outside the high wire fence was jammed. Here and there among the vast throng were refreshment stands, and strolling salesmen hawked souvenirs, balloons and straw hats. At the very edge of the fence a few tents had been pitched by those who had arrived days in advance to be certain of getting a first-rate location. State troopers were moving among the crowd, but their primary concern was to keep the traffic lanes free, for the people were in a quiet and expectant mood. There was no disorder. Everyone was waiting patiently to see the dramatic climax of the International Space Year, a man rocketed up toward the planet Mars.

Within the fenced area, the atmosphere also was calm. Among the cluster of long low buildings were gathered the press and dignitaries, each group occupying its designated location. The television and newsreel cameras were set on a large wooden platform in the center of the asphalt square that separated the Commissary from the Project Headquarters building. In rows of chairs on one side sat the scores of newsmen and magazine writers who had come from virtually every country in Europe and from both the Americas; on the other were seated more than two hundred guests, mostly scientists and political figures. For the more important spectators, a shaded pavilion had been constructed north of the Commissary; these privileged visitors included three Chiefs of State, a dozen statesmen of ministerial rank, and a few members of royal families. Everyone remained quietly in place, anxious not to disturb the scientists and technologists who moved with sober deliberation on their final tasks.

"ZERO PLUS ONE HOUR!"

The loudspeaker system cracked out the phrase like a rifle-shot. Instantly, the crowds on both sides of the wire fence were hushed, and all heads turned east toward the giant rocket that towered on its pad, across the protective belt of sand. In the deceptive haze of reflected sunlight, the slender cone seemed to quiver, as if the initial combustive thrust were already urging it heavenward.

Security Officer Farquhar leaned against the east wall of the Commissary, his thoughts uneasily revolving around the thousand possibilities for trouble. He had been assigned to the security end of a dozen manned space shots before, yet this one was the most nervewracking, for not only was it of top importance, but also it was an international undertaking, involving scientists from a score of nations, who had turned the area into a babel of languages, suggestive of loose ends—even sabotage.

Officer Farquhar frowned, attempting to dismiss his fears. He had done everything possible to guard against sabotage. For many months, everyone connected with the Project, from the Director down to the restaurant bus-boys, had been rigorously investigated and kept under observation, and in the security files there was a thick dossier on each person, packed with the most intimate and revealing details. Nowhere was there the slightest hint of trouble. Farquhar's mind gradually lightened. At any rate, no one could accuse him of a lack of diligence.

"Look, sir," came the amused voice of his jeep driver nearby, "the women are starting to bawl!" The driver grinned and pointed the antenna of his walkie-talkie toward an area twenty yards north, where chairs had been set up for the convenience of the Project staff. Since the scientists were at work at the pad or in the buildings, these chairs were occupied principally by wives, children and a few service personnel not on duty.

The driver was right. Several of the woman were furtively dabbing at their eyes with handkerchiefs. Farquhar smiled tolerantly; the tension of so many months was nearing its climax. Why not tears? It might be better if the men could weep, too, for some relief.

He noticed one of the women in particular, partly because of her unusual beauty, partly because she remained standing, despite the liberal provision of chairs. He squinted against the sun to see more clearly. No, she was not actually crying. Something odd about her, he thought. She stood as stiffly as a statue, with her hands clenched at her sides, staring fixedly out across the sands toward the rocket.

Officer Farquhar recognized her then as the wife of one of the scientists, a physicist named Whitby. To look at the woman, one would think that Whitby himself were about to climb into the rocket, instead of Captain Randazzo. Farquhar shrugged. Tension had varying effects on people. Still he wondered a little . . .

In the main control room of the Project Headquarters building, Captain Miguel Randazzo sat calmly munching a chicken-salad sandwich and sipping a glass of milk, as if he were not in the least interested in what the immediate future held in store or him. Occasionally he would glance with mild amusement at the grave countenances of the top scientific staff members who were busily involved with charts and telephones and the banks of intricate machinery that covered the walls.

In any other man, Captain Randazzo's air of nonchalance would have been properly ascribed to a despairing bravado, or to drugs. But Randazzo was neither desperate nor drugged. His handsome face displayed a quiet smile; the strong and shapely hands that held the sandwich and the glass did not tremble in the slightest, and his slim but powerful legs were crossed with an elegant casualness. One would have thought that he was merely going to travel to New York, or to Rio, instead of to Mars and back again.

If he had evidenced any unease, the fact would have been instantly noted by the two renowned men of medicine who sat respectfully beside him, watching his every move. An eminent psychiatrist stood nearby, but he had nothing to note on his scratch-pad but his own nervous reactions.

Randazzo had been chosen from among some fifty volunteers with previous space-flight experience, and had subsequently confirmed the wisdom of his selection by rapidly mastering the technical skills required for the operation (and repair, if need be of the complicated equipment in the spaceship cabin). The harsh physical trials which had eliminated so many hopefuls had not bothered him in the least, for he was well-rested from the Olympic Games, where he had won four gold medals for his proud little nation. In his spare time, Captain Randazzo pursued his hobbies—hunting kodiak bears alone and unarmed, raising prize orchids, and writing Latin verse plays. On top of these accomplishments, the Captain had an international reputation for romantic gallantry, a reputation which he had not been able to embellish during his recent weeks of semi-seclusion at the Project.

"ZERO PLUS FIFTY!" boomed the loudspeaker system. Every man in the room—save the astronaut—started in automatic alarm.

Randazzo simply smiled, and as the Project Director walked by, he hailed him jokingly in colloquial German: "Don't forget to put plenty of steak on board for me, eh?"

The Project Director smiled quietly but passed on without response. The food supply necessary for the three-month round trip consisted solely of processed concentrates, hardly more than capsules. But even this compressed nourishment occupied more space than he wanted it to have, what with the necessary protective packing and cooling mechanisms.

But the Director was more concerned with another matter at present. The cabin temperature-regulating system had indicated a faint tendency to deviate from its rigid automatic control. It was the single piece of equipment that had not performed to absolute perfection during the months of testing. True, Randazzo could make adjustments by means of the manual control, but nevertheless—

"Get me Whitby at the pad," the Director ordered his communications chief.

As he waited, he gazed through the window at the assembled dignitaries and at the sleek conical shape beyond, on which their hopes and fears were centered.

"ZERO PLUS FORTY-FIVE!"

Too many mechanical intricacies, thought the Director, touching his moist brow with a handkerchief. Too many thousands of tiny interlocking parts—something was bound to go wrong . . .

"Whitby speaking."

The Director responded more sharply than he had intended. "How's the Temp-Reg doing, eh?"

"Seems in perfect order now," Whitby replied.

"Seems!" the Director snapped. "Do you realize that if—" He caught himself. Of course Professor Whitby knew. If Temp-Reg slipped by the tiniest fraction of a degree—and if the manual failed as well—Captain Randazzo would gradually become either parboiled or frozen.

"If you have any doubts, Whitby, now's the time," the Director said, more quietly.

"In my best judgment, Temp-Reg is in proper working condition," came the thin, pedantic voice.

"Good enough," said the Director. "Every expendable in place now?"

"All except food. Wait a minute—here comes Dr. Anders with it now. That's it. We'll have everything tight in two minutes."

"Good," said the Director, and handing the receiver to the communications man, he turned thoughtfully around to survey the room. Too many parts and pieces, he thought, but as his eye fell on Randazzo he felt a heartening optimism. At least the human factor in this gigantic venture was flawless. No wonder the press referred to the fellow as "The Perfect Human."

At the launching pad, Professor Whitby ran his pencil rapidly over his final check-list.

"You're a bit late, you know, Max," he said in mild reproof to a tall, gaunt chemist who was helping two technicians load several long metal cases into the gantry elevator.

"Only eighteen seconds," Dr. Anders replied, with cool precision. He frowned in a preoccupied way at the cases, then gave the nearest one a pat of satisfaction. "All right," he told the elevator crew, "take them up."

He turned to Whitby. "That's everything, I suppose?" It was a purely rhetorical question, for both men knew to the last detail exactly what went inside the cabin and in what order.

Whitby looked up from his check-list. "Of course," he muttered. His eyes were darkly circled. "Well, we're all through now," he added. "Let's go."

The two men climbed into a waiting jeep and, with a final salute to the technicians who would remain at the pad until Zero Plus Ten, they drove across the hot sands toward the group of buildings and the crowd of watchers.

"Everything perfect for The Perfect Human, eh?" Dr. Anders said.

Whitby gave him a quick glance. "Perfect!" He wrinkled his face in distaste. "He's perfect physically, perhaps—and superior intellectually, I suppose, but . . ." His voice trailed off.

Dr. Anders raised his eyebrows inquiringly, but Whitby said no more.

"ZERO PLUS THIRTY!"

Captain Randazzo yawned and stretched. "Time to dress for dinner," he remarked, noting the approach of two Nobel prizewinners from M.I.T. who were bringing him the space-suit they had themselves designed. "Correct that error in the third lining, gentlemen?" the space-traveler inquired, with a wink.

The M.I.T. luminaries smiled back, but the hovering psychiatrist leaned forward with some interest. "If I may ask, Captain, what error?"

Randazzo feigned a look of surprise. "Why, they didn't leave enough room, that's all."

"Not enough room?"

"Room for a space-woman," declared the astronaut, in English that betrayed no trace of an accent. "Three months is a long, long time, eh?"

The M.I.T. men chuckled, but the psychiatrist made a careful note and remarked: "I suppose you will miss the companionship of women, Captain." To which the hero replied with equal gravity: "Correctly stated, sir, and if I may be allowed to abuse the convention of modesty, the reverse will also be true."

"ZERO PLUS TWENTY!"

Security Officer Farquhar winced from the loudspeaker blast as he walked along the corridor of Project Headquarters. His pace was steady but his mind was troubled by two small facts which might or might not be connected—and, even if they were, might be meaningless.

First there had been Professor Whitby's expression as the scientist left the control room after making his final report to the Director. Farquhar had caught only a glimpse of that face, but he would not soon forget its tortured look.

The Security Officer would have dismissed it as evidence of intolerable anxiety about the success of the Project, except—

Except that he still vividly recalled the beautiful young woman who had stood rigid with grief and tension in the Staff area, staring desperately at the distant rocket. Whitby's wife.

There was a third fact, too, or rather, a rumor. Captain Randazzo was said to have indulged his romantic inclinations even in the relative isolation of the Project, although this was hard to credit, for he had been so closely watched in these recent weeks.

Farquhar shivered as he heard the crowd outside break into a sudden rising babble of excitement. He glanced at his watch. Yes, by now Randazzo would have left the building and climbed into the jeep—

He felt weak under the weight of his responsibility. It would be unthinkable to approach the Project Director at this time, solely because of the facial expressions of a husband and wife. And yet he was distinctly uncomfortable about it. Already he had slipped into the security room to check the Whitbys' dossiers. No hint of discord had been inscribed there, but Farquhar had noted down the names of the couple listed under the heading, "best friends at Project," Max and Olga Anders. He needed more information—quickly, if at all. Dr. and Mrs. Anders might know something, assuming there was something to be known.

But thus far he had been balked, for he had searched through the Staff area for Mrs. Anders without success, and her husband, too, was nowhere to be found outside.

Now, reaching the end of the corridor, Farquhar came to a door marked "Nutritional Chemistry" and stepped into a laboratory lined with huge sinks and tables and cupboards. The laboratory was empty, but Farquhar called out Dr. Anders' name anyway.

"Yes?"

Dr. Anders emerged from a refrigerated room at one end of the laboratory, wiping his hands on a towel. "Oh, were you looking for me, Mr. Farquhar?" He carefully shut the cold-room door behind him. "Just cleaning up," he explained. "If you let a mess stand for a while, it's a dozen times harder—"

Farquhar interrupted him impatiently. "I'm going to ask a personal question, Dr. Anders. I hope you don't mind answering. I assure you, I have my reasons."

Dr. Anders shrugged without answering. From the corridor the loudspeaker echoed a fresh warning: ". . . PLUS TEN!"

Farquhar found he was perspiring freely. Now the astronaut would have been strapped inside the cabin . . . the hatch would be closing, the final-check crew climbing into their jeeps—and in five more minutes, the automatic controls would take charge. If there was anything to his doubts, he had better waste no time on circumlocution.

"I'm going to speak bluntly," the officer said. "You and your wife know the Whitbys better than anyone else here. Tell me frankly—do you have any reason to believe that Mrs. Whitby has been guilty of any improper relationship with Captain Randazzo?"

Dr. Anders rubbed his lean jaw reflectively, then turned toward the window and clasped his hands behind his back. "To the best of my knowledge," he said slowly, "yes."

Farquhar did not hesitate, but reached for a telephone.

"One more question," he said as he dialed. "Does Whitby know this too?"

"I'm fairly certain that he does, yes."

Farquhar muttered an oath, then barked an order into the telephone: "Farquhar speaking. Find Professor Whitby at once. Bring him to the nutritional lab—immediately."

He slammed down the phone and mopped his brow. Dr. Anders was regarding him with a curious look.

"I can't believe it," Farquhar said hoarsely. "We kept him under close surveillance. We had him watched, guarded—almost every minute—"

Dr. Anders seemed amused. "Are you really surprised, Mr. Farquhar? Don't you think The Perfect Human could have devised means of evading your vigilance if he wanted something badly enough?" He laughed shortly. "That probably added to the fun of the thing, don't you think? Having not only to woo and win another man's wife—but also to outwit the security men assigned to protect him! What a challenge for a man who strangles bears as a diversion!"

"I can't believe it," Farquhar repeated but his words were lost as the cavernous voice of the loudspeaker cut in: ". . . PLUS FIVE!" Now the automatic controls were operating. The whole system had passed into the shadowy realm of electronics, where cold mechanical intelligences whispered millions of messages at lightning speed, causing levers to drop, gauges to quiver, and microscopic doors to slam tightly shut . . .

Even so, it could be stopped. Farquhar knew that in the control room the Director now stood tensely watching his hand near a button marked KILL.

It could be stopped, but at a fantastic cost. Once the myriad fine-tooled parts began to move—and they were moving now—a stoppage might ruin half of the delicate equipment, would certainly delay the shot for many months, would cost millions. No, he could not ask the Director to wreck everything on a sheer hunch. He stared down furiously at his clenched fists and only slowly became aware of Dr. Anders' voice.

"You can't believe that a faithful wife could be seduced, is that it, then?" Dr. Anders asked, twisting his lips ironically. "Don't be ridiculous, Farquhar! This Randazzo is no ordinary mortal—he is perfect! And beyond that—yes, far beyond that—he is a man soon to vanish on a hero's mission into the sky, perhaps never to return!" Dr. Anders folded his long arms and cocked his head to one side. "What woman could resist the appeal of such a man, a man who comes to her in secret, a man who is already a legendary figure—"

The door swung open. Whitby strode in, his blond hair dishevelled. Behind him were two security agents.

Farquhar stood up. His whole body was trembling; he found it almost impossible to control his voice as he rasped out the brutal question.

Whitby's face colored, then paled. He glanced in bewilderment at Dr. Anders, but Anders had turned toward the window again.

"Yes or no!" snapped Farquhar.

Whitby stretched his hands apart in a despairing gesture. "Yes, it's true—she told me herself last night—but I don't see that it's any of your—"

He was choked off as Farquhar seized his shirt-front roughly with both hands.

"Tell me, Whitby—have you done anything to—to—" The Security Officer was himself almost beyond coherence.

Dr. Anders cut in dryly: "To sabotage the rocket?"

Whitby pulled loose from the hands that clutched his shirt. He staggered back. "I? Sabotage the rocket?" He sank back against a counter and his head tipped weakly against the cupboard above it.

"Sabotage it—*did you sabotage it?*" Farquhar's voice rose to a shout.

Whitby closed his eyes and feebly waved his hands. "Are you insane? You think I would destroy—" He began to laugh, his body stiffening, his head still pressed against the cupboard. "Me?" He gasped the words out through his painful hilarity. "No—no—I knew his reputation, yes—I suspected him—but with other women, other men's wives!" He laughed again. "I never thought it would be with mine!"

Dr. Anders stepped swiftly over to Farquhar. "Look here," he said softly, "the man isn't lying. The only item of importance under his direct control is the Temp-Reg system, and—"

His voice was drowned out by the sudden roar of the loudspeaker system, beginning the final sixty seconds of the countdown:

"FIFTY-NINE, FIFTY-EIGHT, FIFTY-SEVEN . . ."

Dr. Anders had to yell to make himself heard. "It's automatically monitored, Farquhar! If anything is wrong with it, the Director will know at once!"

". . . FIFTY, FORTY-NINE, FORTY-EIGHT . . ."

"There's a monitor dial for everything!" Dr. Anders shouted.   "You must know that yourself!   Call him and check!"

Farquhar seized the telephone and dialed with shaking fingers.   Dr. Anders turned abruptly away and stared at the window's square of sky and sunlight.

". . . THIRTY-ONE, THIRTY, TWENTY-NINE . . ."

Farquhar cursed the loudspeaker's enormous voice.   Suppose Whitby were lying— suppose Anders were lying too.   They might be in it together . . . perhaps Anders had a similar motive—

". . . NINETEEN, EIGHTEEN . . ."

His call was answered.   But the communications officer refused to disturb the Director.

Farquhar swore at the man, begged him, ordered him—

"TEN . . . NINE . . ."

At last the Project Director's voice barked at him savagely from the receiver.

Farquhar screamed the words: "Do you have the Temp-Reg system under monitor?"

"Of course!"

"And is it working properly?"

". . . FIVE, FOUR . . ."

The Director's voice cracked back: "Of course!"

Farquhar dropped the receiver as though its weight had suddenly become intolerable, and as it clattered on the desk, the building trembled slightly and the crowd outside burst into a prolonged roar that seemed to grow enormously in volume, and to roll in upon the men like surf, like vast gray thunderbanks—

"It's off!   It's up!"

The two security agents rushed to the window to see the slowly rising column of steel and fire and smoke.

But the other three remained where they stood; Farquhar at the desk, Anders five feet behind him, and Whitby at the counter near the wall.

"You see," said Dr. Anders, slowly, "It was all right."

Whitby's body was still stretched in painful tensity against the counter.   "I thought of it, Farquhar," he whispered, "Lord knows I thought of it.   But I couldn't do it—no, not even for *that*."

Then his tension broke.   His body relaxed so quickly that he almost fell, and as his head flopped forward, the cupboard door against which it had been pressed swung open.

By the dozens, tiny pellets came cascading out.   They rained down on Whitby's head and shoulders, and spun and rolled upon the floor.   The entire room seemed covered with them, and still more rolled to the cupboard's edge and dropped down.

Wonderingly, Farquhar stooped and picked one up.   It was pliable in his fingers, reminding him of a yeast tablet.

He glanced at Whitby.   The man's face had gone milk-white and he was staring wide-eyed, not at Farquhar, but beyond him.

"Good Lord, Max!" he hissed.

Farquhar turned around, conscious as he did so of the increasing and triumphant cheering of the crowd, and of the loudspeaker voice that crackled now above the roar with a piercing excitement: "STAGE ONE SUCCESSFUL, STAGE ONE SUCCESSFUL . . ."

He looked at the yeasty pellet in his hand, and then at Dr. Anders. The chemist's lean face was oddly contorted; he was smiling in a quiet way, as if anticipating some subtle witticism he was about to utter.

"Was this"—Farquhar waved his hand to include the thousand pellets that lay scattered throughout the room—"was this supposed to have been in the ship?"

Dr. Anders folded his arms and inclined his head almost imperceptibly.

"You mean—you deliberately loaded empty food containers in that cabin? You mean he's off in space to starve to death?"

"Oh, no," said Dr. Anders. "He needn't starve."

Farquhar stared at the man. "But if the containers were loaded empty—"

Whitby broke in. "No! They weren't empty! They were weighed at the pad! They were fully loaded!"

Farquhar shook his head and drew his hand across his face, as if to erase some incredible idea. "Loaded? Loaded—with what?"

But Dr. Anders merely repeated, in his calm and even tones, the phrase he had just used: *"He needn't starve."*

Whitby shuffled forward with the uncertain step of a much older man until he bumped blindly into a heavy counter and could go no farther. When he spoke, his voice was but a whisper, yet the words seemed to take shape almost palpably in the air, like smoke:

"Where's Olga, Max? Where is she? Where's your wife?"

Dr. Anders made no reply. His pale eyes were fixed on the window, on the patch of blue beyond, the great skyway that opened ever wider to where the silent planets circled in the infinite and peaceful harmony of space.

Murder Between Friends

Over their mid-morning coffee Mrs. Harrison and Mrs. Franklin settled down to discuss how they were going to murder their landlord, Mr. Shafer. The day before they had decided that murdering him was the only sane thing to do.

"I believe I'll have a little more sugar for my coffee, please, Matilda," Mrs. Franklin said. At this late date, she was seventy-six, there was nothing she could do about her sweet tooth. "These are the best cheese straws I've ever put in my mouth. You've got to be a born cook to have them turn out this way. Time and again I've followed your recipe exactly, but mine aren't anything like these."

Mrs. Harrison beamed. It was a pleasure to give a little treat to such an amiable person as Mary Sue Franklin, a friend ever since the second grade.

They ate cheese straws and sipped coffee, then wiped their mouths daintily and got down to the business of Mr. Shafer's murder.

"Well, we can't do it with a gun, that's for sure," Mrs. Harrison said. "A gun scares me to death just to look at it. I couldn't bring myself to pull the trigger. Besides, where on earth would we get one? You have to have a permit to buy one and a license to shoot it."

"No, a gun is out," Mrs. Franklin agreed. Then she sighed. "You read a lot about murder, but when you come right down to it, it's hard to plan one."

Even as they talked they could hear Mr. Shafer thundering like a minotaur up and down the halls looking for his next victim.

"I'll take another cheese straw, Matilda, and then I've got to go to the store. Can I get anything for you? I'll be glad to."

"No, thank you, Mary Sue. But tomorrow we've got to get down to brass tacks. Mr. Shafer gets meaner every day."

They finished their coffee. Mrs. Franklin offered to wash up, but Mrs. Harrison wouldn't hear of it. So Mrs. Franklin went back down the hall to her own tiny room and kitchenette to get her shopping bag. She bumped right into Mr. Shafer, who was coming up the back stairway.

"What you old biddies been yakking about today?" he boomed out at her. "Are you planning to overthrow the government?"

Mrs. Franklin liked banter. A woman never got too old to do a bit of discreet, ladylike flirting. But no light exchange was possible with Mr. Shafer. She smiled her sweetest smile and gave a little bow. "No, my dear," she said in the most genteel conversational tone, "we've been trying to decide how to murder you."

Mr. Shafer paid no attention. He never did pay any attention to what anyone said. "Damned old biddies," he muttered, and stalked on past. "Why is the world so cluttered up with old women?"

He turned out the little glow-worm of a light in that part of the hall. He slammed a door somewhere. Even the house shuddered; and he had no business being there at all. The place had belonged to his wife and when she had died it had been willed to their daughter, but Mr. Shafer made the daughter so miserable that she'd left after one of his scenes. Then he had taken over everything.

The next morning the old friends talked again about murdering Mr. Shafer.

Mrs. Franklin asked, as usual, for more sugar for her coffee. She told Mrs. Harrison that was the best apple pie she'd ever eaten.

"It's the cinnamon that makes the difference, that's all," Mrs. Harrison said modestly, "and a little lemon juice."

They finished their snack. They wiped their mouths delicately.

"Well, we can't poison Mr. Shafer," Mrs. Harrison said. "What do we know about poison?"

"We could learn," Mrs. Franklin answered.

"How could we learn, Mary Sue? If we go to the library and ask for books on poison they're sure to remember us. I know all the staff there. Anyway, when you buy poison the clerk keeps a record of it. The police could trace it straight to us."

Over their chocolate cake the next day, Mrs. Franklin said, "We certainly can't drown him." She was so enmeshed in the cake that she wore a chocolate mustache and for the first time since they'd talked of murder she looked a bit sinister.

"No, I guess we can't drown him. There's no deep water anywhere but in the lake at the city park, and how could we get Mr. Shafer there?"

"He wouldn't go with us. He hates women."

"He hates everybody."

On Thursday when they had finished their pineapple upsidedown cake neither of them had any suggestion about how to kill Mr. Shafer.

"I feel so inept and inane, Mary Sue. We've got heads on our shoulders. It looks like we ought to be able to figure out something."

"Maybe we can tomorrow." Mrs. Franklin sounded optimistic.

"What about an axe?" Mrs. Harrison said the next day when they'd eaten every crumb of their cheese cake. "I woke up last night and it came to me plain as day. Why not an axe?" Her eyes brightened.

"Too messy," Mrs. Franklin said. "We'd ruin our clothes and even if we burned them the police would find the buttons and know they belonged to us."

"I don't mean chop him up," Mrs. Harrison said in alarm that her old friend had thought her capable of such an atrocity. "I just mean hit him on the head with it."

"But we don't have an axe, and if we bought one at the hardware store they'd be sure to remember and report it to the police."

"Now listen, Mary Sue, we've got to put on our thinking caps. We've got to figure out something soon. Mr. Shafer put poor Mrs. Grove out day before yesterday because she wouldn't get rid of her cat, and last night he made Mr. Floyd leave because he said he wheezed too much with his asthma."

"Well, have you thought of a way, Matilda?"

"No, I haven't, Mary Sue. But we will. I just know we will. While we're stuck about a method, there're still lots of other things we could be working on. We've got to figure out when the best time to do it will be. In a rooming house full of people we'll have to draw up some kind of time scheme so no one will be around to see us."

They spent a week devising a time schedule, snooping on the coming and going of the other tenants.

They didn't seem to doubt that they would succeed in their plan. They talked as if their murder was over and done with.

"It's sort of sad," Mrs. Harrison said. "Not a soul in this world will mourn Mr. Shafer."

"Not a tear will be shed for him," Mrs. Franklin said.

"Do you think we ought to send flowers to the funeral?"

"Good gracious, Matilda, I never once thought of that. I just don't know."

"Why not chip in together and send a potted lily? A big floral offering might look like gloating."

"Of course, we've got to go to the service."

"Yes, we'll have to or the rest of the people in the house might get suspicious. But don't you think it would look better if we sat more toward the back of the church than the front?"

"I believe about midway would be the best."

"I've thought of it, Matilda," Mrs. Franklin said when she was on her second piece of pecan pie. "It's simple. I'm surprised we haven't thought of it before. Can't you guess?"

"Surely it's not any of the ways we've already talked about."

"Of course not. We couldn't use any of them. We'd be caught red-handed."

"Well, I just don't know. I hate to seem stupid, but I can't even make a good guess."

"A push."

"A push?"

"Yes, just shove Mr. Shafer down the stairs. The basement steps are steep and dark and he goes down there like clockwork every day at eleven. We could take him by surprise. Reach for the small of his back, or use a broom or a mop and give him a shove. The world would be rid of one of the meanest men who ever drew breath."

"Any day at eleven will do?"

"Yes, any day except Sunday, of course. We go to church at eleven then. We couldn't do it on Sunday. I've no intention of missing church just to do away with Mr. Shafer." Mrs. Franklin was flushed over having found their solution.

It made her prettier than ever, almost childlike in appearance. No one would have believed that she had been seventy-six on January ninth.

"I've just thought of something, Mary Sue. That man, Mr. Allen, who moved in last week. He never leaves the place. He'd be here at eleven."

"He's no threat," Mrs. Franklin said. "He's hard of hearing. Besides, he's so engrossed in painting that nothing could budge him out of his room except an earthquake."

"Well, then, we'd better get it over with as soon as we can."

"The sooner the better," Mrs. Franklin said.

Of course they didn't mean it.

Or did they?

They longed for nerve enough to murder Mr. Shafer, but really they couldn't say boo to a goose. Mr. Shafer was mean, he was surly, he made them miserable, exactly as he made everyone else miserable. They wished they could just move out and be rid of him that way, but they'd looked and looked and couldn't find anything for what they could pay; anyhow they liked living where they were, near stores, near their church, near their doctor's office. They loved the old neighborhood, though it had deteriorated from family dwellings to rooming houses. If only they could get rid of Mr. Shafer and his cruelty. But they couldn't. They had just been whistling in the dark with all their talk of murder. They had just been playing with their imagination. It was their game, as if they were two bettors talking about winning a fortune when they didn't have a dollar between them.

Spring came the very next morning after Mrs. Franklin and Mrs. Harrison had decided that a push was the proper way to murder Mr. Shafer. They couldn't ignore the first warm day of spring. They postponed their usual morning coffee until afternoon. Mrs. Harrison said that she was heading for town to see what the new hats looked like, not that she could buy one. Mrs. Franklin sauntered off to see the daffodils and crocuses in the park.

Mr. Shafer heard them leave. "Darned old harpies," he said. "Maybe I can draw a breath with them out of the way for a while."

The only other person in the house then was Lawrence Allen, who lived in the room next to Mrs. Franklin. But he didn't hear the women go out even though the walls were thin. He couldn't hear very well. He didn't mind that he was growing deaf and that people had to shout at him. Nothing mattered so long as he kept his sight and could lift his right hand to paint. He had waited all his life to paint. He had refused to be a Sunday painter or an after-working-hours painter. Dabbling hadn't been for him. He had to be a dedicated painter every waking moment. Now that his youth and middle age and all their responsibilities were over he could try to be a painter. He had supported his parents, then his own family; his wife was dead and his two sons were grown and with almost-grown children of their own. After a lifetime of meeting obligations, Allen owed nothing to anyone but himself. All he needed was a place to paint and painting material. He could get by on one meal a day. Nothing was going to stop him from painting, and after months of looking for a place with a proper light, and one that he could afford on his social security, he had found it. Life in one small room with one scanty meal was paradise.

He had just stretched a canvas and had picked up a brush when the door to his room flew open. Mr. Shafer filled the doorway.

"What in hell's going on in here? What's that stink?"

Even Allen's defective ears were outraged by Shafer's bellow.

"Get that muck out of here. This is a bedroom, not a workshop. I won't have it. It smells like a pigsty. It looks like a garbage dump. I had no idea this was going on. Get this junk out of here at once."

He stalked out of the room and walked down the hall. Allen dropped his brush. His hands jerked, his throat grew dry. He ran after Shafer.

"But you can't do this to me, Mr. Shafer. I've waited all my life to paint. I looked all over town for a room with a good light. You can't make me give it up. I won't go." His voice was a shriek. The dark, empty halls boomed with his shouted despair.

Shafer lumbered down the rear stairway. He shouted back to Allen, "I've told you once and for all. You and that damned muck have got to get out of here!"

Allen pursued him, entreating him to change his mind. Allen was distraught. He was possessed. He had to convince the man. He couldn't be put out. He couldn't. He wouldn't be. He babbled. He yelled. "Listen to me, Mr. Shafer! You've got to listen!"

The emotion in Allen's voice made Shafer turn around. "Get your muck out of here or I'll—" He didn't finish his threat. What he saw on Allen's face terrified him. He ran toward the back porch and when he had reached it he slammed the back door in Allen's face. He charged toward the steep basement stairs. It was exactly eleven o'clock—the time that Mrs. Franklin and Mrs. Harrison had decided would be the safest in which to murder him—when he rushed to descend the stairs, but fear over what he had seen on Allen's face made him falter. His foot missed the first step. He stumbled and sprawled.

Lawrence Allen didn't hear the fall. He was weak with rage and numb from the violence he had felt toward Shafer. But the slammed door had brought his sanity back. Thank God, he was in control of himself now. There was no telling what he might have done if Shafer hadn't shut the door. Allen walked back upstairs. He picked his brush up from the floor and began to paint. It steadied him, brought back his purpose and his optimism. Somehow or other he believed he would find a way to keep his room.

After Mr. Shafer's death Mrs. Harrison and Mrs. Franklin didn't have much to talk about to each other. It was as if they'd talked themselves out in planning Mr. Shafer's murder. Mr. Shafer's pleasant daughter came back and took over the house. It was a happy place then. Mrs. Grove and her cat returned, and Mr. Floyd and his asthma. Mr. Shafer's daughter didn't mind Mr. Allen's painting. In fact, she encouraged him, even sat for him. It wasn't any time before he had two pictures accepted for the Annual State Exhibit.

Mary Sue Franklin and Matilda Harrison were still devoted friends, but a bit miffed with each other. Sometimes Mrs. Harrison's blood boiled a little. Accidental death, her foot, let the poor benighted police think that if they chose. But of course Mary Sue Franklin had done it. Mary Sue's lie didn't fool Mrs. Harrison at all—she hadn't gone to the park that day. She'd sneaked back the moment Mrs. Harrison had left and shoved Mr. Shafer down the stairs just as they'd planned.

As for Mrs. Franklin, she was put out because the method of the murder had been something she'd worked out all by herself, with no help from Matilda Harrison, yet Matilda had gone ahead with it all by herself, as if it had been her own idea. Mrs. Franklin had thought Mrs. Harrison was shy. She was surprised that Matilda had turned out to be the pushy type—not that she meant to make a pun. Well, that just proved that you never could tell about anyone, not even your best friend. Imagine, saying she was going to town to look at new hats, when all the time she had been hiding in the back hall waiting to shove Mr. Shafer to Kingdom Come.

The old friends kept on having their morning coffee together, but they were careful not to turn their backs on each other, and when they looked straight into each other's eyes, each was dead sure she saw a murderer.

HENRY SLESAR

Case of the Kind Waitress

Back and forth, between the kitchen and dining room of the Hotel Gordon Restaurant, Thelma Tompkins kept a worried eye on the empty corner table. Once, in her anxiety, a plate of steaming tomato soup slid precariously to the edge of the tray she carried, and Marian, the hostess, stabbed a warning across the room with her hostile eyes. But Thelma Tompkins hadn't broken a dish in eleven years as a waitress, and her instinct didn't desert her now. Still, Marian couldn't resist a muttered jibe. "What's eating you?" she said.

"Mrs. Mannerheim," Thelma answered, looking again towards the deserted table. "She's almost half an hour late. I wonder if she's okay?"

Marian snorted. "Stop being a mother hen. The old lady'll be here. She always is."

But Thelma continued to look concerned, and the frown lines didn't improve the imperfect features of her drab face. Her stringy brown hair, steamed out of curl by the heat of the kitchen and the coolness of the air-conditioned dining room, became more disordered as the evening grew later. When Mrs. Mannerheim finally took her customary place at the corner table, Thelma looked almost as ill as the old lady.

But not quite. Mrs. Mannerheim, the outlines of her tiny shrunken body not even visible within the loose-fitting black crepe dress, looked especially white-faced and wraith-like. She was a really *old* lady; past ninety Thelma guessed. And tonight it looked like Death was her neighbor.

"How are you, Mrs. Mannerheim?" Thelma rested her hands on the table and put her mouth close to the deaf old ears. "I was worried about you when you didn't come in. Same thing tonight?"

"Yes, dear, yes," the old woman said, opening the table napkin with palsied hands. "Same thing tonight, Thelma. And don't you worry about me."

"You weren't sick or anything?"

"A little," Mrs. Mannerheim smiled. "Just a little."

"Gee, don't you think you should call the doctor? You really don't look well."

"Oh, shush with your doctor talk. I haven't seen a doctor in thirty years, not since that old fool Leverett told me I was going to die." She patted Thelma's hand. "But thank you for worrying, Thelma dear, it's nice to have somebody worry about you."

The waitress blinked back the tears, the same easy tears that could be summoned forth by sad movies, scrawny cats, or her young brother, Arthur. She went into the kitchen, wiping her eyes with the heel of her hand, and told Jeff the cook that Mrs. Mannerheim was there. He didn't require details; in her eight years of residence at the Gordon Hotel, her menu had never varied. A glass of tomato juice, a lean slice of roast beef, a boiled potato, carrots, milk. When she brought the order to the table, Mrs. Mannerheim tried valiantly to cut the meat on her plate. Thelma volunteered, as usual, and reluctantly as ever, the old lady permitted the service.

"You're a good child," she said softly, watching her.

Thelma laughed. "I'm forty-four, Mrs. Mannerheim. I'm not a child anymore. Do you want more butter on your potato?"

"Can you sit and talk a little, Thelma?"

"Oh, gee, Mrs. Mannerheim, I don't think so now; we're kind of busy."

"Maybe later? There's something I want to talk to you about."

"Sure, Mrs. Mannerheim, later."

The restaurant emptied at ten-thirty, and Marian gave her the nod. But before Thelma got out of uniform, she went to the old lady's table and sat down.

"What was it you wanted to talk about, Mrs. Mannerheim?"

"About you, Thelma. Do you mind?"

"About me?" The waitress laughed, and brushed self-consciously at her unruly hair. "Nothing much to talk about me, Mrs. Mannerheim."

"I wanted to know how you're getting on, Thelma."

"Oh, same as usual, Mrs. Mannerheim."

"And that brother you told me about. How is he?"

"Arthur? Oh, he's okay, thanks. He's not making millions or anything in the store, but it's a living." She looked away, her lips whitening.

"You're still worried about him, aren't you? The last time we talked, you were worried about how unhappy he was, having to run that drug store."

Thelma said nothing.

"You love your brother a lot, don't you?"

"I guess so. He's all I have since Pop died, Mrs. Mannerheim. I mean, all those things I said about him that night—well, I didn't really mean them. He's just young; he can't help getting into scrapes. You know how it is."

"Of course." The old lady coughed, and the sound echoed emptily within the hollow crepe dress.

"You want some more water?"

"No, I'm all right. Well, that's not really true." She tried to laugh. "Not really all right, Thelma. For the first time, I really *feel* old. I've been so sick lately . . . sometimes I think the time's coming . . ."

"Oh, Mrs. Mannerheim!" The tears welled again.

"Now don't fret. It's different, thinking about death, when you're old like me. But what I wanted to tell you, Thelma, I mean in case anything should happen to me, is that I think a lot of you, and I want to help you. Do you know what I'm talking about?"

"No."

"I'm talking about money, Thelma.   I'm what they call a rich old widow, more money than sense.   I have a niece in California, and she'll have to get something, just because she's family, but she doesn't care two cents worth for me.   But I wanted you to know that I've taken care of you."

Thelma settled her face, half in bewilderment, half in sudden expectation.

"Taken care of me?"

"In my will.   You've been a good friend to me, Thelma, these past few years. I'm grateful to you.   When I die, you'll be able to leave this place and do what you want.   And your brother—"

Thelma's hand fluttered to her throat.   Arthur!

"Oh, Mrs. Mannerheim, you don't have to do this—"

"But I want to, Thelma, I really want to.   It will be a considerable legacy, believe me.   I don't know why I should be so rich, but since my husband's death the money just seemed to grow and grow.   It's kept me comfortable, and now I want it to make you happy."

She seemed to have difficulty breathing; she clutched her stomach and shut her eyes.

"Mrs. Mannerheim—"

"It'll pass, Thelma, it'll pass . . ."

When her eyes opened again, they were steady and bright.

"I don't have long, Thelma," she said.   "I have dreams about my mother, wearing a long white dress with flowers.   Do you believe in dreams?"

"I don't know," Thelma Tompkins whispered, wondering if this moment were one.

It was only ten past eleven when Thelma arrived home, and Arthur was sitting crosslegged in front of the television set, looking rumpled and sleepy enough to have been ensconced there for hours.   She would have been indignant any other night; now she settled for a milder approach.

"For heaven's sake, Arthur!   What time did you close the store?"

"Only a little while ago," her brother scowled.

"You can't keep shutting up so early, Arthur.   You really can't afford it.   You know what Pop always said, there's an awful lot of business after ten o'clock . . ."

He didn't answer.   He put his beardless chin deep into the collar of his opened shirt until it covered his pouting mouth.   He frowned and rubbed his hand over the stubbly blond hair on his head.   He looked more boyish than ever when he sulked; Thelma could hardly believe he was almost thirty-five.

"Arthur, I have something to tell you."

"Write me a letter."

"Don't be nasty.   This is something important.   More important than television."

"What'd you do, get canned?"

"Arthur, this has something to do with *you*."

The personal pronoun caught his interest. He lowered the sound on the receiver and turned to his sister.

She told him the news. He listened with an attentiveness he had rarely shown any speech of hers before, refraining from puncturing her story with his needle-sharp questions. When she was done, the tension left him like an uncoiled spring, and he sagged into the armchair.

"How much do you think?" he said dreamily. "How much, Thelma?"

"I don't know. There's all sorts of stories about her. Her husband was in the canning business, but he died, oh, years ago. Still, she must have invested the money, that's why it's so much. And she looks so sick, the poor old thing . . ."

"That's the tricky part," her brother murmured. "If she died soon, like in the next couple of months, I got a couple of deals I'm interested in . . ."

"Arthur!"

"Don't get excited, I'm not wishing your girl friend bad luck. But if she's really as sick as all that . . ."

"I don't even want to *think* about that side of it. It's just nice to know that someday . . ."

"Yeah, sure, someday," Arthur Tompkins said. "How old did you say she was?"

"I don't know for sure. Ninety, maybe more."

The man smiled, with his boy's face. He reached up and turned off the television set, but he continued to stare at the blank gray screen as if still seeing pictures there.

For two months of evenings, Thelma Tompkins kept her eyes on the corner table, and night after night, the old lady who had long ago established squatter's rights arrived at varying hours. The last remnants of color were slowly draining from her cheeks, the shuffling walk was becoming a totter. Marian, the restaurant hostess, watched the decline of Mrs. Mannerheim and clucked in concern, not for the old woman, but for her own sense of order.

"Just *look* at the old thing," she said. "I'm afraid she'll die right in the middle of dinner. You'd think a woman like that would go to a *home* or something."

Thelma didn't reply. She had become more attentive than ever to the old lady, spreading the napkin on her lap, slicing her roast beef extra small, filling the water glass herself. But even as she redoubled her efforts to please old Mrs. Mannerheim, she knew that the motive of sheer human kindness had been sullied since the woman's announcement. She knew it was more than that now, that there was selfish purpose in her solicitousness. But Thelma felt no shame or guilt; there was Arthur to consider now too. The responsibility of her love was clear.

But the next step was inevitable. As month succeeded month, as the tiny figure of Mrs. Mannerheim grew more and more ethereal, Thelma found herself unable to keep what was once a fear from becoming an unspoken wish. *Why doesn't the old lady die?*

Mrs. Mannerheim didn't die. Each night it seemed that the fire of life in her shriveled body was going out, but somehow it glowed weakly and burned on. Once, she collapsed over the table, just as Marian had feared, but the fainting spell passed.   For a period of a week, she was too ill to make the journey from her third-floor room to the restaurant below, and Thelma brought up a tray of food each night, expecting with every opening of the hotel door to find the old lady unbreathing and stilled forever.   But Mrs. Mannerheim was alive, if not well, smiling gamely, her tiny head motionless on the pillow of her bed.

Spring passed, and then summer, the winter cold returned to the city, chilling old bones and blood, bringing disease and death to the aged in their hotel rooms and boarding houses.   But each night, the corner table was occupied.

"I'm sick of waiting," Arthur said one morning.

"Arthur!"

"Don't Arthur me, Thelma.   You're sick of it too.   You're getting to hate the old woman."

"Hate?   What are you talking about?   Why, I'm very *fond* of the old lady—"

"Sure, that's what you tell yourself."   He laughed abruptly.   "But you don't talk about her the way you used to.   It's as if you don't like to talk about her. And I'll bet she's giving you a hard time too."

"Don't be ridiculous."   She couldn't look at him.   How could he have known? She *did* feel tension with the old lady.   Mrs. Mannerheim had begun to complain all the time, quarreling over the quality of the food, accusing Thelma of indolence, once even of padding the bill.   One night she had been so vexed with the waitress that she had petulantly forgotten her usual twenty-five-cent tip.   But it was only natural, Thelma thought; when people get old and sick, they get querulous . . .

"I can see it in your face," Arthur said, leaning forward insinuatingly.   "You're getting to hate the old woman more every day.   She's taking a long time to die, isn't she?"

"I won't listen to you!"

"It's almost eight months now.   What makes you think she won't live to be a hundred?"

"But she's so sick—"

"Then why isn't she dead?"

"Arthur!"

"Why not help her along, Thelma?"

He blurted out the words, and from the surprised look on his face, it was obviously without regard for timing.   But the thought must have been simmering for a long time before it was spoken.   Thelma was too stunned to answer, but he took her silence for interest, and went on.

"It would be easy, really easy," he said.   "And it wouldn't even be *wrong,* Thelma, that's the best part.   Think of how the old lady is suffering, sick the way she is.   An old woman like that, why, she'd welcome a little peace.   And you can give it to her, Thelma, so easy!"

"I'm not listening!" she said frantically, but shut only her eyes.

"You could do it so simply, nobody would ever know.   I'd help you, Thelma.

I'd show you how to do it real simply. Everybody who knows the old woman thinks she's ready to kick the bucket; they'll never be suspicious.''

"Stop it!''

He smiled at her. "And you know how we could do it, Thelma? With the food. The food you serve her every night. She'd never even notice it, an old lady like that, her taste buds shot the way they are. Just a lit-tle bit of powder in every dish, Thelma, just a lit-tle bit, night after night, until . . .''

"You're crazy! You're absolutely crazy, Arthur!''

"Sure, sure, only listen to what I'm saying. I have plenty of stuff in the back of the store, Thelma, all we'll need. Then you put a pinch into the food every night. It would be easy for you, wouldn't it? Now wouldn't it?''

She forced herself out of the chair, gasping as if fighting her way out of a whirlpool, and ran from the room.

Arthur didn't follow her. He turned on the television set and remained silent the rest of the morning. He went to the drug store in the afternoon, and returned after midnight. Just before bedtime, he said:

"Poor sick old lady. It's a mercy killing, Thelma.''

Then he went to bed.

Arthur didn't mention his idea for another month. Thelma waited for him to bring it up, but he didn't. Finally, she was forced to say it herself.

"Poor Mrs. Mannerheim,'' she said.

"What?''

"She looks so bad. She can hardly walk. Sometimes, when I see her suffer, I think you were right, Arthur, about mercy killings. I mean . . .''

Arthur had good sense. He didn't smile, or even look smug. He merely nodded, soberly, clucked his sympathy, and then waited a few minutes before saying:

"Suppose I bring something home from the store tonight, Thelma? For Mrs. Mannerheim.''

"All right,'' Thelma said dreamily, almost as if she hadn't heard.

Jeff, the cook, merely nodded at Thelma when she walked into the kitchen; he knew Mrs. Mannerheim had arrived. He handed her the tray; she placed it on the cart.

She paused in the tiny anteroom that led to the stairway descending to the restaurant lounge, and lifted the dented cover of the entree plate. She took the small brown envelope from her apron pocket, and sprinkled a minuscule amount of the powdery stuff over the roast beef. Then she put the cover back and wheeled the cart down the aisle to the corner table.

She hadn't been nervous during the performance of her action, but as she waited by Mrs. Mannerheim's table while the old lady struggled to bring nourishment to her feeble body, her fingers were so tremulous that she had to conceal them beneath the apron.

There was no reaction from the old woman. She ate the meat with the same mechanical lack of interest she always displayed.

When Mrs. Mannerheim left, Thelma dropped the quarter tip into her pocket, where it rested against the small bag of poison.

The next night, it was just as easy.

So was the third night, and the fourth.

But Mrs. Mannerheim didn't die.

"I don't get it," Arthur said. "Didn't she even look worse? Nausea? Anything like that?"

"No. But it's so hard to notice any difference in her, Arthur. I mean, she looks so sick all the time."

"Well, just relax. Better to keep the dosage small; we can't take any chances."

"Yes, Arthur."

"Look what I brought you," her brother grinned. "A present."

She took the package from him and crowed with delight. It was from the drug store, and it was perfume, the sale price still marked in grease pencil on the box.

The next night, Mrs. Mannerheim didn't come down to dinner, and Thelma enjoyed a sudden hope that the ordeal was over. But the old lady returned the following dinner hour, and spoke only of having slept through the evening meal, dreaming dreams of her mother in a long white dress.

Another week passed, and Mrs. Mannerheim didn't die.

"Are you *sure* about this poison?" Thelma said to her brother, no longer afraid to speak the word, now avid for success.

"Of course, I'm sure! But maybe we ought to increase the dose a little. It's bound to get her soon—"

"But it's not, it's not! She doesn't seem any worse than she ever was, Arthur. Sometimes I think she'll live forever—"

"We don't have forever. Increase the dose," Arthur said grimly.

Thelma increased it. Nightly, the powdery stuff went into the old lady's food. For another two weeks, fourteen dinners, lightly seasoned with poison, Mrs. Mannerheim seemed to improve in health, until the dreams of the moneyed future seemed to grow more distant and indistinct, until Arthur began to voice the doubt that was growing in her own mind.

"What if she changes her mind? What if she changes her will?"

"Don't say that, Arthur!"

"It can happen! You told me how nasty she gets to you sometimes. What if she decides you're not such a buddy after all? What if she has a fight with you? What if a million things?"

"It can't happen, it can't!" Thelma sobbed.

"Anything can happen!" her brother shouted, his eyes hating, his voice hating.

"I won't let it happen," Thelma promised. "I won't let it, Arthur."

She reported to the restaurant that evening with a passion for certainty burning in her breast. No more small doses, not bit-by-bit extermination; she wanted something final, conclusive.

At ten o'clock, Mrs. Mannerheim hadn't arrived.

"Where is she?" Thelma asked the hostess, who shrugged.

"Where's Mrs. Mannerheim tonight, Marian?"

"How the devil should I know?" Marian said crossly.   "God, you'd think that old dame owned this restaurant.   She probably dozed off again—"

"Maybe I should check.   Maybe I should call her on the house phone."

"You've got tables to wait on, don't forget that."

"But maybe she's really sick, maybe she needs help."

"Oh, for God's sake, you make *me* sick.   All right, call her, see if I care if the people go hungry."

Thelma went into the hotel lobby and picked up a dialless phone.   It rang twice in the old woman's apartment and Mrs. Mannerheim answered in a barely discernible voice.   No, there was nothing wrong, she said, she simply wasn't hungry.   Could Thelma bring her up a little something?   No, it wasn't necessary.   It wouldn't be any trouble at all, Thelma said, a sandwich or some tea or something.   All right, Mrs. Mannerheim said, a little tea would be nice.

The waitress went to the kitchen and put some hot water into a pitcher.   Then she put a cup and saucer onto a tray, and removed two tea bags from the larder. She went to the hotel elevator and pressed the button marked Three.

When she walked into the room, Mrs. Mannerheim said, "You're a dear girl," and didn't rise from her chair.   "I was too weary to make it downstairs tonight, and my appetite isn't very good."

"I understand," Thelma said.   She turned her back to the old lady and placed the tray on the table near the door.   She placed the teabags into the steaming pitcher, and reached into her apron pocket.

It was empty.   She had forgotten the poison.

"You didn't bring the milk?" the old lady said, struggling to her feet.

"No!" she answered angrily.   "I forgot the milk, Mrs. Mannerheim."

"I can't stand tea without milk, Thelma.   Couldn't you get me some?"

Thelma whirled and glared at the old woman.   "I don't have any milk, Mrs. Mannerheim.   You can drink it without milk!"

"But I *can't!*" the old lady whined.   "I simply can't, Thelma.   I've always had milk with my tea, ever since I was a little girl.   You know how it is, a habit like that—"

"I don't, I don't!" Thelma cried.   "I don't know what it's like!   I haven't always had everything I wanted, Mrs. Mannerheim.   Do you understand that?"

"Why, Thelma—"

"I've had to work for what I wanted, Mrs. Mannerheim.   You think I'm a waitress because I love it, because the restaurant's my *home*?   You think I like greasy kitchens and dirty dishes and complaining old women—"

Mrs. Mannerheim looked shocked.   Then she drew herself up with dignity. "You shouldn't talk to me that way, Thelma."

"I'll talk to you any damn way I please!"

The old lady gasped.

"You're a rude, naughty girl, Thelma.   You're not at all the person I thought you were.   And if you think I'll stand for it, you're mistaken.   I'm calling my lawyer this minute and changing the will—''

"Don't touch that phone!'' Thelma cried out as the old lady reached for the receiver, intercepting the motion with a heavy hand on the bony wrist.

"Now you *stop* that, you awful child!''

"I'm forty-four years old!'' Thelma shrieked, and no longer caring, or thinking, threw herself at the old woman as an animal would pounce upon prey, a primeval instinct guiding her to the throat, the windpipe, the source of air and life.   Mrs. Mannerheim didn't resist beyond a faint touch of her fingers.   She seemed so ready for death, so well prepared for its coming that her withered body went limp even before Thelma's enlarged red hands enclosed her neck with the strength they would need to kill her.   Death came so quickly to Mrs. Mannerheim that Thelma was still holding on when the door opened behind her and the chambermaid screamed the scream that broke the spell . . .

The important thing, Thelma told herself, was Arthur.   Over and over, she said his name in her mind, but never once aloud, not once, throughout the ordeal of arrest and imprisonment and endless questioning.

But then it came out, and all because of what *he* had told her, the tall gray hulk of a man at the police station, who said:

"But why did you have to kill her?   Why couldn't you wait?   A sick old woman like that . . .''

"Sick?'' Thelma repeated, and laughed.   "She wasn't sick . . .''

"But she was, very sick.   They performed an autopsy, and they know.   She had a parasitic infection, dangerous in a woman her age.   Probably the only thing that was keeping her alive was the treatment she was getting.   Small doses of arsenic.''

CARROLL MAYERS

Ghost of a Chance

$\mathbf{I}$n all of County Fermanagh you would likely find no citizen less superstitious than Michael Doyle.   To some, it was imperative to circumvent diligently a black feline or sidestep an angled ladder.   Other precautions were legion.   By and large, Doyle considered such thinking childish nonsense.

Today, though, as he sat in the front room of the neat cottage while Dr. Carmody attended his wife, Doyle's mind was churning with converse speculation.   Could there be anything significant about Sarah's sudden coronary, coming only a month after he'd met Molly Brennan?   Could he look upon the seizure as opportune, even felicitous?   Aside from some funereal fantasies and convictions he deplored, Sarah had been a good wife, tending to his creature comforts all these years.   But never had she fired his blood as did Molly.   Never had her simple touch constricted his chest and set his temples pounding.

Now, and might the good saints understand and sympathize for his harboring such a wonderment, could it be that Sarah's attack meant that soon he and Molly—

Dr. Carmody emerged from the bedroom.   The physician was the best in Aughnacloy and, in the moment of stress, Doyle had considered no other, but had sent a neighbor lass posthaste to fetch him, after Sarah had been stricken while clearing away the supper dishes.

"H-how is she, Doctor?"   Guilt over the macabre pondering which had gripped him made Doyle's query break; he arose unsteadily from his chair.

"She's resting comfortably," Carmody said.   He was a portly man, brisk and efficient, yet with an understanding mien.   "I've given her some medication to ease her distress."

"She'll be all right?"

"I've little doubt of it."   The doctor's smile was reassuring.   "The seizure seems relatively mild.   We'll know more definitely after a bit of checking."

Doyle believed he comprehended.   "A cardiogram, Doctor?"

"Yes," Carmody nodded as he picked up his bag.   "Don't worry, Mr. Doyle; once the medication takes hold, your wife should have a restful night.   I'll stop back early tomorrow.   Try to get some sleep yourself."

After the physician had departed, Doyle looked in on his wife, found her already sleeping.   He went back to the front room, tried to interest himself in the day's newspaper.   He couldn't.   His thoughts vacillated from innate, husbandly concern for Sarah to frank realization such concern was now largely feigned. He kept visualizing Molly Brennan's snapping black eyes and quirking red lips as she dispensed beer and repartee to the patrons of the Cat and Fiddle. Molly had come to town only a month ago, but from the very first week he'd become infatuated, and she had miraculously returned his regard by meeting him clandestinely behind Thompson's Mill.

At ten o'clock Doyle gave up, sought to compose himself for the night on the couch. The endeavor was futile. Censure over his initial thoughts about Sarah's attack (superstitious speculation cloaking a death wish?) engulfed him in waves. Sleep was impossible.

The days immediately following were no better. An examination made with a portable cardiograph he brought to the cottage the next morning convinced Dr. Carmody no extensive heart damage had occurred, and that Sarah would not require hospitalization.

"Complete rest is all she needs for a month, Mr. Doyle," the physician stated. "After that, some buggy rides in the country, a little mild activity, and your wife should be fine. Just be certain she avoids any emotional upsets, any shock or strain."

Doyle knew he should have been delighted with the encouraging prognosis. He also knew he wasn't—and *why* he wasn't—and the clash of conflicting emotions was devastating.

Molly brought the whole smoldering issue to flame one night a week later. The neighbor lass had been staying with Sarah days, getting her meals and tending her wants while Doyle was at work at Jellicoe's farm; and this night he had prevailed upon the girl to remain after supper while he left the cottage "for a bit of a breather." The reprieve had been sought behind Thompson's Mill, where Molly came into his arms with a ready kiss and a fervent sigh. "I wish she had died," Molly whispered.

Shocked despite himself, Doyle drew back. "Don't say that!"

"Why not?" Molly's red mouth pouted as she pressed close. "It's what you're wishing too, isn't it?"

"No! No, it's not."

"Don't be lying to me, Michael Doyle. I know you too well for that."

"Please, Molly," Doyle implored, sorely shaken now that his soul was being stripped bare. "We mustn't be talking like this. Sarah's my wife."

Molly's lips again brushed his. "And you wish she wasn't," she murmured.

"I—I can't wish such a thing."

Molly disengaged herself, but still stood close, close enough for him to catch the intimate scent of her hair, read the unspoken promise in her lovely dark eyes. "I'm not believing you can't, Michael," Molly told him quietly.

There was the devil's own crux of it all; with this breathtaking creature in his arms, Doyle realized he wasn't believing it either.

The sleepless night which ensued was but a sample of many. Though he contrived to conceal his state from Sarah, Doyle's nerves grew wire-taut; his appetite lagged and his strength ebbed. Conversely, with each succeeding day, Sarah's recovery bloomed apace. The fresh air buggy rides which Dr. Carmody had prescribed, and which Doyle had no legitimate excuse against conducting, put roses in Sarah's cheeks and left small doubt of her imminent return to full health. This realization, when balanced against brief moments of consolation with Molly, left Doyle all the more miserable.

And then one night as he tossed fitfully on the couch, the solution presented itself. Full-blown, complete, the very simplicity stunned Doyle, left his pulse racing. Any misgiving, any subconscious moral dissuasion was swept aside in grim recognition of his own intolerable position and what it would mean to be free to take the delectable Molly as his bride. He could do it; he *had* to do it.

"I can't go on this way," Doyle earnestly told the winsome barmaid when they met the following night.

She studied him, shrewdly sensing a subtle implication in his tone. "You've thought of something," she suggested, making it a statement rather than a question.

He drew a breath. "I have."

Molly snuggled against him. "Tell me, Michael."

Doyle hesitated, his arms trembling as he returned the embrace. "The doctor cautioned me against Sarah's experiencing any sudden shock or strain," he said finally. "If she *did* get such a shock, a truly severe one—" He stopped, swallowing hard and averting his gaze. Thinking was one thing, but actually putting it into words—

Molly's dark eyes continued to seek his. "You're saying, if we did the shocking?"

Doyle's reply was barely audible. "Yes."

She pulled back slightly. "That would be murder, Michael," she said.

He stiffened, forced himself to look at her. "I don't want to be talking about that," he answered, his voice abruptly taut. "All I know is, it's our best chance." He drew her close once more, sought her lips. "Our only chance, darlin'."

For a long moment Molly responded; then she resolutely broke the kiss with a simple query. "How, Michael?"

Doyle breathed deeply again. "A scare; a sudden terrible fright," he explained. "Sarah believes in spirits; she's deathly afraid of sometime meeting up with a ghost. If I should take her for a buggy ride and we're late getting back; if we should drive past the cemetery outside town just about dusk . . ."

Comprehension danced in Molly's gaze. "And if I was already there, wearing a sheet and hiding behind a tombstone near the road . . ."

Doyle nodded. "Some wild shrieking and swooping should do it," he said solemnly. "Afterward, there'll be no evidence. I'll simply claim Sarah suddenly collapsed again. There's not a soul in town who will be believing otherwise."

Molly abruptly giggled. "Or suspect our grave undertaking."

He frowned at her levity. "Don't be laughing, Molly. At best, it'll not be easy for me."

She sobered. "I know, Michael," she whispered, slipping into his arms anew. "But I'll make it up to you. You'll see."

Once the seed of decision had been planted, Doyle was impatient for its fruition. Behind the mill two nights later, with the weather cool and pleasant, he told Molly they would make their play the following day.

"Sarah has a sister in Dungannon; she'll be happy to make the trip when I suggest it," he explained. "I've already asked Mr. Jellicoe for the day, and I'll delay our return so it will just be turning dark." He looked earnestly at Molly. "Be certain you time it right, now. Not too soon. Wait until we're almost upon you, so Sarah will be sure to see. Then swoop out with a fierce piercing shriek."

Her lips were soft upon his. "No banshee will ever wail fiercer," she promised.

Sarah was indeed gratified at Doyle's suggestion. An unpretentious woman, she found enjoyment in simple activities and watched her husband hitch the mare to the buggy with obvious pleasure. "It will be good to see Emily again," she agreed.

But if Sarah was pleased by the trip, her sister was even more so. At the hour Doyle had elected for their departure, Emily would not even consider Sarah's leaving. "She'll stay until the weekend," she informed Doyle with firm geniality. "You can drive back for her Sunday."

Sarah's concurrence was characteristically diffident. "A little visit *would* be nice," she suggested.

Some rapid cerebration convinced Doyle to agree reluctantly. Should he obdurately insist upon Sarah's return this day, her sister might very well recall, wonder about it later. While that would be a minor point, and nothing could be proven, still it was better to arouse no speculation, particularly when it meant only a few days' delay until another trip could be undertaken. Further, now that he thought about it, it would do no harm to see how Molly carried it off, how she conducted her ghost act when the buggy approached the cemetery. Sort of a "dry run," you might say.

So Michael Doyle drove home alone.

With a few exceptions, all of Aughnacloy attended the wake and funeral. Molly Brennan was one who didn't. The experience so unnerved her she was forced to take to her bed for a week. She continued to envision that terrible moment when, shrieking and wearing her shroud, she had jumped from behind the tombstone and so spooked Michael Doyle's mare that the frightened animal bolted, throwing Doyle from the buggy to strike a roadside boulder and split open his skull like an eggshell. And all on Friday the thirteenth, no less.

JAMES HOLDING

The Montevideo Squeeze

I called Carlos Olavide, the head of our Drivers Association, from the Sisters of Mercy Hospital in Montevideo.

Carlos picked up the phone in his office and said, "Yes?"

"Fernando Quintana, Carlos," I said. My voice echoed in the little telephone box. I could hear its hoarseness. I suppose the bandage on my neck muffled my vocal cords a bit, too.

"Fernando! What is it?" Carlos asked in the manner of a man expecting bad news.

I lowered my voice to a murmur. "I'm calling from the hospital," I said. "The emergency room. I—"

He interrupted me. "Emergency room! Are you hurt, Fernando?"

"Slightly," I said. "Calm yourself, Carlos. I have a shallow cut in my neck, that is all. Under my chin. Superficial. Five stitches and a small bandage."

Carlos drew a worried breath. "What happened?"

"Two men," I said. "One with a Portuguese accent, almost a dwarf; and a tall, thin fellow wearing a beige-colored hat. I picked them up in my cab at Pereira Rossell Park near the Planetarium. They gave me an address on the waterfront. Halfway there, while they were talking about the weather, the dwarf put his hand over the back of my driver's seat and held a knife under my chin. Very gentle and tender he was about it, but it was a knife, all the same, and I could feel blood starting to drip onto my collar. I pulled up under a tree, as they told me, trying my best, you may be sure, not to swallow or move my head! They demanded my day's earnings, and when I gave them the money, the tall one told the dwarf to cut me a little more . . ." I paused and swallowed painfully before continuing, "just to show that The Big Ones meant business. The Big Ones. That's what he said, Carlos."

"*Terrible!*" Carlos' voice held dismay.

"Yes. And that made it clear they were not just ordinary holdup men. You see?"

"Only too plainly. I am sorry it happened to you, too, Fernando. Did you tell the truth to the doctor who sewed you up?"

"Not after I knew The Big Ones were mixed in it. Of course I didn't. Nor the police, either. He warned us about that, remember?"

"I remember. What *did* you tell the *médico*, then? After all, a knife cut under the chin . . ."

I did my best to chuckle. "I told him I almost tore my head off by walking into my wife's steel clothesline in the back yard. He believed me."

I waited for Carlos to say something, but he remained silent. I asked, "You said you were sorry it happened to me, *too*? Have there been other accidents today?"

"One other, so far. Diego Carnero's cab was blown up this morning. While Diego was not in it, thank God. But his cab was demolished." Carlos spoke bitterly. "They might as well have killed him as destroyed his taxicab. How will he now provide for his family? Diego has twelve children, Fernando. And only one good arm."

I said, "That is a true tragedy. I shall not complain about my minor cut."

"Well," said Carlos, "how do you feel? Will you be driving any more today?"

"I'm going home. My nerves are shaken, Carlos. I'll rest a bit. Perhaps I'll take my cab out tonight."

"Do that." A pause. "I was hoping that Diego's cab blowing up meant nothing. That it was just a chance accident, from gasoline fumes and a cigarette, perhaps. But now that this outrage has happened to you . . ."

"Now it means something, eh? Now we know that man was speaking the truth about his proposal."

"Exactly. And we'll have to present the matter to the membership after all, I believe. Do you agree, Fernando?"

"Emphatically! Having my throat cut is demonstration enough for me, thank you!" I tried to laugh but it came out a shaky croak.

"We have another day before the meeting. Pray that nothing else happens to us meanwhile."

"*Amén,*" I said and hung up.

It was on the previous morning that word had reached me to report as soon as possible to association headquarters off Plaza Independencia. Carlos Olavide wanted to see me. Francisco Guivara, passing the cab rank at the Victoria Plaza Hotel where I was waiting, fourth in line, for a fare, had passed me the message. I pulled out of line at once and headed for the shabby room above a sidewalk café that serves us as permanent union headquarters.

Carlos and Luis Bayeu, the union's *segundo*, were waiting for me when I arrived. Carlos must have sent for Luis, too, from his post out at Punta Carreta Lighthouse.

Carlos handed me a letter. "Read this, please, Fernando . . ."

The letter was written in black ink in a bold and slanting hand. It was addressed to the Montevideo Taxicab Drivers Association. It was quite short. It said:

Dear Sir:

I shall visit your headquarters at three o'clock this afternoon to acquaint you with the terms of a proposal which you must accept at once if you value the health, prosperity and lives of your membership. I suggest that the three top officers of your association be present since prompt action—official action—on my proposal is of the essence. I strongly advise you, in the name of The Big Ones, to give me a hearing.

Manoël Goncalves

I tossed the letter back onto Carlos' desk. "What colossal impertinence!" I said. "It is a sad day when the most powerful association of taxicab drivers in Uruguay can be browbeaten in such fashion by a nervy insurance salesman—or whatever this man is selling! Is *this* why you summoned me, Carlos?"

Carlos Olavide nodded. "That is why, Fernando. As secretary of our association, I want you here for the meeting with this Goncalves."

I said, "The man is an arrogant fool." I looked at Carlos, uncertainly. "You're surely not granting his request, are you?"

Luis was indignant. "Carlos says we must do it, Fernando, whether we want to or not!"

I stared at Carlos. "Why?" I demanded.

Carlos frowned. "I cannot take a chance, that is why," he said. "I would laugh the whole affair off, like you, were it not for one phrase in that letter."

I looked at the letter again. "The Big Ones?"

He moved his head up and down. Carlos Olavide's face is brown and wrinkled, so that when he nodded it was like a monkey nodding. "Have you heard of them?"

Luis and I both looked blank. "Should we have?" Luis asked.

"I have heard of them," Carlos said slowly. "Several years ago, as you will remember, I represented our association at the international meeting. While I was there, I heard references to these Big Ones."

"What references?" I asked. "Who are The Big Ones?"

Carlos' forehead ridged like a washboard. "It was never clear to me, but it seemed to be an organization held in the greatest fear by everyone, even the government itself. Some kind of an illegal business combine, I thought, or a great criminal guild of some description, perhaps. In any case, people whispered the name behind their hands as if terrified of being overheard. So you can understand, if this letter originates with one of The Big Ones . . ."

Luis' eyes were almost out on his cheeks. I felt a cold hand squeeze my heart. Luis said, "Gangsters? Is that what you mean, Carlos?"

"That is what I think they are, yes. In the interests of our members, therefore, can we defy this man Goncalves who represents them, without hearing what he has to say?"

Luis tapped the letter thoughtfully with a forefinger like a sausage. Luis is six and a half feet tall and muscled like Hercules. He was a stevedore before he bought his taxicab and joined our association. "Maybe you're right, Carlos," he muttered in bewilderment. "It could be dangerous to refuse him, I suppose."

Carlos spread his hands. "So. We will see him, then, at three o'clock. Agreed?"

Luis and I nodded, feeling frustrated and uneasy. I stood. "I'll be back at three," I said. "And my own inclination is to see this Manoël Goncalves damned before we—"

"Before you what?" A new voice spoke. "Am I a bit early, gentlemen?"

Our three heads swiveled toward the doorway like three coconuts pulled around by a single wire. Framed there at the head of the stairs was a stranger. He had ascended from the café below without a sound, although he was very fat to move so quietly.

His colorless eyes were childishly round and glacially cold, and they regarded Carlos, Luis and me without expression of any kind in them, although his thick lips were smiling. He carried a briefcase. He stepped daintily into the room, all our startled eyes upon him, and dropped with a sigh into the only vacant chair. "I am Manoël Goncalves," he introduced himself. "I wrote you a letter."

Carlos' frown deepened the wrinkles in his forehead. "Your letter says three o'clock, Señor." He spoke without politeness.

Goncalves waved a hand. "Since you are all here, why wait till three?" He turned his cold gaze deliberately from one to the other of us until each had borne his scrutiny for long enough to become acutely uncomfortable. Then he said, "Since you will not do me the honor of introducing yourselves, I shall do it for you. Carlos Olavide, head of your association. Luis Bayeu, *segundo*. Fernando Quintana, secretary."

"How do you know?" asked Carlos, taken aback.

"It is my business to know such things, and much else besides. I merely sat in the sidewalk café downstairs until I saw you two arrive," he nodded at Luis and me, "and then came up." He took from his briefcase a flat machine and set it on Carlos' desk.

"What's that?" Carlos demanded sharply.

"A tape recorder. You'll need a record of this conversation."

"Why?"

"To play to your membership at the monthly meeting on Friday evening," said Goncalves. He switched on the machine. "Now, gentlemen, I am ready to give you my friendly word."

"Your friendly word," Luis asked, "on what?"

Goncalves put his gaze for a moment on Luis, eyeing Luis' bulging muscles with amusement. Then, imperturbably, he turned back to Carlos. "My friendly word concerns your association of taxicab drivers, as I told you in my letter."

"What is your concern with our association?"

Goncalves answered obliquely. "You are in great danger here in Montevideo, you taxicab drivers."

"Danger?"

"Yes. I have come to warn you."

I noticed now that Goncalves' Spanish bore a faint trace of Portuguese accent.

"About what do you warn us?" Luis was belligerent. "We have been driving taxicabs in Montevideo for many years without any great hazard except, perhaps, *muerte de hambre*, starvation. What threatens us now?"

Again Goncalves ignored Luis. "Danger was the word I used," he said to Carlos. "And danger was the word I meant. *Peligro.*"

"If you will forgive me, Señor, you talk nonsense!" I broke in. "What danger?"

The fat man's lips writhed in his meaningless smile. He explained blandly, "Accidents. Accidents to taxicab drivers and to their cabs."

"I still don't understand." Carlos creased his face in puzzlement.

"I am trying to explain. The accidents of which I speak are promised to you by a group of farseeing men who value money above the welfare of a gaggle of taxicab drivers." Goncalves laughed.

"What group of men is that?" I asked, although I already knew what the answer would be.

"The Big Ones, we are called, or The Corporation. You have heard of us, perhaps?"

"Vaguely," Carlos said, his distaste evident in his tone. He glanced meaningfully at Luis and me. "However, Señor Goncalves, I still do not understand what you are getting at."

Goncalves said in a quiet voice, "Protection, you fool. The Big Ones are offering to protect you from the many accidents that could easily happen to you."

Luis half rose from his chair, clenching his huge fists. "*Por favor*, Señor," he breathed, "do not call Carlos Olavide a fool, or one of these accidents you speak of might happen to *you!*"

Carlos put out a restraining hand. "Wait, Luis. I wish to hear more of this odd protection we are offered by Señor Goncalves. You will explain further?"

"Certainly. I have come here expressly for that purpose. It is very simple. Each member of your association will pay The Big Ones, through me, a small percentage of his earnings. In return, The Big Ones will see to it that nothing of a violent nature happens to your taxi drivers . . . or their cabs . . . or their families. They pay us to protect them, you see, to prevent these unpleasant accidents from happening."

Shocked, Carlos looked at Luis and me. "Do you hear this man?"

"We hear him," I said.

"Is he serious? Or is he joking?"

"It's no joke, *amigo*," Goncalves said.

Luis said, "Do not call Carlos 'amigo,' you scum!"

Carlos' voice drew out into a thin thread of passion. "You dare to propose such a thing? To the Taxicab Drivers Association of Montevideo? A powerful brotherhood with hundreds of members? Let me inform you, Señor, we need no protection, as you call it, from anyone! We are strong!"

"Strong enough, at any rate," said Luis, "to throw you out of this room." Luis reached for the fat man.

Goncalves didn't move. "Before you do something you may regret," he said gently, "remember, I beg of you, the many men—and they *are* many—whom I have brought here to help me protect you. You don't know who they are. Nor do you know, yet, how very expert they are in violence, injury, and yes, even death." He underlined the last word with his voice.

Luis hesitated and looked to Carlos for a sign.

Carlos temporized. "What, exactly, are you asking us to do?"

"Report my proposition to your membership at your Friday night meeting. Play your members the recording of this interview. Tell them it's just a small percentage of their earnings we want. Insignificant. Your members pay dues, I presume?"

"Of course."

Goncalves grinned. "You could pay for my protection, then, by jacking up those dues a mere five percent. Your drivers can't object to that. Everything is going up in price these days. Even the price of safety. Your association will give me that extra five percent each month as a lump sum. In cash. Saves collection charges, eh?" He turned to me. "You're the secretary of this association. You'll be the union's contact with The Big Ones. You'll pay me the protection payment at a spot I will disclose to you each month. In cash, please." He lit a cigarette with elaborate casualness. "And the payment had better be right, my friend. The Big Ones know how many members you have. They know what your current dues are. So we'll know if you try to deceive us. Understand?"

Carlos began in a furious sputter, "Señor Goncalves, if the police of Montevideo hear of this—"

"Try it!" the fat man interrupted fiercely. "Just try it! If any of you goes to the police, I'll know it within thirty minutes. And you'll be dead men within twenty-four hours. I promise you that. We have informers in the police department, you innocent fools!" There was no mistaking his earnestness.

Carlos shivered slightly, the expression on his seamed face very solemn with responsibility. Luis stared hungrily at Goncalves, like a starving tiger at a tethered goat. Carlos looked apologetically at Luis and me. "We won't go to the police."

"You will report the matter to your association?"

Carlos nodded reluctantly.

"Friday night?"

"Perhaps," Carlos said, with a last flare of defiance.

Goncalves laughed. "It will be Friday night, my friends, have no doubt of that. Because by then, you will know with certainty that The Big Ones are very serious about this."

"What do you mean?"

"I am aware that I can't expect you to take my bare word for the dangers that threaten your association members."

"What more than your word can you give?" I asked.

"Some examples of what can so easily happen to taxi drivers in Montevideo who are without protection."

"Examples?" Deep furrows of worry scored Carlos' forehead.

"You'll see," said Goncalves. He stood up, puffing, and switched off the recording machine on Carlos' desk. "Keep this machine and play back the tape for your members. It will help to convince them." He turned and walked out.

We could hear his footsteps thumping on the stairs this time, although we had heard nothing when he came up.

Carlos said to me in a whisper, "Follow him, Fernando!   See where he goes."

I waited a few moments to let him get out of the café below, then slipped after him.   When I emerged on the street among the sidewalk café patrons, I looked around in vain for Goncalves.   Then I saw a stout form disappearing around the corner into Plaza Independencia and hurried after it.

Too late.   When I reached the square, he had disappeared.   For a moment I thought I had him again, driving a battered old Volvo away from a parking place along the curb; but when the car passed me, the driver turned his head my way, and I saw his face was not full and fleshy like Goncalves', but lean, far too lean.

On Friday night, at the monthly meeting of our drivers, Carlos reluctantly reported to them the proposal of The Big Ones.   He played the tape of our meeting with Goncalves, turning the volume up full so that all of us could hear every word of that incredible conversation.

Only now it didn't seem so incredible.   For after hearing the tape, our drivers realized that the blowing up of Diego Carnero's cab had been no chance mishap, but a deliberate destruction of Diego's livelihood.

The stitched knife cut under my chin, from which I removed the bandage for a moment to expose the puckered cut itself, came in for its share of dismayed attention, too, you may be sure.

Then Pepa Lopez, one of our women drivers, reported a mechanical accident that now assumed new significance.   She had driven a fare to the top of the hill which gives our city its name, to show him the magnificent view of Montevideo, the Rio de la Plata and the ocean beyond.   After dropping her fare at a vantage point up there, Pepa had left her cab for a few minutes to use the public rest room. When she started down the hill, returning to the city with an empty cab (luckily!), she found she had no brakes at all.   She'd been forced to bring her wildly accelerating cab to a halt by ramming its nose into a sandstone outcropping on a curve of the road.   Only skillful driving had saved her from sudden death.   Her cab, alas, was wrecked.

Finally, Joaquín Celestinos, with a bandaged head, reported he had been held up the night before by a medium-sized fare wearing dark glasses and a hooded rain jacket.   His fare had knocked him out with a blackjack, and upon regaining consciousness, Joaquin had found his evening's earnings gone, along with his passenger, and his cab immobilized by sugar in the gasoline tank.

In the light of these "accidents," the tape was played again, and the membership was in no doubt as to how to interpret them truly.   When the matter of an increase in monthly dues to pay for the protection of The Big Ones came to a vote, the membership voted "aye" overwhelmingly; and I confess that Luis and I voted with the majority, despite the brave words of defiance we had uttered, in our innocence, before we felt the knife at our throats.

So the following evening, a few minutes before midnight, I parked my cab outside the Hotel Carasco and entered the casino for my usual Saturday night flutter—always modest and usually unrewarding—at the gaming tables.

I played roulette cautiously until fifteen minutes past midnight. Having won enough to convince me I would soon begin to lose, I followed a slender croupier, who had just been relieved by another stickman at the no-limit table, into the casino buffet for a bite of cold meat and a beer.

Finishing my beer five minutes later, I drifted into the hotel lobby and went through to the front steps of the hotel which faced upon the long moonlit beach across the Rambla. I stood there, gratefully inhaling the cool sweet airs that blew against my cheek from the estuary of the Plata. After the smoke and perfume-scented air of the casino, it was a pleasant change.

After a moment, the slender croupier joined me. He lit a cigarette, murmured, "The garden," under his breath, and walked down the steps toward the gardens that flanked the hotel on either side. After a fitting interval, I followed him.

I sat down beside him on a stone bench beneath a *ceibo* tree, whose bright red flowers looked almost black in the moonlight. He turned to me and said eagerly, "How did it go?"

"The meeting?"

"What else?"

I laughed softly. "It went very well. We voted to raise our dues five percent, as you suggested."

He nodded, pleased. "Splendid! And how will you poor drivers possibly manage to pay higher dues?"

I chuckled. "Don't worry about us drivers. We passed the increase along to the consumer, as usual. We also voted to raise taxi fares five percent, you see."

"You have the first payment, Fernando?"

I pulled a bundle of bank notes from my pocket and let him see them. "You were wonderful as The Big Ones' representative," I said. "You could never have put on a better performance in your palmiest days as an actor."

He bowed, a graceful motion with him, even when seated. "Thank you, Fernando. I rather fancied myself in the role, too, if you want the truth. Did my eyes look sufficiently cold and menacing with the gray contact lenses?"

"Terrifying," I said, smiling.

"And the wax wads in my cheeks to make my face fat? And the midriff padding I used to wear when I played Falstaff?"

"Magnificent," I said. "You were a Big One to the life."

He simpered a little, warmed by my praise, a one-time bit-player who still thought of himself as a star. I fed his vanity with more fulsome praise.

At length, perhaps out of a sudden generous impulse of his own, he said, "I was good, Fernando, I admit it freely. Very good. But the idea, after all, was yours, and the idea was the true masterpiece, of course." He laughed softly, rubbing out his cigarette under his heel. "I suppose I am responsible for that bandage under your chin?"

"Of course. A dwarf and a tall man wearing a beige hat are supposed to have held me up and cut my throat, as a warning from The Big Ones. That is what every driver in the Montevideo Taxicab Drivers Association firmly believes at this moment.''

''What if somebody had looked under your neat bandage?''

With dignity I answered, ''Do you consider me a fool? I actually cut my own throat, Manoël. It bled all over my shirt.''

''Marvelous! And what other accidents did you contrive to back up my promises to your colleagues?''

I told him about blowing up the taxicab of Diego Carnero; about tampering with the brakes of Pepa Lopez; about putting sugar into Joaquín Celestinos' gasoline tank.

He clapped his hands together. ''Well done, well done, indeed!'' He laughed until the tears came. Wiping them away with the back of one hand, he held out the other to me. ''Now, the money, Fernando. Is it the full amount?''

''The full amount.'' I began to count pesos into his hand. ''Twenty-five percent for you and seventy-five for me. That was our agreement. I trust you appreciate the true beauty of our arrangement, Manoël. For here we have not just a single small fortune to split between us tonight. Oh, no. We have, instead, a regular monthly income, a delicious succession of small fortunes, one a month, to be enjoyed for years to come, I hope.''

Manoël nodded his head solemnly. ''Genius, nothing less, Fernando. And yet . . .'' he hesitated and looked at me sidelong, ''you could not have brought it off without me, could you?''

''Of course I couldn't.''

''Therefore,'' said Manoël, ''I suggest that my services were worth more than the agreed-upon twenty-five percent of these small fortunes you look forward to so eagerly.'' His voice was no longer soft and genial. It was suddenly threaded through with iron. I said nothing, merely stared at him in the moonlight as though stunned—which I was.

He went on, ''In fact, Fernando, the more I think about it, the more I believe that it is *I* who deserves the seventy-five percent and you, the remaining quarter.''

''Have you taken leave of your senses?''

''Consider for a moment. Could I not go to the officers of your association and expose you as a fraud and a cheat—a man who, in my apt phrase, cares more for money than for the welfare of his fellow drivers?''

''You could do that, yes. But you wouldn't. Because if you do, I'll expose you, in turn, to the police—as a down-at-heels actor turned croupier, who entered Uruguay illegally and is now working in Montevideo under an assumed name on a forged work permit.''

Manoël smiled. ''So? I would be deported, no doubt. That is the worst that could happen to me. But you, my friend, would be killed by your own cabdrivers before the police could intervene to save you! No, we are both vulnerable, I think, Fernando. But you more than I. Seventy-five percent?'' Without a word, I counted pesos into his hand.

The iron had left his voice when he said, ''Thank you, thank you.''

''*Por nada*,'' I said.

Manoël glanced at his watch. "I must get back to my table." He stood up and thrust his bundle of notes into a pocket. "Next month at the same time, eh? I'll see you meanwhile at the gaming tables, I hope."

"Yes," I said. "Good night, Manoël."

"Good night, Fernando." He left me and went back into the casino.

I went out and hunted up his battered Volvo in the Carasco parking lot and wired enough plastic explosive under its dashboard to blow a dozen Volvos and their occupants into tiny bits the moment the ignition key was turned to start the engine.

Then I got in my taxicab and drove slowly home.

MARGARET CHENOWETH

The White Moth

Forrest Blake had been dead less than a month when he first came back.

Janet, his nongrieving widow, elegantly casual in the off-white she usually affected, looking even younger than the forty to which she admitted, was on her way to a small luncheon—just the innermost circle of her deadliest friends, since outwardly she was observing the amenities of mourning—when from the upper hallway she saw him at the foot of the stairs, waiting with quiet resignation, as in life he had waited for her endlessly, patiently, throughout their marriage.

Her first reaction was the quick annoyance Forrest's meekness always had aroused in her, coupled with an unreasoning anger because he looked so frail and old. Descending the broad, deep-carpeted steps, her efforts to control her irritation caused her large gray eyes to appear more prominent than usual and the pulse in her creamy throat to throb noticeably. As she came closer, Forrest extended his thin right hand, and on his wrinkled parchmentlike palm she saw the key. As she reached for it, the key became a white moth which floated away, and at the same time Forrest simply vanished. Janet stared for a stunned moment at the space where Forrest so clearly had been, then began to tremble uncontrollably. What had Annie cried the night Forrest died, something about white moths being poor lost souls?

Supporting herself with both hands on the bannister, she crept down the remaining stairs and staggered across the hall into the library—Forrest's study, actually—where, to the clank of jangling gold bracelets, she poured herself a brandy; then another, and still another to fortify herself for the ordeal of facing her friends who at that very moment she knew were taking advantage of her absence to rehash the events as they knew them before and after Forrest's sudden death. Janet was well aware her activities provided good subject matter for these lively group *dissections,* but she felt sure that even their wildest speculations were not bold enough to guess her dark secret.

Huddled in Forrest's big chair by the fireplace, her expertly maintained pale gold hair luminous against the dark leather, Janet reviewed the nightmare of the past weeks. She remembered that on the day before Forrest died they had driven into the city together, Forrest on business at the bank, lunch at the club and an unexplained appointment later in the afternoon, while she ostensibly planned to attend a board meeting of one of the endless charities she busied herself with since his retirement, vague appointments filling the afternoon before rejoining him.

Janet knew her friends said, among other things, that her "good works" actually were escape measures from the boredom of living with an old man, even one as rich and indulgent as Forrest.   She also knew they were aware of her active interest in young men, but was certain they did not know the full extent of this interest. Rotten luck it had to be Forrest who found her out.   But Forrest was dead, wasn't he?   Well, then, what was he doing over there in the corner, looking at her like a sick dog?

Raising her glass in a defiant salute she mumbled, "Here's to a long life . . . beyond the grave," but Forrest only smiled sadly and shook his head, and when she threw the glass at him, he disappeared.   Shaken, Janet ran from the study and out the front door.   In a moment she reentered and went to the phone to cancel her luncheon engagement.

"You sound as if you'd seen a ghost," her friend Mavis said.

"I have," Janet answered thickly.   "It's Forrest.   He's come back."   She hung up the phone and went back to her room.   Without undressing, she crawled unsteadily into bed and wept.   With her tears came the recurring memory of Forrest's last night on earth.

As agreed, she and Forrest had met for an early dinner in the city before driving home.   As always, she was conscious the Forrest Blakes presented an attractive domestic picture in public as she, the pretty, devoted younger wife, diamonds and dimples flashing, fussed over her distinguished elderly husband, always managing to convey the you're-so-much-older-than-I effect.   Secretly Janet was contemptuous of Forrest's uncomplaining acceptance of his beggar role in this little game, so grateful for the crumbs of her attention.   Suddenly, as if tiring of the endless play, Forrest had reached in his pocket and drawn out a heavy, baroque key which he fingered thoughtfully before Janet's stunned gaze.   Finally he said, "I see you recognize this."

Too startled for denial, Janet whispered, "Where did you get it?"

"I bought it."

"B-bought it?"

"Yes," Forrest said, adding ironically, "and I am wondering if I paid too much. The young man was so anxious to make a deal I am sure I could have gotten it for less . . . much less."

Janet fumbled for a cigaret from her jeweled case but her hand shook so that she could not light it.   Forrest, who had been holding the light for her cigarets for so many attentive years, made no move to help her now, but watched her coldly, his tired old face inscrutable in the candlelight.   Janet started to speak but Forrest cut her off.   "Please . . . spare me the debasement of an explanation."

Finally she whispered, "Forrest, what are you going to do?"

"For the moment, nothing.   Nothing at all.   When I have talked to my lawyer in a day or so, I will let you know."   He then paused to control the quaver which had crept into his voice and asked, "How many of these keys have there been?"

Janet's answer was a stifled sob but her anguish was not regret for her philandering, only that she had been caught.   It was humiliating; so damned humiliating, and dangerous, too.   Forrest might divorce her and, as the injured party, conceivably would not have to be generous with alimony.   That was a paralyzing thought.

Oh, why had she continued this last affair so long!   As a matter of fact, why had she begun it?   Her intuition had warned her the young man was too greedy to be trusted, but he was charming, gay, flattered her so and was such an ardent lover that she had let it drift on against her better judgment.   Then his demands for money became so excessive she had told him she was giving up the apartment in town—rendezvous for so many assignations over the years—that it was all over between them.   This, then, was his dirty revenge, to sell her out to her husband.

On the ride home Janet was too deeply wrapped in her misery and her mink to notice what was happening to her husband, to see that he was destroyed and resigned to his destruction.   It was the next morning she found him dead.

She had waited for this moment so long that when she went to his room the next morning, prepared to throw herself on his mercy and beg forgiveness, then found him quite dead in his big bed, her first reaction was to laugh aloud in sheer relief. "I've always been lucky," she told herself, remembering to turn off her elation before leaving the room.   In the hall she met Annie bringing Forrest breakfast and told her, "I think Mr. Blake is dead.   Call Dr. Walsh and ask him to come at once."

Annie's reaction was more violent than Janet's had been.   She dropped the tray and ran sobbing down the stairs and into the kitchen, so Janet had to call the doctor herself.

After Dr. Walsh had come and gone and they had taken Forrest's body away, Janet had called her best friend, Mavis Carter.

Skipping any condolences, Mavis surmised, "Well, you've waited long enough. Now, with all that money for yourself, I suppose you'll have all of us kowtowing to you for the rest of our lives."

At her end of the line, Janet's answer was an unsuppressed smile which was interrupted by the doorbell.   "Good-bye, I'll talk later," she told Mavis.

Annie was still in the kitchen sobbing convulsively so Janet went to the door. Brightly blonde Olivia Randall, whom Janet tolerated because of her coterie of young men friends, smiled at her archly and piped coyly in her little-girl voice, "Olivia's thirsty."

Janet answered rudely, "Forrest died this morning, the bar is closed," and shut the door on Olivia's shocked white face.

The long day finally ended and Annie came, still sniffling, to turn down Janet's bed.   Going to the window to draw the curtains, she screamed at the sight of a large white moth fluttering against the glass.   Janet found herself reluctantly comforting the girl, who cried, "It's a poor, lost soul trying to find a resting place. It was Mr. Blake himself—may he rest in peace—who told me never to kill a white moth because it was a wandering soul searching for peace."

The next time Janet saw her dead husband was just at twilight a few weeks later. She was hurrying in from an afternoon of bridge to change for dinner with Mavis, whose husband Jeff was out of town.   When halfway up the stairs, she saw the door to Forrest's study swing open and the next minute he appeared, looking sadly up at her, but when she started down the stairs he stepped back into the study and the door closed.   Janet sank weakly to the steps.   It was Annie's day off and she was alone in the big house.   Too frightened to move, she remained huddled on the stairs until the ringing phone stirred her to action.   It was Mavis, and Janet told her, "I'm on my way this minute," and ran out of the house.

Dreading the possibility of seeing Forrest again, she spent the night at Mavis'. She dreamed wildly and woke up calling out so loudly that Mavis came running in, her pink hair in a surprised frizz above her well-oiled face.   Mavis hurried around turning on lights as Janet said hysterically, "I thought when Forrest died that I was free, but he won't let me go.   He keeps coming back, just appears out of nowhere and stands there looking at me.   I know people say dreadful things about me, but don't I deserve something out of life before I'm too old to care?"

At Mavis' look, Janet continued, "Honestly, Mavis, you don't know what it was like, all those years married to a tired, old man.   I know you all think he gave me everything; everything but what I wanted most."

Unlike many of Janet's friends who were watching her gradual disintegration with varying degrees of pleasure, Mavis genuinely pitied her and now tried desperately to think of some way to help her.   "Janet dear, you must get away, forget it all for a while.   We're going to open the house at the lake this weekend.   Why don't you join us on Saturday?   Stay as long as you will, the change will be good for you."   Janet shook her head, and Mavis added, "Think about it, dear.   No need to call, just come up anytime you feel the urge."   She then brought a cup of warm milk spiked with a shot of whiskey and waited while Janet drank it, then tucked her in, turned off the lights and slipped out quietly.

At first the idea of spending time at the lake with Mavis and Jeff Carter held no appeal to Janet, but on reconsideration she decided to drive up, leaving early Saturday morning.   About a hundred miles from the city the freeway abruptly narrowed to an aggravatingly inadequate three-lane road, with Janet trapped behind a big truck and trailer.   She always drove more cautiously than she lived, so her first impatience gave way to resignation and she adjusted to the deadly pace set by the traffic ahead.   In a field to her right, Janet casually observed a cloud of little white moths floating above the sweet-smelling alfalfa.   As she watched, a gust of wind scattered the butterflies, blowing a clustered segment over the fence and onto the highway.   To her horror, hundreds of tiny white wings, beating futilely against the stiff breeze, swept toward her and the next moment she drove headlong into the living cloud.   Janet shuddered at the soft, plopping sounds the frail bodies made on impact with her car.   With the truck and trailer just ahead and a car impatiently crowding her rear bumper, Janet could not stop.   Frantically she rolled up the window but not before one of the tiny creatures flew inside.   Soft wings brushed her cheek momentarily, but as her hand came up to brush it away, the moth flew into her ear where it fluttered to escape.   Fighting panic, Janet drove to the next wide shoulder where she pulled off and stopped.   Probing gingerly, she tried to extricate the moth but it only buried itself deeper, little wings beating helplessly against its dark prison.

In desperation, Janet resumed driving, hoping to find help out of her dilemma. The continuous palpitation inside her head was maddening and she clenched the steering wheel to keep from screaming. Finally she came to a small town where she found a doctor in his office. Deftly, painlessly, he removed the moth from Janet's ear and held it for her to see, its frail wings still pulsing feebly.

Janet said, "There were thousands and thousands of lost souls," and then she fainted.

She revived on a bed in the doctor's office. He was watching her anxiously. "I don't think you should try to drive for a while," he told her.

Janet said, "I have to get back home. Is there anyone here who would drive me? I'd give a hundred dollars just to get home and in my own bed."

Excusing himself, the doctor left the room, returning shortly with a broad-shouldered, bronzed young man whom he introduced as Jack Loren. "Jack says he can use that hundred dollars. I'll personally vouch for him, so whenever you feel up to it you can be on your way."

Ordinarily, the close proximity of a young man, especially one so presentable as Jack Loren, would have intrigued Janet and she would have made the most of the situation . . . and the young man. Today, she was too shaken by her recent trauma even to carry on a conversation. When he reached to turn on the radio with a perfunctory, "May I?" she merely nodded her assent and went back to her own tortured thoughts.

At Burlingame she roused to direct him to her house high in the hills. Jack's low grin and his direct gaze momentarily stirred Janet. It really would be a shame for the young man to start on the bus trip without some show of hospitality in appreciation of his services. She was about to ask him in for a drink, but as they turned into her driveway she saw Forrest waiting for her on the terrace steps. Her hands shook as she fumbled in her purse for the hundred dollars she had promised the young man. Giving him an extra ten, she told him to wait and a taxi would come to take him back to the bus station.

Then she turned to Forrest, still standing on the terrace steps. Suddenly she welcomed the safety of his presence, his kindliness, and she hurried toward him, but as she extended her hand he vanished.

Annie, coming out to meet her, clucked, "Poor lady, the doctor phoned to tell me what happened. He said to put you to bed as soon as you got home."

Once in bed, Janet remained there for days, scarcely eating, refusing to see or talk with anyone; anyone, that is, but Forrest and she was beginning to find his frequent presence such a comfort. She alternately would doze and rouse, and often on awakening she would see him sitting in his lounge chair by the window; "his" chair, because he had ordered it and had it delivered without consulting Janet, one of the few instances he had shown such daring. The chair's capacious bulk was incongruous among Janet's feminine furnishings, but she had tolerated it because it seemed expedient. Now it was reassuring to awake and see Forrest sitting there, sometimes reading the Law Journal, sometimes just watching her with a half smile. At first she tried to talk with him but found that made him disappear, so she quickly learned to accept the settling effect of his silent presence.

One bright day, at Annie's insistence, Janet ventured out of the house and wandered down to the pool where she dropped on a chaise.   Funny, how the crowd around the pool, in the house, had fallen off since Forrest's death.   Incredible that he should have been the attraction when she had always felt she was the magnet who drew them, the ceaseless, senseless swarms.   Strange too, how nobody really liked anybody, yet how they clung together in their mutual dislikes.

She watched in fascination as a white moth skimmed the surface of the water, then drifted toward her in a bobbing flight pattern.   She put out a hand to capture it, but it fluttered tantalizingly just out of reach.   Then she saw Forrest catch it and hold it out to her.   Janet, making a wild lunge that set her drink flying, stumbled and fell, but got to her feet and staggered toward Forrest, following him as he beckoned her on to the middle of the pool.

That is where they found her, face down at the bottom of the quiet pool.   Annie sobbed as they brought Janet out of the water.   Kneeling beside her, she gently pried open a fist clenched around a bedraggled white moth, then screamed hysterically as it imperceptibly moved its bruised wing and, with a sudden convulsive effort, lurched crazily away on the soft afternoon breeze.